DESTINY'S DOOM

THE SUNDERED NATION
BOOK THREE

VAUGHN ROYCROFT

PRAISE FOR VAUGHN ROYCROFT

"Never was a novel more aptly titled. *Bold Ascension* is bold in its narrative choices, surprising the reader with its twists and machinations, not to mention the dark paths on which it takes the characters. And it *ascends* in its widening of the scope and world-shattering stakes of the tale."—**Philip Chase (YouTube's Dr. Fantasy, author of The Eden Trilogy)**

"I love the way that Roycroft subtly weaves the themes he is exploring throughout the narrative, imbedding them in almost every page but in a way that never distracts from the story he is telling... Bold Ascension has cemented The Sundered Nation trilogy as one of my favorite reads of the year, and the concluding novel as one of my most anticipated."—**Quinn Giguiere, Silverstone's Book Blog**

"You could compare [Roycroft] to [John] Gwynn, especially because the prose is able to capture the gravity and the importance of moments, but a bit faster... [I]f you want to read Epic with capital letters Fantasy, *The Sundered Nation* is the perfect series for you."—**Jamedi of JamReads Blog**

Copyright © 2024 by Vaughn Roycroft

No part of this book may be reproduced in any form or by any electronic or mechanical means, including information storage and retrieval systems, without written permission from the author, except for the use of brief quotations in a book review.

Cover art by John Anthony Di Giovanni

Cover design and interior graphics by Three Star Smoked Fish

Maps by Jack Shepherd

CONTENTS

In memory of Miss Helen,
For whom there were never enough books.
I'm a writer because I'm a reader,
And I'm a reader because of you, Mom.

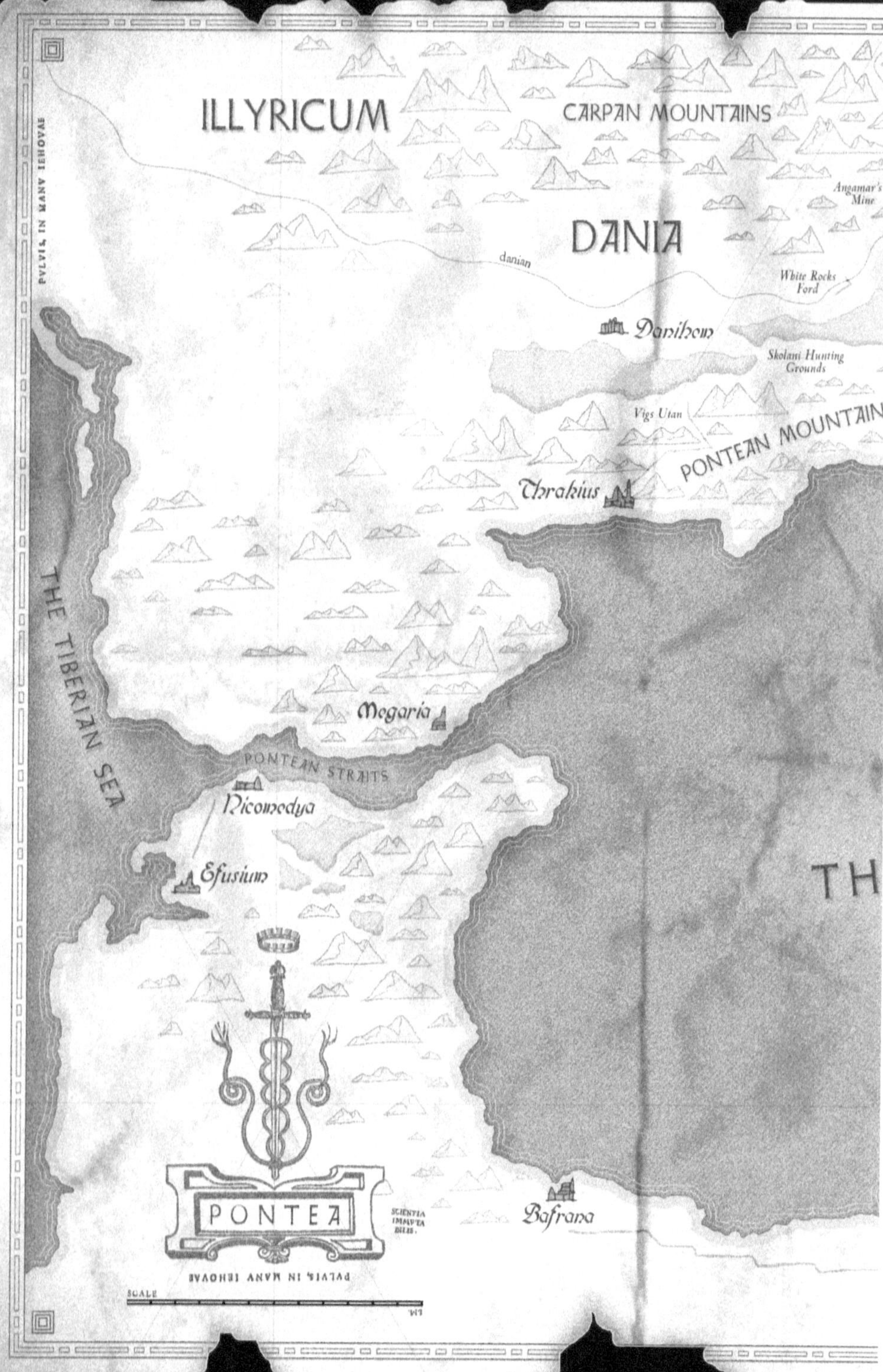

PVLVIS IN MANV IEHOVAE
ILLYRICUM
CARPAN MOUNTAINS
DANIA
Angamar's Mine
danian
White Rocks Ford
Danihom
Skolani Hunting Grounds
Vigs Utan
PONTEAN MOUNTAIN
Thrakius
THE TIBERIAN SEA
Megaria
PONTEAN STRAITS
Nicomedya
TH
Efusium
PONTEA
SCIENTIA IMMVTA BILIS.
Bafrana
PVLVIS IN MANV IEHOVAE
SCALE
FM

IN ATHNAQVE PARATVS
KAUKAZARI STEPPE
OIUM PLAINS
AFLETAM FOREST
berezan
tala vatne
Draughersfen Swamp
Akasas
PONTEAN MOUNTAINS
VNIVERSITAS RERVM, VT
THE PONTEAN SEA
Trazonia
Anissa
Halecz
PVLVIS, IN MANV IEHOVAE

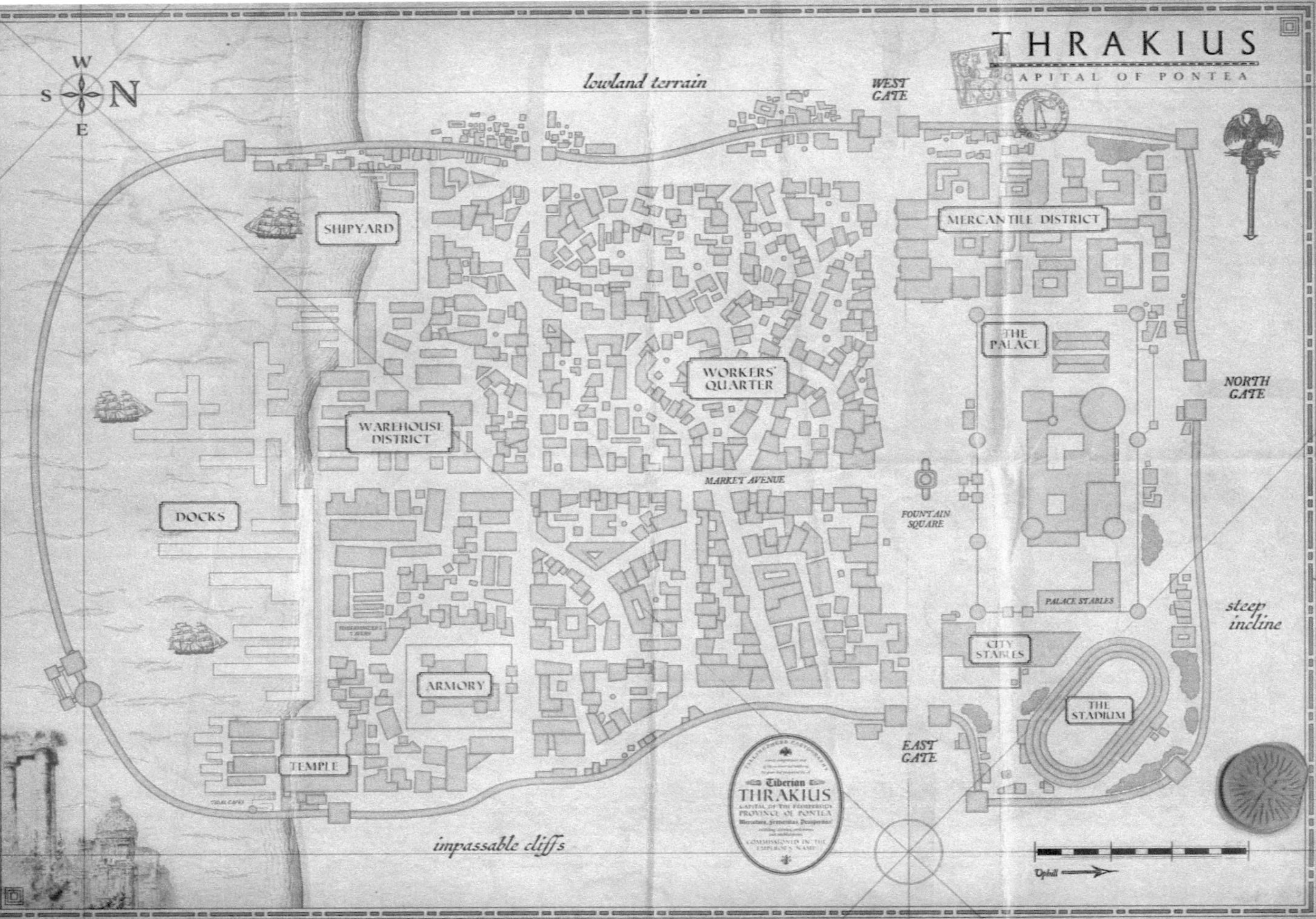

THRAKIUS
CAPITAL OF PONTEA
W N S E
lowland terrain
WEST GATE
MERCANTILE DISTRICT
SHIPYARD
THE PALACE
NORTH GATE
WORKERS' QUARTER
WAREHOUSE DISTRICT
MARKET AVENUE
FOUNTAIN SQUARE
DOCKS
PALACE STABLES
steep incline
CITY STABLES
ARMORY
THE STADIUM
EAST GATE
TEMPLE
Tiberian
THRAKIUS
CAPITAL OF THE FOREMOST PROVINCE OF PONTEA
COMMISSIONED IN THE EMPEROR'S NAME
impassable cliffs
Uphill

CHARACTER LIST

<u>The Gottari</u>

The Amalus Clan (the lions):
    Vahldan (Eldest son of Angavar the Outcast)
    Vahldan's Family:
    Angavar (father, former Lion Lord, deceased)
    Frisanna (mother, wife of Angavar, deceased)
    Eldavar (younger brother)
    Mara (sister)
    Kemella (sister)
    Thaedan (son of Vahldan and Amaga)
    Armesus (son of Vahldan and Harma)

Desdrusan (former Lion Lord, cousin to Angavar, disgraced and exiled)
    Teavar (Rekkr, royal guardsman)
    Jhannas (Rekkr, royal guardsman, deceased)
    Ermanaric (Rekkr, royal guardsman)

Arnegern (Rekkr, right hand to Vahldan, son of Vildigern)
Belgar (Rekkr and captain for Vahldan)
Herodes (Rekkr and captain for Vahldan)
Attasar (scribe and scholar to Vahldan)
Harma (an Amalus woman, daughter to Herodes)

The Wulthus Clan (the wolves):
Thadmeir (Wolf Lord of Dania)
Thadmeir's Family:
Urias (adopted brother and captain of the longhouse)
Aomeir (elder brother, deceased)
Theudaric (father, former Wolf Lord, deceased)
Amaseila (wife, priestess to Freya)
Amaga (daughter of Amaseila and Thadmeir, First Qeins to Vahldan, Priestess to Freya)

Hloed (merchant, prominent member of the wool guild)
Gizar (prominent member of the Elli-Frodei, an order of shamanistic scholars)
Ulfhamr (captain of the Wulthus host based in Danihem, cousin to Thadmeir)

The Ponteans

Malvius (sea captain from Thrakius, son of Decebius, sister to Ligaia, disinherited)
Ligaia (daughter of Decebius, wife of Kluctus, deceased)
Decebius (anax of Thrakius and shipping magnate, father to Malvius and Ligaia, deceased)
Kluctus (husband of Ligaia, named heir to the Thrakian anaxship by Decebius, deceased)
Agoraki (kitchen boy in the Thrakian palace, adopted son of Apontia, known as Ago)

Apontia (maidservant in the Thrakian palace, enslaved during the war in Sassanada)

Despoina (tutor to Brin)

Neveka (a Bafranii woman, partner to Malvius, deceased)

Dexicos (first mate of Malvius, known as Dex)

Sabas (former mate turned overseer of the docks and warehouses in Thrakius for Malvius)

Isidros (anax of Nicomedya, trading rival to Malvius)

Encho (Illyrican right-hand to Isidros, deceased)

Zafan (Bafranii pirate captain, former slave, brother to Neveka)

Dah Arstra (high lord to the Haleez region of the Sassanadi Empire)

The Skolani

Elan (banished to become Vahldan's guardian, former Blade-Wielder, daughter of Ellasan)

Keisella (queen of the Skolani)

Icannes (princess, daughter of Keisella, near-sister to Elan)

Sael (Wise One, a Dreamer/seeress, grandmother to Elan)

Annakha (Wise One, a healer, near-sister to the queen)

Ursellya (healer, daughter of Annakha)

Anallya (Blade-Wielder and royal guardian)

Kukida (Blade-Wielder and royal guardian)

Alela (wet nurse)

Hildeanna (Blade-Wielder, captain of the scouts of the eastern borders)

The Tiberians

Vernius (lord general of the Tiberian mobile reserve legions)

Nicandros (adjutant to General Vernius, known as Nico)

Tullius (captain of the equine division of the mobile reserve legions)

Facerius (master commander of all Tiberian militum branches, including armies and navies)

Mycanius (His Eminence, the Emperor of Tiberia)
Avitus (imperial diplomat, or legatus, based in Megaria)
Horius (provincial governor of Megaria)

PLACE NAMES & GLOSSARY

Places:

Akasas—An ancient, walled city on the northern coast of the Pontean Sea. Located at the mouth of the Berezan River, Akasas was once a prominent port for Hellain traders.

Anaissa—A Sassanadi city on the River Haleez, high seat of Dah Arstra. An important trade center near the termination of the Peshtari trade routes. Because the mouth of the river is controlled by the Tiberian navy, goods are normally shipped from nearby Trazonia.

Bafrana—A port city on the southern shore of the Pontean Sea. Largest city and seat of power for the Bafranii people, a seagoing nation under the rule of their religious leader, the Sadhu.

Cispadaena—A large port city on the eastern side of the Tiberian Peninsula, Cispadaena is the home port of the Tiberian navy.

Dania—A river valley formed by the Pontean mountain range to the south and the Carpan mountain range to the north. Home of the Gottari, Skolani, and Carpan tribes.

Danihem—A stockade-fortified village in central Dania on the

Danian River. The longhouse of Danihem holds the seats of the lords of the ruling clans of the Gottari tribe.

Efusium—The Tiberian Empire's third largest city, a port on the Tiberian Sea, and home to the empire's largest library. A multiethnic city, Efusium is known for its vibrant cultural scene, the center of imperial fashion, art, and music.

Illyrica—The mountainous realm of the Illyrican tribes, located to the west of Dania and north of the Pontean Straits.

Medicia—A river port city on the Tiberian Peninsula and the capital of the Tiberian Empire, it is the seat of the emperor and location of the Militum Academy.

Megaria—A walled city founded by the Hellains at the opposite end of the Pontean Straits from Nicomedya, nearest to the Pontean Sea. Megaria is the seat of Pontea's provincial rector. The catapults of Megaria loom over the vital trade-route for eastern goods to the Tiberian Empire.

Nicomedya—A walled city, largely populated by Hellains, at the opposite end of the Pontean Straits from Megaria, nearest to the Tiberian Sea. A vital trading city, Nicomedya is the center of the Tiberian slave trade.

Oium—A sprawling grassland, relatively featureless beyond its gently rolling hills.

Pontea—A province of the Tiberian Empire, Pontea encompasses the lands adjacent to the northern shoreline of the Pontean Sea, from the Pontean Straits in the west to Akasas in the east.

Thrakius—An ancient, walled city on the northern coast of the Pontean Sea. Due to its enclosed harbor and the marvel of its ancient seagates, Thrakius was long the Pontean stronghold of the Hellain navy. It remains a prominent trading port of the Tiberian Empire. Though Thrakius is but a shadow of its glorious past, it remains the largest imperial city in Pontea.

Trazonia—A port city controlled by Tiberia, once a part of the Sassanadi Empire, on the southeastern shore of the Pontean Sea at the edge of the mouth of the Bay of Haleez. Trazonia serves as the link from the overland Peshtari trade routes, vital to the spice trade throughout the Tiberian Empire. Dispute over control of the port led to the War of Two Empires between the Tiberians and the Sassanadi. Because Trazonia is entirely surrounded by Sassanadi territory, accessible for Tiberians only via the water, tariffs are collected by both empires for the passage of goods.

Vigs-Utan—An aging stronghold at the head of the trail that leads through the Pontean Pass, consisting of a stone tower and ramparts surrounding the gateway to Dania. The tower remains the home of the Elli-Frodei—the order of the Wise Ones of the Gottari.

Glossary:

The Ananth-jahn—A trial in the form of a sword duel, granted to a petitioner to the dais chair and the Rekkr's council, to settle a perceived wronging or a slight of one's honor. The challenged has the right to select a champion to fight in his stead.

Hiatus—An annual period when shipping in the Tiberian Empire's territorial waters is shut down in order to avoid winter storm damage and loss. Sailing during hiatus is punishable by fine and is all the more dangerous due to the free reign of pirates.

The Fulhsna-Utanni—A part of the Mithusstandan (see below), in which the Skolani agree to supply Blade-Wielder guardians to the scions of the Gottari's ruling clans. Considered archaic and obsolete.

Futhark—Technically, any runic missive intended to convey a shared oath or law. To the Gottari, the futhark is the shared oath between the two ruling clans of the Wulthus and Amalus. The runes of the oath are inscribed on rings fastened to the hilts of the two futhark swords borne by the Lion Lord and the Wolf Lord.

The Jabitka—The mobile village of the Skolani. During the time of Vahldan and Elan's tale, the Jabitka is located in eastern Dania, south of the Danian River near the ford at Red Rocks.

Mithusstandan—The ancient oath between the Gottari and the Skolani in which the Skolani agree to safeguard the borders of their shared realm in exchange for Gottari weaponry (primarily the vaunted Gottari blades prized by the Skolani Blade-Wielders).

Qeins—A woman bonded to a Rekkr or chieftain of the Gottari, often of noble or landed birth. A qeins is a wife with rights and an inheritance outside of her marriage. Indeed, some qeins are more wealthy or prominent than their husbands. Esteemed priestesses are also granted the status of qeins.

Rekkr—A Gottari warrior who has claimed his name, pledged himself to one of the two ruling clans, and who owns his own weaponry and at least one warhorse.

The Urrinan—The prophesied calamitous end of the era in which the Tutona peoples shall rise to prominence from the ruins of the so-called civilized world of the imperials. To be wrought by the Bringer of Urrinan, who is foretold to arise from among the Gottari tribe.

DETAILED RECAP OF BOLD ASCENSION

Destiny's Doom is the final volume of The Sundered Nation Trilogy and is preceded by The Severing Son (volume one) and Bold Ascension (volume two).

The Setup—Into a Wider World:

Bold Ascension took up the tale of VAHLDAN of the Amalus clan of the Gottari and his guardian ELAN, a former Blade-Wielder of the Skolani, from the point immediately after the events of The Severing Son. In the first volume, Vahldan had won acclaim during Queen Keisella's War against the Spali for his actions during the final battle fought on the grasslands of Oium. Due to the acclaim won, Vahldan had been able to seize his status as the rightful Lion Lord of the Amalus clan, ousting his father's cousin, the usurper DESDRUSAN. At the war's end, Vahldan had chosen to sunder his clan's host from the rest of the Gottari army in order to pursue a fleeing sect of Spali warriors whose leader had murdered his father.

His guardian Elan had been given the choice of letting Vahldan go and returning to her people or following him, for which she would be banished. She'd chosen Vahldan and banishment, and together they'd hunted the Spali southward, all the way to the Hellain city of Akasas on the coast of the Pontean Sea. When the Amalus had caught up, they'd found the Spali besieging Akasas. The two forces had battled outside the city walls while the Hellain citizens had remained trapped within.

Meeting Malvius:

Bold Ascension opened inside the besieged city of Akasas in the rented bedchamber of MALVIUS, son of Anax Decebius of Thrakius. Malvius was a disgraced scion, disinherited by his noble father and cut off from a fortune and from taking the helm of a shipping empire. He'd been driven into port in Akasas by bad weather on a trading expedition and had become trapped by the Spali siege. This boded particularly ill for him because the timing of his expedition was illegal during the imperial winter shipping hiatus. Another issue of urgency was that his cargo had been procured using illicit funding sources. Worse yet, Malvius's ships had been "borrowed" from his father's fleet without his father's permission. Malvius desperately needed to swiftly win an extraordinary profit. He'd taken an enormous risk, a wild gamble to get back into the shipping game.

When the Amalus host arrived and attacked the city's besiegers, Malvius sensed his fortunes might have shifted. From the top of the city walls he witnessed the Spali's defeat at the hands of an impressive host of Teutonics led by a striking couple—Vahldan and Elan. His hopes were then temporarily dashed when the city fathers denied Vahldan's request for supplies in return for their effort to free the city. Rather than celebrating a reversal of fortunes, Akasas earned a new besieging enemy in the Amalus, which prolonged Malvius's misery, keeping him trapped and further dampening the hopes for his expedition's success.

The morning after the Amalus's arrival outside Akasas, Vahldan and Elan orchestrated a seizure of the cargo ships moored in the city's harbor, most of which were in Malvius's fleet. In witnessing the loss of his fleet and their precious cargo, Malvius thought that all was lost and went on a drinking binge. In a hidden little pub, he encountered the prostitute NEVEKA, whom he'd previously hired. As they commiserated over the city's misfortune, Malvius learned from his first mate DEXICOS that the city fathers wanted to send him out to meet and negotiate with the besieging Teutonics. Because the Teutonics demanded that only one man attend the meeting, Malvius thought himself too drunk to even get himself there. Neveka hinted that she had an idea, and they struck a bargain: If she could get him to the meeting, Malvius agreed to cut Neveka in on the profits of his expedition and take her along when he sailed away.

During the ensuing meeting between Malvius and the Amalus, Vahldan had an epiphany. He'd come to believe that in order to make a difference for his people, he'd need to break the wool guild. He now realized that the best weapon he could employ to do so would be great wealth. Since they possessed these fine ships and a valuable cargo but had no idea how to sail or to whom they might sell the goods, the Amalus could find their way to wealth by becoming the fleet's mercenary fighting force—also for a cut of the expedition's profits. Malvius agreed to partner with forty lions, and Vahldan sent the rest of his host back to Dania after appointing his dear friend ARNEGERN to lead them in his absence.

The forty Amalus struggled to master the ways of fighting on the sea, but they swiftly learned that some battles could be won through mere intimidation. When the expedition arrived in Trazonia, the trading hub for spices coming from the eastern trade routes, the Amalus learned how tenuous and fraught the expedition really was. They were being blocked from the market by the rival trader ISIDROS, the anax of another Pontean city. Without the permission of Malvius, Vahldan ventured to start a fight with the mercenary force employed by Isidros. His boldness was rewarded with a stunning victory, one that gave them access to the market. Not only did the move enhance the expedition's profits, it also foreshadowed the long-term success of their partnership with Malvius.

The Lions' Years at Sea:

Over the course of eight years of sailing together, both groups—Vahldan and his Amalus lions and Malvius and his crews—grew immensely wealthy. In the fleet's home city of Thrakius, Malvius slowly bought up warehouses and ships, usurping his family's empire. When Vahldan learned that Malvius had grown up in the palace on the hill, the grandeur of the place captured his imagination. Just before their last winter hiatus together, Vahldan overheard that the fleet's ship captains had grown wary of their Amalus guardsmen. The Hellains feared they would be led to ruin by the violent recklessness of the lions. He also overheard Malvius's reassurance that, should the worst happen, he had secretly sought the means to have the Amalus captured and sold as slaves. Vahldan was outraged and vowed never to be enslaved.

On their hiatus retreat, while recuperating on a favorite getaway island, Elan learned she'd finally achieved pregnancy. She'd sought it in spite of knowing that Vahldan felt differently. She had been fearing that Vahldan was secretly striving to embody the foretelling of the seeress AMASEILA that he was the Bringer of Urrinan. The seeress had foreseen that he would have a son with her own daughter, AMAGA, who was also the daughter of THADMEIR, the Wolf Lord of the rival Wulthus clan. An heir of the wolf and the lion had been foretold to become the king of a hundred Tutona kingdoms.

Elan had come to hope that hearing of her pregnancy, alongside their astonishing success and newfound wealth, would convince Vahldan to abandon his ambitions and just live the simple life for which she longed. Instead, Vahldan was outraged by her deception and by the fact that—after all that they had gone through and achieved—she would abandon their goals, which he apparently perceived differently than she did. Elan responded to his outrage with her own, vowing to see to it that her daughter would never play a role in the prophecy or in his grand ambitions.

The Return to Dania and the Birth of Brin:
Amaga, daughter of Thadmeir and Amaseila, was eight years old

when she first met KEMELLA, the youngest sister of Vahldan. Kemella came to Danihem to meet Vahldan upon his triumphant return from Pontea. The girls quickly became inseparable friends, and when Kemella met Amaga's mother Amaseila on her deathbed, the seeress had Kemella promise she would remain at Amaga's side. The girls already knew their lives would be entwined as Amaga's union with Kemella's brother had been foretold.

Thadmeir was alarmed by the rumors of Vahldan and his lions as they traveled the Danian countryside and used their newfound wealth to free commoners from debt to the guild, which was swaying scores of new pledges to join his growing host. Thadmeir feared that Vahldan meant to intimidate the Wulthus by marching on Danihem. Rumor also told of Elan's pregnancy and the host's move toward the Skolani home village. In response, Thadmeir sent his brother URIAS out to seek intelligence. He sensed that Vahldan and the Amalus wanted to break the guild and feared that the Skolani would be inclined to aid them in achieving clan dominance.

Urias traveled into the wilderness and met with Vahldan and Elan. Urias agreed to become Elan's guardian, taking her along to the Skolani village, where Elan intended to give birth. She hoped that having her daughter there would ensure that Brin would be adopted into her birth tribe. Upon arrival, Elan was harassed and abused physically by warrior proteges, only to be saved by ICANNES, same as had happened in their youth. Urias received assurances of Skolani neutrality in the Gottari clan conflict, but Elan's hopes for her daughter's adoption were dashed. In the aftermath of birth, Elan felt purposeless and hopeless. Her grandmother, the seer SAEL, arrived to reassure her that both she and her daughter had vital roles to play in the unfolding events of Urrinan.

Meanwhile, Vahldan arrived outside of Danihem. His host had grown so large that its camp engulfed the village. When Vahldan and his Rekkrs entered the village to confront the Wulthus leadership, Amaga and Kemella stood on a bench beside the longhouse door to get a good view. A tussle ensued and threatened to become a riot. Vahldan called for quiet and approached the longhouse door, where he and Amaga spotted one another. Vahldan tried the door but found it locked. He called for Thadmeir, who appeared from out of the crowd. The two argued and in the heat of it, Amaga was accidentally knocked from the bench. Vahldan got to her first, and his touch sent her into one of her spells, at first foreseeing a happy future and then a terrifying aftermath full of blood and fire. Thadmeir was outraged that Vahldan had laid his hands on his daughter and vowed that Vahldan would never touch her again.

Conquest of Destiny:

After the conflict outside of the longhouse, Vahldan held a rally for his followers. He told them that, yes, the guild had been exploiting them, but that who had been behind it all along—who really kept them down—were the merchants of the Tiberian Empire. The imperials kept secret trade pacts with the wool guild. He told them that they could seize the reins to their destiny by striking against those who controlled the means to wealth. His followers roared their approval and vowed to do their lord's bidding, chanting, "We belong to you."

With spring's approach, Malvius won a major contract with the imperial government in Megaria over his sister, LIGAIA, who accused him of stealing it in order to put their family out of business. Moments after the siblings argued, Malvius received word that Vahldan and a host of his men had arrived outside of the north gate of Thrakius. Malvius had feared he'd lost the lions and was thrilled, which made him angry that his father was keeping Vahldan from entering the city. Malvius rushed to the north gate to vouch for his friends. His father warned him that his association with barbarians would bring trouble.

Once inside the city, Vahldan warned Malvius and his father not to interfere in what was about to take place. The Gottari then launched an attack, taking out the imperial soldiers present. In the ensuing action, Malvius's father drew his sword and was struck down by Teavar. Shocked, Malvius fled to the docks in an abandoned chariot, only to find that his ships had already launched. As the Gottari raiders pressed down on the crowd seeking escape, Malvius spotted Neveka. She'd become the love of his life and was pregnant with his child. Malvius watched as she was trampled to death. Enraged and grief-stricken, he fled to his fireproof warehouse and locked himself in. As the mayhem ensued, he vowed to make Vahldan and the Gottari pay for their betrayal.

Living in the New World:

In the springtime after the conquest, a Tiberian diplomatic delegation arrived in Thrakius to discuss the terms of leaving Vahldan in control of the city he had seized. Elan had arrived a short time beforehand with her baby, BRIN, so Vahldan had provided her with a residence and had assigned her a manservant, HESIOD, and a wetnurse. Distraught and feeling unwelcome, Elan had soon sought to flee with the wetnurse and her babe back to Dania, only to have the Blade-Wielders block her from entering the Pontean Pass. On the day of the Tiberians' arrival, in desperation, Elan planned to flee alone by ship, leaving her daughter to be cared for by Vahldan's sisters. Hesiod intervened and convinced her to stay just as Vahldan came to demand that she accompany him to the meeting.

The lead Tiberian diplomat was insulting and threatening but conceded that the Gottari could remain in control if they allowed tariffs and taxes to flow to the empire. Vahldan became the imperially-sanctioned magister of Thrakius. In the wake of the invasion, Malvius's sister, Ligaia, whose husband had been slain before her eyes, had found herself imprisoned in the palace dungeons. She was now brought before Vahldan, who agreed to release her. Not knowing where else to go and concerned over her illegitimate son AGORAKI, who was a servant in the palace, Ligaia instead agreed to stay and work as a handmaiden. She sought connection with her son but was confronted by the boy's adoptive mother, APONTIA, a kitchen maid. Apontia threatened Ligaia, telling her to stay away or she would tell the Gottari who the boy really was, that his father was the Tiberian general VERNIUS.

Eight years after moving to Thrakius, Vahldan followed Elan out of the city. She lured him out to a lush forest setting to confront him about his plans to return to Dania. She suspected that his hidden intention was to seek out Amaga, who had recently come of age. Marrying her would fulfill the prophecy and possibly provide him with a huge boost in military power by gaining the support of the warriors pledged to the Wulthus. Elan made Vahldan promise to abandon his schemes of playing along with the prophecy. He gave her his word.

Amaga was beside herself with excitement over the visit of the Lion Lord and his family. She went out to meet the arriving delegation, first encountering Kemella. From her dear friend she learned that Vahldan's brother ELDAVAR had a son and that his sister MARA was pregnant. She was distressed that there were other Amalus heirs. She considered her divine role to be the wife of Vahldan and the mother of the rightful heir, who would be the prophesied leader of the Tutona. When Amaga tried to get closer to the arriving carriages to connect with Vahldan, she was challenged by Elan, which left her shaken.

Thadmeir agreed to meet Vahldan alone. He was annoyed by Vahldan's bragging about their fine life in Thrakius. He pushed Vahldan to reveal his true intentions and was alarmed to learn that Vahldan sought to unite them to fulfill his military ambitions in Pontea. He became convinced that Vahldan sought to woo Amaga and threw him out, once again vowing he would never have his daughter. After the Amalus left Danihem, Amaga snuck out and ran away with the help of Vahldan's sisters. She went to Vahldan's camp just outside the Danian border, where she was once again confronted by Elan, who threatened her very life. Vahldan intervened, telling Elan that he'd had no part in Amaga's escape and that her part in Urrinan was the will of the gods. Stricken, Amaga was taken to his pavilion. Upon touching Vahldan's futhark sword, Amaga had a seizure and a vision, first of their shared son and then—once again—of blood and fire in their future.

After Amaga's escape, her uncle, Urias, learned that his brother Thadmeir intended to lead a host to hunt and retrieve his daughter. Urias convinced Thadmeir that Amaga left willfully and that he himself should be sent to Thrakius as the Wulthus envoy and to watch over his niece. Urias also had another motive for going to Thrakius. He'd already promised his lover, Icannes, that he would watch over and train Elan's daughter, Brin. Urias arrived in Thrakius to find that the Gottari were all but prisoners in the palace keep, surrounded by a hostile city. He was mistrusted by Vahldan and the other Amalus. He also encountered an alarming state of conflict between his sister and his niece. In spite of the obstacles, Urias stuck to his word and sought to train young Brin. She reluctantly agreed to his plan, and they began their regimen.

With his marriage to Amaga approaching, Vahldan orchestrated his grand plan. He sent trusted allies to seek more warriors in Dania, made a secret alliance with Anax Isidros of Nicomedya on the Pontean Straits, and made a deal with the imperial government to put down an uprising in Bafrana. He made a second, secret pact with the Bafranii pirates, whom the empire had hired him to thwart. During Isidros's visit to discuss the plan, Ligaia covertly met with the anax as well. Agoraki eavesdropped and learned that his birth mother was orchestrating a scheme with the anax to double-cross the Gottari.

Malvius, back in Vahldan's good graces, tricked his former partner into believing that the best path to seizing the Straits—and thereby all of Pontea—was by attacking the empire's fourth largest city, Efusium. Malvius also continued to furnish Vahldan with a special wine that the self-proclaimed king loved and did not realize was fortified with narcotics.

Marital Problems:
Vahldan was drunk on Malvius's drugged wine at his wedding ceremony. He saw his bride morph into the goddess Freya, who

directed him to ignore the bloodshed and mayhem that would ensue, encouraging his war with the empire. At the end of the ceremony, Vahldan's stooge holy man proclaimed him the king of the Gottari. Amaga was outraged and abandoned him at the altar. During the ensuing celebration, Vahldan met a lovely young woman. The two flirted shamelessly and the young lady helped him to his quarters to relieve himself. While in the privy, the two surrendered to lust and were caught at their heavy petting by Amaga. Only as she departed did the drunken groom realize his young paramour was his cousin's daughter, HARMA.

Amaga had realized before the incident that the only thing she wanted from her new marriage was her prophesied son. She had been waiting to seduce her husband when she'd caught him in his tryst. As they argued afterward, her resolve returned and grew. She resumed her plan and the newlyweds consummated the marriage. Afterward she told Vahldan that she hated him and hoped they would never have to sleep together again. Dejected, Vahldan sought solace by visiting Elan, who was still hurting and thwarted his advances.

Seeking Urrinan by Waging War:

The Gottari army was mustered and ready to sail to Bafrana when Elan realized Vahldan intended to leave her behind. Elan gathered her gear and led her horse to the docks. She confronted Vahldan, who was seeking revenge for being rebuffed. Elan drew her sword and challenged the companions among whom she'd fought for half of her life, asking who thought themselves a better guardian for their new king. The disarming moment caused a reconciliation of sorts.

Upon arrival in Bafrana, the pirates presented Vahldan with a gift —the imperial diplomat who'd insulted him in their first meeting and his retinue as bound captives. Malvius tried to convince him to release the imperial prisoners, but the diplomat provoked Vahldan to slay the man publicly, which ensured there would be no turning back from their war plan against Tiberia. Malvius realized he would be named an accomplice, which complicated his own double-dealing.

The Gottari helped the pirates to take the citadel of their sadhu from the imperials. In exchange, Bafranii scouts would lead them across a snowy mountain pass to Efusium. Halfway across, the Gottari realized that they'd been tricked—led into a blind pass, abandoned, and left to freeze. Elan was charged with finding the way out, which she accomplished.

The Gottari raided Efusium, taking the military barracks and burning the docks and fleet, eliminating the protection forces for the vital Pontean Straits. They marched on Nicomedya at the mouth of the Straits and arrived to cheering crowds. The imperial garrison had fled to Megaria at the opposite end of the Straits.

While the Gottari army was at war, Isidros's mercenary fighters arrived in Thrakius and took the palace. Urias tried to save Vahldan's family from capture but failed. Only Brin escaped capture, thanks to Agoraki. The two overheard Ligaia and Isidros planning to wait until the Gottari were beaten. Isidros wanted to marry Ligaia so that they could control all of the trade in Pontea. Ligaia wanted desperately to eliminate Vahldan's family, but Isidros grasped their value as hostages. Still, Ago and Brin feared they had little time to act and sought Malvius for aid.

Vahldan led his army against Megaria, but through discipline and clever strategy, the Tiberians humiliated the more numerous Gottari, nearly trapping and capturing Vahldan in the process. Elan was devastated by the heartbreaking loss of her dear friend, her primary warhorse since childhood, Hrithvarra. The Gottari were forced to retreat to Nicomedya.

With the palace held by his sister, Malvius realized he needed Vahldan to survive for a while longer. He had to thwart Ligaia and Isidros, and he was wanted by the imperials for murder. He took Brin and Ago to the Sassanadi dah to procure a naval ally. Brin managed to convince the dah to join her father's war.

As Vahldan and his host undertook a risky assault on Megaria, Brin and Ago led their new Sassanadi allies in a similar assault on the Thrakian palace. Vahldan's team succeeded, forcing the Megarian imperial commander to surrender. Elan had already procured a promise from him that any captives would be released without harm. Before the surrender, the imperials had managed to fire one of the catapults, hitting a Sassanadi ship. Vahldan learned that his brother Eldavar had been one of the victims and was forced to perform yet another mercy-killing of another loved one.

Brin and Ago freed Urias, and during the ensuing melee, Brin and Urias sought to free Vahldan's family. When they found Amaga, she was being held at knifepoint by Ligaia. While Urias tried to talk Ligaia into surrendering, Brin was able to leap onto the woman. During the scuffle, Brin realized that the only way to save her uncle was to slay Ligaia, and she did so. She was shaken, but she gained an appreciation for what was required of a warrior.

In the Aftermath of Battle:

Vahldan returned to Thrakius and met his newborn son, THAEDAN. He was disappointed that his son had a Wulthus name and that he was sickly and puny. Agoraki had mixed emotions about the slaying of his birth mother and went to the docks to seek a job at sea with Malvius. In their exchange, Malvius realized that Ago was Vernius's son but withheld the information. Elan and Vahldan argued over their complex predicament and came to an impasse in the realization that the past could not be undone. Elan provided Vahldan with the epiphany that Urrinan might occur from within and without the empire. She reminded him that they still held the vital Pontean Straits and that the war was far from over. As they parted, Vahldan met Harma again. Harma sought to console Vahldan about his sickly son, planting the idea that he could yet have a second son who could be more of a lion.

Vernius Stallicus returned to his estate from a campaign in the western empire. He sought out an old flame and thought that perhaps the woman might provide him with a much-needed heir. Without an heir, he was in danger of losing his lands. It wasn't to be, though, as Vernius was summoned the next morning by the emperor. At the meeting, the emperor informed him that the Gottari had taken the Pontean Straits. He made him his second-in-command in a campaign to retake Pontea and wipe out the Gottari. On the way from the meeting, Vernius learned that Ligaia—who he feared had been killed by the Gottari—had given birth to his son.

The events of Destiny's Doom pick up several months after those of Bold Ascension.

"The Bringer wields but half a ring
A scion's get proclaims a king
An exile keeps a nation torn
Of strife and ruin an age is born

Thunder wakes when blades collide
The steed on which Urrinan rides..."
—From The Song of the Severing Son

CHAPTER I
TRUDGING TO LEGEND

"When my mother left to fight with the Amalus army at the mouth of the Pontean Straits as the threat from Tiberia grew dire, she went without my father. In hindsight, it was telling for many reasons. I was beside myself for one simple and selfish reason. We had only just rediscovered ourselves as mother and daughter. I finally had the mother I'd longed for, and I was losing her again—perhaps for good.

Before the war, Elan had brushed aside my complaints over her absences by insisting that it was her duty to be at my father's side. She had chosen banishment to be his guardian. When I gave voice to the injustice of her going to war alone, arguing that my father's safety would not be at risk, it was the first time I heard her say, 'A legend's not a legend until it ends, baby girl.' It was far from the last.

In the throes of my childish outrage, I failed to see. Only years later did I come to fully grasp my mother's fatalism. She had chosen more than banishment or devotion to duty. She had chosen to embrace her destiny's doom."—Brin Bright Eyes, *Saga of Dania*

. . .

BLOODSHED WAS no stranger to her. Still, in all of these years of fighting, Elan had never considered herself a killer. Until today. For on this day, she would kill.

The Skolani killed only when necessary, to preserve life and the safety of the homeland.

Elan was on foreign soil. Truth be told, she loathed this godsforsaken stretch of windswept shore. She certainly wouldn't kill merely to maintain its possession. She knew the killing she was about to inflict would only summon more death.

But none of that mattered now. She was no longer Skolani. And death was inevitable.

The low clouds of the predawn sky lit to gray. The call came down the line. The foe had been spotted. Elan got to her feet and stretched. She tossed aside her bow and quiver and drew her heirloom blade, Biter, from over her shoulder. No bowshots today—not for her.

Her limbs and neck were stiff from dozing through the night in the damp air of the shore. She twisted her torso, swinging the blade to loosen up. Her flexibility was the best it'd been in years. She'd spent the eight months since their seizure of Megaria sparring with the most skilled Rekkrs. She'd been sleeping and eating better, even drinking less. Well, at least until evening. Rigorous training made one hungry. And thirsty. The lifestyle imparted a healthier sort of exhaustion. In the palace, Vahldan had his own guards. Which meant she was sleeping better than she had in all of her adult life.

By the time word arrived that the foe had arrived at Efusium and was poised to attack Nicomedya, Elan's body was lean, her muscles hard, her eyes sharp, and her hands steady. Her reflexes seemed almost as good as they'd been in her youth, although she'd grown wise enough to avoid relying on them.

Icannes had always said that Elan had great intuition and speed, that her deftness with a blade was a gift. But the compliment always preceded the admonishment that she lacked a killer's instincts. The knock implied that she hesitated because of her soft heart.

But those days were gone. Elan's heart, too, had done some hardening.

Pushing herself had not only awoken her gift, it had also made it more lethal. She was as adept as ever and—when it came to Tibairya—she'd become merciless. These were the hard-won attributes she intended to utilize today.

This was finally it. The Amalus army's next test would be its greatest by far. The emperor had sent his most vaunted fighting force. The imperial mobile reserve had sailed east. The Tibairyan Empire intended to reclaim the Pontean Straits.

In the light of what had happened the last time Vahldan left Thrakius defenseless, he'd chosen to stay home, along with a substantial security force. But the elite portion of his army was here. They'd been tasked with maintaining the Gottari hold on the prize they had seized. Vahldan had put his cousin Herodes in charge of Nicomedya's defense.

The Straits were the lifeblood of the empire's prosperity. The success or failure of this Amalus army, defending their most remote possession, would tell the tale of the Urrinan. Somebody had to fight this war. Someone had to strive for the prophecy. Clearly it wasn't Vahldan. Clearly what had once been *their* calling—his and Elan's—had been left to her.

Herodes came down the line, checking on his charges. "Are you ready, Elan?"

"Beyond ready," she said.

"You sure you don't want to lead an attack squad? I can still assign one."

"No. They'd only slow me down. Speed is all. We can't even allow them to form up."

His smile was grim. "Yes. Let's pray this goes as planned."

"It doesn't matter," she said. Herodes did a double take, puzzled. "If I am to be an instrument of Urrinan, I am ready. If killing Tibairya will hasten its coming, today I make it fly. Whoever wins the day, catastrophe is nigh. My destiny demands that I see to its arrival or die striving for it. Prayer won't change a thing. Only action will." The gods were fickle anyway.

Herodes's expression betrayed a flicker of consternation but he nodded and moved on. As soon as Elan settled on her haunches in the scrub, the crimson sails of the Tibairya appeared on the horizon. The warships came in swiftly, riding the spring wind across the calm sea.

She looked down the line in both directions. Every Rekkr lining the crest of the dune had their sword drawn and shield up. She'd chosen the center, hoping to target the foe's leadership. She didn't envy their Gottari comrades on the beach below. They'd been poised and waiting in stillness since before first light. She'd be down there fighting among them soon enough.

The foe's helms in the prow of the ship straight ahead of her came into view. Seeing them reminded her of the Tibairyan garrison at Megaria during that awful first encounter—their straight formations, long spears, and deadly discipline. It was over a year ago now. But in her mind's eye she perfectly saw the Tibairya who'd sneered with glee as he'd stabbed Hrithvarra.

By all accounts, the mobile reserve would be even fiercer. Not to mention inexorable. These were hard men. Men who used any means to kill and maim, who'd do anything to prevail. They would keep coming. Until they won or were destroyed.

She'd heard enough to know that for the mobile reserve this would be but the next in an endless series of campaigns. This wasn't a task to attend to or a hardship to overcome. It was a lifestyle. They never surrendered, never negotiated. Men like these weren't selected or created. They were culled and hardened. Bloodshed was their occupation. Dealing death was both goal and motivation.

The lofty principles of the so-called civilized world did not apply to them. For such men, codes and virtues and pity were weaknesses to be exploited. They were killers without honor. She too must do whatever it took to prevail. She must abandon the weaknesses that had been instilled in her former self.

Only a killer could thwart a killer.

Elan was willing.

Thunar's Blessing filled her chest and thrummed through her limbs. She thought about Vahldan, and what he called his ugliness. This was different. This was clear-eyed. She wouldn't lose herself to this. "If Urrinan is all he'll settle for, he'll get it," she said aloud. She wiped her hand and firmed her grip on Biter's hilt. "As it shall be."

A score of prows hit the sandy beach—this spot having been selected for this very feature. Hundreds of imperial boots splashed into the surf. Still, none of the Gottari moved.

The Tibairya made their way up onto the beach and began to gather into squads. A piercing horn rang and the sands at the very feet of the invaders burst to life. Dozens of Gottari sprang from the ground and were an instant—and murderous—presence among the Tibairya. The exhumed berserkers' blades whirled as the Rekkrs on the dune above launched into a full charge, every Gottari roaring in unholy rage.

Elan led them all, each of her strides a downhill leap. She spotted an officer's crested helm and ran for that spot. The officer was marshaling a squad of about a half-dozen. She arrived before they were able to form up. One of them saw her coming and stepped in front of his commander, raising his shield to block her. She took a final leap and hit his shield with both boots, knocking him into the officer and tumbling the pair as well as a third companion onto the beach. She landed on her butt, knowing those left standing would pounce. She swiftly pushed off of the shifting ground with the face of her buckler and swung her blade as she twisted her torso to regain her feet, slashing an attacker's unarmored thigh.

The imperial squad scrambled to surround her but it only made them easier targets. Elan read their intensions on the fly, seeing their movements before they made them. The openings came as if they were delivered by the gods. She struck—again and again—twirling, slashing, and dodging. Every counterattack was avoided or shield-blocked, each creating an opportunity for the next attack. Again and again, she pulled Biter from flesh to strike new flesh. As she turned to parry a final strike from her right flank, she fell into a low reverse spin, slicing the calf of the last man standing—the officer.

The officer grunted as he fell, but he did not cry out. The man strained to rise and swing again. Elan easily slashed the wrist he exposed in the attempt. The wound sent his sword flying from his hand. She jabbed, hard. The blow pierced his elaborately carved leather breastplate, pushing him to the turf. The sound of his gasp told her she'd punctured a lung. She kicked him and yanked her blade free. She spun to ensure that the entire squad sprawled around her was unmoving.

She ran to the aid of Hjalmar, trading blows with a pair of Tibairya. Again, she saw her opening as she arrived and swung down, cleanly severing the outstretched sword arm of one who'd just struck Hjalmar's shield. Her victim's shriek left his distracted companion to Hjalmar, who shoved the second man to the ground, stepping on his blade and knocking his helm off. Elan delivered the blow that shattered the helmless man's skull. Hjalmar jabbed down into the neck of the one Elan had disarmed, leaning on his sword to turn his victim's scream into a fading gurgle.

Hjalmar nodded his thanks. They turned back-to-back, seeking new targets, only to find a well-coordinated Tibairyan retreat to the ships underway. Within moments, the foe's oarsmen were calling a throaty cadence. The ships smoothly slid back out to sea. The bastards had left their fallen and fled, confirming their lack of honor.

Elan spit on the corpse at her feet. "Bloody Tibairya and their bedamned discipline."

More taunts than projectiles were hurled at the retreating ships. The Gottari knew this was only the beginning. The bastards would keep coming. Next time, they'd hit harder. Next time would be bloodier.

Elan knew it better than most. Destiny was upon them all. It was here in Nicomedya that the Urrinan would be well underway, for all the world to see. At long last.

She scanned the treeless dunes above the shore. The drab stone of Nicomedya's walls rose just beyond. Gods, she hated this place. She strode back to the wheezing officer pathetically crawling from the beach to the dune grass, plowing a bloody rut in the sand.

The bastard heard her coming and rolled to face her. He met her gaze, defiant, resolved to face the violent death he'd surely long known would come. His eyes were cold, his face clean-shaven and full of sharp angles. He was exactly whom she'd expected. She kicked him in the crotch, then stood straddling him, stepping on his wounded right wrist. She pressed Biter's tip under his chin. He gasped, his face contorting in agony. But still he did not cry out. Still he held her stare. Elan had to admire it.

Vahldan always said that the Tibairya stole the cultures of those they conquered. They picked and chose the elements they wished to make their own and snuffed those they disdained. They imposed their will and ways on those who survived and failed to flee. It made Elan wonder. Who was the thief here in Pontea? Who was imposing on whom?

It didn't matter. "I am but an instrument," she told the stoic officer in Hellainic.

"As am I," he said in grim concurrence.

She plunged the tip into his throat. Blood filled his mouth as he gulped for his last breath. "Peace now, Tibairya. A legend's not a legend until it ends. I give you yours."

He seemed to nod in salute even as the life left his eyes.

Elan stuck Biter's blade into the sand, knelt, grasped a clump of his hair, and drew her dagger. She began methodically cutting his scalp from his skull and said, "Mine is yet to come."

A FEMALE SHRIEK jarred Amaga awake and to a sitting position. The drunken laughter that followed was a mixture of male and female. At least no one in the main residence was being terrorized or murdered. Well, the shared laughter made it less likely.

Another thump followed by another female shriek woke the babe. Thaedan's crying incited shushing sounds from the far side of the door, but the laughter continued.

"I've got him," Kemella said, rising from her makeshift bed and heading to Thaedan's crib.

Amaga put on her robe. "This has got to stop." She set a fresh chunk of coal into the brazier, then lit an oil lamp, illuminating the servants' quarters. "First he forces his family out of our home, and now he keeps us awake night after night."

Kemella held the babe to her shoulder and rocked, stroking his back and soothing him. "I told you to take the residence that he offered us downstairs."

Amaga bristled. "I will *not* be moved downstairs. I am the qeins of Pontea. I am the mother of he who is born of the wolf and lion."

Kemella disguised a sigh as a yawn. "Yes, I know. You won't be set aside. And yet, here we are. Again." Kemella rolled her eyes and gestured around at the confining space.

Amaga couldn't bear to lose her only ally in the palace. "I'm sorry I snapped, dear one."

Kemella held out Thaedan to her. "Here, take him. I'll go and talk to Vahldan."

Thaedan's face crinkled in distress again. "No. He's finally settled. I'll go." Sometimes the boy's attachment to Kemella bothered Amaga. But having her son's preference confirmed at a moment like this would only make her feel worse. Besides, Vahldan had already demonstrated how unmoved he was by his sister's appeals.

She moved to the connecting doorway and stopped. It sounded like someone was leaning against it. Rather than lift the bar from its brackets, she turned and went out into the corridor. She raised her hand to rap on Vahldan's entry door just as another thunk and a female squeal issued from within. It was followed by more laughter.

There was no guard. At least not outside. If she knocked, she might be blocked by whomever answered.

Amaga hesitated, her hand on the door latch. Gods, she hated facing them… Facing *him*. The only thing worse than speaking with her so-called husband was actually touching him. The blood, the death she saw in their contact—it was nearly enough to reduce her to the sniveling child he seemed to think her to be. That which he called his ugliness truly was ugly to behold.

She was suddenly unsure what good could come of confronting him. The man grew more defiant, unpredictable, and blusterous with each passing day. He'd become nigh unbearable since his triumphant return from seizing the Straits. She wasn't sure whose idea it was for him to stay back when most of his army marched back to the Straits, but lingering here while others fought for him was clearly having a detrimental effect. Better than most possibly could, Amaga sensed the fragility behind the bravado. Unfortunately, his response had been to indulge his worst impulses.

And, Amaga had to admit, he was even more insufferable without his horrible Skolani bitch. She never dreamed she'd miss having Elan around. Spending her days wondering when the savage might try to kill her again had obviously blinded Amaga to the benefits of living in terror.

Another thud was followed by another female squeal. "Please. Stop!" The female plea was drowned out by more raucous male laughter. Whatever was happening was bad and getting worse. Anger suffused her, overcoming apprehension. Amaga opened the door and strode in.

The lamps were low inside. In the sitting chamber, a pair of musicians sat playing a flute and harp and a scantily clad Bafranii dancer swayed to the music. Cushions were spread across the floor and Rekkrs and women in various stages of dress were splayed in repose. None of the men looked in her direction, all of them busily groping the women.

A cool gust blew through the open doors to the terrace. Outside, the wooden table had been tipped on its side. Another Bafranii woman was being held against the tabletop by two grinning Rekkrs. They knelt to hold her by both her wrists and ankles, pulling her legs as wide as her skirt would allow, while a third man took aim with a knife poised to be thrown overhand. Four daggers were already embedded in the wood of the table between her legs and under her arms, pinning the silk fabric of her frock. One dagger was dangerously close to her crotch.

The poor woman was clearly terrified. Heedless, the dozen or so drunks on the terrace laughed and joked, cheering on the thrower.

Amaga's instincts told her that if she intervened, she might become their next target accessory. Amaga scanned the entire scene. Vahldan was nowhere in sight. Her gaze landed on his giant guardian sitting on a wooden chair, tipped back and leaning on the wall beside the sleeping chamber's closed door, his folded arms and chin on his chest.

She hurried over. "Teavar!" The dozing giant's head snapped up and the front legs of the chair thumped down. His eyes found focus on her, his face contorting in annoyance. "You've got to stop those men. They're about to maim that poor woman." Amaga pointed.

Teavar made a show of leaning to squint that way. "Not my place."

"How could it not be your place? You're a guardian, aren't you?"

He nodded his melon of a head. "I am. But not hers."

Another knife thudded into the wood, and the wretched woman was sobbing between her pleas or prayers in her own tongue. "Where is he?" Amaga demanded.

The big guardian tilted his head at the bedchamber's door. "Can't be disturbed."

Amaga ignored the oaf and hurried to work the latch and push the door open with her shoulder. The big man lunged for her but missed. She slammed the door and flipped the bar into place.

She turned her back on Teavar's knocking. Vahldan lay on his back on the bed, naked. The trollop—his cousin's daughter, also naked—straddled him, slowly raising and lowering herself. Even the slamming door didn't jar them from their inebriated debauchery. She immediately spotted the flask on the bedside table. It was never far from reach and seemed to hold an endless supply of the fortified wine he'd imbibed all through their bonding night. The growing haze it was creating in his mind was nearly overwhelming to her upon their touch. She'd tried to warn him, even by going through his sisters, but to no avail. As obviously debilitating as the effects of the stuff were to her, no one else seemed all that concerned—least of all him.

"Gods afire," Amaga said. The woman finally turned to her, a lazy smile spreading across her cursed pretty face. Unbelievably, the harlot continued copulating with Amaga's husband. Worse, she now seemed to be making a show of it. "Have you no shred of decency left?"

The girl giggled and shrugged. The harlot had always been voluptuous, but Amaga couldn't help but notice she was getting fat. Served him right.

Vahldan raised his head, squinting. He pried his eyes open enough to roll them. "Now what?" Amaga was sick and tired of people rolling their eyes at her. Vahldan pushed the redhead off and gathered the bedding to cover himself. "Don't you knock, woman?"

"I came in here to save one of your *guests* from being knifed just beyond your infant son's bedchambers' door. Excuse me for interrupting the fucking of your cousin's daughter." The trollop snorted a laugh as she casually collected an undertunic from a heap of garments on the floor.

Vahldan's expression clouded. "For the record, it could've been you."

Amaga's bitter laugh came naturally. "You mean being knifed or getting fucked?"

"Take your choice."

"A tough selection, my king, as the two have equal appeal."

"If you're finished now, you may leave, Amaga."

Amaga shook her head. "No. It isn't right. This is not how it's meant to be."

He swung his feet to the floor. "Yet this is how it is. It's as much your doing as mine."

Amaga suddenly felt desperate to reach him. She took a step toward him and stopped, loathing to touch him. "That may be. But is this really what you wanted, my king?" Vahldan opened his mouth to parry. She hurried on. "Is this what you strove for all of these years? Is it really how you imagined the restored Amalus kingship?"

She folded her hands and bowed her head. "I've been harsh, I know. I understand now that neither of us got what we imagined in one another. But can we not set it all aside? Just for a moment? Just to recall what you once dreamed, what we all hoped would come of my mother's augur. Is this how you envisioned an honorable king behaving? Do you imagine you are making your people proud? While your army is away, fighting without you? Do you think there will be songs of your adulterous deflowering of a loyal Rekkr's daughter? And if there are, how could they be anything but mockery? Please remember, my king, that you have a son—one who is preordained to unite the Tutona people. And that he is sleeping in the next room."

Vahldan actually blushed and looked away. The harlot stopped dressing and stood glowering. Had she actually gotten through?

Amaga pressed her advantage. "We are a decent people, my king. A chaste people. Yes, we look to you to bring the Urrinan. Yes, many have welcomed the return of the kingship. But they welcomed it in the hopes that it would raise us up. They so want to believe that they are witnessing the birth of a legend. The Gottari people yearn for honor and respect. And pride. I beg of you, King Vahldan—give it to them. Make them proud. Become their legend."

Vahldan lifted his chin, drew a deep breath, and sighed it out. "Thank you, my qeins, for sharing your perspective."

Amaga bowed, backed away a few steps, turned, and opened the door. She ducked to glide past the surly giant and hurried to the exit. The musicians had gone silent. She felt the stares of the entire room on her as her trembling fingers sought to open the exit latch. She closed the door and collapsed against it, quivering and gasping for breath.

She had been terrified, and was still rattled, but she had done it! She'd made him listen. Amaga composed herself and went through the servants' quarters door to her temporary home.

CHAPTER 2
WAGING URRINAN

"After the war began and things grew fraught, my father often repeated the phrase, 'A Bringer brings.' What I came to understand he meant was that if he had indeed been chosen as the man who brings the Urrinan to fruition, this could not have happened passively. Vahldan believed he was chosen to act. And if his actions resulted in consequences, well, those must have been destined, too.

As a result of this outlook, his passivity faded. My father became convinced that the gods intended him to shape and mold his people's destiny. Even in hindsight, I find I cannot deny the possibility. I sometimes wonder if he imagined the repercussions that echo on to this very day. And if he truly could have—the good and the bad—what he might have done differently."—Brin Bright Eyes, Saga of Dania

THE ANCIENT TOWER's outer door was unbolted. Although Vahldan was sure the Skolani had monitored his host's progress northward through the Pontean Pass, it appeared the Blade-Wielders had refrained from informing the Elli-Frodei of their approach. Or had they?

14

His squad filed silently through the door and the barn-like base of the tower, with Sueridas leading the way to the ladder at the back of the stables. Vahldan followed Sueridas and Attasar up the ladder toward the dark rafters of the first floor. Even with his young guide leading the way, Vahldan was soon covered in cobwebs. It was obvious this route was unused by the graybeards who lived above. Without looking he knew his half dozen guardians were climbing behind him. He hadn't told them all to follow and he doubted he'd need them, but he thought the armed escort would make the proper impression on the old wolves, whether or not they could rouse the energy even to seek to interfere.

Sueridas pushed the trap door open, flooding them in light. In a heartbeat, Vahldan's nimble Elli-Frodei was up and out. Both Sueridas and Attasar were across the main chamber and on the stairs going up before Vahldan even stood upright after the climb. The intrusion finally attracted the attention of the graybeards sitting nearest to the trap door. "What in the gods' names is happening?" one old man demanded. "Who are you people?"

Vahldan didn't bother answering. He led his squad through their primary living chambers, unhurriedly following Sueridas and Attasar up to the third level. Like aging lame hounds, the Elli-Frodei slowly pushed themselves to unsteady feet or sat barking. So easily stirred up, these old wolves. And yet he knew they were toothless.

He arrived on the third floor to find Sueridas already on a ladder, perusing the higher shelves. The young man Vahldan had named as his Thrakian Elli-Frodei drew an ancient leather-bound volume from a high shelf and flipped through it. Below him, Attasar had several scrolls under his arm and another one held open to read. Several Elli-Frodei shuffled up the steps and a few warily descended from the sleeping chambers above. The toothless wolves glared and growled but kept their distance.

A beak-nosed Elli-Frodei stepped up to wave his cane at Sueridas and Attasar. "Who do you think you are? Put those back. This is an outrage!"

Teavar and Ermanaric stepped to block the cane wielder. Vahldan signaled his guardians to stand back and be at ease. "We are here under the authority of the Amalus king, who is sovereign to your order," Attasar replied. "You would do well to show some respect by bowing to His Highness." Attasar gestured toward Vahldan.

The beak-nosed man turned and squinted at him. "King? We have no king."

It didn't matter. Vahldan had expected more verbal challenges than respect here. It wasn't even worth the trouble of setting them straight.

Gizar pushed his way spryly through his doddering fellows and put a hand on Beak Nose's cane-wielding arm. "Don't trouble yourself, Feletheus. They speak of Vahldan of the Amalus. He is no more a king than you or me." Gizar fixed Vahldan with hard eyes and a wry smile. "Though by now he could have been the Amalus lord and helped to restore the futhark. If he so chose."

"Funny you should mention restoring the futhark," Vahldan said. "That's exactly what brings me here."

Gizar glanced at Sueridas and Attasar, then at the armed guardians. "Is it, now? I presume you need some further evidence of legitimacy in order to preserve the loyalty of your pride of deserters? Best to firm up one's own position before asking the rest of us for compromise, I suppose. What's the trouble, my boy? Not certain the nation as a whole will take kindly to the decrees of royal resurrection from a runaway acolyte?" Gizar tilted his head at Sueridas. "Or did you stir some other hornet's nest you need to justify by reinterpreting prophecy?"

Vahldan forced a smile, hating how near the old wolf's arrow had struck. "No reinterpretation is necessary, thank you. We're just facing up to the Urrinan, which is unfolding before those of us willing to crawl from our hidey-holes and step onto the world's dais."

Gizar shook his head. "Facing up is what you call it? I'd call it waving your swords and terrorizing innocent cities. Not to mention provoking a dangerous foe to war. Playing the hero, no matter the cost. It's all just a game to you, isn't it?"

Vahldan let his smile wither. "A game is a good name for it. It's one you wolves invented and long sought to keep us from playing. Now we intend to win it."

"Here it is!" Sueridas called from the ladder, marking a page with a length of ribbon and closing the book. "I have what we sought, my king." Sueridas climbed down and began loading several books and scrolls into the sack hanging from his shoulder.

The beak-nosed graybeard stepped boldly toward Vahldan's Elli-Frodei. "Here now. You cannot simply take those. They belong to our nation's sacred collection."

"Oh, how quaint." Vahldan smirked and turned back to Gizar. "You accuse us of waving our swords, and here you are, hoarding the knowledge you so rightfully cite as belonging to our nation. At least we wield our swords to the benefit of our people. I doubt you can honestly say the same." Gizar frowned but said nothing. Vahldan turned back to Beak Nose. "Fear not, Wise One. We are simply borrowing them. Perhaps you would like to accompany us to Thrakius to see to their safekeeping?"

The man stepped back with a frown, obviously repulsed by the idea.

Gizar stepped closer to squint over Sueridas's shoulder as he loaded the sack. "Ah yes. The Rise and Deeds of the Amalus by Helderith. And a collection of the prescient visions of the Priestess Glismala. Let's see, what do these have in common?" A sly smile spread across the wolf's face. "I have it! Both feature the tales of King Eradaric. Even if both accounts are rather fanciful."

Sueridas cinched the sack closed and stood scowling at Gizar. "Let us be gone from this place, my king. I find I can no longer stomach the smell. Brings back vile memories."

Vahldan nodded and the Rekkrs cleared the way for Sueridas and Attasar to lead the way down the narrow, curving stairs. Vahldan followed, with Teavar bringing up the rear. Gizar trailed them, keeping his distance. "So let me think," Gizar called after them. "What was it about Eradaric? It couldn't be that he defiled half the maidens in his clan, could it? Perhaps what you need is his justification for it. He claimed to seek an heir *of the purest Amalus blood.* Of course that was mostly because he'd come to hate his first qeins. Not to mention her children. Ah, but this is sounding familiar, after all. That's it, isn't it? Perhaps deflowering the Wulthus bride you so coveted wasn't enough for you. Now you seek to supplant her son from inheriting your false kingship."

His squad reached the main floor and Sueridas led them to the platform and whistled to those below to lower away. Gizar hurried after them, still spouting off. "You want to use King Eradaric to justify deflowering all of the fine maidens in your little palace world. And perhaps end up with a young lion just like yourself—a remorseless killer to carry on your quest for legendary status. That's it, isn't it—a legacy of thuggery and depravity seeking legitimacy?"

Vahldan hated that the old fool was able to summon the ugliness. He hardly felt like fighting his own impulses. He got to the platform and turned to face Gizar's smug smirk. His hand shot out, grabbing the old man's robes and yanking him nose to nose. "Here's some advice to the so-called wise. Watch your tongue and stand clear. A footnote to the legend might easily include the unsavory end of the Wulthus domination of the Elli-Frodei order." He smiled. "Think it farfetched? You said yourself that I am a remorseless killer."

Gizar's eyes widened, but the old wolf found neither retort nor apology. The platform creaked and lurched into motion. The descent forced the normally straight-backed Elli-Frodei to stoop, his sour breath coming in gasps. Finally, Vahldan flung the old wolf back. Gizar stumbled clear, disappearing from view as the platform sank to the stables below.

Gods, he hated this place and these smug graybeards. Before they reached the ground, he found himself reaching for his flask.

ELAN WOKE to soft rapping on the door of her sparsely furnished quarters in the palace of Nicomedya. One eye wouldn't open. She realized the eye was not only swollen but glued shut with dried blood from the cut along her brow. The bowl of porridge she'd brought up for her dinner was cradled on her stomach, half-eaten and cold. She hadn't even finished her last cup of wine, though she'd managed to knock back most of the flagon. Her sore knees were propped up on the chamber's only feather pillow, and her head lay on a rolled blanket that smelled of mildew. She poured a bit of the wine on the bandage she'd cast aside earlier and washed the blood from the cut over her eye. The dripping wine and blood mixture made her rumpled tunic look all the more appalling.

The rapping reoccurred, louder. The stub of Elan's candle was guttering in its own melted wax. Her neck, back, and shoulder muscles shrieked in complaint as she struggled to her feet and straightened her frame. Her shield arm was purple and throbbing. Both hands and her bottom lip were swollen. She stood in place for a moment while the wooziness faded.

She stretched, inciting sharp pains that punctuated the general achiness of her limbs and torso. The pain brought the failings of the day back to mind. Despite their months-long success in thwarting the Tibairyan attempts to lay siege to Nicomedya, the Gottari's defense of the shore and the inroads had finally been breached. The failure had come even as they'd killed thrice as many of the invading foe. She herself had killed at least four officers over the course of the foe's campaign. But the bedamned mobile reserve just kept coming, no matter their losses. Fighting the disciplined, well-equipped unit had sapped the Gottari's energy and fighting spirit. Taking on the squat Tibairyan bastards warrior to warrior was like trying to get the best of a tree trunk—possible but laborious and exhausting. None of those whom Elan had faced could be called swift or graceful, but they were all damned stalwart. Surprisingly efficient, too. Damned competent killers.

Thus far, Vahldan's war felt more infuriating and exhausting than glorious.

At the onset of the latest attack, the foe had foisted an astonishing barrage onto the Gottari lines from ships mounted with catapults, followed by a series of massive volleys of flaming arrows that had started vast and swift fires. Everything along the shore and in the neighboring fields had either been smashed or burned or both. Between the smoke and dealing with fallen comrades, the Gottari had lost their cohesion and their verve in the counterattack. Once Herodes had ordered a partial retreat to the city with covering fire, there was no turning back. Actual Gottari casualties had been relatively light, considering. Once inside the walls, they'd put up a resolute counterattack from the wall tops, even managing to sink one imperial warship with a direct hit from a catapult.

Still, by sundown, the Tibairyan encirclement of the city was complete. The imperials had won a foothold in Pontea. For the first time in anyone's memory, the Gottari were trapped under siege. It was a form of warfare none of them knew a thing about.

The victory had cost the mobile reserve much. But as it was from the onset, they seemed willing and able to pay whatever the cost. Day after day, attack after attack, they remained remarkably undaunted. Workman-like, even.

As for the Amalus—besides the exhaustion and withering morale, their supply lines were now completely severed. The region's first grain harvest had yet to be brought in. The Tibairya now controlled access to the city for fishermen and herdsmen. Water was plentiful, but they had a large populace that relied on them for food. A populace whose loyalty was already shaky to nonexistent. It worried her. Summer had just begun. *The war* had just begun.

The third knock on the door was louder still. "Patience!" Elan bent with a groan and used the stub of the floundering candle to light another. She stretched her back again as she shuffled to the door. "Who's there?" she asked before lifting the bar.

"Captain Malvius sent me." The words came in unaccented Hellainic.

Elan opened the door and raised the candle. Even though she was all but certain who was there, it was startling to see the boy so out of place. "Agoraki?" Actually, Ago was hardly a boy anymore. The lad was as tall as a Tibairyan legionnaire—meaning just half a head shorter than her.

Ago took in her bloody tunic and his expression grew alarmed. His own clothes, and face, were filthy. "Sorry to disturb you, Captain. Are you all right?"

Elan stepped aside and tipped her head, inviting him in. "I'm fine, and I'm no captain. Just a soldier."

The lad entered but stood eyeing her warily. "What should I call you, ma'am?"

"Gods, not ma'am. How about Elan?"

"Yes, ma'am. I mean, Elan." Ago furtively scanned the drab chamber, taking in her rumpled bedding and half-finished bowl and cup. "Again, forgive the intrusion."

Elan was too tired to be delicate. "How'd you get here and what do you want?"

Her brusqueness had the desired effect. "I snuck in through a sewage drain that leads from the base of the city's north wall to the Straits. I have a message for Captain Herodes from Captain Malvius. But he told me to deliver it to you first."

"Well, that explains the smell you dragged in. Why me?"

Ago shrugged. "I suppose Cap thought you might help things go... more smoothly."

This couldn't be good. "Tell me," she said.

❧

ELAN SETTLED back in the cushioned chair. May as well get comfortable. She'd come knowing they would meet resistance. She knew the man well enough to know he would need time to work it through. Herodes paced the floor of the anax's formal chambers. "Damn it, Elan. My orders are to hold this city, to keep the imperials out of the Straits. No matter the cost." Herodes turned to Elan. "Would you really have me abandon those orders? On the word of a Hellain boy?"

Elan glanced at Ago. He stood with his head down and his hands clasped before him. "He's no mere Hellain," she said, "and he's no boy. Agoraki is a young man, and he's proven his loyalty. He saved my daughter's life." The lad straightened, lifting his chin. "No need to cross blades with the messenger, Herodes."

"Still, what proof do we have of any of this? Even if Malvius believes it?"

"May I speak, Captain?" Ago asked. Herodes scowled, making the young man wait a moment before giving him a single nod. "On my way here, I saw a man in the market square. I recognized him from Thrakius during the occupation. He's one of Isidros's fighters. The man had a group gathered 'round. A few of them looked familiar, too, but most just seemed like townsmen. Looked like they were trying to rile folk. Seems to confirm at least part of what Cap's heard."

Herodes stopped pacing, clearly bristling. "It matters not who gets riled. None of these city toughs would have a chance against my men."

Elan shook her head. "It *does* matter."

He turned his scowl on her. "Not to me. Not in deciding this. We still hold this city."

Elan tilted her head. "True. We hold the city. But you'd be wise to recognize that we're outnumbered inside these walls. By at least ten to one. If pressed, most of the ten will be more loyal to the anax. We already knew the nobility here opposed us, even before we got this tip that Isidros is maneuvering here again. Isidros is a man who always plays the odds. Makes sense that he disappeared when we arrived and that he would throw in with the imperials once the mobile reserve was sent. Also makes sense that he would never venture to cast his rune stones till we were under siege. Which begs us to remember that we're also outnumbered three to one by the Tibairya outside. We best believe that every local knows it, too. Once the mobile reserve's assault on the city begins, anyone inside who wishes us ill can easily help to tip the balance. The city has five gates, and we have to defend them all, which reduces our strength. The locals know the city better than any of us. All they need do is shoot and scoot. Or worse."

Herodes frowned. "What's worse than shooting us in the back?"

Elan shrugged. "A well-timed, well-placed fire. Nightshade in one of the wells. Those are right off the top of my head. Isidros can be pretty crafty."

"But why?" Herodes asked. "Do these people really love the empire so?"

"Gods, no. But they sure don't love us."

"When we arrived, we were welcomed by cheering throngs."

"Throngs that welcomed the opportunity to shirk their obligations and maybe do some looting. An opportunity that we provided. Think about it. The looting is done. Obligations tend to hang around. We're still foreigners. We brought war to their doorsteps. We've disrupted their lives. We're also the ones who shut down a profitable slave market. Now we're the ones rationing their daily grain. We sure haven't made their lives any easier. Not lately, anyway."

"Even if we believe it's true, even if we decide it's best to go, what then? We would still have to fight our way out of here." Herodes started pacing again. "Even if we manage to get to the shore intact, how can we be sure the damned imperial navy won't discover Malvius's ships and chase them off before we can get ourselves aboard? It takes time to get an army onto ships. Particularly the horses."

"Forgive me, Captain, but Cap—I mean, Captain Malvius—says there'll be no time for horses. In regard to the navy, Cap's planning on having a pair of ships patrolling each end of the Straits while we load. They'll be under orders to lure any approaching Tiberians into a chase, if need be."

Herodes stopped. "Both ends? Why the Pontean end? We control that."

Ago shook his head. "Cap's sure the eastern fleet will soon be coming back around. He says the Tibes will start putting pressure on the comings and goings from Megaria. Especially now that they're sure to take Nicomedya. They outnumber the Sass stationed in Megaria, and both sides know it. Cap says it's a matter of time before the navy is sailing free across the Pontean, even if they don't control the Straits. He wants his ships back to port in Thrakius before then. He hopes you'll be on them. But he says he'll understand if you prefer to be dropped at Megaria instead."

Herodes stopped and frowned. "Would the imperials really risk widening the war by attacking the dah's navy?"

Ago shrugged. "Cap says we can't put too much trust in the Sass to keep them off of us. He sure doesn't. He says he figured they'd put on a fine show as long as it was low risk. But that they'll only worry about saving their own arses once the naval jostling starts back up. The Sass hate the empire, but the dah loves his ships. Top-load that cargo with the fact that they've got no real love for any of us—Hellain nor Gottari."

Herodes pressed the butts of his palms against his eyes. "Oh, this is just wonderful. Not only am I to surrender a city and our position at the mouth of the Straits, I'm supposed to hand over hundreds of our finest warhorses, too?"

Elan felt for him. "There is a bright side. Going out on foot will make fighting our way through their lines easier. We can go through the north gate and head for the shore. Their siege lines are manned lightest there. They'll expect us to go for one of the roads or the harbor. Once we're on the shore, the dunes will give our archers the height to cover us as we get aboard."

Herodes slumped, looking ill. "How in the gods' names are we going to tell the king?"

Elan shook her head. "I'm not sure how *you're* going to tell him. But I'd be sure to mention that losing a city and some horses is a damn sight better than losing a city, some horses, and an army."

CHAPTER 3
OF DUBIOUS INTENT

"When she first entered our lives, I held doubts about the intentions of the courtesan Harma. I presumed that her machinations were preconceived and that her motives were selfish. In time, I came to see that—although Harma was far from dim—there was a girlish naiveté about her. She lacked devious intent at the onset simply because she'd yet to grasp the possibilities.

Much that came to pass may have been due to Mistress Harma's lack of demureness, self-esteem, and restraint. Regardless of the starting mindset, along with Lady Harma's rising fortunes came a much more dubious set of intentions."—Brin Bright Eyes, Saga of Dania

"Ouch!" Harma twisted around to snatch the wrist of the hand that held the hairbrush. She dug her nails into soft skin. "I told you not to yank, woman."

"Apologies, Mistress," Eupheme brayed in the awful accented Gottari that Harma made her use. Harma's father had insisted that she begin learning and using the language of the locals from the moment she'd arrived here. Hence, her Hellainic was better by a

26

bowshot than this mule's Gottari. But why should Harma be the one to sound dumb?

Harma released the woman and noticed the red marks she'd left. She turned back to the looking glass, trying not to smile. The mule's very next stroke through Harma's freshly washed hair snagged and pulled. Harma leapt to her feet and rounded on her. Eupheme recoiled, but then stuck out her proud, hairy chin. "Is too tangled," the mule said. It was growing clear that either her new serving woman was far from sorry or utterly incompetent. Or both.

"Just give it to me." Harma held out her hand, and Eupheme spitefully slapped the brush into her palm. "Go and fetch my frock," Harma commanded as she sat to pull her hair to the front to brush it.

"Your frock, Mistress? Which one?"

"You know damn well which one. The green one. I had you wash it just for today."

The mule stiffened. "You think that one best, Mistress?"

Harma eyed the woman. Eupheme clearly felt no loyalty or gratitude. But Harma was beginning to suspect the mule actually held ill will. Still, she wasn't about to let this foreigner spoil the most triumphant day of her life. "Why wouldn't it be? It's one of the most expensive in Thrakius."

Eupheme puckered her wrinkly lips. "Green one is for courting maidens. Not betrothed lady."

A knock at the door was instantly followed by its opening. "Your wine, Mistress." Unsurprisingly, it was the bold kitchen minx, Apontia. Eupheme looked away and set her jaw.

As the younger woman poured her a cup from the flagon, Harma watched Eupheme twitching in the reflection. "Just what are you implying, Eupheme?"

"You have won, Mistress. The king, he weds you. Why gift the others with rumor?"

"Is there anything else, Mistress?" Apontia asked.

"Yes—take away these dishes and the breakfast tray."

"Yes, Mistress." Apontia set about gathering her breakfast leavings.

"All I seek is to look my best on my bonding day. What of it? I can't summon a care for what the old cows say." Eupheme seemed to be waiting for Apontia to leave. Harma pressed, to annoy her if nothing else. "What sort of rumor do you mean, anyway?"

Eupheme's gaze met hers in the looking glass. "That frock, Mistress—it shows much."

Harma laughed. "As do all of my frocks." She pushed her breasts together with the top of her arms and leaned forward to demonstrate.

Eupheme bristled. "The gods know it is so. I speak of the cut to the form." She gestured at her own midsection and hips with both hands. "Close enough to..." The mule glanced at Apontia and sealed her lips.

Harma didn't care if Apontia heard. Actually, she rather preferred the Sassanadi minx to this old mule. "To what? Speak up."

Eupheme mustered her courage. "To show the swell, Mistress." She gestured with her hands, indicating a round belly. "If they see, they may believe..." The Hellain glanced at her Sass counterpart again.

Harma stood and faced her. "Believe what? That I'm pregnant? I am. And it's the king's—of that you can rest assured. There. Have I properly squashed your rumors? Does that spoil your fun, Eupheme?" Apontia snorted a laugh and swiftly stifled it. Harma smiled and gave the Sass a wink. She'd gone so long without showing, she was a bit relieved her condition was becoming apparent. It certainly helped to mark her claim. It was better than having them all think she was simply getting fat.

Eupheme bowed her head and switched to braying in Hellainic. "I only meant that you wouldn't want anyone questioning the king's reasons... Or your motives, Mistress."

Harma was in the middle of deciding whether to slap the woman's face when the Sass girl piped up. "All the more reason to wear the green one, Mistress. I would." Both women turned to Apontia, who was now holding the full tray. "The frock looks lovely on you. And it'll give the scrawny one something to fret about. As you say, Mistress, let the old cows moo. They already do. The mooing will only grow louder, no matter what you do, yes? Besides, it's mostly because they're all jealous. You have the king. I say let them go fuck themselves, same as always."

Eupheme's hand flew to cover her open mouth and Harma burst into laughter.

Apontia smirked and curtsied while balancing the tray. "Is there anything else, Mistress?"

"Eupheme, take the tray down," Harma said, still wiping the tears from her eyes. "Apontia, stay and help me put on my green frock."

HARMA LED her new handmaiden down the stairway. Apontia had the salt offering and the candle for the ceremony. The Sass would be a fine stand-in for the ceremony's maternal role. Apontia was a mother, after all. Indeed, she seemed to have better maternal instincts than Harma's birth mother.

It went without saying that Eupheme was wrong about the frock. The fabric hardly pulled across the swell of Harma's belly. In spite of it all, Harma had agreed to Apontia's suggestion to carry a fur wrap draped across her elbows and held closed across her midsection. The Sassanadi woman had made a good point, saying that you couldn't be too careful. If Harma needed to sit publicly, for instance, the drape of the fabric would be ruined. Although she didn't plan on sitting before she was lying. By then, the fit of the dress would be moot.

The incident upstairs had thrown the last pelt on the scale. The old mule would no longer haul. Harma had had enough of Eupheme's attitude. She would speak to the head of the kitchens after her bonding ceremony to demand that the Sassanadi girl be permanently reassigned as her handmaid. For her part, Apontia seemed suitably delighted by the prospect. Which demonstrated a far superior attitude to any of the haughty Hellain servants Harma had gone through. They acted as if they thought themselves the masters. Or at least secretly considered themselves superior. Harma was far too clever to miss it.

And Eupheme was the worst of them all. She was almost as dreadful as Harma's mother had been. Thank the gods *that* woman wasn't here to ruin her day.

On the final landing, Harma paused to straighten her skirts over her hips and tug the neckline down. She pinched her own cheeks. "How's my lip paint?" she asked Apontia.

"Flawless."

She patted her newly tied hair. "The hair?"

"Not a lock out of place. You look beautiful, Mistress. You make the perfect bride, yes?" Apontia's smile was forced, but Harma didn't mind. While she didn't speak Gottari—yet—at least she didn't judge or put on airs. It was enough. Better than Hellain condescension in broken Gottari.

Harma made the turn to face the last flight of stone steps to the level of the high hall... And no one was waiting for her below. The entire balcony outside the high hall below was empty and silent. Her perfect entrance to her own bonding was ruined.

She hoisted her skirt and hurried down the stairs and then across the landing to the handrail. A lone servant strode across the otherwise empty main hall below where her bonding ceremony was supposed to take place.

Teavar and Ermanaric stood at either side of the closed doors of the high hall. Apontia stood wide-eyed at the rail. Harma strode to the oversized guardians. "Where is everyone?"

The giants both stared over her head, willfully ignoring her. She stepped to the taller one—the one she'd known almost all her life. "Teavar? I asked a question."

The huge man sighed. "The king sent them away." When he finally looked down, she saw pity in his gaze. Harma would *not* be pitied. Not today.

Harma started to reach for the door latch, but Teavar stepped in front of her. "It's not a good idea, lass. Things are about to happen."

"Things? Besides my bonding, you mean?" What *things* could be so important that he neglected to inform his bride that her bonding was off?

She actually thought she saw Teavar's cheeks pinking under his bushy beard. "The king is waiting for an arrival. One with vital tidings. You'd best go back to your chambers."

She opened her mouth to speak and swallowed back a sob. "But… this is *my* day."

Teavar looked away again. "I'm sorry," he managed.

Harma pushed past him. "I don't need an apology. I need an explanation." She hurried to work the latch and slip inside. Her attempt to slam the door on the giants was blocked by a boot. She sped her step, sensing close pursuit. Vahldan sat at the end of the table with a map spread before him. He had that weasel of an Elli-Frodei and several of the graybeard lions gathered around him, posturing, murmuring, and pointing.

"Forgive the intrusion, my king," Teavar called from behind her.

"Not now, Harma," Vahldan said. His tone was outrageously harsh, considering the circumstance.

"Not now? But, my king, you *do* recall what was scheduled for today, don't you?"

"Of course I do." Vahldan waved a hand like he was sending away the bearer of a tray of something he didn't care for. "We'll have to postpone."

Harma halted with a stomp. "But… I made myself ready. My hair…"

"Thunar's storms, woman, it's just a formality. No need to fuss. We'll do it tomorrow."

A formality? Her bonding was a mere procedural necessity to

him. It felt like her innards had melted to liquid and were beginning to boil. Couldn't he see what this meant to her? She bit back about six retorts. She knew each of them would paint her as a shrew to the others in the hall. Her mother's behavior had taught her again and again how men responded to women who spoke their minds. Especially when it crossed them. She would not become her mother.

Vahldan went back to studying his map. She slumped. The graybeards continued to glance at her. Harma felt her face crumpling. Teavar laid an oversized mitt on her shoulder. It was gently done, but she twisted to pull herself away. He held up his hands in surrender, his eyes sad. More pity. "I'll leave on my own," she said, spinning and heading for the exit.

Before she was halfway there, the doors burst open. Ermanaric led the way. "They've arrived, my king."

Harma was stunned by who followed. "I came as you commanded, my king. But begging your forgiveness, I must be brief. My army needs me."

"Papa?" Harma rushed to hug him. "Thank Freya, you're safe." Herodes stiffened. He returned her embrace but patted her back to hasten her to release him. She couldn't. "Oh, Papa, this means you'll be here for my bonding ceremony." For once, something had gone right!

Another man came in behind her father. A Hellain. Harma had seen him before. Their gazes met; the Hellain smiled. Herodes all but pushed Harma away. "My king, I brought along Captain Malvius as he intends to depart again straightaway. I, of course, would sail with him, with your permission, my king. The foe will likely be—"

Vahldan stood. "For you there is no hurry, Cousin." Harma knew Vahldan well enough to sense he was quite cross. Apparently with her father.

Herodes strode toward the king, leaving Harma standing with the Hellain. "My king, I am all but certain the Tibairya will soon move against Megaria..."

Vahldan held up a silencing hand. "I will not hear another word about Megaria before I've heard what in the gods' names happened in Nicomedya."

Yes, Vahldan was most definitely cross. Restraining rage, even.

Harma felt eyes on her. She looked to find the Hellain captain staring. He offered a resigned smile and waggled his brows. Was the man trying to amuse her? Was he flirting? In the midst of a fight between her betrothed and her father? On what was supposed to have been her bonding day? The nerve.

She frowned and looked away, felt herself flushing. Her father's shame was palpable. It somehow made her feel ashamed. "My king, we thwarted several of their attempts, but they—"

Vahldan slammed a hand on the table. "Damn it, Herodes! I gave you one simple command. Hold Nicomedya. Keep them out of the Straits. Now I want to hear it from you. What came of it?" Her father drooped. Vahldan stepped in close, eyes blazing. "Well?"

"Nicomedya is lost, my king," Herodes said softly. "I... failed you."

Harma's sudden intake of breath was audible in the silent chamber.

"My king." The Hellain captain broke the taut silence and took a step forward. Perhaps the man would speak on her father's behalf. "I feel I really should return to Megaria without delay." So much for that hope. "I'd like to sail at dawn, and there is much yet to attend to today. With your leave, of course. Megaria's supply needs are great, and I smell a storm brewing in the west. Which makes me even less sure what General Vernius will do next."

The crazed smolder in Vahldan's eyes dissipated as he turned from her father to the Hellain. "You'll see to the horses as well?"

"I have only four ships in port. We'll take all we can, my king."

Vahldan nodded. "And Rodulf's men and their gear?"

"They were already mustering on the docks when we left to come here. With any luck, they should be in Megaria by nightfall tomor-row. The next morn at the latest."

"Fine work, Malvius. Go with my thanks. Those are for you to take." The king pointed to the end of the table. "The purse is yours and the packet is for Arnegern."

The Hellain bowed his head and stepped to the table. The purse gave a faint jingle. It was laden with coin. The man stowed it in his belt pouch and put the packet under his arm before turning to leave. This Malvius character actually stopped to face Harma and smiled. He seemed unable to recognize the mood of the hall. "Perhaps, my king," he began, still smiling at her, "I should escort your lovely betrothed out, that you all might speak without fear of distressing her." Malvius bowed to Herodes. "With her father's permission, of course."

Alarmingly, her father agreed without hesitation. "Yes, that would be helpful," he said.

"Thank you again, Malvius," Vahldan said, doubling the insult.

Facing away from the others, the audacious interloper proffered his arm. His russet eyes shone with mirth. Harma glanced at the Gottari men. They all stood waiting for her to leave. She tipped her nose up and took the foreigner's arm. Gods, the man was shorter than her! She stepped briskly to make it clear he was not guiding her. Indeed, he struggled to keep up. Teavar eyed them as he and Ermanaric closed the doors behind the four of them.

Harma wondered just what this little Hellain sailor was up to. Obviously something. As soon as the doors latched, she snatched her hand away and rounded on him. "Distressing me?"

The man remained unruffled and amused. Still, his expression was not unkind. "Forgive me, my lady, but it does seem a distressing day. For all of us—particularly for your father. Worst of all, I understand it was to be your wedding day. A day like this is one no bride should be forced to endure. Particularly one so lovely as you."

"What day this is to me or whether I am distressed is none of your concern, sir."

Her retort only seemed to increase his mirth. "Untrue! I know we have only just officially met, at last. But I assure you, Lady Harma, that from here forward, should I even suspect your distress, my concern will be unavoidable. Whether you are willing to acknowledge it or not, I shall always be at your service." He bowed with the flair of a mummer.

The little show actually knocked her off balance. The only retort she could manage was, "Your concern is duly noted, Captain."

"It's the most I could hope for." Malvius's white teeth flashed. "Or perhaps I should say it's a start." He really was flirting. "I must now leave, but I beg you to summon me to your every whim, Lady Harma. From today forward."

"I am not yet a lady of the palace, Captain. And I assure you that no whim I might have would require the summoning of a man I scarcely know."

"I regret to differ, as you are among the most ladylike I have met within these walls. And that is saying much, for I used to live here." He bowed his head. "I pray your whims will change as we come to know one another better." He spun and strode to the stairs.

Harma felt herself flushing and checked to see if anyone was looking. And there he was, staring right at her: Teavar. Surely the giant hadn't heard any of that. Had he?

Harma kept herself from hurrying as she strode to the stairway to head back upstairs. She discretely looked down into the entry hall before the view was lost to her. Malvius was there, craning to watch her ascend. He smiled and raised a hand. She looked away and kept going.

At the next platform, she met up with Apontia. The Sass girl was wearing a smirk. Had she been watching their little interaction? "Not a word," Harma said.

Apontia bowed her head and fell in beside her. "As you wish. My lady."

Vernius had to admit it, the dried sage that his adjutant Nicandros burned had driven the mildew smell from his new chambers in the

Nicomedyan armory. Or perhaps it had simply covered it over. Either way, it was an improvement. His orders to have the entire armory and barracks scrubbed had rid the place of the moldering whiff the barbarians had left behind.

The mobile reserve had regained control of the entire city. The guard assignments and patrol rotations were set. The gates, temple, and market had all reopened. Order was restored.

He could finally get going on his overdue reports. Not to mention replying to a month's worth of correspondence. Most officers in the militum utilized scribes, but Vernius preferred writing reports and letters himself. His father had never trusted scribes. For him it was more than mere distrust. He'd also learned that misinterpretation led to problems. Writing for oneself offered control. In the militum, information was a commodity and often a useful tool. He preferred keeping very close control of the information he possessed and the means by which he sought and gathered more.

His top priority today was to use every tool in striving to delay the inevitable. The emperor was growing more insistent about traveling to the region. Mycanius was anxious to appear at the head of a victorious army. The man was already picturing a parade of barbarian captives being led to the hill in Medicia to the cheers of an adoring crowd. The fact that the mobile reserve had yet to achieve a definitive victory seemed no more than an inconvenient detail as far as Mycanius was concerned.

Vernius had to walk a narrow beam, first by convincing his superiors that it was still far too dangerous to come, but also that he had everything in hand—that certain victory lay upon the horizon. Preferably before the next hiatus, though he hated to commit to it. After all, it had taken the mobile reserve the entire spring and well into summer just to take Nicomedya. Not to mention the accumulating cost. It wasn't just time that had been spent. He had to admit, his casualty numbers were alarming by any standard. As were the losses of equipment. Neptune's mercy, the navy had even lost a bireme in this endeavor, much to the naval command's chagrin.

Taken as a whole, Vernius knew his standing in Medicia was far from solid. His Excellency was far from the most patient or practical man. Vernius could only imagine how tenuous his command actually was, especially since he'd allowed his sought-for prize—the bulk of the Gottari army—to slip through the net of their siege.

Vernius would not deceive. Nor would he beg for leniency. And he'd never stooped to sycophancy. He'd long ago vowed he would never be critical of the emperor—not even in private. Nor would he display resentment. He'd learned from his father's mistakes. When it came to dealing with the imperial throne, and its underlying bureaucracy, better to do one's duty and flow with the current than to swim against a tempestuous tide of royal politics. Even when it seemed there were those who felt the same resistance to the flow. He knew how deadly that game could swiftly become.

Most any punishment, including demotion, would be better than what his father had received. Vernius was still dealing with the consequences of legacy. Due to his father's defiance, the entire family estate remained in the precarious balance.

The lessons were clear. In Tiberian administrative affairs, justice was subjective. Right was a matter of perspective. Submission to passion was folly. Truth was left to the whim of the final report filed. If Vernius strayed, that report would not be his. Stances in the name of honor that flew in the face of consensus were not just naïve but failures born of a weak will.

Vernius was little more than a few sentences into his report when the knock at the door came. "I warned you about this, Nicandros," he called without looking up.

The door opened anyway. "Forgive me, my lord, but I fear you would be angrier still if I failed to interrupt for this."

"Your life hangs in the balance," he said without betraying a hint of sarcasm.

"It's the anax, my lord."

"They've found him?"

"Actually, he's here. He wishes to speak with you." For almost a fortnight, his men had sought the slippery Hellain noble. Now that the security of the man's city was reestablished, he shows up. Typical. Entitled Hellain ass. Vernius wished, not for the first time, that he could simply ignore the old Pontean nobility. But unfortunately, these families still carried considerable clout within the imperial bureaucracy. Mostly due to the generational privilege and wealth they managed to cling to. The partnership helped to perpetuate a meritless and self-sustaining system built to administer pointless activity—mainly fêtes and banquets. He hated them not because of the waste. There would always be bureaucratic waste. He hated them because they knew they were beyond his reach.

He was tempted to make the ass wait. But he doubted it would help his case, and it might even be risky. This was an eel that might actually slip away again. There were too many unanswered questions, too many unconfirmed rumors. Plus, there was one lingering issue that burned inside Vernius day and night—one that this man may be able to illuminate.

He reminded himself that duty came first. It never paid to reveal anything one cared about to men such as this. "Bring him in," he said.

"Yes, Lord General."

Vernius focused on his work as the ass was brought in, sparing him only a swift once-over. He left the man standing while he gathered his thoughts as he scrawled meaningless notes on a letter he'd received. Patience would guide him to truth.

Of course Isidros's dress was ostentatious, of Peshtari silk, no less. He was graying but handsome, with a trimmed beard that Vernius guessed was worn to camouflage his burgeoning chin waddle. The man wasn't overweight. Just soft. As all such men were. Standing here before him would be the most strenuous part of the ass's day. Yes, the Nicomedyan anax had the look of being well bred —a look that was painstakingly cultivated.

In other words, the ass was also a fop.

The fop started fidgeting. Good enough. If Vernius let him stay too long, his ridiculous perfume would linger. Without looking up, he said, "Something I can do for you, Anax Isidros?"

"Ah, good. You already know me. As I know you, Lord General Vernius Stallicus." Vernius raised his hard gaze. "If only by reputation, of course," Isidros amended. "Which takes care of the first reason I came. I wanted to introduce myself as well as offer you my gratitude and my congratulations on your victory. And offer you my services, of course." Isidros glanced around the shabby quarters. "Which includes the use of my home. At the palace. I can offer you and at least a dozen of your officers accommodations that are... Shall we say, significantly more accommodating?" The fop laughed at his own arrogant joke.

Vernius glared and Isidros fidgeted again. "Tell me, Anax. Where is it you've been?"

Isidros covered his anxiety with a smooth smile. "My ships have arrived in port only this morning, Lord General. I came as soon as I could."

Vernius leaned back. "Frankly, I've already learned more than that from the harbormaster's report." He nodded to a stack of reports on the table. "Could you elaborate?"

"I've been at sea, in the Pontean, Lord General. We left the city before the Gottari arrived and have been unable to return. We alerted the garrison and the bureaucracy as soon as we learned of the coming barbarians. Ask anyone. When word came of it, we celebrated your victory and returned as fast as we could. Even in our haste we took a great risk in passing under the catapults of Megaria. We were forced to do so by night."

Vernius studied his posturing rival. Clearly each of them wanted something. For starters, Vernius wanted to grab him and shake him and didn't mind if the fop sensed it. Patience. The anax was likely more formidable than he seemed. He was a trader—a negotiator with ample practice in thinking on his feet. Vernius guessed the thing his rival wanted most was to be absolved, to be allowed back into the good graces of the imperial apparatus. But absolved of what exactly? That was the question. The anax operated in the shadows, but just how dark had he gone during this uprising?

"In fact, I *have* asked after you," Vernius began. "Oddly, there is a murky portion of the account of your flight from the invasion and your absence throughout the war thus far."

"Which portion is that?"

Vernius gave him a toothy smile. "Where, exactly, have you been since you left port?"

Isidros's gaze narrowed. "My destinations were many. But I suspect what you are keen to hear is a confirmation that I was, indeed, in Thrakius. For several weeks, in fact."

Vernius sought to be casual. "The home port of our current foe?"

The anax stepped to the lone window. "Thankfully, the thug king left with the bulk of his army in tow. Their absence allowed my men to seize the palace."

"You seized the Thrakian palace," Vernius deadpanned.

The fop raised his chin. "Proudly so. With every intention of holding it for His Eminence, of course. Indeed, it was only through the surprise arrival of Vahldan's Sassanadi allies that we were expelled. Their attack seemed to have been simultaneous with Vahldan's attack on Megaria. This additional treachery forced us into ongoing flight. We were left without a home port while we waited."

"Waited while my men bled on these shores in order to liberate your city."

Isidros pressed his lips tight and bowed his head. "A sacrifice for which all Nicomedyans are truly grateful, Lord General."

"Tell me, Anax Isidros. Whatever prompted you to undertake such a risky venture in Thrakius? How did you come to suspect you stood even a chance at success?"

"I was invited. By someone who knew exactly what she was doing."

"She?" Vernius stood, unable to quell his racing heart.

Isidros's smug air returned. "I speak of the rightful anax of

Thrakius, of course. The Lady Ligaia, daughter and heir of the slain Anax Decebius. Have you heard of her?"

The way the man asked it revealed that he knew the answer. "I have," Vernius said. His mouth had gone dry. He feared his expression and his wobbly legs would betray him so he returned to his chair and said no more.

"An amazing woman," Isidros said. "After they killed her husband and father, the Gottari made a slave of her. One can only guess what she endured. But Lady Ligaia came through, stronger and more determined than ever."

"She invited you?" It was all Vernius could manage.

"Through a series of secret missives. You would be amazed by her command of the situation. Both being the heirs to anaxships, we'd known each other all of our lives, naturally. I always found her alluring. But it was in our moment of reunion, when she revealed her plan and pleaded for my aid, that I fell in love with her. Gods, she was a marvel."

Vernius's chest clenched. "Was?" Isidros raised his brow, inquiring. "You said Lady Ligaia *was* a marvel."

The fop composed a rehearsed expression of sorrow. "Have you not heard? I fear Lady Ligaia was killed, Lord General. Murdered by the savages during their violent retaking of the Thrakian palace."

Vernius slumped and stared at the sunlit grime on the window-panes—seeing nothing but her face, standing on the quay as his ship glided out across the Thrakian harbor. She'd implored him to stay with her. When he'd refused, she'd begged to come with him. And he'd left her.

Had she known then that she had been with child? If so, why wouldn't she have told him? Had she feared his response? Had she wished to avoid making him feel obligated? That seemed most likely. If he'd known, would he have been willing to embrace the scandal to see it through?

Then there was the biggest question of all: What had become of his son?

Vernius gathered himself again. He glanced at his rival, whose glee over having gained the upper hand was barely veiled. The fop had known he held the higher ground since he arrived.

"And her brother?" Vernius's voice hardly worked. He cleared his throat. "What came of him?"

"Malvius had already been disowned by their father, of course. He's since gone rogue. The villain fell in with the barbarians long ago. In fact, he was in on their sacking of his home city. Ligaia held him personally responsible for the deaths of her husband and father. Malvius serves the savages still. It was he who secured the Gottari alliance with the Sassanadi dah, which led to the death of his sister—the last remaining member of his family. The man is a monster."

Sorrow he could not reveal constricted Vernius's chest, squeezing his lungs. As he sought to regulate his breathing, he frantically sought for a plausible excuse to inquire over Ligaia's son. How might he happen to know of such a child? Before he thought of anything, the fop went on. "The only small note of solace I have is that my lovely Ligaia honored me by becoming my wife before her life was so brutally cut short. I can, at least, restore the company and the palace that she loved so much to their former glory. Once this mess with the barbarians is finished, of course."

Ah, this was what the man wanted, why he'd come. It wasn't mere atonement or absolution. Isidros came to secure the enterprise and family fortune that he'd risked so much to seize. And he would tattoo the brother as an outlaw to safeguard it. The anax was laying claim to what he considered his spoils of this forsaken war. How tidy for him that Ligaia was gone.

Vernius could do little more than glare. Isidros pushed his advantage. "Which brings us full circle, Lord General. As I said when I arrived, I came to offer my services. Perhaps you now better see why. I can think of no greater justice than your triumph."

"I do see," Vernius managed through gritted teeth. His men's blood was being spent to ensure this sniveling scoundrel's future profit.

"Then with my mission accomplished, I shall take my leave. Please, Lord General, do not hesitate to call upon me." Just like that, the fop turned to leave.

Vernius briefly considered arresting him, locking him up. Alas, it would only lead to trouble. The fop's connections were as good or better than Vernius's. Holding him would be little more than a temporary nuisance. Either way, the man wasn't going anywhere. After all, Isidros had but to wait in order to regain his prize.

Vernius's longing spurred him to impulse. "Wait," he called. Isidros stopped at the door. Vernius had little more to lose. "About Lady Ligaia. Rumor claims she had a bastard—a son."

Isidros regained his rehearsed sadness. "Ah, yes. You are clearly well informed, Lord General. The boy calls himself Agoraki. She hid him in the palace kitchens, among the help. I fear the boy has eluded my grasp. But it's far worse than that, for, like his uncle, the boy too has fallen under the sway of the savages. I myself know Agoraki to be responsible for his own mother's murder. Indeed, several of my men will attest to the fact that she died by his very hand." Isidros shook his head and tsked. "But fear not, Lord General. Once this young murderer is captured, as I'm sure he will be, I shall personally see to it that he's properly punished."

Could it be true? Or was his son just another potential threat to this schemer—another rival who was best tattooed as another villain?

The fop opened the door, his smug smile reappearing. "After all, this bastard can legally be claimed as my heir. With that sort of an attachment to my good name, I cannot allow such a murderous barbarian lover to flaunt justice now, can I?"

The anax bowed his head and closed the door, leaving Vernius in renewed grief for his beloved, terrified for his only son, and utterly unable to challenge a word of the despicable fop's testimony.

CHAPTER 4
SEIZING DESTINY

"*I am near certain that when Amaga first gave voice to it, her threat to raise her son as the Wulthus heir was merely meant to provoke her husband. Few gave the threat much credence, as Gottari custom named heirs from the paternal side.*

But even empty threats can spawn dangerous ideas. Ideas with the power to change the course of history."—Brin Bright Eyes, *Saga of Dania*

VAHLDAN TOOK the steps two at a time, staying ahead of Belgar. He didn't want to talk anymore but he sensed Belgar still coming behind. The man simply wouldn't let it go. He got to his residence, stepped in, and slammed the door. The knock came a heartbeat after.

"Go away."

"Please, my king. May I finish?"

"I thought you were finished. I know I am."

Belgar opened the door and put his head through. "Please..." Vahldan ignored him. Belgar stepped in. "Cousin," Belgar tried. "We've known each other for how long?"

Vahldan plopped down on the chaise, still unwilling to look. "I'm not sure. Years." Belgar's persistence was stirring the ugliness within him. He stared out the terrace doors, seeking calm. "Many years," he admitted. "Long enough that you should know how angry I am."

"True," Belgar said, sounding wary. "I do. And in spite of it, I feel I must ask. In all of those years, have I ever offered advice that wasn't in your best interests? Or in the best interests of our people?"

"Give me a moment," Vahldan said.

"Please, trust that even if I have, today I am certain of this advice. You must reconsider your decree. Herodes is as loyal as anyone who followed you here. He is completely devoted to you and to our cause. Just as his men are devoted to him. Think of the example this sets."

"I am!" Vahldan erupted. "The example it sets is the entire reason for the decree. Can you not see it? I gave the man one simple command. Don't you see how bad this is? His failure is what cannot be tolerated. The Tibairya have a foothold. Herodes handed them a win. If they're winning, we're losing—it's as simple as that. The Straits are everything."

"I do see. But we shall all face the setback together. As we have faced everything till now. Our cousin did what he thought he must. He did so in order to save our people's army. Consider how much worse it might have been."

Vahldan shook his head. "If we accept failing together, if we simply accept defeat and continue to retreat, the war is already lost. Then what?" He would not flee to Dania as a loser. He would never seek shelter from the wolves.

His cousin hardened his gaze. "Then we fight on. Together."

He couldn't accept such a simplistic take. "There can be no more retreat. There can only be victory. Nothing less is acceptable. We must hold the Straits. If we lose them, then all of it was for nothing." Then Eldavar's death was for nothing. He simply couldn't let that be true.

"Megaria still stands, my king," Belgar said. "In order to defend Pontea, we shall need men like Herodes. Please don't send him back. There must be a way to punish him here."

"Gods afire, he should get worse for the loss of the horses alone! Perhaps some time with his wife and her wolf kin will remind him of what it means to be Amalus."

Belgar slumped, looking like a swatted puppy. "We shared a dream, long ago. We cousins. Nothing could've convinced us it would be otherwise. Nor could have come between us. Do you remember? Please say that you do."

Vahldan sighed. "All right. I'll come up with something less harsh. But he will be punished in a way that's visible to all."

Without a knock, the door to the servants' quarters flew open, almost hitting Belgar. Amaga barreled in, clearly ruffled. He'd been avoiding her for days. "Is it true?" she demanded. "You're still going through with this mockery of a bonding ceremony? Even after the disgrace of your little trollop's father?"

Belgar retreated to the entryway. "We can finish this later."

Vahldan held up a silencing hand to Amaga. "No need. Tell Herodes he is to leave only for the winter. I want him back here come spring." Belgar tilted his head. "Have him present himself in Danihem as an Amalus emissary to the longhouse." He looked at Amaga and added, "Remind our cousin of his value to Pontea and to our clan. Also remind him to return as soon as the passes clear as he has a grandson on the way."

"I shall, my king." Belgar bowed and closed the door behind him.

"It's true, then?" Amaga prompted.

"What, my bonding? Of course. It's not only true, it's sanctioned by the Elli-Frodei—a precedent set by King Eradaric."

"Ha! You mean sanctioned by your lapdog priest. Bonding with two women is an affront to the gods."

Vahldan went to the sideboard and poured from his flask into a cup. "Not true. Indeed, it's the gods who demand it."

"I won't stand for it," Amaga spat.

"Stand wherever you like. This is not yours to decide."

"The fuck-bunny's get will still be a bastard."

"He'll be my son, same as yours."

"You won't get away with this."

Vahldan laughed. "I'm the king. Of course I will."

Amaga scowled. "I know what you're up to. You seek to supplant your son yet again. But the goddess chose my womb to produce the first of the hundred Tutona kings, born of Urrinan." She pointed a trembling finger. "Hear me now. If you think to toy with the will of the gods, if you think to name an heir other than your firstborn, there is nothing that will save you from Freya's wrath."

"Ha! She's already named me doomed. What further curse can Freya lay upon me?"

"Only fools tempt the goddess." Amaga's sneer revealed her own inner ugliness.

Which caused his to flare. "Just as the fool who tempts a king? You just said it yourself, woman: Your son is the firstborn. You won! You should be satisfied. And silent. Be grateful for your victory and for the fact that you still have a home here."

"A home? Is that what you call this?" Amaga laughed. She sought to portray bravado but the fact that she was backing to the door spoiled the performance. "Send us away, then, little king. If you do, Thaedan will be raised as a Wulthus heir. You think you have any say in destiny? Pah." The vindictive bitch actually spat on his Saurian carpet. "The true king will ascend; it matters not what you do. In fact, I implore you to send us. That way Thaedan can preside over the Urrinan from Danihem while you flail on toward your precious doom."

Vahldan downed the last of the cup and slammed it down. He faced her and stood teetering on the verge of losing himself. Amaga hurried on to the door. He resisted the impulse to give chase. Once there she looked back, smug again. "You wish to tempt the goddess? Know this, lecher: You also curse all of those you ensnare in this heresy. Particularly every bastard that comes of your unchecked lewd impulses." Amaga laughed again, her eyes flaring with an other-worldly evil.

He took a step toward her. Amaga slammed the door and, of

course, the babe's bawling started up again. His temples throbbed. Gods, he had to have her moved to new quarters. As far from his as possible.

Harma hurried up the stairs toward the king's residence. Her father was being exiled back to Dania. Herodes presumed Harma would go with him. She'd seen his humiliation. As far as she knew, he remained unaware of her condition. Worse, he'd seemed pleased that she had yet to bond with Vahldan—that it got postponed. He obviously hoped to avert it.

Harma had no desire to disappoint or defy her father. But she would not let him make her feel small for having this babe. Nor would she stop until Vahldan made good on his vow.

More than anything, Harma was sure she would never step foot in Danihem again.

Nothing had ever been good enough for the damn she-wolves in Dania. The Amalus matrons of the palace were bad enough, but they had nothing on the Wulthus wives and crones. No matter what Harma had done, no matter how hard she'd tried, to them she'd been too forward, too loud, too candid, too giggly. She'd been too tall, her hair too red, her boobs too big, her dresses too tight. She'd been unserious, too comfortable with men. Too much the opposite of every one of the women who'd hovered around her in judgment.

Gods curse the Danian prudes with a life of cleaning mud from their heavy hems and sweat from their choking collars. No, she would not go back. Her child would not be a bastard.

Her father was going to ruin everything. She'd hoped to give Herodes the news of her pregnancy at the same time that she told him that she and the king were bonded—preferably several months afterward. By then, the starting point of her pregnancy would have been a murky bit of history.

The worse part was, Herodes was not alone in wanting to sabotage her life. Harma knew what the old guard of the Amalus were all whispering in Vahldan's ears—that this was an opportunity to send his little indiscretion packing along with the captain who'd failed him.

She had to make Vahldan understand. It wasn't just her reputation at stake. This was about his Amalus son!

As Harma made the turn to the last flight of stairs and started up, she heard the laughter. Palace enemy number one. Gods, even the laughter of the spooky witch sounded evil. Harma stopped short when the awful creature appeared, slamming the door to Vahldan's residence.

Harma stood frozen. Amaga's beady eyes latched onto her, twisting her mouth to a snarl.

Harma nearly turned and fled, but she simply wouldn't give the witch the satisfaction. They stood locked in a staring battle. A battle that Harma was alarmed to be losing. Normally she used her size to intimidate the waif, but it wasn't working from below her on the stairs.

Gods, she felt like a girl facing her prissy mother or another she-wolf, knowing there was no way to win.

Harma wondered if Amaga knew—not just about her pregnancy, but that her bonding had been postponed. Of course she did. Nothing could be kept secret in this place. It was why the witch looked so smug. Hateful as Amaga was, she actually had allies. Even within Vahldan's family. Harma had none. She suddenly realized that the scheming against her was not only well underway, but perpetrated by a vast network.

The waif's stranglehold was broken when the door to the servants' quarters opened. The squall of Amaga's sickly babe filled the stairwell; Kemella held him on her hip.

"There he is," Amaga sang, holding her hands out for the babe.

"What in the nine realms is going on?" Kemella asked.

Amaga spoke brightly as if to the child. "Nothing but the happy news that your papa has returned to his senses. That's right—your papa agrees that you shall ever be the first and only true heir; the first king of a hundred kingdoms, born of Urrinan."

The boy actually stopped crying and laughed as if in mocking delight.

Harma turned and fled.

Harma half expected to find her father's door under guard. Apontia claimed the palace rumor was that her father was under arrest. At first Harma was relieved to find the corridor outside his residence empty. But when it occurred to her that Herodes might be in the dungeon, she hurried to the door. She knocked but heard nothing. She tried the latch and found it unlocked.

The space was dim—darker than the fading twilight that glowed in the lone window. It wasn't so long ago that she had lived here, but the place already felt dank and confining. "Father? Are you here?"

Rather than an answer, a sigh came from the shadows. It gave her a start. She stared until her eyes adjusted. A familiar figure sat in the shadows, gazing out the window.

"Why are you sitting in the dark?" Harma went back into the corridor, lit a taper from the sconce, and used it to light the lamp on the sideboard.

Herodes blinked and squinted, then looked her up and down. She knew why. "It's true, then?"

Although he'd eyed her belly bump, Harma still wasn't sure which part he meant. She went on the offensive. "I was going to ask the same of you."

Herodes frowned. "Me? Everyone knows what's true of me. I lost Nicomedya. I failed."

"No. I wondered if it's true that you're giving up."

"Giving up? I just said I was defeated."

"Gods, not that," she retorted. "Armies retreat. Wars go on. What I'm asking is whether you're willingly going back to Dania."

"Of course I am." Her father hung his head. "It's better than I deserve."

"Don't be ridiculous."

"My punishment could've been much worse," he said.

Harma loomed over him. "So that's it? That's all you've got?"

"For Freya's sake, Harma, what do you want from me?"

"I want you to fight! Seize our destiny. Win!"

Herodes's eyes flared. Good. She'd roused him. "How?"

"By whatever means necessary. Isn't that what you've always done? What you taught me to do? Rest assured, it's what I've been doing. And I intend to continue."

Her father's gaze fell to her belly again. "Is this what I taught you? That's what you think you're doing—seizing destiny?" He radiated disapproval.

Harma's hands went to her bump. "No." She was right back to feeling like a little girl. It made her angry. "I mean, yes. I am striving for the life I want—for what I love."

"For what you *love*? How could you? The man is bonded. He's just become a father. You've dishonored me."

Harma knelt down before him. "It's not like that, Papa. Vahldan and I simply came to realize our love too late. He recognizes his mistake. He doesn't love her. Even you must see that. That witch has been using him for her own gain. She's been deceitful and Freya has punished her for it by delivering a sickly babe. The goddess shall reward me with the healthy heir that's been denied of our king. I know it. This will be the son of the prophecy—the real heir to Urrinan. Don't you see, Papa? Your grandson is meant for greatness."

Herodes's internal war could be seen on his face. Still, he shook his head. "It's not right."

Tears formed in Harma's eyes. She had to make him understand. She took his hand in hers. "It's like the story you always told me— about the first time you saw him. At the trial, when he was about to face Mighty Teavar. And everyone was sure that he would lose. You said it felt like the gods were speaking to you, through him, about the glory that would come. For our clan. For our people. You said Freya herself compelled you to his side. That is exactly what I felt." His expression softened. "Can you not recall it, Papa? how powerful it was? What happened to you, through him, has happened to me. This is not dishonor. It *is* rightful. Destiny has breathed glory into me."

Her father stared, looking beyond her into another time and place. He looked so tired, so careworn. But a light of the man he'd been when she was a girl returned as he found focus on her. "Do you remember, Papa?"

"Yes." It was as if the word seeped out of him.

"Then you must help me. We must keep fighting. We cannot let destiny slip away. If you won't do it for yourself or for me, seize it for your grandson. Do it for our next Amalus king."

Her father's eyes glazed over. "Even when I chose our king and lost your mother in doing so, I somehow kept you." She glimpsed the pride she always sensed in him, sought from him.

"You would never deny the gods' own destiny. They have ever had a hand in this. Besides, Mother is the one who chose. She doesn't deserve this. The gods summoned us, and she refused the call. Not you and me. We hear and answer."

Herodes laid a shaky hand on her cheek. "You have ever been a gift."

Harma took his hand in both of hers. "Then do as I say. Answer destiny's call. Fight. Take charge—do whatever is necessary. Win."

Before her eyes, Herodes became a captain again. "Tell me how," he said.

Malvius was exhausted but pressed on to finish his final check. He couldn't afford any delays to their departure come morning. He was inspecting the third ship of the fully loaded fleet with two to go. He'd rather be in his bed, but he needed to be gone the moment the gates opened at sunrise. Before Vahldan had a chance to add even a single crate to his overburdened holds.

The lateness was for the best. Malvius preferred to do his inspections alone. Few had ever disputed that his instincts for getting shiploads balanced was unmatched. It had always been so. As a teen, even his father's cranky old shore foreman had conceded it (to others if not to Malvius himself). In the interest of speed, he'd dismissed the other captains and their officers, and most of the sailors had been given the night off. He and Dex moved briskly through the third ship's hold. His first mate raised his lamp and the light eerily reflected from huge, staring eyes in the makeshift stalls to either side of their course. "Gods, it stinks down here," Malvius muttered.

"Horses tend to shit, Cap. Especially when they're nervous."

Malvius disliked horses generally, but particularly when they were aboard his ships. And yet... "I feel for them. I'm nervous, too." Megaria had stout walls, but it was crowded inside. And without a protected harbor, staying aboard ship was decidedly unsafe. He didn't even like to think about the danger to his fleet. He was fonder of his ships than he was of most humans. And the Tiberian war machine was sure to show up soon. Likely even before anyone thought possible. He would need to unload and set sail as swiftly as possible. "After Megaria, we'll have to find a nice load of wine casks to get the stench out." They moved through the stalls and the smell became overpowering. "Maybe make that vinegar."

"Are you thinking of trying to slip out past Nicomedya?" Dex ventured.

"Not yet." Dex sighed. "Don't look so relieved," Malvius said. "Eventually, we will."

"So you're telling me we're eventually going to attempt to slip the Straits with holds full of black-market goods, with the gods bedamned mobile reserve in Nicomedya and half the imperial navy docked in Efusium?"

"Oh no. We won't be doing that." Dex turned to him, trying to read him in the lamplight. "We're going to wait till it's a real challenge. We'll go after they've seized Megaria, too." Dex slumped. "No point in worrying because it's bound to happen. Certainly before hiatus."

"Which one? The imperials retaking Megaria or us running the Straits?"

"Both, of course." He gave his first mate a cheeky smile.

Apparently Dex wasn't in the mood. "I suppose we'll be doing it by night, too."

Malvius slapped his back. "Don't forget to make it stormy. Now, go check the prow, please."

"I can't wait," Dex muttered as he moved on to the fore.

"Trust me—by the time it happens, you'll see why it'll be worth the risk."

His mate turned and came back. "Clear prow," Dex said. At the base of the ladder, Dex stopped. "Seriously, Cap. Where are we headed next? I mean, after we make this Megarian drop."

"That's the good news, my friend. We're headed away from the war for a change. We not only have a full purse from the thug, we have his blessing to spend it. As you said, the western fleet is in Efusium, and the dah's navy is still parked at the mouth of the Straits, blocking them out. The gods know the eastern fleet is stretched pretty damn thin with Zafan's pirates running amok. The gods also know the situation won't last. But for now, it'll be like scooping liver pie with a buttered crust."

"Speaking of the Baffy, I'm guessing pirates like pie, too."

"True. But if we run into any, we'll simply tell them the truth."

"Which is?"

"That we're still happy to pay tribute to Zafan. Same as we did before the war. He betrayed Vahldan, not us. There's plenty of pie to keep everybody happy."

Dexicos frowned. "The thug won't like that."

"He won't mind if he never hears. I mean, I won't tell if you don't." Malvius winked. Dex's only response was to start climbing. "Don't worry, my friend. We're almost to the far side of the storm.

Won't be long now. We'll soon have our city back. Along with our vengeance."

Dex reached the deck and offered him a hand up. "Sure hope you're right, Cap."

They spun to face footsteps on the gangway. It was Ago, coming at a fast trot. "There's a carriage. They're asking for you, Cap." His nephew pointed.

It was one of the thug's carriages from the palace. "Gods spare me, what's he want now? We're already overloaded. Did he come himself this time or send one of his goons to haul me all the way back up there?"

"It's not the king. It's that captain—the one we brought to port this morning."

"Herodes?"

"Him and a woman."

"A woman?"

The boy nodded. "It's that pretty redhead. The one who drapes herself all over the king."

Harma! Malvius had gotten to her, after all. But what would bring her down here at this hour? And with her father?

Regardless, Malvius had smelled opportunity on the wind the moment he had met her—in spite of her potent perfume, at that. He now sensed it was just over the horizon. It wasn't just that he found Harma attractive. Who wouldn't? She was far beyond the usual haul-of-the-nets. Sure, she was well-formed, but gods afire, she made every bloody move seem like part of a Bafranii exotic dance. Even her furtive glances held enticement.

But he sensed something beyond the secret thrill of flirtation. This girl had brought the thug king to the very brink of polygamy. She'd driven the most famous man in her tribe to swim against the strong current of their people's norms. And Malvius found it perfectly understandable. With Harma, Malvius sensed impending conflict. A good sort of conflict, born of her combination of being gorgeous, pregnant—potentially with a Gottari heir—and the daughter of the disgraced commander of the Gottari army. It was a circumstance fraught with intrigue, bulging with possibility. Indeed, the very thought of her stirred him to partial hardness. He couldn't wait to see what happened next.

He strode down the docks with Ago and Dex hurrying in his wake. "You want me to round up a few of the boys, Cap?" Dex asked, sounding worried.

"No need. I think this will be safe enough. You two can hang back here."

"Cap." Malvius turned back. Dex was frowning and fidgeting. "I don't trust them."

"Neither do I." Malvius grinned and lowered his voice. "Nor should they trust me." He winked and strode on alone.

He scanned the carriage as he drew near. The window curtains were drawn. The driver hardly glanced at him as he leaned down to knock on the wooden side. The door opened just as Malvius arrived. Soft lamplight spilled out.

Herodes held the door open. "Good evening, Malvius. Would you mind stepping inside?"

"I'd be happy to." Malvius climbed in and sat across from the father and daughter. He had to resist more than the occasional glance at Harma. It was too dangerous. He could so easily be drawn to lurid gazing. He didn't know Herodes well, but he had known him for years. Well enough to know that the man kept a keen eye open. On Malvius's second glance, Harma dropped her chin demurely. Praise the gods, she was hiding a sly grin.

"Captain. My lady. What a pleasant surprise. How may I be of service?"

"We've come to beg a boon," Herodes said. He seemed anxious, not himself. Understandable after the morning the man had.

"A boon? From me?"

Harma raised her lovely face to him. "You offered. This morning. Remember?"

Malvius had been flirting. And she'd come back for more. "I do."
He smiled.

Herodes lowered his voice. "If you'll have me, I'd like to be a
passenger to Megaria."

Malvius sat back in his seat.

"Well?" Harma prompted.

"Forgive me, both of you. Honestly, I presumed you were to be
punished, Herodes. Frankly, I'm a bit surprised you were allowed
even to leave the palace, let alone set sail."

Herodes flushed. "I am not exactly being allowed."

Harma put her hand on her father's arm. "Captain, my father
wishes to redeem himself in the eyes of the king. The only way to do
this is to get him back to the war."

Malvius leaned in. "You're telling me that the king doesn't know
you're here?"

Herodes sighed. "He doesn't."

Harma rushed to his defense. "But King Vahldan will surely see
how—"

Malvius raised a silencing hand. "Don't tell me too much. Just
tell me this. Will the king be angry if you set sail with me?"

Herodes looked down. "I'm not sure how much angrier he can
get. He's as angry with me as he's ever been. But I hope to make
things right by going. It's a risk, but I'm desperate."

Malvius rubbed his chin. "You're asking me to risk my good
standing with him as well."

"I suppose I am," Herodes said. "And I suspected you might turn
me away. Thank you for considering it. I would appreciate your
confidence."

Harma's face crumpled. Her hands were clasped in her lap, but
they were still trembling. Gods, he hated to see a beautiful woman so
upset. It occurred to him that if he did this, she would be in his debt.
What was one more element of risk to take on? Gods, it was tempting. *She* was tempting. Having something—anything—on Harma

might be worth such a risk. After all, most of Vahldan's ire would be directed at Herodes. If it came to it, he could claim he was duped.

Malvius slid to the door and opened it. Both father and daughter looked dejected. Malvius beckoned Dex and Ago and reclosed the door. He sat back down. "My men will take you to one of the ships that won't have any of the king's men aboard. You'll have to make do in a cargo hold. One laden with the stench of horseshit. And I'm afraid I'll have to ask you to pretend to have stowed away once we arrive."

Harma's face lit up. "You'll do it?"

"Yes, I understand," Herodes said, putting a hand on Harma's to quieten her.

Malvius nodded upward. "What of the driver?"

"I've paid him," Herodes said. Malvius frowned. Men who have already received payment were hardly reliable.

"He's promised me his silence," Harma said, reading him. "I'll see to it."

Malvius wasn't exactly reassured. He tilted his head to her, allowing his gaze to swiftly take in her cleavage. Still worth it.

Dex rapped on the carriage door and he opened it. "Take Captain Herodes to the Pontean Pride. Show him to the cubby at the top of the stem." Dex nodded. "Ago, help the captain with his gear." The boy bobbed his head and started climbing the carriage to fetch the bags.

Malvius climbed out of the carriage as father and daughter embraced in farewell. "I believe in you, Papa," Harma said, clearly holding back tears.

Herodes climbed down, threw his saddlebags over his shoulder, gave his daughter a last nod, and followed Dex. Ago came behind, shouldering his kit.

Harma wiped her eyes and smiled. "Thank you, Captain. This means everything to me. I am in your debt."

Ah. She owed him *everything*. How perfect. Malvius bowed at the waist. "It's my pleasure to serve you, my lady." And to gain her indebtedness. "As I told you, I can't bear to see you in distress." He started to close the carriage door.

"Captain," she called. He reopened it. "I want you to know... This is for my family, yes. For our reputation. But it's also for my son." Her hand went to her swollen belly. "For his legacy. I really do believe he'll be the leader our people deserve."

She'd obviously convinced herself of it. Vahldan was obviously a shitty father, but judging by the warrior girl he'd fathered, he could indeed produce good stock. And the child of this gorgeous creature had a damn fine chance of being attractive. Harma-level attractiveness offered a favorable wind for any child's journey at least.

"You don't deserve what he's putting you through," Malvius ventured. "You are the mother of his child. Never let him forget it." He smiled, and her eyes glowed. "I wish you well, Lady Harma. Until our next meeting," he said and closed the door. He patted the side, the driver cracked the reins, and the carriage lurched into motion.

Malvius watched the carriage disappear behind the ramshackle sheds lining Fishmongers' Lane. "If the thug doesn't have me arrested on sight, that is," he murmured.

THE NEXT UNAVOIDABLE STEP

"*The flow of goods from the eastern trade routes had been reduced to a trickle during the course of Vahldan's war. As it had during the War of Two Empires beforehand. Or perhaps it is more precise to say that the legal flow had been reduced.*

Disruption of a supply rarely weakens a market's craving for it. Indeed, in those days, it seemed that scarcity made the imperial appetite ravenous. As a byproduct, men like Malvius and Isidros not only survived through tumultuous times but thrived. During Vahldan's war, Malvius saw an even greater opportunity—one few would have guessed at, let alone perceived as it evolved.

Fewer still could have foreseen the extent to which a Hellain sea captain might leverage such circumstances."—Brin Bright Eyes, *Saga of Dania*

VERNIUS HAD MET the aide that awaited his carriage outside the doors at Efusium's palace, though he couldn't recall the man's name. "Right this way, Lord General," was all the man said before he spun and led him inside and up the grand staircase. The palace was as pristine as ever. Coming here through the bustling city center, one would never have known that Efusium had so recently been overrun by barbarians. Although the city center had not suffered any damage during the Gottari attack, restoring the docks of the harbor had cost the mobile reserve more than a month at the war's onset, throughout which his men supplied much of the labor for the repair work. Not exactly soldiers' work, but it had been a vital step toward their assault on Nicomedya. Waging war in the Straits would be formidable without the naval support and supply linkage that the waterway's nearest port provided. It was tough enough with those things.

Vernius was surprised when the reticent aide led him not to the throne hall but up a second stairway and through the corridors of the personal residences. The aide opened an unmarked door to a sunny chamber. At least a dozen men reclined on the various furnishings and cushions, with seemingly twice as many mostly female attendants moving among them. Mycanius was prominently seated at the far end. He wore a lounging toga, as did most of the others. Except that the emperor's was of shimmering pink silk. Vernius was by far the most formally attired person in the chamber.

Mycanius's gaze locked onto Vernius. "Ah. Here he is now. Finally." The chamber went silent and all of the loungers turned to watch him approach the emperor.

Vernius bowed deeply. "I am yours to command, Highness."

"Ha. If that were true, I'd be leading our valiant soldiers to victory in Thrakius by now." The tittering that ran through the chamber sounded just like it had at his father's sentencing.

All of the servants scurried out, leaving Vernius as the only one standing. "Forgive me if I have displeased you, my emperor."

Mycanius sneered. "*If* you've displeased me? You have pushed me far beyond displeasure. You've bored me, Vernius." The loungers laughed louder. The emperor's laughter became a coughing spate. "Damn near to death, it seems," Mycanius added as he wheezed to catch his breath.

Vernius would never be so lucky. He bowed his head and stared at the carpet. "How may I better serve you, Highness?"

"Have I really asked for so much? Did I not consent to wait as you plodded to begin this forsaken campaign? Have I not provided you with all that you asked? Have I not committed all of Tiberia's might to overcoming this barbarous rabble? And here we still sit, staring at our flaccid cocks, hoping they'll grow stiff enough to start buggering the bastards."

One of the loungers was bold enough to speak up over the laughter. "Contrary to rumor, these Gottari are no demons from the underworld, General." Vernius recognized the man. It was the insufferable provincial rector, Horius. "They are mere men, I assure you. Undisciplined ones, at that. My own garrison managed to drive an entire army of the savages from the field in disarray. We then held at least twenty times our numbers from taking Megaria for months."

Vernius kept his focus on Mycanius. "As the rector points out, no matter who holds it, seizing Megaria is a formidable task, Highness. And Megaria is the next unavoidable step."

"Have you even begun your siege?" Mycanius seemed to be holding back another coughing spasm. Either that or he'd swallowed a fly.

"We have not, Highness. The dah's navy has made venturing a landing too risky. But we are scouting the heights, securing the roadways, and making the necessary preparations to—"

"I don't care!" Mycanius shot to his feet, surprisingly spryly. "I will not listen to one more excuse. Do you hear me, Vernius? You've managed to fritter away most of the summer, and now another hiatus looms. Do you know how much this is costing me? Gods, man, the empire cannot afford to wait through another winter for shipping to recommence."

Vernius doubted they were considering the same costs. "I understand. I was endeavoring to save lives, my emperor. We lost many in seizing Nicomedya. I only hoped to—"

"Lives? I don't care about your lives. You are soldiers! Your lives are mine. I shall spend them as I see fit. To benefit the greater good. And I am telling you, Vernius Stallicus of Nardium, to spend however many are required to finish this war. Now! Open the bloody Straits and let me lead our men to Thrakius. I want the Gottari wiped from the face of the earth. Come hiatus, I will have either Vahldan's head or yours. Am I being clear enough about how you can better serve me, General?"

Vernius bowed. "You are, Highness."

Mycanius slumped onto his cushioned chaise again, his pink toga swishing as he covered his bony legs. He let out a single cough and said, "Good. Now get out."

Vernius hurried out, closed the door behind him, and leaned on it. Mycanius's voice was muffled but clear enough. "He's as stubborn as the father and a dawdler besides." Vernius strode away with the laughter that had haunted his family for generations still ringing in his ears.

VERNIUS LEANED on the parapet of Nicomedya's wall-walk, gazing out at the wind-rumpled Straits. The crisp air should've been pleasant, but it only reminded him of autumn's swift approach. Which would bring with it the emperor's nigh impossible deadline. The current's relentless flow from the Pontean to the Tiberian Sea was a stark reminder that he'd been tasked with turning a formidable tide.

Perhaps Vernius had always been doomed to his father's fate. He'd spent half a lifetime fighting to avoid it, but to little avail. He could either submit to legacy's doom or find an advantage and continue the fight.

Movement caught the corner of his eye. Nicandros had climbed up with the young officer he'd sent for. Nico pointed and the man strode to Vernius with shoulders back. A confident one. Hopefully not too cocksure.

As unbearable as Horius was, the rector had pointed out a fact that Vernius had failed to appreciate. There was only one Tiberian officer who'd faced Vahldan's warriors on the field and had won outright. And it wasn't Vernius or any officer of the mobile reserve. Reoccupying Nicomedya after the Gottari's astonishing escape could hardly be called a victory.

The approaching officer was fit and tall for a Tiberian. His carriage bespoke athletic grace rather than brute strength. His attire was standard issue, but it was field gear rather than dress wear. He hadn't shaved in days and he wore a belt knife—hardly typical for an officer.

The former Megarian garrison captain had the prominent nose of the Equites but his hair was soil-brown and his eyes were gray. Very unusual features for the highborn. Vernius had it on good authority that he was indeed of noble blood but had grown up in the lower quarter of Thrakius. Unlike the garrison commanders of most prominent cities, he hadn't attended the academy in Medicia. He'd been illegitimate, had come up as a dock rat, some whispered. His mother had been the wrong sort but he'd rejected his father as a youth, said others. In early adulthood, he'd run with a band of Illyrican raiders, they claimed. Although he was a bachelor, Vernius heard he kept a foreign woman and her clan at his remote Pontean country estate.

The officer stopped a span away and stood silently waiting. Proud but patient. "Captain Lauterus Pontus, I presume," Vernius said without looking. "Thank you for coming."

"Is there something I can offer you, Lord General?" Direct. Decidedly not a sycophant.

"Your expertise, Captain."

"I am honored to share what little I have. On what topic?"

Vernius finally turned to him. Lauterus stood straight, formal. "Be at ease, Captain. Several topics, actually. But let's start with the most pressing of them. Megaria."

To his credit, Lauterus did loosen up. "A familiar topic. What would you like to know?"

"Some say Megaria is unconquerable," he said. Again, the man waited. "Your thoughts?"

Lauterus flushed. "We turned back the Gottari when we were outnumbered ten to one, General. We then held the city for several months. Even then, it took trickery to defeat us."

Gods, the man thought he was being dressed down. "I think you misunderstand, Captain. You've actually beaten the Gottari. Having fought them, I can only commend you. I now must accomplish what Vahldan only managed through trickery. I doubt there is a trick that will make the feat possible in such short order as our situation requires. I suspect that a man in your position has had reason to consider the ways in which such a stunning reversal might occur. I brought you here to ask if the means exists through which I can take Megaria, not just swiftly but soon."

Lauterus rubbed his whiskered chin. "There is a way. It could be done swiftly and reasonably soon. But it would be far from easy. And it wouldn't be cheap."

Vernius narrowed his gaze. "I don't need it to be easy or inexpensive." Nothing had been as costly to the imperial coffers as the loss of the Straits. "Tell me precisely what you mean by swift and soon."

Lauterus considered for a moment. "The way I have in mind could be accomplished in a month's time, Lord General. If things went well, the fighting itself would mostly occur on the first day of engagement." The man looked down and pressed his lips tight.

"There's something you'd like to add?" Vernius prodded.

"Regarding expense, I speak not just of treasure. Such a mission would also cost blood."

"Whose blood?"

Lauterus's eyes widened. "Well, mostly the foe's. But also a great many Megarians would suffer. Many would likely die. I speak of civilians, Lord General."

Vernius looked out toward the mountains looming over the Straits to the east. "In this case, I fear it may be an acceptable cost." At least it would be a change from losing his own men. "If I move you to my command, perhaps we could seek the means to best ensure that the bulk of such losses fall upon the foe."

"Of course," Lauterus agreed and then frowned at his feet again.

Was the man displeased by the thought of reassignment? "There's something else you wish to say, Captain?"

"I believe we can manage the campaign by moving overland, my lord. It's just..."

"You would rather we had control of the seas." Lauterus nodded. "You and I both."

The captain joined him in gazing eastward. "Those damn Sass ships are the turd in the trough, all right. Too bad, since their hearts aren't in it."

Vernius looked at him. "How do you mean?"

"My sources tell me that the Sassanadi captains have run out of fondness for the Gottari, and vice versa. It's just that they both still hate us. Rumor says that Dah Arstra is only in this to win back his losses from the last war. It's no secret that he resents the terms of the treaty that ended things or that he believes he's never been properly reimbursed. I have a hunch that Malvius promised he could get Arstra a better take on tariffs for the trade flowing through Trazonia once this war is over. The dah is likely biding time, hoping to get through it without pissing off his xah or reigniting the war with Tiberia in the process. It's too bad we don't have anyone who can get to the dah—maybe to undermine whatever deal Malvius managed to convince him that he'd end up with once Vahldan is gone."

This man was extremely well informed. And clever. Vernius would not be shocked to learn that Malvius was playing all sides of this conflict against the others. He imagined Lauterus would know better than most of such things. His having grown up on the docks of Thrakius was a boon Vernius hadn't fully appreciated. He needed every advantage he could gain.

Vernius looked back out over the cove. A ship was departing the docks, heading into the Tiberian Sea. It was one of Isidros's merchant ships, either seeking a load of freight... Or *delivering* one.

Vernius held no illusions about the anax's trade sources. The most profitable transactions moved goods from east to west. These days, gaining and maintaining eastern sources were the trickiest parts of trading. Isidros and Malvius were two of a kind, both of them very successful traders. If either of them saw an extra coin in it, they would gladly deal with the foes of Tiberia. "Perhaps there *is* someone like that, Captain."

Someone with connections on all sides who wished to maintain the appearance of being an asset to the empire. Someone with a vested interest in keeping Malvius as an imperial adversary.

For the third night in a row, Elan slept poorly. The sky outside her chamber's lone little window finally lit to gray. She kicked off the sweaty blanket and lurched from her pallet to her feet, kicking over the flagon she'd left on the floor. It was empty. Gods, she'd been reduced to Sassanadi sour ale. The thought of it nearly made her retch. She was only mildly dizzy but she knew that once the dizziness passed, she'd be left with a headache. She vowed, once again, that she would never resort to the awful stuff again.

She hurriedly dressed, anxious to escape her stuffy cell. Fresh air would help. She managed to negotiate the uneven steps of the dark stairwell, lifted the bar from the door, and burst out into the alley. She had to hop over the fetid open sewer to get to the lane that led to the gate. It was blessedly brisk, though the city still stank.

Elan hated the way Megaria's brick buildings leaned over the lanes—worse than in Thrakius; the sun rarely reached the ever-damp cobbles. She hurried through the deserted corridor, heading to her usual morning reprieve. She exited the inner keep and made for the outer wall's gatehouse and the stairwell within. The wall-walk not only offered the city's best views, it also got her as far from the stench as possible.

Something was off with the outer keep, though she was in too big of a hurry to bother figuring out what. She got to the top of the stairs, went to the parapet, and drew a deep breath of sea-fresh air and held it. The clouds on the eastern horizon glowed with the coming sunrise, lending an orange hue to the shore and the foothills along the coastline. She sighed it out. It was a daily moment of peace she relished. The rest of the day would be devoted to waiting for war.

Still, the feeling that something was off would not relent.

She scanned the seacoast, then turned to the shoreline of the Straits. Realization struck. The landing was normally lined with Sassanadi ships.

They were gone.

ELAN MARCHED past the guards and into the Megarian palace's throne hall wearing her sword. It was a breach of protocol but her annoyance must've been apparent; the wide-eyed guards said nothing. She was arrayed for scouting, about to depart when Arnegern's urgent summons was delivered. She couldn't imagine why he would delay her mission. They needed answers, fast.

The hall was dim as the torches that lined the walls had yet to be lit. Arnegern sat on a side bench on the dais. Herodes's boots clicked on the stone tiles as he paced the front of the room. She was surprised to see him back but learning more of it could wait.

"What's this about?" She didn't bother to veil her irritation. "My squad is saddled and waiting."

Arnegern cleared his throat. "We called you in to ask you to reconsider, Elan."

"Reconsider what? We all agreed that the navy's disappearance likely means the Tibairya are on the move. The sooner we know what they're up to, the better."

Herodes stood tall and raised his chin. "He means we'd like you to consider allowing me to lead this scouting mission."

Elan frowned. "Out of the question. I'm our best scout. No one can argue it."

Herodes bowed his head. "I would never. It's just that..." He glanced at Arnegern.

"Herodes is looking for an opportunity to redeem himself," Arnegern said. "One that serves both our cause and our king. He's convinced me that this mission can provide it."

Elan turned to appraise Herodes. "Please," he said just above a whisper.

Gods, the man looked miserable. Herodes didn't deserve to be punished for what had happened. No more than she did. Still... "It's not that I have no sympathy. It's just, this mission is so—"

"Vital," Herodes finished her sentence. "Yes, I know. We must know how the Tibairya are coming, with how many, and when. Its importance makes it perfect. I can do this, Elan."

"Besides that," Arnegern began. "There's something else I wish to ask of you. Something that's just as important. To me, anyway. And I'm hoping you'll do this instead."

"What could possibly even come close?"

Arnegern leveled his gaze at her. "Lead a party back to Thrakius, traveling by land."

Elan almost laughed. "That's mad. We need every sword, every bow. Here!"

"Malvius left as soon as he unloaded. Without saying a word. He just slipped away. There's no other way back to Thrakius. The roads are dangerous and growing more so."

Elan couldn't believe what she was hearing. "Send a runner. Send a bedamned squad of runners! Not a warrior. Not your best scout."

"You don't understand. Any day now we could be facing a siege. And..."

"He wants you to take me." The voice came from the benches in the shadowy gallery. A figure rose and approached. Mara was dressed in leggings for riding and a travel cloak. Her bundled little boy was in a sling over her shoulder, resting against her hip. Her countenance was grave. "Me and our son."

Arnegern stepped down from the dais. "Please, Elan. Before it's too late. I can't trust anyone else. They're too precious to me."

Elan sighed. She'd been ambushed. Instead of the foe, it seemed likely that her next unavoidable clash would be with Vahldan. She was far from sure which she'd rather face.

THE SUN SANK BEHIND the Pontean Mountains but the wind off of the sea would not relent. The temperature instantly plunged. Elan rode back down the narrow path to the spot where she'd left Mara sitting ahorse, hidden from the main road by a patch of gnarly pines. Mara had finally gotten the boy to settle. "There's a cove up the hill. It's out of the wind and easily guarded. There's plenty of firewood nearby. It'll do for the night."

"Sorry about this," Mara said softly. She nodded to indicate little Ragnavar, who'd cried and fussed through most of the first day of traveling. "I know we're slowing you dreadfully."

Elan shrugged. "It's just the way it is. Traveling with a little one is never easy." She huffed a laugh. "Reminds me of when we rode from the Jabitka to Danihem with baby Kemella. You probably don't even remember it."

Mara smiled. "Oh, I remember."

"You do? Gods, you were barely waist-high."

Mara's expression grew wistful. "I remember loving the days when I got to ride with you."

"Really? Why?"

Mara grinned. "Don't think I'm strange, but I used to like the way you smelled."

"Used to?" Elan made a show of sniffing under her arms.

"I mean, I'm sure you still smell delightful." They both laughed. "But I'm positive you still make me feel safe. You always have, Elan.

Thank you. For being there for me—for us. Through all of these years. You've been our only constant—our stalwart family guardian. Please know how appreciated you are."

Elan didn't know what to say. Her eyes itched. "Come," she said. "Let's get a fire going."

She led Mara up toward the cove. As they reached the highest point from the road, Elan turned in the saddle to check in both directions. Something caught her eye, out on the sea. She reined in to get a better look.

Three ships were cutting through the water, heading east, their bright sails shining in the setting sunlight. Each had three banks of oars working. There was a golden symbol on each of the crimson sails—an eagle, she knew. "Thunar's curse," she swore.

Mara drew up beside her. "What is it?"

"Bad news," she said.

"Tibairyan?" Mara asked. Elan nodded. "What does it mean?"

"It means things are about to get a lot worse. Much sooner than I'd imagined."

CHAPTER 6
THE REAL WAR

"*Since I have been asked of our relationship often, I feel compelled to plainly state that, yes, my mother was distant. Yes, she could be harsh or cold. Yes, she left me for long durations, often for months on end. Yes, she relied on others to see to my wellbeing. Yes, Elan was often either a mean drunk or a sulking one—sometimes both in the same night.*

Yes, my mother loved me. Yes, she believed in me and in my future role. Yes, I am certain of it."—Brin Bright Eyes, Saga of Dania

VERNIUS COULDN'T HELP but be curious. Thus far he had kept himself at a remove from the real war in Pontea. He'd yet to participate in the actual toil and terror. He hadn't experienced the sweat and blood and piss that he knew had come of confronting this particular enemy face-to-face. He'd been feeling that this needed to change.

These days, many Tiberian officers stayed clear of the action, citing the need for safe leadership throughout a battle and its aftermath. Vernius had always felt that a vital component of leadership could only be gained through sharing the danger. It created a bond

72

with the men. One that fostered a level of willingness and loyalty that couldn't be achieved without it.

Vernius had the proof. He'd witnessed it. As a group, the men of the mobile reserve were all willing to die—if not for empire, for each other. They considered him to be one of them.

Due to the nature of the battles thus far, Vernius had yet to experience direct contact with this foe. He'd seen them from a distance, of course. He'd heard much of them. Among his men, the Gottari had earned a begrudging respect. His men had grown a fierce hatred for them, but to the man they considered the Gottari worthy foes.

Vernius knew that these barbarians, too, would die for one another. And that the Gottari considered their leaders as part of their brotherhood of warriors. Ironically, this seemed particularly true of the Hippomache—the lone female leader among them. She'd gained a sort of mythic status among the mobile reserve. Which only heightened Vernius's curiosity. Not just about the sort of men who fought so voraciously, but about the sort who did so at the command of a woman. He'd gleaned that the Gottari not only fought with her, they fought for her.

Vernius was also curious about the sort of man who falsely proclaimed himself a king and then sends a woman to lead his army in defense of the territory he had illegally seized.

Vernius never placed much stock in the interrogation of captives. It rarely produced any valuable intelligence. The results were often little more than self-fulfilling. He normally left interrogation to others. But the Gottari were still so foreign, so unknown, so legendary to those who'd fought against them. He had to at least see one of them up close.

He exited the armory barracks into the frigid courtyard. A squad of guards had the captives lined up along a stone wall. The Teutonics' wrists were chained to the ends of a yolk across each man's shoulders. They were also chained together by their ankles—quite the caution. The first thing that struck him was their size. Even the smallest of them was half a head taller than the tallest Tiberian present. They were stripped bare to the waist and each was well muscled. Obviously well fed and kept fit. Their pale skin was goose-flesh, and many had cuts and purple bruises. A few were turning blue with the cold.

In spite of the harsh conditions and their humiliating circumstances, each Gottari warrior stood tall, chin high. Their collective countenance was one of proud contempt. If any of them were afraid, they hid it well.

Vernius returned the salute of the ranking centurion. "Which of them is the leader?"

The centurion pointed with his club to the man at the nearest end. He had fair but reddish hair and alert blue eyes. "They won't say, but this one keeps the others in line. I suspect he has some Hellain-speak." The centurion switched to crude Hellainic. "But he still say no much. Will he?" He emphasized the question by punching the butt of the club into the man's stomach. The captive contorted but only momentarily. His haughty glare became a simmering scowl.

"Is it true?" Vernius asked in Hellainic. "You are the leader?"

"Of this host, yes," the man said simply. His Hellainic was accented but better than the centurion's.

"You are under the command of Vahldan the Bold?"

"Of course. He is my king. Though he knew nothing of this patrol."

"You have fought for him for some time?"

The captive appraised him with hooded eyes. "Yes."

"Since before he proclaimed himself a king?"

The man sneered. "I have served him all of my adult life. Just as my father served his."

Vernius sensed this was no mere soldier. He had the bearing of a prominent man. "Forgive me. I should have introduced myself sooner. I am General Vernius, commander of His Eminence's mobile reserve. And you are?"

The captive hesitated, then said, "I am Herodes, captain of the Amalus."

This captain's host had rather stupidly stumbled into an ambush while patrolling the southern shore of the Straits. He'd fallen to the most basic of ploys: The Tiberian captain who'd gleaned his presence had simply sent a pair of scouts to feign blundering into them. The chase that had followed had led the Gottari into a closed ravine with Tiberians lining the surrounding hilltops. None of the Gottari patrol had escaped.

Oddly, the captain didn't strike him as stupid. Which only made Vernius more curious.

"Tell me, Captain—how has this come about?" Herodes seemed puzzled. "Why give such heedless chase? It seems a careless mistake for a man such as you."

The man instantly flushed. "Careless, yes. Even foolish. I was too anxious."

"Anxious for what?"

"For the opportunity to stand where you do."

Vernius glanced down at his feet. "Which is?"

"Looking down my nose at a captive. With a chance to gain vital insight."

Vernius smiled. "Are you saying that I have a chance of gaining such insight?"

Herodes looked over the top of Vernius's head. "No. I am not."

Vernius laughed. "How can you be so certain?"

"Because I am already dead to my king. You may as well kill me. It is what I deserve."

The centurion pulled his belt dagger and put it to the captive's chin. "I will oblige him with happy smile, Lord General."

Vernius touched the centurion's arm. "That's not yet necessary, Soldier." Vernius gazed up at Herodes. "You are dead to him why?"

Herodes paused for two breaths, jaw set. "Because I failed him."

Vernius found he believed him. This man, this stalwart, fit warrior, had surrendered his life to his king. It brought a choking dread, like seeking a satisfying breath in an increasingly smoky chamber. He put his hands behind his back and paced down the line, appraising the other Gottari. They were as fine and fit as their captain. And they looked similarly stalwart. Not a one of them was ready to beg or plead. These were committed foes.

His dread wasn't due to the fact that they would die for one another. It was that they would die for their king—a man who'd revealed himself as beyond reckless.

Oh, he had no real doubt. The mobile reserve would still prevail, as expected. But not easily. This would not be a war of persuasion. Victory would not come through intimidation. Nor through clever maneuvering. Facing men like these, victory would come only through gaining dominion. It was a brutal proposition.

The emperor spoke of wiping the Gottari out. Vernius had considered it hyperbole, an exaggeration to instill the desired mind-set. Until today.

Vernius headed back down the line. "Insight or no, I am sure we can make use of you alive, Captain. I commend you. Your men are hardy. They have fought well thus far." He stopped in front of Herodes. "But I've seen it all before. Iberican horsemen, Baeric slingers, Kelti chariot riders, Illyrican hillmen—you would scarcely believe how many uprisings we have been sent to quell. Each has caused shock and terror. But each has failed and fallen. Would you like to know why, Captain?"

Herodes stared over his head. "You can be brave and strong," Vernius said. "That doesn't matter. You will fail because what you really seek, deep down, is what we already have. You long for the comforts, privileges, and dignity of being a part of the civilized world. Once people like you have seen how we Tiberians live, you cannot help but wish for the same lives for yourselves, for your families. Your desire makes you weak. It saps your will. Meanwhile, we Tiberians have fought to keep what is ours from peoples like yours for centuries. We have known for generations what it takes to ensure it. We in the mobile reserve are the result of generations of ruthless defense of our way of life. Our resolve makes us strong. Our will is relentless."

Herodes's scowl morphed into a sardonic smile. A lone laugh escaped him.

"You find this funny, Captain?" Vernius asked.

"What is funny, *General*, is your arrogance. You are the typical Tibairya—just as King Vahldan has long spoken of you."

Vernius bristled but forced a smile. "Is that so?"

"You have been corrupt for so long, lied to yourselves for so long, that you can no longer even recognize truth. Ours is a society as old as yours. Our Wise Ones are the keepers of writings as ancient as yours. Our elders make and enforce laws which serve justice as well or better than yours. Our warriors have been trained by their sires for as many generations. But there is a difference. Our common men need not scrape for loaves thrown from an emperor's wagons. Those of us who toil are not kept under the whip, on the edge of hunger, as one keeps a pack of dogs. The Gottari earns his food just as he earns his honor. The Gottari does not succumb to lust. His bond to his mate is sacred. He seeks beyond the coveting of coin or jewel. The Gottari strive in the grace that only the gods can bestow. All of this the Gottari does without the crutch of slavery, which is an affront to the gods." Herodes's smile remained, but his eyes hardened. "Can you claim the same for yourself, General? Can any Tibairya?"

Arguing with a man as willful and proud as this would serve nothing. And yet. "Tell me, Herodes, captain of the Amalus: If what you say is true—if the Gottari are so wise and noble and satisfied— why is your king here in Pontea? What does your old friend Vahldan the Bold hope to achieve by subjecting his loyal followers to an unwinnable war?"

Herodes's laughter this time sounded more genuine. "Achieve? King Vahldan does not hope to achieve. War be damned, his achievement is foregone. For what has already begun will now surely come to pass."

"Which is?"

Herodes's expression grew harder still. "Your demise."

The man was detestably insolent. But gods be kind, Vernius

hoped this barbarian did not speak for the beliefs of the rest of them. "Perhaps it will be so, Captain Herodes. Still, I suspect yours will come first." He turned to leave. "As you were, Centurion." Before he reentered the building, he heard the thud of the centurion's club against the captive's abdomen, followed by a gasp. It was far from satisfying.

Urias resisted the urge to smile. The cheering of the boys surrounding the ring was waning, their initial zeal slowly replaced with resignation of a foregone outcome. Brin was in no hurry. She was being neither cruel to nor dismissive of her opponent. But she wasn't rushing. Or worried. She was taking the lad's measure. Not his size; Urias had already forgotten this one's name, Boartusk, son of Bullfart, or some such, outweighed her by half again and had her in height and reach as well. This one also outshined her in apparel: a finely spun tunic—obviously made just for sparring—under a Saurian scroll-laden leather breastplate with boots to match.

Brin wasn't intimidated by any of it. She was probing her opponent's tendencies. She had an increasingly honed ability to focus on what counted in a match. It was only a matter of time.

Sure enough, in his obvious frustration over her elusive speed, Boartusk lunged in for an overhand stroke, opening his chest just enough. It was sloppy. The lad was relying on his power and size advantage. Brin saw it coming and knew how to exploit it. She raised her buckler for the block as she slid inside for a stealthy jab. The blunt tip of her wooden sword struck his shoulder and twisted him painfully. In a flash, Brin was out of range again, dancing along the edge of the circle before the Rekkr's son had even regained his footing.

"Point!" Urias called, stepping between them.

"Not fair," Boartusk cried. "I could've fought on." Even as the lad complained, he was rubbing his shoulder and readjusting his fancy breastplate.

Urias shook his head. "Sorry. If it'd been steel, it would've drawn blood. We both know it. That's two falls to none. One more and it's over." Brin had scored her first within a few heartbeats of the start. It had wiped the smirk off of the lad's chubby face.

The lad's jeering fellows went silent. They realized that a third fall was inevitable. It seemed only Boartusk, son of Bullfart, remained oblivious.

Brin had already gained the respect of the boys in her age group, although it didn't keep them from cheering for anyone who might end her increasing dominance over the sparring rings. He also sensed the growing admiration of many of the older trainees, although it was silent and begrudging. Her matches always drew the largest crowds. Urias had to admit, she was worthy of their study. Brin Bright Eyes was fast and graceful. The other boys whispered about her Skolani blood. But Brin didn't rely on instinct or inherited physique. Her attitude toward training had shifted. She was diligent for her age. She had excellent vision and strategic cleverness. She was harnessing her growing skills into the prescience of an experienced warrior. She had a knack for leveraging her talents to overcome most any advantage an opponent brought against her.

Over the course of her matches in the rings, Urias began to see something else flourishing in his pupil. Her confidence. It pleased him more than any other sort of progress. The first few matches had been difficult for her, even when she prevailed. He saw that confidence had been the missing ingredient, the key to making her a complete and committed warrior-in-training.

Even during breaks, Brin was in perpetual motion, her keen gaze analyzing every detail of her opponent's posture and movement. No potential advantage escaped her notice. "Ready?" Urias asked, hand raised. Brin gave a nod and her opponent reluctantly followed suit. Urias dropped his arm and backed away, taking in his pupil's footwork. They had worked on ideal foot placement during their morning session.

The pair circled a moment, the lad now tentative. The onlookers began to goad the poor boy. He pathetically projected his first attack by shifting his stance. Brin instantly reacted to his predictable lunge. Urias studied her feet as she delivered her strike. She perfectly set herself up for the probable counterstrike. Suddenly there was a third set of boots in the circle, followed by a flurry of chaos.

By the time Urias realized what was happening, Elan had already snatched the sword from her daughter's hand from behind. Brin rounded on the intruder with a snarl, only to find herself facing a mother she hadn't seen in months. Unfortunately, the lad was already in motion. His sword caught Brin on the side of the face, drawing an instant bright pink welt.

Brin's hand flew to her face. "Damn you!" she snapped.

"What?" Elan's eyes flared.

Brin looked stricken. "Nothing. It just slipped out." Urias believed her. Brin never cursed her opponents.

Elan's scowl swept the scene. The former Blade-Wielder was fully armed, her very real sword hilt hovering over her shoulder. Everyone took a few steps back, including Urias. "What folly is this?" Elan demanded.

Hand still on her cheek, Brin shrugged. "Sparring."

"Just a quick match," Urias offered. "Nothing formal."

Elan's glare snapped to take him in. "This is your doing?"

"I approved the matchup." Urias wasn't sure exactly what she was asking, but he suspected she sought more than was offered.

"This ends now," she growled. Elan snatched the elbow of her daughter's shield arm and pulled her from the circle. "Come." She steered Brin toward the palace and the onlookers scurried to clear the way.

Urias hurried after them. "Elan. Look, I'm sorry. Can we discuss this?"

Elan kept going. "We're long past when that should've happened."

"Please, let me explain." She kept going. Brin looked back, her eyes mournful, the welt glowing redder than her flushing cheeks. "What you don't know is that she's good," he said.

"Doesn't matter." Elan arrived at the servants' stairwell door, pausing to fling it open.

Urias caught up. "The girl is a natural. She could be as good as y—"

"No!" Elan rounded on him, her eyes flashing and nostrils flaring. "How dare you?" She stepped nose to nose with him. "This girl will not be made into what I've become. So no more swords, no more shields. It ends this moment. Understood?"

Urias held up surrendering palms. "Understood."

Elan pulled Brin inside, slamming the door behind them.

"Welcome home," Urias said lamely. He went to collect their gear, feeling the same jitters he felt after a battle. Rightfully so. Battles always left him surprised to have survived.

Usually, staring at the stars in the sky over the sea calmed Elan. It wasn't working.

Perhaps it was the cold northerly wind carrying the scent of the coming winter. Perhaps it was the lingering images of the Tibairyan ships she and Mara had seen. Perhaps it was the haunting memories of war that she couldn't seem to banish. It was most likely that the first two were sure to deliver more of the third. She looked down to find her cup empty. It made her realize how she felt inside: empty.

After all Elan had done, all she'd fought for, all she'd sacrificed, here she was, alone and aching and empty. Much still needed to happen, and time was running out.

She went inside from the terrace, retreating from the darkness and the chill. Lamps were lit and coals glowed in the hearth. Still, the residence felt dim and cold. Empty. She went to the dining table. Brin had left her plate untouched. The anger Elan had been nursing all through the day and evening flared. She slammed her cup down, briskly strode to Brin's bedchamber, and flung the door open. The girl was sitting on the floor on the far side of her bed, head bowed to words on a page. Now what was she reading?

"Are you going to eat?" Elan demanded.

Brin didn't bother looking. "Are you?" So damn clever, this one. Elan couldn't even imagine a Skolani protégé speaking to an elder that way. To any elder, let alone her mother.

"Look, girly, I'm still the mother and you're still the child. Remember?"

The girl had the nerve to snort. "How could I forget?"

The chill she'd felt was gone. Indeed, her cheeks were getting hot. The child still hadn't faced her. "Look at me," she snapped. Brin's eye-roll was apparent in her grudging turn. "Say what you mean."

Brin shrugged. "You've made sure we all know that you're in charge. What I want to know is whether you're going to apologize to him."

"Apologize? To whom?"

The girl's brow scrunched. "You know who. Your brother."

"Of course not. Why should I?"

Brin suddenly looked as angry as Elan felt. "He was only trying to help."

"He should've asked first."

"Everything Uncle Urias does for me is because he cares about me. If you knew him like I do, you'd know that you hurt his feelings."

"I know him well enough to know he's a grown man. He'll get over it."

"I guess I understand why you keep checking."

The girl was talking in circles again. "Checking what?" she shouted.

Brin veiled a smile. "To make sure I know which of us is the child."

Elan's chest grew tight. She realized her fists were clenched. What she felt made her aware of what she refused to allow her daughter to become. The flush of her anger turned to shame. Vahldan's blood as well as her own flowed in their daughter's veins. Elan could kill—efficiently and without hesitation. She hated the thought that her baby girl had inherited her aptitude to kill, and that she very well might carry the added challenge of even an inclination toward the ugliness that Vahldan had struggled, and often failed, to resist.

No, pushing this clever child toward anger was as unwise as training her. She spun and slammed the bedchamber door.

Elan went to the table, snatched the flagon, and poured. The liquid burned her throat until the aftertaste hit. The wine was half-gone to vinegar. "Hesiod!" she shouted.

The manservant came hurrying from the servants' quarters. "My lady?"

"What is this vile stuff?" Elan gestured with the flagon, sloshing onto the carpet in the process.

His eye darted to the impending stain. "It's wine, Lady Elan," he flatly asserted. Apparently Hesiod was annoyed now, too. He may as well join the family fun.

This wasn't his fault. Elan adjusted her tone and knelt to wipe the carpet with the hem of her tunic. "It tastes like cooking wine. We had better in Nicomedya while we were under siege."

"This wine did indeed come from the kitchen larder."

She rose with a huff. "Is this the best they have down there?"

Hesiod looked away. "Down there? Yes."

He was trying to tell her something. "Where else would we keep wine?"

Her manservant's eyes fell to his feet. "My lady, of late any fresh wine casks have been delivered... elsewhere in the palace."

Realization struck. "Let me guess. The good stuff goes to the high hall."

Hesiod met her gaze. "More accurately, to the adjoining study."

She and Vahldan had been avoiding one another since her return. Elan had sent several messages, even ramping up the tone of alarm, but they had all gone unanswered. And nothing seemed to be happening in response to the challenges that came their way. It had to end. She'd had enough. Her anger was back, and this time it was focused on the correct target.

"Thank you, Hesiod," she said. She took the flagon and her cup to the basin and dumped them both. "I'll see to this," she said, passing him and heading for the door.

"Lady Elan," Hesiod called. She turned back. "If you don't mind my suggesting..."

"Yes?" she prompted.

"Perhaps a frock?"

Elan looked down at herself. She had on her sleeveless scouting tunic, now damp with wine, and house sandals over stockings. She'd pulled her boots and leggings off. Of course, he was right. She swiftly changed into a frock and a presentable pair of slippers. She opened the bedchamber door and Hesiod was waiting with the empty flagon. At the last moment, she grabbed a scarf and wound it around her neck, hiding the kestrel necklace that the frock partially revealed. She stopped to check herself in the looking glass. The scar over her eye was finally fading, but the bruise on her jaw remained visible. It was a gift from a pugnacious Tibairya. In her most recent skirmish, the walking stump had punched her with a gauntleted fist, even as he had been dying with her sword in his gut. Typical mobile reserve jackass—vindictive to the end. At least the frock hid the rest of her bruises and scars.

Hesiod appeared in the reflection behind her. "May I?" He held a comb.

Elan sighed. "If you must." Once he started, she saw that he was right again.

His tugging though her tangles caused her mind to drift to Icannes. How she'd relished having her braids combed out and retied. She felt some of the tension leave her neck and shoulders. Hesiod smiled as he swept her bangs from her face. He wetted his fingers and gently tucked the excess behind her ear. He adjusted her scarf. "Lovely, as always," he said.

The reflection revealed the smile forming on her face. It was as if her former self ghosted into view. She couldn't recall the last time someone complimented her appearance. "Thank you," she said, feeling like a different person than she'd been mere moments before.

Her anger had melted away again. And with it, Elan lost her zeal to confront him. She'd spent months in harm's way, her life almost constantly on the line. She was safely behind the palace walls, and yet this apprehension was as bad as any she'd felt during her days at the front.

He'd chosen another woman. Again. And another woman's child—this one still unborn.

Hesiod picked up the flagon and presented it to her with a bowed head. When she didn't move, her manservant led her to the door, opened it, and held it for her. "Be strong, my lady," he said. "Remember who you are."

Panic seized her. She spun to him. "Who am I?" she asked, sounding desperate.

Hesiod's gaze hardened. "The woman so many of us are counting on."

Elan pressed her lips tight and nodded. She started down the cold, dim corridor, hating his answer. Maybe if she was wearing a sword.

"I believe in you," Hesiod called after her.

That made one of them.

VAHLDAN WISHED he could just go up to bed. Dinner was long since over. His sister Kemella and Eldavar's qeins, Sairsa, had already left, citing the need to check on children. But Harma simply wouldn't let Mara go. Every time his sister hinted at retiring, Harma launched into a new topic. To complicate matters, every time he offered the slightest critical word, his sister glared. Once, Mara even shook her head. Just what he needed—a marital moderator.

He was aware that pregnant women were prone to stormy emotions, but Harma's was the late-autumn sea of pregnancies. She could be serene one moment, then swirl into a tempest the next. Worse still, she could just as quickly melt into tears. He tried to avoid spending time with her, but she persistently retaliated by finding events that required them to be together. Not so much privately. She was fine with sleeping alone. Harma seemed more keenly invested in being seen together publicly.

All Vahldan had wanted since he'd found out Harma was pregnant was to make their unborn son legitimate. He would have his young lion. His Amalus son would be the countervailing force to Amaga's Wulthus heir, to bring balance to Urrinan. He'd never dreamed how clingy and needy Harma might become. She wasn't even fun in bed anymore.

At least, at the moment, he was pleasantly full. And not just a little tipsy. He considered the tune the Illyrican musicians had chosen to be irritatingly peppy, but at least it was keeping him awake. He settled back into the cushions, drumming his fingers on his goblet to the rhythm. Gods, now Harma was going on about the frock he'd allowed her to have made for their bonding ceremony. There really hadn't been a choice. He had to get her a new one or she would've worn one of her old ones. The woman seemed oblivious to the challenge her condition had begun to put on the seams.

The musicians ended their tune just as the door to his study opened. He craned, annoyed that the guards had let anyone pass. The torchlight from the high hall silhouetted the intruder.

His pulse leapt. The figure was instantly recognizable.

Vahldan held up a hand to forestall the players' next tune. She stepped into the lamplight. Her gaze swept through the chamber and locked onto his.

Elan wore a cloth frock and a silk scarf. Her long bangs were swept from her face. She had a new scar on her forehead that parted her eyebrow. And was that a bruise on her jaw? But oh, Freya's grace, she was beautiful.

Elan stood there, silent. They'd always shared a connection, but it seemed utterly lost to him in the moment. He couldn't tell if she was seething, frightened, or sorrowful. Actually, he couldn't tell which of those he was feeling. Maybe all of them.

"Ah, I've been wondering about you," Mara said.

"Me?" Elan said, sounding like she'd been accused.

"Yes. I wondered why you weren't here with us." Mara frowned at Vahldan again. More sisterly judgment. True, he hadn't sought Elan out since their return. But why was he obliged?

"Because I wasn't invited," Elan said, turning her gaze to take in Harma, her disgust momentarily apparent, then swiftly veiled.

"Please, forgive the oversight," Vahldan said.

"Join us for a cup," Mara suggested, raising hers.

Elan found focus on the tapped barrel and strode to it. "Actually, wine is what I came for." He noticed she was carrying a flagon. "Perhaps you could see to it that some decent wine is left in the larder," she said as she filled it without so much as a *please* or a *may I?*

He was about to say that there was no way to keep the servants out of it down there, when Mara said, "Come, pour a cup. We're toasting the newly bonded couple."

Elan turned, wearing a scornful smirk. "Seems like a recurring theme." Ah, there was no question now. She was seething.

Harma cleared her throat. "That, and Sueridas says my babe will come during this moon." She patted her belly. "The Wise One is all but certain it's a boy. We'll have an Amalus heir at last." Vahldan loathed the idea of Harma speaking to Elan. But he found himself strangely satisfied. She'd managed to say the only thing he really needed Elan to hear.

Elan huffed a laugh in her usual dismissive way as she poured wine into one of the cups on the sideboard. "As it shall be," she said, her tone clearly sarcastic. She raised her cup and drank without waiting for the rest of them. She then tilted her head further, gulped down the rest, and clapped the cup down on the sideboard.

Elan came and stood before him, her chin high. "I came for wine, but I also have a few words for you, my lord. If you care to hear them."

Vahldan braced himself and pointed to the nearby settle. "Sit, then. Speak."

"No, thank you. Perhaps in private?" Her eyes darted to the door.

He couldn't face her alone. Not yet. "I'm sure anything you have to say can be said in front of these two. We're all family here."

Elan's expression clouded. "As you wish. I came to say that you should evacuate the women and children from Thrakius."

Harma's eyes widened. "Evacuate who?"

Elan kept her best Skolani scowl directed at him. "Women and children," she said with emphasis. "You know—your various wives and sisters. Our daughter."

Harma harrumphed. "Gods, whatever for?"

"For their safety, of course."

Mara looked alarmed. "So soon?" she asked. "Is it that serious?"

"No," Vahldan said, continuing to face Elan. "It isn't. Last I heard, Megaria still stands. We are all perfectly safe here. And will remain so."

Elan's eyes flared. "Exactly how long do you think you have? Megaria will be under siege any day. Perhaps it is already. The imperial navy will soon have free reign in the Straits. Soon after that, they'll regain control of the entire Pontean, including shipping. Including our supply lines. In the meantime, the mobile reserve will just keep coming."

He waved her off. "If it happens, we'll just have to stop them."

Elan barked a laugh. "That's what you're not getting. It's already happening. It's been happening, and nothing stops them. Even if we somehow manage to kill every last one of the thousands who are here in Pontea, the empire will only send more."

The ugliness simmered in Vahldan's belly. Damn, had the woman come back just to argue? Was she trying to make him look foolish? Was she really ready to give up? After all they'd been through, she didn't believe any longer? His outrage surged and he leapt to his feet to face her. "Tell us what you really mean. Have you already conceded this war? Because I haven't!"

The chamber fell silent. Elan glared. "Forgive the outburst," Vahldan said to his guests, seeking to calm the storm within. "Elan's concern is misplaced. Our enemy is far away and we are far from defeated. I'm sure that she has her reasons—"

"There's a real war out there," Elan shouted over him. "Real people are dying. Don't you understand? They're coming for us. They don't care how many of their people die, so long as all of ours do."

Vahldan pushed the ugliness down. Elan wanted to punish him. She wanted to goad him so that she could claim the higher ground. "You're exaggerating, Elan. The empire is pragmatic. You're right about one thing. It is a real war now. That's the point. We have but to make it real to them. Which we're doing by strangling trade at the Straits. When the costs grow too high, they will compromise. Same as always. Can't you see that this is all a bluff? We have only to continue to believe and to persevere."

"A bluff? The heaps of bloodied corpses I've seen are no bluff." She stepped in close. "You've faced them, the Tibairyan soldiers. Trust me when I say that these new ones are worse. Open your eyes. Look at what's coming." Elan's gaze locked onto his, imploring now. She lowered her voice. "All I'm asking for is a little caution. Just get the innocents clear. Get them through the heights before the snows make it impossible."

The heights... The Pontean Pass? "To Dania, you mean?" The reality of it crashed into him.

"Yes, to Dania," Elan said. "Where else?"

He suddenly saw it—his subjects arriving in Dania. He saw them entering the gates of Danihem, with a mocking crowd to greet them. They'd be prostrate, utterly reliant on the charity of the wolves, with winter upon them.

Vahldan then saw a picture of himself, sitting penitent in that damn little dais chair. Then he perfectly visualized Thadmeir's smug expression in the grand chair next to him.

The ugliness flared and shot through him. "No, dammit!" he erupted. Elan momentarily shrank back. He composed himself, pleading silently with her for a level of understanding. Instead of finding it, Elan raised her chin again. Typical Skolani obstinance.

"We simply cannot surrender," he said. "We will never be beholden to them. I will defend this city to the last man, if need be." He could hardly breathe.

Elan's fierce façade melted and her eyes grew sad. She spun and headed for the door. He rushed after her. By the time he caught her, she was halfway through the high hall. He grabbed her by the shoulder and she rounded on him, eyes flaring. "What?"

"I didn't ask you to go out there," he said.

"You sure didn't ask me to stay."

Their connection suddenly returned, soothing away the ugliness. Vahldan truly saw her. She was angry, yes. But she was also exhausted and sore. And hurting. "You never gave me a chance," he said hoarsely.

Her eyes filled with that terrible sorrow. "I won't go through it. Not again."

He had to make her understand. "This is about balance. I'm doing this for an Amalus heir. It's about what you said to me that night—about finding destiny within and without."

Elan looked away, shaking her head. "No. Don't you dare lay this on me. And don't think you can whisk it away with your damned broom of destiny." She hardened her countenance. "Please don't speak to me of that night ever again. You misled me. You made me believe again. After I promised myself I was done believing. And then I saw you with... *her*"—Elan's eyes flared toward the study door—"the very next day. I saw you then. You taught me a hard lesson. So don't you dare talk to me about giving you chances."

Elan turned from him and strode off. Vahldan knew he should keep chasing her, keep trying to explain, but he couldn't make himself move. Mara's voice came from behind. "What in Freya's name is going on?"

"She's just upset," he said.

Mara gave him yet another scolding look. "As is your new qeins. I'd suggest you get back in there." His sister indicated the study with a nod. "Good night, my king," Mara curtly said as she followed after Elan.

THE SOUTHERN SHORE of the Straits loomed, a black mass etched against the cloudless night sky lit by a waning moon. Only in such darkness could the Gottari cross the Straits, particularly in a fleet of fishing boats, as they were. It was a level of vulnerability that Arnegern hadn't expected, but it was what they'd been reduced to by the abandonment of the Sassanadi navy.

He rode in the prow of the lead boat. It was the only real way to lead an attack. It was where his king would be if he were here. But this mission was even more personal for Arnegern.

The Gottari army had done nothing but wait since they took Megaria. It had been frustrating and oddly exhausting. But it seemed the wait was over. It was time for the Gottari army to shake off their lethargy. It was time to stand and fight. War had returned to Megaria.

All of the reports he'd received were the same. The imperial mobile reserve had spent days amassing in the hills directly across the Straits from Megaria. Now the foe was on the move again. They'd marched east, likely to the sandy beaches along the western shore of the Pontean Sea. There they would likely board the ships of the Tibairyan navy to be transported to the shores adjacent to the walls. They seemed on the verge of an attempt to besiege the city. Arnegern had sent the last of the Gottari women and children out the prior night. As far as he knew, they were safely on their way to Thrakius, the column taking the bulk of the army's remaining horses. But there was an important mission to be accomplished before the foe's siege began.

Arnegern understood the imperial strategy. Vahldan had attempted to approach Megaria from the west via the road hugging the shore of the Straits. It had been disastrous. The Tibairya had chosen the safer route, moving along the southern shore to muster at a safe distance. They would then rely on their naval superiority to strike. He and his officers supposed they would seek to overwhelm his catapults with sheer numbers. He didn't doubt they had the capacity or the willingness to pay the sort of price such an attack would levy.

What wasn't so clear was why the Tibairya had left their Gottari captives behind.

It had been confirmed that these were the poor souls from Herodes's scouting squad. The squad's lone survivor had reported back that Herodes had been lured into a trap. Several had been killed but over a dozen had been taken captive, including Herodes himself. The imperials had brought these captives along to their mustering.

Arnegern couldn't be sure what the Tibairya were up to, but clearly their methods were wretched and evil.

The mobile reserve had left the Gottari captives on display on the shore, seemingly unguarded. Perhaps it was intended as intimidation, but more likely it was meant to goad the Gottari. The beasts had driven timbers into a series of X-formations along the shore and had mounted their prisoners with arms and legs splayed—some of them upside down. The scouts had reported that the captives' agony had been apparent. The mobile reserve had moved off early the prior evening. Which had brought Arnegern to his decision. They would attempt a rescue, and he himself would lead it. Of course he suspected a trap. Or perhaps a feint to draw a portion of their force out of position. But it was a chance he had to take in order to live with himself.

Arnegern had mustered the whole of the Gottari army, keeping the bulk of the force at the ready in the city's outer keep. The shore-side ramparts were fully manned, with every catapult they possessed ready to fire every last missile that remained. If this General Vernius attempted a landing today, his army would face all of the Gottari's strength. Even if Arnegern's rescue went awry or his team was caught on the wrong side of the water.

The rescue team's fleet of fishing boats reached the halfway point and the pale forms of the captives came into view on the distant shore. Arnegern recognized Herodes's long limbs and long fair hair. The captives' leader was strapped to the center cruciform. He pointed and the boat's helmsman steered toward the spot. He softly urged the oarsmen to speed their pace.

Herodes was nude; his head lolled to one side. His cousin didn't move as the prow hit the sand. Arnegern was the first over the gunwale and onto the soggy turf. The ground rose steeply above the narrow beach. He started to climb, dropping a hand to steady himself. The ground felt oddly sticky. A stench filled his nose. Herodes raised his head feebly. "No, no, no," his cousin pleaded. Arnegern kept climbing. "Go back," Herodes croaked. "It's a trap."

Arnegern could not leave him. Not when he was so close. The terrain began to level. His steps caused crackling underfoot. The ground had been strewn with bundles of twigs. The stench gained pungency.

Arnegern drew his dagger as he arrived beneath Herodes and started sawing at the binding of one ankle. His cousin's feet were shoulder high and blue as a bruise. He'd have to climb to get to the binding on his wrists.

"Arnegern?" Herodes was weeping.

"Yes, it's me. We've come for you."

"Gods, why? Go. Leave us."

"Never." He freed one leg and went for the other. His cousin gasped when his foot flopped down.

"Please. It's a trap. Get your men away."

Other boats hit the shore and his rescue party scrambled to the other captives. Arnegern ignored Herodes's pleas and craned his head, seeking the best way to climb to cut the wrist bindings. Bright streaks appeared, darting across the sky behind Herodes's head.

Scores of flaming arrows picketed the ground around them. Fires instantly flared from the bundled fuel at their feet. Full cognition came—the stench had come from pitch, spread over the entire shore. "Didn't I say?" Herodes cried. "Go!"

The flames spread and rose with alarming speed, driven by the night breeze off the water. One of Arnegern's leggings caught fire and he swatted at it. "You must go!" Herodes shouted. "Now! Get to your bows. Shoot us from the shore."

Tears filled Arnegern's eyes. "No!" he shouted. The crackling blaze became a roar. Another volley of flaming arrows streaked through the sky. More death was about to rain down.

"Arnegern, please. It's over. Grant us mercy, then go. Get out of Megaria. They're coming from on high. Flee to Dolope. Save our army."

"Dolope?" It was a rocky wasteland northeast of the city. He and Herodes had discussed it before, should the worst happen. It was a last resort, a fallback. The heights there could be defended as an army retreated into the mountains.

"Yes," Herodes hissed. "Do you understand?"

"I do," Arnegern affirmed.

"Then go. Quickly!"

"I love you, Cousin."

"Tell Harma..." Herodes could find no more words. His chin fell to his chest.

"I will." Arnegern turned and ran though the flames. "Retreat! Back to the boats!" He and his men hit the cold water, many diving to douse their burning clothes. Arnegern climbed from the water, calling, "Bows! Mercy for the captives!" He flopped into the boat and the helmsman tossed his bow to him. Arnegern fumbled to nock an arrow.

He aimed at his dear cousin's chest as the flames rose to lick at his dangling feet. His hands shook as he took his first shot. The arrow struck but too low, eliciting a wail of agony. Arnegern wiped the tears from his eyes, drew a breath, and fitted another arrow. He could not miss again. A strange feeling of clarity seized him. He released, instantly certain that Freya had guided the shot. Herodes fell silent and still. Arnegern slumped.

The screams of the other captives fell away, leaving only the crackling of the flames. A command echoed from the rocky heights. The words were Tibairyan.

"To the oars," he cried. "Cast off!" The crew pulled the oars and the boat lurched into motion. Arnegern forced himself to look back. His tears blinded him. He rocked on his knees, sobbed, and prayed. "Hel, have mercy," he whispered. "Receive and welcome my cousin and dearest friend. For he was stronger than most and brave to the end."

He turned and moved to the prow, knowing that even with his failure to secure the captives, this mission was far from over. The coming attack would not be what they'd planned for. The sky grayed with the coming sunrise as their ragged little fleet raced for the Megarian shore. "Tibairya!" The call rang across the water. Men in several boats pointed west.

The first trio of red sails glided from the shadows with banks of oars moving in perfect unison. More followed, at least a dozen Tibairyan warships sweeping through the Straits, harnessing the brisk morning wind.

"Hurry, men!" Arnegern urged his rowers. "Get us to shore!" He stood clinging to the mast. "Stay together," he called. "Strength in numbers. Archers, make ready!"

Dawn's light filled the valley as the first of the warships bore down on the fishing boats, coming at an angle, sure to intercept. Arnegern raised his bow, but there was no firm target. The rostrums of the lead warships' bows sliced through the water, targeting their outermost boats. Collision was imminent.

A loud cracking sound resounded over the water's surface. The warships weren't even slowed, and their targeted fishing boats snapped like kindling. The Gottari threw themselves in the water. Tibairyan archers lined the deck rails, firing at the swimmers. If any survived it, they were in for a long swim to safety.

The crackling of rostrums hitting fishing boats continued, punctuated by war whoops and cries of anguish. The only hope for the ships of Arnegern's fleet was that they outnumbered the rostrums. A warship slid dangerously close to his own boat. Arrows thumped the wooden hull. Arnegern drew and aimed but couldn't find a clear target along the taller ship's rail.

"I'm hit," one of his rowers cried. The man dropped his oar and gripped the arrow jutting from his thigh with both hands. Arnegern drew him aside and down onto the deck. He jumped onto the bench and grabbed the loose oar, joining the others in their desperate heaving.

The northern shore grew closer. Behind them, the billowing crimson sails of the warships sailed on, heading east toward the open sea and leaving a broad swath of floating wreckage and bodies in the Straits. The attack had taken at least a third of his fleet. The gods only knew how many he'd lost to the foe's arrows—in the water and on the far shore.

Arnegern watched the ships sail on, angling northeast as they passed the mouth of the Straits. He thought it odd till he remembered Herodes's warning to save the army by making for Dolope. His instincts screamed in warning. Herodes was right. The threat was dire, its scale vast and well-coordinated. This was much worse than the foe seeking to besiege one city. The effort to trap and exterminate the Gottari army was underway.

The helmsman twisted around. "They don't seem to be turning for another pass. Shall we swing back to look for survivors, Captain?"

"No—there's no time. We've got to get to the city."

A heartbeat after he said the words, an ominous boom thrummed, filling the valley. It had come from the north shore. He and the other rowers turned to gape over the prow.

The rocky ridges over Megaria swarmed with soldiers. Astonishingly, a line of catapults had been dragged into position high above the city. One fired as he watched, its huge missile striking the ancient brick of the northern wall. The thunderous cracks echoed down more swiftly after that. The northern wall had never been reinforced. No one had ever anticipated an attack from the steep mountainous backside of the city. The ancient wall would not hold long. In anticipation of a landing, Arnegern had stripped the entire city of its defenses, focusing all of his men and weaponry on the shoreline side and its outer wall.

Flung rock continued to pound the north wall even as flaming missiles began to rain down on the mostly residential lanes and buildings of the upper city. The higher reaches were where most Megarian commoners lived. Arnegern was stunned by the ruthlessness of the tactic.

His boat was among the first to hit the beach. He flung aside his oar and leapt over the side. He ran toward the south wall, crying, "To me! To me, Gottari. Open the gates! To me!"

The men atop the outer wall took up the call, passing it back to those inside. Thankfully, the gates swiftly opened. As he emerged from the archway into the outer keep, a raucous cheer rang down from the heights. Arnegern knew what it meant before he was told. Hjalmar ran to meet him and confirmed his fears. "The north wall has collapsed. The Tibairya are coming."

Senior Rekkrs gathered around him. "Order a full retreat," he called. "Get every Gottari out of the city. Light gear—bring only weapons and necessities. Hjalmar, lead the catapult crews back to the armory. Take the remaining horses and load whatever grain is ready for transport. The rest of you, assemble your men on the inner keep green. Be ready to march."

"Retreat?" someone asked. "To where?"

"Home, eventually."

"To Thrakius?" Hjalmar asked.

"Yes, but not by the coastal road. The Tibairya sail to Kynnya Cove to block our passage."

"How will we get through?"

"We're heading for the Dolope Pass," he said.

"Dolope?" another cried. "With the entire army?"

"Yes, Dolope."

Several spoke at once. "It's so narrow," and "If we make it up, we'll be in a warren," and "We'll be strung out."

"It would take days, maybe weeks, to find our way through," Hjalmar added.

Arnegern nodded. "Yes. But it's our only hope. We must be quick to even try." They all stood gaping. "Go!" he shouted.

They all turned and hurried to their men, calling as they went. Arnegern dropped to his knees to catch his breath. He gazed back through the gate at the smudge of smoke still rising from the south shore of the Straits, with the calls of the celebrant Tibairya echoing down from the heights.

"Forgive me, Cousin," Arnegern whispered to the wind. "Thank you for your council and for your sacrifice. Let us pray you are right."

COMES THE LION, COMES THE EAGLE

"Although the second babe and I shared our father's blood, I felt no real connection to him and never once referred to him as my brother. But I did feel for him.

Harma's son had two parents with their own agendas, to each of which this child was a tool. It was a circumstance for which I had a keen empathy."—Brin Bright Eyes, Saga of Dania

THE KNOCK at the door finally came. Apontia looked to Harma before answering it. Harma nodded her assent. It was about time her husband came to check on her. Harma had been sending messages all day. She'd refused to go down to dinner, even though she was having doubts that this would be the day she'd give birth, after all. She hadn't had one of her birthing spells for some time now. At this point, she wished she could just call it a day and go to bed.

Harma snatched up the embroidery project Apontia was working on and laid it on her belly. It was to be an infant's swaddling fit for a king, crimson silk with gold lions embroidered along the neckline. Harma pretended to be sewing as Apontia opened the door.

"Oh. Hello, um... Captain, is it not?"

Harma stiffened, afraid to look. It wasn't Vahldan?

"Yes, good evening. I'd like to see Lady Harma, if it's possible."

It wasn't Harma's father either. She surrendered and looked. It was Uncle Arnegern. She struggled to sit up.

"Please come in, Captain," Apontia said.

Arnegern took Harma in with wide eyes. Then a sad smile came to his lips. "Wonderful to see you, dear one." Her uncle bent to give her cheek a scratchy peck.

"How is it that you're here, Uncle? Is Father still in Megaria?"

His sad smile faded. "I apologize in advance. There is just no other way to say this. Your father—he's fallen. Slain by the Tibairya. Megaria, too, has fallen."

Dizziness swallowed her. She flopped back. The babe lurched too. She put both hands on her belly, trying to sooth both her son and herself. "This can't be happening."

Arnegern dropped to a knee beside her. "I'm terribly sorry, dear one."

It had to be a nightmare. Harma shook her head, trying to will herself awake. "You're certain? He's dead?"

Her uncle blanched. "Quite certain."

"How?" Such an outcome had never occurred to her, had never been part of the plan.

"Your father led a scouting squad to ascertain the foe's approach. Just as he'd planned when he left you. He came upon the foe, but in the process, his squad was ambushed. He and several of his men..." Arnegern's eyes darted away. "They were killed by the foe."

Harma knew when she was being misled. "What are you not telling me?"

Her uncle pressed his lips together. "You need only remember that your father performed his duty bravely and faced his fate honorably. Hel has surely hastened his passage over the bridge."

Herodes would never see his grandson, never be the grandfather to a king. He'd never be as proud of her as she'd striven to make him.

He'd been disappointed in her so recently, and she never had the chance to overturn it. Harma simply couldn't imagine the future without him.

Worse than all of that, Harma's mother would think she'd been right all along.

Harma had lived with him through half of her life. After his years at sea, Herodes had come back for her. He'd taken her away, saving her from the drudgery and the condemnation of Danihem. He'd brought her to live in a palace. Because of him, she'd gained the chance to become the qeins of the nation and the mother of a king.

He'd saved her, made her who she was. And now he was gone.

Arnegern took her hand. "His last words…" Her uncle swallowed hard. "He wanted you to know how much he loved you. And how proud he was of you."

Harma's vision was blurred by tears. "You saw him? Spoke to him?"

"Only for a few moments. I tried to rescue him." Arnegern looked away again. "I failed. But what he was able to tell me in those moments saved many Gottari lives."

Unwiped tears dripped from her jaw. "Did he suffer?"

Arnegern forced a smile. "Not for long."

Another thought sprang to mind. "The king! Does he know? That Megaria fell, I mean?"

"Of course. I begged King Vahldan's leave to come and tell you."

Harma bit her lip. Vahldan knew.

Arnegern studied her. Her uncle seemed to sense her distress. "The king, he's very concerned about you. He didn't want this to upset you, given your… condition. But he knew that… Well, he understood that you had to know."

Vahldan knew all of this. He'd known that she was near to giving birth. He'd known and he'd sent someone else. Her savior and guardian was gone. And her husband couldn't be bothered.

Harma had recently seen the king's daughter—the Skolani bastard girl—training with the boys in the fighting circles outside.

Though Herodes had taught Harma to stand up for herself, she was no warrior. No one had bothered to teach her how to swing a sword. Now she would have a son to protect. Who would she now rely on? Who would be her and her son's guardian?

Obviously not Vahldan the Bold.

It was all too much. She wanted to be alone. She really should show her uncle out. She lunged, straining to stand. Arnegern grabbed her arm to steady her. Abdominal pain jolted her. Harma dropped back down in a wash of warm liquid. "Apontia!" she cried.

Her handmaiden came running. "What is it, my lady?"

"It's time."

THE COSTS of war surrounded him here, filling him with a heaviness that made the days drag. The results of his decisions also made it more difficult for Vernius to navigate the city they'd seized, forcing him to circumvent the bustle of the masons and carpenters repairing the buildings and replacing the cobbles.

He also had to cross the narrow lane to get around another of the grim wagons, of which he'd seen several this day. Another pile of bodies, which was stacked along the lane like cordwood, was being loaded. Two graybeards unceremoniously swung and tossed one of the corpses, shrouded in what appeared to be old sailcloth, up onto the already burdened bed of the wagon. Where the imperial coroner was having the dead taken, Vernius did not know. Nor did he dare ask. He'd only specified that the city was to be emptied of them. He did not like to consider himself a civil administrator, but some issues were unavoidable. And this one, he knew, was a very important matter of sanitation.

Vernius normally thought of his army as liberators in such cases as this. This time, seeing the cost made him wonder just how liberated Megarian citizens felt.

He finally strode through the outer keep gate of Megaria.

Vernius pointedly avoided looking at the line of already loaded wagons heading to the wharf. Apparently the bodies were being loaded onto a barge of some sort. Where the barge was going, he did not need to know. Post-battle sorting was so taxing. He preferred the planning, and even the battles themselves, to this. He headed straight toward the landing and the cluster of colorfully garbed men and soldiers mulling there. "Which of these peacocks is in charge?" he asked Nicandros, who hurried to stay at his shoulder.

Nico pointed out the most colorfully dressed one—such a surprise. The man was pale and thin. He wore a headband and a wide sash in matching purple, both embossed with shiny wing-spread eagles. The soldiers surrounding the arrivals wore the purple capes and helm crests of the praetorian guard. The lead peacock made a show of being in charge—strutting back and forth, shouting commands, harrumphing with exaggerated impatience.

The man might have been a strutting peacock, but what he was not was most glaring to Vernius: He wasn't militum.

The chaotic scene made it clear. The emperor was coming. The man whose demands had been so costly was coming to prevail over his newly regained prize. Rightfully or not, this peacock would consider his authority to originate from the soon-to-arrive emperor. It was a painful reminder that the costs of this war would continue to accrue and that Vernius was but a minor player in the staging of this grand drama.

The slaves and pages the peacock oversaw were laying hand-painted paving tiles onto the beach. Yes, just moments after the emperor's advance team's arrival, they were installing an appropriately artful walkway from the landing to the road so that the sandals of His Eminence would not be defiled by that most detestable of ground surfaces: packed sand.

Wait till His Eminence got a look inside his rewon prize—the city known as the gateway to Pontea. Vernius doubted the self-proclaimed commander of this glorious campaign would find the wreckage pleasing to behold. The peacock would likely find ways to veil such unpleasantries from the royal gaze though.

The peacock's darting eyes caught sight of Vernius as he approached. "Ah, at last! I've been wondering when some semblance of aid from the locals would finally arrive."

Aid from the locals? Was he serious? "I am General Vernius Stallicus, commander of His Highness's mobile reserve."

The man actually looked him up and down. "Better still. As a general, you well-ought to have the ability to supply the labor we need here. I presume our arrival was not preannounced."

As if there wasn't anything else to be done but attend to a peacock's perceived needs. Vernius knew the type. Putting a man such as this in his place would be possible but exhausting. Probably not worth the effort. Well, maybe just one subtle jab. "And you are?"

"If you must know my name, it's Legatus Putavius. I am the royal liaison of Efusium." Ah—a bureaucrat extraordinaire. "The questions you should be asking next, General, are what I will require to make ready and how little time remains until His Eminence's arrival. But since you've already failed to anticipate our essential needs, allow me to save the precious and dwindling time by simply telling you that I will require at least a hundred men and that our emperor will be arriving far too soon to justify even this discussion."

Vernius clasped his hands behind his back. "A hundred men," he deadpanned.

"Yes, at least," Putavius said blithely. "More will be needed later, of course. Plus we'll need... oh, I'd say about forty staves of three span each driven along the road to the gate."

Vernius's annoyance slipped into his tone. "Staves? For what?"

The peacock raised one brow. "For the banners, of course."

"Of course," Vernius said.

"That will do it for out here. But alas, it will only be a start. I'll soon be inside to see what's needed for the way from the gate to the palace. Of course I can't possibly consider that until we make some sort of progress out here." The peacock rolled his eyes and gave an exaggerated sigh. "Oh, the burdens of backwater towns."

Vernius resisted saying all of the words that sprang to mind and instead repeated, "Of course." He'd seen similar displays before, but they never failed to stun him. The entire bureaucratic apparatus truly was focused on staging the most elaborate show. And this show would have nothing to do with the welfare of Megaria and its citizens. Let alone Vernius's goals in Pontea. Or even the emperor's true goals, for that matter. In fact, this particular staging was almost certain to run afoul of those.

Putavius had already strode off to pester and berate the men unloading various crates and bales of cloth from the ship on which he'd arrived.

Yes, this show would be a distraction. Vernius's father had hated the show. His father had allowed his impatience and disdain to fester into pernicious resentment. Which had been at the heart of his rebellion. Which had led to his downfall and disgrace.

Vernius had learned. The show was a distraction. The show would not win this war. It would not benefit the affected citizenry. But the empire loved—and needed—a good show. Mycanius knew it better than anyone.

Vernius would need to be patient. He must overcome his disdain or suffer the consequences. Consequences he'd learned through legacy. He must suffer the indignities and soldier on. It's what soldiers did. Soldiers who wanted to survive, anyway.

He turned to leave. Putavius shouted after him, "I need those men immediately, General..." The peacock lowered his voice to one of his lackeys. "What was his name again?"

Vernius stopped but didn't turn back. "You'll have them." He nodded to Nicandros. "Get him what he needs."

Nico's eyes went wide. "A hundred men? From where?"

"Pull them from the restoration work on the heights."

"The staves, too?" Nico added.

"Yes, see that he gets all of it." Vernius forced a smile. "The show must go on." He walked back toward the damage and destruction he'd ordered done, all in the name of speed, so that the emperor could come and claim his victory before the hiatus.

Long live the show.

WIND RATTLED THE TERRACE DOORS. Gods, it was getting dark early these days. It made this whole ordeal even more foreboding. Harma just wanted it all over and done.

Concerned female faces hovered over her, their grim expressions macabre in the lamplight. The closest one was the ugliest and most upsetting. Harma wished they would all just go away. Yes, she wanted this kicking, squirming mass out of her. But more than anything, she just wanted to get back to normal. Pregnancy had already played havoc with her figure. Not to mention her love life.

The thought had her wondering if things would ever be normal again.

"Keep pushing, my lady," Eupheme urged. "I can see its head."

"Quit... calling... my son... *it*," Harma growled between panting breaths.

"Forgive me, my lady. Him," the prude amended, sounding more annoyed than she should dare to.

"Where is Sueridas?" Harma asked for the twentieth time.

"It's too late for him. But he's not needed. You're almost done."

Harma was sure the old prude was delighted to preside over her agony. Once this was over, Harma vowed to have her revenge on both Eupheme and the so-called Wise One. It was Sueridas who'd sent the first midwife. Harma had already expelled that one; she'd had such an attitude! She suspected that Sueridas himself was willfully staying clear. The Thrakian Elli-Frodei sought the means to simultaneously take credit and avoid blame. Typical.

"You're doing so well," Kemella said in her damned patronizing tone. How in Hel's name would she know? Harma was certain that Kemella only came down to spy for the pale witch.

Halfway between passing out and shitting herself, Harma sensed it really was nearly over, for better or worse. She would either force this thing out of her or die in the effort. She tried to ignore the fear that her flesh was sure to tear. She pushed again, as they were all now extolling her—as much to shut them up as anything.

The pain intensified. Conscious thought reeled. Then, finally, a wave of relief. Had she merely shit herself? She hardly heard the joyful exclaim of the women. They all seemed far off, irrelevant. She glanced at the bloody mass that had emerged from her and looked away, up at the ceiling. Gods, was he all right? She may as well die too if her son had. Or if he was anything but perfect, for that matter.

Eupheme cleared his tiny mouth and pinched him. He gasped and started to cry.

A surge of joy swept over her. And love. It was the most rapturous she'd felt since her father had come back to Danihem for her.

Which made her realize... her son should be named Herodes. He wouldn't be here without the grandpapa he would never meet.

"It's a boy, just as you always said, my lady." The prude grinned as she wiped her son.

"Give him." Harma held out her hands. Eupheme willfully ignored the command while she took her time swaddling him. "Come, give." The old mule frowned but did as she'd been bidden, laying the warm bundle on Harma's breast.

Harma felt her tears on her face; she'd evidently been crying for some time. The busybodies gathered to coo and natter. Gods, now Mara was among them. Even the fat kitchen matron Heliopa was there, gawping and gabbling. Harma ignored them. Her son was all that mattered now.

A sigh escaped her. Her son sighed in response. Connection. The closest bond she would have in this life. The thought was heavy. It made her sleepy. But how could she sleep? He was everything. Her needs were nothing.

Could this be real? It felt like a dream already. Had her king truly come?

Heliopa filled her field of vision, grinning like an imbecile. "Opa! A fine boy, this." At least the cook had the decency to speak Gottari, thick as her accent was. "This boy is come hearty, milady. He big, this one." The grinning woman held out a fat finger and little Herodes actually grasped it with his tiny hand. Harma gasped in delight. "And strong!" Heliopa declared.

"He already has a fine crop of hair," Mara said, pulling back the blanket hooding his head. "See? Red as flame, just like Mama."

A surge filled Harma's heart. It made him all the more a part of her. Yes. This was real.

Kemella loomed over Mara's shoulder. "May I tell the king?"

Harma stared up at her. "Tell the king?"

Kemella smiled. "You know, your husband. I'm sure he'd like to see his son."

"Oh, him. Of course." Harma had wondered what Kemella wanted to tell a newborn.

Amaga's spy hurried off. Harma suddenly realized what she must look like. Gods, she must look as wretched as the pale witch herself about now. Amaga's little minion probably wanted her brother to see Harma looking like this.

Harma spotted her handmaiden and beckoned. "Apontia, fetch a washing cloth, a brush, and a hand mirror. Oh, and some stain for my lips and cheeks."

Mara, Eupheme, and Heliopa frowned, but Apontia nodded and ran to do her bidding. Apontia understood. Neither she nor her only ally could be bothered to care what these cows thought.

Apontia returned and set about grooming her: hair first, then washing her face, applying her blush, and finally the lip stain—done in perfect order of importance. All the while, the busybodies prattled about what she needed to do for the child. Eupheme actually tried to take him from her, but Harma slapped her hand. She managed to get the serving women out by concocting a tale of how hungry and thirsty she was. Denying anyone food and drink was beyond the cows. As soon as the Hellain matrons left, Mara started in, saying she should try to have the babe suckle at her breast.

Just as Harma freed her breast and set the boy's mouth to the nipple, Vahldan burst through the door. "Where is he? Where's my son?"

The man seemed utterly unaware of the indelicacy of barging in. Kemella shrugged apologetically from behind him. "Sorry. I told him to knock."

"There he is." Vahldan strode right to the bedside, pushing Mara aside. "Let me see him." He held out his big, rough hands.

Harma hesitated. All of her instincts screamed to hide little Herodes away from this ruffian, even to use her body to shelter her babe. And yet, Vahldan's smile was so joyous. She used to find the king so beautiful. It used to melt her. Belying his joy and beauty, his manner was rarely gentle. Vahldan's fierce eyes bore into her. For the first time, she saw the warning his eyes projected. Her husband was more than a mere warrior—he was a killer.

Harma had heard the talk of his rage, his lack of self-control. She'd always laughed it off, thought it all exaggerated, born of envy. She realized now that she'd been willfully blind to it.

What was she supposed to do though? Deny him? She knew the main reason he'd bonded with her was as a means to his Amalus son. She had willingly submitted herself to become his birthing vessel. They had each been a means to an outcome for the other, of course. His desired outcome hadn't bothered her so much... Until now.

Now that she had her son and saw him anew, she felt her heart shifting. Herodes was *her* son. He was not just some Amalus figure-head. He would be a true king, not a mere conqueror who named himself thus.

She saw a twitch in Vahldan's smile, sensed the threat in his veiled irritation. She sighed and gingerly held the bundled babe out to the Bringer of Urrinan.

He snatched the babe and spun away as if she'd handed him a clean tunic to put on.

Vahldan held the babe above him, gazing up at him adoringly. "Ah, now this is an Amalus boy! This is a hale and hearty heir." Little Herodes scrunched up his face, drew a breath, and started to cry again. Which only made Vahldan laugh. "He already roars like a lion."

Harma was grateful that Mara and Kemella hovered nearby. The sisters looked ready to catch her son if he was dropped. Perhaps even to snatch the boy away from their brother if he lost himself. As if she read Harma's thoughts, Mara said, "Here, I can take him."

Vahldan drew the bawling babe to his chest. "Nonsense. I can hold my own son." Harma spotted Kemella's eyes rolling and realized what his sister must be thinking, what everybody knew: The king never held his firstborn son.

Perhaps Vahldan realized it, too, because he added, "Especially a son as fine and strong and healthy as..." He glanced back at Harma for the first time. "Which reminds me. I've come up with the perfect name for him." He held the babe at arm's length again. "You shall be called Armesus. Armesus, son of Vahldan of the Amalus."

Harma's heart lurched.

"Armesus?" Mara repeated, frowning. "Sounds like a Tibairyan name."

Vahldan pulled the boy to his chest and scowled. "So it is. It means son of war."

"In Tibairyan?" Kemella asked.

"Yes, damn it!" Vahldan snapped. Kemella flinched and stepped back. Harma sensed the threat too. Even to his sister.

Everyone went still, breathlessly silent. Wind whistled through the cracks in the terrace doors, causing the flames to flicker in the lamps.

Vahldan sighed. He walked to the doors to look out at the darkening stormy skies, hiding the babe away from them and rocking him in his arms. The babe quieted. Without looking back, Vahldan spoke softly, portentously. "My son... This, my Amalus son. Comes the lion. He brings balance. He shall ascend from within the empire. I have seen it."

"You've seen it?" Mara asked.

Vahldan nodded without looking. "In my dreams." He turned back, eyes wide and haunted. "It is as it shall be. The empire shall crumble. The Urrinan shall come from within and without. This is but the beginning. I have seen..."

He walked to the bedside, his movements wooden. Looking dazed he laid the boy on Harma's chest. She grasped him and clung to him. Vahldan gently laid a hand over his back. "Armesus. My son. Mighty Armesus. Son of war. Sleep and eat and grow, my fine young lion. Your war will come."

Then, looking like a woken sleepwalker searching for his bed, Vahldan the Bold, king of Pontea, turned and walked out.

VERNIUS FINISHED his silent prayers and replaced the necklace with the pouch that held the figurine representing his grandfather around his neck. He pressed it to his chest. It meant more to him than his family torc. Obviously, since he'd given the torc away. It was clearly gone forever now. But that relic had been little more than a way to show off—for him and for his sires. Not this. The pouch represented something deeper, something for him alone. His father's father had been an exemplary soldier. A man with values, who'd lived and died with honor. A man who—unlike Vernius's father—had not only avoided disgrace but had risen above such political pettiness. His grandfather's guidance was essential to Vernius's impending mission.

It wasn't that he sought honor—he'd long set such lofty notions aside. He sought to aspire not just to avoiding disgrace, but to rising above the fear of it.

Vernius rose to his feet. Nicandros was patiently waiting. His attendant had meticulously laid out his kit and stood holding his undertunic. Vernius put his hands through the armholes and let Nico guide it over his freshly sheared head and onto his shoulders.

There was a rap on his chamber doors. "It had best be important," Vernius called.

"Undoubtedly, Lord General," came the gruff reply.

It was Tullius, his captain of the equine. Vernius had no doubt that Tully considered it so. The man's confidence exceeded the point of arrogance. Few would argue that Tullius was an asset to achieving the emperor's goals. But if ever there was someone under Vernius's command who'd consistently goaded him to abandon any last vestiges of honor, it was Tully. "Come."

Tullius was flashily attired and fully armed for their departure, which led to his telltale jingling when he walked. Like the torc Vernius had given away, the balteus Tully wore hanging from his belt was for showing off. It was tied up with the shiny bangles, rings, and earrings favored by the Sassanadi. They were taken from slain corpses—many from women and girls. Tullius considered them trophies of war. Trophies of ruthlessness, more like.

Men such as Tullius were often the first and loudest in naming the Teutonics barbarians. Vernius supposed there was an element of keener recognition among those prone to barbarity.

"Lord General, I feel I should warn you before you emerge."

"Warn me?"

"Yes, of the contemptible state of affairs out on the martialing field."

"The column is not forming up?" Vernius had given the order the prior day.

Tully's most common expression brought a snarling hound to mind. "Forming up, yes. But things are far from being as they should."

Vernius buckled his sword belt. "Out with it, Tully. What's wrong?"

"It's that legatus."

"Putavius." Vernius sighed out the name.

"Yes. He and his *praetorians*," Tully spat, revealing his venom for the royal guardians.

"Now what?"

"They're insisting that the emperor and his retinue take the lead position. They have over a dozen carriages and wagons. I informed him of the need for an advance team—not to mention flanking protection—which was ignored. The praetorian captain says his men will handle it. I strongly objected, of course."

Vernius kept a straight face. "Of course," he intoned.

Tully's sneer tightened. "That prancing prick had the gall to command me to stand down. Worse yet, he called in command to my own men, ordering them to the rear of his procession. Right in front of me. This insolence cannot stand, my lord."

"Bugger us with Priapus's cock. As if ousting the Gottari from one of the most impregnable cities in Pontea wasn't challenging enough." It was bad enough that Mycanius insisted on personally leading the final assault. The terrain made it impossible to simply stage a landing near their objective. There was only one spot that might have served, but Vernius knew a landing at Kynnya would leave an operation of this scale far too exposed for far too long. If they'd been able to sail to Thrakius, the emperor could've "led" the campaign from the deck of a flagship. Gods, if only.

Nico stood patiently holding his chest armor. Vernius nodded for him to be at ease.

"It's worse than an insult," Tully said. "It's foolishness. We know what awaits us out there. This damn road winds through the perfect terrain for ambush. We cannot allow these, these... *dandies* to jeopardize—"

Vernius held up a silencing hand. "I understand, Captain. Your concerns are worthy and noted." Tully tensed but stayed silent. "As you were." Tully tersely tilted his head and spun to leave, clearly less than satisfied. The man was opinionated and ambitious. Before Vernius had taken him in, Tully had already earned a reputation for volatility. He'd also earned a slew of dangerous rivals and no few accusations against his conduct. Tully understood that Vernius was protecting him, not just from demotion but from expulsion and disgrace. It kept the man in line.

Tullius closed the door behind himself, a bit too hard, but not insolently so. Once again, Nicandros held up the chest armor. Vernius waved it off. "Bring the heirloom piece."

Nico's eyes widened. "You're certain?"

"I'm certain. Bring his helm and sword, too."

"The helm makes your head hurt. Your father's head was smaller."

"Today that seems fitting, don't you think?" He gave Nico a wink. "It'll remind me to keep my chin up. And to wish mine was smaller."

"Last time you said—"

"Never mind what I said. Bring the cloak as well. May as well go all the way." His father's cloak was embossed with the insignia of the old republic. It had been in his family since generals had been nearly as revered as emperors. Back then, they had carried more weight with the emperors they'd served than any legatus, besides.

Nico tsked. "Please don't complain to me afterward."

"Sorry. That's a promise I cannot make. Please do it anyway."

Nico bowed his head. "Yes, my lord." He scurried off to dig the items out of their gear.

Vernius knew Nico was right—he might regret this later. Gods, he hated the idea of becoming a peacock for the peacocks. Riding all day in such finery would be irksome. His men had always responded well to his avoidance of putting on airs. But this wasn't for them. He needed to take the reins of this campaign in hand. Better to suffer the ire of the bureaucracy now than to court the disaster that might well bring disgrace later. Perhaps, if he managed to walk the line perfectly, he could even keep some semblance of honor intact. If not for himself, for his station and his family name.

In order to start on the right foot, Vernius would have to put on a show of his own.

VERNIUS MOUNTED inside Megaria's inner gate and dismissed Nicandros to ride with the supply caravan. He'd selected a chestnut gelding named Alacer. The horse—bred by an Equites family friend—was far too spirited and willful to be ridden in a procession all day. Not to mention Alacer being pissed off at having to wear the equine armor that matched his rider's. Vernius could switch horses later. It was these next few moments that mattered.

He leaned to Alacer's pricked ear. "Easy, boy. We're just putting on a little show. It'll be over soon." The gelding tossed his head in retort, forcing Vernius to be firm with the bit.

He rode out along the waiting column, through the outer keep, and toward His Eminence's vanguard waiting on the coastal road. Every head turned and then every gaze followed his progress. Good, he was making the desired impression. Remembering that it was a show, he kicked the gelding to a canter, unsheathed his father's mirror-sheen blade, and waved it overhead, inspiring his men to raise a cheer. He reined to a halt near the vanguard. He kicked and pulled Alacer to rear up. The gelding may have been trying to throw him but Vernius managed to stay in the saddle. The cheering rose to a glorious roar.

Vernius reined to face his primary audience. In spite of the cold and the ominous clouds, the emperor sat in a bejeweled and gaily painted open carriage. Mycanius was alone in the rear seat, with Putavius and a bureaucratic entourage in the smaller row seats behind the driver's bench. The carriage was surrounded by purple-cloaked praetorians.

Vernius drew up alongside the carriage. A praetorian officer grabbed Alacer by the harness while two guards moved to block Vernius's approach. Putavius and his ilk gaped. The bureaucrats looked like bad actors emoting dismay in a comedy. He supposed they were doing well enough for the minor roles in which they'd been cast.

Mycanius, however, refused to look at him. Vernius had seen the emperor wearing this particular expression before. His Eminence was seething. Vernius knew it was but a necessary dark moment—every good show had one, the darker the better. Vernius leapt from the saddle and hurried past the praetorian officers. Still gripping the hilt of the bared steel, he put himself where Mycanius could see him. Before the praetorians could seize him, Vernius dropped to his knees in the cold, squishy mud. He bowed his head till his ridiculous crimson crest almost brushed the ground. He penitently proffered the sword on outstretched open palms.

In his best acting voice, unused since his drama lessons at the academy, he proclaimed, "I am yours, my emperor. As are those sworn to my service." His men cheered.

"Get up, you fool." He rose to meet Mycanius's smoldering glare. "What in the gods' names are you up to, Vernius?" Two praetorians stood by, unsure whether or not to physically restrain a popular general in front of his men. Even one holding an unsheathed sword.

Vernius stayed with the stage voice. "Up to? I strive only to serve and protect our illustrious emperor and through him our mighty empire. I beg of you, Highness—allow me to become your royal knight of the body during this campaign, and together we will vanquish the heathen foe." The line elicited more cheering.

"Knight of the body? This isn't some bard's tale, Vernius. What you should strive for is to be the successful general of my finest army."

"I can think of no finer honor than to strive at the shoulder of my emperor as he leads us forth... to victory!" He raised the sword to the men and, again, they roared their approval.

"End this ridiculous charade. Do what I'm paying you to do and lead this army. Now!"

Vernius bowed with a flourish. "As you command, Highness. To that end, please grant our equine division the honor of leading our valiant force into the hostile territory, that they may suffer the first dart that any barbarian dares to send against us. Our Equites would happily die for the opportunity to keep our beloved emperor safe from harm along the course... to certain victory!" He raised the sword a final time, and his men played their role perfectly to the last, cheering without much noticeable laughter.

Mycanius huffed and faced forward. "Fine. Whatever it takes to end this farce."

Vernius bowed his head. "As you command, Highness." He gave Putavius a wink as he turned, sheathed the blade, and remounted. He urged his spirited mount to prance to the front of the equine column. He shared a conspiratorial grin with Tully. "You heard him, Captain! His Eminence has granted your host the honor of the lead position. Do us proud."

Tully dramatically pulled his fist to his chest. "Yes, Lord General." The captain snapped his reins and signaled his column. With the eagle standard-bearers at the fore, the equine division paraded past the royal vanguard, saluting as they passed their annoyed emperor and his peeved praetorians.

His Eminence's imperial mobile reserve was on the march, off to Thrakius to deal the deathblow to the thug king and his Gottari savages. At long last.

CHAPTER 8
FATE'S FORTRESS

"*Autumn was a season of preparation in Thrakius—of stocking and stowing. Even more so in the autumn of Megaria's fall. Along with the approach of hiatus came an added sense of dread, an unspoken resignation to what could only be an ill fate.*

And yet, life went on inside the palace. For some it was a happy time. With the return of the Gottari army, many families were reunited—no few for the first time in nearly two years, since Vahldan first set sail for Bafrana, two winter solstices prior.

Still, the approach of what had been a distant war became palpable. The imperial navy's tightening grip on the waterways of Pontea severely restricted shipping. The Thrakian docks grew deserted as cargo ships sought alternative ports. Prices rose, as did smuggling activity. Flour, oil, and wine grew scarce. Meat was all but nonexistent. Black market trading flourished. Some law-abiding merchants simply closed their shops and left. Others sent their children away.

In many respects, it was as if the siege that everyone sensed looming had already begun. Whether Gottari or Hellain, the one thing all of us could agree upon was that things would get worse before they got better."
—*Brin Bright Eyes, Saga of Dania*

. . .

AGORAKI WATCHED the sun drop below the mountains over Trazonia from the rigging of *Gullwing*. Since he'd begun sailing, Ago had made this a nightly ritual, climbing up to sit on a spar and gaze out over whichever waters or harbor as the sun set. Other sailors spoke of their longing for home, wondering when they'd be able to return. Ago wondered if he'd ever have a place like that. He flopped back and forth when he thought about Thrakius. Some days he missed his maaman nearly too much to bear. He even missed the comfort of the palace's back passages and catacombs. Other days he never wanted to see that place again.

Tonight, the only thing he was sure of was that Trazonia would never feel like home. This city felt as foreign as any place he'd visited.

He heard voices on the dock below. Dexicos led a small group through the shadows, up the gangway, and then aft. A half-dozen of them. Dex knocked at Cap's cabin door. Light spilled out as the men filed in. The last one turned to grab and close the door, and Ago saw him from the side. It was the captain of *Wavebreaker*—the ship with the largest cargo hold in the fleet.

Ago guessed the other captains of the fleet made up the rest of the group. His curiosity brimming, he scrambled down the mast to the deck, ran to the hatch, and climbed down into the hold. A group of sailors sat in a circle casting gaming stones on a tray propped across the bow beam. Others were already draped in their hammocks. Ago slowed down to keep from drawing attention. Few ever paid him much heed though. Tonight was no different. He slipped down the aisle through the stacks of cargo to the aft.

Ago went straight to the barrel with the bronze hoops—the one that marked his hidden spot. He tipped it slowly, carefully rolling it on its edge before setting it straight again. He crawled through the narrow gap, across his hidden bedding, and up onto the sealed crock. From there he slid up between the strakes, wedging himself in place with his toes on the crock lid. Then he wriggled into the gap between the edge of the deck boards and the strakes till the top half of his head was inside the built-in bench at the stern end of Malvius's cabin. From here he could peer through the slats of the bench's skirt, between one man's legs, and into the lamp-lit cabin. Dex stood by the door. Cap sat at the table. They were the only two faces Ago could see; the visitors were all at the same end of the cabin as Ago—some standing, others sitting.

"All I'm asking is, why take the risk?" Ago recognized the nasal whine of the voice. It belonged to the captain of *Pontean Bounty*. "We've spent months assembling this haul. If even one of us is hailed and boarded, we lose a fourth of what we've worked for. If not more!"

"Yes," Cap replied, "it is a risk. But one I believe we must take. It's also a risk most of your crews will accept gladly, I'll warrant." Malvius was using his patient voice. Ago could tell Cap had already made up his mind about whatever they were debating.

"Every good trader knows that risk is inevitable," another voice said. Ago suspected it was the *Wavebreaker* captain. "The higher the risk, the better the profit. If we make port safely, we can thank the Tiberian navy for what's sure to be a terrific return. Thrakius is bound to be starved for fresh goods when we arrive."

Back to Thrakius! The thought startled a flock into flight in Ago's belly. The crew had been whispering and wagering over their next destination for weeks. Few dared to hope they'd be going home. As always, the thought of home brought other thoughts to mind—thoughts he tried hard to avoid. Thoughts of Brin. Gods, sometimes when his guard slipped, he missed her almost as much as Maaman.

But, as always, the image of her smiling face turned into the pale, grimacing version of that same pretty face. The one from the day he had run back leading the Sass. The one when her big eyes had gone all cat-like and her cheeks had been splattered with gore. He remembered how she had shaken like she'd been cold to the core, how he'd embraced her. How she'd stiffened in his arms and then broken free.

Every time he thought of Brin, her words always came back, too.

"I killed her," she'd said. In his memory it always sounded all husky and hollow, like it came from far away. "I killed your mother." It hadn't been an apology. And one of those never came. Thing was, most days Ago wasn't sure he was owed one.

He shook those thoughts away as the next voice of the cabin piped up. "Well and good if we *can* get there. And once we're there, how long will we be trapped?" This one was the growling rasp of the captain of *Seaswell*. His was a voice that couldn't be mistaken.

"Good point. Hiatus is coming on fast." This last one was the oddly soft voice of the captain of *Dawnseeker*.

Malvius leaned back. "I'm not so certain we'll all be trapped through the whole winter."

"Even so, I can't imagine where else I'd rather be trapped," someone added.

"It's not like we'll be safe anywhere else," one of the captains said. "By aiding the thug, we've gotten crosswise with Tiberia and with Zafan. Not to mention Isidros. The Sass no longer want anything to do with us. Pontea does not exactly hold us in high regard at the moment."

"I still say anywhere is safer than Thrakius," the growly one said. "Once the siege begins, the gods only know what measures the Tiberians will take. You all heard the rumors, same as I. They bombarded Megaria from on high. Wrecked half their own city just to chase out the last of the Gottari army. All they would've had to do was wait. But they're willing to do most anything, including killing innocent civilians, just to get to Vahldan straight away."

One of them harrumphed. "For me that's an argument for going home." It was the *Wavebreaker* captain. "My family's there, as are the families of most of my men. If such an ill turn befalls Thrakius, I would be there with them."

"I've told you all not to worry." Malvius was still using his patient voice. "The Gottari will fall. And when they do, they'll be utterly destroyed. But Thrakius will still stand, as it has for five hundred years and more. Our fair city is more than just a cozy port.

It's one of the finest fortresses of the civilized world. We'll not only survive, we'll put ourselves in position to make her ours again. Finally."

It was silent for a long moment. "I want to believe, Cap," one of them finally said. "But even you've got to admit that it's a little unsettling to face down the whole imperial militum."

"We all know Cap's got this figured out." It was Dexicos, speaking up for the first time. "He's always a dozen steps ahead of both the thugs and the Tibes. Tell 'em what you told me, Cap. About the boy."

Ago stopped breathing. When anyone in the fleet mentioned *the boy*, they meant him. Malvius shot a glare at Dex. "Maybe they should know, Cap," Dex said with a shrug. "After all, we're all in this together." Ago suspected Dex would get a verbal thrashing later, but he'd already let the bird out of the barn.

"I suppose you're right." Malvius leaned back again, his eyes hooded. He lowered his voice. "A few of you already know that young Agoraki is my deceased sister's son. What you don't know is that his father's identity is even more important, especially in regard to our position with the Tiberians."

Ago's heart thumped in his throat. This was it! He'd always suspected that Cap knew who his father was, but Ago had never been able to glean a hint from him.

"Well?" the growly one said. "Who is it?"

Malvius smirked. "The boy's father is none other than Vernius of Nardium, Lord General of His Eminence's mobile reserve. Which is the very army that, as we speak, is marching to besiege Thrakius. My friends, we have in our custody the long-lost son of the man who is about to destroy Vahldan the Bold and oust the Gottari from our home forever."

～

It was Elan's favorite time of day. The girl had left with her uncle, who would—after their so-called *exercise*—deliver Brin into the care of her tutors. And Hesiod was off on his daily errands. Time for her first cup of wine—so much more satisfying than those that would follow.

He'd vowed to stop, but Elan suspected Urias was still training Brin, regardless of whether they actually swung practice swords or not. She also suspected Hesiod was as interested in staying clear of her as he was in attending to household necessities. But none of it mattered. Elan was grateful to have the residence to herself. She could stare off across the sea to her heart's content, without a soul to pester her about how much wine she'd had. Or the state of her attire, or whether she'd washed or combed her hair. Or insist that she eat.

Elan had yet to change out of her nightshift, but if she never got around to it, she'd be ready for bed again whenever she fell into it. She went to the sideboard in the entry hall and poured a brimming cup, ruby red. With one hand still on the flagon, she filled her mouth by rote and swallowed slowly, feeling the warmth suffuse her chest. She refilled it before leaving the flagon, staving off the need to return. Even as she settled into her favorite chair, her first cup was already delivering the return of her old friends: lethargy and haziness. She felt the familiar heaviness slipping into her limbs and her cares sliding from her mind.

She shivered. Damn, it was getting cold. She stood with a groan and went back in for a cloak. She made a quick stop at the flagon. The glimpse of a stranger standing nearby startled her—until she realized it was her own reflection in the adjacent looking glass. She almost laughed at herself, but there was nothing funny about what she saw. Her body was hunched and her hair was a tangled mop. Gods, it hurt to stand up straight anymore. The lines on her face had grown so deep. And those eyes! *Her* eyes, she reminded herself. They were sunken and hollow. And haunted.

To think, she'd once been a Blade-Wielder. Someone to be feared and admired.

Elan had seen that look before, in warriors who'd seen too much —how the fire in their belly had burned down to a smolder. How suddenly they had aged.

But what did it matter? She was doomed anyway. She refilled the cup and turned away. She wasn't in the mood for reflections.

She pulled her cloak over her shoulders and went back out to the terrace. Ah, back to her chair. She had it close enough to the potted fir to occasionally catch a whiff of the forest. The wind was bracing. Hiatus was coming. Winter storms, too. Good.

Elan welcomed winter as she would an old lover to her bed. In Pontea, everything stopped in winter. Which meant there was no one to kill and no one trying to kill her—a temporary reprieve from being what she'd become. She could hunker down and do nothing but wait. Wait for the killing to start again.

She drew the cloak tight and gazed out at the sea, at the coming and going of ships. She filled her mouth again and swallowed, warmth suffusing her chest. Her eyes lost focus. There were only the blue and green water and the gray sky and the relentless, cleansing wind.

Elan heard the slam of the residence's entry door behind her. Without bothering to look, she called, "Did you bring wine, old man?" Hesiod didn't answer. Typical. "You know I'll send you back if you didn't." Her smile drooped from lack of effort.

"Ah, gods. What has become of you, Elan?"

She stiffened. It wasn't Hesiod. Her eyes stung. She blinked and kept them on the sea, unwilling to look at him. She felt his presence drawing nearer. She'd avoided him since that evening right after her return, when he'd turned his ugliness on her. She'd not only been unable to keep him from descending into it, she'd been powerless to bring him back from it.

Gods be damned, how she hated facing this. She'd told him what to do and he'd rejected it. Her voice meant nothing to him now. And it was too late. He wasn't who he'd once been. Neither was she. None of it was fair. But the gods were fickle.

All she could do was shrug. And drink.

"You were the brightest, the bravest—the best among us. How has it come to this?"

Elan shrugged again, wishing he would just leave. "Will of the gods, I suppose," she said.

"You're really going to blame the gods?"

"Why not? They gave me to you. It's either blame them or you."

"Me?" Vahldan asked. "They bound me to destiny, too."

Elan snorted. "But with me you share only your doom. The rest of it you choose to share with others. This"—she twirled her free hand, indicating the wine, the seat, the tree, and the view—"is all that's left to me."

Vahldan's shadow fell over her. She let him take the cup from her hand, afraid he was going to force her to look, terrified that their connection might return. He set the cup on the nearby table. "I need you, Elan. No. Actually, I need the old you."

Her eyes itched again. "This is the only me that's left."

"Come now. You know that's not true."

She drew a breath and sighed it out. "You need me for what?"

"Can you not see? What comes? It's right there in front of you." He went to the parapet and leaned on the rail.

Elan focused on the view. For the first time today, she saw. The ships, they all had crimson sails. Warships. Tibairyan warships.

"This is just the beginning," he said. "They're coming."

Elan stood and went to the rail beside him. The seagates were closed. She finally looked at him. Vahldan was ashen. He looked exhausted. And somehow smaller than he once had.

But Freya be damned, it was still there. She not only saw him, she *felt* him. Their bedamned connection. She couldn't keep herself from grasping it, drawing it in, like a diver sucking in a breath after breaking the surface.

And she knew. Vahldan wasn't just full of doubt, he was rattled. Afraid.

It made her afraid. "We knew the navy would come," she said. "We knew they'd try to shut down the port. Hiatus will—"

"No," Vahldan injected. "Hiatus won't delay this. They're coming. The mobile reserve. They know all of the landings are too easily defended. So they're marching from Megaria."

"Now?"

"Yes, damn it. Now."

Gods, she should've known. Maybe she did. Maybe it was easier to fool herself. "And so?" He cocked his head, puzzled. "What do you need me for?" she demanded.

"They'll seek to set siege."

"I would presume."

Vahldan frowned. "Don't you see? They're not coming to negotiate. They don't want us to surrender. They're sending their best army. With winter coming. They want to destroy us, Elan! They're coming to trap us. They won't stop till they exterminate us."

He wasn't merely afraid, he was lost. It angered her. "Well, didn't I tell you?"

"I... I didn't..."

"You didn't want to believe," Elan finished for him.

He sighed. "I don't know." Vahldan had that look—exactly the one he used to get. The one he'd had that first morning in the aftermath of the Spali raid. He wanted to be strong, but he didn't believe that he was. He wanted to act, but he was letting his fear keep him from it.

"What do you mean, you don't know? We've been talking about facing our doom for half of our lives. What did you think that meant?"

Vahldan looked out over the sea. "Not this. So many will suffer. So many will die."

Her anger only grew. "Gods afire, Vahldan, you're not a teenage lordling anymore. This is it. You led us here. You made yourself a king. Did you think it would be easy? You always said you wanted in on their game, to be a real player. Well, we're all in, and there's no way to bow out. Did you really think no one else would get hurt?"

"I don't know."

Elan moved into his field of vision, forcing him to look into the haunted, puffy eyes of the first victim of his game. "Don't lie to me. You know you can't. Not to me."

"I mean, I don't know what to do." He dropped his chin, unable to hold her gaze.

Elan almost laughed. "That's ridiculous. You're the Bringer!" He glanced up but looked away again. "Did you really imagine the Bringer's role would be to hide in his fortress and await his inevitable doom?"

"Isn't that what you've been doing?" Vahldan glanced archly.

Ouch. "Point taken." She slapped her own cheeks with both hands, seeking clarity. "All right, then. Let's figure this out. First things first. We try to get the women and children away."

"Elan—"

"I know that idea makes you angry. But it's the right thing to do and—"

"I already tried. You were right. I sent scouts. The snow in the high passes, it's already impassable. It's too late to safely get wagons over." Vahldan shook his head. "Besides, almost none of the wives want to be parted from their men. I'm not sure those I've spoken to fully understand. For better or worse, each one I've spoken to says they'll stand or fall together."

Elan stared out at the warships. Her eyes drifted to the west, toward Megaria. The road that would bring the foe wound among the seaside cliffs. She'd traveled the route several times now. Parts of the road were treacherous. She spun back to him. "Let me ask you this: Do you truly believe that the empire is corrupt—that the Urrinan will come and that it will be a boon to our people?"

He firmed his countenance. "I do. You know I do."

Their connection showed her that he believed what he'd said. "Good. Then lead us out."

He raised his brow. "Back to Dania? Haven't you been listening?"

"No. Lead your warriors out against the foe. It's why they followed you. It's why we're all here. If this corrupt foe—the one we wish to supplant through upheaval—is coming to exterminate us, we can't just wait for them to do it. You're right—waiting is what I've been doing, and I hate it. I don't want to do that anymore. If we want to bring upheaval, we have to fight. On our terms."

Vahldan bit his cheek, still unsure. He wanted the old her? Well, she wanted the old him. And he still hadn't become the leader she knew was inside him. "You've sent your army against them. But that's not the same. You and I both know it. This army, these men, they don't care about a Pontean city or an empire. Yes, when it comes to it, they'll say they care about the future of our people. But what they came here for is you. They have always fought for you. They long to do so again. Because they love you."

His gaze hardened and his back straightened. She saw a glimpse of the man for whom she'd given up everything. Elan ran inside to her bedchamber. She flung open her chest, dug out the sheath, and ran back to him. She drew Biter and dropped the sheath as she strode to him. Proffering the blade on her open palms, she dropped to her knees before him. "I belong to you, my lord. Lead me. Lead all of us. Into battle against those who seek the end of our people. Lead us to upheaval, to prophecy. Lead us to victory, even as the world crumbles. But more than that, lead us to honor. Make ours a tale fit for the songs that will echo through the ages."

He nodded. Now she saw it clearly. Vahldan the Bold, Lion Lord of the Amalus, now stood before her. She couldn't keep from smiling. He took the sword by the hilt, swished it twice, and offered the hilt back to her. "Funny, but I don't think I've ever held Biter before. After all these years. It's a fine blade, Elan."

"The finest."

"You've borne it well," he said. "Ellasan would be proud."

This time she couldn't keep the tears from filling her eyes. "I haven't always. But you're right. She will be. I know I will make her proud before I see her again. Just as you will make your parents." He pressed his lips together, blinked away the shine in his eyes, and nodded.

He pulled her to her feet. "I accept your service. On one condition."

"Which is?"

Vahldan's smile was his old, beautiful one. "That you agree to stay at my side, to ride and to fight there. As we once did. Come what may." She opened her mouth to reply, but he held up a silencing finger. "And not in a sleeping frock."

She laughed and sheathed the sword. "I suppose I can find something else to wear."

Elan felt something old stir inside her. Gods, she'd kept this feeling locked away for so long. She loved this version of him. Of them. On impulse, she tossed the sword onto the chair and threw her arms around his neck. She pressed her head to his chest. Rather than hugging her back, he stiffened and grabbed her arms.

She allowed him to take her hands in his. He held them a long moment between his. They were big and warm, and still strong. Gods, the awkwardness came crashing back. Perhaps that version of who they'd once been together was gone forever. Perhaps it should be.

He released her and looked away. "I, ah... I don't want to ruin..." His smile was tight. "We are seeking honor, after all. Maybe I'd better..." He nodded toward the exit.

"I know." The moment had almost been enough to make her forget. He'd bonded with another. Twice. Elan pulled the cloak closed and turned to face the wind off the sea.

Vahldan strode to the terrace doors and stopped. "Thank you, Elan," he said.

She looked back at him, tilted her head. "And you."

"It's good to see you. The old you, I mean." He smiled fondly and left.

IN SPITE of being wedged into the framing of the hull of *Gullwing*, Ago felt like he was in free fall. His head filled with white noise. He only vaguely heard the other captains exclaiming over Malvius's revelation.

Gods, he was half Tiberian. Ago had never met a kind or gracious Tiberian in his life. They were the law, the punishers, the users, the takers. They'd made his maaman a slave, burned her village, killed her family. His father was not just one of them, he was among their elite, a leader of their murderous war machine.

"No disrespect to your sister, Cap, but the boy... He's..." The speaker trailed off.

Cap glowered. "He's what? A bastard? What of it?" To Ago, it almost felt like Cap was standing up for him. It was like a breeze over an ember inside of him.

The speaker cleared his throat. "It's just that I don't know many fathers who celebrate their bastards. How do we know this Vernius will give two shits about the boy?"

"Believe me, he'll care," Malvius insisted.

"Cap's checked the man out," Dexicos offered. "Tell 'em, Cap."

Malvius frowned but nodded. "It doesn't have so much to do with my sister. It's more about the man's personal circumstances. General Vernius is an Eques—born of noble bloodlines. Landed—country estate near the capital, all of that. The father was a general too, you see. But the elder, he got himself in trouble; tangled himself up with a usurper. Proclaimed the last emperor had dishonored the throne and betrayed his people. Together they incited an insurrection. The imperial court convicted dear ole' Papa of treason. So the old emperor stripped the father of his lands and locked him up. I heard he was offered a pardon if he publicly refuted it all. Instead of freeing himself and getting his lands back, this proud prick managed to get himself strangled on the hill of the temples in front of a cheering mob."

Oh great. The proud prick in this story was Ago's grandfather.

"After all of that, they still named the son a general, too?" one of them asked.

Malvius's smile crept back. The only thing Cap loved better than a good tale was being the one telling it. "Ah, that's where Vernius's mum comes in. The woman was also from a noble clan, and by all accounts she enjoyed the finer things. Expected them, even. So much so, when her husband turned traitor, she took young Vernius and left. Went to the palace at Medicia to throw herself at the mercy of the old emperor. Seems the emperor liked the finer things, too. And by all accounts, Vernius's mum had some very fine assets. There were rumors that mercy went beyond mere dalliance. I've even heard tell of a royal bump in her belly. But the emperor had his healers dose her to wash the incriminating evidence away. They say the woman's eagerness to please won the son a spot at the academy. Beyond that, Mum even managed to regain Papa's house and a portion of his lands, which was conditionally bequeathed to Vernius."

The growler laughed. "And the emperor this general answers to is the son of the emperor who humped his mother?"

Malvius nodded. "My sources tell me that our good general has spent his life trying to live down his papa's misdeeds. Vernius has been so busy living it all down, he never married. Hence, no heirs. Which leads me back to that conditional bequeathment. In order to keep his lands and his title, General Vernius will need one. No heir, no estate. And the young heir we happen to have in our possession is from pretty fair stock, if I do say. Believe me, the good general will be interested. Ago is not only born of the Equites. He also happens to descend from an anaxship in Pontea. For a bastard, not a bad get. Wouldn't you agree?"

The pulse at the side of Ago's throat became a stone that he couldn't swallow. Rather than free-falling, he suddenly felt trapped, like his head would never come out of the space beneath the bench. His heart rate soared again. Nearing panic, he turned his head and pulled it down, scraping his ears and pulling his hair. His toes slipped and the crock tipped beneath him. Ago froze, holding his breath and trying to balance. He felt the crock skidding and couldn't do a thing to stop it. It slammed down, hitting the planks of the hold with a resonant thud. It didn't end there. The lid fell off, rolled into the aisle, and made an ongoing clatter before gravity drew it flat and still. The issue left Ago's legs dangling.

"What was that?" the nasal captain asked.

"Someone's in the hold," the gruff captain asserted. Ago gasped. "Indeed, they're right below us."

Stealth be damned, Ago dropped to the platform and rushed back out through the gap in the barrels. Cap's chair screeched and the floor above creaked with the weight of all of the men rising and moving.

No time to right the crock, even to hide his special spot. Instead, Ago ducked his head and rushed down the aisle. Sailors' heads turned as he passed through the bunks and the gaming tables. He stopped short as his uncle's boots came into view ahead, descending the ladder from the deck. He fled on past the ladder, heading for the forward hatch, hoping it hadn't been battened for the night.

"Ago, wait! Let's talk about this." Malvius was in the hold, coming after him.

He saw the blue of the night sky through a gap in the hatch lid. Ago scampered up the ladder, slipped through the narrow opening, and flopped onto the deck. He sprang up and started for the gangway but saw the group of captains talking in a cluster at the top of it. One of them pointed his way and all of their heads turned. Ago spun and ran back to the bow.

The forward hatch lid was sliding back. Ago ran to the prow and climbed up onto the front rail, his arm around the masthead. The taut mooring line to the dock was as thick as Ago's forearm. All of his fellow crewmen said he was the best line walker they'd ever seen. It was fairly steep, but he could make it. He shimmied up the masthead and stepped out onto the line, one hand still on the ship as he gained his footing.

Ago couldn't keep from glancing down at the black water gurgling and slapping at the pilings so far below. The decline felt steeper than he'd imagined. He'd be forced to all but run to keep from sliding. The lump he still couldn't swallow made it hard to breathe.

"Don't go." Malvius stood on the deck, reaching a hand up. "Don't leave me, Ago."

"Why? Because you need me as a prize, to barter with the Tiberians?"

"No. Because it's dangerous." Malvius's smile glowed in the moonlight, but Ago heard the fret in his voice. "Not just walking the line, but that big stinking city out there. Trust me, son, Trazonia is a tough place for a runaway." A few sailors came trotting up, but Malvius held up a halting hand. "Leave us. Ago and I need to talk." The sailors shrugged and stepped back, milling off again. Malvius held his hand back out to Ago. "Come on down, Ago. Let's have our talk down here, where it's safe."

Ago's eyes stung as he huffed a contemptuous laugh. "Our talk? Seems like we've had it. Remember? When I asked you who my father is and you said you didn't know. You looked me in the eyes and lied. Guess that was safer for you."

Malvius let his hand drop. His uncle nodded. "You're right. I lied. And I'm sorry. And I doubt you'll believe me when I say that I did it to protect you."

"Protect me? Don't you mean to keep me from going to him? I'm your betting coin. You couldn't let me slip away. You already knew you'd need me for the deal you plan to make with the Tiberians once they fight the Gottari for you."

Malvius looked hurt. Or was that fear? "I didn't start this war, Ago," his uncle said.

"Maybe not. But you've pretended to side with the Gottari for years now. I finally get it. You did everything you could to make sure it got nasty. And now that it has, my father's going to come after you once he's done with Vahldan. I'm just the gift that keeps you out of the dungeon. Or maybe gets you even better off than free. Maybe offering me up even makes you rich. Or is it richer still? That's what this is really about for you, isn't it?"

Malvius shook his head. "No, son. You don't get it. Please understand. You're all the family I have left. The Gottari, they killed all of the rest of them. Everyone except you. I didn't want you to go to Vernius. I still don't. And I couldn't let you stay in the palace. Look, I'm not going to try to pretend I'm not selfish. I know you know me better than that. Honestly, Ago, I was just so happy when you came to me. Your selfish uncle lied to you and brought you aboard because he wants you in his life. It's as simple as that."

Ago rolled his teary eyes. "Oh, come on, Cap. I heard all of it."

"What I told them?" Malvius threw a thumb over his shoulder. "First, you shouldn't eavesdrop. But you've got to believe me when I say that I only told them what they needed to hear. I never had any intention of bartering with you. But they need to believe we've got a secret weapon. It's not going to come to that."

Ago's legs started to cramp. He hugged the masthead to his shoulder. "How am I supposed to believe you're not just telling me what I need to hear?"

Malvius sighed and slumped against the rail. "You want to know the whole truth? The truth is... I don't have any real plan at all. I'm not sure how I'm going to convince the Gottari that I'm still with them. And even if I do, it may take me until it's too late. After that, I have no idea how I'll convince the Tiberians that I never really was on the Gottari side. It's all a mess, and every time I turn around, it gets messier. I'm just making it all up as I go. I have no idea whether I'm going to survive this war, let alone get rich. Gods afire, if I wanted to get rich, I'd stay here and wait it out. Or maybe take on a load and make a run for the Tiberian Sea."

Ago hugged the masthead and frowned down at him. "Why?"

"Why what?"

"Why risk so much?"

"Because Vahldan betrayed me. In the worst possible way. We

were friends once. Or at least I thought so. But then he deceived me. My so-called friend used me to steal my city. Vahldan stole my life, Ago. He took everything. He and his thugs killed everyone I've ever cared about." His uncle stared out across the harbor. "I lost the only thing I've ever considered precious. And I couldn't save her." Ago had never heard him sound so sad.

But if Malvius was anything, he was a good liar. And a good actor. He knew how to use people, too. "If you have no plan, how come you seem so sure you'll succeed? What if you're wrong? What if we go back to Thrakius and when the Tiberians come, we'll all just get locked up? Or killed? What if we're caught and my father doesn't even want me?"

Malvius faced him again. "Want to know how I'm sure? This tells me." He patted his stomach. "I'm sure because the gods can't betray me. Not again. Not after all I've been through. I feel it in my belly and in my bones. Vahldan will be brought to justice. Even *he* believes he's doomed. And we'll get our due—you and I. We're the rightful anaxes of Thrakius."

Ago suddenly felt exhausted. He crouched to sit on his haunches, hugging the masthead. "What about Brin? She's my best friend."

"Best friend who killed your mother." A sob escaped Ago. Malvius nodded. "Oh, I know. She's just a kid. Maybe it's not her fault. But Brin is one of them. I'm sure it feels sad to realize it, but she can never be one of us."

"I'm just a kid, too. How am I supposed to know who's really good or bad?"

Malvius smiled—one of his real ones. "You're my nephew, aren't you? What does your belly tell you? In this family, bellies are never wrong."

Ago put a hand on his stomach. "Right now? It just feels sick."

Malvius laughed and held out his hand again. "That can happen. But it'll pass. Come on down, son. We don't have to figure it all out tonight."

Ago reached down, took his uncle's hand, and let him lift him onto the deck. Malvius put his hands on his shoulders. "Don't worry, Ago. We'll figure it out as we go. All right?"

His uncle's smile went all sly again. Beneath the queasiness, Ago's belly told him that Malvius was still a world-class liar. But, in his bones rather than his belly, Ago believed that what he'd heard about his father and all the stuff that Malvius had just told him about the Gottari—well, most of that was true. Ago didn't doubt that when it came to it, if Malvius could achieve his revenge or regain his place in Thrakius by using him, he would.

Still, Cap was right. Ago could figure it out as he went. Agreeing bought him time. He nodded. "All right."

CHAPTER 9

ADVANCING HOSTILITIES

"Every Gottari warrior who prepared to ride out to face the approaching imperial army was full of bravado and cheer. Their hearts were lifted upon hearing that their king would lead them once again. As were the hearts of those the army was to leave behind. For days, the palace buzzed with activity. The martial yard resounded with the clacking of swords and the dining halls echoed with laughter and song. After the somberness in the wake of Megaria's fall, it felt like a reawakening.

Seeking courage, I took in every table discussion and eavesdropped on every passing chat. Everyone seemed certain that the tide of the war could be turned, that the foe would be repelled. All but two. My parents.

They sought to hide it from me. Still, I could not help but see. Vahldan and Elan continued to believe that Urrinan had finally arrived. They remained devoted to their duty to it. They were resolved to face their inevitable doom.

As terrifying as the realization was, a place deep inside of me was glad —glad that they had regained the purpose that they had once shared. Witnessing it was new to me, as they had lost it before I'd been born.

Indeed, a part of me believed they had lost it because *I'd been born."*—
Brin Bright Eyes, Saga of Dania

THE MORNING SKY had gone from gray to blue by the time Nicandros returned with Vernius's saddled mount. It seemed the royal grooms were in no hurry to get started. The royal vanguard set the pace and the camp of the mobile reserve followed suit, lethargically forming up to march. As annoyed as Vernius was, he could hardly blame his officers for easing up. This was their emperor—the supposed commander of this campaign—who was setting the pace.

"At least the equine division is ready to set out," Nico ventured. The younger man had always keenly sensed his every mood. And indeed, Vernius was grumpy.

He harrumphed. "Small consolation. None of the rest of us are going anywhere until His Eminence is ready." Although the praetorians had Mycanius's carriages in line, the imperial pavilions had yet to be struck. There wasn't a single indication as to when the emperor might appear to order their departure.

"Perhaps the delay will at least ensure that the supply train is ready when the horns blow, my lord." Ever the optimist, the young man was right that the supply train had been even slower than the plodding army. It made for even later nights, creating a perpetual cycle of woe.

Not for the first time, Vernius considered the ways he might prod the royal caravan to life. He spotted Licinian, which reminded him not to bother. The captain of the royal guard detachment was unbearably condescending, even for a praetorian. The man never missed an opportunity to flaunt the imagined superiority of his division over the remainder of the militum. If Vernius insisted on hastening their departure, Licinian would gleefully seek the opposite.

Vernius scanned the looming hills rising over both sides of the roadway. "Today, of all days, I wanted to get this army moving and keep us together." The scouts reported that, with a good and steady pace, the army could make it through the twisty canyon ahead in the span of one day. After that, the road returned to running along the coast, which would provide them with naval support.

"Shall I draft another missive, my lord?" Nico asked.

Vernius had tried to secure an audience the prior evening. When his request had gone unanswered, he'd sent a message, pleading his case with the emperor. He was being ignored. Again. He shook his head. "Pestering him at this point will only make things worse. I'm going to ride the column. I'd like to see firsthand just how spread out we've become."

Nico bowed his head and held the stirrup for him.

Captain Tullius strode over as Vernius settled in the saddle. Two mounted men walked their horses behind Tully. "These two have been assigned as your guardians for the day, my lord." The guards rightfully looked wary.

"I already dismissed them." And he hadn't exactly been pleasant in doing so.

Tully raised his chin. "I feel it is my duty to tell you, Lord General, that your officers have concurred. Leaving you unguarded has become too dangerous. The raids have grown too numerous. There was yet another raid on the supply train last night."

"I am aware. I'm also aware that yet another wagon has been stolen. I intend to see what in Hades' name is going on back there. There may be little I can do to get us underway each morning, but I won't gladly tolerate banditry by night. Whether or not I'm actually in command of this traveling show, the gods know I'll take the blame for all that befalls it."

Tully squinted up at the hilltops. "May I speak freely, Lord General?"

"Why else do you think I keep you around?"

"Ordinarily, I would never think to argue against your wishes."

Tully's gaze met his. "It's these damn Gottari savages. They have no honor."

Tully complaining about a lack of honor. Ah, the irony. "And?"

"They've been targeting officers since Nicomedya. Especially that Hippomache of theirs. That bitch is a demon from the underworld. It's like facing off with a wild beast. None of them care a wit for their own safety. Which means that none of us should ride alone. Especially in these forsaken hills."

Vernius doubted the bandits in question were actual Gottari. Why would the Gottari risk venturing out this far? Especially since they enjoyed the safety of the walls of Thrakius? But he was tired of arguing. He craned to find the emperor's servants carrying trays to the royal pavilion, finally bringing Mycanius his breakfast. After that, they'd all be awaiting His Eminence's stint on his golden chamber pot. At this point, Vernius could only hope they'd get underway by midday.

"Very well," he said to Tully. "As long as your guards stay out of my way." He swiftly reined around and put his heels to the gelding. His unwanted guards had to swat their mounts to keep up.

As he rode down the column, it only got sloppier. The late starts had established a troubling trend. There was no alacrity about striking camp or making ready. Hardly surprising when each day's starting time was anyone's guess. The rank and file of his infantry snapped to attention or saluted as Vernius rode past. He searched the scene, looking for an officer and finding none. He had already ordered a doubling of the perimeter guard and more frequent patrols. But the difficulty of securing this campaign's massive supply train wasn't lost on him. The train was much more than the actual imperial wagons carrying their supplies. What followed behind was a world unto itself, always in flux. At the termination of each day's march, the two worlds inevitably entwined anew.

An army this size, on any foreign campaign, was bound to attract a civilian supplement. The royal presence only compounded the issue. Those trailing behind seemed to include half of the merchants of both Nicomedya and Medicia seeking to siphon every excess coin. There were butchers and cheesemakers with their goats, egg-men with their chickens, smiths, and fletchers.

Not to mention a virtual battalion of winesellers, odds-makers, and whores.

As he and his guards circumvented the supply train, Vernius finally spotted an officer. It wasn't the quartermaster he sought though. This one led two riders, both seemingly foreigners, down a hillside trail coming in from the north. His guards moved to intercept. Vernius recognized that the officer was Lauterus and called for the guards to stand down. Vernius had kept the Pontean captain for the campaign. The man had been invaluable in seizing Megaria, of course, but his value went deeper still. Lauterus had a better grasp of the local terrain, history, and customs than anyone in his service. Added to that, Lauterus was proving to be an astute strategist and a crack tactician. He preferred scouting alone and Vernius saw no reason to keep him from it.

The pair following Lauterus wore woolen cloaks in Illyrican stripes as well as the caps with earflaps favored by the local hill tribes. Beyond their dress, the two couldn't have been more different. One was dark and handsome with jet-black hair tied into a club behind his neck. The other was massive with long yellow hair and a bristling golden beard that hung down to his chest. The big one rode what appeared to be a draft horse.

The trio halted and Lauterus saluted. "Lord General, I have tidings."

Vernius eyed the strangers. "And companions."

Lauterus glanced back. "Yes, of course. Please meet Khasan, first son of the chieftain of the Hierra." The handsome one bowed in the saddle. "As well as his guardian Burig, who is of the Charaska." Burig grudgingly tilted his head. "They've been aiding me in my scouting."

"That so?" He wondered for whom they were willing to provide such services. Which begged the question with whom they shared what they found. Likely anyone who paid.

"I hope you don't mind my engaging them." Lauterus had noticed his mood, too.

Vernius raised a brow. "We do have our own scouts, Captain."

"I realize that, Lord General. But I've known these two since I was a boy. They know these hills and the region's hunters and herdsmen better than anyone. I was certain hearing what they've seen and heard would be a boon."

Vernius forced a smile. "I presume *we* are paying them well for such information?"

"Not yet, my lord. They came here as a favor to me. I wanted you to hear it directly."

"Well then?"

Lauterus switched to Hellainic. "Tell General Vernius what you told me about the road through Orithya."

The Illyrican's gaze latched onto Vernius. "You are likely marching into a trap."

"You have evidence of this?" he asked.

The man gave him a sly smile. "The road through Orithya is narrow and twisting as a vine. If you enter, your army will be quite stretched."

"That's it? The terrain makes it likely?"

Both scouts scowled. "Of late, many Gotar hosts have been seen in Orithya. They are not merely passing through."

Vernius frowned. "My scouts have reported no such hosts." The big man barked a laugh and muttered in Illyrican. Khasan nodded. "I said something amusing?" Vernius asked.

"Your scouts have also been seen, General. Yet they seem not to see us." Khasan's lip curled. "It makes us wonder for their reliability."

The Charaskan curtly added another quip in Illyrican.

Khasan chuckled in response. "I almost forgot. There are at least two of your scouts who have seen Gotars."

"How can you be sure?" Vernius asked.

The big one grinned, revealing a missing tooth. "We saw them tied up in a Gotar camp."

"And you left them there?"

Khasan frowned. "You speak as if there is something that could be done."

The man was really starting to annoy him. "You could have sought to free them."

"We have no quarrel with the Gotars," Khasan said, "and we have no wish for one."

Lauterus cleared his throat. "There are other routes to Thrakius, Lord General. Khasan and his clansmen have offered to guide the way through the northern passes."

Vernius feigned a smile. "Of course he has." He reached into his belt pouch and extracted one of the sacks of coins Nicandros had made up for such occasions. He tossed it to Khasan. "I thank you for your trouble, young chief."

The chieftain's son leaned in the saddle, letting the bag fly by and hit the ground. The pair scowled for a long moment before Khasan said something in Illyrican. Lauterus briefly replied, and the pair heeled their mounts and rode back into the hills.

Vernius pointed at the coin bag while eyeing one of his guards. The man dutifully dismounted and retrieved it.

Lauterus said, "My lord, I must implore you—"

Vernius raised a halting hand. "I understand your assessment, Captain. Consider it under advisement. One thing I can assure you of is that the imperial mobile reserve will never be led by local tribesmen into the very mountains they inhabit. Whether or not you knew them as a boy."

Urias tapped her arm. "Elbow level. Wrists straight."

Brin released the tension on the bowstring without firing. "Are you sure about this? It feels wrong."

Freya's grace, the girl was actually starting to give him second thoughts. "Of course I'm sure. Your mother clearly said no more practice swords and no more shields. You heard her as well as I did."

"I think what she meant was no more training," Brin said.

"Training? This isn't training. Archery is a fine hobby. It'll help you with your focus. And your discipline. Even Mistress Despoina will be grateful."

Brin rolled her eyes. She drew the bow again. "Feet firmly planted," he reminded. "Now just focus, visualize, breathe, and release."

Brin let the arrow go. She'd moved her arm in the process. This shot not only missed the target but flew off into the overgrown shrubbery bordering the courtyard. Urias had set up the target range in one of the abandoned formal gardens in order to stay hidden from prying eyes. He hadn't considered the prospect of her being so bad that she'd lose half of his arrows.

It surprised him. Brin was such a natural at everything else. Urias wracked his memory, trying to recall his own archery training. He too had struggled initially. He couldn't recall how it had become more natural.

Brin's shoulders slumped. "Can't we just go back to footwork drills? That would be the same thing—training but not with sword and shield."

Urias hated to give up. But he didn't want to demoralize her. They were already up against the daunting challenge of Elan's disapproval. He simply could not let go of his promise. He had to believe that Icannes knew best in this matter. He had to believe that Elan would eventually come around. Besides, his sister had gone off to war, for the gods only knew how long. She'd left it to others to figure out how to best raise her daughter. Again.

He held out the quiver. "One last arrow. We can't quit until they're gone. We're not quitters, are we?" Brin took the arrow and faced the target as she nocked it. He sensed her reaction without actually seeing it. "And please don't roll your eyes at me."

Brin raised the bow and sighted the target. "How'd you guess?"

"I didn't have to. I focused. I anticipated. I visualized. Now you do the same."

The bell from the seagates tower rang before she shot. Brin let the bowstring go slack. "Oh no. I'm late again."

How had the morning gotten away from them? She started toward the target. "Don't worry," he told her. "I'll collect the arrows." The ones he could find. "You get inside, or Despoina will put me in her sights." Brin started toward the arbor and the path beyond it that led back to the palace. Urias glanced at the far edge of the lawn. "Oh, don't forget your cloak and your writing tablet."

Brin turned and ran across their shooting range, still holding the bow with the nocked arrow. "Just leave the bow. I'll clean everything up." As Brin ran, she absently raised the bow, drew it, and released. She tossed the bow on the lawn as she gathered her things.

Urias stood gaping at that last arrow stuck firmly in the target. Alone.

Brin hurried back by him. "What?" she said as she passed.

"Oh, nothing," he said.

She stopped at the arbor. "I know that look. You're up to something. What is it?"

Urias smiled. "I'll tell you tomorrow. Happy studies."

Brin shrugged and ran off.

Urias walked to the target and pulled the arrow. "When will you ever learn, Urias?" he scolded himself. "The girl's a natural. And you've been making this as unnatural as possible."

Vernius continued to kneel beside the carriage and Mycanius continued to stare forward. The pressure of his silence grew. The emperor wouldn't even release him to stand. "All I am suggesting, Highness, is that we use caution; perhaps send the equine through first. Or at least hold for a more thorough scouting report." Yes, Vernius had been annoyed by the delays. Yes, he was willingly suggesting another delay. And yes, he had checked to find that two scouts were indeed missing, just as the Illyrican and his Teutonic sidekick had reported.

"Tell me," Mycanius finally began. "Do we not have the superior numbers?"

Vernius maintained a blank expression. "Superior to the Gottari's? By all accounts, yes."

"Are our men not better trained? Are we not better equipped?"

"Without a doubt, Highness."

"Did I not vow to have this war won by hiatus? That I would free the people of Thrakius and rid the world of these savages by the Saturnalia?"

"You did, Highness."

Mycanius turned his glare to Vernius. "Would you have me break my word? Would you have me appear weak, make my promises to my subjects empty ones?"

"I would never, Highness."

"Well, then. Let us end this nonsense. Let us proceed, shall we?"

"As you command, my emperor." With seemingly no release coming, Vernius slowly rose. He paused, considering a plea that the emperor at least ride in a covered carriage. He'd been whipped enough for one day. He backed up two steps, spun, and headed back to his mount.

"Oh, and Vernius?" He stopped and faced Mycanius again. "Your father was far too proud and obstinate. And mine was too accommodating and forgiving. Do not imagine that I am anything like mine. Nor that you can afford to be anything like yours."

Vernius bowed his chin to his chest and marched through the smirking praetorians. Captain Licinian offered him a bow with a mocking flourish.

Vernius's own officers all sat on their mounts, averting their eyes. Nico stood straight, holding Alacer's reins. Before he mounted, Vernius said, "Select four of our swiftest riders. I need to send messages to Megaria and Efusium. Immediately."

"Yes, my lord."

TWILIGHT BLOOMED in lavender skies and the basin road fell into shadow as Tully's equine division disappeared around another turn in the twisting labyrinth that was Orithya. Licinian galloped up to the vanguard and reined in to ride alongside Vernius. "Seems you've gotten your wish, General. The emperor bids us to continue to the plain." The praetorian captain's smirk claimed that it was a trivial victory. At this point, Vernius was glad for any victory.

Vernius nodded. "It shouldn't be much beyond sundown when we arrive."

"And you've still heard nothing of the foe from those scouts of yours?"

"Nothing."

"Gods be praised," the praetorian said mockingly. The jab only exposed Licinian's inexperience. Every seasoned soldier knew that tempting the fates was beyond foolish. "I'll let His Eminence know." Licinian yanked his poor horse's head around and galloped back to the royal caravan.

"Yes, go and claim credit for mere good fortune," he muttered.

Vernius spotted the next in a series of piles ahead. He turned in the saddle. He'd asked Lauterus to ride in the vanguard, but the Pontean kept to himself, a bit apart from all others. Lauterus had raptly scanned the hillsides throughout the day's ride. "Lauterus!" The captain flinched, his gaze snapping to meet his. He was still jumpy and he was a local, moving closer to home. It was concerning. Vernius beckoned him over.

Lauterus cantered to ride alongside.

"I'm told we are almost through to the plains," Vernius said.

"We in the vanguard are near to it, Lord General. Although the rest of the army will arrive well after nightfall." Even now, the man seemed unwilling to express any optimism.

"Still, it seems your friends' warnings have come to naught."

They rode a beat before Lauterus replied. "Thus far."

The man was proud, unwilling to concede a point until proven wrong. Especially on his home turf. Lauterus being a local reminded Vernius. "Tell me, Captain, what exactly are these interspersed piles alongside the road?" He pointed at what seemed to be the tenth pair of piles of small logs and bundled brush, one to either side of the path.

"The local herdsmen spend the autumn clearing the slopes of saplings and gorse. It encourages the growth of what little grazing the coming spring might produce. When spring arrives and they return with their flocks, they use what they've cut for their fires. The nights can get cold here in the pass, even in spring and summer."

Vernius wondered why they always stacked them in matched piles on either side of the road. It was odd. And the hillsides here were so steep. Hardly seemed ideal for grazing. He realized he didn't care enough to pursue the matter. They came around another curve and the equine division came back into view. Vernius was disappointed to see that the road still did not open to a plain beside the sea. He longed to be out of the saddle, holding a cup of warm wine. "Gods, when shall we be free of this twisting trench?" he asked aloud.

Lauterus didn't reply. When Vernius glanced at him, the man was staring up at the northern hilltops. Vernius followed his gaze but saw only twilit sky over denuded mountaintops. "Something of interest, Captain?"

The Pontean held up a finger. "Listen," Lauterus said, just above a whisper.

They rode on, listening. All Vernius heard was the rumble of hooves and the cadence of the infantry drummers marching behind the royal caravan. "What am I listening for?"

Lauterus continued to scan the hilltops. "You don't hear that?"

"If I knew what—"

"There it is." Lauterus tilted his head. "Low and distant, but definite."

"Captain, I'm not sure what you're implying, but—"

"Shh!" Had this scruffy subordinate really just shushed him? "Hear that?"

Vernius opened his mouth to rebuke him, but then he actually heard something. Almost a musical note. Perhaps the distant howling of wolves. "Yes," he admitted.

Lauterus said, "Now wait for the low note."

It came like the hum of a giant hive—low and menacing. And growing louder.

"Horns," Lauterus declared.

"What do you mean, horns?"

"War horns," Lauterus said gravely. "Gottari war horns. It's begun."

A pair of Tully's men came galloping back, calling and waving. Vernius held up a fist and the call for a halt was repeated, echoing back through the column. As the equine riders neared, Vernius discerned their calls. "Gottari! On the plains ahead!"

The messengers' horses beat to a halt, causing Alacer to bob and neigh. One of them exclaimed, "A host has been sighted, Lord General. We think they're Gottari. They hold the high ground along the northern edge of the plain. Captain Tullius asks permission to ride ahead on the attack."

"Tell Captain Tullius to move onto the plains, take a defensive position, and hold."

The man frowned. "My lord, he bid me to tell you that we have superior numbers."

"You tell Tullius to hold or he will answer to me. Understood?" The pair looked stunned and said nothing. "I asked if you understood!"

"Yes, Lord General." They were as sullen as scolded children.

"Then go!"

Both men saluted, reined around and kicked their mounts to a gallop, causing Alacer to start out in pursuit. Vernius struggled to rein in the spirited gelding and turn him back to the vanguard. It was a poor harbinger, both for his mount and for his overly eager equine division in the battle that now seemed sure to come. And soon. Much sooner than he'd like. Seemed he was even further from that cup of warm wine than he'd thought.

TWISTS AND TURNS

*"*Some say that in the tongue of the Illyrican tribesmen, Orithya means 'the raging of the mountain' due to the fact that the rumpled landscape was formed by the cooling lava from an ancient volcano. Others say it means 'the madness of the mountain' due to the twists and turns of the pathways that run among its foothills. Before the roads were marked and mapped, travelers had often grown confused and become hopelessly lost. Many had failed to survive. Tales were told of those who had gone mad in their futile search for a way out.*

I used to wonder aloud if the name referred to anger or insanity. More than one of those who fought in the Battle of Orithya, through the twists and turns of the fortunes of either side, have assured me that it must be both."—Brin Bright Eyes, Saga of Dania

THE TIBAIRYA at the fore finally trotted into view on the plain below and began to form up, shields up and lances bristling, creating a protective line for their companions that would emerge from the pass behind them. All the Gottari plan required of Arnegern's host was to get the foe's mounted division to move clear of the mouth of the pass.

"Hold the line!" Arnegern called. The Gottari horses stamped and bobbed, as anxious to charge as his Rekkrs. "Nobody moves until my signal."

"Gods, it feels like a chance being pissed away," Belgar said, sitting ahorse beside him.

Arnegern had to agree. Attacking now would be like spearing badgers as they came from the den. Instead, they were conceding their advantage. But not without reason. "We must all play our part," he said. "Ermanaric needs the gap we'll create by holding here."

Even the Tibairyan column stayed true to form, four horsemen abreast in row after row, coming alongside each other to take their places in the assembling battle lines. Belgar harrumphed. "They say these are the Tibairyan elite, do they not?"

"They do," Arnegern said. "They're called Equites, all born of noble bloodlines and trained in their academy. It's said they have the empire's finest horse stock and best gear."

"Look at them prancing, thinking themselves so civilized. But they've shown us who they are." Belgar leaned over and spat. "Our cousin was one of the finest men I ever knew. And they hung him out like a calf to be bled for a feast."

"Don't worry, Cousin. We'll get our chance at them. Once we've split them, we'll even outnumber them. We shall have our vengeance."

"Can't come soon enough," Belgar muttered.

Arnegern did not chastise him. He'd yet to tell Belgar that he himself had fired the arrow that had ended their cousin's life. He'd told no one, in fact. Not even Harma. It was his to bear. Likely unto the coming of Urrinan.

The sky grew darker as the Tibairyan formation grew just out of bow range. The last of the riders came into view, leaving the gap they'd hoped for at the mouth of the pass. There had to be at least two hundred riders—over twice as many as Arnegern led. He looked to the peak above the mouth of the pass. The glint of a waving blade confirmed it. "Well, that's it. Now to keep them engaged."

Arnegern walked his mount out before the line. He knew others felt as strongly as Belgar did, and he had to address it. "Remember, men. We aim to get their dander up. But we cannot press too hard. The time will come to make them pay. It's not come yet. We'll need every sword to finish this war. So no hero stuff. No one loses their focus! Not this time. Understood?" The Rekkrs barked in confirmation. "Listen for the call to retreat," he added. "Remember, we're playing the part of the hare. Getting the hounds to give chase is a win."

He raised his sword overhead and stood in the stirrups. "Rekkrs! Are we ready?" Again, they barked in unison. "Shall we lead them to their doom?" Again, they barked, even louder this time. "Let us give 'em a show, my hares. On my signal!"

Arnegern brought the blade down to point at the foe and kicked his mount. "On, Gottari!"

～

"It can't be all of them," Lauterus said.

Vernius stroked his jittery mount's neck. "Why not?"

"It just wouldn't make sense."

"They know where we're heading. They had time to make ready."

"Exactly. Which means they could've attacked anywhere in Orithya. Why would Vahldan put his army in a position that concedes us the open ground when we're all strung out and vulnerable in here?"

Vernius thought the man almost sounded disappointed. "They obviously hope to avoid fighting a force of superior numbers all at once."

Lauterus maintained his pessimistic frown. "It just doesn't feel right."

Alacer settled a bit. "Perhaps these barbarians aren't as crafty as everyone loves to think them. Whatever the case, let's get this army moving."

Before he could call the command, a light flickered overhead. Vernius pointed. "Enemy fire!" He gaped into the night. It wasn't a catapult as he'd first feared. It was a large blaze, along the top of the ridge. Calls rang out up and down the line.

"It's a wagon," Lauterus said. "Looks like one of ours." He was right. At the top of the northern slope sat an unhitched imperial wagon. Its normally tarp-covered bed was piled with flaming fuel. The blaze reached skyward as they watched. Lauterus pointed down the line behind. "Another! And more beyond!"

Vernius twisted in the saddle, causing Alacer to prance again. The scene repeated itself at least a dozen times at intervals down the line. Wagons, all ablaze, lining the top of the northern slope above his strung-out army.

Vernius then noticed the men silhouetted against the twilit sky between the burning wagons. Most were mounted and all wore helms and were armed with swords or spears. Gods, they looked like demons from the underworld. Their war horns blared again, much closer now—low, loud, and long. The effect created an ominous chorus that only grew louder. Then came the chanting voices, guttural and tribal.

"Shields!" Vernius called. He reached for his sword to find nothing there. He hadn't even worn it. His only weapon was a belt dagger, and the only armor he wore was his lightweight breastplate. No helm, no grieves. How could he be so ill prepared, on this of all days? He'd been sick of wearing his father's heavy, ill-fitting gear. He had let himself get too damn distracted by the royal show, and now the real war was upon him. "Form up!" he cried, riding back against the column toward the infantry, still struggling to hold the gelding in check.

Lauterus rode behind him and took up the call. "To shields! As one!"

The royal caravan was a blur of commotion, with praetorians and servants swarming around the emperor's carriage. Vernius left them to it and rode on toward the infantry. A piercing horn blared over the mournful chorus. At once, the burning wagons began to roll downhill.

Vernius reined Alacer in, forcing the gelding to dance in circles. Incredibly, the nearest wagon looked to be manned with a driver on the bench. The wagon was rolling in a swale that kept it on course to crash into the nearest brush pile. Vernius instinctively knew that all of them were set up this way. "Shoot the driver!" He pointed. "Archers! Take out the drivers!"

As the nearest wagon careened downhill, Vernius noticed the driver's imperial uniform. Worse, the poor man was strapped, arms behind his back, to the bench. "Oh gods," he said. "The missing scouts." It was too late to rescind the order to shoot. Archers were already lined up behind the shield walls, firing at will. He realized it was a mercy.

In mere heartbeats, the nearest wagon hit the brush pile, bursting through spectacularly and sending flames and sparks and burning debris in all directions. But the impact mostly drove the wreckage across the road... to connect with the pile on the opposing side. Alacer reared and screamed. The combination of the two piles and the wagon created a blockade of flames. The strong reek of pitch suffused the valley. Vernius craned as Alacer spun. The phenomenon repeated itself all down the newly sundered line. The Gottari were breaking his already strung-out army into isolated and chaotic fragments.

Alacer finally stopped dancing, leaving Vernius facing what had been the front of the column. To either side, there was nothing but flame and chaos. Where was Tullius? Where was the most mobile and lethal division of the mobile reserve? Their training demanded their return.

Of all of the severance this attack seemed to have wrought, if the mobile reserve had lost contact with the equine division, it would be the most devastating.

Arnegern rode downhill in a controlled gallop, leading the way by several span, just as he and the Rekkrs of his host had agreed. His men roared convincingly, all brandishing sword and shield as if they were fervent to break the Tibairyan line. Arnegern had his sword drawn but left his shield on his back. He needed to focus on riding, not staying safe. He started on course to the center of the enemy formation and slowly tracked to his left, subtly guiding the charging Gottari to the foe's flank.

For their part, the Equites did not budge from their position. Not yet. Even their mounts were disciplined, it seemed. Finally, a Tibairyan officer bawled a command and, in perfect unison, his Equites lowered their lances and drew up their shields. The ones in the back rows raised and drew their bows, angling up over the heads of their comrades.

This was it. As the lead rider, Arnegern knew that many of the foe would target him. Not only did he need to survive, he also had to perform his role perfectly. His ability to react precisely was critical to their success. He would have to trust in the gods. And in his horse, of course.

The Tibairyan commander called out and their bows snapped. Arrows arced toward the Gottari line. He heard horses fall behind him, and one arrow glanced off the leathers of his thigh. But they'd fired too early. The range reduced his host's casualties, thank the gods.

Now came Arnegern's chance to playact as a mummer. He feigned a great display of fearful surprise and in Hellainic shouted, "Retreat!" He pulled hard to the left, leading the charge in a sweeping arc that would bring his force around, briefly exposing the vulnerable sides of their horses before leading them into flight. "Pull back, Rekkrs! To me! Retreat!"

Arnegern's horse was already blowing like a smith's bellows, but he urged him to keep galloping uphill. Arrows fell around them and a few horses screamed. After several long strides, Arnegern allowed himself to turn in the saddle to look. At least two Gottari horses were down, but both men were up and running. Several Rekkrs had ridden close enough to the ends of the line to swipe at the lances of the foe, causing a stir in the Tibairyan ranks.

Those who'd physically engaged the enemy line had disobeyed their orders, but Arnegern couldn't deny the possibility that their boldness might become the decisive factor. Indeed, starting with a few of the impacted Equites peeling off in pursuit, the effect he'd sought was set in motion. Like a crumbling dam, the discipline of the entire imperial equine formation steadily collapsed. More and more of the foe broke away to give pursuit until finally the entire division succumbed to the lure of the chase.

Gottari horns echoed in the distance, coming closer and closer. The attack within Orithya was underway. And the hidden remainder of Arnegern's host appeared at the hillcrest ahead. As did Ermanaric's force atop the hill to his left at the mouth of the pass.

The vaunted Equites had taken the bait. The Gottari trap had sprung.

THE THROATY CHANT of the barbarians continued to build, pulsing with relentless menace. The Tiberian shield wall just beyond the nearest fire was swiftly crumbling, with some soldiers backing away and others rushing to the aid of those whose cloaks had caught on fire. Some brave fools broke formation and charged uphill at the steadily advancing foe, only to be struck down. The Gottari ambush was succeeding. Against the most highly trained fighting force in the civilized world. What Vernius had once considered indelible discipline was bleeding out and draining away.

Gods, could he have led his army—the subject of his life's devotion—into disaster?

Vernius's mind reeled. "Your orders, Lord General?" Lauterus had stayed with him. The captain had not only kept his head, he'd also rightfully implored his stricken commander to action. Vernius stood in the stirrups, looking east. "Ride to the fore, Lauterus. Get to the equine. Have Tullius lead them back. Rally everyone along the way to get back to shields. Remind every officer that we stand as one."

Lauterus saluted and rode off. Another blare of a Gottari horn pierced the deepening darkness. Calls echoed down their lines. The Gottari were about to charge. A centurion bellowed, gathering a cluster of infantry to form up inside their segment between the fires. "To me! Stay together!" The centurion's voice was cutting through the chaos, returning them to cohesion.

"Mobile reserve! As one!" Vernius exhorted them.

He turned to check the royal caravan. A cluster of praetorians had arrayed themselves around the emperor's carriage. Despite it being an open carriage, Vernius couldn't see Mycanius. His Eminence had likely been advised to lie down. Licinian was directing the emperor's driver to steer away from the northern slope, which was lined with advancing Gottari. The praetorian captain had dismounted and was standing on the sideboard of the carriage, calling orders. He was drawing the carriage and the bodyguards into a cove on the southern edge of the canyon. A rocky precipice rose steeply around three sides of the spot.

Vernius wasn't sure it was the wisest move, but he'd have to leave it to Licinian.

He turned back to the nearby centurion. The man had done an admirable job of getting his squad into a unified shield wall. The Gottari were moving closer, making a lot of noise, but hardly seemed to be in a hurry. The barbarians leading the way held their position just above the valley floor, content to hurl more insults than spears.

Something was amiss. The attack was unlike Teutonics, let alone the Gottari. They should've pressed their advantage, made use of the terror they'd instilled and the momentum their height provided. Instead, they dawdled. Now that they were in view on the hillside, Vernius began to doubt they had the numbers to press the attack to completion. His army might just survive this.

In spite of the hopeful sign, something still seemed off. What did Vahldan hope to achieve here? Was this merely about the parsing of his equine to take them on separately? If so, it was a shortsighted strategy. He could easily lay siege without them.

With a niggling unease growing, Vernius turned to check on the royal caravan. As he twisted in the saddle, Alacer screamed and started bucking, catching Vernius off guard. He lost his seat and his grip and instinctively kicked free of the stirrups. He hit the turf hard, jarring the base of his back and rattling his jaw. He had trouble drawing a satisfying breath and could only watch as Alacer danced off into the night with an arrow jutting from his hindquarters.

Vernius wheezed to catch his breath and pushed himself to his feet. He was on the roadway between the Tiberian shield wall to the north and the royal caravan to the south. His right leg and arm were both wrenched and painful. He had no shield and no desire to catch another stray arrow. He limped toward the emperor's caravan, hoping the praetorians could provide him with a mount.

The sky was sliding from deep blue to black and the rocky cove surrounding the caravan was etched in shadows by the flickering light of the fires. Movement above caught his eye.

Could it be? Surely it was too steep.

Vernius stared and sped his limping steps. A moment later, he was sure. Riders were swiftly descending from the heights. They came into the light, horses all but tumbling down the precarious slope with their riders leaning back in the saddle. It would've been an amazing feat for one rider, but this was a small host!

The attack from the north was a ruse, a distraction. *This* was the

Gottari objective. The words of Tully rang in his head. *"These Gottari, they have no honor. They target the leaders."*

The praetorian guards had arrayed themselves around the emperor's carriage but on the wrong side. Worse, they were facing the wrong way.

In spite of the pain, Vernius ran. "Behind you! Another attack! Protect the emperor!" His voice was drowned out by the clamber of the feigned Gottari attack. That pompous idiot Licinian stood gaping at him, clueless.

He tried again, louder. "Attack!" He pointed at the hillside. Licinian said something to another officer. Incredibly, several of the praetorians broke their formation and came jogging toward Vernius. "No, fools! Behind you!" Vernius pointed above them more frantically.

The stealthy riders gained the valley floor and sped up. A trio led the attackers, the flames gradually illuminating them. The leader was helmless and wore a savage grin. His long golden hair was unbound, flying behind him, his broadsword held low but ready.

Vernius instinctively knew. This could be none other than Vahldan the Bold.

At one of the leader's shoulders rode the largest man Vernius had ever beheld. He was also brandishing a sword.

Ah, but the third, riding at Vahldan's right, confirmed the trio's identity. This was the Hippomache, Vahldan's deadly warrior-woman guardian. Gods, even the campfire tales did not do her justice. The three rode in perfect concert.

Just as a few praetorians became aware, turning and raising their shields, the trio hit the royal guards' formation. The Gottari warhorses toppled the praetorians like toys. Vahldan and his deadly duo swung their swords, leaving a swath of Tiberians falling in their wake—one's head even toppling to the turf, severed by a scything whoosh from the giant. All Vernius could do was watch in horror and hurry on toward the scene.

The trio was through the defenses and a host of about a dozen of

Vahldan's followers fell upon the frantic praetorians. Vernius ran through the outer melee, racing to get to the carriage before the three assassins came around to strike at their target.

Vahldan got his feet under him on the saddle as his horse approached the backside of the carriage. The assassin leapt from the horse onto the driver's bench, towering over the royal passengers. Licinian was the only praetorian left between the murderous Gottari king and the Tiberian emperor. The praetorian poser likely hadn't swung a sword at an opponent since he was in training at the academy.

On Vernius ran, expecting to be cut down at any moment. All he could do was try to get to the carriage and intervene—the gods only knew how.

Vahldan snarled and raised his sword. Neither the attacker nor Licinian bore a shield. The praetorian foolishly stepped up, brandishing his gladius as if to trade blows. Vahldan struck the instant Licinian stepped into range, knocking the gladius from his hand. Still standing on the bench, the Gottari took a deliberate, measured, and lethal stroke, chopping into the base of Licinian's neck. With a thunk, the blade buried itself in flesh like a newly sharpened axe into a fresh pine log. Vernius was near enough to watch Licinian crumple to the carriage floor.

Vahldan yanked his blade free and raised it. The assassin stepped over the body, his every muscle flexing to strike. The next sword stroke was a heartbeat away. Vernius spotted the targeted victim lying in the fetal position on his side on the cushions of the rear seat. The emperor was frozen in place, like a rabbit hoping the swooping hawk might somehow miss.

Vernius hit the sideboard at the open passenger door and his sore leg almost gave out. He feebly leapt just as Vahldan swung. As if he were diving into water, Vernius stretched and turned in the air to put his body between the attacker and the attacked. Vahldan's sword chopped audibly into his chest, knocking him backward and down.

Vernius crashed into the far side wall of the carriage interior, crumpling like a flung wet towel.

Vahldan landed on his feet and loomed over him. It was only when the barbarian yanked his sword back that Vernius realized the blade had been lodged in his breastplate. Time seemed to slow. Vernius perceived the blood on the blade, felt the wetness of his tunic and leathers, and all he could think was that his father's fancy armor wasn't so ridiculous, after all.

Vahldan seemed momentarily stunned, but he swiftly recovered. The barbarian grinned and uttered what was surely a curse. He raised the blade again. The only weapon Vernius had was his belt dagger. He drew the short blade and pathetically brandished it to parry, which only made the barbarian's grin widen.

As Vahldan brought his sword down, he abruptly lurched and twisted, causing his blow to miss and thunk into the deck a finger's width from Vernius's head. Licinian, amazingly still alive, had kicked Vahldan's leg. Vernius blindly swung his dagger arm and Vahldan roared. The Gottari king drew back, stumbling and growling, his free hand clutching his side. Vernius's blade had punctured a leather spacer under the sleeve of Vahldan's mail armor. The dagger was wet with blood. Against all odds, he had stabbed the flesh of the rampaging barbarian.

Two more praetorians arrived at the open carriage door wielding swords and shields. Now the wounded assailant was fighting for his life, parrying left and right in retreat, still holding his side wound. Vernius was reduced to watching from his back on the carriage floor.

"Vahldan!" It was the Hippomache. There was fear in her cry. Vernius propped himself up, gasping for breath. More praetorians were closing in on the carriage. The Gottari host was in flight. Vahldan cursed again, stepped up onto the carriage side rail, and leapt, disappearing from Vernius's view. He craned to see. The barbarian had landed on the rump of the Hippomache's horse, clinging to her as they fled the scene.

Vernius rolled onto his side to face not a majestic emperor, but a sickly man-child. Mycanius was terror-stricken—wide-eyed, hugging his knees, and visibly quaking. "Are you unhurt, Highness?"

"Bloody gods," Mycanius gasped. He started to wheeze and cough.

Relief suffused Vernius. He slumped to his back, head lolling, suddenly exhausted beyond belief. A warm wooziness overtook him. He lay on the carriage floor, thinking how wet his tunic had become. It was sticking to his chest and stomach. "Apollo's grace, I'm bleeding out," he whispered, staring at the starry sky.

Several faces appeared over him, looking concerned. A praetorian said, "Hold on, my lord. Stay with us. The medicus is coming."

But Vernius didn't have the strength to hold on. All he wanted was to sleep, to let go. He briefly wondered if he had a choice. How does one keep from bleeding out? He couldn't feel his hands or feet but he had to tell them. He could do that much. "Get to the seashore. Protect the emperor. I sent for them. They'll come..."

"Shhh. Save your strength, Lord General. His Eminence is safe now."

But, gods, was he? Had Vernius really saved the emperor? If so, hopefully his final effort would secure his estate. Perhaps somehow the boy would find his way to it. Bastard or no, Vernius's newly revised will made clear that Ligaia's son was to be his heir.

Sleep was like a siren, beckoning and alluring, drawing him under. He shuddered. So cold. Damn, everything was spinning, fuzzy. Vahldan yet lived. Nothing was settled. But then again, who could know? Maybe his little blade had dealt Vahldan a mortal wound. Wouldn't that make a fitting tale? Even in death, Vernius Stallicus, general of the mobile reserve, had managed to save the emperor and kill the barbarian king, thereby ending the war and saving Pontea.

Even as he drifted toward oblivion, he recognized it as wishful thinking. And yet, he found he was relieved—relieved to imagine that he'd actually restored his family's honor. Vernius closed his eyes, allowing himself to slip into that contented dream, more hopeful than ever that his grandsires would be pleased.

ARNEGERN REACHED the hilltop overlooking the plain beside the seashore. He reined in his horse to look down on what their army had wrought. Those who'd led the Tibairya pulled up, not quite halfway up the hill. They'd perceived the trap, but too late. Ermanaric's host had ridden down onto the foe's right flank, blocking their return to the pass and their trapped infantry column.

Already, their commander was barking orders, calling them into formation for a retreat. A squad of about a score of Tibairyan riders formed a protective crescent while the line reformed and moved back downhill. At the hill's base, another crescent was already forming, allowing the line to pass while the first crescent filed in behind their comrades. It was the very model of discipline under duress.

Time for a bit of disorder.

Arnegern raised his sword overhead. "Now, my brothers! Now is the time to take our vengeance! Let this terrible invading foe know our wrath!"

A thunderous cheer arose from his men, eliciting an echoing cheer from Ermanaric's force. Horns took up the call, long and low, sending a shiver of excitement down his back. "Archers! Let us begin by lighting the way to the foe."

The archers who'd waited out of sight in the heights rushed out with torches to light the pitch pots. They lit their tar-smeared arrows. "Fire!" he cried. The volley streaked across the sky and down onto the retreating foe. Horses and men cried out as patches of gorse and dry grass caught fire and spread. The vale swiftly filled with smoke, which was pushed against the mountains by the brisk sea breeze.

Arnegern pulled his shield around and slipped his arm through the straps. Once again, he pointed his sword at the foe. "To blades! This time without relent or mercy. On, Gottari, on!"

He kicked his mount and started downhill. His division filed out across the hillside, joining with Ermanaric's cascading Gottari riders. They became a closing pincer, their hoofbeats drumming thunder to the horns' call.

The Tibairyan rearguard stood their ground, their lances leveled. Arnegern tucked in behind his shield and kicked his mount. His fellow riders closed on his sides, connecting him to an overwhelming wall of horseflesh, oak, and steel. Just before impact, several of the foe's rearguard lost their nerve and turned to retreat. Arnegern slipped by one of their lances and delivered a sword blow that practically pulled his arm from the socket. He turned just enough to glean that his victim had been knocked from the saddle.

The retreating imperial column shattered, with a sizable portion turning to face the oncoming charge and the remainder breaking into flight. Arnegern was no longer at the fore and he sensed his horse was nearly spent. Movement and torches caught his eye and he drew up. The footmen of the foe were marching from the mouth of the pass. Ermanaric's force was turning to block the two forces from merging.

Arnegern smiled. Even if they did merge, where would they then go? They would be surrounded, with the coast at their backs. Even as the thought occurred to him, he saw the shooting star arcing toward his men. Then another, and another—coming from dark shapes out on the calm sea. The first star exploded, bursting into tumbling fireballs, sending dozens of Gottari horses and men flying and shrieking. Other stars flew in, coming further inland, this time falling directly among his host.

Arnegern had seen this before, in the Pontean Straits at the first battle for Megaria. "Ships. Their gods bedamned navy." He waved his sword overhead. "Hold! Pull back!"

Crimson sails loomed at the edge of darkness, prows heading toward shore with catapults affixed at their bows, firing as they came. His men didn't need convincing. As the fireballs increased, once again they found themselves in full retreat.

The foot and horse divisions of the Tibairya merged at the shoreline just as the first ships slid to the beach, still firing. A great cheer went up among the foe.

The battle had turned yet again.

He gathered his men at the hillcrest. Ermanaric had done the same along the hilltop over the mouth of the pass. Belgar rode to Arnegern. "Most of the mobile reserve is still trapped and strung out in the pass. They're reforming and gathering strength but it'll take time. How many more missiles could these ships possibly be carrying?"

Arnegern looked out at the scene. Soldiers were disembarking from the ships, even as the catapults were being reloaded. He scanned the field below, still burning and strewn with the twisted corpses of horses and men. There seemed as many Gottari as Tibairya. Some of his men crawled uphill and others lay, calling for help. "I don't want to find out," he said.

A group of riders came galloping around the backside of Ermanaric's position and toward his. Arnegern instantly recognized several of them. He scanned the group. The figure he sought was slumped, hugging the neck of his mount. His guardian rode directly beside him, her arm outstretched as if to catch him if he fell.

Arnegern started toward them. Teavar came in the lead and called as they arrived, "Sound the retreat. The king is wounded. We must get him back to Thrakius."

UNFINISHED BUSINESS

"*I clearly recall the night the army returned from Orithya. I remember the clamor, the underlying fret. I remember the blood so many wore. I remember Teavar carrying my father up the stairs as if he were a sleeping child, with my mother leading the way and a stream of retainers at their heels. I remember women crying and Amaga leading prayers for a man she did not love. I remember solemn Rekkrs, still armed and armored, mulling about the palace, unsure what to do.*

But through it all, as bewildering and frightening as the night had been, I remember my mother's steadfast, purposeful, and strangely calm demeanor. When I tried to follow them into our chambers, she stopped me at the door. Elan sensed my fear. My mother put a hand on my cheek and said, 'Don't worry, baby girl. It's not his time. We're not done yet.' Then she closed me, and everyone else, out."—Brin Bright Eyes, Saga of Dania

VAHLDAN STIRRED AND GROANED. Elan sat up and watched him. He'd woken once before but only briefly, and he'd hardly been lucid. This time his eyes twitched but didn't open. It was the bedamned knocking that had agitated him. Gods, these intruders were persistent. It almost made Elan miss having Hesiod here. Having anyone else inside was out of the question though. She still had to have him to herself.

Nothing else mattered right now. There was nothing else. This threat to his very existence laid everything bare. In spite of all of it—of everything that had happened till now, all of the mistakes they'd made, all the ways they'd hurt one another, all the time they'd wasted being at odds—Elan clearly saw the truth of it. Her life was his and his was hers. Their shared destiny overruled all the rest of it.

The knocking resumed. Why was Teavar allowing this? Elan brushed the hair from his forehead, then ran her hand down onto his cheek. His fever still hadn't broken. "Just rest, my love," she whispered. She rose and carried the lamp to the door. "Go away," she hissed through the crack at the jamb. She wasn't about to unbolt it.

"Elan, please." It was Kemella again.

"He's resting. Please stop disturbing him."

"You can't keep us out forever."

"I can for now." Maybe forever, if that's what it took.

"She's the mother of his firstborn son, Elan."

"I don't care. Go away."

"However you feel about her, whatever else you feel she might be, Amaga is a healer first. She can help to ensure that he lives."

Elan glanced back at Vahldan. He looked peaceful. She wasn't even sure how many days it had been. The foul-smelling unguent the Elli-Frodei had brought her to apply to the wound seemed to be staving off infection. As ugly as it was, the gash looked slightly better. He even swallowed the water she trickled into his mouth. But he would need to eat something soon. "Please," Kemella pleaded. "Just let her take a look."

Elan sighed but said nothing.

"He does need nourishment." That addition came from Amaga herself. Elan shuddered. She hated to think that the spooky little witch could read her thoughts through the door. It was bad enough that she sensed things through touch.

"You are alone?" Elan demanded.

"Yes, it's just us," Kemella replied.

Elan would take no chances. "Teavar?"

The giant's deep voice reverberated. "They're alone. The corridor is empty."

She unbolted and opened the door and backed away, offering them a wide berth. Kemella stood a head taller than the little crank and outweighed her by half again. Something was strange about them. Elan realized it was the first time in over a year that she'd seen them together without the boy. The contrast between them reminded Elan of Icannes and Sael. She wondered if her grandmother yet lived. The image, and the thought, suddenly made her homesick for the first time in a long time. Horsella's grace, how she loved Dania in autumn.

Kemella started through the door, then realized she'd left her companion behind. She went back and wrapped a protective arm around the waif and practically pulled her in. Amaga was ridiculously wary. The woman's unblinking eyes never left Elan as they passed through. Elan grudgingly admired Amaga's courage for even coming. "In the bedchamber." She pointed, then followed them with the lamp.

Amaga's bug-like eyes finally strayed from Elan to Vahldan. "He's pale." Vahldan's first qeins started to reach for the bedding, then stopped. "May I see the wound?" Elan moved around the bed and reached across him to draw back the blanket. The wound was purple and puckered. "It's healing well on the outside. I fear for within." Amaga's beady eyes came back up to Elan. "Tell me about afterward. How long was he awake?"

"Not long. Soon after we fled, he fell unconscious. The few times he woke, he was very weak. And his speech was slurred."

"Did he vomit?"

"Yes."

"Was there blood in it?"

"Yes."

Amaga held her trembling hands over him. "May I?"

Elan was as frightened as she'd been since it had happened. She reluctantly nodded her assent and the priestess laid her hands on Vahldan's abdomen, one to either side of the wound. Vahldan's body tensed and heaved and Amaga gasped. As Vahldan settled again, the waif squeezed her eyes tightly, seemingly in agony. She looked much the same as her mother had while touching him at his trial all those years ago.

Amaga finally withdrew her hands. She was breathing hard and nearly crumpled. Kemella caught her under the arms and held her upright. "It's his spleen," Amaga said between breaths. "It's been pierced, but cleanly. He is strong and Freya is with him. He is mending." Amaga tapped a drinking skin slung over Kemella's shoulder. "Does he take water?"

"Yes, some."

Amaga nodded to Kemella. "Give him this. As much as he'll take. Until it's gone." Kemella lifted off the strap of the drinking skin and proffered it. Elan eyed it suspiciously. "You know he needs nourishment," Amaga said. "This will provide it. Along with some healing herbs." Elan finally took the sloshing bag. It was warm. She stared at it. Amaga said, "If I wanted to poison him, Elan, I'd have done it long ago."

Elan had never heard Amaga say her name before. She nodded. "I'll give it to him."

Amaga turned and headed out. Kemella followed. The priestess stopped at the door. "Aren't you going to ask me if he'll live?"

"There's no need. I know he won't die. Not yet."

"Is that so?"

Elan nodded. "His doom is mine. We're not done yet."

Amaga actually smiled. "Clever deduction."

Elan followed them from the bedchamber to bolt the entry door behind them. Kemella opened the door and Amaga stopped again. "I sense that you're right."

"About?"

"I have seen his doom for many years now. And I sense that you are right that you will share in it. Somehow. But you will not share his fate. Freya has never shown me yours. But the goddess reassures me you shall each play your own vital role in destiny."

Elan stiffened. Gooseflesh bloomed on her arms and rushed up her neck. She'd only ever imagined dying at his side. "I'm his guardian. It's all that I am. All that I want."

Amaga's laugh was genuine, the first like it Elan could recall ever hearing from her. "Even a fool can see that's not true. May I give you some advice?"

"If you feel you must."

"Perhaps you should set your wants aside and begin to recognize what else you are. And to whom. Ask yourself what your destiny demands you to become." Amaga grinned. "As I said—it's vital. For the old world shall not merely fade away. What's to be born shall be fragile, the linkage vital to its survival." The spooky witch spun and led her keeper off to the stairwell.

Teavar shook his head after them. "That girl never fails to give me the creeps."

"Me either." Elan looked down and saw his weapons and helm, alongside his hauberk and bedding rolled up beneath his chair next to the door. Gods, the man was still wearing his rumpled armor leathers and mud-splattered leggings and boots. "You should go change. Wash up. Get something to eat. And some sleep. I've got this."

The giant raised a brow. "*We've* got this." Elan opened her mouth to argue, but he held up a silencing hand. "Don't worry. They bring me food. And you know I can sleep anywhere. Now get back in there. He needs you."

She nodded and closed the door, grateful—as always—for his presence.

∽

Everyone was talking about the Battle of Orithya but Malvius couldn't discern truth from rumor. Not on the docks, anyway. The tales varied wildly, from the thug king being dead to the utter decimation of the mobile reserve. He seriously doubted either of those extreme outcomes.

Malvius needed to know more. Everything depended on it. Which is how he found himself shivering on the bench of a merchant's open wagon on a dark, windy day, heading up the hill to the palace of Thrakius.

The imperial blockade of Thrakius had become more porous at the ideal moment. His fleet had ridden the same wintry winds into port that had driven the Tiberian navy from their vigorous patrol of the coast. The clamor over the goods he'd brought home was even greater than he'd anticipated. Which, of course, made his cargo all the more profitable. He dearly hated leaving the docks during the ongoing bidding. But at the moment, gathering information was crucial. Not just to his profitability and planning, but to his survival.

The merchant who drove the wagon, a graybeard named Tabaeus, was an old friend. Tabaeus specialized in delicacy foods and wines, which made these difficult times even more difficult for him. Malvius had been selling the man items of dubious origin since he'd been in his teens. He'd made a point of supplying vendors such as Tabaeus with the bulk of his higher priced items from this current haul, mostly to be resold to the Gottari on the hill. The transaction was a boon to everyone involved. Easy profit all the way down the supply line, as all knew the Gottari had more money than sense.

The Gottari guards at the gate eyed them suspiciously before letting the wagon pass. It was beyond annoying to be judged with suspicion for returning to the home of his forebearers. Particularly when the judgment came from the thugs who'd stolen it. Outside the door to the kitchens Malvius reached back to grab the stoppered jug he'd brought along. He thanked his old friend, reminded him that he had urgent business to attend to, and slipped away. Ideal timing in that he wouldn't be asked to help unload. He entered through the main entrance, crossed the echoing hall to the stairs, and headed up to the high hall. A crowd had gathered on the broad balcony above.

Malvius reached the top of the stairs. Thrakius's current magister—a man named Elpides, formerly a staunch ally of Malvius's father—was on his way out of the high hall. Malvius pulled his cloak over his left arm to hide the jug and bowed as they came together. "Magister."

"You ought to be ashamed of yourself," Elpides hissed.

"Trust me, I often am."

"Never more so than you should be now. You disgust me. Seeking to profit off of your fellow citizens during this time of hardship."

Malvius tilted his head. "Your regrettable disgust aside, I've found that fewer times are more profitable than the hard ones." Elpides walked on with an audible huff and stomped down the stairs. "Somewhere else you'd rather be?" he called after the man. Without slowing, the magister offered an obscene gesture over his shoulder. "And just when seeing you again was getting fun," Malvius said.

Malvius supposed the magister was particularly peeved in regard to the bidding war that had developed over his grain cargo. He'd wisely devoted an entire hold to it. By chance, the city was already dipping into the winter stores for breadmaking. And the real siege no one doubted was coming had yet to begin! Talk about poor planning. Malvius guessed that Elpides had come to plead for Gottari intervention. Talk about resorting to extreme measures. The magister made no secret of his hatred for Vahldan and his ilk. It was one of the man's few redeeming qualities.

A line of petitioners milled about, waiting for an audience, but with whom? Malvius headed for the closed high hall doors. One of the guards stationed there was a Rekkr who'd sailed with him in the days of ignorant bliss before Vahldan's betrayal. Malvius knew him only as Hook, though he was sure it was a nickname. He strode over. "Hallo, Hook. What goes?"

"More beggars than I'd care to recall. Scores have come, and they all want inside one at a gods-bedamned time." Hook stretched his neck. "Been on my feet since breakfast."

"So the king is well enough to receive petitioners?"

Hook shook his head gravely. "Oh no. Those who attend him say the king heals well, praise the gods. But it's Captain Arnegern taking them on today—the poor lad."

Well, there was one rumor disproved. It seemed the thug was indeed wounded, but not mortally. His improving health could be a cover story, but Malvius sensed no deceit. "Praise the gods," he offered with as much sincerity as he could be troubled to fake.

"It's the first time we opened the high hall since we got back from Orithya. That magister's been hovering around yowling like an unfed housecat since your ships docked."

"Doesn't seem like his audience went too well."

Hook grinned. "And to think that was his second try. At least his departure means we're nearly done here."

Malvius threw his cloak back and proffered the jug. It was the special concoction he normally saved for Vahldan, but it didn't seem likely that the thug would be imbibing anytime soon. "Here, Hook. I doubt the captain would be too happy to see me. Why don't you take this and share it with him and your fellows." He nodded toward the other guards. "You've all earned it." He hoped it led to as much troubling behavior as he suspected it did for their leader.

Hook's eyes widened as he accepted it. "Say, that's much appreciated, Cap."

"Go easy, though. This is the good stuff. All the way from Sauria." Now that he'd oiled the hinges… "I'm just glad to hear the king is recovering so well. Not to mention that my brave friends have driven off the Tiberians."

"We'd have finished the job but for those damn ships of theirs showing up when they did. The bastards are still sitting fancy in Megaria, strangling the Straits. Just waiting for a chance to try for us again, no doubt."

So that was how the ambush had failed. The navy must have landed at Kynnya. Evidently, the mobile reserve was far from decimated. There was only one last major rumor to check out. "Ah well. They won't be back any time soon since the king killed that general of theirs."

Hook nodded. "Aye. That's the best bit to come of that bloody night. King Vahldan would've gotten the emperor himself if that damn fool general hadn't thrown himself in the way. I hear Bairtah-Urrin sliced the bastard's fancy breastplate from one armpit to the other. Dropped him like an anchor from a greased winch."

Damn. It was true. Vernius was dead.

Malvius had to force himself to keep smiling. "Serves the old prick right for trying to save that wheezing mouse." Gods, this changed everything. Malvius had always envisioned sealing his final deal with Vernius.

It wasn't so much that Ago would no longer be of use as a bargaining chip. Vernius Stallicus had just always seemed so methodical, so pragmatic. The man's death not only left the coming victory further off. It also left Malvius facing more bureaucratic protocol than he could imagine overcoming, even in victory. However it came together, his endgame just got trickier.

The doors to the high hall opened and another petitioner exited. Hook stepped over to usher the next in line inside.

Feeling gloomy over the news, Malvius decided to make himself scarce before someone asked him for favors. Learning that the wrong one had survived had ruined his mood. Besides, there was much to do on the docks. Maybe squeezing some excess profit from his imperiled city would brighten his spirits.

Malvius waved farewell to Hook and the others and turned for the stairs. A sensation overcame him, one that he'd learned to trust. He was being watched, he could feel it. He casually continued toward the stairs and, without being obvious, began to glance about the palace, seeking his watcher.

It didn't take long. She was that obvious. In an instant, both his apprehension and his foul mood dissolved, giving way to a completely different sensation.

The tall redhead stood at the top of the next flight of stairs to the residences. Harma wore a wry smile. She made no attempt to hide her surveillance of him. He stopped and offered a sweeping bow. Her smile grew. Malvius had been around long enough to know that not every woman was susceptible to his charm. But he'd also been around long enough to recognize one who was.

He went to the base of the stairs, cupped a hand to his mouth, and called, "You have often been in my thoughts, my lady."

Harma feigned a look of surprise and pressed her fingertips to the bare skin above her ample cleavage, mouthing the word, "Me?" Then she pretended to swoon. It was a sardonic delight. Gods, with this one he didn't even need to fake it. She entranced him.

"May I come up?"

Her demeanor instantly changed. She subtly but forcefully shook her head. Instead, she started down the stairs, her chin high, scanning the guards as she came. Malvius should've known better. It would hardly be appropriate for the king's wife to be seen speaking to a man alone on the stairs to the residences.

When Harma arrived on the balcony, she hardly glanced at him. She headed for the handrail overlooking the entry hall below. She surveyed the space, finally turned to him, smiled, and nodded for him to approach. Malvius casually walked over. He tried not to stare at her cleavage as he bowed his head. Gods, her height made it difficult. Well, that and its alluring glory. "Apologies, my lady."

"What brings you to the palace, Captain?"

Searching for a clever quip, his hand fell on his belt pouch and it came to him. "I came to ask after you. And to bring you this." He opened the pouch and drew out the tiny ceramic jar. He'd brought it as a backup gift for Vahldan in case he'd really have been forced to face the thug himself. The gods knew how much the man loved the stuff.

Harma accepted it, opened it, and gave it a sniff, causing her eyes to instantly water. "Careful. That's some of the finest pepper cultivated. It came all the way through a war zone."

"You could've warned me before I stuck my nose in it." Gods' grace, there was laughter in her voice.

"Again, my apologies."

She raised a brow. "And what exactly did you learn by asking after me?"

Gods, how had he forgotten to ask after her? He'd allowed the news about Vernius to get to him when he should've been thinking about the next opportunity. It felt like the gods' grace that she had appeared right when he needed her. It revived his certainty that he was going to win.

"I learned that you are well. And as beautiful as ever. I have been blessed to see it for myself." Malvius tilted his head again. When his gaze rose to hers, he was pleased to find her blushing. "May I offer my sympathies over your father? Such a tragedy." Tragic that the entire Gottari army hadn't been crushed due to the man's hubris and incompetence.

Harma swallowed and blinked back emotion. "Thank you, Captain," she managed.

It seemed like an opportune moment to take a greater risk since he'd heard little of the babe since its birth... "At least you have a fine son to help in displacing your grief."

"There is some comfort in motherhood."

"May he always bring you the joy you deserve. I'm sure Herodes would be proud."

"Armesus would've shared his name, but..." Harma frowned and looked away.

Armesus? That didn't sound like a Gottari name. "I'm sure King Vahldan is proud, too. You must both be a comfort to him as he recovers."

Harma's lip curled. "Hardly. She doesn't allow a soul to see him."

Her detest was apparent. "Amaga? At least she's a healer. Or so it's—"

"No, not her. The little witch isn't allowed in either. Which is one of the few consolations in this mess. No, it's her majesty of the blades who's playing at queenship now."

"Who? Elan?"

"They're all too terrified to remind her that he's not her husband. The selfish bitch. Thinks she's more important than all the rest of us."

Malvius repressed a smile. So Elan had reclaimed him. It made sense. Even a fool could see that theirs was a special kind of love. One that could never be replaced. Especially by marriages for political alliance or to make new heirs. And how wonderfully Elan's bold move played to his advantage. It almost made him think fondly of her again.

But gods, he wasn't doing a very good job of charming his target. Harma had gone from looking like a wild, beautiful Teutonic queen to a lost teenager. It made him wish he could take her in his arms. He could perfectly imagine how soft and yet firm she was. In all the right places.

How could he cheer her up now? "I brought food," he blurted. "And wine." Harma's eyes widened. He could find Tabaeus and pay him back for some of the finer items, so he could claim them as gifts. "Enough for the makings of a fine feast. You've all been through so much. Just a small token of my appreciation. I hope you enjoy it."

Harma brightened. "You'll be joining us, then, won't you?"

"Oh, no one here wishes for my company," Malvius said.

"No one?" Harma's eyes shone and her wry smile reappeared.

"I've gotten the impression that the first qeins and the king's sisters dislike me, my lady." Not to mention Teavar, who remained the most suspicious—and dangerous—of all.

"Ha. The first qeins dislikes everyone. And I've grown to dislike the company of most of the rest of them." Harma gazed out over the rail. "Gods, this palace is driving me mad." Her eyes darted back to him and her smile became sly. "Perhaps I should come down to dine with you. Aboard your ship. That way we wouldn't be dining with anyone who shares our mutual dislike."

"It sounds perfect, Lady Qeins, but I fear it would not be seen as—"

"Proper?" She pouted.

"I'm afraid not."

She raised a brow. "Why? Are your intentions... impure, Captain?"

Malvius opened his mouth to deny it, but no words came before she laughed. "Fear not, Captain. I'll bring an escort. You can invite anyone else you like—you know, for the sake of appearances. But you need not bother. I promise you, none of those who'd get themselves in a lather shall know of it. Can we set a date?"

"I... Of course I have no wish to refuse—"

"Good. I'll send word once I've made the arrangements."

Harma eyed the guards, and Malvius saw that their long chat had gained a bit of attention. "Are you sure that we won't be creating an issue?" he murmured.

"I've found there are few advantages handed to a second qeins, Captain. Even one who is the mother of the more fitting heir. So I've decided I need to make my own. I'll send word."

Malvius found himself grinning. "I am your most willing servant, my lady."

"How pleasing of you. And so nice of you to ask after me, Captain. But I must be going. Thank you for bringing some spice back to my life." He felt himself flushing when she held up the pepper crock. She leaned in, close enough that he could smell her musky skin. "You can't know how long I've been craving it," she purred, raising a brow and her wry smile.

Harma spun and sauntered back up the stairs—gods' grace, the way she swung her hips on each step, once again leaving him partially hard. With all of the Gottari guards now staring! Gods, she was fearless. Malvius held his cloak before him and rushed to the stairs, then down and through the entry hall. He didn't allow himself to smile until he made it out the palace doors.

CHAPTER 12
AWAKENINGS

"*Hiatus came shortly after Orithya, and with it came a spate of wintry weather. The mobile reserve had withdrawn to Megaria and the imperial navy was forced to stay near to their ports in Efusium, Nicomedya, and Trazonia. Thrakius seemed to breathe a collective sigh. For the Gottari it was of relief over the reprieve. For the Hellains, it was one of resolve, that even though their conquerors had yet to be expelled, at least peace could prevail for the coming months. In spite of the weather, the day-to-day activities of the city slowly rebounded.*

Then word came of imperial troop movements. Tiberian squads were seizing and occupying every Illyrican settlement and every Hellain fishing village in the surrounding territory. It seemed the mobile reserve would not risk repeating the mistakes of the past. Clearly, the imperial army was in no mood to hunker down in safe ports and wait through the winter. For Gottari and Hellain alike, that sense of relief or resolve was swiftly replaced by dread."—Brin Bright Eyes, *Saga of Dania*

. . .

Agoraki slid his last crate onto the wagon his crew was loading and tucked his freezing hands under his arms to warm them. Cap had left the docks without a word. Ago suspected he had gone to the palace, so he'd be gone for some time—perhaps all evening. Ago had originally been assigned to loading pallets for the winch in the hold, but trading for a spot on the docks, unloading the winches and loading wagons, had been easy. He was asking for a harder job, not to mention a colder one.

He scanned the dock for his other marks. He spotted Dex talking to the captain of *Seaswell* at the bottom of that ship's gangway. Ago didn't see any other officers; no one who had the choice to be elsewhere was enduring this biting wind.

This was it. His first real chance to slip away. Although he'd spent the days sailing from Trazonia telling himself that he not only could do this but would, he still hesitated. When it came down to it, liar or no, Ago liked Cap. He liked his fellow sailors, too. He had seen much since leaving the palace. Sure, the work could be hard, but he always felt good about what they accomplished together. The sailing life was a fairly secure and sometimes exciting one. Rather than take a risk, he could simply hunker down for the winter. He was sure visits with his maaman could be arranged. Maybe he'd even get a chance to see Brin in the course of things. Maybe he could simply ask Cap if he could go on up to the palace—he wasn't at all sure that the request would be denied.

But a feeling in the pit of Ago's stomach told him that he couldn't stay. Since he'd found out about his father, his sense that he was indeed his uncle's hostage—a mere tool for Cap's use—had only grown. He wasn't sure what would happen to him if he were caught and brought back, but he doubted it'd be good. Manacles came to mind. He also had his doubts as to whether he'd be welcome to openly walk through the palace. If he were caught up there, the Gottari were likely to hand him right back to Malvius. He had not a clue whether he'd be welcomed by his father, but he doubted it. After all, if anyone had the means to find their bastard son, it was a high-

and-mighty Tibe general. Didn't matter what Malvius thought about the man's need for an heir, the general obviously never had a care.

Whether Ago weighed all of it or none of it, he knew he had to go. It was as if he'd woken up in a strange life and he no longer knew where home was. He had to do *something*.

There was a lull while the dock crew waited for the next skid to be lowered. The others stood talking amongst themselves by the brazier, warming their hands. Indecision became impulse. He simply turned and started walking. *Gullwing* had taken the first quay. The skinny alleyway that led to Peddlers' Row—the avenue that ran uphill along the city's eastern wall—was just a hundred or so steps away. He and Brin had taken the route in what seemed like another life.

Ago pulled his cloak hood down, bowed his head, and sped his step, waiting to be called back. The call never came. In mere moments, he was in and through the little alleyway—the few old drunks sleeping there didn't even wake when he tiptoed past them. He headed up the nearly empty cobbled roadway.

The cold was evidently keeping the usual slew of shady vendors and slave recruiters indoors. He was only beckoned by one hawker, inviting him to enter old, boarded-up guards' quarters. Ago simply shrugged, miming that he didn't speak Hellainic, and kept moving.

He arrived at the upper stables, just outside the palace keep walls, to find the aisles even more deserted than the streets. He strode through the place as if he owned half the horses there and the boys mucking the stalls hardly glanced as he passed. He made it to the tack storage stall. He looked around before slipping inside. One of the grooms—a teenager—spotted him. "Hey, you there." The groom headed his way. Just then, an arriving patron led his horse in. The groom signaled for Ago to wait. As soon as the older boy looked away, Ago slipped into the tack room.

Thankfully, there was only a single broken bale of straw atop the trap door. He lifted the lid partway, straw and all, wide enough to slide in feet first. He used his shoulder to hold the door while he found his footing on the ladder. The last thing he heard as he silently lowered the lid was the groom asking the stall muckers where the stranger had gone.

Ago descended by feel, in complete darkness. At the bottom of the steps, he felt inside his tunic along the top of his belt for the stubby candle he'd stolen from the ship. It was unbroken. Rather than try to strike a spark here, he moved till he found the side wall and then felt his way along the tunnel that ran under the keep to the palace. He repeatedly wiped the cobwebs from his face and tried not to let the sounds of scurrying rodents give him the creeps.

He made it to the intersection that led to the various catacombs under the palace. From here, pressing ahead in the dark was risky. As well as he knew the way, there were too many turns, storage areas, and dead-ends—even a few open pits. It took what seemed like a hundred flint strikes to set a flare in his wad of damp tinder, but he finally got his little candle lit. He was able to move faster now. He found the right ladder and climbed up into the wall behind the larder shelves. His old collection of candles was still where he'd left it. There were a few lamps left elsewhere. He'd get to one eventually. He lit one of the longer candles and left it burning. He crawled to the vent and slowly and silently slid aside the same old crate on the bottom shelf.

A welcome wave of heat washed over him from within. Ago breathed in the smell of roasting meat and onions with a hint of yeast from the morning bread. The kitchens were bustling with the upcoming dinner preparations. He smiled to hear Heliopa barking orders and to see her minions dashing to and fro. It made him realize that if any place could be called home, it was this dreary cellar kitchen and the always fragrant, forever-too-hot-or-cold servants' bunkrooms and cells adjacent to it.

He didn't see his maaman among the kitchen workers, but finding her was only a matter of time. Ago thought it best to stay unseen until he spoke with her, so he settled into his old spot on the back of the middle shelf at the kitchen-end of the larder. From here he could monitor the comings and goings while staying hidden.

Time passed and Ago grew concerned. His mother was one of the most prominent, not to mention vocal, kitchen workers. He neither heard nor saw her throughout the frenetic dinner prep. His neck was getting stiff and his legs were getting cramped. His old spot had been more comfortable when he was smaller.

He finally heard her before he could see her. "Well, fatso, what's the excuse tonight? Where in the seventh realm is Lady Harma's dinner?"

"Right where it always is," Heliopa called without looking. "In the pot, waiting for you to come and dish it and deliver it."

"I told you I'm not a serving girl anymore."

"If Mistress Cleavage wants her dinner in her quarters, someone's got to haul it up there. There'll never be a spare server to do your running, girl."

Ago tried to get into position to get Apontia's attention, but she kept walking right by on her way from the stairs to the kitchen. Apontia slammed the lid back on the pot with a clang. "I also told you no more mutton! The Lady Qeins prefers fish."

"Then tell her to get a net and catch some. I've got no fish!"

Ago found he was smiling. He'd forgotten how much these two enjoyed their bickering. Apontia finished making up her tray and headed back through the larder. He wriggled to the front of the shelf, then glanced at the other kitchen workers and back at the stairs. All clear.

Ago stuck his face and one arm out into the corridor, waving at his oncoming maaman.

"Aah!" She nearly dropped the tray. Her mouth fell open, eyes wide.

"What now?" Heliopa shouted down the corridor. "You drop it, you clean it!"

Ago shrank back. Apontia gave him one of her mock scolding looks and called over her shoulder. "Mind your mutton, woman. And keep your damn cats out of the aisles. I almost tripped! This beasty is lucky to not be kicked."

Heliopa waved her off and went back to work. "Would you rather have cats or rats? Without one, we're sure to have the other."

Ago signed for her to step deeper into the larder. He slid off the shelf and stood to face her. His maaman came around the shelves. She seemed so... *small*. He was almost as tall as her. She still wore her mock scolding look, but her eyes were shining. He wanted to embrace her but the tray she held was in the way. "What are you doing here?" Apontia hissed.

"I need to talk to you," he whispered.

She glanced back. "Third floor linen locker. Go. I'll be there as soon as I can."

He nodded and she headed for the stairs. Ago was only a little surprised that she knew that the vent in the linen locker was one of his entry points to the inner wall passages.

It seemed to take forever to make his way up through the labyrinth of back passages. Ago wondered whether he could've just cautiously made his way up the servants' stairs. But then he reminded himself that Cap was supposedly here in the palace somewhere. At least the trip gave him the chance to retrieve one of his old lamps. He'd even left it with plenty of fuel.

Once he was in the locker, he set his lamp on a shelf and made himself comfortable. If someone else came in, there was nowhere to hide and no way to flee other than revealing how he got there. Thankfully it was Apontia who arrived.

"I heard you were in port. I've been trying to find a way to visit you," she said with a smile. She wrapped him in a warm embrace and then drew back, holding his hands. "Let me see you. You're so tall, so strong. Such a man you are becoming, yes?"

"I'm not so sure. Some days I just wish I were small again, living with you."

Apontia's eyes shone. "As do I." She clucked in laughter. "Ah, my little pink baby boy." She hugged him again. When she drew back, she raised her chin, gathering herself. "Now. Tell me. Why have you come? And why so secret?"

"I ran away. No one knows I'm here."

Her dark eyes narrowed. "He is your uncle. You are the one who went to him, yes?"

"Yes, Maaman. But..."

"But nothing. You tell me why you need to run."

Ago couldn't hold her sharp gaze and looked down. "I overheard him—Uncle Malvius. I know why he brought me on. He knew how he could use me, and it wasn't as a sailor."

"How, then?"

He thought he would start with a stunner. "Malvius is secretly planning for the fall of the Gottari." He paused for a reaction but it didn't come. He went on. "He's sure they will fall once the Tiberians come. Once that's happened, he wants to use me as a bargaining prize. I overheard who my father is. Malvius knew all along. It's why he took me in. The man is an important Tibe. Malvius thinks he can offer me up to save himself."

"Ah." Apontia sighed it out. She released his hands and nodded. "Now I see."

"You do?" Ago didn't understand how she could. Unless... "You knew, too... who my father is." Apontia turned away without answering. "You did, didn't you?"

Her gaze met his. "For a long time, I suspected. One day, I finally got her to admit it."

"Her? My real mother?"

Apontia nodded. "After Ligaia became a slave, we could better see one another, yes?"

"Why didn't you tell me? You knew I wanted to know."

Apontia's gaze lost focus and her lip curled. "Because I hate him. I thought I might lose you to him. And I could never forgive him for what he did. I could not bear the thought."

"You knew him? What did he do to you?"

Apontia drew a deep breath and released it. "Your father, he led the soldiers. The ones who came and burned my village. They killed everyone… My dear maaman." Her eyes hardened. "They killed everyone but me. Me, they took. They…" She swallowed hard. "They kept me, for a time. Till their army was shipped here. They sold me because they'd tired of me. For I was as a feral cat—either growling and hissing and scratching or yowling and whimpering. Some found it amusing, at first." Her eyes narrowed. "By the time we came here, I had seen to it that none were still amused."

"Weren't you afraid? They could've killed you."

She nodded. "Most nights, I prayed for it."

His eyes stung. "This Vernius, he knew of this?" His voice quavered with sudden rage.

"Of course. They only did what he ordered or allowed. In the end, it was he who sold me to Ligaia's family." Apontia's anger melted when her gaze came back to him. She reached up and put a hand on his cheek. "But as much as I hated them all, they gave me you. And now that all of them are gone, I find I cannot keep hatred in my heart for them. It costs me too much to cling to it, yes?"

"Wait. All of them are gone? Vernius is dead, too?"

"Oh, my son. I thought you knew. The king, in the battle, he killed your father himself."

Agoraki leaned back on the shelf behind him, mouth open, gulping for air. He'd been so angry. But now… "Both of my parents are dead?"

"Yes, dear one," she whispered.

"Then I truly am an orphan. For good this time." Gods, he'd gone from not knowing what an orphan was to being one, to learning who his parents were, and then back to being one. He didn't know what he felt anymore.

"You have me," Apontia said.

"Do I? I mean, do you really think I can come back here?"

Apontia paused, her forehead creased, considering. She finally shook her head. "No. You must go back. Back to your uncle."

"But I just told you he was going to—"

"Let him. Let him use you."

"What are you saying?"

"He's right—the Tiberians will come. I have seen it. They will keep coming until they win. No matter how many they must kill to do so. But not you. Malvius will see to it. He will make them see that you are one of them." Ago shook his head but she went on. "You must listen to me, Agoraki. You must wake up to this. This is who you are, yes?"

"Maybe by blood," he conceded.

"Blood is what matters to them. Your blood means you can claim your place among them. And then you will be safe. Safer than I can keep you. Do you understand?"

"But it won't work anymore. My father's dead. I have no proof."

Apontia held up a finger and became very still. "Ah, but there is proof," she whispered.

"What kind of proof?"

She nodded like she'd decided something. "Wait here. I'll be back as soon as I can."

Apontia opened the door partway, peeked out, and then disappeared. Ago found himself pacing the tiny space, trying to absorb it all. His maaman returned before he knew it. She held something cupped in both hands. It was gold. She held it up. It was some sort of torc, designed to fit around the neck, made up of two joined pieces. He leaned in. It was shaped like two curved serpents, their tails connected at one end and each holding a clasp in their fanged mouths. A round medallion hung from the clasp. The gold of the medallion was shinier than the serpents.

"What's this?"

"A trophy of war. It belonged to your father. The man who was your great-grandfather won it fighting in the far north, what they call the hinterlands. Your father was very proud of this man—more so than his own father, whom he hated. Ligaia said Vernius even prayed to him. This was very precious to him."

She gestured for him to take it, and Ago did. It was heavy. There was an eagle on the medallion. And some letters. "What's the medallion say?"

"It's supposed to say a family name. *Your* family name."

"How did you get this?"

"Your mother. Your father gave it to her when he left Thrakius. Because it meant so much to your father, it meant much to Ligaia. She hid it from her husband. After the Gottari came, she found it was still where she hid it. She showed me the spot."

"Why would she do that?"

"She surprised me, too, your mother. It was when Isidros was here with his men. Ligaia was afraid. He wanted her to marry him, but she wouldn't. Isidros grew restless with her. He was getting angry. Your mother, she needed Isidros's men, but she refused to marry him. I think it was because she held out hope for your father." His maaman smiled and put her warm hand on his cheek again. "It means you were born of love, yes?"

Ago drew a breath and sighed it out. "Maybe so," he said.

Apontia nodded as if it were foregone. "Anyway, your mother, she told me that if anything happens to her, I should find a way to give this to you. At first, I told myself that I would never do it. But now I see—it is the only way. Ligaia says this will prove to the Tiberians who you are. She knows this because no other such trophy exists, yes?"

He nodded absently, trying to absorb it all. Apontia looked back at the closed door. "Put it away; keep it hidden. Take it with you when you go back to your uncle."

"But I can't—"

"Yes, you must," she said firmly.

"But I know him, Maaman. He won't—"

"He will. Your uncle was up here, at the palace, until a short while ago. He will be looking for you. If you go to him now, he won't stay cross." She didn't understand. Cap only cared about people for what he might gain from them. He would now know that Vernius was dead. It meant Ago was worth a lot less to him.

But still... He looked down at the golden torc. He tucked it into his belt pouch. He could never show it to Cap.

Apontia opened her arms and Ago fell into them. His tears wet her tunic as she rocked him. "When I go to Tiberia, you can come with me."

Apontia huffed a laugh. "No, sorry. People like me are only slaves there."

"I don't care. We'll just pretend you're my slave. No one has to know." She drew back from his embrace, smiling. She didn't believe him. "It'll work. I'll come back and I'll buy you and take you to my estate. You'll see."

"All right. I will say I believe you. But if your plan is to work, you have to get back to your ship." He bit his cheek, trying not to cry. Her smile grew warmer still, full of love. "Do not worry, my son. Until the soldiers come, we will still see one another. We have a bargain, yes?"

Ago knew he couldn't go back to Malvius. But he also knew he couldn't tell her that. It was far easier to tell his stubborn maaman what she wanted to hear. "We do," he lied. He consoled himself that the first part wasn't a lie. Somehow, someday, he *would* come back for her.

"**WHAT DID I TELL YOU, VAHLDAN?**"

Vahldan tried but couldn't open his eyes. "I don't remember."

"Yes, you do. I told you to take them back. Why haven't you?"

He twisted but his arms were trapped. Was he tied up? Why couldn't he open his eyes? "Father? Can it be?"

"Is this really what you thought I meant? To lead them away? To sunder our people? You had them, son. All of the herdsmen, the farmers— they were yours. And you threw it away."

His head lolled back and forth. "No. It's all for them." Vahldan forced his eyes open, blinking against the bright light. It took a minute to figure out that he was in Elan's bedchamber. He was in her bed and couldn't move. The silhouette of a figure loomed at the foot of the bed, limned in brilliance. The figure took a step closer, revealing Angavar's face. His father still wore a bloody hauberk and a look of consternation—the very ones he wore on the day that Vahldan had killed him. "You told me to lead them back to glory."

His father's eyes flared. *"You call this glory? Waiting here to die?"*

"I became a king. I did what you bid of me."

"What I bid? Did you ever listen?" Angavar drew Bairtah-Urrin from the sheath. *"Do you know what this is?"* His father held out the hilt, pointing to the ring dangling from it.

"It's the futhark ring."

"It's** half **of the futhark ring!" Angavar flicked the ring with his finger, making it clatter. *"Do you know what it says when it's made whole?"*

Vahldan shivered and turned his face from Angavar's wrath. "Two..." He couldn't form the words, even though he knew them. "Two become one, Together to stand, Forever to lead, Brothers unto Urrinan." Elan was sleeping beside him. Why wasn't she waking? She was still his guardian, wasn't she?

"You never even sought the bridge." Angavar's disgust was apparent.

"Bridge? What bridge? To where?"

"Where is the other half of the ring, Vahldan?"

He squeezed his eyes shut, his head lolling back and forth again, trying to will it all away. "I don't know."

"You do! Look at me, son." He forced himself to look. *"Where is it?"*

"In Dania. In the longhouse of Danihem. On Thadmeir's sword."

"Take them back."

"But I can't. The snows."

Angavar bent closer. *"Take... them... back."*

"It's too late."

"That's ridiculous. It's never too late. At least not for the few who are vital." A woman's voice, coming from right beside him. Vahldan recognized it from a distant past. She rolled to him. Gods, it wasn't

Elan. The Skolani queen's strong hand caressed his face almost mockingly.

"The boy's right—he's ruined everything."

"Nonsense," Keisella said. "No more than you did. This is as much your fault as his. After all, his ugliness has ever been your legacy."

"Stay out of this, Keisella."

Gods, were his father and the queen really arguing across the bed from which he couldn't rise?

Keisella's smile grew arch. "I told your son he could only seize his greatness if he avoided your folly. Seems he's never really woken up to that. And after all I did for him. Indeed, he still hasn't recognized it."

Vahldan tried to focus on her, but Keisella's image kept morphing, changing from one Skolani face to another, ever-changing yet always familiar. "All you did for me?"

"The first gift was obvious. But we've been with you all along, Vahldan. Right there beside you. Yet time and again, you turn your back on us."

"I don't understand," he said. "Who have I turned my back on?"

The queen's smile grew sly. "We are the old. Always you seek for the new, forsaking the link between. But the link is the only way forward. Neither side can prosper without it. We gave her to you, yet you both ignore her."

Vahldan's head spun. "I don't know who you mean or what to do? What can I do?"

*"Take. Them. **Back!**"* Angavar thundered.

Vahldan thrashed, trying to rise and flee, but couldn't. "I... I don't know how."

Keisella sat up and leaned over him. "Calm yourself. Of course you do. All is not yet lost. Urrinan is not yours alone to shoulder. There are those who share in it. Others have seen to her fostering. The link thrives. She and the heirs are yours. You have but to wake up. Wake up and come to me."

"Come to you how? I see no link, no bridge. It's too late to cross. I was always doomed."

Angavar harrumphed. *"Listen to him. He's beaten already. He wastes all that's been given."*

Keisella moved closer, nose to nose. "It's not too late. Not for those who matter. Not for Urrinan. Your doom is beside the point. Simply wake up and come to me." The queen gripped his shoulders and shook him. "Do you hear me, son of Angavar? Wake up. Come to me."

Vahldan squeezed his eyes tight. "I don't know how," he repeated.

"You do! Just **wake up!**" The words boomed and thrummed. He was jolted as if a bolt had struck with a flash, and his eyes shot open.

"Vahldan? Are you awake? Darling? Have you come back to me?"

The light was dim. The air was cool. And she was there.

Elan's smile sent relief rushing through him. Her touch was gentle, her voice soothing. "There you are. Thank the gods."

"You? Thanking the gods?" Vahldan smiled. "The gods are fickle, remember?" Elan laughed and leaned in, just as the queen had. She was so close, so beautiful. Her lips touched his, deliciously soft. He longed to wrap her in his arms, but she was sitting on the blanket, trapping him. "And now you're stealing a kiss. From a man who can hardly move."

Elan's smile grew sly. "The gods favor the bold, remember?"

RUNNING TO OR FROM?

"During my years in Thrakius, I often stood gazing from the top of the north wall into the misty depths of the Pontean Pass. That view, and what lay veiled beyond it, intrigued me more than that of the sea, so vast and empty. I came to liken the pass with the Skolani, who I was told guarded it—ferocious and ruthless, relentless and resolute.

At first, the idea of traveling through the pass terrified me. As did my image of the Skolani themselves. My thinking began to evolve once my uncle began to train me. In hindsight, I see that it was the incident with Ligaia that completed my transformation. That day, there was no choice. It was either scheming Ligaia or my kind Uncle Urias. I could either wield power or be subject to it.

Against the approaching threat of war—one to be fought against such an immense force as the Tiberian Empire—I grasped for any semblance of control and self-reliance I could find. My uncle had whispered of the possibility of becoming one of them—of being as ferocious and relentless and feared as the Skolani who lurked just beyond the treeline in the misty depths of the Pontean Pass.

I came to realize I had never wanted anything more."—Brin Bright Eyes, Saga of Dania

FROM THE COVER of the haw thicket, Brin scanned the overgrown gardens at dawn. She saw nothing. She couldn't see the targets or the prize. Worse, she saw no sign of him. She tightened the straps on the little shield. Urias had made it from an old pot lid borrowed from the kitchens. It was so small that at first it had made her laugh. Urias insisted that if she were grown, it would be about the size of those the Blade-Wielders wore. Although Brin had never seen her mother wearing a shield, she'd seen a smallish disk with straps among her mother's gear. She gripped the bow and double-checked that the arrow—one of only three that she was allowed for this exercise— was nocked and ready.

She blew out a breath of steam and focused. Training wasn't just about muscles and practiced skills. According to Urias, it was about finding a special belief in herself and surrendering to it.

Her uncle called it Thunar's Blessing and said focusing would help her find her way to it. She'd learned that Thunar was some sort of war god. Supposedly this blessing would come during moments that demanded the best of her—as in life-or-death situations. It all seemed a bit backward but she was willing to play along. If there was even a small chance of meeting any Skolani in her future, she wanted to learn everything she could about them.

According to her uncle, powerful feelings, like concern for loved ones or even anger or sadness, could be gathered inside her and focused into a sort of emotional strength. The sort that could fuel her and serve her purposes. The rage she'd felt at the end with Ligaia had been scary. She'd been so out of control. It made her want the ability to stay in control, no matter what kind of crazy stuff was happening. She could see how focusing like this during training might help her with that. According to Urias, the greater the emotion, the harder it was to control. But also, the more powerful the blessing would be.

Today, she had to admit, her simmering anger at her mother might be pretty useful.

Elan had shut Brin out of her own home for days now. Her mother hadn't so much as bothered to ask about her, let alone send word as to how Brin's father was doing. She'd gotten the news that he would survive from Amaga, of all people, who *had* been allowed inside. Brin couldn't imagine a more upside-down world.

It really wasn't surprising, but the way Uncle Urias had instantly taken her in made her all warm inside. He'd even taken in Hesiod. Living with Urias only made her appreciate him all the more. He was so steady. He was firm and yet gentle. She felt even luckier to have him in her life. She suspected her mother had known he would take her in.

In the moments when Brin forgot to stay mad, she could imagine how worried her mother must be about her father. As much as her mother fought and denied it, she knew Elan cared more about him than just about anything else. Particularly now that Hrithvarra was gone.

That didn't keep her from being mad though. And sure enough, she did feel something weird growing inside her as she scanned the field. The squirming in her belly was filling up her chest, which she figured was good. Maybe this Thunar wasn't such a backward god, after all.

It was time to decide and act. Brin decided and launched from the thicket of haw bushes. She ran for the low stone wall along the cobbled path, avoiding the wild lengths of thorny rose vines but using the crumbling archway as cover. She paused and cleared the edge of the archway, bow raised, just starting to run again when it caught her eye: the first target, wedged in the border shrubs. She hardly paused as she drew and shot. She moved on, reaching for a new arrow even as the satisfying chink of the first arrow hitting the crock came to her ears.

Brin let her eyes roam across the overgrown gardens as she ran. She'd learned that her wandering eyes would let her brain know when they came across anything strange. Stuff like a glimpse of color or movement. Any clue might alert her to the second target, the prize, or—most importantly—her opponent's position. Moving in a crouch, she slipped along the low wall lining the path and carefully peeked over the top. She didn't spot the next target but she saw something else. There it was, sitting atop the post that held the rotting wooden gate on the far side of the field, which was planted with rows of carrots. The prize.

It was a small red vase pilfered from the entry hall. Her job was to retrieve it unbroken. The first level of failure meant she lost the day outright. The second level would require her to tell Hesiod that she'd broken it. A pretty thing like that wasn't as easily explained as a few broken crocks. Brin supposed Hesiod would know how old it was, how irreplaceable, and would make it clear—for at least a few days —how disappointed he was in her. No fun but survivable. Hesiod could be tough on the outside, but she knew his heart was as soft as a winter-stored apple.

She'd rather risk some old vase and suffer the consequences with Hesiod than suffer her mentor's smug satisfaction. Brin hated losing, and she'd done too much of it lately. Her uncle was getting too cocky.

It was well and good that she had spotted the prize, but she still had no idea from where its defense would come. And getting the trophy would only be half as sweet if she didn't take out the second target. She firmed herself in her anger and launched herself again, bow up, leading with her pot lid shield and heading for the sagging trellis.

The first dirt clod zipped by her and crashed into the brush. She turned in the direction it had come from and barely raised the lid in time. The second clod crashed into her pretend shield, spraying soil over her head. She lunged for the cover of the vines that weighed down the trellis and landed hard but out of his sight. Her instincts called to her. She scrambled to a knee, turned to face away, sighted, and shot. Clink. She dropped down again. She'd been right: The second target was in his line of fire.

Her trainer's words rang in her head: *Never relax. Trust your instincts, but never trust that you're safe. Always expect the worst.* She couldn't stay here—not for long.

With both targets knocked out, she shed the quiver from her shoulder and laid it, along with the bow, at her feet. She fleetingly peered around the corner of the trellis. A clod exploded on the post next to her head. He had her position locked down, but now she was clear about his position, too. He was at the end of the shaggy hedge that separated the garden from the martialing grounds. She peered through the vines. There wasn't much cover between the trellis and the prize. He had a commanding view and the range to strike the entire carrot field. She could try running for it and hope to avoid getting hit. Maybe take an odd tack, make a few unexpected changes in direction.

No. Her anger surged. Trusting to luck wouldn't do. He would not beat her again. She was her mother's daughter.

What would Elan do?

Almost instantly, she knew. Brin knelt and selected a fairly firm clod of soil at her feet. It fit perfectly in the coil of her index finger and thumb. She couldn't dally. Surprise would be everything. She drew a breath, visualizing her opponent's position and the outcome she sought.

She launched herself again, sprinting not toward the vase but back into the garden and then on an angle toward the overgrown hedge. It was the opposite of what best suited him. Once in the open, she sped her step, taking long, full strides along the low wall. She leapt over the wall with scissor steps and kept on, staying veiled from his throwing arm. She came to the end of the hedge and kept running around it, knowing her footfalls were audible to him now.

As she came clear, Brin raised the shield and lifted the clod in her cocked throwing arm.

They were both right-handers, and, just as she'd guessed, he had to fully expose himself to get a decent throw. Her new position rewarded her with the better angle. As Urias stepped out to raise his arm, her clod was already on its way. It exploded on his chest as he released, and her pot lid shield blocked his weakest throw of the morning.

"Got you!" Brin ran by him and snatched the vase from the post.

"Hey!" Urias brushed dirt from his tunic. "Coming after me was never part of this game."

"Says who?" She couldn't keep from grinning.

"Says the trainer."

"Well, if the trainee is dead when she's hit, the trainer should be, too. It's only fair."

"I suppose. This time. Next time we lay new ground rules." Urias was hiding one of his secret smiles. The kind that told her he was proud of her.

"Yes! I win." She held the vase overhead in triumph and pumped her shield arm fist.

"All right, winner. As a bonus, we'll be using the paddle for your wall work."

Brin groaned and slumped. She hated that bedamned boat paddle. She often considered hiding it, maybe throwing it over the palace wall. It was so much worse than the broomstick.

By now, Urias's promise to her mother about not training her seemed to have come down to a few specific details: that they didn't use wooden swords or spar with the boys. But clearly the swinging of lengths of wood was not off limits. Nor were shields. Well, if you could call a pot lid a shield. She even had her own bow and quiver now, gifts from Urias and kept at his residence.

Brin took the lid, bow, and quiver and put them with her cloak and tablet. She snatched up her cloth and wiped the sweat from her face. It didn't pay to let sweat get into your eyes. Especially not for this. She hopped up on the wall. Urias came over with the paddle. "Begin," he said, trotting out ahead of her as she began to straddle-hop along the wall top.

"Where's the guard?" He always started with the guard, but that was the easiest of late.

"East wall, near the corner tower," she said and quickly glanced to make sure she was right. Since the army had left, the Amalus boys had been gathering in the gatehouse and the stables each day. They liked to pretend they were patrolling the keep, but they were mostly just showing off. It gave them the chance to boast about what they would do if they were allowed to go to war.

"There's a raven," Urias called, still moving ahead of her progress.

"Not fair!"

"War isn't fair. And this one's not in flight. Find it."

She immediately looked to the old cherry tree. There wasn't much fruit left but the ravens still loved whatever they could find. Damn, no raven. She scanned the garden and finally saw a flash of black movement. "Shed roof," she called and swiveled back. Too slow. The swinging paddle was already coming. Instant reaction. She leapt but just barely cleared the top edge of the paddle blade. She landed awkwardly, regained her feet, and straddled on.

"Sloppy," Urias said, tsking. "Stay mindful, even as you search." He strolled along but didn't run out ahead. She would be safe until the return journey.

Brin came to the wall's end, turned to face the other direction, and headed back. She hated it when he was behind her but it was part of the drill. At least she knew he wasn't much farther along than the spot where he'd swung last.

"Gray squirrel," he called.

Damn. Squirrels could be in trees or on the ground. She'd seen one digging earlier, under the haw that separated the garden from the stables. She glanced over her shoulder. Urias still hadn't moved. She had a moment. Brin focused intently on the area of the haw... and saw feet. She followed the legs up, peering into the shadows. A face! Watching her.

Recognition struck. It was a face she knew well. His eyes went wide and he ducked.

A tingle ran up her spine, then alarm. Her eyes darted back and she leapt, but too late. The paddle hit her anklebone even as she sprang, knocking her foot astray. She managed to push off of the wall with the other foot, hard but clean. Her last effort allowed her to land on her shoulder in a thick layer of leaves. It was painful but she'd learned landing on a tucked arm was better than throwing out a hand to catch herself. Even as she scrambled to regain her feet, she was checking herself, shaking her limbs. She hadn't wrenched any bones or joints, and she doubted she'd be bruised. She'd allowed a surprise to distract her. It was a mistake but it could've been worse. Plus, she knew she could temporarily put off dealing with the surprise.

She sprang back up onto the wall, wincing when her ankle hit the top. Damn. It was worse. "Is the ankle all right?" Urias asked. He was a keen observer, just as she aspired to be.

"It's fine," she lied. It ached with each step, but she kept straddling. Sometimes you could shake off stingers like this, which would be better than having him fret.

Brin sensed Urias easing back. He was testing, watching. She resisted the urge to look for her distraction again. "You never found the squirrel," he said. She resumed her search and found it.

"Ash tree branches," she said.

"Berserker!" he shouted as he swung. Saying it as he did it was his way of going easy on her. She leapt over the oar with no trouble, trying not to show favor for the ankle as she landed. She went on to the starting point and hopped down, taking most of the impact with the sound ankle.

Urias threw her a towel. "I don't know. You may have won the prize, but that wall work was pretty shoddy today."

Brin pushed the pot lid under the nearby bushes with her toe as she wiped her face and then bent for the vase. "It's such a lovely prize, though." She grinned and held it next to her face and stroked it as if it were precious. "I bet you wish you'd won it."

"I still say you cheated," he scoffed.

"I didn't cheat. I improvised." She handed him the bow and

quiver, donned her cloak, and tucked the tablet under her arm. "Isn't that what a Blade-Wielder would do?"

They headed toward the door to the servants' stairwell and Urias gave her a side glance. "We'd better hurry. I've been warned again about your tardiness."

"Ha! You're changing the subject. You know I'm right. Admit it."

"I'll admit it if you agree to soak that ankle tonight," he said.

Brin had to admit, the man was sharp. "All right."

"Have Hesiod salt the water and get it good and hot."

"I know." They arrived at the door, and Brin stopped. "Wait. I forgot my shield."

Urias waved it off. "It'll be there tomorrow."

"Oh no, a good warrior would never leave her gear out to rust." She winked. "Go on ahead and start your tea. I'll get the lid, then I'll bring up the breakfast tray."

"All right, but don't dawdle, or you know what we'll hear."

"I know, I know."

"Captain Urias," he began in a high-pitched imitation of Despoina. "If there's one thing I will not abide, it is tardiness."

"If you ask me, all the man is training you to be is unladylike," Brin added in her own Despoina impression. Urias laughed and started up the stairs.

As soon as Brin closed the door, she set down the vase and tablet, spun, and ran, snatching up the lid as she passed. She came around the haw from the backside of the stables. She scanned the low branches as she moved, finally spotting him. He was faced the other way, watching a pack of Amalus boys in the stable yard. He was probably waiting for the chance to sneak to the trap door in the tack room.

"I would ask what you're doing here. But what I really wonder is why you're hiding?"

Ago spun, clearly startled. He released a breath and came through the branches. Brin wanted to embrace him but his expression stopped her. Apparently things were still awkward between them. He looked as flustered as she felt. She nodded, beckoning him to follow. She went to the old benches that faced one another along the palace side wall. The high-backed seats were practically swallowed by leafy vines that continued up the wall, offering a mostly hidden spot for them to sit and talk together.

Brin sat right away, but Ago remained standing. He'd grown! Not just taller. He was bigger all over. Which made him seem oddly out of place. Odd because he'd always been a built-in feature of the palace. Particularly in all its nooks and crannies. "Well?" she prompted.

"I ran away."

"From your ship?" Ago nodded. "What about your uncle?"

"He'll be angry. I can't go back."

"Can you stay here?"

"No. It's the first place Malvius will look. And your father would make me go back."

Those both seemed likely, all right. "Why'd you run? Where will you go?"

Ago looked at his feet. "I found out who my real father is."

"Who?"

Before he'd say, Ago quickly explained how Malvius was secretly waiting for, and possibly actively working toward, the eventual return of the Tiberians. Brin was momentarily stunned but quickly recovered. It was troubling but really not surprising. She'd come to see that everything Malvius did was in Malvius's best interests. She suspected that went beyond his survival. Any alliances, or even friendships, would come second to his success.

Ago told her how Malvius wanted to use him as a bargaining chip. Then he told her that his father had been the Tiberian general that her father had slain in battle.

That surprised her.

It meant that both of Ago's blood parents were dead. Worse, Brin had killed one and her father had killed the other. He stood in sullen judgment as she worked that through. She didn't know what to say.

Ago lowered the figurative blade from her chin. "Never had them anyway," he said wistfully, looking away. "And this way Cap can't use me. Guess I never really had him either."

She was beginning to understand his predicament. She had instantly sensed something different about him. She realized that part of it was a lonely sadness. It was a burden that people hauled around with them, whether or not they wanted others to see it.

"But my maaman, she gave me this." He withdrew a heavy golden piece of jewelry—maybe a necklace—from his belt pouch. He quickly shoved it back in. "It was my father's. It'll prove I'm his rightful heir. There's an estate. In the country, somewhere in Tiberia." Brin's surprise and doubt must have been evident. Ago raised his chin. "It's rightfully mine."

"So that's where you'll go?"

"I think. I mean, I'm going to try. Sailors who've seen it say Tiberia is beautiful. It's my family's home. And I don't really have one."

Ago sounded more certain than he looked. Did he want her to say it was the right thing? She found she couldn't. "Is that what you want? Or do you think it's your only choice?"

He frowned. "Maybe it's both."

"You don't even speak their tongue."

"I can learn. And Cap says most of them can talk regular, like us."

"How will you get there? I mean, you're in here and the Tiberians are out there." Brin pointed west.

"I have a few ideas." It sounded like a dodge. "You could come with me if you want." Brin laughed and he frowned. He wasn't joking. "We'd finally have our own place. You could live on my lands, even in my house, for as long as you like. Forever maybe. Like a real home."

Brin took his hand. He tensed but didn't pull away. "Ago, that sounds really nice. But think about it. You know how the Tiberians feel about my family."

"We could hide that."

"Hide this?" She held up one of her red braids. "Someday, some way, they'd find out. I'm guessing it's just like here. None of them look like me. I'd be a stranger there, too."

"Except slaves—lots of them have red hair. We could pretend you were mine."

She shook her head. "We'd always be hiding, always keeping secrets."

Ago pulled his hand away then. He looked off to the west. "The Tiberians *are* coming, you know. Their armies are huge. They never lose. Everyone says so. It's just a matter of time."

Brin looked down at the pretend shield in her hand. "I know." She brightened at a thought that occurred. "We could run away into the pass. No way the Tiberians would follow us there. No one can. We could live in Dania, maybe even build a cabin. That could be a home, too."

Ago took a length of his short brown hair in his fingers and scrunched the nose that she now realized must have been his father's. "And nobody looks like me up there. You said yourself, the Skolani guard the pass, and—"

"We'll tell them I'm one of them. My uncle's been training me. I'm getting good, too. I was even beating the boys till my mother made me stop sparring."

"Brin, no. You're not listening." His cheeks flushed and his words came faster. "I'm trying to tell you that I'd take care of you. *I'd* keep *you* safe. I'd take you where no one could hurt us or leave us or use us. We'd always be there for each other. And even if we pretended you're my slave at first, I could marry you after a while. And I'd never marry anyone else. And if we had a kid, that kid would always know we were his parents. His real ones. His only ones."

Brin leapt up to face him. "Gods, what are you talking about?"

"I mean, it wouldn't be how our parents did it. It would be for real."

"Skolani don't get married, Agoraki. They don't pretend to be slaves either."

Ago stuck out his bottom lip. "Too bad you're not a real Skolani then. You told me yourself, you're nothing but a ghost to them. Same as your maaman."

Brin took a step closer, stretching to her full height and raising her chin to look him nearly nose to nose. "I am *not* the same as my mother. I'll never be. They'll take me if I try hard enough. Because I'm not her. I'd never throw my life away for a man."

Ago couldn't hold her gaze. He laughed but there was no mirth in it. He stepped out from the space between the benches, shaking his head. It was concession, withdrawal. But he kept shooting as he retreated. "Sorry, Brin, but I'm afraid you are. You're exactly like her. And if you're not careful, you'll turn out just like her—unmarried and alone and mean. And sad."

Tears filled Brin's eyes. "I'm late. I've got to go." She walked past him, heading for the servants' door.

"Me too. I can't be seen here."

She glanced to find him heading for the haw thicket. In spite of herself, concern flared. "Ago? How will you get out? Those boys..."

He stopped. "There's an old gate, through the thicket. One of the bars swings free."

He started walking again. "Ago, wait!" He stopped again but wouldn't look. Brin ran to the thicket and he turned to face her. "Take care of yourself. Thank you for keeping me safe. I'll never forget you."

Ago smiled, his cheeks still ruddy from their skirmish. "I'll never forget you either."

Brin lunged to hug him. It took a moment but he hugged her back. She released him and his smile brought back the boy she once knew. "Be careful," she said. "All Tiberians care about is treasure. And you're not like that."

Ago's smile faded, but he nodded before he turned and disappeared into the haw bushes.

～

Elan was already awake when Vahldan stirred. He leaned over her for the water cup and drank. As soon as he set the cup down, Elan pulled him down on top of her. He kissed her bare shoulder and tried to lift himself off, but she held him there. He laughed into her hair. "I am feeling better, Elan, but I don't think I'm quite that much better."

She closed her eyes. "Just for a moment. I need to feel the weight of you. I've missed it."

Vahldan relaxed onto her and she tightened her grip. "Seems like you ought to be used to it. You've been carrying me for so long." He drew back and looked into her eyes. "Keisella gave me a mighty gift in you. And she's right. I've never properly appreciated it."

Elan ran her fingers through his hair. "What do you mean, she's right?"

He laid his head on her chest and sighed. "Oh nothing. Just a dream."

Which reminded her. "Before you woke up the other day, you kept saying something about it being too late. You were clearly still out of it but do you remember what that was about?" Vahldan rolled off of her and stared at the ceiling. He was pale, grimacing. "I'm sorry. We overdid it. Are you're in pain now?"

Vahldan shook his head. "Well, yes. Feels like the good general broke his bedamned blade off inside me, truth be told. But that's not..." He glanced over, looking sheepish. "I'm sure you could guess —about the dream, about being too late." He shook his head. "Anyway, I'm awake now and fully aware that you were right."

Elan gave him a lopsided grin. "Which time?"

"Every time. Especially about the Tiberians. And my selfishness, my stubbornness. My recklessness, my ambition. My pride. All of it. You tried to get me to do the right thing. You said I should send them back before the snows came to the heights. And I wouldn't listen."

Elan propped her head on her elbow to face him. She'd kept him so isolated. Rightfully so, but she owed him an admission or two. "You probably don't realize this, but by all accounts, we won."

"Won?"

"At Orithya. Yes, their navy showed up and they got away. But they lost hundreds while we lost dozens. And you got Vernius. Those who know about the mobile reserve say he's the driving force behind their success. You damn near got their mouse of an emperor, too!"

Vahldan went back to staring at the ceiling. "Proving what?"

"Proving that *you* were right. We can win! They're not unbeatable. This war isn't over."

He shook his head. "I've done so much wrong. So many are dead because of me."

"I've told you before—people die in wars. They believed in something. They died honorably seeking to serve that belief."

"You told me that about Eldavar. It made me feel better then but it just keeps happening. Because of me Herodes is dead. And Jhannas, and on and on." He shook his head. "My father told me to lead them back to glory. Nothing about this feels glorious anymore."

Elan huffed a laugh. "I think we've both learned that war is only glorious to those who've never experienced it."

"It took me too long to learn it. I've not only been a selfish ass, I've also been a fool. Even in seeking to prove my worth to my father's memory, I've failed. He never asked me to conquer an empire or proclaim myself a king. He considered the prophecy to be a tool, which is all I ever should have done." He squeezed his eyes shut. "I thought, if I could just raise myself high enough, I'd be above it all— above all my weaknesses, all of my shortcomings. All of my mistakes. I thought I could absolve myself of guilt by proving that I was bigger than the man Angavar bragged I might become."

Elan couldn't argue with that. "Sounds about right."

"Worse than that, I was so focused on proving myself to everyone who admired my father that I failed to honor what my mother implored me to do. In order to ignore it, I wouldn't allow myself to grieve for her. Because grief felt like an admission. I even stole her legacy from my siblings. I blocked them from even speaking of her, just to absolve myself. If I'd honored her, we'd all be better off. Again and again, she warned me not to buy into it. Even the last time I spoke to her. That night she made me vow to put family first, to ignore those who sought to harness me with prophecy. Gods, I failed her so miserably.

"I let Eldavar die. I've placed Mara's husband in harm's way again and again. I even sent Mara out there. To a bloody war zone. With a babe! Then there's Kemella. Freya's grace, my mother sacrificed her very life to give Kemella hers, and what have I done since? First, I abandoned my sisters to the care of others. Then I put my poor baby sister in a position to become the surrogate husband to a wife I don't love and the father figure to a son I don't deserve. Now they're all trapped here with me because I failed to listen to reason."

He wiped tears from his eyes and wouldn't look at her. Everything he said was too true. And very sad. Elan hadn't the slightest idea what to say.

Vahldan finally turned swollen, sorrowful eyes to her. "But the worst thing I've done is push you away. I did it purely out of selfishness, knowing you would block me from doing the wrong thing. I thought the ugliness would aid me, that it was actually a boon when deep down I knew it to be a curse. I willingly lost myself to it. For years. I knew better. My mother taught me better. I ignored what I'd learned, which is a betrayal—not just to you, but to Frisanna. You were my anchor and I cut you loose. I treated you awfully and you didn't deserve it. And yet, here you are. I don't deserve you."

Elan gave him a smug smirk. "Well, I hope you don't expect me to deny any of this."

"How could I? You've suffered too much for that nonsense. I'm so angry with myself. I mean, damn, we had them. They were ours— the herdsmen, the farmers. No few of them had once been loyal to the Wulthus. They switched sides, left their homes, followed me. Fought for me. Because you stood by me. Because of what I promised them. And I betrayed all of it. Mostly by betraying you."

"Stop this. No more bemoaning the past. It's time to start seeking to make good on your mistakes. You can't erase them. But you can still honor both of your parents. This tale isn't over. Not yet." Seemed she'd gotten a head start on coming to terms with their fate. She'd had to look past his betrayal just to ride out with him again. "Face up to it. I have. You are the Bringer." He made a harrumphing sound.

"Oh no, you don't," she said. "Don't you dare dismiss it. We're far past being able to decide whether it's true. All of us. Think about it. Because of you, every one of us knows what we're capable of. We see what we've wrought. However you choose to define it—as prophecy, destiny, divine, or just compelled by our will, the world shall be changed. It's already well underway. We are a people to be reckoned with. Those of us who continue to follow you have to choose to keep believing. Every day. Don't you dare try to take that away from us. Not now."

Vahldan pressed the butts of his palms to his red eyes. "This war... I made my followers think we're invincible. I even let myself believe it. All we've done is lose."

"I said *stop it*. What's done is done. It's what got us to this point. The war is here. We all knew that was what it would take to bring Urrinan. Each of us knew it when we set out from Akasas all those years ago. None of us can run from it—certainly not you. The civilized world has been forced to see. No matter what comes of this war, our people will rise." She leaned to get him to look at her. "Did you get that? I said the Tutona shall rise. It's been set in motion by us. By you. That's no small thing."

Vahldan met her gaze, his countenance grave. "If they do, they'll have to rise from the rubble of the calamity I've wrought. And maybe that's as it shall be. But I've come to see that there's more to being the Bringer than wreaking havoc. I can't just set this thing in motion and then submit to its doom. Or worse, expect anyone else to. Doing nothing now would mean it's all been for nothing. If there is a future, it's a future that I need to look to—to strive to create."

"All right, then. What else is there, Bringer? What future should we strive toward?"

"I'm not sure. But I love that you said 'we.'" He grinned. "And I think we should find out." He sat up, surprisingly spryly. He paused on the edge of the bed, put a hand on his wound, and took a breath.

"Easy there. You're going to have to take it slow. Healing takes time."

"Healing will have to wait. There's much to be done before the siege begins."

"Such as?"

"I'm the one who let this thing get out of our control. I need to wake up to it and make up for it. I need to make sure I'm doing all I can to ensure the destiny the seers foresaw." He faced her. "I need to see the queen, Elan."

"What? That's impossible."

"I don't think so. In fact, I believe she's been speaking to me... somehow. She's demanding that I come to her. I'm not sure how but there are things she still needs to tell us. About our destiny, about our progeny. I must speak with Keisella, and I need your help to do it."

"*My* help? You're the bedamned king. And she banished me."

"Neither of those things matter. What matters is that we do it soon and in secret. You're the only one who can pull it off." He actually stood, hissing through gritted teeth as he did so. He was shaking, but he stood tall at the side of the bed. "Never forget, my dear: You are the Skolani's gift to the Urrinan."

"Ha. Some gift. I'm a ghost to them, remember?"

Vahldan raised a brow, smiling through his evident pain. "You're a ghost to *most* of them. But not to the ones who matter. Come." He beckoned with both hands for her to get up. "Before it's too late."

She got to her feet. "There's just one thing I need to do first," he said.

"Which is?"

He took her hands and faced her. "Please don't say anything. And know that I don't expect you to accept it or for it to change anything. I'm not asking for anything in return. I just need you to know it. And hopefully believe me." He looked deeply into her eyes. "I am so deeply sorry, Elan. For the way that I treated you, for all I put you through. It is my deepest regret—one that I will live with until I draw my last breath."

He held her gaze. She didn't want to react. Reaction was too close to acknowledgement. And acknowledging how badly he'd injured her by lacerating the couple they'd once been was simply too dangerous. Paralyzing even. As evenly as she could, she said, "I believe you."

She turned from him, pulled his arm over her shoulder, and led him toward the door and to Teavar, who would be just outside of it. In trio, they might find sanctuary from the couple they struggled to be.

SEEKING BEYOND

" *I have mentioned my great-grandmother's influence on the course of events many times, and not without reason. I can think of few who had a larger impact upon the story of the coming of Urrinan than Sael, Wise One of the Skolani. Before Sael's rise to prominence, above all else, the Skolani were a solitary people, scornful of intrusion and suspicious of change. Sael's foresight changed everything.*

Her vision thrust the Skolani into their role in the Urrinan. Like the Gottari, the Skolani's submission to destiny provided an inexorable push toward the undoing of many traditions. Both tribes would be transformed by what Sael foretold. In spite of it, Sael continued to insist that the Skolani would forever serve as the link for the Tutona to the old ways. Indeed, I came to learn that she had passed down the responsibility of maintaining that link to me. It is a legacy I have never taken lightly.

Gone is the old world Sael was born to. Still, as with the old ways she sought to enshrine, my prescient ancestor shall not soon be forgotten. Some, including my mother, have said that she exerts her influence even from the beyond. I find I cannot refute it. Though I was far too young to recall our sole meeting, I often sense her presence in my life."—Brin Bright Eyes, Saga of Dania*

. . .

AGORAKI SAT IN THE SHADOWS, peering down at the docks from the charred and abandoned loft, huddled in the woolen cloak his maaman had given him. The spot was above one of the last burned-out warehouses yet to be restored in the aftermath of the fires of the Gottari invasion. Although the lower floor was a refuge for drunken sojourners, no one had bothered to climb to the loft since Ago had started using it. Why would they? The floor beneath his feet made a better roof than the holey one over his head. Besides that, the ladder was a ruin, making it a challenge to get up here.

His spot was fairly safe, but better still, it afforded him a view of the docks without being seen. Cap's ships dominated the quays, particularly since the onset of the imperial blockade. The majority of the workers and sailors here worked for his uncle. Ago should have been anywhere but here. He had to risk it though. There was someone he needed to see. And he had to speak to them alone without being seen. The future would not be simple or safe. The odds were against him but he only had this one plan.

Nightfall came early these days and the crowds thinned as it grew darker. There was some moonlight through the clouds as well as a pole-mounted lamp outside the entrance to The Fishmonger. Ago's eyes were starting to adjust when a carriage rolled down from Market Avenue onto the docks. He harrumphed audibly. This wouldn't help. In fact, it might complicate his mission. The carriage was from the palace. There was a lone driver on the bench, an armed Gottari guard.

The odd sideshow continued as Malvius and Dex emerged from Cap's cabin and hurried to the gangway. Cap actually walked down to welcome their mystery guest. Ago had presumed it would be the king or one of the senior Rekkrs, so he was surprised when a lone woman emerged. She wore a fancy frock, a fur wrap, and a matching hat. Cap bowed and offered his arm to his guest before escorting her to the gangway. The lamp Dex carried revealed the visitor's red hair, but Ago had already figured out by her saunter that this was Lady Harma.

The show was all the odder that she was there without her husband. Or any other escort, other than the guard, who'd already pulled out a skin and settled in to wait.

It dawned on Ago that Harma was the new him. Rather, now that he was of no value to his uncle, Cap had found someone new to use. This new chip provided a new advantage: She could get to his nemesis. Winning Harma over didn't strike Ago as being all that hard to do. The woman never heard a compliment she didn't love. And Cap could spout some pretty smooth talk when it suited him.

Just moments after Cap and Harma went inside, a pair of men exited the tavern. They bid one another farewell. The one Ago had sought for days strolled down the docks toward him, alone. It had taken time to learn that the man he sought lived in one of the warehouses at the west end of the docks—one of the few that didn't belong to Malvius.

He hurriedly but carefully climbed to the ground floor. He came to the partially open door and slid his hand into his belt pouch. His bargaining chip was the only thing in there. He didn't know the man's name. He doubted the man would know who he was. He had nothing to offer and everything to lose. But Ago had to make this work.

Ago peeked out. The carriage driver had already moved to the inside of the carriage. Smart if he didn't get caught. The wind was brisk. His mark, walking from the tavern, had almost arrived at Ago's position. He didn't want to startle him, so he stepped out into plain sight.

The man slowed, looked him up and down, and then steered to take a wider berth.

"Good evening." Ago bowed.

The man grunted in reply, pulled his cloak tight, and kept on.

Ago hurried to walk alongside him, staying more than an arm's length away. "Forgive me, but I have a favor to ask."

The man stopped and turned to him. "Sorry, boy. I got no extra coin."

"Oh, I wasn't going to—"

"And I got no food. And nowhere for you to bed down neither." The man started walking again. "Still plenty of jobs unloading."

Ago glanced to make sure no one was paying heed and fell in behind him. "I don't need a job or a place to stay. What I need is a way to get to Anax Isidros. I think you work for him."

The man stopped and stiffened. He turned slowly, his gaze narrow. If he was wary and irritated before, he looked downright dangerous now. "Look, wiseass, I don't know what you're about or where you got your—"

Ago cut him off, speaking fast. "I mean no offense. It's just that I think I saw you with him. In the palace, back when he seized it. I used to work up there, in the kitchens. I have something for him. Something I know he'll want." Ago held out his open palm, showing him the medallion from his torc.

The man started to reach for it, but Ago closed his hand and stepped back. "I'll show it to you again in better light if you like. But I need your help getting to Isidros, so I can deliver it. I'm sure he'll be pleased. He'll likely make it worth your trouble."

The man smirked. "Maybe I should just take it from you."

Ago backed away another step. "Maybe you could try. But I'm pretty fast." The man flinched and Ago danced away. The man laughed and Ago saw that he was too drunk to actually give chase. "Besides, that sounds like a lot of trouble. For both of us. This medallion is only part of a valuable necklace. The anax would want the whole thing. The other part is very old. And very rare."

"Where's the rest of it?"

"Well hidden. Trust me, this is a rare opportunity. Together they're priceless. The piece is Tiberian. It belonged to a noble. A dead one. His kinfolk will want it back. This will win Isidros much favor with them. He'll know it right away—as soon as he sees it."

The man sneered and laughed. "Horseshit." He started walking. "Go home, boy."

Ago stayed with him, keeping his distance. "It's not horseshit. And the reason I'm offering it to your boss is for that very reason. I want to go home."

"If it's so valuable, why not sell it here? I'm sure Malvius would pay a hefty sack for it. Or maybe go to one of them Gotars on the hill. They still got plenty of loot."

"I don't want it to go to Malvius or the Gottari. I want it to go to its rightful owners. And I'm sure they'll pay best for it."

"You said yourself that it sounds like a lot of trouble. Trouble's the last thing I need. It's no simple thing, getting to Nicomedya these days."

"That's why I came to the best."

The man stopped again, outside a warehouse door. He turned and leaned down, face to face. "All right, let's have it straight. No twisty words or japes. Why're you thinking to take this treasure of yours to Anax Isidros?"

Ago glanced at the carriage and lowered his voice. "It's as I said. I want to go home. More than that, I have to get out of here. I hate the Gottari and I hate Malvius."

"Why's that?"

"Because of them, both of my parents are dead." The man stood thinking, but his eyes were still mean-looking. Ago risked pressing. "The Tiberians are coming. It's just a matter of time. I want to be on the right side of this war. It only makes sense to be in good favor with those who're sure to win. I'm guessing Anax Isidros feels the same. And you do too, I'm guessing."

"Come on in, boy." The man turned to unlock the warehouse door. When the door came open, the man stopped, blocking the door. "This better be the real thing, sonny. Or I'll make up for it by selling not just your bauble, but your skinny arse to the slavers too."

Ago swallowed hard and raised his chin. "It's the real thing," he said and followed the drunk into the dark and rank-smelling warehouse.

～

ELAN HELPED Vahldan into the saddle. His face was ashen and he stifled a groan as he settled. He nodded that he was ready but looked miserable. "Is the pain too much?"

"Can't be," he said through clenched teeth. "No amount will keep me from this."

Elan and Teavar exchanged a look. The giant shrugged. They both knew there was no point in arguing. They'd already tried. She nodded for Teavar to take up his position on the other side. She wasn't taking any chances that he might fall.

Vahldan frowned. "I still don't see why we aren't all riding."

"I told you. This way is less likely to alarm the Skolani."

Vahldan said nothing. He tapped Druzana with his heels. Druzana was an aging dun mare Elan had befriended in the palace stables and had selected for him to ride. The old girl was sturdy but unlikely to jostle her wounded rider. They emerged from the gateway and headed down toward the treeline of the Pontean Pass at an easy pace.

Soon enough, the climbing would begin. And with it, the danger.

The stars began to wash out with the coming dawn as they entered the forest. The air was crisp. The smell of pine needles and fallen leaves filled her nose as the trees closed in around them. It was the first time in over a year since she'd ventured into an actual forest. It would've filled her heart with joy if it weren't for the dread that was already there. For the last time she'd ventured into this particular forest, an arrow had missed her nose by the width of her hand.

The morning waned and the road became snow-covered, slowing their progress. Still, no warning arrows appeared. Although they continued to climb, the forest rose even steeper to each side. The trees—mostly hemlock and cedar—began to lean in, causing a tunnel effect. It was cloudy above the trees and the way ahead fell into deepening shadows.

A tingling sensation ran down her neck. "This is where it will begin," she said softly.

"I presume we're already being watched?" Vahldan asked.

"Since we left the gate. But this is where the pass truly becomes theirs."

A gust of wind stirred the trees, sending clumps of snow down around them. Teavar grunted, his big head swiveling. "Hands off hilts," she hissed. The giant frowned but complied.

"We did request this meeting," Vahldan said. "And it seems the request was accepted. Or at least acknowledged."

Elan barked a lone laugh. "None of that means those who guard the pass will make it easy. Or cordial." Particularly for her.

As if on cue, a long yowl rode the wind. It sounded like an angry cat. Elan swore she heard laughing afterward. Next came growling and signaling whistles, from behind and ahead.

"Eyes forward. Hands off weapons," she reminded them.

Next came the wailing of a ghost echoing through the trees. And finally, spoken word. "Ghosts are not welcome here." More muffled laughter, then, "Especially not ghost whores."

"Remember, it's me they're taunting," Elan said. "Whatever happens, do not defend me."

"Elan, you can't expect—"

"You promised. I told you not to bring me, but you insisted. Now you must do as I say."

The crunching of snow and stirring of brush surrounding them became more heedless. "Lions should choose their companions more wisely." Open laughter followed the quip.

"I come to see Queen Keisella!" Vahldan shouted. The laughter stopped. Elan moved to make him look at her and scowled. He sighed and nodded. They'd had several conversations about how vital it was for him to maintain his grip. Even the slightest concession to the ugliness could cost all three of their lives.

The boughs on both sides of the road rustled and then stopped. Elan held up a halting fist. Only the wind could be heard for a long, tense moment.

A voice came low and clear, very close, very menacing. "The lion is far from home. And even farther from our queen. We defend the realm. No one stays the hand of those who stand vigil. Trespassers should be polite."

Elan instantly recognized it. An old fear she'd thought dead and buried shivered through her. "Do. Not. Defend me," she whispered. "Let it play out, or it will escalate."

The brush began to stir again. At last they appeared, from every side, all with bows drawn and aimed. Their faces were painted for battle rather than scouting. Most even wore breastplates. Not good signs. Elan counted six, which meant twice that many remained hidden. She didn't recognize a single one. They were so young!

Once they were completely surrounded, the leader stepped forth from the brush, standing tall, no bow. Just a buckler on her arm and her blade hilt over her shoulder. She had two daggers sheathed on her broad belt, along with at least a dozen Spali scalps.

"Because courtesy matters, wouldn't you agree, Lord Vahldan?" The blood-bitch strode toward them. Keeping her focus on Vahldan, Anallya abruptly veered toward Elan, throwing out her buckler. The shield struck Elan's midsection hard. It surprised her enough to send her sprawling. Elan cursed herself for not expecting it. She got to her knees and braced herself but stayed down. She tried to poise herself without appearing provocative.

Both Vahldan and Teavar put their hands on their hilts and all of the Skolani bows creaked. The circle of Blade-Wielders leaned in, bows taut and eyes hard. "Hold!" Elan called. "I'm all right. Let it go."

"What was that?" Anallya held a hand to her ear. "We keep hearing ghosts in the woods today," she added with an amused sneer. If anything, the blood-bitch looked even bigger and tougher. And meaner.

The hateful woman clearly hadn't changed. Adding insult to

injury, there wasn't a single crease on her face with the exception of a new purple scar extending from the corner of her mouth almost to her ear. The sides of her head were newly shaven, emphasizing the mass of braids that rode over the top of her head to trail down her back. Her fur-collared cloak was thrown behind her shoulders, revealing a finely scrolled doeskin tunic with matching leggings and knee-high boots. Two silver torcs rode on her bare muscular arms.

The blood-bitch had done well for herself.

"I hadn't noticed," Vahldan said. "But then again, ghosts have never troubled me."

Anallya's lip curled. "Clearly. Alas, you may find them an impediment yet."

Vahldan glanced at Elan. She shook her head and slowly rose, keeping her hands in sight.

Vahldan drew another breath and sighed it out. "Forgive us, Blade-Wielder. If we've caused offense, trust it was not our intent."

Anallya smiled and stepped back, though her eyes continued to scowl. "Anyone who knows our ways knows that bringing a ghost forth is anything but polite. Surely the lord of lions knows us this well?" She still hadn't even so much as glanced at Elan.

Vahldan tilted his head again. "Fairly spoken. I humbly request your forbearance. I am anxiously seeking an audience with your queen. I flatter myself that she will be pleased to receive me. But I will forgo the honor if my guardian is harmed or blocked from accompanying me. I will not be parted from her. It is as simple as that."

Anallya actually laughed; Elan didn't think she'd ever heard her laugh at anything that didn't involve cruelty or harassment. "Your stubbornness does not surprise us. For this ghost of yours is known to us. She too has ever been stubborn. It seems that over long years, she has inflicted her poorest trait upon the lord of lion's will. Keep her if you must. Only know that our queen will not abide any ghost in her presence. Ever. Do we understand one another?"

Vahldan looked to Elan again and she nodded. His eyes were

clear. They were going to get through this. "We understand one another," Vahldan said.

Anallya tilted her head. "You may proceed in safety. If you can manage greater haste than you've shown thus far, by nightfall you may yet come to a place where Skolani often camp. We will make it ready for you. From there you shall be a bit more than halfway to our queen. Once you draw near, I will meet you again and take you to her. She will greet you for tomorrow's evening meal. That is, if you can keep from dawdling. If not, you will miss your chance. With or without your visit, the queen shall withdraw come the next dawn." Anallya glanced up at the sky. "More storms are coming."

Without awaiting a reply, the blood-bitch signaled. She and all of her Blade-Wielders melted into the trees. Neither Anallya nor any of her charges had so much as glanced Elan's way. It was a stark reminder of how much it stung to be invisible to those who had once been her people. She reminded herself that she had left almost a lifetime ago.

The day remained gloomy and they walked into blowing flakes riding a north wind. The higher they climbed, the deeper the snow became. They struggled through the afternoon to maintain their pace, trying to heed Anallya's warning. It was indeed too late for wagons to traverse the heights. Soon it would be all but impossible to cross with or without a wagon.

Night fell early and swiftly. Elan smelled the fire before she saw the trail that led to the first Skolani camp. They proceeded into the blind warily. A fire burned brightly beside two small tents of aurochs hide, but the camp was deserted. Elan knew they would need no watch. They were as safe here as they were in the palace. The snow let up as they unloaded their packs. Their boots and cloaks were soaked through, and the three of them quickly huddled around the fire in their stockinged feet and tunics, drying their gear on propped branches. A small pot was left on the fire for them. She lifted the lid to find a hot broth with chopped parsnips and a few chunks of rabbit. To that they added their own strips of dried goat, a sliced green apple, and torn chunks of a travel loaf. The resulting supper was warming and sustaining.

Elan must have dozed off. Vahldan woke her and nodded to the tent. He looked exhausted. It made her feel guilty. Teavar was already snoring in the second tent. She brought in her mostly dry cloak and put her arms around Vahldan, wrapping them both in wool. He was shivering at first but swiftly fell asleep. His nightmares started soon after. Suddenly feeling wide awake, Elan lay listening to him murmur, holding him through his terrors and relishing the feel of him and their shared warmth. She remembered her dream—the one that had started it all for her. It wasn't that it hadn't come true, not in the specific details. But the reality was far from what she had imagined when she had first had it.

She wanted to blame him but knew she couldn't. Not completely. Had her dream been a trick of the gods or was it her own choices along the way that had shaped her days?

As for Vahldan's part in it, she had to admit, at least to herself, that she could've seen the signs and avoided much of the damage he'd inflicted. At least to her. She lay wondering how things might have been different—how their dreams might have been shared and full of bliss. Could she have somehow dissuaded him of his ambition?

All she knew was that it was too late. Too late for what-ifs. They would never be who she'd hoped they would become—not in this life. The thought filled her with a melancholy, but she couldn't ignore what the days since she'd claimed him had reawakened. She hated even to admit to herself that she still loved him. She kept it shuttered and guarded. She'd sought to live a life devoid of love. Love had caused her so much pain and sorrow, after all.

She found it harder and harder to deny though. She couldn't keep it out of her heart. How could she deny her love for her daughter or for her brother? And if she acknowledged those forms of it, could she turn away from her feelings for her oldest friend and the father of her daughter?

She found the truth of it more and more difficult to ignore as the danger that had been awoken by the Bringer closed in around them.

Yes, Vahldan had made terrible choices. As had she. His had led him to treating her horribly. And yet, an undying love for him dwelled deep within her. Her awareness of it only grew. It was beyond renouncement.

Their lives together had been anything but easy. As Urrinan drew nearer, things would get much more difficult. But didn't all love have value? Even of the sort that had caused pain, that she had sought to renounce and upon failing had locked away? Love was what had started it all. Love for her people had always been central to her dream. Love had been behind her choice to leave her tribe. Love had led her to seek to have Brin. Love had kept her at his side, kept her believing that the Urrinan would ultimately lift up their people.

After all that had happened and all that still loomed, she saw it more clearly than ever: Love might be the only thing that truly mattered. She realized it might be the only thing left to her, the only reason to continue to strive.

It seemed half the night was gone but with acceptance came resignation, which sent Elan sliding into a deep, peaceful sleep. She woke alone to the smell of tea brewing. It was nearly dawn. Vahldan handed her a steaming cup as she emerged from the tent. He looked better. The best he'd looked since he had been wounded. Teavar had already fed, watered, and saddled Druzana. They ate chunks of travel bread crisped in the flames and spread with sheep's milk cheese they'd softened by the fireside. Best of all, Elan had dry, warm boots when they set out. They were making steady progress before the sun was over the eastern peaks.

The snow continued to deepen, but they worked to keep their pace up. Cold as it was, she began to sweat with the effort. The Skolani had broken the trail, which helped. It also helped that they now faced nearly as much downhill walking as uphill. The snow stopped falling and the afternoon grew colder. The snow underfoot grew crusty as the daylight waned.

They descended onto a high plateau rimmed by bare rock ridges. Elan knew the place. The far northern edge of it was the last fallback of the Skolani in the pass—the place where, if necessary, they would make a stand to defend Dania. The Skolani kept a camp in a series of hidden coves beyond the plateau. The scouts used the spot as a base of operations—a sort of home away from home. A stream ran through the center, and besides offering a commanding view of the approach, in season, the plateau floor became a fine grazing meadow. She liked it here. The spot reminded her of simpler times.

They stopped to fill their skins and let the horse drink at the stream. Elan wasn't too surprised when Anallya appeared before they reached the northern ridge. She was more surprised that her old nemesis appeared to be alone—though Elan suspected Anallya's gang lurked nearby.

The blood-bitch said nothing as they approached. She only turned and led them around the base of a hillside. Once they were out of the wind, a quiet cove opened before them. Elan smelled, and then spotted, a blazing fire. As with the prior night's camp, there was no one else in sight. Unlike the prior night, there was only one tent pitched. The snow had been cleared from a span surrounding the fire and there were dry logs for seating.

Anallya stopped and turned to Vahldan. "This camp the Skolani have made as a tribute to a ghost—one who is missed by many of her former sisters. It shall be guarded along with the queen's campsite. It is the hope of those who miss this ghost that she will find comfort and rest here while the lord of lions visits with our queen."

"Our thanks to you all," Vahldan said with a bow of his head.

Anallya paused a long moment. "There are some among the Skolani who once failed to recognize the sacrifice this ghost made. Some once thought her selfish. They did not appreciate how this ghost suffered, nor did they consider how... *difficult* it must be to be parted from her old life. At least one of those who thought thus now better sees the ghost's intentions for her people, for Urrinan." For the first time, Anallya turned, her gaze fully upon Elan. "Though I still cannot condone the betrayal of one's sisters, I have come to better understand this instance of it."

Elan stood stunned and awkward, a lump in her throat.

Before she could respond in any way, Anallya turned and walked away. "Come, lord of lions. You and your tall guardian must be hungry and thirsty. Food and drink await you both in the queen's camp."

Elan stood gawping. She'd never imagined such a thing. It was as close to an apology as Anallya would ever give—to anyone, let alone her. Vahldan cleared his throat, jarring her back to the moment. She hurried to pull her bag and her blanket from Druzana's back. He held out his hand and she took it. "I'll come back later," he offered.

"No. Stay. You are Keisella's guest. It's an honor. Don't tarnish it. I'll be fine." Anallya stopped at the crest of the ridge but didn't look back. "Go," Elan said. "She won't wait long."

Vahldan nodded, drew her hand up, and kissed it. The pair led the horse on. He gave her one last wave before they disappeared over the ridge.

Elan threw her gear into the tent, shivered, and went to warm herself by the fire. She spotted the food that had been left for her. Besides the pot of broth and vegetables, there was a perfectly roasted hen on a spit. The fowl appeared to be fully cooked and set in place to keep it warm. There was a drinking skin, too. They'd even left her a cup. She poured and took a sip. It was mead. Memories rushed in along with the smell and taste of it.

She sat. Twilight slid to a darkness that fell like a curtain around her little camp, closing her off from the world. Alone. She realized she should be drying her soaked boots and cloak. She stripped them off and set them up to dry, still feeling stunned by it all. The camp, Anallya's almost-apology, the food and mead—it felt so close to being home. She could almost smell it but she still couldn't get there —and likely never again would. She felt full of unshed tears. Her mother had always said that you couldn't drink and cry at the same time, so she poured a brimming cup and drank.

Half her cup was gone and a tear still slid down her cheek. It wasn't working. She couldn't remember ever feeling so isolated. The fire gave off plenty of heat but she couldn't stop shivering. She looked down at the hen, golden skin glistening. It looked good. Maybe eating would fill up some of the emptiness she felt. She took her belt knife, wiped it, and cut a chunk of crispy skin and soft flesh. She stuffed it in her mouth. Warmth and memory suffused her as she chewed. What was that herb tucked under the skin, marjoram? She hadn't tasted its like since leaving Dania half a lifetime ago.

Elan filled her mouth with mead, swallowed, sawed off another hunk, and took another bite. "Damn, that's good," she said aloud.

"Everything I know of cooking, I learned from you."

Elan froze. No. Could it really be? She stood and turned.

Icannes stepped into the firelight looking like a goddess in a dream. Her first beloved smiled and opened her arms. Elan rushed into her strong embrace. The tears came again but she let them flow. "Is it really you?"

"Of course it's me. I told you, didn't I? You'll never be a ghost to me. Our love is beyond any of that nonsense. Didn't you believe me?"

"I wanted to. I mean, I did. I just... It's been so long."

"I'm sorry, dear heart. I wish it could've been more often."

Gods, there was nothing like it—the intoxicating musk of the cleansing paste, the power of her old protector's arms and hands, the soothing sound of her throaty laughter... just, the warmth and strength of her. "Horsella's grace, I've missed you so much."

"Me too. Here, let me have a look at you."

Icannes tried to draw back but Elan tightened her grip. "No. Just a moment longer. I don't ever want to forget what this feels like."

Icannes laughed and stroked her back. "You'd better not forget." Elan finally relaxed her grip and Icannes drew her back. Elan saw a few new creases, a few faint scars, but her hero had never looked so beautiful. Her eyes were unchanged—so fierce and yet so full of love. Icannes ran her fingertips along Elan's jawline. "I think about you every day." Icannes's fingers moved to push her bangs from her forehead, tucking the excess behind her ear. Her smile grew. "But your hair! I always forget."

Elan tried not to sound stung. "What do you mean?"

"It's just that I still picture you in braids."

"Well, it's easier to wash this way. And to comb. I don't have anyone to retie braids, you know."

"I'm sorry. I promise not to forget it when I picture you. It actually suits you."

"My princess?" Elan leapt from their contact, heart trilling. It was the second time she'd been surprised by someone's approach. She was definitely out of practice.

A graying Skolani woman came into the firelight, carrying a small child. "Oh yes," Icannes said. "There's someone I want you to meet." She strode to the woman and held out her arms. "Thank you, Alela." Gods' graces, it was indeed the wet nurse who'd cared for both Kemela and Brin, all those years ago.

Elan waved hello to the woman as the child changed hands. Alela smiled shyly and gave a slight wave as she backed to the edge of the firelight and averted her gaze. At least she hadn't totally ignored the ghost. Icannes brought the cheerful child to Elan, carrying her on her hip. The girl had bright yellow hair, big blue eyes, and rosy round cheeks. She was about two.

"Say hello to Ainsela."

Elan leaned in, smiling. "Hello, Ainsela. You are such a beauty. Just like your mother."

"Ainsela, say hello to your Aunt Elan. Can you say Aunt Elan?"

"Ahn E-lah," the girl ventured. Elan widened her eyes and opened her mouth, emoting her delight. Ainsela put her chubby hands over her eyes and turned to hug her mother, abashed.

"Ainsela, eh?" Elan said. "If my memory of the old tongue serves, she's the chosen one?"

Icannes rubbed the girl's back and rocked her. "More like the special one. Or as I like to think of it, the one who was long sought."

"Long sought? What about the older one? Doesn't she count? And where is she? Did you bring her along?"

"Haelya? Oh, Horsella knows she counts. That girl will have it no other way. But no—I knew from the day I first felt Haelya stirring in my tummy that she wasn't the one we sought. And gods no, she didn't come on this trip. Haelya is back at the Jabitka, terrorizing her guardians, I'm sure. Mother would never have abided bringing them both, but I so wanted you to meet Ainsela." Her daughter turned back to Elan. She made faces to get the girl to smile again. Icannes nonchalantly said, "You really are her aunt, you know."

Elan kept making faces. "Of course I am. We're near-sisters, so—"

"No, Elan. By blood."

Realization dawned. "Freya's tits! Does Urias know?"

Icannes actually blushed. "I was hoping you would tell him for me."

"Of course." Elan knew there was a time—not so long ago— when such a revelation would've caused her to feel jealous. But now she only felt amazed and happy. "I'd be honored," she said and knew it to be true. Maybe she was actually gaining maturity as well as age. "He'll be so pleased."

"I hope so. Tell him she's perfect—exactly as I'd hoped. Tell him that I know in my heart that she'll be everything we all hoped for."

"Which is?" Ainsela started to fuss and twist.

Icannes beckoned. "It's her bedtime, I think." Alela hurried over and took the child, bowing her head and carrying her off into the darkness.

"So?" Elan wasn't about to let such an auspicious comment go unexplained.

Icannes sighed. "Come, let's sit. Pour me some of that." She reached for her belt pouch and drew out a cup. Still always prepared. Elan filled the cups as Icannes settled in. "Oh, and eat if you're hungry," Icannes said as she accepted the full cup.

The silence stretched. "Well?" Elan prompted. "You know I'm not going to drop it."

"It's not that. I just can't decide where to start."

"How about the beginning? That usually works."

Icannes huffed a laugh. "You haven't changed a bit, I see. I suppose, as most things do, it starts with Sael. She was the one who revealed Urias's role. I mean, I was already fond of the man, but…"

"But what?"

Icannes pressed her lips tight for a moment. "You know as well as anyone how much of this has been your grandmother's doing." Icannes took a sip.

Elan suddenly knew. She saw it in Icannes's eyes. "Is she…"

Icannes gave a nod. "She spoke of you, just moments before she passed."

Elan swallowed hard and wiped her eyes. "What'd she say?"

"She asked me to lend you strength. I told her I wasn't sure how. She said I'd know when the time came, which was so like her. I'm still not sure, but I hope to convey a bit of it tonight." Icannes reached and took Elan's hand, rubbing it with her thumb. "Sael also asked me if I'd heard anything of Brin."

"Brin?"

Icannes solemnly nodded. "You and your daughter were among her last thoughts in this life. But I hadn't heard anything of Brin in some time. So, how is she?"

Was she changing the subject again? "Brin's fine. Growing like a vine…" And then it hit her. The pieces were swiftly assembling in Elan's mind. "It was you," she breathed.

Icannes raised a brow. "Very likely. Is this an accusation or an accolade?"

"It was both of you." Elan remembered her grandmother coming to her, right after Brin's birth. "Sael may have been behind it, but you were the one who put him up to it. Watching over her, befriending her… training her. Telling her all about the Skolani, filling her head with wild ideas. *You* sent Urias to Thrakius. You put him up to all of it."

Icannes's smile was sly and her gaze drifted. "I may have made a suggestion or two."

Unsure what else to do, Elan leapt to her feet and stomped to the edge of the firelight.

"There's nowhere to go, Elan. We're surrounded. As always."

Elan stopped short, knowing she was right. As often as she'd run from facing things, she was always still surrounded by them. She stood facing the last bit of light on the western horizon. "Gods, how could I not have known?" she said. "I should've seen it, sensed it."

"Is this really what you want to do with our night? We may only have one, dear heart. Come. Sit."

Elan turned to face her. She opened her mouth, but no words came. A sob finally escaped. Tonight, it seemed, there was no end to her tears. They ran down her cheeks to drip from her chin.

Icannes stood and came to her. "What is this really about? Tell me."

Icannes tried to embrace her again, but Elan raised her hands to block it. "You knew and I didn't. I mean, Sael told us both but I didn't want to hear it. And you knew I'd ignore it."

"What are you talking about?"

"You knew I'd be a terrible mother. Sael told us Brin would be the link, but I didn't want her to have to play any part in it. The queen rejected her and I didn't want her to be used, so I held her back. You knew I'd be awful so you sent my brother to make up for it."

"Oh, don't be silly."

"Silly? You were right! I am. I've been awful. I'm a terrible moth-er." The words were pouring out between sobs and gulps for breath. In spite of Elan's attempts to push her away, Icannes pulled her in and held her tightly. "You saw it—that I had no hope left, that I wouldn't have enough hope to offer to my baby girl. And I didn't. And she's so beautiful. And so strong. And so... good. I should've recognized it. It's so clear how vital she can be. And she will be.

Because of Urias. Because of you. And in spite of me!" She buried her face against Icannes's chest and wept. Icannes held her in place and rocked her.

Icannes's mouth was right beside her ear. "Shhh, quiet now. Sael asked me to lend you strength because she knew that your lot in this has been the hardest. Mother knows it too."

Elan shook her head. "No. Keisella tried to warn me, tried to tell me. She said I'd be a ghost, that my daughter would be a ghost. Then Sael told me Brin would still be a bridge, but it didn't seem fair. It felt like they were blocking her but still wanted to use her. They told me but I wouldn't listen. Because I was angry. Because I'm selfish."

"They told you because they knew you were brave enough to know. You and Brin have been given your roles because you're both strong. Keisella and Sael said what they did because they knew you had the strength, the will, to follow your heart. They always believed in you."

Icannes hooked Elan's chin between her fingers and thumb and tilted her head. Her beloved gazed intently into her eyes. "I knew it too. I knew you would be brave and strong. But you have borne so much. I sent Urias because I couldn't go. I sent him because I wanted to help you, however I might. I sent the only one who loved us both, almost as much as we love each other, to be at your side. And, yes, to be at Brin's side, too. I sent him *because* I believe."

Elan had run out of tears. Icannes wiped her cheeks with gentle swipes of her fingers. She hadn't thought of Icannes's sacrifices. Or Urias's. It made her realize anew. "He loves you."

Icannes's smiled and her gaze grew distant. "I like to think so. And I him."

Elan finally felt the pangs of jealousy. So much for maturity. She realized she was as jealous of his role with her daughter as she was of his relationship with Icannes. "I still can't bear the thought of Brin being..."

"What?"

"Of being like me," she said, looking down.

Icannes raised her eyebrows. "Competent? Skilled? Quick-witted?"

Elan shook her head. "A killer. A mean, spiteful, selfish killer."

Icannes made a face. "That's ridiculous. But Brin does need—"

"Does she really?" Elan didn't want to hear it. "She's so caring, Icannes. And so smart. She has a tutor. And she knows her letters. She's always reading. The girl speaks three languages! Must she really swing a sword? Must my baby girl play a role in the bedamned Urrinan? Am I not enough?"

Icannes laughed and pulled her by the hands to the fire and sat her down. She went to the tent, pulled out the blanket, laid it across the log, and sat. Icannes unlaced and pulled off her own boots, then stretched her long legs out and leaned back on the log. She reached back and pulled Elan down to recline beside her and put her cup in her hands. "Now listen to me. I've spent half of my life thinking about how unfair it's all been. I've been bitter. I've had regrets. I, too, hate the thought of my daughters living through this chaos. Chaos I have had a hand in creating. It was Sael who first told me what I've finally come to see as truth. She said that change *is* upheaval. She said that the gods chose us for this because we were meant to live epic lives, vast in scale. Think about it—without change we are kept small. Sael knew that our role as a people, our place in the world, will only grow larger. Because of our effort—our pain and perseverance—our children and our children's children will live lives grander than our minds can grasp."

Elan sighed. "Sometimes I wish I'd chosen a small life."

"No, you don't. You've always been larger than most. You couldn't have done it." Elan sulked and Icannes laughed. "You know it's true! You're the one who actually demanded to be trained. They beat you for it and still you wouldn't relent. And that was just the start of it. You've all but carried the Bringer to his duty on your back. You, my love, are like a flaming star streaking across the night sky." Icannes swept an arm in an arc above them. "Even if you'd tried to stay still, you'd have burned brightly. If you'd not lived the life you chose, you'd have burnt to a cinder."

"Maybe so. But I still wanted that for Brin. I wanted her to be small and quiet. And happy."

Icannes leaned over, making Elan look into her eyes. "Sorry, but no. She is to be the best of us all. We both heard it. Brin will be the link—the lodestar shining to guide us through our darkest days." Elan shook her head, unwilling to accept it. "Search your heart," Icannes softly implored her. "Deep inside, you know it to be so. The Skolani are the keepers of the old ways, and she will bring her gathered knowledge of the new and be as one with her people. Brin may not be exalted as queen or commander, but she will ever be there, at the shoulder of those who will wield change, imparting wisdom, courage, strength. Everything about her is as it was meant to be: her parents, her upbringing, her tutors, her letters, her mastery of tongues—everything. With her guidance our people will be lifted to our rightful destiny. Without her we might well falter. For Urrinan is but the start. She is vital to the future of any actual ascent. Brin is a guardian, same as you. She is fierce, same as you. But unlike yours, Brin's fire does not flare, it glows, endures. This daughter of Horsella is keen, caring, steadying." Elan shook her head, stunned. "What? Do you deny it?"

"No," Elan whispered, blinking. "I just... How can you know so much of her?"

Icannes gave a secret smile. "How can I not? I lost you to Vahldan. The gods owe me. I know Brin because I need her. My daughters will need her. Ainsela will need her. Do you really not see?"

This realization hit Elan like a punch to the chest, stealing her breath. "You're saying she... Brin will be Skolani?"

Icannes laughed. "Of course! Brin already has the heart of a Skolani, does she not?"

"I... I don't know." Gods have pity, she really wasn't sure.

"Then you're still choosing not to see. This has always been our destiny, my love. Best open your eyes to it."

"Gods, how have I not seen? I guess I was too busy swinging a sword."

Icannes huffed a laugh. "You and me both. Ours is the easy part: to swing a sword and cause upheaval. Our children will face a much greater challenge: to build a new world on the ruins we wreak. But I, for one, have faith in them. Don't you?"

Elan wasn't sure yet. She wasn't sure she wanted to look too closely. It was wonderful to believe that Brin would be Skolani. But it hurt, too. They'd put her and her daughter through all of this, leaving her in doubt for years. Elan hated herself for the resentment that kept rearing up.

Icannes was waiting for a reply. Rather than give it, Elan finished her cup.

Icannes laughed again and pulled her close. "Oh, don't be like this. We spent all of our lives saying that Urrinan was coming. I think it's time we recognize that it's here. That's what Vahldan came to hear from Mother, isn't it?"

Elan nestled in close and hooked a leg over Icannes's, entwining their feet. They still fit together so perfectly. Urrinan may have come, but it wasn't here in this camp. In the here and now there was only her first true love—her dear near-sister. The biggest regret of her banishment. She didn't want to spend another moment contemplating the echoing chasm of the future, for fear their moment might be yanked away as she fell into it.

"I suppose so," was all she was willing to say. Elan closed her eyes and pressed her ear to her beloved's chest, to feel her warmth and listen to the steady rhythm of her mighty heart.

ANALLYA HELD the pavilion flap open for Vahldan while very pointedly blocking Teavar from entering. He nodded to his guardian to stand

down and remain outside. The thought of the blood-bitch and the giant outside in a silent stare-down was almost comical. With those two he doubted there could ever be an actual victor.

It was dim inside. A lamp burned low in the corner next to the entry flap, but the queen sat further back, in shadow, lit only by the glowing coals of the brazier before her. Keisella did not raise her face. "You came," she said.

He bowed. "As you bid, my queen." He felt his cheeks flush, remembering that she'd bid him in a dream.

She did not refute him. "Sit, Young Lion. You must be weary. There is wine." Vahldan sat gingerly, holding his hand against his side. "The pain is great?" she asked.

"The wound?" he asked. How would she know of it?

She softly barked a lone laugh. "That and the reckoning."

He instantly understood. Keisella was talking about his having to face up to his regrets. "Both continue to ache. Though I sense that the first will fade, I fear the second may not."

"An astute observation," she offered. She still hadn't raised her face to him.

He took the flagon and poured wine into the nearest of two cups. "Will you have some?"

"Of course."

"May I fill your cup?"

"Of course." Vahldan leaned over the brazier, trying to see into her cup in the shadows. "Oh, forgive me, Young Lion. There is another lamp and dry tinder, just to your right. Light it if you will." He put one of the slender twigs into the coals until it flared, then lit the lamp, bathing the space in light. The queen's normally colorful wardrobe had been replaced with functional tanned doeskin. There wasn't a single tapestry in the pavilion, which was so unlike her.

"I have little need of lamplight these days." Keisella finally raised her face to him. He gasped. Her fierce blue eyes had become gray, rheumy, and bulging. He instantly knew whose eyes these were.

She smiled. "I gather no one told you?"

"Forgive me, my queen."

"There is nothing to forgive, Young Lion. I, too, was startled by it. It came on very suddenly, on the day after she passed."

"Wise One Sael," he acknowledged.

Keisella nodded. "She's still with me, guiding me. For this new form of sight is yet a bit of a mystery to me. And, I must admit, I still miss my old sight. Sael comes seeking to comfort me." She grinned. "But I think the old trickster is enjoying my new lack of poise." Her smile faded. "Sael has yet to cross Hel's bridge. I doubt she will until…"

"Until Urrinan has come," he finished.

"Ha! I'm sure if you are truly willing to look, you'll see that Urrinan is already here. As you of all people well know, the tumult has been unleashed." Keisella's eyes locked on his face and narrowed, as if she could suddenly see him. "What we must now seek to take are the next steps. Which is the thing for which Sael bides."

"Next steps?"

Keisella cocked her head, her smile wry. "From tumult to ascendancy, of course. Does the Bringer not agree?"

"It's why I came. I needed to be sure. That I hadn't…"

"Hadn't ruined it for our children—for our people?"

Vahldan hung his head. "Yes, my queen." His eyes started to sting.

Keisella's stern countenance softened. She smiled fondly at him. "Ah, there is the lad I once knew. No, Vahldan," she whispered, and he couldn't recall her ever having used his given name. "You could not ruin this. Indeed, because of you—through all you've done, the good and the bad—they have all three arrived."

She'd lost him again. "Who has arrived?"

"The heir to the old, the heir to the new, and the link who shall bind them unperceived. And they all have been born to you."

Her expression hardened. She raised her chin. Although she had aged, she remained a handsome woman. "Still, nothing is certain. Choice yet plays a role. Tumult was required, but there is much to overcome. For you have done much to bring ruin, have you not?"

"I have. But I wish to make up for it."

Keisella nodded once. "As is fitting. As I knew you would."

"You knew?"

She cocked her head again. "Did I not make myself clear? All is not yet lost. Urrinan is not your burden alone."

"You really did," he said, marveling. They were her exact words from the dream.

"Once I underwent the change, the first thing I *saw* was that my days are numbered. Shortly thereafter, I came to know that you shall be one of my final duties in this life."

"Thank you," Vahldan said, tears blurring his vision. "I want to make it right."

"Ask, then," Keisella demanded. "I will reveal what I can."

"I waited too long, I know. My pride..." Shame nearly choked him. "It kept me from sending out the women, the children. They should not suffer for my stubbornness. If only—"

"What is it I told you when I first saw you, long years past, Young Lion?"

Vahldan sighed. "That I had but to grasp my greatness. And that I should not fall prey to my father's folly."

Keisella offered him a wry smile. "Very good, Vahldan." The second ever use of his name felt like a reward. "And of course you know you did the first without avoiding the second."

"I do now."

"Then you know it is folly to speak of sending your women and children out into the heights in winter. You have learned that hubris has its price."

"I suppose I have."

"Ask what you really wish answered, the questions you keep buried in your heart."

Vahldan leaned back. He drank deeply and relished the burn,

summoning his courage. "If we could find a way, if all of us could flee, if we, the Amalus, simply leave it all behind... The Skolani, would you..."

Keisella shook her head. "No," she whispered. "This is too great a foe for the Blade-Wielders to withstand, even in the pass, where we have long held dominion. In choosing not to face what you have wrought, you would bring death and destruction with you to Dania. Such a flight would curse your homeland and your people forever. You would be reviled and mocked in songs that echo through the ages."

"And if I stay and fight?"

For what seemed like the first time, Keisella closed her eyes. She tilted her head back. "Long have you known of your doom, Lion." He heard a note of Freya's voice in the queen-come-seeress. "The price was long ago set."

"But must my doom become theirs?" Keisella nodded. "Even the women, the children?"

"You have foreseen what comes of this for them, at least in snatches, have you not?"

He had. And now the certainty of it lay heavily upon him. It was something he'd dreaded for himself and his close kin through all of his adult life. "Slavery," he whispered. "A great many will become slaves because of me. They will suffer the exile of my father. The fate I evaded shall be theirs."

Keisella nodded in confirmation. She sipped her wine, stolid.

Tears filled his eyes. "So many will suffer. For so long. Because of me. I have truly sundered my nation."

"Do not despair, Young Lion. For even in doom are the seeds of Urrinan sown. Ascendancy must come at a price. The sundering is but a step. Among those who endure, even in slavery, shall the prophecy—and your legacy—play out." Keisella's eyes seemed to find focus on him again. "You still have not asked that from which you hide."

Vahldan drew and released a breath. "The boy. The wolf. He is meant to rise?"

The corners of her mouth curled. "Ah. The heir to the old. You sought to reject him, to look only to the new, did you not?"

"I did, my queen," he said. The shame that had choked him now burned on his cheeks.

"The young wolf is meant to restore the futhark. For only through restoration can ascendancy be realized. But this, too, you know."

"I do," Vahldan whispered. "I have seen it in my dreams. More often of late."

"As have I," Keisella said, her eyes unseeing again.

"It's just, the Amalus—"

"Shall ever be half of the futhark," she firmly interjected. "Only with roots firmly established in the fertile soil of the old world can the vine grow into the light of the new."

"As it shall be," he said in submission.

"Then you know what you must do."

Vahldan got to his knees and bowed his face to the rug. "I do now, my queen."

"Good. Then rise and face what comes."

He rose to sit on his feet. "And the rest?" he ventured. "The gift of legacy? It is not a mere dream, I hope."

Keisella's small smile returned. "I once made a promise to your father. One of which I have never spoken to another living soul. Though of course Sael knew of it." Queen Keisella reached to place her hands on either side of his face. Warmth radiated from her touch. "Rest assured, Vahldan, son of Angavar—my vow shall not be broken. I see that of which you dream, and the goddess affirms it. The Skolani will ever strive that your legacy shall endure. We remain with you, resolute. Through my progeny and yours.

"Should you continue to choose wisely, even in doom, you may rest assured that a true king comes. And yes, a queen as well—the mother born of the old world who shall give birth to the new. Together they shall seat the throne of the first of a hundred Tutona kingdoms. If all continue to strive, Urrinan wrought by you, fostered by your progeny, shall sow the seeds of ascendancy. And the world shall be made anew."

CHAPTER 15
BESIEGED!

"*Thrakius is a city that is not simple to besiege. Its sheer size and the scale of its ancient walls are only the beginning of many problems to be solved by any who seek to do so. Its access to the Pontean, via its famous seagates, demands control of the Pontean coastline by any who aspire to blockade. Thrakius is served by many freshwater wells replenished by underground mountain streams. Its catacombs provide ample storage for ice and fresh foods. Its eastern walls are dwarfed by rocky heights, but they are heights that are unattainable for the positioning of siege machines. The terrain to the north and west is inhospitable, to say the least.*

None of this seemed to daunt the Tiberian mobile reserve. Within days of their encircling of the city, it became clear that the imperials were content to settle in, assured that time was on their side."—Brin Bright Eyes, Saga of Dania*

ELAN COULDN'T BELIEVE IT. The imperial noose was already tightening. From the safety of the heights, she peered through the boughs across the open canyon bottom and sloping ground outside of Thrakius's northern wall. The snow had yet to accumulate down here by the sea. Instead of snow, the canyon floor teemed with imperial soldiers. Things were happening fast now.

The imperials had already erected scores of tents and pavilions behind their busy lines, set just beyond firing range. The Tibairya were assembling siege machines despite being hopelessly out of range on vastly lower ground. Gottari Rekkrs lined the wall top overlooking the spectacle. The slings atop the wall were loaded and drawn, though there was no evidence that any shots had been fired.

At last, the rivals were poised on the brink of their inevitable violent climax.

A bit beyond a bowshot from the treeline of the forests surrounding the pass, the foe had built a corral for their horses and goats, though they had only managed to bring a half-dozen wagons over the difficult terrain from the western coastal road. These were arrayed in a semi-circle behind the Tibairyan lines, creating a perimeter around the corral. The imperial soldiers were busy cutting trees, digging trenches, and hauling rocks. The crafty bastards were constructing battlements opposite the city walls. Beyond those, they were clearing the area of cover, even denuding a portion of the forest. They were proofing the terrain against Gottari flight, she realized.

The empire wished to trap them—to eliminate a recurring problem once and for all.

The sun sank toward the western ridge and the cookfires of the foe foretold a hearty evening meal for the laboring besiegers. The imperials seemed to have been there for a day or two. This was anything but an urgent attack. Thorough preparation was the order of the day. Once again, the mobile reserve was methodically striving toward their grim goal of extermination.

Elan rushed back uphill to the copse where she'd left her companions. She passed Druzana nibbling on the remnant grass along a rivulet of water coursing through the rock. Vahldan and Teavar reclined on a lichen-spotted outcrop, sharing a skin and gnawing on strips of dried goat.

"And?" Vahldan prompted as she pulled the stopper on their water skin and drank.

"They're here, all right. Making themselves at home, too. Busy little shits."

Vahldan nodded. "I guess this is it then. The final press." They all sat absorbing the statement. Vahldan had been reflective since departing the Skolani camp. Elan supposed she'd been the same. And Teavar rarely spoke anyway. Made for a damn quiet trip home.

Oddly, the giant broke the silence. "So we fight our way in?"

"Since it's our doom they're planning, I suppose we should be there to face it," Vahldan quipped. "Do we wait till dark, try to sneak in?"

Elan shook her head. "I vote no. We need the guards on the wall to see us. Or, more precisely, to know it's you. If we try to get their attention after dark, we're more likely to get the Tibairya's attention instead. That or attention in the form of Gottari arrows."

"I'll go," Vahldan said. "Once inside, I can lead a sortie out for you two."

"Not a chance," Teavar growled.

"Well, we only have one horse."

The giant crossed his thick arms over his chest. "If anyone goes alone, it'll be me."

Vahldan laughed. "Hey, I'm the king. That's supposed to carry some weight. Besides, how would it look if I sent someone else? It's bad enough I went missing the moment a besieging army showed up."

"It would look like you recognized your role as a leader," Teavar deadpanned.

"All right, you two," Elan intervened. "Maybe there's another way."

"I suppose a king should be willing to hear other ideas," Vahldan said.

"Now he tells us," Teavar said with an eyeroll. It took both her and Vahldan a beat to realize the big man had made a damn fine joke. Even Teavar joined their laughter.

"All right, now listen," Elan said, trying to get serious again. She turned to Vahldan. "You used to be pretty fair at riding bareback. Think you're still up to it?"

His hand drifted to his injured side. "I suppose it would depend on the horse."

Elan gave him a wry grin. "How about one you've never met?"

Vahldan narrowed his gaze. "Just what do you have in mind?"

"Did you ever notice how besiegers tend to focus on keeping folks in?" she asked.

MALVIUS KEPT his cloak hood up and his head down as they rolled to a stop in the gatehouse archway of the palace keep wall. There was only one Gottari guard in sight. Likely, the bulk of the thug king's men were out on the walls of the city, monitoring the Tiberians as they set their siege. Dexicos tipped his head to the guard. "A gift for the king." Dex turned in the wagon seat and flung aside the tarp. "Wine and fresh fruit from our Sassanadi allies. Courtesy of Captain Malvius."

The guard glanced at the barrels and crocks and waved them through. Malvius doubted the man spoke a word of Hellainic.

It seemed that riding in a merchant's wagon was the perfect way to arrive at the palace. He had presumed the Gottari would get much stricter about who came and went now that the siege had begun. Still, the savages relied on Hellain merchants for many necessities, and the siege would only increase that reliance. The current circumstances made fine foodstuffs and drink the best sort of gift. Malvius had selected the very best of his warehouse stores to provide it. He figured he may as well gain some goodwill while his supplies lasted. With everyone's stocks dwindling, he guessed it wouldn't be long before the Gottari began taking whatever they pleased.

Although he wanted credit for the gift, he thought it might also be wise to remain discrete. At least until he could gauge the mood within. He directed Dex to steer them to the servants' entrance. The last thing he needed was for one of Vahldan's thugs to start questioning his presence in the palace. Especially considering the primary goal of his mission here.

Malvius couldn't stop obsessing over Harma's note. It had arrived sealed, delivered by a kitchen boy. The actual text wasn't as damning as it could've been: *"Must see you. Please come."* It was signed only with the letter H, all in Hellainic. He wasn't certain but he doubted she knew her letters. Few of the barbarians did. It was risky enough that she seemed to trust her serving girl and her driver so implicitly. He suspected neither of them was literate either. Which made him suspect she'd brought yet another into her confidence, someone to act as a scribe.

Damn, the woman made him terrified and exhilarated at once.

The wagon rolled to a halt and Malvius leapt down. "Give me a chance to get upstairs before you unload." Dex nodded. "Don't forget to let them know it's from us."

"Will do, Cap."

Malvius opened the door far enough to peek up and down the servants' stairwell. Seeing no one, he slipped in and closed it behind him. Loud voices from the kitchen gave him suspicion and hope. He stole down a few steps till he could see, keeping to the shadows. The kitchens were bustling. Dinner preparations were underway.

He spotted whom he sought amongst the commotion. Perfect! One of the loud talkers was indeed the Sassanadi serving girl, the one to whom Ligaia had given her son. His hopes rose. The Sass girl was ambitious. And moving up in the world. He found it an admirable trait, but also one that made her worthy of his caution.

Malvius dashed up the stairs, stopping at each floor to peek out into the halls and then hurry up the next set of steps. The palace was quiet. About three floors up, he heard footsteps coming down. Heart thumping, he slipped into an empty corridor before he saw who came. The descender was a maidservant. The girl continued down past him, heedless. Another good sign. He wasn't sure how many serving girls there were, but at least two of them were now downstairs.

He came to what he hoped was the correct floor, popped his head into the corridor, then walked softly and swiftly to the door. He pressed his ear against it, hoping to hear her or her son. Silence. Damn. He was fairly sure he had deduced through their conversations which residence Harma lived in, but short of hearing or seeing her, he had no way to be sure.

Malvius straightened, calmed his jittery nerves, composed his face—and the lie he'd tell if it wasn't the right door—and knocked. "I told you to leave it open!"

The scolding voice was Harma's. His lucky streak continued.

He spoke low into the crack at the jamb. "Harma? It's me."

He pressed his ear to the door. "Just a moment." It was followed by shuffling and muttering, much of which sounded like Gottari curses. It seemed to take forever. He tiptoed back to listen at the stairwell. The Sass girl would eventually return.

Harma finally opened the door. Her cheeks were almost as red as her hair. And the hair was as disorganized as Malvius had ever seen it, a wisp hanging across her forehead and one eye. And she was wearing a rumpled evening frock. He guessed she'd pulled it on after his knock. Gods, even the top of her exposed bosom was flushed pink and rising and falling rapidly.

Once again, he marveled. This creature wasn't just potentially useful, she was gorgeous.

"Praise Freya," she breathed. "Thank you for coming." Gods, she was practically begging him to entangle himself. His hopes soared— so high that he knew he should rein them in.

"I came as soon as I could." Harma stood gazing into his eyes. He still wasn't used to standing face to face with a taller woman. "May I?" He pointed inside.

Harma's eyes widened. "Oh shit. Of course." She stuck her head out and looked both ways as he passed her in the doorway. She closed the door and latched it. Good instincts.

She turned to face him. Malvius was just about to ask her why she'd sent for him when she launched herself at him. It was either catch her in a hug or be knocked over. She clung to him so tightly, he felt not only each breath but her racing heart. Her cheek was pressed to his ear. "You're actually here," she said huskily. "Thank the gods. I don't know what to do."

He wished he didn't have to ask, but he had no idea. "About what?"

Harma drew herself back but kept her arms around this neck. "We're trapped. The fool has doomed us all. Now no one even knows where he is. Vahldan left us here to die. The Tibairya will kill us all. Just like they killed my father."

"I won't let that happen," he lied.

Her eyes shone. "My son." She turned to the crib behind her. The babe was fast asleep. "He's the rightful heir. Armesus didn't start this ridiculous war. He shouldn't be blamed for his father's sins."

Of course Harma had married the thug some months after he'd started his *ridiculous war*. But Malvius wasn't in a position to quibble. "He won't be. I'll see to it. You can trust me."

"I do," she said with a relieved sigh.

Someone tried the door, found it latched, and knocked. Harma flinched and audibly gasped. "Lady Harma? How did the door get latched?" It was the Sass girl.

"She shouldn't see me here," he whispered. "Send her away."

Harma frowned. "I trust Apontia, too."

More knocking. "My lady? I have your afternoon wine. It is your favorite cup, yes?"

Malvius shook his head. "We shouldn't trust anyone else." Particularly her.

Harma gave him a look of exasperation and hurried to the door. Malvius went to stand where he'd be behind the door when it opened. Harma took a breath. Another knock. She opened the door but blocked Apontia's entry. "Here, I'll take it." Harma grasped the tray. "That will be all for now, Apontia. Leave me."

"Leave?" The girl was incredulous. "What about dressing for dinner? And your hair?"

"I can manage."

"What about the babe?"

Harma lowered her voice. "He's sleeping. Please leave me till dinner is ready. I wish to be alone."

"As you wish." The Sass girl sounded suspicious, but it would have to do.

Harma used the edge of the tray to push the door closed. Malvius took the tray from her and she swiftly latched the door and blew out a relieved sigh.

"You did well," he said. Better than he would've guessed. He sat the tray on the table, turned, and nearly ran into her. "Some wine?" he asked, not knowing what else to say.

Harma wrinkled her freckled nose and gave him that sly smile he loved so much. "No. I want something else." Gods' glory, the gorgeous creature aroused a whole new sort of hope.

Urias slumped against the parapet at dusk. What a day. It seemed the Tibairya had already settled in for the night. They had left a line of soldiers to guard their new defense works, but most had retired to their camp behind the lines. Urias envied them. He was exhausted. It wasn't just the bustle of preparation. These invaders controlled the agenda. Which left those in the city in a state of heightened anxiety and lacking sleep. It was clear the circumstances had taken a toll.

Several high-ranking Amalus Rekkrs huddled down the wall, glancing his way as they spoke. Arnegern left the conclave of lions and strolled toward Urias. Seemed he was in for yet another interrogation. "Exactly how sure are you that they went north?"

"As certain as I can be," Urias said with a sigh. "Which isn't saying much. All I know for sure is that my sister came to say goodbye to her daughter. Elan told Brin not to worry, that they were going into the pass and would be back shortly."

"Shortly," Arnegern muttered, gazing out beyond the imperial siege lines. "And you didn't see them leave?"

"I didn't walk them to the gate, if that's what you mean." He'd told them all of this already, and his annoyance was starting to show. "Look, Elan may be a lot of things, but a liar isn't one of them. Nor is Brin."

Arnegern frowned. "I would never say so. All anyone wants is answers. And it seems Brin is the only one they told of their plans. People are rightfully upset."

"I'm sorry," Urias said, rubbing his eyes. "The day's been a long one."

Arnegern looked out at the foe again. "Now we face not just a siege, but another night without a king. We don't even know if he's dead or alive. The man couldn't even stand on two feet the last time anyone laid eyes on him. No one knows what to do. Some are suggesting we begin firing the catapults. There's talk of trying to escape, which makes little sense now. Some say we should commandeer all of the ships in the harbor to sail off to the gods know where. A few have even dared to mention seeking to parley."

That was startling. Urias glanced at the restive lions, who'd resumed their grave discourse. "What will you do?" he asked.

Arnegern shook his head, looking exasperated. "A growing group of Rekkrs thinks we should at least send out a host to break through the lines and go looking for him. Some say the sooner the better. Now even. I'm not so sure I should continue to resist the idea. It's more reasonable than most of what I'm hearing. Although I think we should at least wait till morning. Those who argue against it say the loss of even one sword is reckless."

"That's hard to argue, too."

"Trouble is, I'm sick and tired of arguing. The worst is the rumors. I hear there are whispers in the palace, wondering if he's abandoned his people and fled to save his skin. Others gossip that he was stolen away. I consider it all nonsense, of course. But there's one thing we can all agree on: No one wants to find out what happens if the foe attacks before we learn what became of him."

Urias still felt rattled. "There's really been talk of parley? To what aim? Surrender?"

Arnegern scowled. "Trust me, it would be a mistake. A deadly one. The Tibairya have made it clear that they want nothing for us but death. The best we could hope for is slavery, and that would mean dishonor on the way to death. Still, there are those who say our people haven't the heart to fight this war without our king."

It had never been clearer to him. The Amalus were lost without Vahldan. He was why they were here. For the lions, none of this made any sense without him.

But Urias realized something else, too. "He would never abandon you... us. Vahldan would never forsake his people." Vahldan could be called many things, but cowardly was not among them. He valued his vision of his place in history too much.

Arnegern sighed. "I agree. But I fear his ability to return to us may now be beyond him."

A lone call rang through the valley below, coming from the Tibairyan lines. Movement caught Urias's eye. Horses galloping toward the city walls. In the fading twilight he made out the auburn hair of the lead rider. He pointed. "Look."

Arnegern leaned over the parapet. "By the gods. Is it..."

"It is!" Urias cried. "Never underestimate Vahldan the Bold. Especially not when he has his best two guardians alongside."

"The king!" Arnegern called. Others took up the call, pointing and exclaiming.

The foe had noticed, too. The bastards began firing arrows.

"Give them some covering fire!" Belgar called, running to the catapult crews.

Within moments, several of the preloaded pitch-laden missiles were alight, aimed, and fired. Explosions lit the night and imperial soldiers scattered and ran from the raining flames. The trio of riders were well beyond the foe's lines, galloping across the void.

"They're going to make it!" Urias shouted. Cheers rang out along the wall top as the catapults were reloaded.

Arnegern ran to the gatehouse stairwell. "Open the gates! Make way for the king!"

The rattle and clang of the portcullis echoed across the martialing yard as Urias hurried down the stairs from the wall-walk.

The gates hadn't even finished opening when Elan ducked to gallop through, soon followed by Vahldan. Both of them rode bareback, holding on to what appeared to be wagon harnesses. Teavar rode in last, the only one sitting in a saddle. The giant's mount seemed aged and ornery about the effort and the fuss, but they made it unscathed.

The trio came to a halt as the gates closed behind them. Elan was grinning, which only filled Urias's heart with more joy. He bowed to Vahldan as they dismounted. "Welcome back, my king."

Vahldan winced as he straightened. He looked a little unsteady but otherwise hale. "Thank you, Captain." He seemed in pain but otherwise buoyant. Others came running and calling. Young grooms ran to collect the horses. The saddled horse compliantly headed for the stables while the two unsaddled ones were confused and jittery. The calls of the archers and catapult operators faded. It seemed the Tibairya had settled in again. No additional fighting would come tonight.

Urias turned to find Elan right behind him. "Sister." She surprised him by lunging into his arms, hugging him tight. Her spirits seemed to be soaring as high as his. Her mood was as strange and surprising as running siege lines in order to get back into a war. So perhaps it was fitting. "Oh, I can't wait to hear the tale behind this," he said.

Elan drew back, her eyes alight. "There is much to tell. Tomorrow, all right? I'm sort of wrung out."

Urias didn't press. "Tomorrow it is," he said.

"How about after your training session with your niece?" She smiled archly.

He squinted at her. "Is that a trick question?"

"Why should it be? You're still training her, aren't you?"

"Well, yes. And while I do recall promising to stop, I haven't exactly agreed with your reasons. Hence, I've been very careful about—"

Elan raised a silencing finger. "Brother. I said we'll talk after you're done training my daughter." Her smile brightened. "Speaking of Brin, I'd better go and let her know we made it."

"She's probably been among the least worried occupants of the palace. She never doubted you'd be back safe. Not for a moment."

Elan laughed. "Strong girl. Still, I miss her. And I hate that I wasn't there for her when the Tibairya arrived."

It shouldn't have surprised him—particularly tonight—but it did. "As you wish, my lady." He bowed.

Elan made a mockery of doing a curtsy. "Captain." She started off toward the gates to the palace keep, then stopped and turned back to him. "Urias?"

"Elan?"

"Thank you. For everything." Her smile was sincere, although her old, veiled sadness remained. He sensed an apology and perhaps a bit of regret beneath the gratitude. He bowed his head and watched her hurry off, full of wonder and admiration for his amazing sister.

MALVIUS'S LOINS were stirring even before Harma hooked her fingers in his belt and pulled him to her, tilting her head and parting her mouth. Her lips were so full, so inviting. He went in for a soft kiss but her response gave it instant ferocity.

Almost involuntarily, his hands slid to her buttocks and squeezed. Gods, it felt as wonderful as he'd been imagining. His action seemed to spur her hands to roam and one swiftly found his swelling shaft. She returned the favor, sliding and squeezing. Her motion became a teasing stroke. He couldn't recall ever getting so hard so fast. She abruptly broke off their kiss and backed out of his arms. He was distressed until he saw the wicked look in her eyes. This was definitely more teasing.

Harma backed away until her bottom hit the table. She beckoned him with a finger, and then her hands went to her hips. She slowly drew up the hem of her frock until it bunched at her waist. She tantalizingly slid the skirt back and forth across the front of her hips, offering fleeting glimpses that made it clear she wore nothing underneath.

Malvius unbuckled his belt as he went to her. She dropped into a squat to pull down his leggings and drew her frock up to her ribcage as she rose and sat down on the table. Before he could wrap his mind around her swiftness, she wrapped her legs around him. Then his cock was in her hand and she was guiding him to her sex as she scootched to the edge of the table. Gods, just the sight of their connection drove him mad with desire. "How perfect," she purred, rubbing him against her. "I'm already as wet as you are hard."

He was beyond holding back. She wrapped him in her arms as he entered her and started humping, urging him on by pulling and softly moaning in rhythm. Their increasing intensity caused the table to buck and bump. Harma's moans turned to gasps, which grew louder with each stroke.

The cup of wine spilled on the tray and the babe started to cry. Malvius stopped and started to withdraw. Harma's arms and legs seized and trapped him. "No," she whispered. "He can wait. Finish this." She pushed her hips forward, engulfing him again, then, undulating, coaxed him back to a frenetic pace.

His legs started to tremble. He groaned. "Not inside me," she hissed. He withdrew and she adeptly dropped to her knees, grasping his quaking shaft and stroking it to completion, popping him into her mouth just as he released. He saw stars and... Was that an explosion? Had the war suddenly started as he came? He swore the stone walls shook.

Harma hadn't seemed to notice. She wiped her mouth and smiled as she stood, obviously pleased with herself. Malvius had only ever seen such behavior from whores. Perhaps this gorgeous creature wanted something else from him, same as they did. Same as he wanted something from her, he supposed. Seemed fair. Besides, he liked whores. One always knew where one stood with them.

She leaned in and kissed him as she straightened her frock. Malvius watched her fuss with her hair, fascinated by her casual acceptance of their new normal. Realization of the precariousness of the situation hit him and he found himself hurrying to dress. She leaned toward the looking glass and her hand flew to a wet spot on the taut fabric between her breasts. "Oh damn," she said, rushing to the water basin on the sideboard.

The babe had settled somewhat, but seeing his mother rush by the crib prompted the boy to revive his wailing. "Just a moment, Armesus," Harma cooed as she dabbed at the stain.

"Let me try," he said and went to lift the wriggling infant from the crib. "Here we go, little man." He held the bawling babe in the crook of his arm against his chest and rocked him, smiling down as he danced across the chamber. "It's just us sailors now. Rocking on the sea." He swayed bigger, imitating the motion of a ship. It worked. The boy quieted, his apprehension swiftly morphing into astonishment and then a pudgy-cheeked smile.

Malvius worked his way around until he was facing Harma. She stood staring, eyes full of either shock or adoration. He hoped it was the latter. "What?"

"You're a natural." She beamed.

"It's not my first time. Though it's been a while." A fleeting sadness hit him at the thought of how much Neveka had longed for a moment like this. The irony of it struck next. This woman had married the man who'd ordered the attack that had killed his only true love and his unborn son. In his arms was that very murderer's son.

"You're better at it than his father. Though the man has rarely bothered himself."

Malvius looked down at the infant's ruddy cheeks and wispy red hair. This babe was innocent. For now. "He's a fine boy. He'll be a fine man if he takes after his mother. Especially if his father stays out of his life."

Harma started toward him and he momentarily wondered if he'd gone too far. She gazed pensively down at the babe in his arms. "He *will* be a fine man. I know it. He is our people's heir. No matter what his father's done, even if the Gottari come to renounce him, they will always accept Armesus as the Amalus heir. I know it in my heart. He is a lion, through and through. My son shall be the man his father should have been." She grabbed Malvius's arm. He glanced over to find her searching his eyes. "Save us from him," she whispered.

"From whom? Vahldan?"

She nodded, evidently mustering her courage. "Save us," she said, "and my son will deliver the Gottari people to you—to your service, forever. Just as I will ever be yours—at your service, forever."

Malvius was stunned. He had no idea what to say, so he just gazed back into her eyes. Whether or not she knew what she was saying, she was clearly serious.

Stranger still, it actually wasn't a bad idea. This opportunity could be more than he'd dared to dream. Malvius had relished having this secret, covertly holding sway over the thug king's possession. But having such a powerfully connected woman and the king's son in his power could be so much more valuable to the endgame than mere sexual comeuppance. And not just because he seemed to have misplaced his nephew. Perhaps this was a divine gift. The gods knew he deserved one. Perhaps this was their way of offering him the weapon that would bring him the victory he'd long sensed was rightfully his.

The gods knew, come what may of this war, there would always be more Gottari to contend with. Malvius could never let another treachery like Vahldan's happen again. He could imagine how possessing this woman and her royally bred son would help him to ensure it.

Either way, what could it hurt to make a promise? The gods knew Vahldan had broken all sorts of promises. Malvius had learned that one's broken promises only mattered when one no longer had the upper hand. "I will," he said softly. "Trust me. I will save you both."

Harma's blue eyes shone. She leaned in to kiss him.

A loud knock at the door made them both jump. "Harma? Are you in there?"

"It's Mara," she whispered.

"Answer her," he mouthed more than spoke.

"Yes?"

"Come quick! The king is back. We're all going down to greet him."

Harma's eyes went wide. "I'll be right there!"

THE WHITE WITCH

"The start of the siege, after such a fraught wait, created a strange atmosphere in the palace of Thrakius. The fear and dread did not go away, not exactly. But I suppose many of us had already felt ourselves under siege. Once the Tiberian soldiers and their siege engines were actually in sight, there was a shared sense of acceptance.

The war had been going on for two years but it felt like decades. Until then, most of us had never laid eyes on a Tiberian soldier. And yet we all knew we must inevitably face them, that the war would eventually touch us all: man, woman, and child.

I think for many of us, the sight of the Tiberian lines made us feel giddy that the wait was over. We were drunk with our resignation to fate. Not to mention that many were also drunk with the wine that was freely dispensed. For there was no longer a call for either scrimping or temperance."—Brin Bright Eyes, *Saga of Dania*

MALVIUS SENT Harma out of her residence ahead of him to make sure the corridor was empty and to listen at the servants' stairwell. She held up her skirts to run back. "It's clear. I heard nothing."

He stepped out, brushing past her in the doorway. She grabbed him by the shoulders and pulled him in, kissing him hard on the mouth. "Thank you," she said breathlessly.

"Not a word to anyone. And no more notes. Understood?" Harma nodded. "I'll be in touch." Gods, that face. She looked like a pup left waiting past feeding time. Could she actually be in love with him? It was either true or she was a damn fine actress. He had to admit, he was feeling fairly smitten himself. He gave her full lips a parting peck and hurried to the stairs.

Malvius descended several flights before he heard laughter and talking below. He stopped. They were clearly coming up. He turned to retreat, but before he started, he heard footsteps coming down as well. He had to get out of the stairwell fast. Where in the seven realms was he? He'd rarely used the servants' stairwell. Not since he was a boy gallivanting through the palace. He thought he was on the second floor. If he took the corridor, he would come out behind the main stairwell on the terrace outside the high hall. It would have to do.

Malvius hurried into the corridor. He heard distant voices, likely servers coming up from the kitchens. If he was right, they'd follow this same route. He couldn't dally. He cracked the door to the terrace. Voices. Many people. The reunion Mara mentioned. The servers' voices from behind him grew nearer.

He had no choice. He strode out across the terrace, trying not to act suspicious but keeping to the shadows of the main stairway. He didn't look too closely, but at least two dozen Gottari, mostly women and youngsters, were gathered and chattering on the terrace. They mulled at the bottom of the main stairs up and the stairway down to the entry hall and the exit, blocking his escape routes. Going back and running into servants would lead to questions.

Again, Malvius had no choice. He headed for the open doors to the high hall. All the torches and dozens of candles were lit and several servants worked to set the long table inside. Too conspicuous. He slowed his step. Men's voices rose behind him. Women replied. A garbled gaggle of Gottari honking. He pushed his cloak behind his shoulders, smoothed his tunic, and turned to wade through the crowd, heading for the stairs down. He strode as if departing from the high hall just prior to dinner were perfectly natural.

He stopped short. Gods, here came the thugs. Rekkrs, by the dozens, heading for the stairs to come up. Malvius turned and painted on a smile to blend in with the meandering crowd awaiting them. He skirted the crowd, trying to look natural. The thug king himself led the newcomers, limping and pale but looking cheerful. It certainly didn't seem the man would be succumbing to his wounds anytime soon.

Vahldan arrived on the balcony and his sisters rushed to greet him. They fawned over the thug king as Arnegern and Elan's brother stood at his shoulders grinning. Vahldan's elder sister was apparently pregnant again. Malvius sensed he was being watched. A quick scan revealed a head looming above the jubilant scene. Of course, the first one to pick him out of the crowd and stare him down was the bloody giant. Malvius feigned a brighter smile and Teavar's eyes narrowed. Always suspicious, that man.

Vahldan embraced his pregnant sister and caught sight of Malvius over Mara's shoulder. "Ah. At the very mention of Loki! Here is our benefactor."

Malvius held his hands up. "Here I am." He realized the pose might make him look guilty and swiftly lowered his hands.

"Where have you been, little captain?" Teavar's voice always conveyed a level of threat.

"I was..." Gods, how could he not have prepared a lie? "We brought you wine, my king," Malvius blurted, seeking to put the focus on Vahldan. Damn, he was out of practice.

"As we heard," Vahldan said warmly. "And much more, I'm told. Having the best trader in the Pontean call Thrakius home has ever been our boon. You have our thanks, old friend."

Malvius bowed deeply, smiling in the knowledge that having the most murderous barbarians call Thrakius home had ever been the city's bane, but that the end of that circumstance was drawing near.

More and more thugs filed onto the terrace. Gods, were any of them left out on the walls?

Vahldan embraced Kemella and called to Malvius, "You'll stay for dinner, won't you?"

"Oh no. Dexicos is waiting downstairs. I have much yet to do. But thank you—"

"Stay! You've supplied the wine and the makings of our feast, after all."

Malvius fought a rising panic. "I'm hardly dressed for dinner, my king." Damn, that was lame. Why was he so befuddled?

"Come now, Malvius. I've never known you for a dandy. You look fine. Come! It'll be a homecoming feast. For all of us. You've never even met my sons." Vahldan looked up the stairs with knitting brows. "Wherever they might be."

Mara piped up. "Harma said she'll be right down."

Kemella said, "I'll see to it that Lady Amaga comes down for dinner, my king."

"Then it's settled." Vahldan wrapped an arm around Malvius, pulling him to the high hall. Gods, even the familiar smell of the man curdled Malvius's innards. "You must stay and come to know my sons and their mothers."

"It'll be an honor," he said, suddenly terrified that Vahldan might catch a whiff of his wife's lingering scent on him in turn.

Once inside the high hall, a cluster of young Gottari men gathered around Vahldan to offer their welcomes and the thug released Malvius. He started to sidle back toward the exit. Vahldan noticed and interrupted the well-wishers. The thug pointed to the far end of the table. "You'll sit by me, Malvius, at the head of the table. Have some wine." Damn, he was being directed to go as far from the doors as possible.

Vahldan was instantly distracted again. Dozens of Gottari began surging into the high hall, all talking at once. Malvius felt like trapped prey. He kept his distance, wandering into the depths of the chamber. A cask and several full flagons were laid out on the sideboard. May as well drink as invited. He went to the seat adjacent to the head of the table and grabbed the cup from the place setting. He poured from the nearest flagon. It was some of the Saurian red he'd brought. He found himself sucking down the first cup. Way too swiftly, he realized as it hit him. Of course the barbarians had served it unwatered.

He stood with his empty cup, surveying the crowd. Harma entered. He didn't even want to be caught looking her way. He turned to pour another cup.

A trio of Hellain musicians struck up a song in the nearby corner of the hall. At first, Malvius was relieved to have the distraction. Until he noticed the looks on each of their faces as they played. The players were all glaring at him. They recognized him and they resented him. To them he was a traitor, an ally of the barbarians who'd brought war to their city. The trader who blatantly profited from the shortages they suffered.

Someday they'd find out how wrong they were. They'd all be thanking him soon enough.

Malvius turned from their harsh stares. Alarmingly, Harma was walking directly toward him. Worse, besides a fresh frock, she was wearing a sly little smile. Yes, it was sexy. Thus, all the more alarming. Her hair was freshly combed and tied back. She had the boy propped on her hip. The Sass girl hovered behind her.

"So nice to see you, Captain."

Malvius bowed. "And you, Lady Harma." Apontia hung close, watching Malvius with feral eyes. She seemed almost as suspicious as the giant. "Ah, so this is your son," he said. "Such a handsome lad." Malvius made a show of bending to smile at the boy. Armesus leaned to him, reaching, begging to be held. Malvius laughed and put a finger in one of the boy's reaching hands.

"Already he seems to like you, Captain," Apontia said. "You must have a way with children, yes?" The Sass smiled but her narrowed eyes judged. Impudent girl.

"So it seems." Could she suspect? Had she been listening at the door? The gods knew she was a clever one. Apontia had evidently found a way to contend with Ligaia, which was no small feat. This one may be more dangerous than he'd surmised. Because Armesus wasn't getting his way, the babe wiggled and strained. Then the infant started to whine.

"The king wanted you to meet him." Harma turned and held the boy out to Apontia. "Now that you have, I think Armesus had best be getting to bed. Take him up, please."

Apontia had no choice but to do as she'd been told. "My lady," she said with evident disgruntlement, giving Malvius the side-eye as she left.

"Funny," Harma said, "I had an incredibly satisfying snack earlier, but I'm still ravenous." She had that adorable crinkle to her nose. "How's your appetite, Captain?"

He glanced around and lowered his voice. "I've recently found it insatiable, my lady."

"Shall we see what we can do about it?" His alarm soared until she indicated the table. "Come, Captain. Join me for a feast that's sure to satisfy, won't you?" She tilted her head as if she were inviting him to kiss her. He gave a scolding expression. Flirting was one thing, but this was just plain dangerous. Harma took the hint but went to her seat wearing a secret smile.

Harma sat at one of the table's three settings at the end, on the corner toward the spot Vahldan had directed Malvius to take. As they got settled, Vahldan came to the end of the table. The thug took a spoon and tapped his ceramic cup. "Come, my friends! Let us sit together."

No one paid any heed till Teavar barked, "Seats!" The music abruptly stopped and the roar of conversation fell to a restrained drone as Vahldan's cadre of killers and their ilk slowly found their way to their seats. Other than the ruddy-cheeked, drunken grins and tangled beards of the menfolk, the rabble almost looked civilized.

The giant took the seat directly across from Malvius, Arnegern and Mara sat next to the giant, and Kemella came to sit on Malvius's right. The seat to Vahldan's left remained empty—presumably for the other wife. Malvius hadn't seen the woman since their wedding ceremony. That spectacle had been odd enough to convince Malvius to avoid being in her presence. The gangly child bride had seemed harmless enough till then. Such a spooky little thing. She'd left the ceremony in the midst of a hysterical fit. Odder still, the revelry had gone on afterward as if nothing out of the ordinary had happened. Observing the strange bride and knowing the Gottari, perhaps nothing had.

Vahldan remained standing, again raising his hand for quiet, and it eventually arrived. "My friends, I apologize for being absent. I had no idea our unwanted guests outside would be arriving so soon or I would've changed my plans." Low laughter came from around the table. "And yet, I'm glad I went. I learned much. More than I would impose upon you before you've had your dinner." Louder laughter at that one. "But I will say that I am more convinced than ever that Urrinan has finally arrived." This one elicited a murmur of awe.

Gods, the madman was going to spout off about their bloody prophecy again. But his audience was lapping up the slop he was dishing. Malvius nearly jumped right out of his chair. Something had grazed his leg, moving upward. He looked down into his lap. A bare female foot was tracing along his thigh, toes wiggling in the process. He looked at Harma, ready to visually scold her again. She had her face raised to Vahldan, although a corner of her mouth curled up wickedly. He kept his hands folded on the table in front of him, unwilling to risk making a move that might be noticed.

The thug droned on. "Your sacrifice provides a great service to our cause. Know that the highest glory of our people is nigh. It will ring in song through the ages. It is as it shall be."

From the periphery, Malvius sensed more than he actually saw Kemella looking. He turned his torso to block her view, scooting closer to the table in the process. But the move only gave the naughty vixen a closer reach and a better angle. The persistently playful toes caused an immediate, involuntary swelling. Harma's smile only grew.

Malvius had to do something. Without moving suddenly, he reached for his cup with one hand and slowly moved the other to his lap, carefully pushing the mischievous foot away. The foot simply hopped over his hand, softly knocking on the table in the process. Malvius froze, hoping no one had heard it.

The thug's voice rose. "And so, it is in your honor, my brothers, that we feast tonight. And speaking of our feast, we owe the plentiful bounty we are served, both on our plates and in our cups, to Brother Malvius, the finest captain in all of the Pontean. We would never have come this far without his enduring aid." Vahldan raised his glass, grinning down at him. "Stand and say a few words, old friend."

Gods, no! "Oh, I couldn't, my king." Not like this. "I am happy to be of service," he said without standing. "Please, enjoy your dinners." Vahldan made a face. He had to think this time. Before Vahldan could insist, Malvius raised his cup. "To the king," he called out.

Arnegern chimed in. "To the Bringer of Urrinan!"

They all toasted and drank to their foolishness, and Harma's foot retreated. The danger seemed to have passed. Malvius's gaze drifted back to her to give her a scolding glare. Gods, her smile. He couldn't remain angry with that face. His glare faded to a warm smile. She pushed her cheek out with her tongue. He had to look away before she made him laugh.

Platters of food began to arrive and the drone of conversation grew raucous, punctuated with loud laughter. Before the pork, gravy, and mashed turnips had been completely devoured, several Rekkrs noticed that all the table's flagons were empty. Boisterous complaints rang out from up and down the table. Vahldan rose. "For the gods' sake, remain calm. I'll go and see about another cask of wine." The proclamation roused a cheer.

On his way past, Vahldan leaned down between Malvius and Kemella. Malvius's heart raced, but Vahldan spoke to Kemella. "Well, Sister, where is she?"

"I'll go and see." Kemella sounded annoyed but she didn't hesitate, pushing back from the table and striding from the hall.

The platters empty, several Rekkrs stood, seeking the dregs from the cask on the sideboard and talking and laughing loudly. In response, the musicians increased the tempo and their volume. Amidst the growing revelry, he felt Harma's stare. He looked, and she wrinkled her nose, mouthing the words, "I want you." At least she'd done it in Hellainic. Gods, and they called Vahldan bold. He had nothing on his second wife.

All Malvius could think of was escape. He wondered if he could slide out. He didn't dare. Not without thanking the thug. What if he ran into him? He leaned to check the door. No sign of Vahldan's return, but Kemella came in carrying a baby boy, obviously Vahldan's firstborn son. The king's sister strode back to her seat. The boy looked around as if in terror and pressed his face against Kemella's chest, his tiny hands clutching her frock.

Kemella sat with the boy on her lap and spoke to him in a high and lilting voice. "Thaedan. Thaedan, I have someone for you to meet. Come on, let us see that handsome face. Come out and meet Captain Malvius." Her efforts were for naught. The boy would not unbury his face.

Harma harrumphed. "Stubborn as his poppa," she offered unhelpfully.

Kemella ignored Harma and started tickling the child, which caused a strange reaction.

Malvius was startled. Rather than laughing, the boy responded to the tickling with a look that seemed to border on fury. Malvius had never seen such an expression on a baby before. As if sensing his startlement, the boy's gray eyes met Malvius's stare. His little face was gaunt and wrinkled, his flaxen hair wispy. This was more of a grouchy old man than a happy babe. Besides that, he was so oddly tiny. The child was older than Armesus, wasn't he? He looked far too thin for a babe—sort of like a miniature adult.

"It's an honor to meet you, my prince," Malvius ventured and held out his hand.

If a babe could sneer in disdain, that's what this child did before turning back to his aunt, once again pressing his face to her bosom.

The noisy hall abruptly fell to near silence. Malvius presumed Vahldan had returned and leaned back in his seat. The king's first wife stood near the open entry doors, her eyes darting over the crowd. Now he saw who the boy took after. The woman's countenance was one of annoyance verging on wrathfulness.

Several Rekkrs backed away, like pups yielding to the dominant bitch. Once she'd cowed the entire chamber, the woman lifted her priestly robes clear of her feet and swept in, her skirts and her unbound white hair fluttering behind. She looked like a wing-clipped raptor appraising a room full of rodents. Her face was nearly as pale as her hair, making her unblinking eyes and blood-red lips all the more garish.

Harma snorted. "There goes my appetite for dessert." She stared into her cup.

"Well, have they met?" The woman was at Malvius's shoulder. Irritation radiated from her. He felt it without even looking.

Malvius gathered himself to stand. He made himself smile, turn, and bow his head to her. "Greetings, Lady Amaga. I am Malvius."

As he tried to concoct something pleasant to say, the woman's eyes latched onto him. Her appraisal felt hostile and invasive. All he could think about was getting away. He pushed aside his chair, instinctively clearing a path to flight.

Amaga put up her hands. In the moment, he didn't interpret it as the defensive reaction it likely was. Desperate to make a better impression, he grasped her right hand, thinking he would kiss it.

Her hand was cold, bony, almost claw-like. Her eyes flared, causing him to look away. It took great effort to bow but he found he couldn't release her hand or kiss it. He felt oddly compelled to lift his gaze back up to meet her fierce eyes again. Her stare locked with his again and she clenched her jaw. His hand went numb, and then a cold vibration ran up his arm from their connection. Her grip tightened and her muscles locked. She was having some sort of fit.

A piercing ache squeezed his head at his temples. The black centers of her eyes dilated, her scrutiny digging and clawing, prying into and plundering his secreted soul. Gods, it was agony.

"I *see* you," the relentless witch hissed.

Malvius's pulse raced. He couldn't draw a satisfying breath. With herculean effort, he all but threw her hand from his, yanking it to his chest protectively. He forced his head to turn away and, once released from contact, gasped for breath.

He became aware that the conversation had resumed in the hall. He didn't know how long the assault had lasted, but only Kemella seemed to have noticed it. The king's little sister looked suspicious as well as silently alarmed.

Malvius warily glanced to find the white-haired witch still glaring as she backed away. She seemed to be summoning a spell or devising a curse. "Take Thaedan away," she snapped.

Kemella's alarm increased. "Amaga? Is something awry?"

The white witch's eyes darted to Kemella. "Do as I say. Take Thaedan up to our quarters." Kemella frowned and the boy started to cry. "Please," Amaga added stiffly.

Kemella went pale, evidently miffed, but she rose, pulled the boy to her chest, and left.

Vahldan met her in the doorway. "What's happened?" he asked Kemella as they passed.

"Your qeins happened," Kemella said and kept walking.

Vahldan looked their way with a frown but then directed the servants he led to set up and tap a new cask of wine. The white witch slowly moved around to the end of the table, her eyes never leaving Malvius. Amaga sat, her back stiff and her chin high.

Once the wine was flowing, the thug took the first flagon filled and brought it to the head of the table. "Cups! Raise your cups, all of you." Malvius's head still throbbed. He lifted his cup from the table and held it out, willing his hand to stop trembling as Vahldan filled it. "Come, come, family. Have some wine." He beckoned them all over and filled Harma's, Arnegern's, and Mara's, then came around and filled one from the table for the white witch before pouring the last of the flagon in his own cup.

Vahldan held his wine up in a wordless toast. Everyone followed suit and drank. "Now, all of you sit and someone tell me. What's all of this about?" Malvius reluctantly sat, his body angled slightly toward Kemella's vacant seat with his instincts screaming for flight.

Amaga didn't hesitate. Her voice resounded like a priest's in a temple. "Perhaps, my king, you should tell us." The entire chamber fell silent.

Vahldan looked pained in a *here we go again* sort of way. "What should I tell, then?"

Amaga suddenly stood. "I wish you would tell us all why it is that you keep someone who hates you so very much this near to your sons, your family."

The others glanced his way. Malvius felt like he was naked and shrinking, becoming a little boy again. He slid down in his chair as if there was a way to hide in plain sight.

"*Now* what are you about, woman?"

"Your sea captain. Your so-called friend. His heart is black with hate. Hatred for all of us. But for you most of all, my king."

The chamber emitted a collective gasp. Now every gaze fell upon him. Malvius had to convince himself that dropping his cup and running out was a foolish idea.

Malvius forced himself to look at Vahldan. He couldn't read him. Was the thug a bit embarrassed? Was he in denial? Or was he actually considering her accusation?

Malvius made an expression of exaggerated incredulity and shrugged. It seemed to help. "That's nonsense," Vahldan said. His tone lacked conviction. "Malvius has only ever been my stalwart ally. Why, he even supplied us with tonight's feast. Including the very wine we drink."

"An ally?" Amaga's eyes flared again. "Nay, my king. This man is no ally. Everything he does builds to a single-minded purpose—to see to your downfall and demise. He dearly holds ill wishes for all of us and eagerly awaits our riddance."

A loud snort of laughter shattered the stunned silence. Harma covered her mouth, but another laugh escaped. She dropped her hand, tried to straighten her face, and then actually fell into an uncontrolled fit of giggling.

Amaga's glare swept to her rival, then back to Malvius. "Well, perhaps not *all* of us." The witch grew an evil and knowing little smile.

It was as if Harma had released the table from a spell and everyone else in the chamber began speaking at once. Malvius spoke over their honking and Harma's ongoing laughter. "My king, I assure you, I would never wish—"

"Enough!" Vahldan slammed down his cup, spraying wine. The thug leapt to his feet.

"Please," Malvius whispered. "You can't possibly believe this, this..."

Vahldan leaned on both hands on the table, hanging his head. "I think you'd best leave."

Malvius wasn't sure whether the thug was referring to him. It didn't matter. He slid from his chair and strode for the door, keeping his gaze on the floor, feeling all of their suspicious stares. He was only able to draw a decent breath when he cleared the high hall's open doors. He skipped down the stairs to the entry hall. He felt dizzy and found he was panting.

He burst through the palace doors, sucking in the cold air. His head began to clear. It was all he could do to keep from running to the stables. Thankfully, Dex had the carriage ready and was already seated on the bench. His first mate had brilliant instincts and patience. Malvius swung himself up onto the bench next to him and said, "Get us the fuck out of here. Fast."

Without a word, Dex slapped the reins onto the team's backs and they lurched into motion.

CHAPTER 17

PLAYING THE FOOL

"Though not as populous as the capital in Medicia, Efusium has ever been known as the more vibrant and cultured city— undeniably the most refined of the Tiberian Empire. Efusium has the larger port, is more ideally located, and is more central to the eastern trade routes. By all accounts, it is the city most hospitable to all of the empire's various ethnicities.

They say Efusium has the larger library and the more vital theater and artistic community. I have even heard that it boasts twice the number of brothels as Medicia. Hence, Efusium has an air of irreverence and a decidedly independent flair in regard to imperial decorum."—Brin Bright Eyes, Saga of Dania

ISIDROS LEFT AGORAKI standing in the entry hall of the huge building. Throughout the carriage ride from the ship in the harbor, Ago had been amazed. The stone in this city was so smooth, like it had been cut by the gods. Like divine cheese sliced with a keen blade. Efusium made Thrakius feel old, even shabby. The city seemed bigger than Anaissa in Sassanada, although it wasn't as crowded. It

273

felt so modern, so spread out. The gods knew the cloth most folks here were garbed in was finer, either than folks wore at home or anywhere else Ago had been. It was as if every citizen was highborn.

The outside of the fancy building offered no clue as to what went on inside. The halls and corridors bustled just like the city streets, but it was so quiet! Still, it had Ago wondering what all these folks were about. Everyone was endlessly in motion. It almost made him feel lazy. He found himself craning and gaping, which caused him to bump into one of the fast walkers. He didn't understand the man's words but he suspected they were nowhere near as fine as the man's robes.

Ago backed against the wall to look up again. Every bit of the soaring ceiling was carved with details as tricky as those on a statue. It was incredibly colorful, too, with windows at the tops of the walls to light it all up. The floors were so shiny they made him think of the ice stored in the Thrakian catacombs come summer once it started to melt. The shine made everything brighter, like there were no dark corners anywhere. That thought made Ago uneasy. He usually sought the spots where he could stay out of sight. This place didn't seem to have any.

Ago spotted Isidros between the columns at the far end of the hall, talking to a fit young man in a crisp militum tunic and knee-high boots. Isidros gestured toward Ago and the young man strode straight for him. The man's pace caused the shorter-legged trader to hurry to keep up. "Agoraki?" The young man's voice and expression made him seem mean.

"Yes?"

"You are from..." The man spoke with a Tiberian accent.

He made it seem like he knew the name but couldn't recall it. "Thrakius," Ago supplied.

The young man nodded. Now he seemed less mean. "And you gave this man something?" He gestured to Isidros, who nodded and smiled.

Ago wasn't sure what he meant. "Well, not to keep. It belongs to my family."

The young man's mean face came right back. "What was it?"

Ah. He was checking Isidros's story. Maybe he was mad at Isidros. That wouldn't be a shocker. "A torc," Ago offered. "With dragon mouths holding a medallion. The medallion has my family name on it."

"And that name is..." Again with pretending he couldn't recall it.

"Stallicus."

The young man finally offered the trace of a smile. "Thank you, Agoraki." The man turned to Isidros and handed him a sealed pouch of stiff parchment. "The first charter you requested, with our thanks, Anax." Ago knew he'd been used again. But it didn't matter this time. After all, this time Ago had used Isidros, too.

Isidros bowed his head as he accepted the parchment. "Happy to be of service, Nicandros. And the second charter..."

"Is still with the rector's review committee." The young man looked like he tasted something sour. "I expect today's gesture"—he nodded at Ago—"will go some distance toward securing it."

"Please pass along my thanks to your master for any help he may provide with the rector." Isidros tilted his head again but he didn't seem as happy as he had a moment before.

"Agoraki, please come with me," this Nicandros fellow snapped, and he spun and started for the end of the hall, boots clicking on the shiny floors.

Ago wondered what he'd gotten himself into. It seemed like he'd landed in the middle of something sneaky. Maybe even a little scary. He considered his escape routes, craning his neck to look over his shoulder. Isidros was almost back to where they had come in. Funny, the anax had tried to seem like he'd been in charge but he was always disappearing when things got tricky or risky.

No one was looking. It occurred to him that he'd gotten himself free of Malvius *and* Isidros. Not to mention the Gottari and the war. He could run, carve out a life in this big, shiny city.

No. That thought seemed even scarier. This place had no dark corners. He didn't even speak the language. After all he'd done to get this far, it wouldn't make sense to not see his plan through. Plus, he had to get the torc back. The whole point was to see if he could still get what he should rightly have coming to him, no matter how long it took. If things got worse, there'd be other chances to run, to try again. He had to believe it was true, anyway.

Ago hurried after snappish Nicandros, who kept on without so much as a glance back. Ago caught up just as they reached a wide staircase leading down. They stepped down into what almost felt like the shadowy corridors of his old home. But unlike the lower levels of the palace of Thrakius, the air grew warmer, stuffier. Funny, warm as it was, he still had the shivers. Maybe the icy shine of the smooth stone was tricking his mind. Or maybe he was about as scared as he'd ever been, even when the anax's men had held the palace. Might as well admit it, at least to himself.

Nicandros led him down a corridor lined with lamps that gave off an odd sort of light. There were dozens of open doorways along either side. All the chambers were lit, too. The whole place seemed to glow like moonlight. The air grew damper. Men in various states of dress strolled from chamber to chamber, most wearing robes or simple wraps, many with wet hair. His guide even led him over a little indoor bridge with clear water flowing beneath it. He caught a glimpse off to one side of men lounging at the edge of the water.

Ah, that made better sense now. He'd heard of bathhouses but had never been to one. There were baths in the palace of Thrakius, but they weren't this fancy. And folk didn't tend to bathe together. It happened, but not on purpose.

Next, snappish Nicandros led him into the biggest bath chamber yet, with columns along the edges, painted tiles underfoot, and a barrel ceiling over the top. There were fountains tinkling and the air was steamy. Everyone in here was nude except for a dozen attendants, who all wore matching sleeveless tunics. The attendants all had light brown skin like Maaman.

The young man walked right on through the big room, finally taking Ago into a tunnel that led to a smaller space. With another damn bath! How many could there be? This one seemed all but empty. The far walls were covered in tiles painted with fish swimming. It was brighter in here as there was a high, arched window that let sunlight in. A curly pipe had water trickling from it, and the sound of it hitting the bath made Ago wish he'd peed one more time before they'd come.

"This is Agoraki, my lord," Nicandros said. He sounded a lot less snappish now. Ago's gaze found and locked onto the man sitting in water up to his clean-shaven chin. Seemed the mostly submerged man—or lord—was the only one in this smaller bath chamber.

"Thank you, Nico," the submerged lord said. "Leave us." His voice wasn't kind, but it wasn't mean either. He had short gray hair and a stern look about him. Ago couldn't tell how old he was. He seemed older than Isidros but not ancient or wrinkly. The lord stayed low in the water, staring at him for a long moment. Then he nodded his head. "Your property. It is there on the table." His Tiberian accent was thick, formal.

Ago went to the table. Beside a couple of rolled parchments was his torc. He stood looking down at it. "It's all right," the bathing lord said. "You may take it."

Ago snatched it up and held it close to his stomach. He wanted to hide it away inside his belt pouch, but the lord was watching and he was afraid it would seem rude. Unsure what else to do, he checked it. It felt heavier, if anything, but looked the same.

"Do you know the history of it—your torc?"

Ago shook his head. "My maaman said it was a family heirloom."

"It was a trophy of war, given to your great-great-grandfather. For his victory over the Kelti in the far northlands. It belonged to a Kelti chieftain whom your ancestor defeated. The Kelti were very brave, very proud—particularly this one. This chieftain left your torc with his wife before his last heroic chariot charge into the Tiberian lines. The man told his wife to surrender herself and the torc to the man who could rightly name himself the victor of the day. The wife gave it, and herself, to your grandsire. In so doing, she became a fore-mother as well."

"A Kelti woman?" Ago thought they were barbarians. He couldn't help but think of Brin.

"Yes," the man said. "Did you say your mother gave it to you?"

"Yes." Ago didn't look up.

"The mother who adopted you?"

"Yes."

"Do you know who your birth mother was?"

"Yes." Ago finally looked up. The bathing lord gazed at him through the steam. He gave Ago a nod to prompt him. It was another test. "She was Ligaia, daughter of Anax Decebius of Thrakius."

Ago dropped his gaze to his feet, avoiding the lord's searching eyes.

"Your mother was a good woman. A good and loving woman in bad circumstances."

Ago looked him in the eyes. "You knew her?"

"Very well. I loved her. As I believe she loved me. But I, too, was in bad circumstances."

He sounded nicer so Ago studied him now. The lord offered a half smile. "If I had known, I would have sent for you sooner, Agoraki. Or should I call you Vernouthus?"

Ago had heard the name before. He didn't care much for it so he hoped not, though he said nothing.

The bathing lord grimaced and slowly stood, his square torso finally rising from the steamy water. He took a step forward. Ago backed away, matching his steps and clutching the torc to his chest. As the naked lord moved into the sunbeam from the window, Ago's gaze locked onto his chest. Just below his nipples, a perfectly straight line ran from one side of him to the other. It was some sort of welt, like a long finger of purple, swollen flesh.

The lord winced as he bent for a long white bandage lying on the raised rim of the bath. He noticed Ago staring as he wrapped it around himself, fastening it over the ugly scar. His smile was grim. "Your old friend Vahldan the Bold gave me that."

Ago shook his head. "He's not… King Vahldan is no friend of mine."

"But you know him, do you not? Him and his family?"

Ago didn't want to talk about Brin. "I guess you could say. As well as a servant can."

The man put on his robe and sighed once he had it tied. "There. That's better. Tell me, Agoraki, what is it you want from me?"

Ago backed up until his backside hit a marble bench. "Nothing."

"Come now. You sent that snake Isidros with your torc. You must have wanted something." The lord came and loomed over him. He wasn't as tall as a Rekkr, but he was just as imposing.

Ago looked down at his sandaled feet. He supposed it was time to admit that he had a good guess who the bathing lord was. To himself as well as to… his father. "I'm sorry. I didn't think… I thought you were dead. I didn't know…"

His father placed a hand on his shoulder, gentle but firm. "Come now. Don't be afraid, son. You are a Stallicus, same as me. Tell me what it is you want?"

Tears filled Ago's eyes. "A home. Just a home."

Vernius put his fingers under Ago's chin and raised his face to meet his gaze. His father's face became kind. "That's what I hoped you would say. Because it's what I want as well. But first, there is something I must do. My duty. If you're willing, you could be a help to me. It would likely make doing my duty easier. Would you help me, son?"

"H—how?"

"Tell me everything."

"Everything about what?"

"About Thrakius. About the palace. About Isidros and Malvius. About the Gottari. About Vahldan the Bold. Everything you can think of. If you can do that, and I can finish my duty—our duty—then we can go home. Just you and me. Then we can tell each other about your mother. And about ourselves, our hopes and dreams. Would you like that?"

Ago wiped his eyes with the backs of his hands and nodded.

His father smiled for the first time. "Good. Let us talk, you and I."

Vernius carefully bent his knees, lowering himself while keeping his torso perfectly straight. He kept his chin level and looked down his nose, reaching for his sword belt. He grasped it and started to lift and... He winced and dropped it. The entire belt tumbled off the bed to the ground. He straightened, hissing through his clenched teeth, his head swimming from the pain. Gods, it had been weeks. He simply had to get beyond this wound—a wound that no one could see. A wound that shamed him even more deeply than the sword had cut his flesh.

He had to get past it simply to keep his men from knowing how much it weakened him, humbled him, shook him to his core.

Although they couldn't see it, every man in the mobile reserve had heard about it. Perhaps every soldier and sailor in the militum had. Not to mention those he answered to. Vernius had to make it seem as though it was but a trifle. He had to rise above it, to stand taller than his barbaric rival—the man he had to be allowed to bring to justice. He would make it his life's mission; he couldn't live with himself if he was kept from it. Which was why he couldn't afford to appear unready, let alone unfit. Particularly not today.

Vernius pressed his shoulder against the wall, his eyes squeezed shut and his arms crossed over the wound, trying to slow his breathing. Each intake of air was excruciating, which only caused him to hiss it out slowly, leading to his body demanding another.

"He's calling for you, my lo..." Nico saw him and rushed over. "General!" His loyal adjutant gripped his hand and slipped an arm around his lower back, helping him to straighten.

"My belt." Vernius pointed to the floor.

Nico was reluctant to let go. "Can you stay upright without aid?"

Vernius nodded and Nico rushed to retrieve the belt and buckle it onto his hips. He pointed at his father's crimson garment laid out on the bed. "The cloak, too." Nico scooped it up and fastened it at his shoulders with the two-headed dragon clasp. "Where's the boy?" he asked.

"Waiting in his chambers," Nico replied. "He's packed and ready. I took the liberty of finding Ago some suitable clothing. I hope you don't mind. It's going to be a cold voyage."

Trying not to take too deep a breath, Vernius said, "No, of course. Thank you, Nico."

"Are you going to be all right?" Nicandros looked more concerned than Vernius wished was warranted. It wasn't a good sign in regard to how healthy he appeared.

"I'll be fine. Lead on. You know how much he hates to be kept waiting."

Nicandros reluctantly led the way through the luxurious palace of Efusium. Vernius knew Nico would prefer to help him walk, but that wouldn't do. Every eye in the place was watching. More so today than ever before. They came to the stairs and started up. Each step made Vernius clench his jaw tighter. By the time they arrived outside the royal residence, Vernius needed a moment to catch his breath and compose himself.

Nico patiently waited. Vernius nodded and Nico knocked. A royal attendant opened the door. Both attendants stood aside to allow Vernius inside. The cavernous sitting chamber was empty. The attendant hurried ahead and led him to a sleeping chamber.

Mycanius sat upright, propped on uncountable pillows, in his oversize bed. His Eminence wore a purple silk sleeping gown and had several shimmering blankets pulled to his waist. Scrolls and parchments were sprawled on the bed around him. Sitting in a lounge chair beside the bed was Vernius's superior, the master commander of the militum. This was not good. Facerius had come all the way to Efusium during hiatus. Worse, he hadn't bothered to speak privately with Vernius when he'd arrived.

This might be it, the moment he'd long feared.

Vernius sucked in a breath, held it, and bowed. "Highness," he managed. He turned and tilted his head. "Lord Commander. Forgive me. I didn't realize you were here."

Facerius looked anxious but said nothing. Mycanius spoke up. "I'm told you plan to depart for Megaria, Vernius."

"Yes, Highness. The ship is ready to sail and the seas seem as fair as we could hope. We'll leave as soon as possible—with your permission, of course."

"That's just the trouble. I gave no such permission. Nor did I offer any command at all."

Vernius stiffened. "I seek to finish your bidding, Highness. I assumed that you would—"

"Jupiter's thunder, man!" The outburst caused the emperor to cough and wheeze, but he continued in spite of it. "You... of all people... should know better than to assume."

"There's something you need to know, Vernius," Facerius said, evidently seeking to steer clear of the rising storm. "Perhaps you should sit." His commander gestured to a nearby chair.

Damn, the thing was low. And cushioned. "I'm comfortable standing, my lord."

"Gods of patience, Vernius. Sit!" the emperor demanded.

Vernius went to the chair, stood facing away from it, clenched his jaw, and slowly lowered himself, trying to keep his torso straight and catch himself on the chair's arm. A wince escaped him as his tailbone hit. He pulled himself upright to keep his chest and stomach flat and forced a smile.

"Are you even well enough to be out of bed?" Facerius actually sounded concerned.

"Of course. Just a bit of indigestion." They both stared suspiciously.

Mycanius finally waved dismissively. "He's a grown man, able to decide for himself what's best for him. Let's get on with it."

Facerius looked out the window and said, "I've sent for Verrio. He's on his way."

Vernius's eye twitched. General Verrio Etruscus. They'd been at the academy together. To compensate for his diminutive stature, the man practically lived in the saddle. Verrio was so pompous, he'd given himself the moniker *The Provosta*. "Doesn't General Verrio have the command in Gallica?" Perfect place for him—distant and cold enough to cool his ridiculously quick temper.

"He happened to be in Cispadaena," Facerius said. "If the weather holds, he'll be in Pontea within the week."

"Why bring him to Pontea?" Vernius leaned forward, winced again, and dropped back.

Mycanius cut through the clutter. "We're giving Verrio command of the mobile reserve."

"The mobile reserve is mine," Vernius spat without forethought.

"Excuse me?" Mycanius's eyebrows rose almost to his hairline. "Yours?"

"Forgive me, Highness. I meant—"

"You're wounded," Facerius swiftly interceded. "You should acknowledge it. Get some rest. You've been on campaign now for, what, five years running? Take some time. Gather yourself. Settle your affairs at home. Another command will arise, given time."

Vernius didn't dare wipe the moisture that escaped the corners of his eyes. He sought to compose his face. He'd rather plead than whine. "Please. I beg you both to reconsider." Just the thought of losing his army was like a punch to his already throbbing torso. His pride was at stake, of course, but this would cut him so much more deeply. If he lost his commission, his hold on his father's lands were at risk. There were so many—in the provincial bureaucracy and even in the Senate—who still longed to punish his family and humiliate his father's memory for his crimes. All at a tidy profit. And Vernius had just found his son, which in time might reaffirm his grip. If he lost his estate, his mother's shameful sacrifice would be for naught.

Through all of his adult life, Vernius had been fighting to regain some semblance of legacy. His ancestors were relying on him. But this would decimate it. After all his grandsires' achievements, his father's disgrace would become synonymous with the Stallicus name, to be engraved in Tiberian history. His shame would be complete.

Facerius's expression was full of pity. "I'm afraid it has been decided."

Vernius faced the emperor, who refused to meet his gaze. "Why, Highness? I've sought to do all you've ever asked. I did things—endured things—that no other would or could. I gave all of myself to—"

"I will not be mocked, Vernius." Mycanius turned his fierce gaze on him.

"I would never, Highness."

"Not *by* you. Because of you."

"I don't understand. I seek only to honor you in all that I say and do."

"Would you call this honor?" Mycanius snatched up a scroll and slung it to the end of the bed, an arm's reach from Vernius's knees. Gods, he really was being punished.

Vernius drew and held a breath, clenching to lean and reach to take it. He managed to lean back silently, though the pain momentarily blurred his vision. He unrolled it and sighed.

It was a crude drawing in the style of a bill for public posting. The central caricature was unmistakably of himself, with his sires' square jaw and jutting nose, not to mention his father's crested helm and arcane cloak. In his caricature's left arm was slung a babe and with the right he brandished a centurion's gladius. His caricature was crossing swords with a bearded and shaggy assailant holding a sword twice as long as his own. The assailant was drawn with the animalistic features that many satirists used to depict Teutonics.

This one wore a crooked crown. Vahldan the Bold. The babe also wore a crown, one of gilded laurel leaves. In addition, the babe was bawling and had close-set eyes with bushy eyebrows and a weak chin—unmistakably a caricature of Mycanius.

"It's utterly ridiculous, Highness."

"Ridiculous? It seeks to portray *me* as ridiculous! Even the mummers in the market square are now crafting skits that make me the pathetic fool. How long before this sort of excrement makes its way to the capital? Would you have me return home a fool, Vernius?"

He instantly knew what had to be done. Without hesitation, Vernius fell to his knees at the side of his emperor's bed. He boldly took Mycanius's hand in his. "No. Never." Mycanius seemed to want to pull his hand away but Vernius clung to it. "I would have you return as the people's great hero. At the head of a procession that includes your foes either in chains or in the form of corpses piled on wagons. I would have your people rightfully cheer you as you signal for our empire's most vile and murderous foe to be strangled for all to see. I would have the people of all Pontea, and particularly those of Thrakius, sing your praises unto the ages as their savior." The pain brought tears back to his eyes but he did not blink or turn away.

Mycanius stared deeply into his wet eyes. "Then we are of like minds. Unlike our fathers."

"We are, Highness. Which is why you must let me see to it. Verrio simply cannot make this happen. Not as I can. My men, they and I— we see one another. We have known one another. I would do anything for them. And they know it for truth. And because of it, they will do anything for me. So, too, do I know this foe. I have come to know how he thinks. Verrio cannot possibly know what's at stake. Not as you and I do. Making this right is my passion. It burns within me. Please, trust me, Highness. These are the makings of our victory."

Mycanius continued to look into his eyes but did not speak. Vernius laid his hand on his wound. "That savage," Vernius said softly. "He did this to us, Highness. To you and to me. It is a matter of honor. I can only save mine by affirming yours. Verrio has no such investment."

Vernius bowed his head and drew a deep breath. He thought of the boy, the motherless son who only wanted a home. For him to find it, he needed a father. A father with honor. Or homeless he would remain. "Indeed, I wish to vow to it. I will deliver you the victory you deserve. There on the hill, you shall have the thug king's body. Or mine shall take its place. Should I somehow fail, make me the fool, the one to be mocked and scorned unto the ages." Without this chance, it would happen anyway.

Vernius blinked till his tears ran down his cheeks and raised his face. Mycanius's eyes were now shining, too. Vernius actually thought he saw pride in them. "So be it," his emperor whispered.

CHAPTER 18
SMUGGLING RETRIBUTION

"*It is said to be the wisdom of my paternal great-grandfather, Beremund of the Amalus, that one's greatest foe or ally in war is the weather, that in but an instant it can turn from one to the other.*

It was the early cold and wet of autumn that pressed the Tiberians into their first, hasty campaign. It led them to march on through dense fog and thus to defeat at Orithya. That same early cold and wet weather also fueled early snows in the heights of the Pontean Pass, trapping the Gottari in Thrakius. A subsequent warming trend at the onset of hiatus led to unimpeded winter movement for the Tiberian navy and troops, which seemed to cement their advantage as the war settled into the Thrakian siege.

Still, Beremund's truism could not be denied. As the siege lingered and our uncertainty grew, none of us could guess whose ally the fickle weather would be by the end."—Brin Bright Eyes, *Saga of Dania*

MALVIUS STOOD on *Gullwing's* deck, watching the carriage rolling away from the docks, only to see another carriage from the palace rolling in. He groaned to himself. Gods, he'd just gotten rid of

Harma's driver, who'd come to find out if he planned on abandoning her. The driver had also discretely indicated that if Malvius should be thinking of flight, she would consider joining him. He'd finally assured the man that he was indeed returning to Thrakius.

The two carriages were barely able to squeeze by each other in the narrows at the end of Fishmongers' Lane, sending passersby hurrying to clear the way. Malvius briefly entertained the idea of having his men rush to cast off before the second carriage arrived. But the ship was too far from ready. Besides the fact that the seagates were closed. The timing of their opening was critical to his running of the Tiberian blockade. The northwesterly wind was perfect and showed no sign of slacking. The seas had worsened, as he'd predicted in his message to Vahldan, but weren't rough enough to send all of the Tiberian ships back to port. A seeming misfortune that was actually critical to Malvius's plan.

The second carriage rumbled across the docks. Shit. It was his father's old carriage, the most ornate of the four, indicating it was probably the thug king himself. Could Vahldan have changed his mind about opening the seagates and letting him leave?

The carriage door opened and out crawled the giant, arms and legs first, like an immense spider from a too-small hidey-hole. Teavar fixed his glare upon Malvius. It was as if the giant thought he could compel him to stay as one would a hound.

Teavar clomped up the gangway, causing it to bend and creak. "Who rides the other one?" The giant jerked a thumb over his shoulder at the retreating carriage.

"The qeins sent a request. She wishes to surprise the king with another cask of his favorite wine. I bid the messenger tell her that I will seek it."

"The first qeins or second?" Teavar asked, narrowing his eyes.

"The second. What of it?" Seemed a foolish question. He couldn't imagine the white witch bestowing a gift upon Vahldan, let alone venturing to reach out to Malvius. Unless it was with a curse, or maybe a threat.

Speaking of threats, the giant squared himself and said, "We need to speak." If anything, Teavar's deep voice had only grown more menacing in the twenty years since Malvius had first heard it. Today he sounded like a malevolent demigod.

Malvius swallowed. "Sorry, old friend, but we're about to cast off." Couldn't hurt to try.

Teavar's grin actually grew more menacing. "That is what we will speak of, *old friend.*"

Malvius had to admit, the giant's Hellainic was improving. Finally. It had only been two decades. "Oh really? The king seemed pleased by my suggestion to make a run for supplies. He even made suggestions as to what we should seek."

"The king has many cares. You are not among them. But you *are* among mine."

"Oh really?" he repeated. "I'm flattered." His nonchalant act grew less effective with each new higher octave his voice involuntarily achieved.

The giant stepped closer, casting him in shadow. "You made an oath to serve our king. Only the gods can know how, but he yet trusts you. Your fleet is our only navy—gods help us."

"Of course. He trusts me because he knows my heart. Just as I trust him." With difficulty, Malvius made himself stare back.

The seagates tower bell rang once, signaling that the gates would momentarily open. They'd been watching for the two patrolling Tiberian warships to reach their far turn.

"Hear that? I'm afraid we must be going." Teavar continued to loom. Malvius turned his head and called, "Dex! Be ready to cast the lines! Remember, the aft is last." Damn the quaver of his voice.

"Aye, Cap!" Thank the gods Dex was near enough to hear. He hadn't even checked.

Teavar squinted. "Something is not right. Of this I am sure. But of this *you* can be sure: If you forsake him"—Teavar jabbed his chest painfully with a finger—"you will have me to reckon with. I now make you an oath. I will not rest or die until it is so. Understood, *old friend?*"

"Of course." The damn mountain of flesh still wouldn't move. "We really must haul the gangway. Or we'll never get clear. So, unless you'd like to sail with us..."

The giant slowly turned and lumbered back down the gangway. Malvius hadn't felt more pleased to gain distance from another human being since he'd left the feast with the white witch. His men scrambled to haul the gangway and cast the proper lines.

Malvius strode the deck, barking orders as the rowers pushed off at the fore and *Gullwing's* prow drifted into the harbor, still tethered at the aft. He climbed to the tiller just as the gatehouse bell rang again. "Ready to cast off!" he bellowed. The great chains rose from the murk to tightness, and the seagates began to creak and groan as they crawled apart.

"Hoist sails," he called and raised his hand to signal to Dex. "Release," he cried as he dropped his arm. The last aft line released, and in moments the ship gained the clearance the oarsmen needed. He signaled again for the caller to start them. The sails fluttered a moment, then snapped taut. The ship leapt into motion, heading across the harbor for a gap in the gates that was currently too small.

The gates continued to creak but almost seemed to slow down as the ship gathered speed. Why did he always have to torture himself like this? He stood at the tiller, pretending not to fret, fantasizing that this would be the last time he'd try a stunt like this.

With a few heartbeats to spare, Malvius called for the oars to be pulled in. The prow reached the opening to the seagates and it almost seemed the gap widened just ahead of the growing width of the ship. The starboard side grazed the gate, but several of Dex's men were there to push from the rails and guide them through. The prow sliced the first wave of the open sea and Malvius called for the rowers to resume, though he knew they'd hate hearing it. He needed just a bit more speed.

He steered to the perfect angle to fully harness the wind, looking east then west to monitor the two Tiberian ships. Even a glancing blow from a Tiberian rostrum would doom a ship like *Gullwing*, built for speed and a maximal hold. One trireme was headed away, eastward. The other had just come about on their starboard side. The western one spotted them. He heard the calls for pursuit from the Tiberian officers. Their oarsmen had been working for the entire westward run. The imperials didn't have the muscle or the wind. Malvius was riding the waves hard, but he had the ideal angle to harness the gusts.

Dex came up beside him. "Call in the oars," he said. Dex gave him a wary look. "They can't help us now. May as well rest them till we see if it gets close." Dex ran to do his bidding.

A trumpet sounded from the eastern ship. They'd come about. Malvius steered slightly toward the eastern side of the gap, gauging where he would lose the wind and readjusting back to fully harvest it.

The first Tiberian captain drew a wide, curving course, seeking the angle to intercept *Gullwing's* inevitable next tack. The man was no novice. This was going to be close. Malvius doubted they would try a catapult on waves like these, but the bastards just might end up in bow range. His crew would survive that, though. If they could just avoid that rostrum.

As *Gullwing* gained depth, the waves became less of an obstacle. He trimmed the sails again. His fastest ship leaned and gained speed, slicing the water perfectly. The distance from the Tiberian prow grew. The trireme was too squat to keep pace. The few arrows the Tiberians fired fell short in the water. As the distance between them grew, the echoing curses of the Tiberians told the tale's end.

They'd gotten away. Again.

Malvius slumped at the tiller and sighed. No matter how many of these races he ran, the thrill—and the terror—never lessened. Dexicos appeared at his shoulder. "Here, take the helm," he said to Dex. "Keep us heading south-southeast. Come around after we're beyond the horizon. Then head for the drop just east of the mouth of the Straits."

"Aye." Malvius started down the ladder. "Where're you off to, Cap?"

"To change!" He indicated his sailing togs. "I need to look my best. Might even comb my hair. You know how judgmental Tiberian officers can be." He winked and continued down.

Malvius stripped and washed his face and armpits; Teavar's visit had incited a cold sweat with a powerful stench. And indeed, he even combed his hair. He then donned his finest silk tunic and the blue cloak his father had given him before Decebius had disowned him. The collars were adorned with the symbols of the anaxship. He fastened the clasps shaped like suns and threw it behind his shoulders. Once he was suitably groomed and attired, he filled a cup with the last of the strong brandy and took a gulp. He checked himself in the looking glass. "This is it," he told his reflection. "Pull this turnabout and the rest is a downwind drift." He finished the cup, tossed it on his bunk, and headed back out to the deck.

The trireme had become a speck on the horizon. They'd given up and turned back for Thrakius. His plan was still on track. He turned to the helm and saluted Dex, who smiled and pointed to the west. The spires of Megaria were visible in the distance. He beckoned two crewmen to come and ready the launch.

As the crewmen hoisted the launch, he climbed to Dex on the aftcastle. "Remember, the dah will only do so much to protect you. Leave Anaissa if you sense trouble, but don't come for me until you receive the message we agreed to."

"Aye, Cap."

"You remember the words, right? Tell me."

"The sun shines above the soaring eagle."

Malvius nodded and the two men grasped one another's forearms. "Thank you, my friend." Dex bowed his head, obviously moved. "It will all be over soon now," he assured his most dependable and loyal ally.

"Aye, Cap. We're with you. Till the end."

Malvius clapped his first mate on the shoulder and climbed down to the rail where the crewmen held his launch steady over the side. A sailor helped him to climb in and Malvius signaled Dex to come about. The men started cranking down the winch. When the ship had turned enough, the sails went slack and Malvius hit the release. His little craft fell the remaining distance to splash into the surf. The first wave that hit him sent him bumping into the side of *Gullwing*. Thank the gods, he didn't capsize. In mere moments, the ship was away and resuming course, sailing on. A sailor at the stern swept an arm overhead in farewell.

The waves continued to hit broadside and Malvius was soon drenched in frigid seawater. He fumbled with the oars and finally managed to put the prow to the oncoming waves. Once he'd righted himself, he was able to look around. It didn't take long for the Tiberians to spot him. They launched a patrol ship in mere moments. Malvius kept swiveling on the bench, craning over his shoulder to track the Tiberians' progress. For a moment, he feared they hadn't seen him or would simply continue to pursue *Gullwing*. But soon, it was clear they were coming for him. Their approach was so swift that he feared they intended to sink his tiny craft. He drew the oars in and held up his hands.

"Stay where you are!" an officer shouted needlessly in Tiberian. The officer was flanked by a half-dozen archers, their bows loaded and aimed.

"Believe me, I'm not trying to get away," Malvius called, still holding up his hands.

"Take the line," the officer yelled, and another sailor tossed him a rope with a pre-tied loop. Malvius caught it and pulled the loop over his head and shoulders, putting his arms above it and holding it before him. Feet spread, he managed to stand in the rocking dinghy and nodded.

The line cracked tight and he was viciously yanked up. He flailed and crashed into the planking of the ship's side. He bumped and scraped all the way to the rail. He reached to grasp it, but before he could get a hold, strong hands grabbed his wrists. He was pulled over and flung to the deck. Pain shot through him as he scrambled to rise, slipped, and fell again. Laughter rang out around him. He got to his hands and knees and gathered himself. They grabbed him by both arms and jerked him upright, wrenching his shoulders.

"Peace, brothers," Malvius said. "I come to be of service to the empire." More laughter. The grips on his arms were cruel as the officer appraised him. The man's bearing and dress named him the ship's captain. Malvius bowed his head. "Greetings, Captain. I am—"

"We know who you are, traitor," the captain interjected. "We saw the ship that left you." The officer spun away. "Chain him to the mast."

"But I come to offer valuable aid."

"Still your tongue, smuggler, or I'll have you chained to the rostrum instead." The captain strode off, calling to his men, "Stations. Make ready to port."

Malvius was all but dragged to the mast and pushed to a sitting position. One of the sailors put his wrists into shackles already in place on the mast. Malvius watched his bobbing dinghy growing smaller in the distance, wondering if he'd made a fatal error.

The ship sailed into the relative calm of the Straits. The rowers guided the vessel to a newly built dock. Sailors threw lines to waiting soldiers. At the helm, the captain spoke to a group of four sailors, all of them glaring his way. Two of them came and unchained him while the other two hurried to shore. They put his wrists into chained cuffs and pulled him to the dock.

The two sent ahead were waiting for him with a rope. As they dropped a knotted loop over his head, he briefly wondered if he was to be hung without a trial. Such things were not unheard of in a war zone. Instead, they cinched it tight around the tops of his arms and pulled him up toward the city gates on a newly laid path of pavers. They walked so fast that Malvius stumbled and would've fallen a dozen times if they hadn't continued to yank him back upright. Tears ran down his face, his nose, and into his mustache. His arms and hands went numb.

Just inside the outer keep wall, they pulled him to the left rather than to the inner gate. They came to a guard standing outside an iron door in the stone wall. Malvius had never noticed it before. "Who do we have here?" the guard asked his bearers.

"Smuggler. His ship ran the blockade. Captain says he'll put in a report later tonight."

The guard took out a large key and opened the iron door, holding it wide. It was dark inside. The two dragged Malvius to another door within. The guard opened it as the sailors removed the rope and flung him in. He tripped on the rough cobbles and fell on his face. He gasped and the reek of urine filled his nose.

Malvius scrambled to his feet and turned to the door, which slammed shut in his face. He fell against it, slapping it with stinging hands. "I must speak to an officer! Please, I have valuable information for the commander of the mobile reserve."

The guard laughed. "Best save your strength, smuggler. You'll need it for whatever the sadist you think you want to see has in store for you."

"No, please! You don't understand." The guard's laughter faded as the outer door clanged shut, throwing him into deep shadow.

Malvius turned back to survey the cell. Slivers of pale light shone from a set of gaps in the stone overhead, probably there to vent the space. His eyes began to adjust. The far wall had a bench of cantilevered wooden slabs. A pail sat in the nearest corner. A shuffling sound came from the opposite corner. Malvius spun to face it. He made out a shape at the end of the bench. "Who's there?"

"Your mother. Come give us a kiss." The voice was almost as menacing as Teavar's.

A snorting laugh came from behind him. He spun again. Another shape, at the other end of the bench. His eyes continued to adjust. Another male. This one sat with his feet on the bench, hugging his knees. His clothes were tattered rags. The first one—his *mother*—

stood and moved closer. The man was stout, had short hair and no beard. He held his shoulders square and his head high. His pale tunic looked to be militum—probably a deserter. Or, considering Malvius's current streak of luck, arrested for drunkenness or brawling.

"That's fine cloth you have there." Malvius detected an accent but couldn't place it. The soldier moved closer and reached to touch the embroidered edge of the cloak his father had given him. Malvius shuffled back a step. "Looks warm," the soldier added. He smelled of sweat and sour wine. One of his hard, unblinking eyes was blackened. Definitely a drunken brawler.

The soldier still held on to Malvius's cloak. Malvius yanked it away and tried to back up further. His heel hit the door. The soldier smiled and reached for the cloak again, rubbing the fabric between his fingers and his thumb. "This is fine indeed. Lucky they let you keep it."

Malvius pressed his back to the door. "Thank you." Once again, he slowly pulled the cloak from the man's hand and took a sidestep to gain some distance.

"They took my cloak away," the soldier said, hovering close. "Yours is even thicker than mine was. I've been so cold at night. You must want your mother to be warm at night, don't you, my son?"

The soldier flicked Malvius's clasp, detaching one side of his father's gift. In a flash, the man yanked the cloth, pulling the cloak from one shoulder before Malvius could catch it. The man tugged, pulling Malvius into a stumbling step toward him and bringing them face to face. The man grit his teeth and raised the fist clutching the cloak, letting out an animalistic growl. Malvius's shoulder ached. Gods, he wasn't sure he could handle more pain in more body parts. Particularly not his face. He hadn't been punched in years, but the moment conjured a vivid memory of the sensation.

Spinning to unwrap himself from the cloak, he abandoned his father's gift just as easily as he'd abandoned the man himself.

Malvius hurried to the door and pounded, using his shackles to clank on the bars. "Guard! Guard! I've been robbed! Guard!"

The disgraced soldier laughed as he wrapped himself. Thank the gods, the key rattled in the door. The guard stood silhouetted in the light. "What's all this? Already with you?"

"He's stolen my cloak," Malvius whined, pointing without looking.

"He said I could have it," the soldier claimed with laughter in his voice.

Malvius looked to the third man huddled in the corner. The man looked Bafranii. "Tell him," Malvius implored. The third prisoner hid his face in his folded arms. Malvius repeated the request in Bafranii. The man shook his head without raising it.

"Aye, it does look like a fine cloak." The guard stepped inside. "I suppose I'd better settle this fairly." He yanked the cloak from the soldier's shoulders.

"Thank you," Malvius said, holding out his hands for it.

Wearing a grin, the guard pointedly folded and rolled his father's beautiful gift and tucked it under his fat arm. He shoved Malvius harshly as he headed out. Malvius tripped on the cobbles again and fell against the wall. He landed within arm's length of the pail full of excrement, the reek of it assaulting him as overtly as the guard's shove. The outer door slammed shut, muffling the departing guard's laughter.

"Now look what you've done, you little shit." The soldier kicked him in the midsection. Malvius rolled on his side, unable to draw a breath. "You'll keep me warm tonight, one way or another." The man went and sat heavily on the bench. "Best figure out the way you'll get that done and get yourself in the mood for it, smuggler."

Malvius crawled across the filthy cobbles to the far wall opposite the pail. He sat leaning against the wall, gasping to catch an even breath. He'd avoided a punched face, but now he hurt everywhere else. In mere moments, he found himself hugging his knees, just like the Bafranii.

The soldier muttered, cursed, and even growled. Malvius sat like that for the gods only knew how long. As the vent slots dimmed, he both longed for and dreaded nightfall. He knew he had to keep an eye on the soldier, but exhaustion born of pain finally won out and he dozed off. He woke with a start at the sound of the key in the door and voices on the other side.

The outer door swung open. It was clearly evening, but he still had to shield his eyes against the light. The guard came in and pointed at Malvius. "You. Up."

Malvius sat cowering, certain that it was a trick. The guard was looking for an excuse to hurt him again. "Now!" the guard blared. Malvius struggled to his feet, arms up, defensive.

The guard took his elbow, pinching but merely steering him through the door. Amazing that a pinch could feel like a mercy. "Can't image why the old man would want the likes of him," the guard said.

"Hard to tell." It was a pair of sailors. They looked like the pair who'd brought him here, although he wasn't sure if they were the same two. "Wasn't long after he got the daily roster that he asked for him," one said, appraising Malvius with a grin. "Doesn't seem like a good sign. I'm guessing his troubles are only beginning."

The sailor who spoke to the guard took Malvius by the opposite arm. "Come on, troubles," the sailor said. The pair walked on either side. The second sailor never laid a hand on him. Malvius tried to be as compliant as possible, hurrying along in spite of his aches and pains.

The pair led him to the Megarian palace. Rather than taking him into the hall where audiences were granted, the sailors steered him to a minor set of stairs. Malvius had never noticed them or visited this part of the palace. On the second floor, they led him down a long, austere corridor. Malvius surmised it had once been the quarters for the palace guards. At the far end, one of the soldiers knocked on a door. "Come."

The sailor opened the door and the pair ushered him into a

surprisingly large series of chambers. The space was well lit and comfortably furnished. The near side was set up as a study, dominated by a table strewn with maps and parchments. Behind the table were shelves filled with bound books. A man sat beside the table, but his chair faced away, toward a window to the palace's courtyard. His cropped gray head was bent, focused on reading. Malvius scanned the space. The adjoining chamber had a simple cot for a bed, a wardrobe, and a bench strewn with the gear and garb of a Tiberian officer. There was an open-arched doorway beyond, also lamp-lit. Another bedchamber? He couldn't tell.

The guards stood silently at Malvius's shoulders. They were patient, respectful. The officer eventually rolled up the scroll he was reading and set it aside. He drew a deep breath, slowly stood, and finally turned.

Malvius gasped aloud. "You?"

One of the guards cuffed his head. "Quiet. Speak only when the general bids you."

Malvius kept gawping as he rubbed his stinging ear. He hadn't seen the man in years—not since he'd been garrisoned in Thrakius and courting his sister Ligaia. But there could be no mistaking him. This was none other than Vernius Stallicus, general of the mobile reserve, the man Vahldan had supposedly killed.

"Well, well. So it's true. Malvius of Thrakius." A grim smile spread across Vernius's face. "I've been waiting a long time for this."

CAPTIVE ATTENTION

"Thrakius has impressive walls, an enclosed harbor, and a history of being nigh unconquerable. Despite those truths, actually maintaining the defense of a city of its size against a besieging foe is no simple matter. The mobile reserve devoted few resources to the eastern half of their encirclement; rightfully so, as the east gate is hardly an efficient point of attack or a viable route for mass escape. Still, a Gottari force was required to defend the east gate, just as the north and west gates required manning day and night. In addition, a squad was needed to guard the seagates and an experienced, mostly-Hellainic crew to man the machinery that operated them. And let us not forget the necessary routine patrols of the wall's entire perimeter.

Complicating the issue, the Amalus occupiers had always been all but besieged within the city itself. The majority of Gottari lived inside the palace keep walls, either in the palace itself or the barracks buildings on the grounds. The armory compound, on the city's lower east side, was manned by mostly young and bachelor bannermen. Only a few score of the lesser Rekkrs with large families lived in the commandeered merchant houses on the city's hillcrest, just west of the fountain square.

Commanding this disjointed force into a cohesive defense on a day-to-day basis was not my father's forte. Vahldan had long since ceded such routine chores to his close kin. With Herodes's death and Belgar's return to Dania to attend his ill wife after the Battle of Orithya, the tasks of daily operational command fell to Arnegern, perhaps his most competent captain. Alas, it was a burden that proved cumbrous for one man, however competent."—Brin Bright Eyes, Saga of Dania

VAHLDAN RELUCTANTLY APPROACHED Druzana to mount. He grimaced, lifted a foot to the stirrup, and lunged, heaving his leg over and landing in the saddle with a groan. He settled in, waiting for the searing pain to fade. He wiped away the tears the effort provoked and turned to find Arnegern mounted and waiting, looking concerned and impatient in equal measure. He nudged the mare to walk out onto the path from the stables to the palace keep gate. He shielded his eyes to look back up at the palace. It was never difficult to spot her, with that mop of auburn hair and standing on the only terrace overhung with greenery, basking in the winter sunlight.

Elan waved. He returned it then shrugged, pointing to Arnegern. She shook her head and went back inside. He refused to admit it to her, but she was probably right. He should at least show himself. After all, the Gottari were at war and he was their war leader. Not to mention their king. He was hale and whole. Well, for the most part. At least he could play the role well enough to appear that way. Hopefully it would help to settle the city's nerves.

Arnegern followed until they cleared the archway leading from the palace keep out onto the fountain square. He circled wide of the statue, looming over the fountain and the city. He tried to resist, but then gave in and looked. As usual, the stone version of Malvius's ancestor glowered in judgement.

"Remind me again why you wouldn't let me tear down that bedamned statue," he said to Arnegern. "That and this gnarly old tree." He nodded to square's the only massive tree, still shedding its leaves, befouling the fountain's basin.

"You decided to avoid disrespecting the Hellains of the city when I reminded you that these are two symbols of their heritage. Symbols that preexisted imperial rule." Vahldan shot him a look. "My king," he added.

"How benevolent of me," he dryly intoned.

Arnegern hid a righteous grin and trotted into a slight lead, guiding him toward the lane to the west gate. His wise first captain had inquired about bringing guards along, but Vahldan had made his irritation clear and Arnegern had dropped it. More than ever, they were all in this together—Gottari and Hellain—prisoners in their own city. Vahldan refused to be guarded from his fellow prisoners.

It was a brisk but otherwise fine winter day. The dusting of snow that had fallen overnight was melting off of the cobbles and the steeper tiled roofs in the sunshine. As they proceeded west the lane narrowed and they rode into cold shadows. A loud, crashing thump came from ahead, echoing between the buildings lining the lane. Vahldan flinched but Arnegern didn't react. Shouting followed. The west gate came into view as well as a crowd bustling with activity in the broadening corridor leading to the gatehouse. Rekkrs from atop the wall were calling down to men on the ground. Those below were loading large stones into a sling that was attached to a winch on top of the wall.

"Make way for the king!" Arnegern cried as their mounts waded into the crowd.

A team of horses blocked their passage. Arnegern led him to the mouth of an adjacent alley, so they could watch without dismounting. Amalus soldiers whipped the poor team, urging them to tug a massive chain attached to their yolk. The team didn't budge. Vahldan traced the chain to find it fastened to a stone lintel over the doorway to the large house adjacent to the gatehouse. Vahldan remembered the place. It was a shambles compared to its former grandeur. The columned portico had already been torn away, as had the terraces from the upper floors. The crowd watching appeared to be mostly made up of Hellains. Sullen Hellains. Many of them redirected their moody glares onto him.

"Tell me—if we wouldn't tear their statue down, why are we tearing this house down?" Vahldan asked.

"For stone," Arnegern said. Vahldan gave him a questioning look. "For the slings, my king. Ammunition is in short supply these days."

"Why this house?"

"Proximity, mostly. The roof had already been severely damaged by enemy fire. We relocated the old couple who lived here. The husband was the former gatekeeper, appointed by the anax. Their children are grown and living elsewhere."

"So, we just seized their home?"

Arnegern raised a brow. "We seized the entire city, my king, remember?"

Vahldan frowned. Gods, was this a necessary part of the glory he'd sought for his people? Was this what his father had envisioned? "Then tell me this, Cousin. Why are we flinging so much stone? Didn't you say the Tiberians were fairly well settled into siege lines? That they seemed content to wait us out?"

"Fairly well settled is perhaps a misleading summary. Each night they move their catapults a bit closer to each gate. Each morning, by the day's first light, they take a few shots at the gate. I suppose it's just to see if they get lucky. In turn, we fire from our higher position to force them to back off. It's a bit of a tiresome routine. But, as you know, the mobile reserve are stubborn bastards. At this point a tiresome routine feels preferable to a full assault."

Vahldan scanned the faces of the locals, most glowering like the statue that symbolized their heritage. All of them looking miserable. It was one thing for him to be doomed. He could even come to terms with having those who willingly followed him risking their lives for a cause. But what of these poor souls? Did they deserve what he'd wrought? "If the house belonged to only one old couple, why have so many turned up to watch?"

"Oh, they're not here for that," Arnegern replied. "They're here for the loaves wagon." His cousin turned in the saddle to peer up the avenue. "Which should be arriving soon. They just pass the time by jeering us. It seems to provide a nice outlet for them. Which beats insurrection." Vahldan shot him a look. "Don't worry. Once the wagon comes, they tend to disperse quickly."

"The loaves wagon? This is a regular thing?"

Arnegern gave him a side glance, struggling to not look pained. "Aye, my king. Very regular—as it must be. We supply the city's bakers with grain and in turn each distributes the loaves they produce to their neighborhood. Hunger is as big a foe as those besieging soldiers."

"How long has this been going on?"

Arnegern didn't bother trying not to look pained anymore. "Since the siege began."

"Who's paying the bakers?"

That one produced a near eye-roll. "We are, my king, of course. It's a siege, remember. No food coming or going. Your subjects must be fed. Trapped people tend to be troublesome. But hungry trapped people often become outright dangerous. It's why I keep warning you that the grain stores are growing dangerously low."

He vaguely recalled being warned, but... "What about all of that grain in the catacombs?"

Arnegern nodded as one would to a child. "Yes, the stores. They're getting low."

It stunned him. "That massive stockpile? It's almost gone? Already?" He'd only been down to see the stores once. They'd seemed so vast. Like they'd never run out.

"It's why I advised you to allow Malvius to run the blockade when he offered. And why I bid you to have him devote most of his hold to grain."

"Well, I did do that much," he said, hoping he'd put enough

emphasis on it. Malvius tended to hear what he wanted to hear. And there'd been a longer discussion about some special ales, wines, and foods. After all, he needed to keep his army's morale from sagging. "I'm sure he'll come through for us." Sure, hopeful—there wasn't that big of a difference between them.

Arnegern scowled. "Ask me, even if Malvius never even tries to come back, it will be for the best. At least we'd be rid of the shifty bastard." Everyone in the palace had been grumbling and rumor-mongering over Malvius since Amaga's foreboding assertions the night he and Elan had returned from the pass. He had trouble himself, deciding how he felt about his so-called friend and his first qeins' wild allegations. It wasn't that he doubted Amaga's spooky connection to the spiritual so much as that he habitually suspected her motives. He felt like he had to hope for the best in regard to an offer from Malvius that felt like an attempt to prove his loyalty and worth. But he certainly wasn't going to argue with Arnegern's sentiment.

They sat watching as a huge chunk of stone from the old couple's former home was being strapped to the winch to be raised and loaded in a catapult. A stone which would be flung at invading soldiers that the poor couple might actually consider a liberating army. Vahldan scanned the grim, angry faces of the denizens of the last remaining city of his fleeting empire as they waited for bread they needed because commerce had been halted. Many of them continued to glare at him.

Never before had Vahldan been so able to imagine how the city's original inhabitants must feel as he did in that moment. His face grew hot. Damn, he had caused some major tumult. All of these years he'd seen it all through his own distorting prism. It wasn't just that he'd thought only of himself, though selfishness had been central to his actions. He'd actually convinced himself that he was the liberator, freeing this city from the corrupt. He'd never even bothered to try to see it from these humble folks' eyes. Eyes that now looked so hollow.

Vahldan spotted a little girl clutching an old woman's hand—probably her grandmother. She was about Brin's age. The girl's face was alarmingly gaunt. But her eyes! Gods, what did he see in them that haunted him so? Suddenly, he knew. An image of himself, at her age, appeared in his mind's eye. His family had been on the run, fleeing from Desdrusan's thugs—always fleeing—all along the fringes of Dania. Eldavar had been so small and Vahldan had been bidden to watch over his little brother, to help him keep up. Ever had he felt Eldavar's eyes on him. And in them he'd seen the terror reflected from his own. The memory of what had come of that seemingly endless terror caused the ugliness to stir, deep in his belly.

He saw that same grim and endless terror in this little girl's eyes. What would it wreak?

It was why the mining compound had meant so much. Safety. Reassurance that all had been well, that the love of their parents had actually provided sustenance, nourishing their souls and psyches. It was why the Spali attack had been so shocking, so devastating.

Freya's grace, it was an endless cycle. One that he was perpetuating.

Arnegern brightened his tone. "Well, this will take some time. Shall we ride to the docks next, my king?" Unbidden, Druzana began to follow Arnegern's horse. "In any case, we'll likely run out of time before we run out of food," his captain quipped. Vahldan twisted for a last look at the girl. She was so thin! A sharp pain shot through him from his side wound. Her haunting eyes narrowed, and in them he saw the resentment terror brings. He turned away.

Arnegern reined back toward the fountain square through the glowering crowd.

He might have awoken from his own delusions, but what he'd learned along the way was still real. "Malvius won't run," he said. "He'll bring the grain."

"How can you be so sure?" Arnegern asked.

"Without us, he'd have no fleet, no warehouses, no wealth. He knows he owes it all to us." Arnegern nodded but didn't seem convinced. Vahldan found that he wasn't, either. From a certain angle, Amaga's accusations did not sound so outrageous. They'd also killed the man's father. And his sister, come to think of it. Nine realms, he lived in Malvius's family home.

The resentment was all but assured. Still... "Even if Malvius forgets what he owes us, he knows how much trouble he'll be in if the imperials ever get their hands on him." Yes, Malvius could be relied upon to act in his own best interests. Yes, the lessons were still real. And he needed them now as never before.

BRIN SLIPPED from the table while Despoina gathered her things to leave. Hesiod had been gone all afternoon. She suspected he'd gone to attend to her mother. Uncle Urias might still be up on the north wall and before it got dark she wanted to go and see what progress the Tiberians had made out there during the day. Each day the foe's numbers grew, the forest receded, the lines grew more entrenched, and any chance of an escape to Dania seemed all the more impossible.

She tiptoed though the entryway, grabbing her woolen cloak and quietly working the door latch. She heard the tutor say something, obviously not realizing no one was there to answer. Brin held her breath, backed into the corridor, and silently pulled the door closed behind her. The latch softly clicked. She sighed in relief, turned, and gasped. A large male form loomed in the dim torchlight, completely blocking her in the doorway.

"Sorry, I didn't mean to startle you." The strange thing was that her father actually did sound sorry, a sentiment she didn't genuinely sense from him often.

Brin shrugged and nodded at the same time. "Mother isn't here. I think she's upstairs."

"I came looking for you," he said. Which was even stranger.

"Me? Why?" she squeaked, sounding like a toddler caught stealing a tart.

King Vahldan's mood grew serious. He drew a deep breath and sighed it out. She braced herself. "Well, I saw some things today. Out in the city. What I saw made me think. And remember. What I remembered made me realize that I should speak to you. Would you mind?"

These were among the strangest things she'd ever heard from him—mainly because he was saying them to her. She opened her mouth but no words came. Instead, she shrugged.

"We could do it another time," he said, sounding apologetic again.

"Oh, no." She glanced back at the door, afraid Despoina would come out and scold her in front of him. Not that she cared what he might think of that. Well, not so much. It was more that her tutor's intrusion might cause this strange meeting to come to an end. She wasn't sure how she felt about it, but it made her insides all bubbly, like the water that shot out of the spigot down in the baths. Which helped to ease her apprehension, leaving only her growing curiosity.

She glanced at the door again. "I was just going to check on Uncle Urias. Down on the north wall. Want to come?"

Her father actually smiled. "Lead on," he said. He seemed surprised when she led him to the servants' stairwell but he followed without saying anything. When she exited through the ground floor door to the gardens, he looked back at the door and scanned his surroundings. Brin marveled that he didn't seem to recognize one of her most-used routes. It was like they lived in two different homes. She supposed it was sort of true.

She started down the path that led to the small gate out onto the martialing courtyard, pretending that she didn't notice that he didn't seem to know the way. The path got wider and he fell in beside her. "So, what did you want to talk to me about?" Talking while walking was something that felt perfectly natural to her. She realized that was Urias's doing.

"Well, mainly I wanted to ask you how you're feeling."

"How I'm feeling?" Gods, where would she begin? "I'm well," she offered.

"Oh. That's good. But I meant, you know, about the war. The siege. How you're feeling about things like that."

Oh no. Did he want her approval? "Does it matter?" She realized how snappish it sounded. She glanced to find him looking stung. "I mean, I'm a kid. There's nothing I can do about it. And my tutor says I'm too young to grasp all of the layers to a conflict like this. So what does it matter?"

"Fair enough. Although I'm not sure I agree with your tutor." She glanced again. It was so odd. He didn't look cross. He seemed like he wanted something from her but couldn't figure out how to get it. The weirdest part was, he seemed to actually care. About her! Whatever he wanted, he seemed to know he couldn't just fire off one of his commands, like he usually did.

They arrived at the small gate and he stopped and turned to her. "It's scary, though, right?"

"What, the war?" He nodded. She studied him for a moment. "Are *you* scared?"

Her father huffed a laugh, sounding just like her mother. "So scared." The way he said it made him seem younger, almost like a fellow child.

Brin couldn't help but smile. She gave him one of Elan's firm, single nods. "Good. Uncle Urias says that the match that doesn't scare you is the one you're most likely to lose."

"I've known your uncle for a very long time," he began. "But I don't think I'll ever know him well enough to stop being surprised by his wisdom."

She nodded again. It made her chest warm. Like she was proud of Urias, even though she had nothing to do with how wise he was. They passed through the gate and started across the martialing courtyard toward the stairs to the wall walk.

"Which reminds me," he said. "I hear Urias has had you doing some sparring. Even matching you with older, more experienced boys."

Uh oh. "Not for a while now. Mother doesn't like it, so we stopped sparring."

Vahldan seemed to already know it. "But when you *were* sparring, did the boys ever taunt you or try to bait you? You know, to get your blood up?"

She gave him one of her mother's crooked smiles. "Have you *met* the Amalus boys?" Her father slowed and looked at her, seeming unsure how to counter the stroke, so she finished the point. "Of course they did. Every time. It's who they are."

They got to the bottom of the stairs and she took the first step before she realized he'd stopped again. Seemed he wasn't coming up. She looked to the top. Uncle Urias was in sight, talking to a group of Rekkrs. Her uncle spotted them and gave her one of his puzzled-but-amused expressions. She waved and he waved back and resumed his conversation.

She was closer to her father's face now. She'd never realized how handsome he was. Worn, but handsome. He put his hands on her shoulders and looked at her really hard. "When the boys did that— taunted and baited you—how did it make you feel?" She shrugged. "I mean, it made you angry, right?"

"Of course. But I learned that it was best not to let them know it. Whether I won or lost, if I kept them from thinking they got to me, it made the next round easier. And the next. Trying to keep them from knowing helped me to focus. Uncle Urias made me realize that the better I focus, the more I win. Knowing all of that kept all of their nonsense from getting to me."

His eyes grew wide but he didn't look away. "Did you ever get flustered or overwhelmed or feel out of control? Did things ever get blurry or like your head's under water?"

He was really intense. She sensed his veiled fear, but it wasn't like an opponent's fear. She sensed that he was telling her something about himself—something that he actually feared he'd passed along to her. The fact that he was afraid made it clear that he was concerned for her. It made her chest warm again. And it made her want to reassure him. "No," she said. "Never. I mean, I get angry, and Uncle Urias says I'm not as good when I'm rattled. I don't like that. I like to win. Or at least give myself the best chance. So I just... set it aside."

Her father pressed his lips tight and nodded. "That's..." He swallowed. "Really good."

She'd never seen him like this. She could almost swear that he looked like he was on the verge of tears. It made her feel humble. And a little ashamed. Not *for* him. It shamed her that she had never imagined him having such feelings. It shocked her that he was having them over her, but she couldn't deny that it made her happy. So happy she felt like she might cry. That wouldn't do. Not with all of this being so fresh. She shook it off. And yet, once again, she felt a strong impulse to reassure him. "I swear it's true. Never." She smiled. "One less thing to worry about."

Vahldan smiled back and nodded, gathering himself. He actually bent so they were nose to nose. She'd never seen him this close. His eyes! It was like she'd never seen the person inside them before. She actually saw the kindness in there, almost like Urias's eyes. "I'm not as wise as your uncle," he said, "but can I give you some advice?" She nodded. "I can tell you that you will keep getting angry. Really angry. Especially when things get scary, like they are now. You'll find someone to blame and you'll put your anger on them. It's natural. We all do it. When it happens, you've got to remember how you handled it when you were sparring and set it aside. Trust me, it won't always be easy. But holding onto it, well, it'll cost you too much. Understood?"

She'd heard this last part from Urias. Her father had said it like the Skolani queen and princess did. "Understood," she barked in reply, chin high, as warrior-like as she could manage.

He stood straight but kept his hands on her shoulders. "Oh, and please remember this: No matter what they say about your mother and me, no matter how you feel about us, even if we're no longer there with you, you have nothing to prove. To anyone. Not us, not anyone. Even if what you think you need to prove is that you're different than us. You don't owe that to anyone. Not even yourself. You're your own person, now and till your last day."

Still drinking it in, she nodded. "All right," she said.

Looking awkward, her father gave her shoulders a squeeze. "I can see that your great-grandmother was right. You're going to be the best of us, Brin Bright Eyes." He chuckled and muttered what sounded like, "Load star indeed." She had no idea what that might mean.

Vahldan looked up the stairs and waved to get her uncle's attention. When he had it, he laid his open hand on his chest and bowed his head. As he looked back up, he raised his open palm to Urias like it was some sort of salute. Urias raised his the same way and bowed his head.

Her father looked really young again when he turned back to her. "Thank you, Daughter. You've eased my mind." He really did seem grateful. She realized that she was too. Without waiting for a reply, he turned and headed back to the palace keep.

Brin almost felt dizzy as she ran up the stairs. Urias reached to offer her a warrior's shake, grasping forearms. "What was *that*?" he asked her.

Brin released her uncle and turned to see her father's broad frame filling the keep's smallest gate before he disappeared from view. "That... was really something."

Malvius dropped to his stinging knees and bowed his head. "I have long looked forward to meeting you as well, Lord General."

He rose up to find Vernius smiling. "You have, eh?"

"Oh, yes. Long have I looked to the day when I could serve you in bringing the invader Vahldan to justice."

Vernius sat, looking bemused. The meeting seemed to be going well. "For the gods' sake, stand up, man." Or not.

"Thank you, Lord General," Malvius said and struggled to his feet.

"I admit you've made me curious, Malvius. If you've long wanted to serve us, what has kept you from it?"

Malvius blinked. "Lord General, I have only just escaped the clutches of our foe—a man who plundered my city and killed my family. As soon as I was able, I came right to you."

Vernius barked a lone laugh. "You came right to me, eh? Did you not also send your ship on to Anaissa, the port of dispute with our Sassanadi foe? A certain dah with whom I gather you've had previous transactions? Transactions which I seriously doubt benefited the empire in any way. Indeed, no few report to the contrary. Come now, Malvius. I suspect you're being modest about all that you've been up to besides coming to me."

"I, well, yes, it's true. But please understand that I have ever labored in the service of the empire from behind the scenes, unbeknownst to our shared foe. Trust that I have been playing out a lengthy deception. One which I hope to continue to see through. A deception that will soon serve the fruition of our shared goals. With your permission, of course. There is so much I have to offer, Lord General."

"Ah, so now I am to trust you." Vernius reached for the scroll he'd been reading and unfurled it again. "I was just going over what's been recorded of your efforts, as you say, *from behind the scenes*. Let us review, shall we?"

"Review?" Malvius was suddenly more terrified than he'd been back in the cell.

"Yes, from the beginning. Perhaps we could start with your... *association* with Vahldan of the Gottari tribe. Let's see." Vernius ran a finger down the scroll. "Seems your first ties formed during the many years Vahldan and a gang of mercenaries were in your employ —ostensibly as guardsmen, but let's face it, Malvius: They were hired thugs. You paid them to intimidate and to coerce. Even to spill blood, when necessary."

"I realize how that must sound to you, General, but those were lawless days. And more importantly, that was before Vahldan betrayed me." Malvius could feel his pulse racing.

Vernius held the finger up. "Ah, his betrayal. I presume you refer to the sacking of Thrakius." The general scanned his document again. "Let's see… Here it is. Afterward, when the first Tiberian delegation arrived, it was duly noted by the new harbormaster that one Malvius, son of Decebius, had taken over operation of the vast majority of shipping services and the warehousing in the city, including those of the fallen anax." Vernius looked up from his reading. "Meaning you gained this new status due to the murder of your father and sister. How fortunate. All of this with the sanction of the barbarian who'd declared himself the new magister. Of course that was before he named himself a king, but I don't want to get ahead of our little tale."

"Where was I to go? I would've been ruined had I fled the city." He was getting dizzy.

"So, self-preservation. I see. All right. You merely sought to preserve your fortune. Who wouldn't? Still, in fact, you have enhanced it by all accounts, have you not? More mere happenstance?" Vernius smiled as if they were discussing how pleasant the weather had been.

"I may have done well, yes. But if you look at the circumstances, you'll see that—"

"I'll see what? That betrayal is not always so bad as it may seem? That I should always be ready to reap opportunity, even when it's wrought through bloodletting?"

"No, I'm begging you. You must believe me. I was always striving to—"

"Simmer down. We'll get to what your striving has led to." Vernius used his finger to scan the parchment again. "Ah, here we are. After your betrayer married and named himself a king, it seems the fleet of Malvius of Thrakius served to deliver the Gottari barbarian's army to Bafrana." Vernius lowered the scroll and shook his head. "I suppose it's needless to say, some pretty damning things happened in the insurrection that followed. Not least of which was the murder of one Legatus Avitus."

Malvius sat up straighter. "I had nothing to do with that murder!"

Vernius's gaze hardened. "So your answer is yes, you did deliver your so-called betrayer's army to Bafrana. Whereupon they overthrew the reigning monarch—a man loyal to the empire—to install the current insurgent government controlled by a pirate and his allies."

"This is true, but..." Malvius tried to swallow. Gods, his mouth was dry.

"But what?" Vernius spat.

"Please, you must understand. I had to do a few things. Things I wish I had not needed to do. As I said, I have been attempting a lengthy deception."

"A deception that included transporting the attacking army for their seizure of Megaria?"

"I—I had no choice. There was a conspiracy against me. My rival, Isidros, he—"

Vernius slapped a hand on the table. "Jupiter's balls, Malvius! I sincerely hope you made an ample profit through this period. I mean, with the Straits in the hands of those you were supposedly deceiving, you controlled virtually all of the trading in the entire Pontean—including the steady flow of black-market goods into imperial markets from the eastern trade routes. All while you played out this *lengthy deception.*"

Malvius's chin dropped. He felt exhausted. "Please. I only did what I had to in order to keep Vahldan believing in me. I wish to now utilize a long and carefully built advantage. I came here to help, I swear it."

"I see," Vernius said more mildly. "Tell me, did keeping Vahldan believing in you really require your delivery of his daughter to Anaissa? Was it necessary to arrange an audience for her with the dah? I know we've already mentioned your role in the sack of Megaria, but we certainly shouldn't skip over the part where Vahldan's new ally—secured by you—seized Thrakius from your own sister, a sister who was loyal to the empire and sought to hold her city until imperial troops could arrive."

How in the gods' names did he know so much? "There is much that you cannot know about what went on with my poor sister, Lord General. She too had been deceived. Ligaia was being manipulated by a rival of mine."

Vernius shook his head. "Fear not, Malvius. We know all about your old friend Isidros. He can be a slippery fellow, all right. I only wonder: Should I trust you over him? I mean, Isidros claims to have not only aided the sister you betrayed, but to have married her."

Malvius's head snapped up. "Married her?" Could Ligaia really have gone through with it?

"This is his claim. Can you refute it?"

"No," Malvius whispered. "I mean, I wish I had proof. But it can't be. Ligaia made some poor choices, but she wouldn't..."

"Marry in order to save her city, her people?"

He shook his head. "Ligaia knows Isidros is a snake. She'd see through him."

"Ah. So you acknowledge deduction, the study of character and motive. Yet here you stand, expecting me to believe your intentions have been true all along. That you still wish to make this right. Funny, but Isidros has made very similar claims. And yet his association with the barbarian king seems positively tame by comparison."

Malvius hung his head again, his mind reeling. Had he really come all this way only to be unable to take the final step? "Please, Lord General. I beg you to listen. You cannot know what you're up against—how fragile it's all been for me to stay in Vahldan's good graces. I have put myself and my men in grave danger. For years! This

I did so that I could come to you now, at this vital moment, to see to his downfall. I wish to lessen the loss of imperial lives."

Vernius's fist hit the table so hard that Malvius felt the thud in his chest. "Loss of lives? Now that I have him trapped? Gods, man, do you have the slightest guess how many men I lost at Nicomedya? At Orithya?"

Malvius shrank back a step. One of the guards nudged him to stay in place; he'd almost forgotten they were there. "I am truly sorry about the loss of lives thus far. But please, you must know how dangerous this might still be. I speak of staggering loss. Loss of civilian life, inside my city and elsewhere. Damage and bloodshed that can be avoided. Please hear me out. I know where all of the Gottari are housed. I can show you ways to bring men inside. I know how one or more of the gates can be taken and how to keep the thug's forces divided and leaderless in a swift strike."

Vernius smiled mirthlessly and settled back into his chair. "Oh, you're going to have to do much better than that, Malvius. I already know how I could send my men in. Just as I know where the Gottari are housed. You had better do *a whole lot* better. Or you're going to get a whole lot more familiar with that cell. I presume you've had a chance to get acquainted with your new living companions, have you not?"

Tears filled his eyes. No. He couldn't go back. After all he'd worked for—his plans, his men, his city, his reputation—he couldn't fail now. "You can't possibly know how much I hate Vahldan—how much I hate them all and long to rid my city of them."

Vernius harrumphed in laughter. "You speak of Thrakius as being *your* city."

"Of course it's my city. As it has ever been. As it was my father's before me. Thrakius is my home. Its people are my people."

Vernius rolled his eyes. "As Isidros considers Nicomedya his city, I suppose. You anax heirs are all the same. Coincidentally, His Eminence recently saw fit to reissue Isidros's trading charter for Nicomedya. Surely you've guessed that your fellow anax would lay claim to Thrakius's charter as well. And since you are complicit with the foe, it seems inevitable that Emperor Mycanius will—"

"No!" Malvius erupted. Vernius's glare smoldered. Malvius hung his head again, petulant. "Please, General. You cannot know how long I've planned not just for the Gottari's downfall, but for their utter destruction. You cannot know how dangerous they truly are. I did everything I did, over so many years, to ensure their demise. You must believe me when I say that Vahldan and his ilk—they may be some of the worst, but they are only the first."

He looked up, meeting Vernius's hard gaze. Though it seemed the man might finally be listening. "I swear," he went on, "what has happened has been the only way forward. They must be destroyed. The only way we could have gotten to this precipice is by the awful path which we have already trod. But things can and will get worse —much worse—if this is left unfinished. You can't know how carefully I sought to ensure that this never happens again. Please. I'll do anything to help you defeat and destroy them. Anything."

Malvius dropped his chin to his chest and slumped, utterly spent. After a long moment, Vernius called, "Well, Vernouthus, what do you think? What shall we do with him?"

"I do believe one thing." The familiar, youthful voice came from the dim recesses of the adjacent chamber. Malvius spun to face a boyish silhouette in the doorway.

"What's that?" Vernius asked.

"We can't possibly know just how much he hates Vahldan and the Gottari." The figure strode forward into the light. "I think it's the most honest thing I've ever heard from him."

"Ago?" Malvius whispered. "Is it really you?"

"Hello, Uncle."

His head reeled. "I—I've been so worried."

Ago gave a little laugh. "Don't bother, Cap. I know you've had a lot on your mind."

Malvius glanced back and forth from Vernius to his son. Yes, he was definitely Vernius's son. And Ago was certainly his nephew and

Ligaia's son—nimble and cunning. He'd actually forgotten how connected he and the general were. It should count for something. "This is perfect, Lord General. Of course I now see how you know so much about getting in and about how the Gottari are arrayed inside the city. It's wonderful."

Vernius raised his brows. "Oh? How so?"

"Why, Agoraki, or rather, Vernouthus, can show your best team to the caves that lead inside. And then the boy can stay back where it's safe, of course. But I can take over from there. I can show them to the gates and direct your officers to swiftly divide the Gottari force within. We'll make a wonderful team." Malvius rubbed his hands together.

Vernius's little smile became a wicked grin. "Oh no. That's not going to happen. None of my men are going to risk their lives to open your city. Nor is my son. No, if you want even a sniff at a chance to redeem yourself, to avoid going back to spend the rest of your days in a cell, you're going to have to do much better than that."

Malvius looked back and forth between them. The resemblance really was strong, especially with both of them grinning. "How... How will we open the city, then?"

Vernius reclined and laced his fingers on his chest. "*We* have a better idea. If you really wish to ever have the chance to call it your city again, *you* are going to open it."

Vahldan followed Arnegern and the guard to the dungeon door. The guard put the key into the lock and the massive door swung open with a screech. The space was dim and reeked. The stone of the cell was massive and close—not just confinement but oppression, as if it were devised to smother the last embers of the human spirit. He'd never imagined a dungeon cell as a part of his doom and he was glad for it. Facing it would be much more difficult. As dark as it was, there was a high stone chute emitting a soft glow of natural light.

Arnegern's lamp revealed the cell's lone prisoner sitting on the only bench, which likely also served as a bunk. He sat leaning against the adjacent wall, knees drawn up and hugging himself against the damp chill, face angled to the chute like a winter sprout seeking the sunlight. He didn't even glance at the intrusion.

"This is the only officer we took?" Vahldan asked, speaking Gottari.

"As near as we can tell," Arnegern replied in the same tongue. "He never has confirmed it. I'd find a more suitable place to lock the damn fool up if he'd speak." He raised his lamp, gazing around the dreadful little space. "Still, we gave him one of the nicest cells down here, believe it or not."

Vahldan studied the profile and stretched back his memory. The day and its monumental events were fuzzy. After all, he'd been imbued. And yet, his recollection of the imperial officers and the rector came clear, sitting ahorse behind the phalanx, baiting him. He'd been so focused on getting to them. "I think you're right. It's him. Not such a damn fool, after all. Probably imagining what we'll do to him if we realize who he is and what he's done to us."

Arnegern snorted. "That might do it."

"You are an officer?" Vahldan asked, speaking Hellainic for the first time. The man didn't move, let alone speak. "I ask only because we wish to treat you accordingly." Still nothing. "There are still ways you can be of service to your people, even in captivity. I would like to explore them with you." The man blinked and sighed but still didn't turn to them. Vahldan switched back to Gottari. "Maybe he is a damn fool." He turned to leave.

"The damn fool understands much." The Gottari was formal and accented but clear and confident. Vahldan turned back to find the man sitting with his feet on the floor, facing them, squinting against the lamplight. "What he cannot understand is how speaking with murderous raiders might help his people."

Vahldan hid a smile. "So it seems it's true, is it not, Captain Lauterus Pontus?"

The Tiberian tilted his head, curious. "What's true?"

Face to face Vahldan saw it in him, both the classic Tiberian features—particularly the prominent nose—and the long limbs and light eyes of the Tutona. He switched back to Hellainic. "All of it. Every rumor I've heard about you. That your mother was Gottari—a slave freed by the noble son who loved her. How your father vouched for you when you were caught riding with Illyrican outlaws. I suppose that he also saw to it that you were accepted into the academy. How generous of Papa."

"Not all is true," Lauterus said in Gottari before switching back to Hellainic. "I did not attend the academy. My father had nothing to do with my rank. I earned it. The hard way."

Vahldan allowed himself a slight smile. "Tell me. What way is that?"

The Tiberian raised his chin. "Dedication. Loyalty. Brotherhood. Common sense. A grasp of other cultures and customs." Vahldan raised his brows. Lauterus switched back to Gottari. "Oh yes, including that of the Tutona."

"And yet it did not save your army in Orithya."

The Tiberian looked away, frowning. "The mobile reserve is not my army."

"Well parried! I suppose it explains why you were riding alone, seeking to warn their foolhardy equine unit that a trap was about to spring. Which would also explain why you're in here and not out there with them."

Lauterus raised a hard glare. "You still have not explained why in the gods' names I would ever aid you."

Vahldan glared back. "Because I know that this city is your home. And I would hate to see what happened to Megaria befall your home city."

Lauterus lowered his chin and fell silent. Vahldan waited. He saw it written upon the man—the death and sorrow in which he'd played a part, for which he felt responsible. Vahldan knew the burden all too well. Finally, he asked, "What would you have of me?"

Vahldan turned to Arnegern and held out his hand for the lamp. "Give us a moment, Brother." He said it as prosaically as possible but he sensed his old friend's surprise. And perhaps that he felt stung. Still, Arnegern did as he was bidden and closed the cell door behind him.

He gestured to the far end of the bench. "May I?"

Lauterus sneered. "As you will, *my lord.*"

It was sarcastic and perhaps unwise, but Vahldan couldn't really blame him. He didn't dare ask what had become of his mother in the seizing of the city. Right now, he needed information. He sat with a sigh and set the lamp between them. "What I seek is to minimize unnecessary injury and death in what comes. Particularly for Thrakian civilians and for our own women and children. They followed me here, but they don't deserve what I have brought upon them."

Lauterus was looking at him now. He thought he sensed some sympathy. He decided to take it a bit further. "I have seen, all too clearly, how war perpetuates itself through the very hatred it spawns. Even from one generation to the next. I wish to do all I can to bring an end to the cycle."

Lauterus had a pensive expression. Vahldan waited. This couldn't be forced and the man was hard to read. "You do know how much they respect you, do you not?"

"Who?"

"The mobile reserve, of course." Lauterus must have sensed his surprise. "Oh, don't get me wrong. They hate you. All of you. They won't hesitate to kill you all. For that is what they do best and it is what they have been bidden to do. But they respect the Gottari, as much as any foe they have ever faced." Lauterus actually smiled. "Particularly your Hippomache, of course."

"Of course." Vahldan mirrored the smile. "As do those of us who strive beside her."

Lauterus looked away and grew serious again. "What you have achieved with them—well, to the men of the mobile reserve, it's as close to a shared form of honor as is possible. However this war reflects on you to the rest of humanity, you have shown these elite, merciless killers that you are their equal." The Tiberian met his gaze again. He spoke more softly and in Gottari. "It is why you cannot surrender. Nor would it bode well for you to try to flee. Particularly without your women and children. That would be a terrible mistake."

"I understand," Vahldan said in Hellainic.

"In order to preserve what you have earned, you must not only face them but face them well. It will be bloody—perhaps very bloody. But by doing so you might contain it among those for whom a bloody ending is foregone, thus sparing those for whom you now speak."

"And still, for them I have... *foreseen* slavery. As has a Skolani Dreamer." Lauterus studied him but did not seem taken aback. "This they also do not deserve, but I am beyond giving them anything resembling the lives they deserve. I now seek to provide them with, well, hope. Hope for their children, at least." The next step was risky, but it was one he felt he had to take. He switched back to Gottari and added, "Hope like your mother had."

Lauterus went very still. In the lamplight Vahldan saw his Tutona blood flushing his cheeks. He waited a moment, long enough to feel confident that no angry outburst was coming, then went on. "I understand there are better and worse forms of bondage in the empire. I speak of seeking for the better for my followers and their children, if that is possible."

Lauterus finally nodded. "You have heard of Federati?"

"Foreign fighters in the imperial militum?"

The Tiberian gave him a wry smile. "In this, too, there are better and worse forms. In my early days as an officer, I served as a translator and was often sent out as a liaison between leadership and Teutonic Federati. I have heard many tales. I can tell you of Federati who serve in units made up only of their kinsmen—even of those who once opposed Tiberia. I think I can give you a few ideas on how these units came into being. Would this be to your liking?"

"It would," he said, not veiling his relief.

Once again, Lauterus raised his chin and met his eyes. "And in return?"

"How about your freedom?"

"Even should I return to my command and serve those who besiege you?"

Vahldan gave a lone laugh. "Depending on what you tell me, that just may turn out to be for the best."

THE PRICE OF HARD BARGAINS

"*Over the years, many have asked me how—in light of its toll —I could continue to believe in the prophecy of the Urrinan and live for so long in perpetual response to it. It is precisely because of the very dear price I paid that I continue to believe and live as I did then. For I cannot bear to believe that I paid for nothing or that vital change has not come of it. I live now as I always have, with the same mantra: It is as it shall be.*"—Brin Bright Eyes, *Saga of Dania*

VAHLDAN WOKE to a clamor coming from beyond the closed bedchamber door. He sat up in bed, sweat-soaked. Voices cried out in anger and there were thumps and clangs—clearly the sounds of battle raging. There was turmoil outside the palace, but also as close as the corridor, just beyond his residence door. Had the battle for Thrakius somehow begun without him?

He was alone. Where was Elan? Was he to face his doom without her after all? Nothing terrified him more.

There was a thump on the outer door. Vahldan held his side wound and climbed out of bed. He wore only a loose nightshirt. A louder thump was followed by a splintering crash. The residence door was broken. Boots thumped into the sitting chamber. Where was his armor? Even more importantly, where was his sword, Bairtah-Urrin, the futhark sword of the Amalus?

The bedchamber door was not barred. He scanned the chamber, looking for anything that could be used as a weapon. Too late; the latch clicked. Vahldan turned to face his fate.

In strode a tall Tiberian—an officer. Alone! The clamor beyond faded to a dull roar. The officer wore a fine crimson cloak and a colorful crested helm with cheek pieces that covered all but his bright, curious eyes. The officer led with his shield and entered. He then halted and stood spear-straight, just beyond arm's reach. His gear, posture, everything about him spoke of the Tiberian nobility. Vahldan knew—this was a member of the vaunted Equites.

The officer had a sword in his hand but it hung slack at his side. The weapon caught Vahldan's eye. It was no legionnaire's thrusting sword. This was a great broadsword, a weapon of the Tutona. Its familiarity called to him. Gods help him—the intruder held *his sword*. This elite Tiberian officer had possession of Bairtah-Urrin. No one but the blood of the Amalus kings of old should bear it. The gods would not abide this insult. Worse, the blade was red with gore— likely the blood of slain Gottari.

The officer stood transfixed. "This cannot be," the intruder said in accented Gottari.

Vahldan's eye locked onto a golden chain that held his cloak in place. Each end was a clasp fashioned into a snarling lion's head, their mouths gripping the cloth. That, too, was his.

The officer took a tentative step. "Is it really you?"

He raised his chin. "I am Vahldan, son of Angavar of the Amalus. Who are you?"

The Tiberian sheathed his sword and slowly reached up, grasping his helm and pulling it off. It revealed a young man with a head of short but bright red hair. His face—it was so familiar.

Eyes wide, the officer said, "Father? Is it really you?"

Vahldan backed away. "Who are you? What do you want?"

The intruder reached out his hand. "Father, it's me, Armesus."

The shock jarred him. "No. It cannot be. You... You are Tiberian. You are the enemy!"

The man who called himself Armesus smiled. "Yes, a general now. In command of the finest imperial army. I am as a brother to royalty. We have risen from within. It is just as you wished it. As it shall be."

"I wished this?"

"Of course! It is the way of Urrinan, the will of the goddess."

"Freya, please, help me," Vahldan prayed.

"Almost instantly, the handsome face of his grown son morphed and grew, replaced by the fierce apparition of the goddess, hair curling and twisting around her head. Her voice filled his head. ***"Thunder wakes when blades collide, The steed on which Urrinan rides!"***

"Tell me what it means," he pleaded.

Freya laughed. ***"The roles are set, Lion. The old and the new. As you sought. A blade for each. One for the wolf..."*** She drew and raised the Amalus futhark sword before her wild eyes, her grin filled with bloodlust. ***"And one for the lion!"*** She flung Bairtah-Urrin at him. Vahldan threw up his hands to block the oncoming blade.

In a flash, he found himself sitting in bed again, sweat-soaked and panting. And alone.

"A dream," Vahldan gasped. "It was a dream."

He was in Elan's bed. It was morning, silent and still. He sat back, catching his breath, and spotted it. There on the blanket near his feet lay Bairtah-Urrin, naked and gleaming.

VAHLDAN HAD to ask four people for directions before he found her. He left the north gate of the palace keep, insisting on going alone, much to the fret of the guards stationed there. He crossed the martialing courtyard and climbed the stairs to the wall-walk. A cluster of young bannermen sat talking near the catapults, while two actually walked the wall as sentinels. The sitters all leapt to their feet and stood straight, murmuring honorifics and apologies. He spotted Elan down the wall, bid the men to be at ease, and left them scrambling to appear diligent.

Elan was leaning on the parapet, gazing northward. Before he arrived and without turning to him, she said, "Seems they want to make sure we stay put."

Vahldan followed her gaze. The area beyond the gate was a plateau. It sloped down to the Tiberian lines but rose to rocky heights on either side. The foe's lines filled the entire base of the plateau, from one rocky rise to the other. They'd denuded the forest at the base of the pass to where the road rose steeply into the foothills. They'd used the felled timber as a bulwark, fortifying a trench they'd chiseled from one side of the plateau to the other. Even the flanking hillsides were stripped of shrubbery. Behind the foe's lines were rows of tents, and behind those were larger pavilions and unhitched wagons. The corral from which he and his guardians had stolen the horses had only grown.

"Looks that way," he said.

Elan turned to him. The rising sun lit her hair like a halo, yet her smile still shone brighter. Her eyes were sad but her tone was resolved. "As it shall be."

"As it shall be," he replied. She looked out again. "You're up and out early," he added.

"Didn't sleep much." He waited. "After what you told me—your meeting with her—I went to see her. I just wanted to look at her while she slept." Elan huffed a laugh. "She woke up almost immediately. Asked me what was wrong. I told her nothing was wrong, and I guess she believed me. She lay back down and was instantly asleep again." She turned to him. "I used to be able to do that. Every good Blade-Wielder can." She shook her head with a weary smile. "No longer. Guess there's little left of who I used to be."

"What else?" Vahldan knew there was something much larger here.

"I know what it is," Elan said without looking.

"It?"

"My destiny. I know what I must do. I've sensed it for a while now. I've been fighting it, but I…" She glanced at him. "I always wanted it to be at your side. But it's out there. It's her. She's too vital to it all. I have to stay with her, out there." She tilted her head northward. She shivered. "I'm afraid. For all of us."

Vahldan fully grasped it. He'd been fighting it, too. But he knew she was right. It all fit. Brin was the link. It was too vital to leave it to chance. "I'm afraid, too," he said softly. "But as I look back, I really don't know how we came to be so sure."

"Of what?"

"That you would share in my doom." Elan started to react, but he hurried on. "We were inseparable in those days, but… I betrayed you. I betrayed the gift of you. I surrendered to the ugliness. You could have kept me from it, but I cast you aside." She turned to him, brow furrowed—always ready to fight for him, always his guardian. "I made some hard bargains with the goddess," Vahldan said. "There's a price that I must pay. But not you."

"I chose you," she said softly but vehemently.

"But we both know where that choice now leads." He looked north, into the pass. "The Urrinan must split, to the old and the new. The sundered nation shall continue. It must. So…"

"So the link must survive," Elan finished. She gazed northward too. "And thrive."

"And thrive." He swallowed hard. "I don't know how I'll face it without you."

Elan surprised him by wrapping him in her arms. Gods, she was strong. "You won't have to," she whispered, her breath in his ear. "Not really. I'll be there. Just as you'll be with me."

Vahldan hugged her back. "And one day, we will be together again."

"As it was always meant to be," she confirmed. It felt like a pact. It was contrition, forgiveness, and acceptance. It was timeless, soul-deep love. It was the truest thing they had ever shared—the only thing that really mattered. Embracing it again, they could face their duty.

Their amazing daughter was the living embodiment of it. *She* was all that mattered.

HARMA CARRIED Armesus on her hip as she followed Mara back upstairs after dinner. Mara was carrying her own son up the stairs in spite of how round she'd become with her next child. So Harma made a point of carrying her son up, too, even though she preferred to have Apontia carry him. She doubted she'd ever get used to all of these stairs.

Mara gained several steps on her, the show-off. As they came around to Harma's floor, a voice called down from above. "Vahldan? Come quick!"

It was her husband's Skolani bitch. The woman never came to dinner. Elan seemed to hate everyone in the palace, save one. She'd obviously won Vahldan's favor. For the moment, anyway; Harma, of all people, knew how fickle the man could be. She supposed Elan knew it, too. Which would explain the tight grip she'd been keeping on him—practically holding him hostage in her chambers.

"Come quickly, *my king*," Harma said, correcting her.

"The king is dawdling," Mara called up. "I'm sure he'll be on his way soon."

"Send a runner for him," Elan replied. "Tell him there's a ship!"

A ship. Malvius! Harma felt like her innards had turned to liquid, swashing at the top of her chest. She suddenly could hardly bear the weight of her growing boy. She stood calming her breath, letting her innards settle, regaining her strength. Thank Freya. He'd come back for her.

Just as she reached the landing to her floor, Vahldan came running up the stairs with Arnegern close behind. The king smiled at her. "Come and see," he said, beckoning Harma as he passed. "Bring my son."

Thank Freya. He'd included her. That he'd seen her carrying their son was a bonus. Harma tipped her head for Apontia to follow and headed up. Unfortunately, handing the squirming babe off to her handmaid now was out of the question.

She arrived on the floor of Elan's residence. The woman's door was open. Harma went in. A cold breeze pulled her attention to the open terrace doors. Vahldan, Elan, Arnegern, and Mara all stood at the parapet, gazing out. Harma signaled for Apontia to wait at the entryway.

Harma took her time checking out her surroundings. The entry chamber was much larger than hers. Elan had some fine furnishings as well. How had she gotten all of these potted plants up here? How did she rate, when Harma was actually the mother of Vahldan's son?

Harma looked over the items on the sideboard. There were several unwashed cups and a half-eaten tray. What a slob. And wasteful, too—there wasn't enough food to be picky. Where was that manservant of hers? She drifted to the bedchamber door and leaned to look in. The bed was unmade. No surprise there. The lazy bitch. She moved on, heading for the terrace. She stopped short, startled.

Elan's child was there, standing perfectly still, staring. The girl was always staring.

"Oh, I didn't see you," Harma offered.

The child had the nerve to snort. "I figured."

The insolent girl strode out onto the terrace ahead of her. Brin went to the end of the line of spectators, all but hiding in the boughs of an absurdly large potted evergreen. Such a little spy!

Vahldan cupped his hands and bellowed, "Come on, Malvius!" He grinned and clapped. "Gods, get those gates open! What's going on down there?"

Harma came up alongside Mara, as far from Elan as she could be. The view nearly stole her breath. The white sails of Malvius's ship glowed in the evening sun. As did the crimson sails of the imperial warships—two of them, both slicing through the water toward him, one from the southwest and one from due east. Malvius's ship had no rowers, just sails. Both imperial ships' oars were working. And yet the imperials didn't seem to be gaining—not fast enough. The massive gates parted slowly. Malvius would arrive just as they came open far enough. Their racing had her heart doing the same. She hid a smile, flush with pride for him.

Harma wondered if Malvius had struck his deal with the Tiberians. If so, they certainly were making a good show of it. It was going to be a trick to get the seagates closed again to shut the warships out.

"Yes!" Vahldan shouted as Malvius's ship passed through the gates.

The outburst startled little Armesus, who began to cry. Elan leaned back from the parapet, glaring at Harma. She hurried back to the terrace doors and signaled to Apontia, who ran to her. "Take him down and put him to bed. I'll be along shortly."

Harma hurried back to the parapet just as the gatehouse bell rang. The seagates began to close. Malvius was inside the harbor. One of the two catapults from the walls surrounding the harbor fired, splashing several lengths from the nearest imperial warship. The white wakes of both ships revealed they were turning away. It was over. The sound of cheering rose from below, echoing through the city.

Even the townspeople were celebrating her man. Harma's heart swelled. All would soon be well. Even after this bloody war was over, Malvius would still be loved by his people. And he would see to it that she and her son were accepted, too. It was all happening. Everything Malvius had promised her was coming true.

Vahldan suddenly seized Harma and embraced her, jarring her from her daydream. "What do you think of him?" he asked.

"I... I don't know," she stammered.

"That Malvius is really something." Vahldan released her, still beaming. "That'll show those who doubted him. The captain of our fleet has done it again," he called. "Come! Let's all go down to the docks and give them a warm welcome."

"He better have brought wine," Elan quipped. "All we have left is shit." She threw the remains of her cup into the pot for the tree.

They all headed for the terrace doors. All except the girl. She was staring at Harma. Again. Harma gave her a smug smile of the sort she always gave to the jealous females in her life and spun to follow the others out. Standing at the door was the giant. Also watching her.

"Coming along, Lady Harma?" Teavar said in his usual beastly growl.

"Of course," Harma snapped and hurried past him to the corridor without looking back.

MALVIUS FELT JUBILANT. He was back on top of his game. The destiny he'd envisioned, for himself and for the Gottari, was being brought to fruition, after all. The price was high. Great risks yet lay ahead. But this city would be his once again.

Even as *Gullwing* was being tied off to the quay, Malvius was directing his men to hoist Vahldan's cask of Saurian red, along with several barrels of ale, to the deck to be unloaded first. He sent Dex to fetch some taps and a mallet. He and Dexicos would still have their work cut out for them once the ship would be unloaded, but the crowd was in a festive mood. May as well put on a little show for the citizenry—to rewarm their feelings for the anaxship he would soon again embody.

Once the gangplank was secure, Malvius grabbed two of the fancy bottles of potent spirits he'd bought from the Saurian wine merchant and went to the top of the gangway. It wasn't the laced stuff he'd been supplying to Vahldan, so it was safe for all to drink. Well, safe enough if sparingly imbibed.

The gathering crowd on the docks spotted him and started to applaud. Among the throng were dockworkers, Hellains of the upper city, and even a few Gottari. This was even better than he'd imagined possible. It had been a long time since he'd felt this optimistic. A bottle in each hand, he raised them overhead and the applause became a raucous cheer.

Before Malvius descended the plank, the back of the crowd began to stir. Those clogging the base of Market Avenue hurried to clear the way. Moments later, a gang of Gottari thugs appeared on horseback, barking at the crowd to make way. Right behind them came a line of carriages. The thug king was coming. The gods only knew whom he'd brought along.

The procession slowly parted the press. Malvius turned to Dex. "Get the kegs tapped and start pouring for the townsfolk. Lure them out of the way as you do. We need some space if we're going to get unloaded by nightfall." Dex gave a knowing nod. They both knew how important it was to get *Gullwing* clear of the main quay.

He was annoyed that Vahldan would complicate the matter. But as the thug and his retinue emerged from the carriages, Malvius's annoyance faded. The smile that replaced it was difficult to suppress, though he would have to be careful not to reveal who incited it.

As soon as their eyes met, Harma's smile matched his. She looked away, abashed and hiding her radiant joy. Gods, he really had done it. His plan was proceeding smoothly *and* he still had her.

And, he had to admit, she had him.

Vahldan started up the gangway, leading his entourage. Two of his men were about to head down with the final barrels and had to back up onto the deck and wait. Malvius beckoned the impeding Gottari to hurry up to the boat. "Welcome aboard, my king!"

"You're missing the point, Malvius. We're here to welcome you. You did it!" Vahldan slapped him on the shoulder and moved past him. The thug went to peer down into the hold as men stood by, waiting to unload the winch. "Well done," he said, oblivious to his obstruction.

There was nothing Malvius could do so he turned to Vahldan's companions. "Hello, Elan. It's been some time." She replied with a scowl. How original. "Lady Mara, Captain Arnegern, welcome aboard."

Then she was before him, wearing that adorable sly smile. He couldn't keep from glancing to take in her curves. She always made him feel like a baying hound. Just a glimpse and he was lusty as a teenager. "Good evening, Lady Harma." He was about to take her hand when the giant's head appeared over her shoulder.

"So, you came back after all," Teavar said. The man had a knack for making every utterance sound accusatory.

"Of course!" Malvius turned to Vahldan. "I found some of the Saurian red we discussed." He nodded to the cask at the top of the gangway. Then he raised one of the bottles he still held. "Plus, I was able to get some of the distilled stuff—two bottles! If you like, I'd be happy to open one, my king."

Rather than politely declining as Malvius had hoped, Vahldan distractedly said, "Why not? Bring cups for everyone."

Since he'd already sent Dex out into the crowd, it was left to Malvius to run and find a stack of cups. He hurried to his quarters. He wasn't sure the cups were clean but they were good enough for barbarians. He rushed back to find the Gottari meandering around the deck, impeding the men scrambling to unload before their light was gone.

Malvius opened a bottle and managed to get filled cups into the hands of Vahldan, his sister and brother-in-law, Elan and Teavar. Vahldan sipped and was obviously pleased. "Teavar, load that cask into the carriage."

Teavar frowned. "My king?"

"I'm sure you can handle it. Or shall we have Malvius help you?"

Teavar gave Malvius an arch glance. "I have no need for Malvius," he said as if it were a general statement, which was fine with Malvius. The giant lifted the cask as easily as if it was empty, hoisted it to his shoulder, and headed down the gangway.

"I'm hungry," Elan randomly announced.

"The rest of us just had dinner," Vahldan said.

"That's all right. I'll go see what those vendors have." She pointed to carts along the edge of the docks.

Vahldan frowned. "You'll need coin. Food is still in short supply. I'll go with you."

Arnegern and Mara were talking among themselves at the stern. Malvius glanced to find Teavar looking conflicted on the docks. He'd already delivered the cask. The giant gave a last look up to the deck, then followed his king into the crowd. Malvius turned to Harma. She was alone. And beautiful. His grin reappeared. "Would you like a tour of the ship, my lady? You'll be amazed by what we've managed to bring back. The gods are with us."

Harma raised a brow. "Are they? I'm sure I'll be delighted, Captain."

He held out his hand. She glanced around and put hers into his. She was trembling. He led her to the ladder to the hold. Harma gave him a wry smile. "Has anyone ever fallen?"

"Oh yes. I've fallen. Hard. Allow me to go first, so that I can be there for you if you should fall the same as I have."

"I'd like that."

Malvius scrambled down and glanced around. A dozen sailors were all focused on loading sacks of grain onto the winch platform. He craned just in time to catch a tantalizing glance up Harma's skirts, taking in her lovely white thighs.

Malvius led her aside, down the aisle between the crew's empty bunks. A lone lantern hung aft of their position. He put his hands on her waist. Harma wrinkled her nose. She ran a hand up his arm and hooked it around the back of his neck, holding her wine cup off to the side. He kissed her, pulling her deeper into the shadows.

Her tongue slipped around in his mouth and then out and over his lips. "The wine is delicious, Captain," she said breathily.

"I've never tasted finer." She really did taste like fine wine. "Soon we can taste it daily." His hands slid down over her hips. The feel of her only made his hunger more voracious.

Malvius kissed Harma's neck and she tilted her head back. "You came back for me."

"Of course." His hands slid down to cup her buttocks and pulled her against him.

"And it's all going to happen? You'll save me? And my son?"

He drew back, smiling. "Of course. I told you. I have everything in hand." He squeezed.

Harma squeaked and giggled.

Malvius stretched to nibble her ear. Movement caught his eye over her shoulder. He focused to find a large figure poised on the ladder, the huge head just below the deck, eyes narrowed, intently watching. The giant's face contorted into a snarl. Teavar pointed and mouthed, "You die," and then continued to climb down.

"Teavar," Malvius hissed and pushed her away.

Harma spun, sloshing her wine down his front side. "It's not what you think," she started. Malvius knew it was too late for that. He set out running.

Malvius had a lifetime of experience moving below deck. He slipped through a gap between bunks and headed to the fore. A quick glance was enough to tell him pursuit was coming. Which meant Harma was safe for the moment.

But his own safety? That was definitely in question.

DISSIDENT MEASURES

"*Word of Malvius's return raced through the palace. From the moment I heard it, the evening and the night that followed took on a portentous feel. I clearly recall thinking that a monumental change was occurring. I was certain that nothing would ever be the same again.*

I have never since had a premonition so strong. Nor have I ever had one turn out more accurately."—*Brin Bright Eyes, Saga of Dania*

MALVIUS FLEW DOWN the center aisle. The winch ahead was loaded and the full platform was already slowly grinding upward. Malvius leapt and hit the stack of grain sacks and started climbing it even as the top rose to the opening in the deck above. He made it to the top of the stack just as it violently tilted and stopped rising. The giant had gotten ahold of the platform. The sailors working the winch crank had stopped. Malvius got his feet under him atop the rocking load. The platform lurched again. Teavar was pulling himself up. Malvius leapt again. He landed his upper body on the deck and slithered to pull his legs up. He scrambled to his feet.

"What in the nine realms?" Arnegern strode toward him, confused but ready to help.

"Sorry, Captain," Malvius called as he darted past. "It's just a misunderstanding."

Malvius was at the bottom of the gangway before he heard Teavar bellowing in Gottari. He didn't catch all of it, but the raging giant clearly wanted Malvius stopped, and likely worse afterward. He darted and wove through the crowd, startled faces all around.

"Malvius!" It was the thug king. "What's going on?"

He beat to a halt. Vahldan and Elan were four or five span away, just off the docks and at the edge of the crowd. Elan held a meat pie in her hands. "Forgive me, my king," he called. "It's not what it seems." The pair was as confused as Arnegern, but not for long. They stood blocking his path to Fishmongers' Lane. There was no way to get back to Market Avenue or to his warehouses. And Teavar was coming. Fast.

Malvius offered an apologetic shrug and waved farewell. He spun and ran east, running away from the main quay. The old temple blocked the end of the docks, and the way through to East Wall Avenue was narrow and twisty and often used as a hiding spot for drunks to sleep in peace. The oldest warehouses in Thrakius were built on pilings out over the water, adjacent to the temple. They were decrepit and mostly empty and likely locked up. Beyond them was the wall and another dead end. He had an idea. When he'd worked on the docks for his father as a teen, he'd often explored the area below the docks, if only to avoid work. A potential escape route sprang to mind. As long as he could get to it without being seen.

The temple loomed ahead. The walkway out to the old warehouses was empty. The commotion behind him intensified. He was definitely still being pursued and had definitely attracted a lot of attention. He headed to the edge of the docks. At the entrance to the walkway between the old buildings and the back temple wall, he dropped to his butt at the edge of the docks, hoping that in the past two decades nothing had changed about what lay below the spot.

Indeed, the large rock was still there, a span below his dangling boots. He glanced back. The top of Teavar's head was moving through the crowd, wending toward him. He dropped to the rock and turned to climb down, fairly certain he hadn't been spotted.

With the tide out, the area beneath the old warehouses was made up of mossy stones of various sizes. The far end was a sheer rock face that served as the foundation of the city wall. Malvius squinted in the shadows and spotted the opening in the craggy rock. It looked smaller than he remembered. The crowd noise echoed through the cavernous space. It was impossible to run across the slippery rocks, but he did his best to make haste, thankfully avoiding a fall. He finally made it to the rocky face and moved along it. He got to the waist-high foothold and stepped up. Chest to the rock, he reached. His hands hit the ledge overhead and he pulled. Gods, this was harder than it had been for the teen version of himself.

Huffing and straining, he managed to pull himself up to get his torso over, gain a new handhold, and pull his legs up. He wriggled forward till he knew his feet were out of sight. The cave was so much snugger than he'd recalled. His body blocked the light from the entrance. The way ahead was black as night, and the stone was cold. The air was stale and damp.

Malvius lay there, seeking to calm his breath and his racing mind. Why was he feeling so damned panicky? Well, there was a murderous giant chasing him. But this was something more. Something primordial. He didn't use to mind confined spaces, did he? Using his elbows, hips, and knees, Malvius shimmied forward, moving little by little into the blackness, reminding himself that the cave would keep him from being murdered. He sought to comfort himself by remembering the cozy little cavern that he used to hide in. He'd been able to sit upright there and it was not so far ahead. As long as nothing had shifted or changed. Caves didn't change in a mere twenty years, did they?

No. The cave would be the same. He *would* be able to turn himself around. Indeed, if necessary, there was even a way through to the outside of the city's walls. He just had to keep moving. Even if Teavar found the cave, the giant would never fit inside. That didn't mean he couldn't send someone else in, but all of that would take time. Time he could use to escape.

Between the sounds of the city behind and the echoing of the waves on the rock, Malvius kept imagining he heard voices. Several times he stopped and held his breath, listening. He couldn't discern what he was hearing, but before he reached the cavern, he smelled something recognizable. Wood smoke.

He stopped, afraid to move forward and doubting he could crawl all the way back out backwards. In the cavern ahead would be an ancient ring of stones for fires. The spot was perfect as smoke vented up and out. When he was a teen, he imagined men from the age of legend hiding there. He'd even had his own fires in the spot. He realized there was nothing to do but to move on and face whoever was there. It made him feel like a trapped snake waiting to be speared.

Malvius finally gained some headroom. The crawling became easier. Just as he was able to get to his knees, he heard the voices more clearly. Male and female. He moved slowly, feeling his way. The light ahead was so dim at first that he thought he was imagining it.

He came to a kink in the course and remembered it. The cavern was very close, just beyond a narrow, vertical opening that grew broader at the base. If he sat on his butt, he could swing his legs under and move his torso through the top sideways. The light was definitely brighter on the far side. The voices were more audible, too. There seemed to only be two of them. He got to his butt and slid up to the outcrop that obscured the way. Once he pivoted he'd be visible to whomever was there. Before revealing himself, he sat and listened.

"There it is again. Hear it?" The female voice. They knew he was there, too. The female sounded more frightened than angry or fierce. It didn't mean they wouldn't turn out to be dangerous, but it was better than the opposite.

Malvius slid and bent his torso, trying to peek before exposing himself. He checked for his belt knife, then pulled his tunic down over it. He smiled to make his voice sound friendly and called, "Greetings, friends. Forgive the intrusion."

"What do you want?" The male voice. Just the couple? No way to be sure.

"Only to warm myself for a moment. It's cold out there tonight. And the damn Gotars have ousted me from my home." That last part was a bit of a risk, but not a large one. He didn't detect an accent, so they were likely locals. Most every Thrakian hated the Gottari.

They whispered among themselves. Then he heard shuffling. The light grew. A bearded man of about 40 came into view, holding a candle in a bony hand. His hair was long and matted and his beard unkempt. His clothes were filthy. Worse than the man's state of hygiene, he looked shifty. His beady eyes, broken nose, the twist of his mouth—everything about him spoke of deviousness. His candle was of the type used in the nearby temple—surely stolen.

Malvius smiled. "Greetings."

"How did you find this place?"

"I've known it since I was a boy. I used to work in the warehouses." He threw a thumb back toward the entrance. "As I said, I was just looking to get out of the wind for a while."

"Invite him to the fire," the woman said. Her decency instantly put the man to shame.

The man remained suspicious. He held up the candle. His lipless frown and the wrinkling of his crooked nose became a caricature. "He stinks of wine. He's even spilled it on himself."

Malvius looked down. His cream tunic was splattered with Harma's wine. He pulled his cloak around himself to daub at the stain. "It was spilled on me. Maybe that's why I got so cold."

"Got any more?"

"Any more..."

"Wine," Lipless said incredulously.

"Oh," Malvius said. "No, sorry."

"Just invite the man to the fire," the female repeated.

Lipless retreated, muttering indecipherably. Malvius presumed it was as close to an invitation as he would get and crawled into the cavern. The fire was small but warm. They had a pile of broken wreckage and driftwood nearby as well as a large pile of rags over straw, which he could only presume the pair used as a bed.

He tried not to stare as he settled and appraised the female. She was little more than a scrawny girl. His daughter? No, she'd be even uglier. Malvius inclined his head to her. "My thanks for your kindness."

She forced a smile and averted her gaze. Her eyes were wary, flitting like one who expected to be struck at any moment. Maybe learned from Lipless? Malvius leaned to hold his hands to the fire. It provided a better look. No, she wasn't his daughter. She was older than he'd thought. And her years had not been kind. She bore the shadows of bruises and fading scars on her hollow cheeks and neck. Her hair hung in uncombed ropes. "Are you hungry? We have a little bread."

Her soiled shift was shoulder-strapped and a bit too revealing for everyday wear. Likely a garment that one of the dockside brothels provided. The male grunted in disapproval of her offer. Malvius shook his head. "No, thank you. I have already eaten today."

Lipless scooched to block Malvius's view of his companion and hugged his knees. His little eyes roved over Malvius, prying and judging. "Huh," Lipless scoffed. "Looks like you can afford to eat, all right. That's a fine cloak."

"The man's lost his home," the girl scolded. "War is cruel, so we must be kind."

She was wise, if naïve. Malvius felt for the girl, to be stuck here with that man. "The gods' truth," he murmured. He rubbed his hands together and focused on the fire. "I'll be out of your way as soon as I thaw out."

He couldn't risk going back the way he'd come. Not yet, anyway. The driftwood said they knew the way through the cave that led out to the beach beyond the wall, but he wasn't sure how they'd react if he headed out that way.

Malvius felt the male's stare. Perhaps he could offer them some coin. Although revealing his belt pouch was probably a foolish idea. The girl said, "Stay as long as you need..." She didn't know his name. "I am Semele, by the way. And this is Kleitos" She indicated her counterpart. Kleitos turned his scowl back on her momentarily.

"Call me Pupa," Malvius blurted. It was Tiberian, short for puppet, a nickname the imperial sailors had recently given him.

"Pupa, eh?" Kleitos grunted. Malvius glanced at him. The man's appraisal was getting more intense. His expression read of his suspicion, which made him all the more loathsome. "That name doesn't spark a flame but you do look familiar. What else do they call you, Pupa?"

Malvius gave him a weary smile. "Well, it's not the name my mother gave me. But few have known me by that one since her passing, which was long years ago." He pulled his cloak tight as if to keep warm and let his hidden hand drift to his hilt.

Kleitos nodded and stroked his tangled beard, his eyes growing sly. "That home the Gotars ousted you from wouldn't happen to be a ship, would it... Captain Malvius."

Malvius grinned but tightened his grip on the hilt and coiled his muscles. "Very clever, Kleitos. You got me."

"Ha. I knew—"

Malvius drew the knife and sprang from his coiled feet with a suddenness that startled even him. "And I got you," he said as he plunged the dagger into Kleitos's neck.

Semele screamed. Kleitos's beady eyes and lipless mouth went wide. The man locked his grimy, bony hands onto Malvius, one on his wrist and one on his cheek, fingers pushing down on his jaw. Damn, it hurt. Worse, the man had a wiry strength in his arms. Malvius had meant to stab him in the throat but he'd obviously missed the windpipe. Pain and fear spurred Malvius to push harder on the knife, causing blood to spurt and flow. Malvius pulled on the wrist of the hand that clutched his face. He eased off and pushed the blade again, all the way to the hilt. Kleitos gurgled and wheezed and his bedamned grip finally slackened. Malvius yanked away his hand and glanced at the girl, wondering how she'd react. He couldn't let her flee back toward the harbor. Luckily, Semele crawled further into the recesses of the cavern, eyes wide, panting like a terrified hound.

After what seemed a goat's age of gushing an unfortunate amount of blood, Kleitos slumped. Malvius yanked the knife free and slapped aside the despicable hands. Lipless was apparently deceased, though Malvius was loath to touch him to make sure.

Malvius cleaned the knife on the man's ragged clothing. He turned to Semele, touching his raw chin to find a series of ragged, stinging gouges. He worked his sore jaw back and forth. Not broken, at least. "Gods, he was stronger than he looked," Malvius said. Semele huddled back further, making herself small. "I'm sure you are well aware of that, though, aren't you?"

"Please," Semele whispered, her lips trembling.

"Well, he'll never hurt you again," Malvius offered cheerily. The nice thing about her defensive reaction was that she'd trapped herself. He could easily block any attempt she'd make to flee. He rose to his knees and edged around the fire.

"Please. I won't say a word." Her tears streaked the dirt on her hollow cheeks.

Malvius slowly edged toward her. "I appreciate you, Semele. You've been kind to me tonight. Here's the issue, though—"

"No, please. There's no issue. I'll go away. You can have the cave. I'll disappear."

He was almost close enough. "See? More kindness. Damn, that makes this hard. But there really is an issue. You see, tonight is a crucial night. And tomorrow—oh, tomorrow. It'll be the day of days."

Merciful gods, Malvius couldn't stand to see her terror. Best to get past the inevitable. He lunged, landing on her. She kicked and hit and shrieked. It was like grappling with a sack of bones and wriggling fish. He pinned her with all of his weight—which was about twice of hers, thankfully.

Semele shrieked endlessly now, slugging his sides and his back as he fumbled to get the knife to her skinny neck. He managed to get his free hand over her mouth. "I'm sorry," he said as he slid the blade across her throat. Her shriek became a mewling whimper. That sound and those eyes, so mournful.

Even as she gasped for her final breaths, Malvius tried to convince himself he'd mercifully ended a sad existence. "I really am sorry. But no one can ever find out about this. Tomorrow is just too important. And it's just the beginning. Well, for me."

Her struggling slowed and ceased. Her mournful eyes were left staring in horror. Damn, that image was going to stay with him.

Malvius released her mouth and closed her eyes. He sat back to catch his breath. It wasn't enough. He went and turned her head away. He found a skin of water and cut a chunk of fabric off the bottom of his cloak. He sat again, wiping his hands and face, trying not to look at her.

It couldn't be helped. Just like the fact that he couldn't stop looking at her. Crumpled and frail. And bloodied. A victim. His victim.

Too bad. He liked to picture himself as the savior of the good folk of his home city. He reminded himself that Semele did not seem to have been a member of that category.

"Tomorrow's just too important!" he shouted at her. His voice echoed in the recesses of the cavern. Gods, he had to get a grip on himself. He took her by the feet and dragged her back into a dark dead-end passage, out of the firelight and out of sight.

But, just as he'd suspected, not out of his head. "Tomorrow is everything," he muttered. "I worked too long for this, damn it! Tomorrow is the start of the rest of my life."

ADULTEROUS REVELATIONS

"*During a war, one should seek to anticipate the possible outcomes. During a war, one should seek to forestall the foe. During a war, no one should be surprised when battle begins.*

And yet, when the assault on Thrakius finally came, the Gottari of Thrakius seemed surprised. No one seemed to have truly considered the unavoidable or exactly how they should react to it. No one seemed prepared for what came. No one, that is, except for my parents."—Brin Bright Eyes, *Saga of Dania*

THE MOON HAD SET and the stars were fading when Vahldan finally returned to the palace. The ugliness, simmering in his belly, kept exhaustion at bay. He hadn't lost himself to it. But then, they had yet to find Malvius. The gods only knew what would happen then.

The palace stables were silent and dark. No groom emerged to meet them so Teavar led their horses off into the shadows. "Don't go up without me," the giant called over his shoulder. Vahldan wasn't sure the demand was born of fear for his safety or fear of what he may do if left unaccompanied.

Vahldan scanned the residences. Several were lit, including Harma's. But Elan's was dark. Good. He was glad Elan had left before anyone had fully gathered what had happened. It was all so ugly, even without the ugliness. Much of the fault was his, he knew. Bonding with Harma, trusting Malvius—he'd never felt more foolish. Imagining how it all would look to Elan only made him more ashamed. It only made him angrier, which made him all the more foolish. Such an endless cycle.

Elan might be the anchor that would keep him from losing himself, but at the moment he'd rather face his rage than face her. She'd just begun to trust him again, to let him back in. It was so fragile. The thought of losing her again, at a time like this. He couldn't bear it. And yet it felt damn near inevitable. In spite of her fragile trust, he obviously didn't trust himself to have fully changed.

Teavar returned and led him to the main entrance. A guard opened the door for them. They trudged up the stairs in steady silence. Teavar had to be exhausted. He'd started the pursuit by running the docks for some time before Vahldan even realized what was happening. Only then did the search begin.

They arrived at Harma's door. Ermanaric stood outside the entrance, awake but seeming to struggle to stay that way. The Rekkr bowed his head. "My king."

"Is she in there?"

"Of course. As you commanded."

Vahldan reached for the door latch. Teavar laid a hand on his forearm. "My king, may I speak?" The ugliness momentarily flared. But his loyal guardian's earnest expression helped him to push it down. He nodded. "Please remember that she is the mother of your son and the daughter of our fallen brother."

A lone laugh escaped him. "The last person I expected to defend her is you."

Teavar shook his head. "Her actions are indefensible. And yet..."

"She knew what she was doing," he said.

"As did I, back when I stepped into the ring to fight my rightful lord. I had been corrupted. I nearly killed that young lord. Still, he was wise enough to forgive. Even in the heat of the fight, he saw clearly enough to offer me another path. To this day I live in the grace of it."

The giant withdrew his hand. Vahldan actually felt calmer. He nodded and entered. Harma stood by the terrace doors holding Armesus to her chest. She spun to face him. Her expression was fraught. She'd obviously been crying.

And yet the sight of her fueled the flare. "Gods, you disgust me." His vision blurred. He couldn't allow himself to make this worse. He looked away and pushed it down.

"Only now? You've hardly given me a second glance since our son was born. You won't even look at me now." Her voice quavered but she clearly wasn't penitent.

Vahldan made himself face her. He drew a breath and evenly released it. "Where is he?"

Harma stepped back, holding the babe closer. "I don't know."

"You must have an idea. Where would he be?"

She stepped back to the terrace doors. "I said I don't know." She raised her chin.

More fuel. The heat increased. Vahldan's face grew numb. No, it wouldn't help. He had to get to the bottom of this. "All right. Then what's he up to?"

"I have no idea." This time Harma looked away.

The ugliness flared again. He stormed toward her. "Don't you dare tell me you know nothing! What betrayal is that little shit scheming?"

The babe started to cry. "You're terrifying our son," she said. "And me."

Vahldan realized his fists were clenched. He stood back, shaking his hands loose. "Where is she?" He strode to the bedchamber doorway.

"Where is who?"

"The Sass girl, damn it! Where is she?" The ugliness slid to the top of his chest now, constantly threatening to seize him.

"Sleeping." Harma pointed to the servants' quarter's door.

"I doubt that." He strode to the door and flung it open. "Get up." The Sass sprang from the bed, obviously awake. "Come and take the babe."

He had to admit, the handmaiden was obedient and efficient. In mere moments, she was into a robe and striding by him toward Harma.

Harma was shaking her head. "No. Please. Don't take my son from me."

"Take the boy," Vahldan told the Sass, nodding to assure her.

"I've got him, my lady," the handmaiden whispered. "His well-being is all, yes?"

Harma reluctantly handed Armesus to her. His son's mother was visibly trembling. The Sass bundled the babe to her chest and carried him back to her quarters, rocking and shushing him. The woman barred the door audibly. Vahldan couldn't say he blamed her.

Harma crossed her arms over her chest and hung her head. Her whole face was wet with tears and snot. "Please, Harma. Just tell me. What is Malvius planning? You've betrayed your husband. That's one thing. Don't betray your people too."

She shook her head. "All I know is that he was trying to make a deal with them."

"Who, the imperials?" She nodded. "What kind of deal?"

"I'm not certain. He promised to keep us safe. After..."

"After my defeat, you mean?" Harma shuddered and a sob escaped. Vahldan laughed, venting off a bit of heat from the forge. "And you believed him?"

"I was afraid," she said.

"Why would he save you? Because you fucked him?"

Harma's face crumpled. "He was kind to me. He cares about your son."

"You must think yourself one marvelous fuck, my dear. I can't believe you fell for that slippery little Hellain's self-serving mummery."

Harma looked up. For the first time, there was anger in her eyes. "Like I fell for yours?"

"I bonded with you! I went and found a bedamned Elli-Frodei to make it happen."

"You bonded with me because *you* were afraid. Afraid that your firstborn son was weak. That it would reflect on you. You wanted me because you wanted a healthier son. You used me for my womb, same as you used that bony witch upstairs."

The ugliness struck like a bolt. Vahldan took three steps to close the space between them. Harma stuck her chin out. "Go ahead. Hurting others is what you're best at, Bringer." He realized his fists were clenched again, this time with his arms cocked back. A fighting stance. Gods, he still couldn't be trusted.

He relaxed his arms and took a step back, shame burning on his cheeks. "Gods, how has it come to this?"

Harma snorted. "You really don't know? You of all people."

He closed his eyes and shook his head. "Just tell me why?"

Harma's sneer melted to sorrow. "You never said a word when my father died. Not even 'I'm sorry for your loss.' Herodes gave you everything. And your enemies killed him. They killed him because of your goals, your schemes. You expect us all to die for you. Even your son." She shook her head. "I just didn't get it. How could you go to so much trouble, just to let him die? My father loved you. He was honorable. But it did him no good. His loyalty didn't save him. It won't save any of us."

Vahldan stared out the terrace doors. His shame smothered the flames of the ugliness to choking smoke.

She went on. "The blood of the Amalus kings flows in our son's veins. He should be the king our people have longed for, the king they will soon need. But you trapped us here. Your ridiculous war has trapped us all. Why? Must all of us face your doom? Must we all pay for your pride with our lives?"

"That's enough," he said without looking.

"You used to act like you were skeptical. Like you were one of us—a king in name only. A king merely to serve us. But you willingly surrendered to it all. Secretly you not only believed the whole prophesy, you cherished it. You thought it reflected so well on you. You strove to put yourself above us all. And as a bonus, you thought it exonerated you of your father's death."

Vahldan stiffened. "Please, you've said enough."

Freya's mercy, the woman kept talking, her tone all the brasher. "You do see that the imperials must make an example of you and all your kin, do you not? How in the nine realms is that going to reflect on you, Bringer, if you and all your progeny end up dead or enslaved? Some legacy."

He feared the ugliness was about to flare. "That's enough!" Vahldan shouted.

"It *is* enough. Enough for me to have sought to save our son, to save the rightful heir. For the sake of our people. I saw a path to save him and I took it. It's more than I can say for you."

Something strange happened. Vahldan felt deflated. But also relieved. Unburdened. He suddenly realized what had changed. He turned to her and she shrank back, completely misreading him. Harma had actually broken through. The ugliness remained snuffed out. She'd shown him, as never before, how slim his chances had become, the wealth of fortuitous chance the gods had bestowed. The ugliness, his pride, his selfishness—his failings had been a necessary part of bringing them here, to this moment. Even Harma's conceit and desperate need for adulation. But she'd also reminded him that love and honor remained vital to the legacy he hoped to provide.

The pieces and the players had all been set. But nothing was certain. There was still a chance it could all have been for nothing. All that he'd sought still teetered on the precipice. Even with the ugliness defeated, it was all so fragile.

There was much yet to be done. Things would happen fast now.

They stood staring at one another. Hers was just one more life that he'd ruined. Betrayal became second nature for the betrayed. Hurt people made hurtful choices. As necessary as their failings had been, Harma didn't deserve the pain and the fear that had come of what they'd wrought.

The tolling of a bell rent the awkward silence between them. Vahldan went to the terrace doors. The predawn twilight lit the rooftops and the sea. The dark smudge of a ship on the water beyond the seagates caught his eye. Then another, and another.

Teavar burst through the door. "There's fighting, my king. Down at the docks."

He turned to Harma. "Take it or leave it as you will, but I *am* sorry for your loss. I loved him, too. It's too late for us to come to terms with all of this. For that, too, I am sorry." He didn't wait for a response. "To the horses," he said to Teavar and strode to the exit.

"Shall I continue to guard her?" Ermanaric threw a thumb to indicate Harma.

"No. Get your gear and come," he barked over his shoulder. "Find Arnegern, too!"

"What shall I tell him?" Ermanaric called.

"Tell him the battle has begun."

RATHER THAN SLEEPING, Malvius felt like what he'd managed was a smattering of semi-conscious worrying. He'd crawled to where he could see the mouth of the cave at some point during the night, lying still, waiting for a sign of the coming dawn.

Malvius wondered if he ought to pray. Pray for his plans to be set in motion, for his allies to come through as promised, for his survival —of the morning, let alone of the battle. But he'd never been the praying type. If the gods were actually paying heed to this pitiful little war, or were inclined to take sides, he imagined that such a desperate prayer would only incur their spite.

Once he gleaned the slightest bit of light, he stuck his head out of the cave and listened.

It was quiet; there was just the distant thunder of the waves against the seagates. A good sign?

Malvius crawled out the way he had come in the previous day, emerging with his butt on the ledge and his back to the rock above the cave's mouth. A cold gust of wind lashed him. Gods, it was cold out here. He clung to the rock and slowly, awkwardly, lowered his dangling feet. Malvius realized too late that the last time he'd emerged this way, he'd been much more flexible and agile. Not to mention thinner. He scraped his hands and butt as he slipped to drop heavily and clumsily. He splashed into frigid water, slipping on the rocky bottom. He pitched against the rock face to keep from falling, jarring a leg and shoulder. His hands stung and his boots and leggings were soaked but he'd managed to avoid splitting his skull. Another good sign?

Well, it was a start.

He limped off the stinger in his leg, rotating his arm to check his shoulder. Malvius was no warrior. Yet he was being asked to act as one today. Gods, he'd just killed his first human beings. Well, with his own hands, anyway. All that killing with his own hands had shown him was that he wasn't made for it. He still vastly preferred hiring others to do his ugly work. His run-in hadn't bolstered his confidence for what came next. It only added to his burgeoning cargo of guilt and self-loathing.

But whatever getting through the day would require of him, it would be worth it. He had to find a way or die trying.

The tide was high. He cautiously sloshed through thigh-high seawater, which numbed his feet. With stinging hands he climbed the rock on which he'd descended and reached to pull himself up by the edge of the planking overhead. He peered over the docks. Not a single lamp or torch burned. Pushing a foot off of a support timber, he managed to squirm up onto his belly. The docks were veiled in shades of gray. Blessedly, *Gullwing* had been moved from the quay. He spotted a dark shape, a squat figure hunched atop a pile of coiled lines. Staying on his stomach, ready to drop back down, he did his best imitation of a gull cry. The figure stirred. Then came the answering call—a much better mimicry.

Dexicos! Gods, how he loved the man.

Malvius got to his feet, scanning his surroundings as he stole across the frost-coated planking toward Dex. His first mate stood, still wrapped in a blanket from the ship. Dex's toothy smile shone in the growing light. "I've been worried, Cap."

"Me too. I've never been happier to see anyone."

Dex leaned in, studying the front of his tunic. "What's all of that? Blood?"

"Spilled wine." Mostly. "I'm fine. Freezing but fine." Both were at least partly true. "Where do we stand?"

"I found all but two captains. They were all willing to ask their men. I heard back from two. So far just over thirty have agreed to join us. There will likely be more."

Relief suffused him. "Thank the gods." The plan was still on course.

"The men from *Princess* are gathering in the kitchen of The Fish-monger. The others are meeting at Phlaron's house. It's pretty close to the east gate. They've decided Kynas should lead. He's had some battle experience."

"That all sounds good." Amazing, actually. Dex had not only waited for him through his shameful night, he'd been striving to accomplish their mission. In spite of Malvius's blunder, his amazing first mate was keeping their hopes alive.

"It gets better. Kynas used to serve in your father's city militia. He's put the word out to his old comrades. He says there could be as many as a hundred militia that will join in. He was going to send the best-armed among them to The Fishmonger. Not sure if any have shown up, though. Once the docks cleared out, I slipped down here to watch and wait for you. The place was swarming with Gottari for half the night." Dex sighed. "I knew I'd find you, though. We need you, Cap. I don't think those we recruited would try this without you. Rightfully so. A lot of them were worried when you disappeared. Having the Gottari riding around all night didn't help. I kept telling them it would work out. I said you'd come through." His dear friend smiled. "I'm glad I was right."

"I'm honored by your faith." Malvius gripped his shoulder. "Well, shall we go and see who's still in?" Dex nodded and turned to lead to the tavern. "Dex?" His loyal mate turned back to him. "Thank you, my friend. For everything."

Dex beamed. "You said it yourself, Cap. It's our city. And you've never let me down."

This would be the riskiest moment of his life. On top of that, he was willingly putting this loyal friend's life—along with many others—at risk. "For you, gods willing, I never will," Malvius said solemnly. It was as close to a prayer as he dared offer up.

Malvius gathered his newly acquired host at the bottom of the stone steps to the wall walk that led from the docks to the eastern harbor gatehouse—the one that housed the mechanism and crew that operated the seagates. He hadn't decided whether it was a pleasant surprise or not, having so many who were willing to follow him into this. A pleasant outcome was far from assured. He couldn't believe how many old codgers—men of his father's generation—had shown up. He'd known some of them his whole life. It surprised him because aging militiamen were as quick to talk big as they were to find excuses for their own inaction. Still, he suspected they were as likely to be a curse as a blessing. The eldest among them would slow the attack. But they had also supplied more than half of his host's actual weaponry, including every last one of their few shields. Most of his own sailors who volunteered had shown up with little more than knives and cudgels, pike poles and harpoons.

Malvius bid his team to wait on the docks and climbed to the wall walk alone. It only took a moment to spot the first Tiberian trireme, not too far off to the southeast. He spotted a second beyond that and knew it would be enough. His allies had come as promised.

Now to get them in.

He hurried back down the steps to his host. "It's on. Remember, speed and silence. We get to the gatehouse door and make room for the ram." He nodded to the pair of sailors carrying the sawed-off mast they'd brought from the shipyards. "Those with shields lead the others. Everyone ready?"

They looked as terrified as Malvius felt, but most nodded and no one turned back.

He wasn't sure what else to say. Nothing could be gained by dallying. The sky was growing lighter by the moment. The Gottari stationed in the gatehouse would likely consider a mere pair of passing ships to be part of the ongoing blockade, but his host had to strike before they sensed something was amiss.

Malvius ran back up the stairs. From the landing the wall curved to the gatehouse. There was no cover from here on out. He was already winded and it looked like such a long way. He beckoned his followers and started running down the wall walk. The host's boots were drumming on stone and their sketchy weapons rattled and clinked. There was a light in the gatehouse windows, but no faces appeared and no warning bell rang. Not yet.

Malvius looked back. Gods, his force was woefully spread out. As he'd feared, the elderly militiamen were lagging behind. A squad of his youngest sailors ran right behind him. He slowed his pace so the laggards could catch up. As he looked back, one of the young men running right behind him jerked and let out a small yelp. The lad's eyes bugged before he stumbled and fell. Malvius spotted the arrow the lad gripped protruding from his chest.

Everyone beat to a halt as the poor young fellow flailed against the harborside parapet, gasping and coughing. From ahead, a call rang out. In Gottari. Damn.

Another arrow whizzed by Malvius's nose and another of his men shrieked and dropped to his knees, clutching an arrow in his thigh.

"Get down!" someone cried. They all crouched but there was nowhere to hide.

"No," Malvius cried. "We must keep going! Onward!" He ran on, hoping someone would follow, and scanned the gatehouse windows. He spotted the archer in an upper-story porthole. What could he do? The only escape lay ahead. He sped up, arms crossed over his chest, sure that an arrow would skewer him at any moment.

"Shields! Archers and those with shields to the fore!" It was Dex. Malvius hated that he hadn't thought to say these things, and his gratitude for Dex soared from an already incredible height. Running in front was the only idea he'd come up with in regard to leading a host. At least it's where Vahldan and Elan had always been during the most violent fights that he'd witnessed. He should have known better than to take lessons from barbarians.

The gatehouse was getting nearer. All he could think about was running and breathing. The earsplitting clang of the gatehouse bell hit him almost as a physical push. He kept going and it kept on ring-ing, alerting the city of an attack. Within moments, the bell in the palace keep's gatehouse joined in. Gods, this was really happening. Malvius was in the very heart of a battle.

He looked up. An arrow struck, just missing the open porthole. An attempt by one of his men seemed to be making the Gottari shooter wary, at least. He probably should've called for that as well. Gods, he really wasn't cut out for this.

Malvius got to the building first. He pressed his back flat against the wall, panting. He wanted nothing more than to slide to his butt and sit to catch his breath. No, they had to get in. He slid along the wall and stupidly tried the door. Of course it was barred. But he was heartened to be reminded how weather-beaten the old wooden door was. His host started arriving, with shield bearers at the fore. He beckoned the pair with the ram as the team gathered around him, heads swiveling and looking vulnerable. He didn't think the archers among his host had hit anyone inside, but they'd evidently come close enough to slow the Gottari arrows.

Dawn was about to break and Malvius could see across the harbor to the docks. He scanned the ends of the city's downhill avenues, looking for what he feared even more than what they would face on the other side of the door—galloping Gottari Rekkrs. Nothing yet.

The pair of sailors with the mast finally aligned themselves to strike the door, then turned and stared at Malvius. "Hit it!" he cried. This time it didn't seem like a command that needed to be voiced.

They drew back and swung. They hit the door with an echoing thud and the mast flipped out of their hands. They both danced out of the way as it thumped and bounced at their feet.

Malvius leaned to look. There was only a small scrape in the door. Not a heartening start. As the pair scrambled to lift it and try again, Malvius couldn't resist scanning the docks again. The Gottari would come. The only question was when. His legs were frozen and leaden and his chest was so tight it ached. They had to speed this up. How could he take charge and help to move things along? "We need more power. Come on, let's get some muscle in on this. You and you, you two as well. Get in there and grab ahold." The mast was now lined with men. "All right, how about a running start? Archers, cover them. Keep your aim on those windows. All right, one, two, three, charge!"

The collision caused a deeper boom this time. And the beam wasn't dropped. Progress! Malvius leaned to look. "It's working." The wood was dented and cracked around the center latch. "Again, harder! One, two, three, charge!"

The third strike broke one of the door's vertical planks. Malvius bent to peer inside. Luckily, whoever was taking the shot from within missed the gap and their arrow thunked against the inside of the door next to his head.

Malvius beckoned to one of the lads nearby. "Give me your cudgel." He took it and, keeping out of line of the gap in the wood, used the cudgel to pry at the inner crossbar, now visible in the center of the gap they'd created. The crossbar rose a bit, then slipped back into place. He pried at it again, this time lunging to knock it free. The crossbar disappeared from view, audibly clattering onto the floor inside. "Hit the door again," he called.

The beam holders swung, hit, and the whole door fell in. A flock of arrows instantly hissed out. One of the two at the front of their ram fell back yowling. Once again the mast bounded loose, causing everyone who'd borne it to flee. Malvius pressed his back to the wall beside the door. "Shields!" he called. "Out front!"

A half-dozen of the militiamen with shields hurried to the fore, holding them edge to edge. "Those with pikes or swords, right behind them," Malvius called. He edged over to peek inside. The interior was dim and deep. He had no idea how many they faced. Still holding the cudgel, he pulled his dagger. "Charge!" He waved for them to lead the way.

The shield bearers moved in, but too slowly. Once the first few cleared the door, the Gottari appeared from the shadows, bellowing as they counterattacked. The more experienced Gottari warriors hit the shields of the mostly elderly militiamen with a resounding crash, knocking apart the Hellain formation. Malvius leapt clear as several of the codgers toppled over backward in the entryway. Malvius feared he'd just initiated a slaughter.

The fallen codgers scrambled and crawled back. The Gottari pressed the next line of his men, barking like beasts, pushing them back, and slashing with swords and axes. Malvius's entire host was on their heels, terror in their pale faces. For some it was too much.

Several of his volunteers turned and fled. In mere moments, it seemed at least a third of his host was bloodied, fallen, or fled.

Malvius found himself on the flank. Good fortune had pushed him from harm's way. One of the codgers lay at Malvius's feet, a bloody mass at the crown of his wispy white head. He wasn't sure if the man was dead or dying. Didn't matter. Either way, he was out of the fight. Malvius grabbed the fallen man's shield and yanked it from his arm. Moving further inside, he realized that there were only about a half-dozen Gottari inside. As he'd surmised, his Hellains had the gatehouse crew greatly outnumbered. And yet his squad was floundering, slowly falling back toward the ruined door. The Gottari stayed in a cluster, consistently hacking at his host's shields and bellowing gutturally to intimidate. It was a ruse! A desperate one, at that.

"Come on, men!" Malvius called and moved to the fore. He tripped on an old rusty sword. He dropped the cudgel, snatched up the sword, and raised his borrowed shield. "We have them outnumbered! Forward! For Thrakius!"

Several of his young sailors cried out and ran in behind Malvius. In a heartbeat, the Hellains had reversed the attack, pressing the defenders. His spirits soared. So this was how an actual fighter felt!

The Gottari were too close to effectively swing with their broadswords. Malvius's new weapon was a short thrusting sword. It came naturally to use it as intended. He plunged between shields with a low jab. The nearest Gottari's eyes went wide before he vomited blood into his mouth and it leaked through his gritted teeth. Malvius pulled back the blade. It felt dreamlike to see his victim stagger off into the darkness.

Malvius had stabbed his third human being. Gods, he was a killer now—a warrior, drunk with battle lust. As bad as those he sought to oust. He instantly knew it was what was needed. Nothing would change until these barbarians received as they'd always given.

Now the Gottari were backing away, their faces wary and their postures defensive. Their baritone calls faded to the sound of shuffling boots. "We have them," Malvius called. His host surged ahead, with more gathering behind. Those who'd stayed back were joining in. The small space was filling with determined Hellains. Realization had dawned among them. Victory could be theirs.

They pushed the foe deeper within. Torches lit the broadening circular stone chamber behind the Gottari. Surprisingly, the ringing of the bell was less deafening inside. Malvius beckoned and called again. "Let us finish this. For Thrakius! Strike them down!"

This time the Gottari scattered and fled. "After them!" Malvius cried. The Hellains cheered and rushed on in pursuit. The chamber was mostly filled with large metalworks, gears, and shafts. The Gottari ran to a steep wooden stairway. A few of the foe with swords formed a rearguard, backing up the stairs and slashing at any who challenged their flight.

Malvius realized the defenders really didn't matter anymore. He'd spotted their objective.

He called to those nearby. "Help me with those mules!" They hurried to the row of stables adjacent to the turnstile. A trio of padded harnesses hung in pairs around a huge iron shaft. The group quickly pulled the jittery and complaining mules into place beneath the padded harnesses around the wooden wheel that drove the huge iron shaft. Once the mules were coaxed into place, they clearly knew their role. The beasts of burden merely stood waiting to be hitched.

Two of his men hitched the final mule and gave him the signal. Malvius found a whip and cracked it behind the nearest pair. That was all it took. The turnstile lurched into motion, causing the gears to grind. A loud clanking rhythm gained speed, followed by a resounding groan that nearly drowned out the bell and the fighting above.

Finally, the bells stopped. His men upstairs must have prevailed. The groan of the machinery faded as the shaft gained speed. Malvius ran out the door and leaned on the parapet. Water churned at the base of the gatehouse, but nothing else happened. He feared something was wrong, but a moment later the seagates lurched and began to separate.

"It's working!" he cried. The men inside cheered.

Malvius ran down the wall walk to get a better view outward. He scanned the sea. The Tiberian ships had seen. Rowers were rowing and sails were unfurling. They were coming.

The attack was on. The battle to take his city back had truly, finally, begun.

CHAPTER 23
THE ENDING BEGINS

ELAN WAS DREAMING of bells and fire—relentless clang and smoke and danger. The resound of the bells was broken by a sharp thumping. "Elan! Wake up!"

Her eyes sprang open. Consciousness came with a steady throbbing at her temples. Worse, the bedamned bells kept ringing. The latter was worsening the former. She sat up. Gods, it wasn't just her head. She ached all over. Even her face hurt. She was so parched she felt like she'd swallowed paste. She looked for the water Hesiod always left at her bedside. There was only an empty wine cup.

And an empty flagon.

It started coming back to her. At nightfall, she'd returned to the palace in the carriage. With the wine cask. Worse, the bedamned thing had already been tapped. She'd finished one flagon and there'd sat the bedamned cask, handy as could be. She'd refilled her flagon. At least she'd still had the sense then to bar herself in her bedchamber. Alone.

Elan had been angry down at the docks. Nothing fired her thirst for wine like anger.

She hadn't been angry for the same reasons as everyone else, though. She might have even burst out laughing when she first heard it. Everyone had been in an uproar, but Elan wasn't the slightest bit shocked that Malvius and Harma had been fucking. They were perfect for one another.

How could anyone be surprised? The trollop had delighted in luring Vahldan to cheat. Harma had even convinced him to turn his back on his firstborn son. The woman would stoop as low as her necklines to have her way. Being outraged by Harma for fucking was like being outraged by a wild colt for bucking.

No, what had angered Elan was that Vahldan had tried to hide it from her. It had happened when Arnegern had pulled Vahldan aside on the docks and whispered in his ear. They'd both seen Malvius fleeing and Teavar chasing him. Vahldan could've just told her what had been happening and they could've dealt with it together. Especially since she had seen the shadow of the ugliness in his eyes. He'd only just renounced it. He'd only just reaffirmed that she was his anchor. And then the very next time he'd felt it, he'd sent her away.

"Elan! Even *you* can't be sleeping through *this*! Open the door."

Now Vahldan was here. And the bells could only mean one thing. Duty called.

Things were supposed to be different now. She'd been so hopeful that things had changed. She hadn't drunk herself to sleep in weeks. She'd been too busy repairing her life. And he'd been central to it. But Vahldan had reverted to his old, less admirable self. Worse, she'd used it as an excuse to do the same. She should've been ready for something like this. Such a pathetic relapse. And so soon after coming to terms with their awful past lives. Gods, she hated the old them.

Now battle was upon them again. In spite of the siege, Elan had hoped for more time. Time with him, finding their way to a new understanding of who they were, not just to one another but as a couple and as parents. Apparently their time was up.

Elan swung her legs over the side of the bed and sat. The spinning would subside if she sat still for a moment. More bedamned thumping. "I'm coming already." Her voice hardly worked. She stood, limbs creaking, old wounds shrieking. She'd never fully realized it, but the wine that she'd thought dulled the pain of all of her old wounds ultimately enflamed it. She drew a deep breath, stretched her sore limbs, and shuffled to the door.

Elan pulled the bar out of the brackets and set it aside. She turned from the door, stepping out of her frock and pulling her undertunic over her head.

The door opened partway. "May I come in?"

Was he really asking now, after such a rude awakening? "Suit yourself." She turned to splash her face in the basin. She heard him enter, sensed his impatience. She continued to wash.

"How in the nine realms have you been sleeping through all of this?" Vahldan had the nerve to sound incredulous.

"Practice," she said. She snatched up a wiping cloth and dried herself. She finally turned to face him. *Now* she was surprised. She focused on his eyes, just to be sure. Indeed, Vahldan was free of the ugliness. Rather than impatient, he looked earnest. Maybe even contrite. So he hadn't murdered the trollop, at least. Elan refused to ask about it. She didn't want to waste any more of their precious time on such distractions. She threw aside the wiping cloth and moved on to her gear. The drinking skin from her saddlebag still had water in it. She pulled the stopper and drank—stale but she gulped it gratefully.

"There's fighting," he said. "It's begun."

"Who would've guessed?" She wiped her mouth and thrust the skin into her saddlebag.

"Are we really going to start off like this? Today?"

He had a point. Last night's relapse aside, they really were in this together. "The west gate?" Elan asked.

Vahldan came and helped her into her cuirass. "No. Down at the docks."

"Shit, that's not good."

"Why?"

"I'm sure you'll recall since you were just there, but it's a long way from here. Making it tougher to respond to. I'm sure your dear friend Malvius thought of that, too."

Vahldan grimaced. "I suppose it's a good reason to get moving."

"Go on ahead without me," she said, feeling annoyed.

"I would never."

"Belt." She held out her hand.

Vahldan handed her the belt and then held up Biter's harness as she donned it. "You really think Malvius could've pulled this off?" She made a face. "Not just the betrayal, but a coordinated scheme? I mean, he and the imperials have always hated each other."

Gods, she was the one that was hung over. But then, she'd never been as willing to buy what Malvius had always been selling. She also knew better than Vahldan that the mobile reserve would do whatever it took. "Yes." Now her tone was incredulous.

"Freya's cats' claws, maybe I *should* go without—"

Elan held up a silencing finger. "What's that?"

"I don't hear anything?"

"That's what I mean. The bells have stopped."

"I'm not sure if that's good or bad," he said.

Elan sat and bent to pull on her boots. "I doubt it's good." Vahldan knelt to lace the boots while she laced her arm guards in silence. They stood and faced one another. Sobriety was taking its toll. Dawn brought reality home, as it always did. This time more cruelly than ever.

"This really is it, isn't it?" she said.

He drew a breath and sighed. "I think so." His hand drifted to the wound on his side.

"After all of these years, it's finally here." Like water from a tipping well bucket, emotion started to spill and then flowed. "We didn't get to—"

"Don't," he said, perfectly reading her. "It won't be today. I mean, it's come. But we still have time. Not as much as we'd like, but enough."

"How can you be sure?"

"Because. There's too much that's unsettled. We simply can't allow it. Not yet." She wrapped her arms around him and he pulled her tight. "I need to apologize," he said.

Elan didn't feel up to it. Plus, gods, where would he start? "We can't go there."

"But I need to. About last night, I mean. I pushed you away. After I swore that I wouldn't. But I—"

"Stop," she said, still holding him. "I can't do this. Not now."

"It's gone, Elan," he said softly.

Something about his tone made her draw back and appraise him. "What's gone?"

"The ugliness. It's just gone. I'm not sure how I know, but I do. I feel different. It's like the gods keep whispering to me, telling me that it's so."

She wasn't sure how, but it made her feel... jealous. "You beat it without me?"

"I'm sorry," he said. "None of it has ever been fair to you. I didn't want you to have to deal with any of it. And, well, I was ashamed. It's funny, but I think the shame was the start of it. It sort of shocked me into facing things."

Elan's chest started to ache. "What things?"

"While we were arguing, Harma said that I've been trying to exonerate myself for my father's death. She told me that getting everyone killed would be my legacy. It terrified me that she might be right. So much has to go just right."

Elan released him and stepped back. "So Harma made you ashamed? Enough that you were able to change, just like that? You're telling me that's what beat the ugliness?"

Vahldan looked away. "No. It's more than that. It's always like being hit by a wave—one that would carry me helplessly along, just as it was last night. And for once, I made myself face the fact that I've willfully surrendered to this thing. Since the beginning. And it very well could kill me. Which is one thing. And then there's Urrinan and our people. But then I—"

"But then you decided to change," she said sulkily. "Because Harma shamed you."

He faced her again, eyes hard. "But then I thought of you. I thought about how you were there that day with my father. I thought about how you told me that what I did was brave and how much strength it required of me. I thought about how you've not only been my anchor against my ugliness, but how you've been my only real constant, my only true home. I thought about how you've always been there for me, no matter how horrible I've treated you. I thought about how now that I finally see how much that means to me, our time is almost up. I thought about how I spent half of my life chasing other things when the most important thing was always right there, at my shoulder, watching over me.

"So yeah. I thought of you and it shook me. And I regained my footing. The same footing you've always provided for me. The footing that's enabled me to achieve everything I have so far. And once I had that footing again, I realized I wasn't dead yet. This may be the beginning of the end, but we're not done yet. Thinking of you, my love, made me see how I can still shape the future for our people. But more than all of it, thinking of you made me realize that I needed to be sure. That you and I... That we're..." He pressed his lips tight, his eyes shining now.

"That we're as one," she said. "As it was always meant to be."

"Yes," he whispered. "That means more to me than any of it." Vahldan's smile was so boyish—uncertain but sincere. She saw him just as he had been when she'd first laid eyes on him.

"So," Elan said. "What are we going to do?"

His smile was wry. "First things first."

"The battle?" She nodded to the terrace doors.

He nodded and straightened into his resolve, shoulders back and chin high. "Through it all, we're going to believe. And strive." He looked out at the growing light of the sky. "I said it was shame that brought this on. But it was more than that."

"What else?"

Vahldan grinned. "Hope. Hope that good truly can come from bad—even my bad decisions and my awful behavior. Hope that love can prevail. That change can ultimately be for the better. The gods keep showing it to me in glimpses. If it's true, then Eldavar's and Jhannas's and Hrithvarra's deaths mean something." He shrugged. "I decided to believe again, Elan. To truly believe that my legacy can still lead to the ascendancy of my heirs, of our people. That Urrinan's toll will be worth paying. That even after all of this, there will still be a new beginning."

Elan strode to him and wrapped him in her arms again. "I believe, too."

Vahldan held her in silence. "Time's up," he finally said. "Hope is one thing, but there's still much to be done."

"What's happening?"

Elan pulled from his embrace and spun to face the intruder. Brin stood in the bedchamber doorway. Their daughter's newly muscled arms were crossed over her chest. Her hair was tied in Skolani braids and she was dressed in her crimson sparring tunic and black leggings. Brin even wore the fine leather boots and arm guards Elan had recently learned that Urias had procured for her.

"The imperials have attacked." No point in dissembling.

The girl didn't miss a beat. "Where do you want me?"

"Here!" Vahldan's tone was absurdly sharp. "You are not to leave this residence." Now he was going to play papa?

"Please stay and help keep the others safe," Elan amended.

Brin pouted. "That's stupid. I can help. I can at least patrol the keep. I'm better than most of the boys who'll be out there."

Vahldan shook his head. "We can't risk your safety."

"Till when?" Brin asked. "Seems like the risk is only going to grow."

"Maybe so, but it's not here yet," she said. "Not for you." Brin was outraged but there was no time to argue. "We have to go, so please do as I say." Elan walked past her to the entry chamber.

"Listen to your mother," Vahldan added lamely as he followed.

Brin marched right behind them. "You both think this is just about you. But it's not. I was born of the wolf and lion, too, you know. I heard you talking about your legacy. Well, if I'm not a part of your legacy, I don't know who is."

"She's got a point," Elan said, turning back. Vahldan stood staring at them both, dumbfounded.

Brin put her fists on her hips and addressed her father. "Think about it. If you're so sure you're destined, then I'm destined, too. If it's true, then maybe I'm supposed to fight, same as you. The Urrinan is here, isn't it? Neither of your sons is ready to fight. This is it. And I'm part of it."

Elan knelt and took her daughter's hands in hers. "Listen to me, Brin. I believe you *are* destined. You have definitely been chosen. In fact, I think your destiny is the most vital one. Trust me, you will be called upon to fight. But not right now. This one is not your battle. You've been chosen for far more. Your role is yet to come and you must live to perform it. For if you don't, the Urrinan—all we've endured and fought for—might all have been for nothing. Neither your father nor I can bear the thought of that. Which means we need you to stay here, inside the palace. I truly believe you can help to protect those who can't protect themselves. And that's what we need you to do. Understood?"

Brin looked hurt. She dropped her gaze, pressed her lips tight, and nodded.

Elan forced a smile. "Don't fret, baby girl. You *are* destined. Your wise great-grandmother guaranteed it when she held you on the day you were born. I admit, I didn't want to see. I tried to keep you from it. I'm sorry about that. But now I see it inside of you. So clearly." She tapped her daughter's chest and gently drew her chin up. "Your people will one day need you—more than you can know. Stay true to them. For me." She nodded up toward Vahldan. "For us. You are our most important legacy." She hugged her daughter and stood. Brin gave a stoic nod and Elan returned it. They'd fairly sparred to a draw. She turned and led Vahldan out.

Brin called down the corridor. "Promise me you'll come back."

Elan smiled at the routine. "I promise," she sang in reply. "And do you know why?"

"Because you're good at this," Brin replied in kind. "Damn good."

Elan caught Vahldan's astonished expression. "We'll both be back," she added. "Because we're even better together." She headed down the stairs and Vahldan wordlessly followed.

"Form up!" Arnegern cried from the saddle. "Those of you with horses, mount up."

Ermanaric came to mount his own horse. "All the lads under sixteen have been assigned to the walls of the keep, and I sent a messenger to the armory with orders to muster."

"Surely they know we're under attack." Ermanaric raised a brow and Arnegern nodded. "Wisely done," he acknowledged.

Through the commotion on the grounds of the keep Arnegern spotted them. "Gods afire," he murmured. Even in the morning twilight, they were stunning to behold.

Ermanaric followed his gaze. "Sometimes I forget," the big man wistfully said.

Side by side, Vahldan and Elan strode down the palace steps toward the vanguard, fully arrayed and walking tall. Vahldan wore his father's hauberk with the roaring lion's head crest newly emblazoned in red on his chest. The lion's mane sprouting from the crown of his helm fell into the flaxen hair that fell onto his shoulders. He wore the futhark sword on his hip.

Though Elan was no longer Skolani, she radiated the pride of a Blade-Wielder. She exuded a contempt for danger. Her cuirass was polished to a glow and her heirloom blade rose over one shoulder. In spite of the cold, her muscled arms were bare. Her doeskin leggings were tucked into her knee-high Saurian boots.

Striding together, side by side, they looked unstoppable.

"If that doesn't stir hearts to a fighting spirit, nothing will," he said.

"Aye," Ermanaric agreed.

The scattered cheers started as the grooms held their mounts for the pair. Vahldan mounted his new favorite horse, the dun mare Druzana. He drew Bairtah-Urrin and raised the bright blade overhead. The cheering rose to a roar.

Arnegern had to smile. Gods, they still loved him. Vahldan had led these men into this dismal war. He'd stubbornly put them into one impossible situation after another. Through it all, he'd sloughed off all of the day-to-day duties of leadership. He'd disappeared without a word just before the besieging foe had arrived. He was a womanizer, often volatile, and occasionally petulant. He flaunted Gottari custom and morals and often seemed to consider himself above Gottari law. He'd broken every rule a leader could break. But the rules didn't apply for a man like Vahldan, son of Angavar, Bringer of Urrinan.

Through all of their lives as warriors, Vahldan had been the first into every battle. Vahldan had come a blade's width from slaying the emperor of the mighty Tiberian Empire. Every man here knew that their chosen leader would die for them. Every man believed Vahldan would die to bring about the ascent of their progeny. And they in turn would die for him. He was their captain, their chieftain, their king. He was their hero.

Vahldan of the Amalus was a living legend. No one could doubt the truth of it. Who wouldn't want to be a part of a legend, to live on in song?

Vahldan kept the futhark sword overhead as he trotted the mare down the line. "My lions!" the king shouted and the cheering faded. "These imperial bastards have come in arrogance. They think to subdue us! But their arrogance is folly and their mission is doomed." The Amalus lions roared in agreement. Vahldan reined back to the vanguard and stood in the stirrups. "Come, my brothers! Let us show these invaders the error of their ways."

As always, Vahldan rode at the fore, leading the way. Once they cleared the palace gate, Vahldan beckoned Arnegern to ride beside him and Elan. "What do we know?" Vahldan asked.

"The seagates were opened. I suspect by force. The imperial navy was waiting to sail in."

"So it's a setup," Vahldan said, sounding unsurprised. "How many ships?"

"At least a score. Fewer than half have cleared the gates. Sadly the main quays were empty. Still, the foe can only dock and unload four ships at a time. But there's room for several others to wait at anchor inside the harbor."

Vahldan gave a single nod. "We need a division to retake the harbor gatehouse and reclose the bedamned seagates. The rest of us can try to contain those who've made land."

A resounding boom startled the horses. It startled Arnegern, too, truth be told.

Vahldan scowled. "What in the gods..."

"Catapult strike," Arnegern said.

"Sounds like the east gate," Elan added. "Looks like it's a two-pronged attack."

Vahldan turned to him. "At this point, I'd be a fool to doubt her. Take a detachment."

"How many?" Arnegern asked.

Vahldan looked back over the column, its tail end emerging from the keep. "Take all of those on foot. Elan and I will lead the riders to join with those at the armory. In haste! Let's ride!"

The king led the best of his Rekkrs, around a hundred mounted fighters, down Market Avenue toward the harbor, leaving Arnegern with mostly their sons and bannermen—all of those whose horses were kept in the city stables.

Arnegern called to those marching, regaining their attention. "Everyone afoot follows me!" He pointed and led them east. The sun had yet to crest the ridge ahead. The occasional missile strikes against the east gate were the only sounds. It was oddly still and the city streets remained deserted. Would the Hellains hunker down and wait this out? Or was there something more sinister at work?

For the first time, movement caught his eye. A boy ducked down behind the low stone wall of a courtyard ahead, in front of one of the largest merchant's houses to their right. Arnegern urged his horse to the edge of the lane to better see. The boy ran in a crouch and disappeared down an alley. Arnegern scanned the area more intently. More movement higher up. Faces disappeared from windows. He saw another form silently duck behind a roof parapet.

Their progress was being monitored.

"Stay alert," Arnegern called to those in front. "Shields at the ready. Pass the word."

He smelled smoke. Had the foe launched flaming missiles at the gate? They'd done it before. The lane ran straight from the fountain square to the east gate. He saw no smoke rising from the area around the gate.

Arnegern spotted more lurkers ahead. A pair of young men. One of them held a bow. They both ran north, up the lane that ran to the stadium.

As the column reached the crossroads, the source of the smoke came into view. It was billowing from the backside of the massive city stables near the stadium.

Arnegern halted the column. The terrified screams of horses echoed down the lane. At the end of the lane straight ahead, the Gottari detachment stationed at the east gatehouse was scrambling to reload their only catapult. He'd minimized their defensive presence here because there'd been almost no Tiberian activity on this side of the city. The eastern coastal road that led to the gate was narrow and the nearest landing was a long march away.

Clearly they had done things exactly as the foe had wished. Now Arnegern had to choose. Should he save the horses or hurry to attempt to thwart the attack on the gate?

Before he came to a decision, another missile crashed into the gate. This time the impact was accompanied by the sound of wood cracking. The iron portcullis was compromised. He was all but certain: The gate was about to fail.

Vahldan rode out ahead of even Elan and Teavar. He was the first to turn onto Armory Lane. He instantly reined in as Tiberian bows snapped and arrows flew.

A phalanx of the mobile reserve blocked the way. They had the walled armory compound besieged and had been waiting.

"How can this be?" Elan shouted as the vanguard's horses clomped to a halt and tried to turn to retreat down the lane. Horses reared up and snorted and neighed in complaint as they bunched together and arrows clattered to the cobblestone lane before them.

The rows of imperial shields looked like the scales of a dragon that had lain across the entire junction ahead. They filled the entire lane, staying just out of bow range from the only archers' nests to either side of the gate in the armory's surrounding wall. At least a third of his Gottari army was trapped inside. The Tiberians had established positions to rain arrows onto any attempt to escape the compound. They also blocked Vahldan's force from gaining access to their trapped comrades. Additional mobile reserve members continued to arrive, marching in a steady stream up the narrow lanes from the harbor.

"We must charge, my king," Ermanaric called. "Scatter them before it's too late!"

"No!" Elan cried. "Look. Their pikes! Remember? These devils target the horses."

The foe's lines bristled with the long spears they'd faced on the plain outside Megaria during his worst defeat. "We've got to get those seagates closed," he said.

"We can't leave so many trapped in the compound, can we?" Teavar asked.

"It would cost the bastards dearly to attack the armory," Elan said. "He's right, we may outnumber those left on the docks. If we don't stop them from arriving, we'll be outnumbered no matter what we do."

Vahldan raised his sword to gather attention. "Leave a squad of archers to keep them occupied. The rest of us will double back and ride to the harbor. We'll split up there and send a division to retake the gatehouse. On, Rekkrs!"

He waved the sword and rode back through the press. Getting the vanguard back to the back of the column was painfully slow. They cut through the city just north of the armory, winding through in order to bypass the foe. Once they were back on Market Avenue, they sped to a canter. Within moments of riding downhill, the next obstacle came into view.

"How have these walking stumps done so much so quickly?" Elan said, riding at his shoulder as Vahldan slowed Druzana. At the base of the avenue, between the last two corner warehouses, a barricade had been constructed. Closer inspection revealed stacks of shipping crates, barrels, and even overturned wagons. The obstacle stood twice the height of a man. Just as with the barricade outside Megaria, an opening was left at one end. The roofs of the warehouses above were lined with archers.

Ships lined the main quay and filled the harbor beyond. An acrid smell filled the air. He could almost taste it. Pitch burning. Elan pointed out into the harbor. "Look! The walkway to the gatehouse." A raging fire roared, belching black smoke from the wall walk between the docks and the gatehouse. "We won't be attacking that way any time soon," she said.

Vahldan's focus dropped to the avenue ahead. Before the barricade stood an imperial phalanx, shield to shield. But there was something else among them. Interspersed across the roadway were a half-dozen unusual wooden contraptions, about chest-high, each sitting on a base. "What do we have here? They have a new set of toys?"

"Are those tiny catapults?" Teavar asked.

"More like huge crossbows," Elan said.

He knew she was right. "They're horse killers." And he was leading them into range.

"Do we charge or pull up?" Ermanaric shouted.

Gods, Vahldan wanted to drive these bastards back into the harbor. But the memory of the first attack on Megaria provided a warning too clear to be ignored. "Pull up!" he cried as he reined in Druzana.

They beat to a halt, but too late. A cry went up from the imperial line, followed by a loud snap and whoosh. In a heartbeat, Druzana was rearing and shrieking. The mare tumbled to the cobblestones, struck in the chest by the largest arrow he'd ever seen. Vahldan was able to jump clear of her as she rolled, gasping for breath and writhing. He staggered to keep his feet beneath him and pain from his side wound pierced him. It felt like he'd been stabbed anew.

He got into a defensive stance, shield up, and surveyed the lane. Several other horses suffered the same fate and the entire Gottari column roiled in chaos. And then the arrows from the rooftops began to fall.

"Shields!" he called. "Form up to retreat!"

A guttural call echoed from the foe. Suddenly Elan was beside him. Teavar came up on the other side. "They're coming," Elan said, peering between their shields. "We've got to charge. Too many horses are down. If we run, they'll be on us. We can't let them break us apart."

She was right. "Dismount, men! Horses to the rear! Form up to attack!"

A line hastily gathered around him and his guardians. Vahldan huffed to catch his wind, each breath like a dagger to his side. He had to push past the pain. "Together, lions! Charge!"

ARNEGERN KNEW there was no time to waste. He didn't know the extent of the fire in the stables, but he knew that the Gottari army without horses was a severely weakened force. He went to a senior bannerman at the front of the column. "Take a score of archers and hurry to reinforce the gate."

"Right away, Captain!"

"The rest of you, follow me!" Arnegern turned and started up the alley to the stables. The bannerman drew aside those with bows and quivers from the column as they passed.

Arnegern rode as quickly as he dared. It wouldn't be wise to get too far ahead. Smoke poured from the northern doors and windows of the stables, but he saw no flames. The roof was made of clay tiles and the walls of stone, but the stalls were wooden. Based on the smoke, it seemed likely to be a straw fire. It also seemed likely to have been deliberately set.

As they closed in his eye was drawn to entry doors, flung wide. He peered in to see open stalls. He scanned the other exterior doors and the visible stalls. All were open. Which begged the question: Where were the horses? He dismounted in the courtyard outside of the stadium. "Hurry, men! Shields up! Form a perimeter. Some of you start drawing water from that well."

Arnegern drew his sword and beckoned a group of spearmen to follow. He headed to the main entrance, peering through the smoke.

He was right—mostly small straw fires. But he was also right that the horses were gone. Every stall gate had been left open.

A neigh drew his attention. He crouched down to get out of the thickest smoke and moved to look down the length of the main corridor. There was movement at the far end of the building, near the exit closest to the stadium. Two men with torches were shooing horses out.

The doors opened to a causeway that led into the stadium arena. The arena itself was enclosed but for a few narrow stairways that led into the surrounding stands. He could only hope that the horses were all contained there. That they were still safe.

The smoke forced Arnegern to retreat, much to the relief of his coughing guardians. Outside his men were drawing water and passing buckets to put out each blaze but their progress was slow. The fires were small but widespread.

Arnegern had to check the arena for their horses. He was about to mount to call out the orders when an arrow struck his horse in the hindquarters. The bucking horse pulled the reins from his hands and went kicking in flight down the alley. "Shields!" he cried.

Several more arrows landed among them. His men rushed for cover, several hunching against the low wall that lined the courtyard. Arnegern spotted a lone figure atop a house along the city wall. "Archer on the roof," he shouted. "Those with bows, return fire!"

Another arrow struck the ground, angled to have come from behind them. The shots were terrible, even with so many targets in the open. He spotted the second archer on the stable's roof, behind the ridge of the peak. He got a better look at this one. The man was no soldier. None of them were. They were Hellains in workmen's garb.

Realization struck. "It's a diversion!" Holding his shield high, Arnegern ran through his men, shouting as he went. "Back to the gate! We've got to get back to the gate!"

Before they were able to form up to march, the resounding boom of another catapult strike shook the very cobbles beneath his feet. It was soon followed by a thunderous chorus of male voices crying out in unison. It sounded like hundreds, if not thousands.

Arnegern couldn't see what had happened but he still knew. The gate had been breached. The eastern prong of the Tiberian assault was under way. And by the sound of it, his horseless detachment was outnumbered.

AT LEAST VAHLDAN had one thing going for him. The pain in his side faded as Thunar's Blessing pulsed through his veins and thrummed in his limbs. It was the clean burn of the forge. He remained clear of the ugliness, thank Freya. He knew it was because he was out in front, leading his host. He was acting in the name of his people. This was honorable, rightful. Fear held no sway in this. He ran harder, taking advantage of going downhill, and his two trusted guardians kept pace. He knew that his lions would stay with him, which made them formidable—a lethal force bearing down on an invading foe.

The Tiberian phalanx tightened and braced, shield to shield. The unified Gottari attack struck and immediately pushed the imperials back several steps. One of the long spears of the foe slid between Vahldan and Elan. She growled, quickly and deftly slashing it with Biter, snapping the wooden shaft like a dry twig.

Teavar roared and pushed, carving a gap into the enemy line. The yielding imperial line provided Vahldan and Elan access for lateral strikes. A thick-necked soldier slammed into Vahldan's shield, jamming the top rim into his jaw. Vahldan spotted the opening the move had created and jabbed. His blade bit into Thick-Neck, sliding past his chest armor into the meat adjacent to his shoulder. His victim howled and fell back and Tiberians scrambled to fill the gap. The foe's phalanx was straining, about to break. At the apex, the three of them worked in concert. Elan brought Biter down, hacking at a man that the giant had shoved back. Teavar bellowed and heaved again, sending another pair toppling back into those rushing to repel the Gottari gain.

They had broken the dam. The center of the phalanx broke and more Gottari burst through the void, slashing and jabbing. Tiberians preferred to stay close, utilizing shields and one another. Now the Amalus had made the space to fight the Gottari way. A doughty centurion came at Vahldan, leading with his shield. Their shields hit and the crafty centurion thrust low with his short blade. Vahldan was prepared for a tendency he'd long noted and parried with a down-slash. Once the centurion's blade was forced down, he yanked up, his pommel cracking the man where his chin ought to be. Vahldan pushed the off-balance soldier, creating the distance to swing the broadsword. The stroke severed the centurion's sword arm at the elbow. He jabbed as his victim contorted, piercing him alongside his breastplate. He yanked the blade back and the doughty centurion dropped to the cobbles like a felled log.

Trumpets sounded and Vahldan looked up to find that he and his companions were standing among the fallen. Tiberian discipline was on display again. He marveled. The foe had reformed their shield wall even as they hastily retreated. Marching backward, all on guard as row by row they slipped through the gap in their barricade.

"Damn you!" Vahldan spit a mouthful of blood. His side wound began to throb again as the threat receded with the foe disappearing through the gap.

"Who practices that?" Teavar huffed, watching their backward retreat incredulously.

"We're charging again, right?" Elan said, chest heaving.

"No," Vahldan said, surveying the archers lining the rooftops further down the lane. "Stand your ground, lions! Reform!"

"We were winning," Elan spat, her unsated rage apparent.

"We need to regroup. We're divided. This is how they want us."

Elan let out a roar of frustration. He put himself in front of her, making her meet his gaze. "Maybe I should anchor you today, eh?"

Her eyes cleared. She actually huffed a laugh. "Don't worry about me," she said. "Just work on keeping our hopes alive." Elan was back to herself, much faster than if the situation had been reversed.

The ground at their feet was bloodstained and scattered with bodies, mostly of the foe. The last row of the imperial phalanx stood guarding the opening at the side of the barricade. There were three mounted imperials visible through the gap. Officers, he knew. This was all being closely monitored and directed. He couldn't let them seize control of the events of the day. He had to get his army together, keep them off balance.

"Fall back," he called. "Help the wounded and bring the fallen."

He turned and cried, "Ermanaric!"

"My king?"

"Send a pair of messengers to find Arnegern. We need a plan for a coordinated attack on the Tiberians who are besieging the armory. Quickly!" The big Rekkr nodded and left.

Vahldan studied the foe as his men withdrew. "What of their fallen, my king?" someone asked.

"Leave them. No harm, no looting. Allow them to collect their dead and wounded."

Within moments of their withdrawal from the space, Tiberian soldiers scurried out to take up their fallen comrades.

Vahldan started uphill. He had a niggling sense and turned back for another look at the mounted officers. Only Teavar and Elan stopped with him. "Is that..." The one in the center removed his crested helm. It seemed willingly done, just to confirm his suspicion. And it did. "It is him," he said.

"Well, well," Elan said. "So he survived, after all. It explains much. The crafty bastard. He's tougher than I thought."

"Who?" Teavar asked.

"Their bedamned general." She grinned. "Got himself a new breastplate, though."

It was true. Vahldan would know him anywhere. That solemn expression. It felt like they were somehow tethered to one another. He knew neither of them would escape this without going through the other. The ache in Vahldan's side sharply flared at the thought. He'd long felt as if a part of the man's knife had been left inside him.

Vahldan had heard that the two of them were of an age. He'd always supposed Vernius to be older. Their rivalry had been so much different than his with Auchote. The mobile reserve had been so methodical, Vernius himself so detached, almost inhuman. Even so, the Tiberian leader had proven far from craven. He'd willingly sacrificed himself to save his emperor. Even when he'd thought him slain, Vahldan had been left with a begrudging respect for the man. The feeling was a bit less like respect now that he was no longer dead. Which left him with begrudging.

He and Vernius had been staring at each other a long moment when Vernius pulled his gloved fist to his chest and offered a tilt of his head. Vahldan held up Bairtah-Urrin before him, blade parallel to the ground, and tilted his head in reply. Without rushing or looking away, he wiped the futhark blade on the end of his cloak and sheathed it. He could've sworn that Vernius smiled before he pulled his reins and rode to disappear from view.

Vahldan turned and trudged uphill. Elan and Teavar stayed with him. He stopped over the poor fallen mare and knelt. He put his hand on her neck. Druzana was still. He stroked the soft mane. "I'm sorry I got you into this, old girl. You didn't deserve it. You served me well."

Elan stood over him. "Seems they wanted to make a point."

"Which was?" Teavar asked.

"That horses will not avail us," Elan said.

Vahldan stood and sighed. "Just as they've always wanted us to believe that our longer swords will not avail us. But they do not hold sway in this city. Not yet. Horses may yet have a part to play in this fight." He raised Bairtah-Urrin slightly in the scabbard and thumped it down. "Either way, I'm certain this sword will."

AGORAKI'S FATHER had told him to stay in their cabin below the top deck. Vernius had said the ship would soon be anchored in the harbor. As soon as it was unloaded. Ago couldn't see much through the portholes, but he could tell they were still alongside the quay. It was the smell of smoke that first lured him to the cabin door. He wondered if the whole city was burning. The thought was alarming.

Ago kept telling himself that his maaman would stay safe. For now she was behind stout walls. She had survived war and battles again and again. Even if his father's troops seized the palace, they weren't going to harm the servants.

He had to admit, at least to himself, that Apontia's safety wasn't the only reason he was troubled. There were others he cared about here who would be in harm's way. Indeed, there were others who would be targeted for harm.

Ago tried to convince himself that his worst fears were silly. The Gottari would ensure that the women and children were kept safe. Then he told himself not to worry about anyone whom he'd never see again.

It couldn't matter that one of those people was the only human who had never claimed to care about him. Well, without saying it because they wanted something from him. Other than his maaman, that is. It didn't matter. He reminded himself that she'd told him straight out: They were from different worlds. And neither of them fit into the other's. Their friendship had been a fine thing, but it was in the past. They had said their goodbyes. It was over.

Having Brin in his life was impossible now. And even if it wasn't impossible, their friendship would always be complicated. Besides, Brin was a survivor. She didn't need him, not for anything. He was sure of that much.

Still, he was having trouble shutting it all out. Imagining never seeing her again, without knowing what happened to her—well, that was what seemed impossible at the moment. Keeping thoughts of her from his head was like keeping the smoke from seeping into the cabin. Damn, it was stifling in here. Maybe he just needed some fresh air.

The cabin door wasn't locked. Ago peered out. The hold was empty. He started out the door, then hesitated. If there was even a chance he might not be able to convince himself to come back, he refused to be seen as a thief. He released the clasp on the torc hanging around his neck and laid it on the table his father used for his maps and papers. He rushed to the door, filled with crushing doubt and exhilarated at the same time.

Ago slipped out into the hold and stole to the nearby ladder steps. He popped his head up to survey the deck of the flagship. All of the soldiers were gone. Only a few crewmen remained, all busily unloading gear. There wasn't much left on deck. The sailors paid him no mind. They would be pulling in the lines soon, casting off to make room for the next vessel to unload.

From the steps he couldn't see over the gunwales, but a column of thick black smoke billowed into the dark clouds, coming from the walkway to the harbor's gatehouse. The day had started under clear skies, but Ago recognized clouds like these. A storm was coming.

The sounds of fighting had ceased. Ago stealthily climbed up onto the deck and moved aft, keeping low and out of sight as best he could. He squatted behind the dingy and peered over the side. The docks bustled with soldiers and sailors moving among stacks of gear. The mobile reserve was here to stay. This was an occupation.

Ago scanned the city sprawling across the hillside. He spotted a smudge of smoke rising from the northeast quadrant. It wasn't the palace. More like the stables. He sighed. Why should he care? Much of the city would probably burn again before this was done. Same as it did when the Gottari had come. This time he had a chance to stay clear of it. He really *should* stay clear of it.

Movement in the water caught his eye, just behind the ship. A fishing boat. Four men rowed and one stood at the prow. It was Malvius. The fink kept reappearing in Ago's new life.

His uncle scanned the docks as the fishing boat approached the quay. Ago ducked behind the gunwale. He peeked again a few moments later. Malvius's boat was tied off and his uncle was already at the top of a piling ladder and on the docks. "Lord General!" Malvius waved and Ago followed his line of sight.

Ago's father was mounted and riding from the end of Market Avenue toward Fishmonger's. The end of the avenue was mostly blocked by a giant pile of overturned wagons, barrels, and crates. His father was flanked by two other riders—the jingling captain with the horse-tail helm, Tullius, and another officer Ago didn't know by name.

Vernius kept watching Malvius. Even from here Ago could see that Malvius wanted something. He could also see his father's annoyance, from just his posture and expression. Vernius continued to speak to his companions as they walked their horses east along the edge of the docks. Malvius started to run, calling as he chased them.

Ago noticed the crew was untying the lines at the bow. They would cast off soon. He hated the thought of being isolated out in the harbor, so close and yet so far from things. Things that were happening so fast to his home city.

The gangway had been hauled. The aft line was the only one still tied; the dockworkers were strolling to release it.

Ago hadn't walked a line in ages. Why would he risk such a thing now? Gods, he couldn't be stuck on this damn ship. Not now. A powerful impulse seized him. He jumped up, gathered his balance, and started tiptoeing down the fat, taut rope.

"Hey!" one of the dockworkers shouted. The pair ran toward the dock-end of the line.

As soon as Ago was over the dock, he jumped. It hadn't looked far but his landing jolted his legs, sending darts from his stinging feet to his chattered teeth. "Hey!" someone shouted. Ago ran without bothering to look. "Stop! Grab that kid!" He wasn't about to turn back now.

An empty wagon rumbled by, heading east. Ago leapt and caught the large rear gate, got his feet on the edge of the bed, and held on. He looked back. The wagon had rolled behind a massive stack of crates, blocking him from the view of the ship and the dockworkers. He didn't know if he'd been recognized or whether they'd keep after him. Since he was out of their view, he leapt off and strode into a crowd of soldiers milling near the barricade at the end of Market Avenue. A few looked surprised but no one said anything or seemed all that interested.

Ago wove through the soldiers till he came clear of them near The Fishmonger. "Please, I need but a moment, my lord!" Malvius was just beyond a stack of barrels. Ago dropped to all fours and crawled into a gap in the lowest level of the barrel pile.

"Yes, Captain, what is it?" His father's annoyance was even clearer now that Ago could hear him. Ago crawled further into the pile until he could see through the gaps on the far side. His father had dismounted and Nico was leading his horse away. Captain Tullius and the other officer rode off.

"I was just wondering if the barbarians have been contained. Do you have them trapped in the palace keep yet?"

"Things are going well, Captain," Ago's father said. "All is on schedule. Thank you for your part in starting us off, but you and your followers may stand down." It was a dismissal. Vernius turned to leave. He'd heard that they were making the tavern a command post.

Malvius lunged to block him. "You've left the city's north side blocked?"

"As I said, all is in hand." His father's tone indicated he was getting hot. Ago leaned forward to peer out at them.

"Please, you mustn't forget the catacombs. They can be accessed from the palace."

"If the Gottari make the mistake of going down there, it will be a relief. We could trap them and take our time rooting them out. Even if I have to flood the damn things. I'll reduce the palace and everything beneath it to rubble if I must. Trust me—Vahldan will not escape."

Malvius stayed in front of him. "It's not just him. None of them can get away."

"Of course. Now, if you'll—"

"Particularly the family." Malvius grabbed his father's arm. Vernius looked down at Cap's hand with contempt. Cap removed it. "It's just... I know these people. They're obsessed with their prophecy. They believe they are the beginning of the end of our empire. They consider it a divine directive to ruin us, our very way of life, by any means possible. They care about that more than they do for their own skins. You must trust me, if any member of his family— particularly his children—is allowed to escape, this won't be over. It will start all over again. They simply must not survive this."

Vernius gathered himself. "As it happens, our emperor agrees with you. My orders are very clear. *No* Gottari are to escape this city. At the end of this campaign, no Gottari man, woman, or child will be left alive without being locked in slaver's shackles. As for Vahldan the Bold and all of his kin, I am to return to the hill in Medicia either with all of them in chains or with their corpses. Does that ease your concerns, Captain Malvius?"

Malvius backed off a step. "Yes, of course."

Malvius remained standing there as Vernius stalked into the tavern. Malvius wandered off, muttering, probably to go check his warehouses. Ago crawled back to the far side of the barrel stack. He scanned the docks. His father's flagship was gone and another was in its place. The dockworkers who'd chased him were tying it off.

He climbed out and started walking. He was already in trouble. He should go inside and surrender himself to his father. He strolled east and looked up the hill toward the armory. The top of the avenue was clogged with Tiberians. The mobile reserve had surrounded the armory square. They'd built more barricades on the side alleys. Along the avenue, doors were smashed and windows broken. Black smoke rose from the hilltop beyond the scores of foreign soldiers.

Gods, it was ugly. His city was being assaulted, defiled.

No. This wasn't Ago's home anymore. He had a new home. An

estate in Tiberia. He would inherit his own land. And these soldiers here weren't foreigners. They were *his people.*

Those things might have been true. But they didn't feel right.

He'd finally found his way to a future with a permanent home. But he'd never felt more off-kilter, more alone.

Although she wasn't his blood, nor even of his race, his mother lived in that palace. As did his only true friend—the only person who had accepted him as he really was.

Images filled his mind's eye: of the palace being reduced to rubble and the catacombs flooded. Of so many whom he'd known all his life either dead or in slave chains. He knew he should go to his father. It was the only route to his new homeland. Instead, Ago found himself walking past The Fishmonger, past the locked food vendors carts, and on into the gap between the warehouses to Peddlers' Row, heading uphill along the east wall.

Heading home.

CHAPTER 24
DESPERATE MEASURES

"In regard to those final days of the war, I have been asked about morale. Folk wonder how, as the mobile reserve's grip tightened, my father kept the fighting spirit among his followers so high.

The answer is far from simple. From my perspective, perhaps the prevailing morale of the day is better described as a fervency. But spirits inside the palace were far from high. I think the fervency was born of a dogged resolve. It must be remembered that everyone who followed Vahldan to Pontea believed in a very specific version of the prophecy. A version that foretold how this stage of the struggle would result in defeat and loss. But they also had faith that only in defeat could the Urrinan come to its providential fruition.

Their resolve was rooted in the belief that only through loss and suffering could their people ascend. Only through carrying out this final fight would their glory live on through the ages in song."—Brin Bright Eyes, Saga of Dania

IT WAS near midday by the time Hesiod finally left the residence. Once the manservant was gone, Brin hurried into her mother's bedchamber and closed the door behind herself. She went straight to the chest at the foot of her bed. With most of her mother's gear gone, the small shield was easily spotted. Brin grabbed it and pulled. The straps were tangled with the horse-hoof scallops of the breastplate, but she finally disengaged it.

The shield's chipped and pitted face was as green as the forest of the Pontean Pass. The bronze edge was dark with age. The wood was surprisingly light—not much heavier than the pot lid she'd been training with. The straps had grown stiff, almost brittle, but the buckles still drew them tight on her forearm.

Before closing the chest's lid, an overwhelming impulse compelled her. She just had to try it. Brin carefully lifted the breastplate from the chest and held it up. It too was surprisingly light and more subtle than she'd imagined. The top formed a simple loop. She dropped it over her head and it settled onto her shoulders. There were two straps that buckled across the back. She was able to reach to pull the lower strap through its buckle. The buckle hit a kink in the strap—obviously the spot where it fit her mother. It was too loose for Brin though. She pulled it tighter—all the way to the end of the coupling strap—and the scales grew snug on her hips. She couldn't reach the middle strap so she left the ends dangling. Instead, she slid her leather tunic belt out and tied it over the scales at her waist.

Brin went to her mother's looking glass. The sight sent a chill over her skin. She held up the buckler and lifted her chin. She gathered her braids and draped them over the breastplate in front of her shoulders.

Other than her mother, she'd never really seen a Skolani. Still, she was surprised to see how close she looked to what she had always imagined. The only thing missing was a sword hilt rising from over her shoulder.

Brin didn't own a sword. Yet. But her bow and quiver would finish the look fairly well.

The rattle of the outer door latch jolted her from her reverie. Hesiod was already back. She reached for the bottom breastplate strap. She couldn't pull it loose. It was stuck. It was only a matter of time before he came looking for her. Brin gave up on the strap. She'd just have to wear it. She crept to the door, listening. She heard the door to the servants' quarters and opened the bedchamber door to peer out. He'd gone into his quarters but left his door open. It was adjacent to the exit.

Brin glanced around the living chamber. The terrace. She needed to retrieve her bow, anyway. Ago had shown her how to climb from terrace to terrace. And this situation called for desperate measures. She crept out of the bedchamber and hurried to the terrace doors. In a mere moment, she was out and had the door closed behind her. She tiptoed to the corner of the parapet, behind the potted fir's branches, and looked down. Her uncle's residence was two floors below. All of the terraces below were empty. There was no one in sight.

Brin looked out over the city. The sky was dark and the harbor was crowded with ships. The seagates were still open. Dark smoke rose from several spots around the city below and on the hill toward the east gate. Brin couldn't be sure if the distant cries she heard on the wind were men's battle calls, seagulls, or both.

She took hold of the woodiest vines and scrambled over the parapet, seeking a foothold and moving down. The breastplate and the shield added to the challenge but she made steady progress, quickly growing accustomed to the new gear. A few times she was forced to let her legs dangle, using only her hands and arms to repel. The terrace below belonged to Arnegern and Mara. Too risky to stop there. She moved on. When Urias's terrace seemed close enough, she swung and dropped. It was farther than she'd judged and the landing stung her feet. Thankfully she'd learned how to flex her legs to absorb the impact.

Brin ran to the stone wall of the palace, beside the terrace doors. She peeked inside, scanning his quarters. No Urias in sight. No lamps were lit. Surely on this day of days, he'd have gone to command the patrol of the north gate. He'd been there most days since the siege had begun. Brin felt bad about sneaking into his quarters but the bow was hers. It had been a gift. When her mother had locked everyone out, Urias had said she should consider his home hers.

He'd forgive her. Well, eventually.

The click of the latch was alarmingly loud as the terrace doors closed behind her. She stole into the empty bedchamber. The bow and quiver were normally in the corner with Urias's gear, but the entire corner as well as the adjacent rack was empty. She spun, scanning the space. Both bow and quiver were leaning in the corner opposite his bed. Weird.

Brin hurried around the bed to grab them. She hastily strung the bow and slipped it and the quiver strap over her head, one on each shoulder. She headed for the exit, stopping at the main door to the corridor, listening for a moment. She opened it a crack to peek out.

A hand grasped the latch and pushed. Brin gasped and jumped back. Urias filled the doorway before her. Her uncle calmly stepped inside and closed the door behind him. He was wearing a polished hauberk with green and gold leather trim. There was a howling wolf's head etched at the center of his chest. A sword hilt was at one hip and a dagger at the other. He wore laced leather wrist guards and his hair was bound behind his head.

Gods revealed, her uncle was a warrior! Brin had never seen him look so formidable. Besides that, it reminded her just how handsome he was.

He took her in. "What's this about?"

"Sorry. I thought you'd be out on the north wall." She pulled at the bowstring and quiver strap across her chest. "Just came for my bow and quiver."

"I see what you came for. I'm asking what you intend to do now that you have them."

"All of the boys are patrolling the keep and the palace walls." She hated how whiny it sounded.

"You intend to join them?" She nodded. "So my next question is, does your mother know?"

"She's out fighting with my father."

"That's not what I asked and you know it. Have you two spoken about this?"

Urias's eyes hardened on her. Brin simply couldn't lie to him. She sighed. "We have."

"And?"

"I said I wanted to patrol the keep. Mother bid me to stay and protect the families in the residences."

He moved past her, then around her, looking her up and down. "Tell me why you decided to disregard your mother's wishes."

Brin recognized his tone. He wasn't admonishing her. Not yet. He was asking her to explain her thinking. "Because I know I'm better than them. The boys, I mean. I have better instincts. We're at war. Things are likely to get dangerous around here. I can be more useful out there than in here. Besides, our two biggest leaders are my parents. I have as much or more at stake than any of the boys down there. And..."

"And?"

"And, well, I'm afraid. For my mother. I... If there' a chance, any chance, that I can help her, save her... Up here I just feel so help-less. And useless. I want to help. I want a chance to make a difference."

Urias came back around, blocking her from the door again. He crossed his arms over his chest. He was weighing what she'd said, at least. Or was he just concerned? He didn't seem angry, thankfully. He finally spoke. "I understand your mother's concern. If the palace were to be breached, the king's family would need protection. Partic-ularly his young sons and their mothers, who are all but helpless. To be honest, it's why I came back from the north gate."

Urias drew a breath and sighed it out. He beckoned her closer, then took her by the shoulders and turned her to face away. "But I also understand your feelings." He took up the middle strap of the breastplate and started to fasten the buckle. "Truth be told, I too was feeling afraid and useless down on the wall. And I believe you are correct. You are better than the boys out there. Indeed, you do have better instincts."

The breastplate grew nicely snug on her. Urias turned Brin back to face him. "I will stay and protect the families, relieving you of the duty to which you were assigned."

She couldn't keep herself from smiling. "Thank you, Un—"

"On one condition." He held up a silencing finger.

"Anything," she said.

"That you promise me you'll never abandon your duty again."

"I promise."

Urias nodded. "Remember. Focus. Visualize the outcome. Do not let fear control you. Decide and do not hesitate."

Brin rushed to embrace him. Her uncle patted her back, then put his hands on her shoulders and held her out at arms' length. "Be mindful, my pupil," he said. "Remember what you've learned but trust your instincts."

Brin nodded and hurried to the door. Before the door closed, he called, "Brin." She stopped and turned. "Your mother... She may not often say it, but you are very precious to her. Please don't place me in the position of explaining to her why I put you in harm's way."

"I won't." She smiled. "Thank you, my mentor." She bowed and Urias tilted his head in reply. Brin closed the door, pumped her fist in victory, and ran for the stairs.

THE EXHAUSTED GOTTARI gathered on the fountain square outside the keep. From here Vahldan could see all the way to the harbor down Market Avenue. It was almost surreal, how quickly the odds against them had spiraled to new heights. He plopped down on the low stone rim of the fountain, their horses crowded around him, drinking from the lower basin. The breath of Rekkrs and horses came in steam that hovered like a low cloud over the square.

A gust of cold wind rattled the last of the brown leaves, hanging from the limbs of the damn tree, a few falling and drifting to the slushy pavers underfoot. The ancient tree had supposedly been planted in commemoration of the anax ancestry which was also celebrated by the adjacent statue, towering over them. Malvius insisted the man depicted was his forbearer. Vahldan recalled thinking when they first conquered the city how fitting it was that the decrepit tree seemed all but dead, just like the anaxship. And yet each year its leaves budded and flourished anew. No doubt it would flourish again come spring. It was more than he could say for his own reign.

It had been a long day already, and it was barely midday.

"What's your status?" Vahldan asked as Arnegern dismounted. The host his first captain led back dispersed to rest and talk among Vahldan's men that were already loitering on the square.

Arnegern pointed east. "The gate collapsed but I left a division to hold them from advancing on the palace. We're trading bowshots but the Tiberians aren't pressing. They seem more interested in forming a connection route to their fellows downhill."

Vahldan stepped up on the rim wall of the fountain, gazing east down the avenue. "Content to keep us separated from those in the armory?"

Arnegern shaded his eyes and looked south. "That and to begin their encirclement. I'd guess they sent the local militiamen they recruited against the stables because, yes, they want us disjointed. But it seems they also prefer to keep us afoot."

"Not to mention trapped," he added. "What's their end game?"

"I reckon that when they come, it'll be up from the harbor. Their main thrust will likely come right up Market Avenue. Still, they'll want to cover all other routes, to keep us from flanking. It'll take time to set up. The forces to the east and west are merely to make sure we stay put."

"Why Market Avenue? We can easily focus our counterattack on such a direct and obvious advance."

Arnegern nodded. "True, but it's still the broadest route, with the least potential for ambush. The bulk of their force can be formed up to advance right off of the ships. If they can keep containment on those in the armory throughout, all the better."

Elan stepped onto the fountain's rim, shading her eyes to gaze down at the harbor. "With us up here, they can take their time getting ashore and forming up. I'd say things are going pretty well for them, so far. They only grow stronger as the day wears on."

Ermanaric exited the palace keep gate and came to them. "What did you find out about the horses?" Vahldan asked.

"The Hellain militiamen drove them out of the stables and into the equine arena, but all the gates were open. Half of them wandered out to the north to get as far from the fires and the noise as possible. But there was nowhere for them to go from there. Most are just grazing on what little grass they can find between the wall and the arena. The rest have wandered into the martialing courtyard and have huddled together. Just looking for safety and to get out of the wind, I suppose. Can't say I blame them. I've got some lads herding them into the keep."

"Did you happen to check on the bastards outside the north gate?"

"I did. Our sentries have seen no new activity. I asked if the foe has reduced their numbers there. They said if anything, it looks like there may be more of them."

"Making sure we stay put," Arnegern repeated.

Elan huffed a laugh. "As I've long said, they don't want to drive us out. They want to crush us. Their way of ending this war is to end us."

Arnegern smiled ruefully. "Then I guess it's a good thing we're looking to begin something. Are we not, Bringer?"

Vahldan clapped his old friend's back. He looked to Elan. "Didn't you also say they wanted to make sure that horses wouldn't avail us?"

"Feels that way to me. Why? What are you thinking?"

"I'm thinking that they think they're succeeding in every way—that we've reacted exactly as they've expected, at every turn."

"And?"

"I think it's high time we did something they aren't expecting." He turned to Ermanaric. "Take a squad back and round up every saddle and bit of tack you can get your hands on." The Rekkr bowed his head and started to leave. "And we'll need the pikes we used at Efusium, too."

"Right away, my king."

ELAN SCANNED the dozen or so horses Ermanaric had brought out for them to choose from. The first mare to catch her eye was as brown as burnished leather with black socks. She was notably calm, standing alone, unconcerned by the bustle. A young groom held her lead.

Elan looked down and offered her hand to humbly greet her. "Do you know her name?"

"Aye, my lady. She is called Ainsjót. Though I've no guess what it means nor how she came by it."

Elan laughed. "Horsella's shiny bare ass!" The mare bobbed her head and snorted, miffed to be laughed at. "Forgive me, Ainsjót. It is a very fine name. And I am honored to meet you." The mare then deemed Elan worthy of stroking her neck. The groom's eyes went wide. "Her name is from the old tongue of the Skolani," Elan explained. "It means *the chosen spear*. It also means that I am meant to choose her. She shall lead the final charge on this day of days."

Vahldan came over. "You've found one already? I presume she's the best here."

"I have and she is. Shall you ride her or shall I?"

"Oh, she should bear the best rider we have."

"I can't argue with that logic."

He grinned. "So now pick the one least likely to throw me. Then we can get going."

"I have the horse for you, my king." It was a young Gottari woman. Elan had seen her many times but they'd never spoken. Elan thought she lived in the barracks building. She led a sleek stallion toward them. He too was dark brown with jet-black mane, tail, and socks.

"Whom do we have here?" Vahldan asked.

"We have Luith-Anthar—the song of battle." She bowed.

"And you are..."

"I am Afredya, daughter of Fredebrand, my king. My father fell at Orithya."

"I'm sorry for your loss," Vahldan murmured.

"It was his honor to serve both you and Urrinan." The girl stroked the stallion's neck. "Lu here has not been himself since that day. He misses my father, yes. But Lu knows he is at his best in battle. He and I have feared he is fated to a life of grazing. Both of us know that would be far from fitting. He will serve you well, my king. It is meant to be. I know it in my heart."

Vahldan bowed his head to the young woman. "I thank you for your sacrifice. It's a mighty gift. Your family has served our people well. You have their gratitude and mine." Elan saw that Vahldan was genuinely touched, as did Afredya. It was clear how proud he made her feel. He'd always had a knack for connecting with people. He really was a born leader. It made Elan wish things had been different. But it was far too late for regrets.

Vahldan introduced himself to the stallion while the grooms briskly worked to saddle the mounts and the Rekkrs readied their armor and gear. Gottari horns echoed through the city.

Ermanaric rode in through the keep's south gate and spurred across the grounds to Vahldan. "Arnegern's men have made contact, my king."

"It's time," Vahldan said. He mounted Lu, who immediately showed his spirit, tossing his head and strutting proudly to the fore.

Calls to mount up rang through the keep. All told, they were just over a hundred. They'd be vastly outnumbered. But they would also be unexpected.

Elan settled into the saddle and Ainsjót started a jittery little sideways dance. She leaned over the mare's neck. "Fear not, brave one. I will not let them target you. Together we will make them pay for what they did to Hrithvarra." The mare instantly settled. Better still—and unbidden—Ainsjót instinctively headed to the front of the column. This one knew her place. "The chosen spear, indeed," Elan said aloud.

Vahldan drew the futhark sword and rode along a waiting column for the second time that day. "This is destiny, my brave brothers. Be proud! For together, we face our fate. Together, we ride for the good of our people, for their future. At long last, Urrinan is here, waiting only for us. Together, we ride unto the prophecy's fulfillment."

They were grimmer words than those normally said to those riding into harm's way. The response was equally somber. But they were spoken to, and accepted by, those who grasped that they rode to destiny.

Vahldan trotted the dark stallion up to halt beside Elan. "Ready?"

"If I'm not after all of these years, I have no one to blame."

The sky had grown darker all afternoon and a gust of wind blasted them as they reined to file through the narrow north keep gateway. Light snow swirled around them. "The storm comes," she said once they were abreast again.

Vahldan smiled. "In more ways than one." They cantered east and followed the curve of the wall around the backside of the stadium. The lane narrowed as they came about, heading for the top of the avenue, between the city stables and the east gatehouse. The avenue broadened beyond the east gate. The Tiberians had formed a line a bit west of the gateway, toward the fountain square. A few men could be seen loitering in the distance near the gatehouse. "They don't look like soldiers," he said. "Maybe militia?"

"All the less likely to slow us down," she said.

Vahldan twisted in the saddle to check the column winding through the maze of lanes behind them. "Shall we gallop?"

Elan gave him a nod. "May as well get warmed up."

He leaned to one side. "What say you, Lu?" The horse instantly responded to his heel taps. Vahldan raised the bright blade overhead, pointed forward, and started to gallop. Ainsjót carried herself well, easily falling into the rhythm of breath and stride. Those in the roadway near the gate turned and gaped before scrambling out of the way. "They're carpenters," she called. "Already repairing the gate, I suppose."

Vahldan nodded. "No need to call up the lances, then." They led the first riders past the gateway. Elan glimpsed a few surprised Tiberians on the wall near the gatehouse but they rode past without incident, out onto the downhill avenue that many called Peddlers' Row. Vahldan beckoned the column on and pressed Lu for more speed. The mare she rode was competitive, unwilling to allow the males to get too far ahead.

She glanced back to find the rest of the column had passed the gate. The avenue ahead was empty. They rounded a slight curve and headed down Armory Lane. The corner of the compound wall came into view. A roar of voices echoed down the lanes—men shouting battle commands. Arnegern's feinted infantry attack was well underway.

A pair of Gottari sentries stood on a platform at the nearby corner of the wall. Vahldan waved the sword. "Ready your brothers! Call them to battle!"

One of the guards cupped his hands and cried, "We are ready, my king! On your call!"

Good. Those inside the armory had gotten the message. Color and motion lay ahead in the square at the far corner of the armory, outside its main gate. Vahldan signaled and he and Elan moved aside. He beckoned to the lancers. Two dozen of his finest Rekkrs rode out to the fore, lowering their long weapons.

Elan and Vahldan kicked their mounts and rode into the gap left for them, behind the lancers but ahead of the remaining host. She drew Biter from over her shoulder, twisting her neck and rotating her right shoulder. The old aches faded as Thunar's Blessing pulsed anew.

The chargers gained speed. Though she couldn't see much around those riding ahead, she felt it. Battle was upon them. The very air thrummed with it. Ainsjót sensed it, too.

The lane broadened and lancers fanned out. The imperial formation sprawled before them—straight and tight, shield to shield. As they'd sought, and dearly hoped, the foe was near but faced away, oblivious. Arnegern's footmen initiated their retreat. The imperials cheered, thinking they were winning.

But they were heartbeats from finding out differently. Collision was imminent.

Agoraki popped up to peer over the low wall he'd vaulted to hide behind. He took several deep breaths to settle his thudding heart as he watched the last of the Gottari riders disappear downhill into the swirling snow. Shock didn't seem like a strong enough word to describe the feeling he'd had when they'd come charging around a bend on Peddlers' Row, heading straight for him. He'd thought for sure they'd been coming just for him. It seemed silly now that they'd passed him by, heading down to turn onto Armory Lane. He'd seen the troops there and had realized that the fight had been on. He'd also recognized the opportunity. Both sides were about to be busy. This was his chance to get to the palace.

There was no turning back now. Ago was behind the Gottari lines.

He hopped over the wall onto Peddlers' Row again, heading uphill. He just had to get to the city stables. He came around a light bend, stopped short, and jumped into another courtyard. This time the way was blocked by dozens of imperial troops. They filled the crossroads at the east gate, all bustling and calling to one another. The Gottari's passage must have stirred them up. Continuing that way was out. He couldn't afford to be stopped or even seen by an imperial soldier. Many of them would recognize him as the general's son.

Ago sat down and leaned on the inside of the wall to think. The stone was cold and the wind off of the sea was even colder. He tucked his hands into the pouch on the front of his tunic. He should've thought to look for a cloak before he'd left. Snow swiftly covered his lap. Perhaps the situation was a sign. Maybe he should do exactly what he was trying to avoid—go to the soldiers and turn himself in. He could say he got lost. They'd likely escort him to safety and shelter. They would probably even have a cloak or a blanket for him.

The mobile reserve would not be losing this battle after all. That was unthinkable. This war would soon be over. He might not even get to the palace in time. This was a fool's errand.

His father would return to his home a hero. Ago would go with him. Home. The home he'd never had. Vernius had already told him of it—of the hillsides lined with grapevines and the dew on them in the mornings; of the cottage and the gardens; of the ancient brick oven in the cooking shed and the wonderful bread that was baked in it.

An unbidden image came to Ago, of the Thrakian palace being swarmed by these very soldiers. Images of the fires and blood, of the catacombs being flooded or the entire building being reduced to rubble. Images of the people who lived there suffering, dying.

He thought of his maaman, how she hated the Tiberian soldiers, how they'd slaughtered her family and burned her people's village.

No. He'd already decided. He knew the palace's hidden ways and the catacombs better than anyone. He could make it there safely. And swiftly. Once inside, he might be able to save lives. He should go home. Home. The only one he knew.

He just had to get to the stables. Ago scanned the houses. Their terraces were empty. All of the shutters and drapes were closed. He spotted a walkway between the two nearest houses with an iron gate. In this quadrant, each house along the avenues and lanes housed multiple families—mostly vendors from the marketplace and their workers. He knew each would have a back courtyard, likely shared by several houses. The walkway would lead to the courtyard, and on its far side would be another walkway, leading to a gate that opened to the next lane over. He could utilize the walkways to make his way to the arena alley, then head north. He got up and ran to the gate. It wasn't locked.

He slid through, peering down the narrow passage. Empty. The courtyard was in sight. He quietly closed the gate behind him and jogged into the shadows.

THE LANCERS HIT the Tiberian formation with a resounding crash followed by a grinding sound—their armored victims being knocked down and shoved across the cobbles. Elan watched in awe as the foe's phalanx shattered into pieces. Human screams were drowned by the roar and horns of Arnegern's men, who turned back to rejoin the fray.

A moment later, more horns and a chorus of voices rose behind them. Elan turned in the saddle to the new sound. The armory gates flew open and Gottari warriors poured out onto the streets.

Elan moved to ride just behind Vahldan's raised sword arm and raised her own. Vahldan targeted a handful of Tiberians scrambling to form up to face the onslaught. Vahldan's swing clanged an imperial helm, sending its wearer sprawling. Elan spotted her target—a soldier drawing back his spear to jab at Vahldan's mount. The soldier twisted to thrust, baring his unarmored side. Biter's edge found the gap. For her part, Ainsjót barreled right through the remaining soldiers, knocking two over and trampling over them as she galloped on.

Tiberian centurions bellowed commands and the remnants of the scattered imperials hastily retreated downhill toward the docks. Vahldan retreated from the slaughter, calling back those who rode in pursuit before they ventured too close to the dockside imperial barricades. He needed cohesion to have their newly-won momentum make an impact.

He raised the futhark sword. "To me, lions! To me!" He pointed down the lane. "Together! Together we can push these demons back into the harbor!"

Once the riders were reassembled, with Arnegern's foot soldiers and the newly released men from the armory lined up behind them, Vahldan pointed the sword and spurred his mount downhill. Elan hardly needed to heel Ainsjót to follow. Heading along the armory wall, they galloped through the swirling snowflakes with the thunder of a hundred sets of hooves and a raucous cheering behind them. It was beyond exhilarating.

Vahldan looked at her, his eyes and smile bright. The thrill of it made her spirits soar even higher. For he remained free of the ugliness.

Time seemed to slow and everything beyond them seemed to blur. This was it! The sights, his face, this feeling. It was seared in memory. Elan suddenly realized she was living a part of her dream —the one that had revealed her destiny all those years ago. She hadn't had it in years, but the images that had repeated until they'd been etched in memory came flooding back. Dream and waking life became one. It filled her heart with a surge of joy, unlike anything she'd ever experienced. And yet, it was a melancholic joy.

She suddenly knew, then. By revealing the dream as real, the gods were whispering that this was almost over—that everything that had led her and her truest love to this moment was about to culminate in a fated ending. Destiny was nigh.

Still, Elan knew she'd gotten here by choice. She'd chosen to leave her tribe, chosen to follow him here, chosen to stay at his side through it all. She'd chosen him. In this moment, she knew, too, that she'd chosen love.

This was the ending of a story so vast, so swift, and so damn powerful. The sweep of their entire lives together suddenly felt like a dream, and the dream was a river running to the sea, carrying them with it.

All along, this had been it. Whatever came of it for their people, she and Vahldan had been borne along by the flow of love. Even the hurt and the agony during their long struggle had been powered by the flow of love. A mighty and unstoppable love, beyond what ordinary folk would experience or even dare to seek.

The moment ended when they came around the south end of the armory and turned the angle onto Fishmonger's Lane. Vahldan reined in and cried out, "Halt, Rekkrs! Hold!"

Elan pulled on Ainsjót's reins and focused ahead, taking in the barricade at the base of the hill. But the entire barricade was moving, being drawn aside as if by magic. As it was pushed aside, it revealed a sight that her eye, at first, could not quite comprehend.

Men. Rows and rows of them. Not just men, soldiers. Tiberians. Thousands of them filling the docks. Their crisp ranks filled the entire space to the quay's edge. All of the thousands of lookalikes bore the same shields, their spears bristling in perfect rows. She'd seen imperial legions before, but never like this. This was an awful, almost incomprehensible sight.

Elan's joyful dream had turned into a nightmare.

The mounted Amalus beat to a halt, horses neighing in complaint, many bumping and rearing and bucking.

A lone, resonant call was followed by the thunderous reprise from a thousand baritone voices, and a thousand spear-butts thumped the wooden docks. The resound seemed to still the very sea. The Rekkrs and the Gottari footmen behind settled to stillness on the avenue.

Vahldan looked over at her, his eyes a little wild. It wasn't the ugliness. This was Thunar's Blessing morphing into temptation. He wanted to ride through them—to kill as many imperial invaders as possible on the way to the doom he'd long known he would face.

Such a feat would be sung of through the ages.

But she knew it couldn't be. This wasn't it. There was more. There was Brin.

Elan shook her head. "Not yet," she said.

He seemed to come to himself. "Yes, you're right," he said.

Vahldan the Bold turned reluctantly and called for a retreat. The gods were fickle, indeed.

CHAPTER 25
ECHOES OF HONOR

"It is odd, is it not, how certain moments stay with us? They are carved into memory just as a chisel etches runes onto a ring. They are not always moments we wish to save. Indeed, some we dearly wish we could change or take back.

Some have the power to summon the cheek-stinging flush of shame, fresh as the day it was first invoked.

The years have caused my memories of my father to fade and blur, like pages crumbling and falling from an aging book. But in one such memory, etched by my shame, I see him fresh, vibrant as the sundrenched evening on which the incident occurred. As a consolation to the enduring shame, I have come to realize it is perhaps the moment in which Vahldan's love for me was most vividly revealed."—Brin Bright Eyes, Saga of Dania

VERNIUS AND NICANDROS sat on their mounts, side by side and behind the lines, watching the phalanx march another agonizing ten paces up Market Avenue. The snow had ceased but not before it had coated the cobbles, making the footing treacherous. At least the wind was from the sea, which put it at their backs. Each time Vernius thought they'd finally established enough momentum to send the Gottari into full retreat, the stubborn barbarians turned and counterattacked. Again and again, the shield walls of the two sides slammed together, mashing and sliding, bellowing and cursing. Each time, he was forced to call his lines back to reform.

He had to admit, each time the Gottari not only took their dead and wounded with them, but also kept a respectful distance, allowing the Tiberian dead and wounded to be retrieved. Vernius had thought he was done with honor—at least for the duration of this war. But it seemed there was some honor left among these barbarians after all. He wondered if it was his ancestors intervening, trying to keep him off balance.

Although the casualties continued to mount, at least Vernius's plan was back on track. His army might yet take this city by sundown. He had to admit, they'd suffered a stunning blow at midday. It was more than a minor setback. Vahldan's strike had reunited the Gottari. Which was precisely what was making the rest of this uphill drive so brutally difficult.

Over the course of this war they'd passed through many dark moments, suffered loss, pain, and angst. Much as the two sides reviled one another, the mobile reserve's begrudging respect for the Gottari remained. He suspected it was mutual. Still, Vernius had to admit that his respect had only grown through this awful day. Gods, these warriors were doggedly determined, even in what could only end in defeat.

He had seen Vahldan the Bold several times that day. Each time, his rival was not only dashing and charismatic, but valiant and honorable. The man evidently would never ask anything of his men that he would not risk doing himself. It seemed so discordant from everything Vernius had been led to believe—not just about this backwoods raider come self-proclaimed king but about this particular tribe of Teutonics in general.

Tullius and Lauterus appeared from the lane that crossed from the armory and rode to Vernius. Much to Tully's chagrin, Vernius had assigned Lauterus to serve as his equine captain's second-in-command. The man had been captured, found his way to gaining honorable release, and reported back with solid intelligence. He'd proven himself unshakable. Vernius had never admired him more. Plus he was a local. Lauterus was the perfect foil to Tully's reckless and somewhat brutal tendencies.

Just as Tully saluted, a gust of wind blew the ridiculous red horse's tail at the back of his helm into his face. "The push continues on each of the uphill lanes, Lord General. The lines at the east gate and the west gate stand firm. We outnumber the savages on all fronts now. I ask that you allow me an equine charge from the armory. The barbarians are weaker there and we might find a way to thrust westward, flanking those you press here. It would speed a break-through, I assure you. The bulk of Vahldan's army would then be trapped between us."

Vernius continued to gaze at the Gottari line, grudgingly reforming a few span uphill from their prior position. They looked exhausted, but so did his own veterans. These were proud men. On both sides. The Gottari knew they were giving ground. But they were unbroken. Unbroken and unbeaten. They would yield this city on their own terms. Seeking a swift end through sly maneuvers might cause them to behave erratically.

It would likely lead to the abandonment of the semblance of honor both sides clung to.

"No. My orders stand. Maintain your positions and continue to press. There's no need to get clever. If every unit keeps the pressure on, soon enough we'll have the Gottari encircled in the palace square."

Tully looked like he was about to burst into flames. "But, my lord, we can cut them in two. We might even prevent them from fleeing into the palace keep. If we trap them, they would be ours to slaughter at will. We can end this!"

"I said no," Vernius snapped. Both Nico and Lauterus went wide-eyed. "Only trouble comes of whipping an aurochs that's already backing into the pen."

Tully's lip curled. "As long as you intend to slaughter the beast in the end."

Just as Vernius opened his mouth to reprimand him for the insolence, a host of mounted Gottari galloped crosswise behind the Gottari line, taking the crossing lane east toward the avenue up from the armory. It was Vahldan and a dozen of his fiercest warriors, including the Hippomache. They'd been doing this all afternoon— flying back and forth, striking wherever his warriors needed the aid. Their efforts were evidently keeping the fighting spirit of the foe high, their lines unbroken.

This time they were headed for Tully's unit's position. Lauterus nodded back the way they'd come. "Seems we'll have our hands full without attempting a clever maneuver, Captain."

Tully's jaw clenched. "I wish my lord would consider that these are savages. Our orders are to exterminate the ongoing threat."

Vernius took a beat. "Never question my grasp of my orders again." He'd kept his voice low, even. Tully dropped his chin to his chest. He brightened his tone. "Now, I would suggest, Captain, that you hasten to ensure that our containment holds. I shall hold you accountable for any such failure."

The man gave an obsequious salute, causing his ridiculous bangles to jingle. "As you command, Lord General." It might have been sardonic and irreverent, but Vernius knew that a man like Tullius needed to assuage his ego. He let it go.

As Tully rode away, Lauterus actually rolled his eyes before he bowed his head. Although Vernius sympathized, he kept his expression hard as he returned the gesture with a tilt of his head.

Navigating the end game of this war would be tricky indeed.

THE ALLEYS that had led him here had been a maze—one that Ago couldn't easily retrace—but he finally peered out onto the broad avenue that led from the east gate to the fountain square. He sensed movement at the corner of his eye. Someone was peeking out the shuttered window of the house next to the alley. The shutters snapped closed when he looked.

Ago stepped out to the edge of the avenue. To the west the roadway was blocked by dozens of soldiers facing the other way. He couldn't see much beyond them, but he gleaned they were standing off with a line of Gottari defenders, holding them out of the fountain square. Back toward the east gate there were more imperial troops, mostly mulling about as carpenters worked to restore the gate. There was no one directly in front of him. Across the roadway were the stables—a complex of buildings and lean-tos that had been added onto dozens of times over decades, if not centuries.

Ago wasn't sure if anyone was looking, but he saw no reason to wait. He ran.

A man's voice called for him to halt, but he kept on running into the shadows of an alley directly across the way. He ran into the open doorway of a lean-to shed and hid among the bales of straw stacked inside, his heart thudding. At last he was north of the battle, on the same side of the gate roadway and square as the palace. Progress. He worked his way through the back of the shed and into a maze of connected storage sheds that lined the exterior walls of the main stables. He came out on the eastern side and hurried along the line of rickety donkey pens and their carts, ducking behind a series of chicken coops and piles of coal.

Ago turned the corner at the north end and stopped, panting to catch his breath and straining to listen for sounds of pursuit. A rattling sound caused him to jump. It was only a cat. He hurried on, working his way to the stables' main doorway on the angling northeast side of the complex, across from the stadium. He finally saw it. He'd made it. He spotted a group of imperial soldiers patrolling the roadway along the wall on the far side of the stadium. But the entrance was near. Better still, the area between the stables and the stadium was empty.

Staying to the shadows, he briskly strode toward the open doorway. The smell of wet charcoal and burnt kindling filled his nose, growing stronger as he went. He began to taste it. Just within the open doorway he saw it. Smoke hung in the air. A noise behind him startled him to hurry into the dark interior. He instantly started to cough. He pulled the neckline of his tunic up over his nose and mouth. The courtyard outside the stables was churned to mud.

Ago gazed down the hazy corridor lined with stalls. The piles left in the open straw storage bays still smoldered. There wasn't a horse in sight. Here and there, the wood of the stalls was charred black. His eyes stung and he could hardly draw a breath without coughing. The spot he sought wasn't far. He couldn't give up. All he needed was access to the catacombs. All he had to do was get to the trapdoor in the tack room.

Continuing to breathe through his tunic, he hurried to the tack room door. If anything, the smoke was thicker inside. He gagged and nearly retched. He dropped to his hands and knees, held his breath, and crawled in. Through the murk he perceived that the racks that held the saddles had fallen. The entire back half of the floor was a smoldering heap.

Ago felt dizzy and knew he needed air. Heart thudding, he scrambled for the exit. Once outdoors, he drew his first breath and fell onto his side, hacking, unable to stop or catch his breath. He felt miserable. Not just because he had to keep swallowing to stave off vomiting.

The smoldering heap of leather lay directly on top of the trapdoor. He couldn't even get back to it, let alone move it. The way home, to his mother, to his friend, was blocked.

All of this way, all of the danger and cold—all Ago had sacrificed in order to run away—had led to nothing. It seemed no matter what he did, he was trapped between two worlds.

THE SNOW STOPPED, which was good. It made it easier for Brin to keep her bow dry. A thin layer of white covered all the grass and plants. It was pretty but it had made the paths through the palace keep gardens muddy. The sky remained cloudy, but the sun behind the clouds had sunk to the western hilltops, casting the entire keep into shadow. It got dark early these days. Brin meandered in the area she and Urias used for training. She slowly retrieved her arrows, listening to the distant horns. Gods, it seemed like they kept getting closer. She tried to control her fears but this was scary.

Earlier, Brin had made an appearance on the wall-walk. The bully-boys clustered around the southern gatehouse had whispered and snickered. Their nonsense didn't bother her all that much. Having beaten most of them in the sparring rings made them pretty easy to dismiss. But it was so boring up there! Nothing in sight but distant columns of smoke. She figured she'd go back when there was something to see.

Brin counted her arrows. All there again. She returned to the firing line and forced herself to stand in place, to straighten her wrists and firm her arm. She sighted the target properly, forced herself to breathe, to focus, to visualize, and to smoothly release.

And she missed. Again.

Gods, this version of archery was frustrating. Her uncle kept telling her it was fine that she was better at shooting on the move. He'd even laughed and mused that it was probably more useful than standing and shooting with proper form.

But Brin couldn't let it go.

Why couldn't she stand, aim, and shoot? It should be so simple. Seemed like a skill that would come in handy up on the wall. Soon now, actually. She drew and shot again. Another miss.

Brin lowered the bow and sighed. Just as she drew another arrow from the quiver, Gottari horns sounded. The blast was one was the closest yet. She held her breath and listened for more. She felt more than heard the hoofbeats. The bully-boys on the wall scurried to line the parapet closest to the gatehouse, chattering and pointing.

This was it.

Brin scanned the top of the south wall adjacent to the garden. Not a single one of them was patrolling the end of the wall-walk nearest to her. Which was absurd since it overlooked the eastern end of the fountain square. Rather than heading for the main stairway by the gatehouse, she threw her bow over her shoulder and headed for the southeast corner of the keep. There was a crumbling old stair that ran along the east wall up to the mini version of the gatehouse that sat on the corner. No one used the stairs to it because of the missing steps. That and the fact that the ancient stone slabs seemed likely to collapse underfoot.

On the way to the stairs, she snatched up the two arrows she'd shot. Keeping herself flat to the wall, Brin pranced up the stairs, hopping over the worst of the crumbled treads, to arrive safely on the empty ramparts. The defensive shield wall across the avenue that led to the east gate was still there but behind it the square was filling with Gottari. Riders on horseback circled the square, shouting commands. Gottari warriors on foot poured from the alleys and smaller lanes into the square. In several spots, they reformed into shield walls, but she could tell they were all in retreat.

She leaned over the parapet. The main shield wall holding the line to the east was slowing stepping back to the fountain square.

Then she saw them. The most Gottari yet appeared, moving slowly in retreat up Market Avenue. Behind them were rows on rows, all on the march, coming up the avenue, pushing the smaller Gottari force backward. The Tiberian formation was so neat, their rows so crisp. They held their rectangular shields just so—as neat as shingling tiles on a roof.

The commotion and the awesome sight of the foe sent a wave of terror through her.

The Gottari lines at the tops of all the alleys and lanes, along with those coming from the east gate and west gate avenues, all came together with the retreating army coming up Market Avenue. Every outer edge of the square bustled with Gottari now. Trumpets blared and the foe on Market Avenue released a guttural bark as they came to a halt. In comparison, the Gottari lines looked messy as they came together. Behind the shield walls, mounted Rekkrs and runners scurried back and forth across the fountain square, shouting and pointing, directing the Amalus army to gather and hold in a giant arch-shaped line. The Tiberian commanders' cries echoed up to her. Just behind their front lines she saw archers raise and draw their bows. Their moves were just as precise as the way they marched. She glanced to find the Tiberians to the east and west were doing the same. The Gottari at the front all raised their shields overhead and those behind the line gathered into clumps and raised theirs together, too. From above they looked like a centipede crawling around a cluster of flowers.

When the Tiberians fired, Brin swore she heard the thrum of hundreds of bowstrings snapping at once. The arrows looked like strange flocks of diving seabirds angling down to fall like hail onto the Gottari shields and the cobbles of the square. Several Gottari horses screamed and one was sent bucking so wildly the rider was thrown.

Then Brin saw him—her father, riding behind the lines. He was moving from the thickest part of the formation at the top of Market Avenue to those holding the line coming from the east gate. And there, riding at his shoulder, was her mother. They each sat so tall in their saddles. There was beauty and grace to their posture and form. Her heart swelled with pride even though her hands were shaking. She was so scared for them. Her father had his shield with the snarling gold lion's head on a red background slung over his back. He waved and pointed his famous sword as he called to his warriors.

At Vahldan's call, the eastern portion of the men began stepping in unison, backing more smoothly and rapidly. A deep-voiced call pulled Brin's attention to her right toward the gatehouse. "Open the gate! The king commands it!"

It was Teavar. The army was withdrawing into the keep. This was the final retreat. To their last stronghold. This would be their last stand.

The realization suddenly struck Brin like a stray arrow falling from the sky. The Gottari of Thrakius were about to be trapped. Night was coming. Perhaps their last night of freedom. Or, perhaps, their last night alive.

Agoraki crept along the eastern wall of the palace keep in the shadows of the evening. The bottom of the wall was lined with old overgrown decorative shrubs and portions of the wall were covered with vines. He briefly wondered whether he could climb it. It was a long way to fall and the vines at the top grew pretty sparse and thin. Didn't seem like a good idea.

He got to where the rounded corner rampart and the stables' storage building grew closer, making the end of the lane no wider than a carriage. As he came around the curve of the wall, he could see the fountain square. Within a heartbeat, a rider flew across the gap. Staying in the shrubs at the base of the wall he crept closer. The entire square was bustling with activity. Right in front of him, the Gottari were clustered, holding their shields edge to edge, bellowing to one another as they backed up to a called cadence.

Ago had hoped to make his way along the front wall of the keep to the little gate with the loose bars. He'd used it the last time he'd been here. The base of the front wall had what he supposed had once been a decorative hedge. Many of the plants still bloomed, but besides being overgrown, it was mixed with wild weeds. He tried to see around the curved corner. He might still be able to make it without being seen. He got on his hands and knees and crawled through the thicket until he made it past the curve of the corner rampart.

The shrubbery was thickest here at the eastern end of the front wall. The extra cover allowed him to stand. He flattened himself to the stone and slid along it, keeping behind the foliage. It was slow going but he thought he could make it. Through the limbs and the last of the brown leaves, he could see the warriors on the square. It was as many Gottari as he'd ever seen in so small a space. They were clearly falling back. He caught a glimpse across the square and through the Gottari lines to a formation of Tiberians coming up Market Avenue. His father would be among them.

Time was running out. He had to get inside the palace keep, fast.

Ago slid until he got to a tangled thicket of barberry and holly, full of prickers and burrs. The vines were growing right up the stone wall, making his way forward impassable.

He figured the little door with the loose bars was only about thirty paces from the spot. So close, and yet there was no getting through without stepping into the open. Gods, the scene was hectic. Who was going to notice him? They were all facing away from the palace.

The imperial trumpets rang and the calls of the centurions went up. Something big was about to happen. The Gottari seemed to sense it too. They were backing up even faster now, all of the lines closing in, moving closer. Off to his right, a deep voice cried, "Open the gate!"

This was it. He heard the clanking of the portcullis as it opened. The Gottari were heading into the keep. The palace would be surrounded on all sides. He was on the wrong side of the Tiberian lines. Would they shoot him if they spotted him? What if he called out to them? Outside of the officers, very few imperial soldiers spoke Hellainic.

However the battle and the war turned out, at the moment it seemed like things would be a lot safer inside these walls. It was where he'd been trying to get to, anyway. Now it was hard to imagine another choice. Let alone figuring out how he might get himself back behind the imperial lines without getting shot or speared.

Ago spotted King Vahldan riding behind the Gottari lines, calling to his men to stay in formation as they pulled back. Groups of Gottari warriors on horseback began riding through the open gate. The lines of men on foot, shield to shield, slid back faster now, coming nearer by the moment. It wouldn't be long before the Gottari on the east side of the formation moved past his position, leaving him caught between two warring armies.

His time was up. It was now or never. Most on the Gottari side would understand him if he called out. Some of them might even recognize him from his days as a servant. He still thought he could get to the little door unnoticed. He leaned and tried to see the top of the wall. He couldn't see anything. Even if someone on the wall happened to look down and spot him, would they really shoot an unarmed child running behind the Gottari lines?

Another bellowing call came from the Tiberians and a thousand spears thumped the cobblestones. The calls of the centurions signaled the rhythmic thump of a thousand boots.

Desperation filled him. He felt frozen. Staying put was not an option. He had to go.

A group of about twenty Gottari riders broke away from the lines at the top of one of the lanes, riding across the square, angling for the gateway. The riders would come within ten span of him as they came around the backside of the fountain and the ancient tree.

He made his decision, poised as the galloping horses approached. As they drew even with his position, Ago pushed through the brush, out onto the square, running alongside their progress.

Brin raised her arrow-nocked bow, aiming at nothing. She was still off by herself at the east end of the palace wall-walk. The Gottari retreat on the square was getting hectic. Her parents rode back and forth behind the closing formation, hollering at everyone to stay together, to hold the lines. They were doing their best but it was getting out of hand. Parts of the formation were backing up faster than others.

Her parents were at the west end when a group of mounted Rekkrs broke through the eastern corner, coming from an alley to gallop for the palace gate. Brin thought one of them might be wounded, riding slumped in the saddle. They angled toward the backside of the fountain. Their disruption made things worse. The east end of the line started to form gaps, with some rushing to follow the galloping riders. Brin was trying to see who the wounded rider might be when movement between her and the horses caught her eye. A lone runner burst from the shrubs below and sprinted west, toward the gate.

It was a boy dressed in a fine gray tunic. If he was a local, he was from a noble family. Or was he Tiberian? Brin raised her bow to aim. The running boy's face turned her way, scanning the shrubs right below her. Brin gasped and dropped her aim.

It was Ago.

Just as Brin was about to call to him, an arrow clacked off of the cobbles near his feet. She hadn't been the only one to spot him. Ago froze where he stood, but the riders went on. Another arrow zipped by him, clattering on the square. It was the bully-boys lining the walls near the gatehouse.

The riders made the gate and Ago stood alone and exposed. He gaped at the wall top, looking terrified. "I'm a friend!" he shouted toward the boys in Hellainic. He was forced to dodge another arrow, which sent him running, heading away from the wall!

Just then, the Gottari lines holding the east end broke. Clusters of warriors turned and ran. Suddenly hundreds more were running.

Ago heard and saw them coming right at him. He ran for the fountain and leapt over the low wall that rimmed it, sloshing through the thigh-deep water to the raised plinth at statue's feet. The roar of those retreating and the rush of the steady advance of the eastern portion of the Tiberian lines drowned out everything. Ago cowered beneath the plinth, huddling in the shadows beneath the stone skirts of his carved ancestor. He wasn't exactly hidden, but his position made a bow-shot from the wall nearly impossible, at least.

The Gottari retreat became chaotic. The entire square became filled with fleeing warriors.

Brin couldn't look away from her friend, terrified and alone. And trapped. The Tiberian lines closed in but rather than giving chase to individuals, they formed up and halted in a new line. Calls rang out and the archers loaded and drew again. They were about to rain arrows down on those in flight.

Brin had to do something. It was now or never.

She stowed her arrow, looped her bow over her shoulder, and ran to the crumbling stairs. She took them in leaping bounds, unable to think of anything but getting to the bottom.

Brin found the gap in the haw where she and Ago had last met. The little gate he used, with the broken bars, was just beyond the tangled branches.

She pushed through, arrived at the rusty little door, held her shield against her shoulder, and rammed it.

Vahldan rode on, too exhausted to worry about catching a stray arrow.

"Stay together! Shields up! Fall back as one!" He'd shouted himself hoarse. The pain in his side-wound flared with each shouted word. Worse, he wasn't even sure anyone could hear him anymore.

A roar erupted behind him. Vahldan reined his horse around to find the lines at the east end of the square breaking. This could get bad, quick. He needed the center to hold—particularly the men who'd fought their way back up Market Avenue. They were the only thing keeping the bulk of the imperial advance from the open gate of the palace keep. He galloped to them. "Stay where you stand! No one moves!" Thunar's grace, they held.

The imperial centurions called off the push on the left flank, drawing their lines up for a volley. For once that bedamned Tiberian discipline was working in his favor.

Elan and Teavar rode between him and the lines of the foe, both with their shields up. "It's getting tight!" Elan called. "Might be time to let them go."

"Not yet! Let's get them back to the fountain before we call it for those on foot. The mounted Rekkrs can cover the final retreat."

His guardians both nodded and went to spread the word. The centurions called out again, and again the foe marched twenty paces forward. Their front edge was tightening. All of the gaps between their divisions had been filled. Their cohesive wall became an engulfing phalanx, pressing in on the remains of his army.

Elan led a dozen mounted Rekkrs to him and he pointed to the last of the Gottari shield wall. Teavar shouted, "Let us pass, men! Make ready to withdraw to the gate."

The shield wall parted and he, Elan, and the senior Rekkrs rode through. Vahldan turned back to the warriors on foot and called, "Stay together, brothers! Nobody runs. We give ground on our terms. Understood?"

The exhausted men barked in affirmation. His mounted Rekkrs spaced themselves at intervals in front of the Gottari lines, shields and swords at the ready. Vahldan raised the futhark blade. "Lions! As one! Retreat!" He brought the blade down, and those on foot turned and marched for the gate.

For the first time, the Tiberian soldiers on the front line bristled and fluctuated, looking ready to burst. The centurions shouted and thumped their anxious soldiers' helms with batons. Again, the foe's lines straightened and held.

Thank the gods for small mercies.

The imperial commanders did, however, then call for another volley from the archers. "Shields up!" The cry ran through the ranks. Most of those on foot were streaming through the gate. Only a handful of the Gottari horses caught an arrow, riders either jumping off or coaxing them back to the gateway.

Vahldan looked to find the way was clear. "Rekkrs! As one, we ride. Now, retreat!"

His men turned around and rode from the front, circumventing the fountain and filing in through the gate. He and Elan and Teavar stayed at the center, facing the foe, until every last Gottari was inside.

Again, the Tiberian lines held. Before Vahldan turned to leave, he sought the rear of the foe's vanguard, at the crest of Market Avenue. A cluster of mounted officers sat at the rear of the phalanx. He spotted the red-crested helm. Vernius sat tall in the saddle, surrounded by his officers.

Vahldan held Bairtah-Urrin high, then sheathed it. He held his open palms to either side and bowed his head to his rival. He knew. His army had been allowed to retreat into the keep.

It was a show of honor. The honor of the imperial commander, at least.

This Tiberian war chief, who'd so steadfastly and patiently pushed him to the verge of defeat, and hence unto Urrinan, put his fist to his chest in recognition. In that moment between the two of them, it was as if they dwelled in another age.

Vahldan turned and rode for the gate with Elan and Teavar at his shoulders. He knew the respite could only last so long.

Once inside, Teavar called to close the gate. He and Elan leapt from their exhausted mounts as grooms rushed to take their reins.

"To the walls!" he shouted. "Every archer, every spearman, onto the ramparts!"

Vahldan ran among those rushing up the stairs adjacent to the gatehouse. "Keep them back! Keep them off the walls!"

Gottari bowmen lined the parapet and scurried down the wall-walk to fill the gaps. Teavar shoved the shoulders of those at the top of the stairs who were blocking Vahldan's way. "Make way for the king. Make way."

For the first time that day, the setting sun dropped below the ceiling of dark clouds, oddly illuminating the massive phalanx of the foe lining the square and filling the adjacent avenues, leaving only the long shadows of the leaf-barren tree and the adjacent statue on the open cobbles that separated the two sides.

The clang of the portcullis echoed and the palace gate thumped closed. A moment later, Tiberian trumpets rang out. The calls of the centurions followed.

"They're coming!" someone cried.

"Be ready but hold your fire!" Vahldan called.

AFTER BRIN'S shield struck the iron bars, she drew back to look. The door was intact. Her shoulder ached and the bars held firm. She was trapped. The clanging of the closing main gate reverberated in the stone wall. She grabbed with her fists and shook the bars, a growl erupting from her lungs. One of the bars moved slightly. She pushed again. The fastener that held the bottom of it was rusted through. The whole bar pivoted on the radius of the top fastener, leaving a gap wider than her head at its midpoint. She took off her bow and quiver, set them on the outside, then turned her shoulders and slid her torso through. She gripped the remaining bar, holding herself in place while she pulled her legs through.

She was out! Better still, she was surrounded by overgrown juniper bushes, hidden from everyone. She dropped and crawled, pushing through the brush. Finally, the sun lit the cobbles before her. The Gottari were gone. Brin spotted Ago in the shadows, still hovering beneath the fountain's upper plinth, evidently forgotten or unnoticed by both sides. As Brin surveyed the square, the Tiberian trumpets blared. Commands rang out and the imperial lines began to march. If they continued closing in, they would overrun the statue. Soon!

Ago was directly ahead of her. The only way back inside was through the little door behind her. Brin had a bow and a shield. Aiming the bow with the unwieldy shield on her arm would be difficult. She had on her mother's breastplate. With the bow, she might be able to keep a few of them away long enough to give Ago a chance to run for it. But only if she got into position before the approaching imperials reached the fountain.

It was now or never. Her uncle's words echoed: *"Remember. Focus. Visualize the outcome. Do not let fear control you. Decide and do not hesitate."*

Brin decided. She dropped the shield, nocked an arrow, drew a breath, burst from the shrubbery, and ran.

Vahldan gripped the wall and grit his teeth, hoping the pain in his side would fade as he watched the foe's lines close in. He wondered how far this would go. He hoped they were merely establishing a siege line, just out of bow range. Someone down the wall fired an arrow, causing two more to fly out. The shots fell hopelessly short. "Hold!" he called. "Don't waste another arrow till they charge the walls!"

"Who's that?" Ermanaric called, pointing down, almost directly below them.

"Looks like a child!" someone yelled. Through the empty branches of the tree, he spotted small figure, racing toward the fountain holding a nocked bow. As the child emerged from the shadows, bright red braids were lit to fire by the setting sunlight.

"Brin!" Elan shrieked. "No!" Elan pushed away from the parapet and ran for the stairs. "My horse!" she cried as she ran. "Bring my horse! Open the gate!"

"Bring them up!" Vernius called, and the trumpets rang, calling for a halt. "Keep them out of range," he said to Tully. "Send divisions to either side of the keep to maintain containment. Have the men rest in place until nightfall. Then reestablish the siege lines. The Gottari aren't going anywhere."

Tullius glared. "But, my lord general—"

"You have my orders, Captain." Vernius glared back until Tully sullenly saluted.

Before Tully started off, Nicandros pointed out across the square. "What's that?"

A lone figure was splashing into the fountain, holding a bow, trained toward the center of the southern line. "It looks like a girl," another officer said.

The officers all watched as the girl waded to the statue plinth at the center of the fountain. Still holding the nocked bow with one hand, she deftly vaulted herself up onto the upper plinth. She took a firing stance next to the statue, drew the bow, and took aim towards the Tiberian vanguard. The sight provoked scattered laughter among the ranks. "Uh-oh! We're in trouble now," a soldier called out, inciting more laughter.

"Should we shoot her?" one of the centurions asked.

Vernius shook his head. Tully shouted, "Hold your fire!"

"Look—there's someone else," Nico said, pointing.

Vernius shielded his eyes. He spotted movement below the girl. Indeed, someone was skulking in the fountain behind her.

"Looks like another child," Nico said.

The girl momentarily glanced to the second child, evidently commanding her companion to retreat from hiding under the cover of her threat. Suddenly, the palace gate clinked and groaned and started to rise.

The girl stood tall, holding her aim as the other child moved in a crouch, sloshing to the outer rim of the fountain. The second child turned to look back, his face suddenly illuminated by the setting sun. Vernius's chest lurched. "No."

Nicandros gasped. "Gods, is that—?"

"Vernouthus!" Vernius shouted. "Make way!" He kicked his

mount, but the horse couldn't move past the ranks of men lined before him.

Tully appeared beside him and grabbed his arm. "No, General! You must see that you cannot. Let me go!" The intense man nodded, insistent.

Vernius realized Tully was right. He couldn't risk it. He was responsible for an entire army. He couldn't risk being shot by a child right in front of his men. "Go!" he cried.

"Make way, make way!" Tully called, urging his horse as men scrambled to clear a path.

"Save my son!" Vernius shouted as Tully broke through to the open square. "Save my heir," he murmured in plea, to the gods and his ancestors.

VAHLDAN HEARD the gate gears grinding and the chains clanking, but the damn thing hadn't even started to rise yet. The boy had just climbed out of the fountain when a commotion drew his eye to the Tiberian lines directly ahead. A lone rider emerged and kicked his horse, heading for his daughter, still standing at aim on the plinth. It was an officer Vahldan had seen many times that day, the rider with the red horse's tail flying from his helm. The bastard had thwarted their counterattacks several times.

The gate still wasn't opening. Something was wrong. This was taking too long. Elan wouldn't be able to make it.

Vahldan leaned over the parapet to look down. A man stood watching on the other side of Ermanaric, holding a short spear. "Give me that." Vahldan snatched the spear from the man's hands, drew a deep breath, and vaulted over the wall.

Freya help him, but it was a long way down. He crashed into the shrubbery below, one stick jamming him in the back but not puncturing his hauberk, thank the gods. He'd barely hung on to the spear but he was able to use it as a staff to push his way free of the shrubs. The moment Vahldan started to run, he knew he'd ruptured something inside him that hadn't quite mended since Orithya.

It didn't matter. His legs still worked. He pushed through the flaring pain and ran for his daughter. The oncoming Tiberian hoisted a javelin over his shoulder, poised to throw.

Vahldan realized he couldn't get there before the Tiberian was in range. Brin's stance and aim remained fixed but he saw the fret in her expression. She was frozen. "Shoot," he cried. She fired.

And completely missed. Horse-Tail came on grinning, his arm cocked to throw.

"Equites!" Vahldan bellowed, running at an angle to make himself seen. He had to draw the bastard away from his daughter. "I am Vahldan the Bold!" he shouted in Hellainic. He raised the spear. "It's me you want! Come and get me!"

He'd drawn the dandy's attention, all right. Horse-Tail reined his horse and fixed his aim on him. Vahldan drew back his borrowed spear, feigning an imminent throw. The man bore down on his position. As the Tiberian released, Vahldan threw himself into a roll across the slushy pavers. Horse-Tail's javelin missed and the Gottari on the wall cheered.

Better yet, Vahldan still had his spear.

He grunted and pushed himself to his feet. The man pulled his mount around for another pass, drawing a sword as he came. Vahldan threw as the rider approached. Horse-Tail contorted backward in the saddle and the spear narrowly missed. Now the Tiberians cheered.

"To your left! Fly!" It was Elan, her blade held ready to swing. He threw himself again, just as she galloped by. The Tiberian had drawn his own sword. Blade met blade in a mighty clang and Horse-Tail tumbled to the cobbles, his horse prancing away.

Elan came around and charged again as the officer scrambled to his feet. Vahldan saw the front lines of the Tiberians reacting. Horse-Tail's men were about to break ranks to save their officer. Which would doom him and Elan. A bit too early, by his reckoning. Not to mention the danger to the children.

"Hold!" Vahldan called.

Thank the gods, Elan looked. He beckoned and shook his head. "Let him go!"

Elan roared her rage as she pulled up, turning from her target and coming around. Vahldan started to run even as she drew alongside, holding out her hand to him. Vahldan caught her hand and leapt. He grunted in pain as Elan yanked him high enough to land on Ainsjót's rump, head on one side and legs on the other. The pain in his side flared again. She spurred the mare on to the gate, sending shocks of new pain through his innards with every step.

The children ran in just ahead of them and the gate immediately started to drop as the horse galloped through. Vahldan slid off as they slowed. He bent, hands on his knees, panting to catch his wind and clear his blurred vision, waiting for the excruciating pain to subside. Elan called his name. He managed to straighten and found himself facing through the bars of the portcullis. The imperial officer was surrounded by a dozen shield-bearing men guarding his retreat to their lines—Tiberian lines that still held.

The Gottari in the keep and on the walls were cheering. He turned to the keep. Brin was hugging the boy, her bow tossed aside. It was Malvius's nephew, he realized. He went to take a step and nearly crumpled. Elan was there, wrapping an arm around him, bracing him upright. "You all right?"

He laughed, which caused him to wince. "Wasn't one of my better landings, was it?"

Vahldan took a limping step and gasped. Elan held him firm, pulling his arm over her shoulders. "You could've killed yourself, jumping off the wall like that."

"It wouldn't have been as though I don't deserve it," he said. "But the risk was for a worthy cause." He nodded to their daughter. Brin never ceased to amaze him. She'd risked her life for her friend.

They approached Teavar, who was standing at the mouth of the gateway with his great arms folded across his chest. "I really wish you'd stop pulling stunts like that."

"If I try it again, please stop me." He forced a wry smile. "There's got to be a less painful path to destiny's doom."

Teavar harrumphed and hid a smile as he wrapped an arm around him from the side opposite Elan, bracing him upright, easing the pain.

Arnegern rushed over. "Your orders, my king?"

"Set up patrols on all the walls, but send them in rotation. Let everyone get some food and rest. I'm guessing that once they set their siege lines, the foe will be done for the night."

"Yes, my king."

"And you, Captain. Go see your family. Tell Mara I'd like to see her whenever she's able." His most loyal captain bowed his head and started for the gatehouse. "Arnegern." His friend stopped and turned. "You've done a fine job defending this city. That, and so much more. We'd have long been lost without you. *I'd* be lost without you. Thank you, my brother."

Arnegern bowed at the waist. "It's been an honor." He smiled and hurried off.

Brin and the boy strode arm in arm, sort of clinging to one another in the fading light. Both seemed a bit stunned. Elan steered them toward the youngsters. His daughter's gaze met his before her chin fell to her chest. Her anguish was apparent.

The boy bowed. "Thank you, King Vahldan. I am forever in your debt."

Vahldan kept his eyes on the girl and said, "I may hold you to that, lad."

Brin glanced furtively and looked away. "And *you*," he said to his astonishing daughter.

"I know," Brin said. "I'm sorry. I failed you." Her tone was full of woe.

Vahldan was stunned anew. "Gods, no. You have nothing to apologize for. Not only did you not fail me, you taught me something important. Something I should've learned a long time ago. And so it is I who must apologize. For I have long failed you. I owe you so much more than can ever be repaid." He bowed, trying not to wince.

His guardians had to help him straighten. Brin was wide-eyed. He smiled and winked.

Elan said, "Come on, heroes. Let's get you all inside so we can have a look at Papa." She led him toward the palace doors.

PARTING WAYS AND MEANS

"Looking back on the aftermath of the fall of Thrakius, though it may sound strange, I consider it one of my father's finest moments. I have mentioned the shame I felt as night fell on the besieged keep. But I was also frightened and bewildered, and I dare say I was not alone in feeling that way.

Though Vahldan was injured—the gods only know how severely—he was calm. Serene, even. He was thoughtful and deliberate, not to mention oddly practical. He eased an immense anxiety that threatened to overwhelm the rest of us. All through his downfall, he provided hope to his people. Not that they would prevail, or even that all would be well. But that all had not been for naught—that what they were enduring was worthy of their struggle and sacrifice.

It felt as if he'd prepared for that moment all of his life. And, of course, he had."—Brin Bright Eyes, Saga of Dania

VAHLDAN LEANED HEAVILY on the parapet of Elan's terrace, clutching his side and gazing out at the city he'd lost and the new siege lines of the imperial army that had won it. Every painful breath reminded him that time was running out. His doom had arrived, regardless of what came of the siege.

The clouds had parted to reveal a gibbous moon and the wind had died down. Townsfolk had joined the Tiberian troops, bringing out food and drink to share. Groups were singing and dancing. There was laughter and hugging. Indeed, they considered the invaders to be liberators. The city was alive as it hadn't been in years, from the fringes of the torch-lit square and on down the market lane. Thrakius was celebrating his defeat.

Had he really darkened their lives so?

Vahldan knew the answer. His rule had been darker than he'd realized throughout it. He'd given himself over to his ugliness to achieve it. He'd remained absent and inattentive. Lost in selfishness. His many failings, his willful blindness to human suffering—some were saying it was necessary to Urrinan. He had his doubts. And regrets. The gods might be that cruel, but divine intercession and searing physical pain aside, he was grateful that he was awake now —that he'd found himself again before the end.

Elan appeared at his side. She handed him a cup. "It's not as good as what they're having." She nodded toward the celebrant victors. "But it'll warm you up."

He took a sip and sighed steam. "The whole bedamned city is festive."

"Really can't blame them. I'm sure there will soon be more and better food for their families. Perhaps there is already. Not to mention better wine." She held up her cup.

"I know. It still…"

"Stings? That they're so glad to be getting rid of us?"

He nodded and drank. "You're right. Who could blame them? I've been a shitty king."

Elan huffed a laugh. "You've been a shitty soul mate, too."

Vahldan put a hand flat on his chest. "Ouch. That stabs me deeper than Vernius's knife did." The mention of a knife reminded him: He should be finishing his gift. It was a bit late for that, too. "I suppose we'd better add shitty father to the list."

"You've had your moments. One of them was today."

He smiled. "I have never understood my father better. On that day of days, he didn't hesitate. I get it now. His hopes for me made it easy to do what he did. It really is all about the next generation. Preserving that... It's an honor. Never a sacrifice."

"You might not have been a good king or a remotely loyal partner. But I can better see it all now—the breadth of it. All that matters now is that you've been a good Bringer." Elan's smile was wry as she took his hand in hers. "Sometimes it seemed like you were doing your best to fuck that up too. But somehow you always end up doing what you're destined to do."

She'd done it again. As somber as he felt, she made him laugh. "Some consolation." He turned to face her. "I'm sorry I put you through so much. Thank you. For saving me."

"In fairness, I rode out there for Brin."

"No, don't." Vahldan squeezed her hand. "You know I mean more. Thank you for bringing me back to myself. You've always been there for me. Always. Which is saying a lot."

Elan's smile grew. "Songs will be sung." She drew his hand to her lips and kissed it. "I never thought I'd say this, but I wouldn't trade it. I believe. It'll mean something. My dream was a divine gift."

A knock preceded the terrace door opening. "They're all here, my king," Teavar said.

Vernius followed Nicandros up the stone steps, leaving the celebrant officers of the mobile reserve in the well-lit living quarters of their commandeered mansion. Vernius was exhausted. Troubled and exhausted. He knew he should get some sleep, but he doubted sleep would come easily. The house Nico had selected for him and his officers was a bit worse for its recent wear and tear. But it was large enough to provide him with some privacy. Besides being near to the siege lines. This war wasn't over, after all.

Nico led Vernius down the upstairs corridor and opened the door at the far end. A lamp already glowed within. It was a palatial bedchamber, extraordinary for a residential home. Vernius sniffed the air. "It's sage," Nico said, noticing his noticing. "They say burning it cleanses the air. The gods know it needed cleansing." Vernius didn't have the heart to tell him he could still detect the stench of the barbarians who'd last occupied the place.

Nico lit a twig of tinder in the lamp and lit another on a table near the impressive front-facing window. The place had a view! Except the dozens of windowpanes were steamed. Which made him notice the source of the steam. The sight prompted Vernius's first smile of the day. "Oh, Nico," he breathed. "You've outdone even yourself." Nicandros had actually found a house with a little gilded bathtub right in the bedchamber.

His adjutant smiled down at the full tub. "I put it at the top of the list. Thought you might need it. Best hurry, my lord. The water will only grow cooler." Nico came to take Vernius's helm from him and strode to his trunk, already at the foot of the bed. "I had your gear brought up from the ship," Nicandros said as he started to unfasten his breastplate. "They found this." He reached to a pouch at his belt and produced Vernius's grandfather's torc. Nico laid it at the foot of the bed and finished with the buckles of his breastplate.

Vernius sighed and slumped. Nico lifted off the breastplate and Vernius's hand drifted to the pouch that hung at his neck in the torc's place, with the figurine of his grandfather inside it.

"Your son is confused, is all," Nico offered. His aide set the breastplate with the helm and torc and bent to unfasten Vernius's greaves.

Vernius shook his head. "That's absurd. You know as well as I do that the boy's too clever to be confused. My son seems to have gotten too large a dose of his barbarian grandsire's blood, just as my father did. It gave them both passion. But also a misguided sense of honor."

His grandfather had won that torc by defeating his most worthy rival, just as Vernius hoped to do. But the story went that Grandpapa had also won love and honor. At least that was what Vernius had been led to believe. That was what his father had believed.

Vernius had already found love here in this forsaken city. But love had spurned him. As for honor, he had but to look at what having honor had done for his father. Seeking honor had incited betrayal and delivered death. It had been a death that felt anything but honorable to Vernius. "No, my very clever son simply went back to those who've shown they care about him. He recognized that I was more interested in him as an heir than as a son." His laugh was sardonic. "The gods know I showed him what I thought. The very first thing I did was ask him to help me defeat the only folk he ever really knew."

Nico laid his greaves with the rest of his armor and the torc. It left Vernius stripped to his under tunic. He lifted the necklace with the figurine off and tossed it onto the bed beside the rest.

"May I speak freely, my lord?" Nico asked.

Vernius wasn't sure he wanted to hear it. But how could he deny the only person he cared for who remained loyal to him? "If you feel you must."

"It is an item, yes. But it holds great meaning for you, for your family." Nico gently laid a hand on the torc. "You gave it as a gift in order to bestow that meaning upon its receiver. Only deep feelings can spur such a gesture. The boy is the product of those deep feelings. He is more than an heir. You both know it. I still say he is confused—and yes, clever. Such feelings cannot die, my lord. Not truly. Not even when we lose someone special. But such feelings can be kindled to live on in another. Particularly in one who shares the same loss."

Vernius held himself very still. "I understand," was all he was able to say.

Nico bowed his head, averting his gaze. "Is there anything else I can do, my lord?"

"Pack it all in my trunk," Vernius said, nodding at his fancy, inherited gear.

Nico frowned. "My lord?"

"Find some plain but sturdy armor for the morning, will you? I'm done with the show."

Nico bowed again. "Of course, my lord." The lad stowed the gear and started to close the trunk.

Vernius went and picked up the torc and the figurine Nico had left out. "These too." Nico raised the trunk lid and stepped back. Vernius stared at the torc for a long moment. Even the thought of allowing himself to start again—to finish the task which duty commended—while carrying such feelings was too painful to contemplate. He tossed both in with his father's flamboyant armor and slammed the lid.

"No more," he said and strode for the bath, pulling his tunic over his head as he went. He stepped into the steaming water and sat, instantly feeling his ill humors being cleansed and rinsed away, his heartache being soothed. "No more hearth tales, no more honor, no more weakness. No more estate, no more heir. No more." He settled into the small tub till his chin touched water.

Nicandros pursed his lips, veiling his disapproval, and fled to the chamber door. "Is there anything else you'll be seeking for tomorrow, my lord general?"

"Order," he said. "Order and empire. I intend to cleanse this city till that's all that's left, by whatever means are necessary." His loyal adjutant evidently knew better than to reply. Rather, Nico pointedly looked down as he backed out and closed the door behind him.

Vahldan led Elan back into the residence from the terrace. She closed the door, muffling the sounds of the celebrant city below. Kemella stood behind the settle holding his firstborn son, with Amaga lurking behind her. Urias stood near them, looking affable but out of place.

"Captain. Welcome." Vahldan strode to clap Urias on the shoulder. "Please, everyone sit," he said as he passed through the seating area. "Make yourselves comfortable." He went to the sideboard and refilled his cup halfway, then topped it with water. It was helping with the pain but he needed to keep his wits. And stay awake. Wine had not been his friend during the dark days that preceded his awakening. "Elan, please pour our guests some wine."

Vahldan spotted Brin sitting on the guard's chair near the door to the servants' quarters, staring at the carpet. His daughter looked miserable. He left his cup on the sideboard and went to the table. He knew what he had to do first. He grabbed his gift and strode to her. "I'm going to start this evening's agenda over here." He knelt down before his daughter, grimacing against the shooting pain. Brin startled. Gods, she'd been lost in sadness.

"The first thing I need to do tonight is to ask you, Brin, to forgive me. Will you?"

"Forgive you for what?"

"For being a terrible father, for a start. Your mother and I were just talking about it. This morning you reminded me that you were born of the wolf and the lion. It's never been clearer. I was so fixated on my own preconceived notions that I totally ignored what should've been obvious. I let you down. I didn't see the amazing gift that was right in front of me, and it's truly my loss. Luckily, even coming through my foolishness, we seem to still be on the Urrinan's rightful path. I'm told you're to fill an important role, which makes perfect sense. But that doesn't make it fair. It's the same for many of those I love, but it's particularly unfair for you. And I'm truly sorry about that."

Brin shook her head and tears filled her eyes. "No. I thought I was worthy, but I'm not. I thought I could be a warrior, but I'm not. I failed. I failed you, and I failed my trainer." She glanced up at her uncle. "I failed my parents' legacy."

Vahldan gently laid a hand on the side of her lovely face and wiped a stray tear with his thumb. He sighed and took one of her hands. "Sorry, but you're wrong. I know from experience. If you're at all like me—may the gods keep that from being too true—it may take time for you to see. Still, I need you to believe me because you've got a lot to do. You are to be not just a guardian, but a guardian of guardians. And of queens." He smiled at Brin's puzzled expression. "After today, I've never been more certain that it's true. You proved it out there."

"I was so... bad. I disobeyed you. Worse, I froze. When I finally shot, I missed."

"You proved it not by shooting but by going out there. You didn't hesitate to try to save your friend. You proved that your heart is true. And fierce! For now, that's more than enough. A lot of us freeze— particularly the first time." Vahldan chuckled. "I sure did. I also know it won't happen again. Not as long as you stay true to who you are."

Once again tears welled in her big blue eyes and rolled down her cheeks.

Vahldan brightened his tone. "Beyond the apology, I have a gift. And a favor to ask of you."

"A gift?"

He held up his carved pieces. "They're not quite done. I had hoped to polish them up. Seems I've run out of time."

Brin reverently took the two pieces in her hands.

"What are they?" Amaga asked, sounding peevish.

"A writing stylus and an inkwell," Urias said with warmth. "You made these, my king?"

"I carved them, yes." Vahldan smiled at Brin. "Carving soothes me—helps me think."

"You came up with the idea?" Urias asked. Her uncle seemed surprised.

"I did. Seems training her as a warrior was already taken." He gave the wolf a wink.

Urias bowed his head. "I'm impressed."

Brin flicked the nib he'd procured from her tutor with a fingertip, then held the stylus as she would to use it. "I don't write," he said, "so I'm not sure if they're quite right. How does it feel? Will they suffice?"

She bit her lip and nodded, clearly still brimming with emotion.

"What's the favor?" Brin managed.

"I ask only that you'll consider doing something for me, nothing more. Just consider it. I wouldn't dream of having you make your father a promise. I lived that. And I would never put such a thing on you."

Her big eyes met his. Gods, they were amazing. Gorgeous and keen. How could he have not appreciated them like this before? They were her namesake feature, after all.

"What is it?" she asked.

"It's clear that you're clever. And observant. You take everything in, don't you? You've seen much already, and—for you—this really is just the beginning. So the favor starts with this. Stay alive." Brin tilted her head, puzzled again. "Stay alive and remember."

"Remember what?"

"All of it. All of this, and all that's yet to come. It's going to make an amazing story one day. The Urrinan has come. The world is about to change. In ways that are rarely seen. By the end of it, no one will clearly remember how it happened. Everyone will have their own version of it, but you lived it. Without you, folk might never know what we went through. You'll be the only one who can truly tell the world how it came to be. And since you're already the best among us —both in spoken tongues and with your letters—I hope that someday you'll consider writing it all down." He nodded down at the stylus and inkwell in her hands.

"Like one of the sagas?" Brin asked.

"Yes, exactly. *The Saga of Urrinan*," he tried. "No. Sounds too dreary. And it doesn't bring in what comes next. I mean, this story's far from over. How about *The Saga of Dania*?"

"Of Dania?"

"Yes. It's our home. It's where it all started. And it's where the next part of the story takes place. And you'll be there to witness it."

"Will I?"

"I plan to do all I can to see to it," Vahldan said. "And you're going to stay alive, remember?"

Brin surprised him by lunging to hug him. Gods, she was strong. "I'll remember," she whispered. "I'll remember everything." Now his eyes were itchy. How had he allowed himself to miss out on this?

Vahldan eased his daughter back and gave her hands a squeeze, firming her grip on her gift. He grunted, straining to stand and straighten. He went to retrieve his cup, hoping to dull the pain. He had to get through this.

He took a drink and turned to find Urias, Kemella, and the now-sleeping boy on the settle. Elan was sitting across from them, with Teavar standing behind her, arms folded over his chest. Amaga continued to hover behind Kemella. Everyone was staring. They all seemed stunned.

He smiled brightly and raised his cup. "That brings us to our next agenda item."

"Which is?" Urias asked.

"Getting most of you to Dania, of course."

Amaga surprised him by being the one to ask, "Exactly whom are you *getting to Dania*?"

The first qeins was obviously animated by the prospect. "You and Thaedan, foremost."

Amaga leaned in, her raptor-like eyes narrowing. "How would this happen?"

"I'm taking you," Elan said. Amaga visibly recoiled, her eyes darting to her nemesis. Her mouth opened, but no words came. Elan grinned. "Surprise!"

Amaga found her words, but they came in a stricken rasp. "This isn't possible. Not her."

"On the contrary, my qeins," he said. "I can't think of anyone I trust more to make sure of it." He looked down at Elan and gave her shoulder a squeeze. "Indeed, I believe it's destined."

Before Amaga could complain again, Vahldan stepped to Elan's brother. "Although I have no right to ask anything of you, Captain, I was hoping you might join them. It couldn't hurt to have a wolf along to smooth the way back into the good graces of Dania's powerful."

Urias bowed his head. "I don't know how much help I'll be with that. But I'd be honored to be at their side to try."

Amaga came around the settle, hands on her hips. "In case you hadn't noticed, we're trapped. You might recall how you waited too long. Just how do you now suggest we escape to Dania?" Her terror was showing through the testy façade.

"This is where our daughter steps to the fore," Elan said, looking over at Brin.

Brin looked almost as startled as Amaga. "Me? Where am I stepping, now?"

"Besides being the destined link between our nation's two worlds," Vahldan began, "you're the only one here who's made it out of the city via the catacombs and the caves."

Brin sat on the edge of her chair. "That was over a year ago. I honestly doubt I can remember the way. And last time, even once we got out of the palace keep, we had to sneak through the city to the docks. Is that even possible now with all of these Tiberians about?"

"Of course not," Amaga snapped. "We can't risk having them get their hands on my son. They seek to kill us all. Especially those who are related to you." She glared at Vahldan.

"I have to agree," Urias said, frowning. "We can't go through the city. There must be another way."

A door latch clicked. "There is."

Everyone turned to the new voice, Teavar with his blade halfway out.

The boy, Ago, stepped in from the terrace and bowed. Seemed he'd gotten right back to his old ways, sneaking around and eavesdropping. "Forgive me, my king," Ago said in accented Gottari. The lad switched back to Hellainic. "But I do know the way. Through the catacombs and caves. Out of the palace *and* the city. I wish to lead them."

"HURRY, SISTER," Kemella urged her, staying several steps ahead on the stairs.

But Amaga didn't feel like hurrying. It felt like hurrying to her final judgment. Although she'd already been sentenced—into the custody of the one person who least cared for her wellbeing in all the world.

By the time Amaga made her way into the residence, Kemella was already in the bedchamber. Her near-sister held Thaedan on one hip, even as she bent to dig in their shared chest of clothing. Thaedan clung to Kemella, eyes wide with fright. But still he didn't cry. Amaga certainly felt closer to crying than her little boy. She was frantic with worry.

"You'll need to put on this." Kemella threw Amaga's heavy woolen tunic onto the bed.

"I can't wear that. It itches like Hel's curse."

Kemella threw her own cloak beside it, then a woolen blanket. "There's no time to argue. You must dress as warmly as possible. You'll need to wear my boots as well."

"Your boots? They're far too big. And what will you wear?"

"I won't be needing them as much as you will." Kemella laid Thaedan on the bed and bent to pull out leggings. "These, too. There's a lot of snow in the pass by all accounts."

Amaga forgot herself and reached to grab Kemella's shoulder to turn her. A flash as brilliant as lightning jolted Amaga. It was the glimpse of her dearest friend's unavoidable agony that Amaga had often experienced in their touch. It had never felt more intense. Which terrified her all the more.

"Tell me," Amaga said, her voice breaking. "Tell me what you're saying, Sister."

Kemella threw her boots onto the pile and kept digging. "Surely you've *seen* that I can't come with you. It's time to face up to our parting, dear heart."

Amaga instantly knew Kemella was right—she'd just been hiding from the truth again. "I... dearly hoped it would change. Freya wouldn't do this. She knows I can't. I can't do this alone."

"Freya provides, then," Kemella said. "You won't be alone."

"You can't mean that horrible savage. She'd as soon kill us."

"If Elan wanted to kill you, why would she be offering this gift?"

"Gift? Ha. I'll bet she wants to get us alone out there, away from anyone who'd stop her. Her and that awful daughter. You heard Vahldan. Elan's been whispering in his ear. He just admitted what they're plotting. They're claiming that the daughter was born of the wolf and the lion."

Kemella came and pulled off Amaga's frock like she was a child. "Seems they think Brin has a special role. But that doesn't mean they're plotting. Arms up." Kemella held the tunic wadded and ready to place it over her head.

Amaga raised her arms and Kemella pulled it on. "Why don't they speak plainly of it? They're up to something."

Kemella made that tsking sound she so often used to scold her. "What about your uncle, then? Sit." Her near-sister pushed her to sit and dropped to her knees to pull on Amaga's leggings. "Surely Urias wouldn't be partner to a plot against you, would he?" Kemella pushed the first boot onto her foot and started lacing.

"I don't know. Vahldan's invitation was obviously a surprise to Urias, so perhaps it was a surprise to the savage, too. But she'll figure out a way around my naive uncle. She's vicious but she's also cunning. Anyway, you must come. To make sure."

"Amaga!" Kemella shouted. Her dearest friend sat back on her haunches, closed her eyes, and drew a deep breath. Amaga couldn't recall ever seeing her like this. "You *know* I can't come. My place is here. With Mara. She's due any day. Would you really have me leave our sister alone at a time like this? And what about her babe, brought into the world amidst the terrors of war? Would you deprive them out of your own selfish and unfounded fears?"

Amaga pressed her lips tightly. She wanted to snap back. Then Kemella's hard glare softened and Amaga wanted to apologize instead. A sob escaped when Amaga opened her mouth. She gasped to catch her breath and Thaedan started to quietly cry with her. She shivered and hugged herself into the itchy wool tunic. "How will I do this without you?"

"I told you. You're in good hands. And I'll be with you in spirit. You and Thaedan will make it safely to Dania, I'm sure of it."

Amaga shook her head. "No, I mean all of it. How will I raise him? How will I go on without you by my side? I'm too afraid. Too weak."

Kemella leaned in, narrowing her eyes. "You're not," she said fiercely. "You are stronger than you know. I believe it and now you must. You are the mother of the king of Tutona kings."

Amaga wanted so badly to embrace her. "How will I ever let you know how grateful I am? How much you mean to me? How much I love you?" She started to open her arms, then stopped and shrank back.

"I know, dear heart," Kemella said. "I'm here." She put one hand on her heart and the other a finger's width from Amaga's chest. "And I always will be."

Amaga couldn't bear it. She grabbed her dear near-sister and pulled her into a tight embrace. Kemella's power and strength surged through her, briefly filling her with warmth and confidence. And love. As if she'd been underwater and reached the surface, Amaga opened her mouth and sucked in a breath. Then what she'd dreaded struck. The horrible agony. The terror and the piercing pain. And the blood—so much blood. Worst of all, it was all so near.

Amaga pushed her away and gasped for breath. Kemella drew back, looking hurt.

"I'm sorry," Amaga whispered.

Kemella nodded. "I know," she sighed.

"I know how you feel about it, but I feel I must—"

"No!" Kemella's hand flew up, hovering close to Amaga's mouth, ready to physically silence her if need be. "We've spoken of this dozens of times. I cannot know."

Amaga kept her mouth closed but couldn't keep her tears from flowing again. "As Freya wills it," she managed.

"As it shall be," Kemella replied in refrain. "Now come. We must get Thaedan ready and get you both on your way."

VAHLDAN GRASPED Urias's arm as the captain departed. "Thank you," he said simply. He wanted the words to convey more than he could express.

"As I said, it's been my honor." Urias smiled. "My king." The Wulthus envoy had never avoided using the honorific. But it was clear that Urias, too, wished to convey more. Vahldan nodded his understanding and Urias turned and left them.

Elan had already sent Brin and Ago to the kitchens to fill all of their skins and gather some traveling food. That left Vahldan alone with his two guardians. The two people he trusted most in this world.

Vahldan and Elan exchanged a look. "Well, I'd better go and get ready," Elan said, heading for the bedchamber. She quietly closed the door behind her.

"Come and sit with me, my friend," Vahldan said to Teavar. "I need to ask a favor." Teavar sat as stiffly as Vahldan did. Neither of them leaned back.

"You need not ask. I am yours to command."

Vahldan shook his head. "No. This is too big a favor for that. This is something that can't be promised lightly, even to a king. Not even because you have been my loyal guardian for more than half of the days of my life. It can't even be sworn out of our long, close friendship. It is something I would only ask a brother. But you must remember: I would never resent my brother's denial of this. Though I do hope our closeness will help you to decide. Am I being clear or just babbling?"

Teavar finally leaned back. "Clear enough. Go on."

"This is a favor you must agree to grant not just for me, but out of a deep love of our people. It will require the greatest sacrifice imaginable—greater even than all your years of loyal service. Greater even than the sacrifice of an honorable death. And, as it was with my daughter, I will not ask you for an oath to bind you to this duty. It must be sustained out of an abiding sense of devotion. Devotion that is yours to keep. Devotion that can only be born and maintained out of love."

"I confess, you've made me damn curious. Not to mention a little frightened."

Vahldan held his side as he rose to fetch the sheathed sword leaning by the sideboard. He'd already removed the scabbard from his belt. "It has to do with this."

Teavar frowned. "Surely you don't intend—"

"I *do* intend." Vahldan grimaced and kneeled before his guardian. He held Bairtah-Urrin on open palms. "I won't be carrying the futhark sword into battle tomorrow."

"Oh no. I'm not worthy of—"

"And neither shall you carry it, my friend. In fact, if you accept, you won't be accompanying me into battle at all." Teavar vehemently shook his head, already set to refuse. "Please. Just hear me out. This is far more important than any battle. It will mean more to the outcome of Urrinan than participating in my doom ever could."

Teavar clenched his jaw. "As you wish. I will listen before I refuse."

"What I want you to do is to stay alive. Beyond the battle. More than that, I want you to live so that you can submit yourself to the victors."

"But if the Tibairya prevail, I'll be killed or enslaved."

Vahldan nodded. "I'm hoping enslaved, obviously."

"You're *hoping* I am enslaved?"

"Yes. If all goes as planned, you would be enslaved and then placed in the service of the anaxship. You would remain in this palace, held to a bond by the imperial magister of Thrakius to the service of his future wife. But you would secretly become the guardian of her son."

Vahldan grunted, then rose to take his seat on the settle again to wait. He laid the futhark blade across his lap. The giant didn't often reveal much about what he was thinking or how he felt. Now Teavar wiped his face and pulled on his beard. "Forgive me, but I'm confused. Who is this wife and her son?"

"The wife is Harma, daughter of Herodes. And the son is Armesus, son of Vahldan."

Teavar scowled. "She… she means to… marry him?" Vahldan nodded. "To be clear, we're speaking of Malvius. The shifty sailor who betrayed you and everyone else who ever trusted him." Vahldan nodded again. "And just how does the little shit think to become the imperial magister?"

"The deal has already been struck. The title, his return to this palace and the anaxship, all of it. It's been offered in return for his services in aiding the mobile reserve in their retaking of Thrakius and our ousting from Pontea."

"He made this deal?" Vahldan nodded. "In return for your downfall." He nodded again. "You knew?"

"I first gleaned it shortly after Malvius and his cohorts stormed the gatehouse and opened the seagates to the imperial navy."

Teavar stared down, working his mouth like he was swallowing an atrocious potion. "She betrayed you." The giant's glare rose to him. "And you didn't strike her down on the spot?"

Vahldan huffed a laugh. "It's part of how I came to see what was really happening. I had already spoken to the captive officer, Lauterus, of seeking to make the best of circumstances afterward. Then this. Trust me when I say that it really hit me how it might all come together. I mean, with a wallop. The final piece, I think, was when my ugliness left me. It was as if Freya herself delivered the blow. She made sure I knew it was gone. For good this time. I haven't seen things this clearly in long years. What's happened with Harma since I found out only serves to prove it to me. This is all ordained."

"So... Malvius traded your life for his enrichment, he's taking your qeins in the bargain, and you think it's ordained?"

Was Teavar outraged? Disgusted? Both? Vahldan shrugged. "A hard bargain, I know. But a worthy trade for being awakened—for a chance to seek what's best. Besides, it's not as though I haven't wronged each of them. Or used them. From a certain perspective, I had it coming. Plus, we can't overlook the fact that my life is already forfeit." As if on cue, the pain flared and he put his hand on his side. "Believe me," he said as he winced.

Teavar tilted his head back to stare at the ceiling. "I'm just trying to sort this all out."

"Maybe I can help. This all started some time ago, going back to something Elan said about how the empire couldn't possibly be made to crumble by our little war. She said that perhaps our people were meant to rise both from within and without the empire. Freya's grace, I instantly recognized it as truth. It's been as if the gods have whispered to me, directing me toward it ever since. For instance, do you know what came to me after I heard my qeins confess her infidelity and then watched the imperial navy coursing toward my city's harbor?"

"Since my thoughts would be only of rage and vengeance, I cannot imagine."

"I thought of these words." Vahldan flicked the ring dangling from Bairtah-Urrin's hilt. "Two become one, Together to stand, Forever to lead, Brothers unto Urrinan."

"You thought of the futhark," Teavar deadpanned.

"My hand drifted to my hilt as we left Harma and the line about the brothers just popped into my head." He fingered the futhark ring and smiled. "It's funny, but I was so upset about Thaedan. About how his name sounded like a Wulthus name. About how little he resembles me. Even then, deep down, I think I knew. The boy is a wolf. He's much more his mother's son than his father's. And then Armesus came and, well, no one will ever be able to deny his Amalus blood. I've only become more certain of it since. Thaedan will be the Wolf Lord. Amaga will see to it. Which will make Armesus the sole and true Amalus heir."

"By Freya's will," the giant murmured, finally sounding awestruck. "Wolf and lion—one in each world."

"As it shall be," Vahldan said wistfully.

He closed his eyes. "Looking back on it all, it's like a lingering vision from Freya—one that's haunted me for years. I dream of my lion son often. Yes, Armesus will be a credit to his sires, but he'll be much more. He will find his way within the imperial fold, ascending to heights unheard of for the Tutona. And Thaedan." He chuckled. "Well, he may struggle, considering his mother's influence. But the queen has assured me that he will always have the guardianship of the Skolani—the same gift that so greatly benefitted me. I have to believe it will see him to his ascendancy. Thaedan will be forced to choose. But there is much in place to keep him on his destined path. Armesus—on the other hand—will have no such guardianship. He too will face choices. But I fear if he's left alone in the imperial world, he may not remember his blood or even recognize his destiny. The gods know Harma cannot be relied upon."

Teavar stroked his beard. After a long moment, he drew a deep breath and sighed it out. "I belong to you, my king," he said. "The gods have long ago willed it. What must I do?"

"Submit to the imperials. Strive and hope to be placed in the service of Malvius—"

"As a slave," Teavar interjected.

"As a slave."

"Belonging to Malvius," the giant deadpanned again.

Vahldan huffed a laugh. "Yes. Sorry. But Harma has vowed to do all that she can to see you are granted access to Armesus to mentor him in the ways of the Gottari and of the Amalus. In addition, you must attend to this." Once again, Vahldan proffered the sword on his open palms.

Teavar looked distressed. Vahldan gestured for him to take it. He did. "What shall I do with it?" Teavar asked solemnly.

"Later tonight, you shall hide it. Tell no one where. Perhaps tell the boy, Ago. Have him point you to the palace's most secret places, but do not tell him why. No one can know of your mission. Then, when the time is right, retrieve it and bestow it upon the Amalus heir. See to it that my son understands its significance. Seek to have him use it in the pursuit of the restoration of the futhark. The futhark that his father renounced by sundering his people."

Teavar drew it partway out of the sheath, gazing into the bright blade's reflection. "If I hide it and tell no one where and the imperials kill or imprison me, what becomes of Bairtah-Urrin then?"

"Such would become as it shall be," Vahldan said. "We shall have to surrender to fate and have faith in our people's destiny in Urrinan. And even though Elan might advise us against it, we must trust in the providence of the gods."

Teavar nodded and slid the blade back into its sheath. "As it shall be."

"Then you'll accept? You'll do me this great favor?"

"I will," Teavar said.

"Excellent! Now, although I said I would not ask a vow of you for myself, may I suggest you take a vow to the sword?"

The big man frowned. "How would I go about such a thing?"

"Hand me the sword and kneel."

Vahldan held his side, gritted his teeth, and struggled to stand. He unsheathed the blade and stood over the kneeling giant. He laid the blade gently on the bowed head of his guardian. "Teavar, son of Skaldan. Do you vow to protect this blade, to keep it as a symbol of our clan's heritage, to bestow it upon its rightful heir in due time?"

"I do."

"Do you also vow to pursue the restoration of the futhark and to seek the reunification of the Amalus and the Wulthus, that they might stand as brothers again, that the Gottari might ascend to their rightful glory as the high kings of a hundred Tutona kingdoms, and that the old world and the new might link, thereby creating a wider world for our people—one that is free from tyranny and slavery?"

"I will."

Vahldan tapped his head, then turned the sword, offering him the hilt. "Then arise and begin, guardian of Armesus of the Amalus, sworn steward of the futhark of the Gottari in Pontea."

Teavar took the sword hilt and rose. Vahldan extended his right arm. His ally, guardian, and dear friend grasped his forearm tightly and warmly. "Thank you, my brother. May the progeny of our people forever praise your name."

The bedchamber door opened. Elan's smile was wry. "Are you boys finally done plotting your secret pacts?"

"Yes, we're done," Vahldan said.

"Well, praise be to Freya's tits. Can you come and do me up?" Elan turned to reveal the unfastened buckles of her cuirass and sword harness.

Vahldan bowed stiffly to Teavar. "May I have a moment alone with Elan?"

"Of course." Teavar mirrored the bow. "I remain at your command, my king. Always."

THE DOOR CLICKED CLOSED behind Teavar. One by one Vahldan drew Elan's buckles tight and fastened them. He leaned in to sniff the back of her neck and then couldn't resist kissing her beneath the ear.

"Unfair," she said. "How am I supposed to leave if you do that?"

"Gods, that takes me back. Is that the old Skolani cleansing paste I smell?"

"Icannes gave me some when we went to see the queen. To

cleanse myself of the battles here. I took it down to the baths while you all were at dinner."

Vahldan turned her to face him and put his arms around her waist. "You're one to talk. How am I supposed to let you go when you smell so good? Like Dania. Like the old us."

She raised an eyebrow. "You can never really be rid of me. Haven't I proven that?"

"Thank the gods," he said. "It's a gift—having you here, so close to…"

Elan's eyes shone in the lamplight. "I'm afraid again."

Vahldan drew a deep breath. "Me too." The words came as a whisper of exhaled breath.

"Can this actually be happening?"

"How could it not?"

"You know what I mean. I still wonder if maybe there's another way. I mean, maybe we can talk to them—strike some sort of bargain. Vernius doesn't seem like a monster."

He shook his head. "You heard what the boy said he heard. And Lauterus confirmed it. This is out of Vernius's hands. His orders are to exterminate us. It's been decreed by the emperor himself. And his men will turn to butchery if we show any sign of cowardice. We're beyond any sort of surrender. I'm sorry that I got our followers into this but we need to look to a future for those who survive. We have to fight for the best form of slavery. We have to fight to keep the fires of hope burning."

Elan frowned. "Maybe we should still try to fight our way out of here, flee into the pass."

"We've been over this. I vowed to the queen. I won't lead our foe to them. Dania must be left apart from this world. Plus, I don't want to endanger your mission. It's a matter of facing our duty with honor."

She drew back from him, looking out into the dark night, her expression fierce. "I hate this. You've finally come back to me and now you're being taken again. There must be a means of escape that we haven't—"

"Elan." Vahldan grabbed her hands and gripped them. "It's done." She found focus on him. He swallowed hard. "The wound. Something ruptured. I can feel it. It's close now. I don't know how long I have. I think I'm being granted extra time. To see to..."

Her eyes shone. He saw that she knew it for truth. "I always thought I'd be with you, right up till—"

Vahldan shook his head. "We've already agreed. You said the plan feels rightful."

"I agree that the goal feels rightful. But the plan... Gods, the plan is tearing me apart."

"You're going to make it," he said fervently. "You'll get them through. I know you will."

Tears sprang from her eyes. "That's what I'm afraid of. I'm afraid I'm going to live. Without you. I don't think I can do that—not again. I've already tried. And this time there would be no hope that you'll come back to me."

"You can," he hissed. "And it's you who'll eventually come to me. I need you to stay alive. I want you to promise me."

Elan wiped her eyes. "What are you saying? We've always known we share this doom."

He drew a breath that made the wound ache. He'd have to confess. "I need you to say the prayers to Hel to convince her that I'm worthy. After all of my failings, all of my crimes. There's no one else... no one I've truly loved who has returned it. Not like this."

Elan took his face in her strong hands. "Oh, my darling. You are so worthy. Hel will have no say—not in this. The Valkyries will come for you."

Now his eyes filled. "No. There can be no redemption for the Bringer. Too many have suffered. Too many have died. There are more to come. It's too many, too much, for redemption."

Elan's gaze hardened. "Now you listen to me. No matter how you cross over, no matter when I follow, I will come for you. I've never been more certain of anything. I'll find you. We are destined to be together. After all we endured, I will not be cheated of it. Consider it a futhark between you and me. To death's door and beyond, my love."

"And beyond," he repeated. She kissed him and he felt all the intensity of all the years of their love in it.

As their lips parted, Vahldan pulled her tight. He held her till the pain faded. Time seemed to stop while they stood hugging for the gods only knew how long. A rap at the door broke the trance. "They're waiting for Elan, my king," Teavar said through a crack in the door.

"It's time," he said. She didn't move. "You have to go." Her grip didn't slacken. "It's destined. You're *their* guardian now." He hated saying the words but knew she wouldn't leave without hearing them. "I release you from the Fulhsna-Utanni. Your duty to me is done."

Elan abruptly released him, turned, and hurried for the door. "Elan." She turned back in the doorway, pressing her lips tight, her cheeks wet with tears.

"Now it's my turn." Vahldan smiled. "Kestrel."

Her hand went to her chest, pressed over the talisman he knew hung beneath her cuirass. The corners of his true love's mouth curled into a loving smile as she closed the door and left him alone. More alone than he'd felt in long years—since before they met, a lifetime ago.

CHAPTER 27
FATED FLIGHT

"There are few things in this life worse than being hunted. Prolonged predation pushes the victim beyond terror. Flight consumes the pursued, mind, body, and soul. To become prey is to have all other aspects of one's being stripped away. In food, there is no nourishment, only sustenance. In sleep, there is no rest, only recovery.

In love, there is no shared joy, only cooperative survival. Or sacrifice."
—Brin Bright Eyes, Saga of Dania

AMAGA HELD Thaedan against her chest with his head over her shoulder. His soft crying had finally faded to exhausted snoring. It made her realize how badly she longed for sleep, or at least rest.

Freya's trials, but she hated it down here in these forsaken tunnels. The air seemed too thin and the cold seemed to penetrate to the bone. She couldn't stop thinking she'd somehow be trapped, left to die down here. Every bedamned rocky passage looked the same. Even the periodic timbers that apparently held the tunnels from crushing down on them all looked identical. And insufficient. It didn't seem possible that they resisted collapse beneath the weight of an entire city. Nor did it seem likely that the foreign boy could somehow remember the way. She wondered if it was all a ruse—if this Tibairyan son was willfully leading them nowhere. He was Ligaia's son, too, after all. Perhaps Ligaia was whispering to guide her son from the other side of the veil, just to torment Amaga.

Amaga's arms were long past numb, her leg muscles burned, and her side ached. She'd gone through so many cobwebs, her entire face was coated, forcing her to blink their stickiness out of her eyes and off of her eyelashes. She stumbled again on the uneven footing, then somehow caught herself, twisting her ankle in the process. Kemella's boots were too damn big.

She slowed to a limp. The torches disappeared around the turn ahead of her, plunging her into blackness. Freya's mercy, she just wanted to give up. A scurrying sound came from the floor of the cavern, off to the side, made by the gods only knew what. "Wait," she called, trying not to reveal her panic and upset her son.

Amaga limped around the corner to find the group stopped and waiting. Ligaia's boy stood with a hand on his hip, disdainful. Worse, the only one who'd started back for her? The savage. Loki's torment, she didn't know if it was worse being left behind or relying on Elan. "Are you all right?" the savage asked, appraising her gait. The woman managed to make concern sound scolding.

"I twisted my ankle, is all. I'll be fine," she lied.

"Why don't we let Urias carry the boy?" Elan beckoned Amaga's uncle.

Urias strode to her. "No, please," Amaga pleaded. "He's already frightened."

"Time is running out," Elan hissed. "We must be well into the pass before it grows light."

Her uncle handed his torch to Elan and took Thaedan from Amaga in spite of her reluctance. Then the damned super-siblings started off again. Amaga reached down to straighten the boot on her foot and tighten the laces. Thaedan's eyes went wide over Urias's shoulder and his face wrinkled up, ready to erupt. "He's very sensitive," she called after them.

Thaedan's renewed crying was the loudest since their flight began. Amaga hurried to catch up. She would simply have to take him back. Urias pulled him from his shoulder, holding her son in front of his chest.

"Thaedan, did you know that we're going to meet your grandfather? He is as big and as cuddly as a bear." The voice was childlike, soothing. It was working. Considering the source, Amaga would never have imagined it.

Elan bent before Thaedan, gently holding his hand. "He is known as the Great Wolf. Isn't that funny? A wolf who is a bear? He will love meeting you so much. And he'll always keep you safe. But we have to hurry to meet him. All right? Shall we keep going and meet your grandfather?"

Thaedan's gray eyes fixed on the savage. Amazingly, he'd stopped crying and settled. He seemed to gain an uncanny grasp of the situation, even giving Elan a little nod. The reaction didn't surprise Amaga. She'd seen many such instances with Thaedan, in which the goddess whispered to him. Still, it was shocking that Freya had responded to anything Elan said or did.

Urias lifted her solemn son back against his chest and nodded. "Let's go," Elan said.

Thaedan's eyes met Amaga's over her uncle's shoulder. She forced a smile and waved. Her son laid his head down and sighed. On they went, into the endless black of the catacombs.

"DEAD END," Brin's mother said, sounding both annoyed and worried.

Brin sensed Agoraki's relief when the rubble appeared, virtually blocking the catacomb tunnel ahead. "No. This is it," her friend said.

His tone made Brin suspect he'd been unsure he was on the right course till now.

Ago immediately started to scramble up the pile of rubble, causing small stones to tumble. As Ago's torch came to the top, near the ceiling of the tunnel, Brin saw it—an opening off to the side. Ago stuck his torch and his head through the gap, then drew back again. "Sorry, but it gets a little tight in spots. Might be worse than I remembered."

"What do you mean, *a little tight*?" Elan asked.

"You'll have to crawl. It'll be harder for some than others. But it isn't far till it gets better."

"Can I manage holding him?" Uncle Urias indicated Amaga's son in his arms.

Ago looked forlorn and shrugged. "Not easily. Sorry, it's the only way out into the pass."

Even as Ago spoke, Urias handed off the boy to his mother and unfastened the clasp to his cloak. He folded the cloak in half, then into a triangle, and slung it over his shoulder. He gestured for her to bring the boy nearer. "Hold him like this," he instructed Amaga. He slipped Thaedan, feet-first, into the folds of his cloak, like swaddling, then tied the loose tails of the triangle around his neck. The cloak now held the boy snug to her uncle's armored chest.

Amazingly, through it all, the boy didn't cry.

"Lead on," Urias said.

Everyone sensed the growing urgency and even Amaga didn't recoil or complain when Brin's mother helped her up the pile of rubble. Once Amaga was inside the cave behind Ago, Elan stopped at the top. She beckoned Urias up and awaited him in case he needed help. He scrambled up like a crab using one hand and held Thaedan with the other. Brin went in next and her mother came last, holding a torch.

The narrow passage was oddly muffled, the only sound being their heavy breathing and the echo of an occasional grunt or the click of armor or scrape of boot on stone. The floor was sometimes jagged enough to cause Brin to wince and change how her hands or knees touched down. She sensed they were beginning to climb and the floor of the cave became sandier. The headroom grew, too, and even though the adults had to stay on their hands and knees, Brin was able to get to her feet and use her hands only to steady herself and move on in a stoop.

A gust of fresh air came to her face. The cave suddenly grew and the air got colder. The mouth was obviously near. The rock opened overhead, angling to reveal a bit of sky. There was a hidden space on the steep hillside, wide enough for them to gather in a group. Though there were still stars visible, Brin could see the first hint of the coming of dawn.

Ago signaled for them to stay put. Her friend stuck his torch in the sand and crept into the clear. A moment later, Ago crawled back to them. He put a finger to his lips and then whispered, "The Tiberian camp is below us. There is a path that leads up to a ridge, just above us. The ridge runs downhill to the north. You should be able to get clear of the camp if you follow it down without being seen. Once the ground begins to level, the trees are not too far."

Elan stuck her torch with Ago's and crawled past them all. "I'll take a look around. Don't move until I return. If I don't return, go back." Her mother pulled her bow from over her shoulder, nocked an arrow, and disappeared.

Urias untied the wrap that held Thaedan and handed the boy to Amaga, who shushed and soothed him back to stillness. Brin crawled over to Ago. His face was all angles in the torchlight. He looked older. She saw the man he would soon become. "You can still come with us," she whispered.

Ago shook his head. "It's your homeland. I still have my own to discover."

"What about your father? If you go back, won't he be angry? What if he turns you away? Or worse, locks you up?"

Ago smiled and his features softened back to the boy she knew.

"It's a chance I have to take. Same as you." He was right. She had no idea whether either of her parents' tribes would accept her.

Her mother returned and beckoned them close. "Ago's right—the path is a dozen steps up. If we stay along the top of the ridge, it leads us right down to the flat. The forest is just beyond. There are three sentries near the corral, less than fifty paces down. So we must be completely silent. Brin, you lead the way. Amaga, take the babe and follow right behind her. Just keep moving, no matter what. Urias and I will bring up the rear."

Brin turned to Ago. "Thank you for saving us. For saving me. Again."

Ago's smile widened. "I think we're even."

"I hope you find the home you've always wanted. And the wife you deserve. You know, one who's a friend first."

"Gods alive, let's go, girl," Amaga hissed.

Brin's patience for the waif snapped. "You wouldn't even be here if not for Ago and me."

A hand clapped over her mouth. "Enough." Her mother's whisper was a growl in her ear.

Her mother released her and Brin nodded. She knew she deserved it. It was time to act. She turned and started to go. She glanced back. In spite of it all, she couldn't just leave him like this. She nudged past Amaga to go back and raised herself to her knees to hug her dear friend. Ago hugged her back, tight.

"I'll never forget you," she whispered in his ear.

"Me either. Never."

Brin broke from his arms and scrambled past her glaring companions, ready now to lead the way into the unknown.

ELAN'S DAUGHTER pulled her own bow from over her shoulder. Brin swiftly and adeptly nocked an arrow. Elan inwardly cringed, almost telling her to put it away, then stopped herself. Brin was leaving the child behind, and tonight, they needed the young warrior she was becoming. Elan had to leave the child behind as well. Elan bowed her head in thanks to the boy and followed this new version of her baby girl out onto the rocky mountainside.

She pointed out the steps she'd taken up to the path for Brin. "Just keep moving," she breathed to her. Brin nodded. The path along the ridge was better suited to goats than to humans, but it would have to do. Amaga emerged, clinging to the boy. The waif gasped, eyes wide at the Tibairyan camp sprawling across the vale beneath them. The rows of tents and dozens of campfires were indeed enough to take one's breath. It was a stunning confirmation of Vahldan's assertion—the imperials meant to end this war in extermination.

Elan put a finger to her lips and then helped Amaga to her unsteady feet. Gods, the waif was moving clumsily. Urias had his sword drawn when he emerged. "Stay close to her," she whispered, indicating Amaga. He nodded and climbed after his niece.

Brin pranced silently and gracefully along the ridge above. Amaga struggled to follow, causing a gap to form. Although the coming dawn tinged the sky to gray, Elan's hopes began to rise. She kept watch of the camp, which was silent and still.

She heard a shuffling sound, then the rocks tumbling. Amaga had slipped. With her arms around the child, she lost her balance and fell onto her hip. She slid downhill a span. Elan stopped and raised her bow, gritting her teeth and scanning the camp below. She was about to breathe again when the squalling cry of the boy rent the night.

Sentries' calls rang out across the camp. Elan drew her bow, sighting for movement as she hurried toward Amaga. A pair of sentries ran from the corral toward the base of the ridge, carrying spears. One pointed up at Amaga, who was struggling to climb back to the path. The man called to his companion. Elan loosed her shot at the one who was pointing. He fell with a yowl.

Brin had returned to help Amaga to her feet. Elan called, "Get them out of here!" She nocked another arrow and shot. The second spearman raised his shield and her shot thumped wood rather than flesh. The man peered over the shield, calling for help and pointing.

Urias ran downhill, heading for an inbound squad of five soldiers. "Damn it," Elan hissed. She started after him, paused, and aimed. The bastards had shields. She shot and the lead runner fell with an arrow in his thigh. It was the best she could manage. The turf grew less steep. Arrows weren't going to resolve this. She dropped the bow and reached for her blade.

The remaining four Tibairya slowed and clumped together, forming a shield wall. On the approach, she and Urias split up, forcing them to separate. Urias took on the two on the left. She ran past him to engage the pair on the right. The first one thrust a spear, wild and early. It left him overextended and she hacked his right wrist. She swung from the strike into a backhand for the second, who jabbed with a thrusting sword. She easily parried, knocking his blade hard enough to set him off balance. She slammed her buckler into his shield, knocking him to the ground. Her roundhouse follow-up struck his armored shoulder the moment he hit the turf.

Sensing the wounded spearman behind her, she spun into a swing. His left-handed thrust was weak and off target. He'd lost his helm and Biter smashed the side of his skull. He dropped like a stone from a bridge.

Elan turned back just as the one she'd knocked down regained his feet. She swung, but he shield-blocked her blow and countered low. She parried and dropped to a low crouch, looking for a way to flee, sensing that time was running out. Other foes were surely coming. Urias arrived behind her opponent and landed a downward stroke, felling him.

The first five were down but the camp boiled with calls and commotion.

"Time to go!" She ran and Urias followed.

Staying in the vale would keep them too close to the camp, so she led him uphill. They scrambled across the face of the hillside, angling toward Brin's progress above. Her daughter pulled Amaga by the hand, hurrying down to the flat.

Imperial trumpets blared. As if in response, long, low blasts from Gottari war horns sounded, echoing from the city walls above. Elan glanced back to see flaming missiles arcing from the north wall onto the Tibairyan camp, setting tents ablaze and causing horses to dance and neigh. Vahldan! The Gottari had abandoned the north wall at nightfall. But because of its nearness to the walls of the keep, the Tibairya hadn't sought possession of the north gate or the section of the wall adjacent to the palace. Vahldan had led a squad out there to ensure their safe escape. Now they were sowing chaos in the foe's camp, doing their best to aid their flight.

Brin and Amaga had reached the final steep drop, which slowed them. She and Urias would meet up with them on the slope that angled to the roadway into the pass. The treeline was less than fifty paces beyond that. The footing became a treacherous scree. The terrain forced her and Urias toward the gentler slope. Their pursuers would take an angle to intercept—one that would bring them too damn close, too damn soon.

Elan ventured a look back. A half-dozen soldiers ran after them. Worse, behind the runners came a trio of mounted Equites, gaining at an even more alarming rate.

Brin and Amaga hit the level ground. Brin wisely demanded that Amaga put the boy on her back. She held his legs with one arm and her bow in her free hand. It sped their pace. Elan hurried on after her daughter. She sensed her brother falling behind. She looked to find that Urias had stopped. He faced the foe in a fighting stance, his blade held high.

"Urias, no!" Even as Elan cried the words, she knew it was their only chance. The horsemen had overtaken their running companions. The riders would catch them before they made the tree line.

Urias looked over his shoulder. "Go! Take them."

She stopped and reached for her blade hilt. "I'm staying too."

"Elan, do your duty!" His stern face shone in the twilight. "This is mine. I know it. Go!"

Urias turned from her, standing ready again. The horsemen bore down on him.

"I love you, Brother!" Elan turned and ran, her eyes stinging and a sob caught in her throat.

The galloping hoofbeats grew thunderous as she ran and over them came her brother's clear call. "For the futhark!" A horse screamed, followed by a chorus of angry shouts punctuated with the resound of steel clanging.

Tears blurred Elan's vision. She could not—would not—look back. She would do her duty, as he'd bidden her.

Amaga faltered as Elan caught up. Elan grabbed the waif by the hand, pulling her to the trees as fast as her little legs would carry her. "Come on, Amaga," she urged. "You can do it."

"I...I can't."

"You can! Do it for your son." Her face contorting, Amaga sped her step.

Brin made the trees with the boy still bumping along on her back. Hoofbeats drummed the ground behind them. Elan flung Amaga forward. "Brin, your bow!" Elan snatched the bow and a single arrow from her daughter. "Now run! Both of you."

Elan spun back, hiding herself among the fir boughs. She sheathed Biter and drew Brin's bow. The lead rider appeared in her sights. She fired, turned, and ran on.

They scrambled through the lashing branches. The hoofbeats still came on but they were slowing. Elan managed to take a look. Her target's horse had continued into the forest, the rider slumped over the neck of his mount, his hand gripping her lone arrow protruding from his neck. Her victim was the only one of the three to make it to the treeline. Urias had somehow managed to take two out of the chase. The half-dozen foot soldiers who'd been in pursuit were clustered in the area where Urias had made his stand.

No. She couldn't look. The slumped rider was near, wheezing for his final breaths. Elan shouldered the bow and moved carefully but swiftly to the confused horse, speaking to him with a soothing voice. He was a stallion and wasn't skittish. Elan drew her belt knife and came around behind. She snatched his dangling reins, holding the knife at the ready. But the rider's body was slack now. She easily pulled the lifeless Eques from the saddle and sheathed the knife. She stroked the horse's neck as she dislodged the dead man's boot from a stirrup. "There, that's a fine fellow," she said softly. "Maybe you can help us now, eh?" The stallion didn't resist as she led him deeper into the forest.

Elan soon caught up to the others. Brin and Amaga both spun around, startled. "Just me," she assured them. "I made a friend." She led the stallion to Amaga. "Can you ride?"

"Oh no," Amaga whined pathetically.

Elan stepped closer. "It may just save him." She nodded to Amaga's mewling babe.

Surprisingly, the waif nodded. "All right. I'll try." After all these years, Elan had finally found the means to handle Amaga's negativity. She helped her into the saddle and Brin handed the boy up. Amaga wrapped her arms around Thaedan and gripped the pommel. The boy wasn't as terrified as his mother, and his crying fell to a soft whine of disgruntlement, thank the gods.

Elan handed the reins and the bow to Brin and drew Biter. "I'll blaze a trail. You lead them." To Amaga she said, "Watch for low branches and try to keep him quiet." Amaga set her jaw and nodded. Something had come over the woman. Whatever it was, it might just save them.

Elan turned and picked out a trail heading up, away from the roadway and onto the snowy slope. Up higher, the hemlock and cedar would give way to pine and maple, she knew. They obviously couldn't cover their tracks, so they'd just have to take on more difficult terrain instead.

If they had any chance at all, it would be due to her superior ability to navigate the pass.

They wouldn't even have had this chance without the sacrifice of her brother. The thought put an instant lump in Elan's throat and an ache in her chest. No. She would not cry. She would mourn later. Urias wouldn't have it any other way. He'd given them a gift. She refused to squander it.

Elan would make it. She'd lead the Wulthus heir to safety and provide their people with the link from the old world to the new. She'd do it in her amazing, loving brother's honor. She'd do it for her daughter and for Vahldan's son. They would help to remake the world.

Malvius awoke to voices. It wasn't the first time that night. Interruptions were to be expected by someone seeking to snatch a bit of sleep on the ale-soaked floorboards of The Fishmonger Tavern. Particularly since an invading army had been using it as a command post during the prior day. But these voices were different—stern and insistent, tinged with menace.

Something was happening.

He raised up to look over the blanket-wrapped forms of the dozens of townsfolk who'd been swept up in the action—wounded or made homeless by the battle—and were softly snoring around him. Overnight, the tavern had gone from command post to makeshift sanctuary, its refugees all drawn to the hearth at the far end, away from the door. Another dozen of the men Dex had recruited still sat at tables, still drinking. He'd been meaning to tell them that their premature celebration might curse the outcome, but he'd left it alone. They'd risked their lives and rightfully considered their part of this war over and done. He hoped they were right.

The menacing voices belonged to a pair of Tiberian soldiers. They were brusque, evidently interrogating the drunken militiamen. Malvius heard his name and without hesitation one of the gray-beards jerked a thumb toward him. Of course. How could he expect compassion or aid from his father's friends and followers? He swiftly lay back and closed his eyes. Boots clomped through the sleeping bodies and tables, coming closer.

One of the soldiers kicked his boot. He sat up. "You Malvius?" The nearest refugees startled awake, wide-eyed and edging away.

"I am. How can I be of service?"

"You're coming with us," the soldier said. His tone brooked no argument.

Malvius stood, unwrapping himself from the blanket Dex had found for him. It made him wonder about Dex. Where was he, anyway? Malvius recalled his first mate engaged with one of the dozens of whores that had swiftly appeared once the battle had moved uphill. It was rare for the man to seek carnal distractions. He supposed he couldn't begrudge it. After all, Dex often covered for him through his own carnal distractions. Dex had been more than loyal and attentive. As he had been for years, but unbelievably so since the siege had begun. He owed all of their success to his first mate's exceptional competence.

The Tiberians led Malvius out into the brisk wind. The sky remained clear and betrayed signs of the coming dawn. A merchant's closed carriage sat outside. A Tiberian soldier sat yawning on the driver's bench. The remaining snow was crunchy under their boots as the soldiers led him to the carriage door and knocked.

The general's adjutant opened the door—Nicandros, Malvius thought he recalled. The young officer scowled. "What do you know of Vernouthus, Captain?"

"I know much. Can you be more specific?"

"How did he end up in the middle of the battle outside the palace gates?"

Malvius swiftly overcame his surprise. The boy was sneaky, that was sure. And unpredictable. Ago tended to turn up in surprising places. "I hadn't heard. Is he all right?"

"The boy said nothing to you of this?"

"Of what?"

"Of why he might leave the safety of the general's ship?"

The young officer's accusatory tone was getting annoying. "In case it's not clear, trust that I'm not exactly Agoraki's favorite relative right now. I haven't seen him since Megaria."

Nicandros sighed and beckoned him inside. "Come with me, Captain. The general will want answers."

Malvius glanced at the soldiers flanking him. "I doubt I'll be able to supply them. But I suppose it'll save me the trouble of finding a way to check your progress."

Nicandros frowned. "My progress?"

"Not yours specifically," he said. "No offense, but I happen to be deeply invested in your army's success. I'd like to know how this war is coming along."

The young man leaned back without reply, glowering. Malvius climbed into the dark carriage and they lurched into motion. The adjutant's peevish disposition did not abate. "I'm also concerned for my nephew, of course," he said to break the sullen silence.

Nicandros continued looking out the side window. "I'd strongly suggest that you avoid any indication to Lord General Vernius that you are... *checking on our progress*. Or that his son was an afterthought to that."

Malvius smiled. "Thanks for the advice."

They rode up the hill without another word, finally arriving at one of the largest old mansions in the northwest quadrant. Until one of the Rekkrs had seized it, the place had belonged to the family that had owned the city's old sailcloth weaving operation adjacent to the shipyard. The owners had long since fled the city. As they stepped out of the carriage, a distant trumpet call came floating on the wind. It was almost immediately answered by more trumpets, then by Gottari war horns. It all seemed to be coming from the direction of the north gate.

Nicandros hurried up the mansion's front steps. Malvius lingered, listening to the shouts that drifted down, obviously from the palace walls. "This isn't good," he said aloud.

The soldier who'd woken him spun and fixed him with a look of warning.

Within moments of Nicandros entering, the mansion's doors burst open again. Vernius led a gaggle of his officers and attendants down the stairs. "Bring the horses," the general called. Soldiers snapped out salutes and scurried down the side alley to the mansion's stables.

"We could take the carriage, my lord," Nicandros suggested, gesturing.

Vernius stood, irritably donning his gloves. "No. The city avenues will take us too close to the palace keep walls. I'm told there's a path that can be taken outside the city walls to the northern camp."

The general's gaze finally found Malvius just as the grooms brought up three saddled horses. "You stay here," Vernius said stiffly. "We still need to have a conversation."

"I'd prefer to go with you, Lord General."

Vernius mounted. "No." The general turned to the soldiers who brought their mounts. "See that our guest is made comfortable. And that he doesn't stray off."

Malvius rushed to Vernius's stirrup. "Please, my lord. I can be of service. I know the trail you mentioned well."

"We'll find it, Captain, thank you."

His three companions mounted and they started west on the avenue. Malvius ran after them. "I may know why Ago ran away," he blurted. Vernius reined to a halt and scowled. "He *has* run away, hasn't he? Straight to the Gottari?" Malvius was guessing. Even if it was true, he had little insight to offer. But at least he had a better guess than these foreign stiffs.

"I suggest you tell me," Vernius said, sounding even more hostile than usual.

"It's complicated. It will be much easier to explain as I guide you to the northern camp."

Vernius turned to the others. "Nico, give the captain your horse."

The adjutant's peevishness flared, but the young man instantly did as bidden.

Malvius mounted, rather awkwardly. The horse danced in a circle and Malvius held his breath and stayed as still as he could. Finally, the beast settled. Gods, he hated riding. "This had better be good," Vernius said and kicked his mount to canter out ahead of them, heading down to the city's west gate in the growing twilight.

The general's gaggle dismounted and Malvius was relieved to slide out of the saddle in one piece. He followed Vernius into the northern camp. Before they reached the command post, the camp's commanding officer rushed to meet them. After a bit of low murmuring, the officer led them all to the northernmost end of the path that led to their corral. A row of male bodies—six in all—was laid out on the snow alongside the path. Five were clearly Tiberian soldiers, reverently laid out on their backs, arms crossed over their chests. A half-dozen soldiers sat on the ground or leaned on the fence nearby. The Tiberians slumped in dejection. A medicus was treating the wounds of one. Malvius couldn't tell if the others were awaiting treatment or judgment. Both, perhaps.

The sixth corpse, at the far end and apart from the others, was face down, his arms stretched overhead. He'd obviously been dragged there and unceremoniously dumped. His green-gray Gottari cloak was smeared with mud, as were his corded boots and leggings. His tangled golden hair was matted with dark blood.

Malvius strode past the Tiberians and bent to roll the Gottari over. In spite of having half of his head caved in and half of his face chopped to a meaty gore, Malvius instantly recognized him. "Urias," he whispered. His stomach lurched, followed by a wave of fret.

"Who is he?" Vernius barked.

"He is the brother of the one you know as the Hippomache. He is also the uncle of Vahldan's first wife." Malvius rose and faced the camp commander. "Who was with him?" Urias could be an imposing figure, but he wasn't a thug like so many of the others. Malvius doubted he could have inflicted this kind of damage by himself.

The camp commander looked pained and turned to Vernius. "Yes, I'd like a report," Vernius said.

The man gestured to one of those leaning on the fence. "Centurion, report to the general."

The centurion stood and snapped to attention. He cleared his throat. "We spotted a group of the foe climbing along that ridge, coming from beneath the city's walls. They were sneaking toward the forest road when the alarm went up. One of them was the Hippomache, who ran down to attack a squad of sentinels along with this man. The soldiers who responded had never faced the like of her, and she, well, she's a very dangerous savage, as you can see." The centurion glanced at the bodies. "Murderous bitch," he added, full of scorn.

"How many of them were there in total?" Malvius prompted him.

Vernius offered Malvius a stern side glance but then nodded for the centurion to go on. "Besides the dead man and the Hippomache, there were at least three others. One I saw clearly seemed little more than a girl."

"Brin Bright Eyes," Malvius said. "The daughter of the thug king and the Hippomache."

The centurion went on. "Another, a woman, was almost as small as the child. But this one was carrying an infant. It was the babe's crying that gave them away."

"The white witch," Malvius hissed. "Carrying her child, the thug king's firstborn son. Where are they now?"

The centurion looked to his commander. "Answer the question," Vernius ordered.

"Other than him"—the centurion nodded at Urias—"they all escaped into the forest."

"A girl and a woman carrying an infant." Vernius deadpanned the question but his disdain was apparent.

"Aided by the Hippomache," the man retorted. "My Lord General," he quickly added.

"Was there a boy?" Malvius asked.

The centurion scowled, obviously considering him a meddler. "We saw no boy."

"It's a long way to Dania," Malvius said. "How many men did you send after them?"

The centurion's scowl grew baleful. "Answer it," Vernius said.

"We are under strict orders not to enter the surrounding forests."

"The orders were given back in Megaria, Lord General," the commander added. "To avoid inciting the local tribesmen."

Malvius turned to Vernius. "Lord General, please. This situation must be rectified immediately."

Vernius raised a brow. "Two women, a child, and an infant? It's winter, Captain. And that is a mountain range. Their chances of survival are not worthy of taking men from this battle. You recall that we're fighting a battle, do you not?" The general turned and started back to the horses, his gaggle toddling after him. "Speaking of which," he said to the camp commander. "Our final push is about to resume. I expect that you'll not allow another soul to slip past."

"Of course, Lord General."

Malvius rushed around the gaggle and stopped in front of the general, impeding his progress. "My lord, I beg of you." Not a bad idea, considering the ire on Vernius's face. Malvius dropped to a knee. "You must order those who've escaped to be hunted down and eliminated. I don't think you understand what's happening."

"I understand that Vahldan the Bold is not among them. He is the one I am charged to defeat and bring to Medicia, dead or alive."

Malvius laced his fingers before him and looked down. "My lord, there is reason to suspect that your son is with them."

In the silence that followed, Malvius glanced up to find Vernius stricken. "What would make you say such a thing?" the general growled.

Malvius bowed his head. "It's as I told you on the way here. The girl among them, Brin Bright Eyes—Agoraki is smitten with her. She's why he ran away to them." He ventured a glance. The general was considering it. "Ago is the only one who could have led them out here via the catacombs."

Vernius stepped around him and kept walking. "Those who saw them saw no boy."

Malvius leapt to his feet and hurried after him. "Please, Lord General. You must try to understand. They claim the infant they're stealing away is to become the king that unifies the two ruling clans of the Gottari. The prophecy of these savages tells of the conquering of the empire. They will not stop until that happens or they are utterly defeated. I know that Ago once harbored a secret desire to marry Vahldan's daughter." Vernius stopped, bringing his little entourage to a halt. Malvius hurried on. "If there's even a chance that he went, that he could have ended up with some twisted belief in their superstitious nonsense, then we must rescue him. Please seize this last chance. Not just to be sure about your son, but to stop it from happening all over again. You can put an end to what could become an endlessly recurring war simply by ordering those few hunted down."

The general sighed and spun to face Malvius. His scowl was fierce but instead of a reprimand, he called, "Captain Tullius."

"My lord general." It was the sly-looking officer with the ponytail on his helmet and the jangling Sassanadi bangles on his belt.

"Select a squad of your finest Equites. You may finally hunt down your Hippomache rival. If my son is with them, bring him back. Alive and unharmed. As for the she-devil and her companions, bring them back dead or alive, whichever suits."

The officer's sly grin became a wicked one as he saluted. "Yes, Lord General."

URRINAN'S LEGACY

"In the early pages of this text, I made an assertion about my parents. I claimed that theirs was one of the world's great loves. I went on to describe it as deep and potent, as pure as can be shared by two beings in this life.

Having experienced more of their story in the ensuing pages, one might be forgiven for acquiring a sense of doubt. I admit that I have doubted their love. Through much of my early lifetime, in fact. I spent years resenting my father for what I saw as his betrayal of love. Just as I resented my mother for so willfully devoting herself to a man who treated her callously. I resented them both for their shared obsession with a destiny that foretold their doom.

For those who doubt, I offer a final item of evidence, one that helped me at the time to better see. Vahldan and Elan chose to separate in the service of destiny. They believed and sacrificed for their shared belief. I knew then, seeing their agony in making this commitment, that only a love of depth and purity could inspire such sacrifice. Mere obsession would never have sufficed.

Perhaps only those who beheld them together those last nights in the palace, who gleaned the strength required of them, who knew of their faith *that their love would always reunite them, can truly grasp it. Indeed, perhaps I alone could've truly felt the power of it all. As for me, it is more than enough. I long ago chose to forgive their poor choices and accept that the beauty and power of their love is what made me—and saved me.*

Perhaps in this life, my parents' love story is mine alone to preserve and hold dear. A legacy to strive to share, that it might echo through the ages."—Brin Bright Eyes, *Saga of Dania*

As DAWN BROKE, Vahldan made his way to the palace doors. He drew a deep breath and took his hand from his aching wound, dropping it to his side. He nodded and the guards opened the doors. The applause was instant and only grew louder as he emerged. The blast of cold air braced him. It felt like it would freeze his hair, tied back but still wet from dunking his head to stay awake. He drew another painful breath, trying not to cough as he moved to the top of the steps to stand and look out over the last of his army—those so loyal they could not be persuaded to leave his side—gathered in the keep. Their cheering became a chant, which became an echoing thunder. *"On, Gottari, on! On, Gottari, on!"*

He raised his hand for quiet and the chant faded away, leaving only the whistle of the wind off of the sea through the leaf-bare trees.

Vahldan firmed himself, stood tall, and began. There was no need to shout. Grim determination was written upon them. "My brothers. Today we embark upon much more than a battle to quell an invader. Today we fight for more than just a home or a foothold in the so-called civilized world. Today, we fight for our people's place in history."

Rather than cheering, his Amalus followers grunted and nodded in grim concurrence. "The foe that now comes against us is not merely coming to kill or capture. No, what this foe seeks is to quash the Urrinan itself." Scattered boos and hisses rose and swiftly faded.

Vahldan went on. "The Tiberian Empire has ever feared us, as they fear all of those they hope to keep subjugated. Ever have they hunted and enslaved our children. Ever have they hated the Tutona as they rightfully see they are destined to be supplanted by us. They instinctively sense that we Gottari shall be the beginning of their end. Today, born of their desperation, they seek to snuff the flame that shall soon consume their decadence. As you have seen, they spare no expense or effort to do so. Already they have seen that the fires of Urrinan have been lit. They know that you, my brothers, are not just the spark but the wind that propels what comes for them. For we are the leading edge of the firestorm that shall now engulf their empire."

Guttural hoots punctuated his point. "Today, we fight for the ascension that *shall* come. Not just of the Gottari but of the Tutona. Today, we fight for the reign of the first king of a hundred Tutona kingdoms."

The chant began again. *"On, Gottari, on! On, Gottari, on!"* As the chanting spread and grew, Vahldan pressed his hand to his wounded side and descended the steps, heading through the parting warriors who would hold the shield wall once the foe breached the keep. The lions already manning the battlements raised fists or bows overhead in salute as he crossed the keep to the old gardens.

Arnegern stood awaiting him, holding his own mount and Luith-Anthar, the magnificent stallion he'd ridden the prior day. Behind Arnegern was a column of about fifty Rekkrs, already ahorse, waiting to ride in the final charge of the Amalus.

"My king." Arnegern bowed. Vahldan held his breath and mounted. He landed in the saddle with a groan and sat waiting for his blurred vision to clear. His captain proffered the battleaxe Vahldan had asked him to bring. "Are you well, Brother?"

"Well enough," Vahldan said. For one more battle, anyway. He didn't voice the rest of the thought. He took the axe, gritted his teeth, and swung it to check its weight. "This should do." Ermanaric handed him his helm, which he donned.

Warning calls rang out from the battlements. Men on the wall walk turned to face out, nocking their bows. The Tiberian trumpets sounded. Loud, low Gottari war horns swiftly drowned out their soprano peal.

Arnegern and Ermanaric mounted, moving to sit ahorse on either side of him. Vahldan turned to Arnegern. "I have one final favor to ask of you, Brother."

"You have but to ask."

"Once I fall, surrender," he said softly.

Even with Arnegern's helm obscuring much of his face, Vahldan saw his shock. "What are you saying?" Archers from both sides began firing their volleys and the sound of the mobile reserve's attack rose from outside the walls.

"Exactly what it sounds like. My fall, my doom, is ordained. The Urrinan demands it. Once that happens, I want you to save yourself and as many of our people as possible."

"But... this is for our people, for Urrinan."

"Your eventual submission is the only means to ensure it. You must stay alive to see that it all comes to fruition."

Arnegern stared ahead, his lower lip quivering and his cheeks turning red. Vahldan couldn't remember ever seeing him so enraged. "You would say this now? To me? After all of these years? After dedicating my life to staying by your side, pursuing your ends."

"Yes. I'm sorry. I can only hope you will one day find your way to forgiving me for asking even more of you."

"You're asking me to submit to slavery. Or worse." It was the harshest tone his oldest friend had ever used with him. Ermanaric scowled as well. Evidently he'd heard, which was just as well. It saved Vahldan the trouble of repeating himself.

"Listen to me, both of you. The best of the next generation of lions is in those dungeons and catacombs. Including your sons and Eldavar's. And mine. We need them to survive this. The day will come when they shall fulfill the futhark. I know it in my heart. I want you both to guide them to it. The goddess has spoken to me. I sense this must be done from within the imperial system."

"As slaves. All of us. To work for them. To fight for them."

"Yes," Vahldan admitted. "That is what I'm asking of you." He felt himself flushing. Hearing the words aloud made it sound like so much more to ask.

Arnegern looked away.

"It is a command I cannot obey," Ermanaric growled. "I would rather die fighting them than to ever fight for them. Or to see a single one of our sons do so."

Vahldan didn't rebuke him. He focused on Arnegern. His sister's husband sat rigidly, his chin high, facing the gate. His friend seemed to vibrate with outrage. The archery commanders ceased their volleys and called for their men to fire at will. The bowmen fired straight down over the parapet. The foe had reached the gate.

The first thump rattled the portcullis. The horses behind them pranced and pawed in anticipation. The Rekkrs on the ground called for the forming of the shield wall.

He prompted Arnegern. "How about you, Brother? Will you seek to carry out my will?"

Arnegern's glare snapped to him. "A score of years ago, I swore an oath. I committed myself not just to my rightful chieftain, but to my best friend—my brother. I swore to stay by his side till his death or mine. It is an oath I will not abandon. Even when the one to whom I swore dares ask it of me. For I fear that my friend, my brother, is not of sound mind."

"That's just it. I am not of sound body. But I am of sound mind. I see it all. I beg you—"

"I said no!" Arnegern looked away again. "I will not stand by as you fall. I will fight beside you. Till your death or mine. If I somehow survive and you do not, I will consider myself dishonored. I will never willingly submit to the disgrace you would put upon me now."

The thumps grew louder. A clanking sound rang out, indicating the imperials had pulled the portcullis away, likely with teams of horses and chains. The commanders on the wall called for the withdrawal of those manning the walls. They ran down the staircases, streaming to join the ranks forming up in the keep.

Time was running out. "I will not beg." Vahldan nodded in concession. "I ask you only to keep the thought in your mind. Trust that I have heard the will of the goddess, that I believe it is the path to Urrinan's truest fulfillment. I will only say two more things. First, you, my brother, can never—*never*—be dishonored. You have ever been the most honorable, the very best of us. Also, I can never truly tell you how grateful I am, nor how honored I have been made by your loyalty. And by your friendship."

Arnegern faced him, his expression softening. The flare of anger left his eyes and he gave Vahldan a single nod. It was enough. The final thump came with terrific splintering sounds. Then came the roar of Tiberian voices.

The ranks of mobile reserve marched swiftly out through the gateway, their huge shields on all sides and above them making them resemble a scaled snake emerging from its hole.

"Hold!" Arnegern called to the riders, raising his sword. "Hold for my signal."

The flaming arrows slashed down from those left on the battlements. The last of their pitch-covered catapult missiles, broken up and mixed into the thick gravel at the invaders feet, erupted into a wall of flame. Dozens of Tiberians shrieked as they found themselves engulfed.

Amazingly, the men of the mobile reserve continued to push their way in through the narrow gateway, pressing their own comrades into the conflagration, such was their fervor.

The Gottari shield wall shook and recoiled but held in place. Even as the burning soldiers writhed and rolled, the Tiberians who came behind them used their shields to douse and trample the center of the flames. Soon a pathway began to emerge. The wounded among the foe were pulled to either side of the fray, as there was no room in the gateway for them to be taken out.

"Leave their wounded be," Vahldan called to those around him.

The center of the Tiberian lines reformed and charged again. The Gottari shield wall responded, running the short distance to reengage. Shield slammed shield audibly, even over the roar of ragged throats from both sides.

The foe's numbers grew, causing a backup and a press, both to get to the fight and to get out of the lingering fires. Vahldan nodded to Arnegern.

"Lions! For Urrinan!" Arnegern brought his sword slashing down. The Amalus Rekkrs kicked their mounts and galloped out of the garden, coming at the flank of the foe's phalanx—charging against those inside the gate but behind those engaged with the Gottari shield wall.

"For Dania!" Vahldan raised the battleaxe. The bronze stallion, Luith-Anthar—the song of war—raced out ahead, heading for the heart of the attacking foe's ranks.

Elan hunkered back into the hillside crevice, pressing her back into the cold snow till she felt the stone beneath it. She kept her sword held tight to her shoulder and grew still, waiting. The hoofbeats slowed as they grew near. Her pursuers had gleaned that the canyon she'd led them into was a dead-end—potentially a trap. She only needed them to come a bit further.

It wasn't to be. Instead, they stopped. She still couldn't see them. Elan strained, listening to hear over her thudding heart. She wished Thunar's Blessing would imbue her but she felt only fear—for her mission, for those in her protection, for her people's legacy. For her daughter.

If Elan failed, if she was killed or captured, their chances of survival grew thin. If her mission failed, all may be lost—for her people, for the old ways she hoped to preserve, that they might live on beyond her days in this newly remade world.

She heard boots hit the turf. One of them had dismounted. The pair exchanged a few softly spoken words. Footsteps. One of the Equites finally came into view, examining her misleading trail. The feathery hemlock boughs did not fully hide her. He would eventually look up. She would be spotted. Elan had to act before he did, but if she acted too soon, she would fail.

Just a few more steps and her target would be within striking distance. Without looking up, parting the ferns protruding from the snow with the tip of his halberd, he took one slow step, then another, and...

Elan leapt. Her foot slipped and her leg cracked a hemlock branch. The man's head snapped up. He brought his long weapon around with startling swiftness, blocking her swing and pushing, sending Elan off balance and falling.

She hit the rocky turf hard. Her opponent brought his halberd slashing down. Elan parried but sent the weapon's blade sliding. The blade hit the backside of her right forearm guard. She wasn't sure if it had sliced through the leather but it felt like it. The Tibairya loomed over her, raising his halberd for another strike. She lashed out, springing up and swinging backhanded. The space was too limited. The man easily parried with the shaft of his weapon. Worse, he caught Biter and pressed down, trapping it against the turf. He had a boot on her thigh and pushed his weight against her body and her trapped blade, holding her in place, calling to his companion.

The hoofbeats told her the companion was coming. The Eques growled, his face contorting. She wriggled, working her way up the rising slope of the ravine to slide out from under his weight. The man pressed harder, straining to keep her beneath him. His mounted companion appeared over his shoulder, spear poised to be plunged into her.

Elan reversed, pushing herself down, using the pressure he was providing to slip beneath him, which put him into the path of the plunging spear. The man atop her cried out and grunted, his warm blood spilling onto her. He'd been run through by his own partner's spear, its tip hitting the rocky turf just over her shoulder.

Elan pushed the wriggling victim off of her and scrambled to regain her feet. The enraged spearman yanked back his weapon. He jabbed again before she was able to pull Biter free. She turned as steel hit her right shoulder. Her cuirass kept the tip from penetrating flesh. But damn, it hurt.

The moment he drew back to strike again she leapt up. The soldier yanked his reins, seeking to ride her down. Once horse and man faced her, the Eques kicked his mount to charge. She surveyed the field. The ravine was too steep to flee. The first man's horse had wandered away. The very prize Elan had sought was their horses. It defeated the purpose to stab the horse. Besides that, he had the longer weapon.

The odds were steep but she had few options. She set her feet to make a stand.

A jolt of pain pierced her as she raised the blade. The shoulder wound was bad. The charger neared. His spear thrust came too early. She whirled the blade, sweeping the oncoming tip aside as she leapt, grabbing his leg and pulling him off his mount as it galloped on. The horse's back hoof thudded her head as they both tumbled down, dazing her. Biter slipped from her grip and clanged to the bed of the ravine.

The Tibairya was up first, his spear already on its way. She rolled aside and the tip struck rock next to her ear. The man kicked her as she lunged for her sword. She gasped. The air was knocked from her. The man loomed over her, grinning, confident of his victory.

Elan knew he was right. She could hardly draw a breath, let alone get to the blade.

His head suddenly jerked. He staggered a step and dropped to his knees, screeching. Elan couldn't comprehend it until he twisted, revealing the arrow shaft sticking from the back of his bare neck. Elan lunged again, snatched up Biter, and drove the tip up into his crotch. The Tibairya's yowling ended in a grunt as she pushed the blade up into his abdomen.

The second Eques fell over, twitching and gasping as he died.

Elan withdrew the blade and scanned the hillside, trying to catch her breath. Brin stood frozen, holding the bow that had saved Elan's life in firing position. Brin gaped, her jaw slack. Her daughter was in shock. Elan searched for the horses. One had trotted from the commotion but lingered up the ravine.

The animal was closer to Brin. "The horse," she called. Brin didn't move. "Wake up!" It jarred her daughter from her stupor. "Get the horse." It was harsh but necessary.

Elan straightened and stretched, checking herself. Her body shrieked with pain from multiple spots.

Brin ran heavily down the hill and set the bedamned horse in flight. "Easy," Elan said. "Nice and slow. Talk to him." This city child hadn't grown up with horses. Elan cursed herself for it. Some fine link to the old world she'd raised.

Voices echoed in the ravine. Then hoofbeats. More horses. The foe was coming. Brin was having no luck approaching the horse. "Leave it. Time to go." Elan wiped Biter on her victim's cloak and sheathed it.

Brin ran to her. "Which way?" she asked.

"Away from Amaga. Up this way. Follow in my footsteps."

Elan started up the rocky hillside, seeking footing that would disguise their trail. She had to bend to steady herself with her hands and was swiftly wheezing for breath. She heard Brin right behind her. Gods be cursed—they were still on the run. Worse, Elan had earned two new wounds and had gained them no horses.

It was fast approaching midday. Elan hurt everywhere. They'd seen no sign of the Skolani. And gods afire, these bedamned Equites hunters were good.

Their escape was not going well.

Worst of all, her brother had given his life for them to have this chance. Failing him now was unthinkable.

❀

Vernius Stallicus sat ahorse in the fountain square, watching his troops file in through the archway of the palace gatehouse. The screams of the fallen echoed through the archway and the smell of burning pitch mingled with the faint whiff of burning meat—likely the flesh of his men.

There were no Gottari archers left on the walls. As the last of those assigned to the mobile reserve's attack squad entered the gateway, he urged his mount to move up behind them. He peered through the smoke to see the melee unfolding inside the keep. The shield wall his men had created was pushing in toward the palace, creating some space behind them.

Vernius hadn't been able to stop thinking about his son—about what Nico had said of their shared loss, the way they might find the path to completing one another. It wasn't about the estate—though his father's land might be a fine place to end up with his son. No, Vernouthus was his blood—perhaps the only family he might yet have in this life. As they strove to retake the home of the lost love of his life, he realized his son was the last and only link that remained to her.

The thought that he might somehow find the lad, that there may still be a chance to repair how he'd left things between them, was as great a motivation as completing his assigned task and bringing an end to this war.

"No, my lord," Nico called, riding to catch him. "It's too dangerous."

"For whom?" he snapped. "We're at war. I am still a soldier, am I not?"

Nico bowed his head and fell silent.

Vernius nudged his mount to walk on through. Just as he cleared the archway, the thundering riders appeared out of the smoke to his left. Vernius instantly reined his horse to the right and Nico followed. His men scrambled to reform the shield wall to their flank, but too late. The dozens of Gottari riders slammed into and through the disintegrating phalanx. The Gottari warriors either swung blades or pushed through with lances to devastating effect. Scores of his most seasoned veterans were instantly trampled or struck down.

"We must flee, Lord General," Nico called.

But there was nowhere to flee to. The way back to the archway was blocked. Along the keep wall to the east was a thicket of overgrown shrubbery and moving inward led back into the thick of the battling shield walls.

Vernius drew his gladius and reined around to face the mounted onslaught.

The lead rider came through the haze on a bronze warhorse, wielding a battleaxe. Recognition instantly struck him and Vernius felt a deep, visceral terror flash through his innards. The scar tissue across his chest seemed to come alive, throbbing anew.

The red shield with the snarling lion, the flaxen hair flying from beneath the helm, the clarion voice—once again he would be facing off with Vahldan the Bold.

Vahldan had clearly spotted him. The thug spurred his mount straight at Vernius.

Tiberian centurions cried out and his men rushed to reform, seeking to ward off the charging thug king. His men managed to slow the raging barbarian but could not seem to stop him. One by one, Vahldan chopped down those who intervened. In a flash he had parsed the entire line of Vernius's protectors. As Vahldan's horse came clear, a spear slammed into the charging beast's shoulder, causing the horse to stagger to one side. The slow-down led to another spear strike—this one to the horse's throat, stifling a scream. The sleek animal tumbled to the turf, throwing his rider from the saddle. Vahldan was instantly on his feet, swinging his axe to gain the space to advance on foot. Vernius's men swarmed, surrounding the whirling warrior.

Somehow the Gottari king kept them off, bellowing and hacking and shield-blocking his way to step after step. The amazing warrior simply kept coming. He seemed unstoppable. If it hadn't been such a terrifying sight, Vernius would've found it astonishing—brave even.

There could be no doubt that Vahldan had earned his legendary status.

Then it happened. A pike slipped through Vahldan's defenses, slamming into his hip, causing the barbarian to stumble and stagger, just as his noble warhorse had a few moments earlier. The thug king stayed upright but was limping heavily. Still Vahldan came on, growling and snarling. Another spear jabbed his chain-mailed chest, knocking him back. Though the man had made it to within five span of Vernius's position, Vahldan was utterly surrounded again, crippled and fighting for his life.

Horns blew and calls rang out. The Gottari were rallying with vigor all along the Tiberian lines that surrounded their king's position. The Tiberian lines held this time. The Gottari charge slowed. The remaining foe were outnumbered. Their king was doomed. Vernius's attack would prevail after all.

In spite of a terrifying late surge by the foe, the end of this terrible war was within reach.

A discordant note caught Vernius's ear. A shiver ran up the back of his neck. His head snapped around and he strained to listen. "Vernius Stallicus of Nardium! Vahldan of the Amalus! Hear me!"

"Oh gods," Vernius said aloud. He removed his helm and scanned the grounds, then the palace itself. He spotted his son in mere heartbeats. The lad stood on the parapet of the lowest terrace, five span directly above the palace doors.

Vernius's hand flew to his father's torc. Out of a desperate hope for his son, he'd retrieved it and hung it around his neck again that morning. "Agoraki!" he shouted, though he couldn't say why. Till that moment he'd adamantly refused to call him by that name.

"Hold!" Vernius cried to his men. He turned to Nico. "Blow the cease fire."

Nico stared wide-eyed at the boy but had evidently heard his command. Nico drew up the small horn he carried and blew the notes, causing the disciplined mobile reserve to cease and back into a defensive shield wall. Centurions and Gottari leaders alike took up the call, and astonishingly swiftly, the battle halted. An odd silence fell as the confused fighters of both sides looked around, gasping for breath, unsure what would happen next.

"Go back, Son!" Vernius shouted. "Keep yourself safe and I'll come for you!"

Agoraki shook his head. "No, Father. Let them gather their fallen. Let them retreat."

"The Gottari are beaten! Go inside. I am coming for you."

"No! Let them retreat. Let them say the prayers to their goddess." Agoraki raised a short blade out before his chest. "Or I will jump, right into the fight below! If I survive the fall, I will fight you. I will fight for them. Your men will be forced to kill me right before your eyes."

Vernius had already learned that the lad meant what he said. His son never spoke lightly. "If I do as you say, what then? What if Vahldan here will not surrender?"

"Then do as you must, for the honor of all. But if the king retreats with honor, you must allow it. You must also promise that, once you prevail, you will leave those who surrender—especially the women, the children, and the servants—of this palace unharmed. You must vow to do this in spite of what your orders demand. In spite of what is to come next for the Gottari king himself. For he has accepted his own fate."

Vernius looked down to Vahldan. His nemesis stood leaning on his battleaxe like a cane. Vahldan nodded once. "On my honor," he huffed.

The man was clearly beyond exhaustion. He was badly wounded. Their battle had been vicious, at times ruthless. Both sides had reason to mistrust, to hate. And yet, Vernius believed this man.

Vernius called to his son. "You must promise me that you will be among those we spare. You must agree to return to me afterward. Promise you will come back home with me, my son." Vernius pointed the sword at Vahldan. "And you," he said to the thug. "If I let this happen, you must promise that my son will not be harmed."

Vahldan nodded again. "My word," the thug said.

Agoraki raised his chin. "I too agree." His son turned and hopped from the parapet back to the terrace. Vernius sighed with a relief he could not have imagined before he'd met and come to know his son. Or perhaps it was a relief found in having imagined living with the loss of him.

ANOTHER GROUP of four Equites hunters rode past, following the false trail Elan had created. She crept back down from the precipice above the trail and moved into the spruces, passing the hobbled horse nibbling from the ends of boughs. She ducked into the blind copse where she'd left her charges.

Brin was on one knee, aiming a drawn bow at her. Elan held up her hands. Her daughter sighed and released the tension. Brin collapsed back to a sitting position, leaning against the outcrop on the uphill side of their blind.

Amaga was slumped against the base of a spruce trunk, head bowed over her son in her arms. Both of them were sound asleep. "Shall I wake her?" Brin whispered.

"No. Let her rest. We'll make a final push for the Skolani camp before nightfall. She'll need all of her strength for it."

Brin laid the bow across her legs and bowed her head. "This is bad, isn't it?"

"Yes." Dissembling would gain them nothing. She'd long known the girl was too clever for it anyway.

"We won't make it," Brin said.

"That is *not* what I said. If you're going to be a warrior, you have to learn to avoid being ruled by your fears. Setting them aside is the first step in doing one's duty." Her daughter looked up with one of her equivocal expressions. "What?" Elan asked.

"It's just... I've never heard you say that I might be..." Brin looked down and shook her head.

Elan huffed a laugh. "If I've learned anything, it's that you, my amazing girl, will accomplish whatever you set your mind to. Urias tried to tell me that you're a natural. I finally see how right he was."

Brin's face crumpled and tears ran down her cheeks. "I can't believe he's really gone. He sacrificed everything—his whole life— for me." Her words rose into squeaks at the end.

Elan knew Brin meant much more than Urias sacrificing his life to ensure their escape. He'd willingly left his life in Dania. He'd moved to a palace full of lions. To a foreign city, where he'd been surrounded by rivals and foes. He'd devoted years to training Brin, mostly in secret and with limited resources. Elan's brother had taken her daughter into his residence whenever it had been needed. Urias had been Brin's mentor, her protector, her safe harbor. Her home. Brin's uncle had shown her nothing but trust, belief, and love.

Elan swallowed back emotion. "Then you must honor his sacrifice," she managed.

Brin wiped her tears with the backs of her hands. "How?" Brin's voice quavered.

"By striving. No matter the odds against you. By seeking to fulfill his hopes for you. By living the life he foresaw for you. That's what he would want." Her daughter bowed her head. "Understood?"

Brin brought her gaze back up to meet Elan's. She firmed herself. "Understood."

In that moment, dappled with late afternoon sunlight, Elan saw the Blade-Wielder in her beautiful child. A deep sense of pride bloomed within her. She remembered Sael telling her how vital Brin would be to the future of their people. Elan had never been more certain it was true.

She leaned, straining to reach behind her back, pulling free the buckles on her harness. "I have something for you." She pulled the harness over her head, extracting herself from the straps. She got to her knees and held the sheathed heirloom blade out to her daughter.

Brin's big eyes grew wide. "Mother, no," Brin breathed. "I can't."

"You not only can but must. It was my mother's. Now it must go to you."

"But you're the better—"

"Don't be so sure," Elan interjected, pointing to the bandaged cut on her forearm. It was clearly worse than a flesh wound. Not to mention the shoulder wound. She honestly doubted she could raise her right arm over her head. Elan nodded at the weapon lying across Brin's lap. "We'll trade. I'll take the bow and quiver."

Brin drew a shaky breath as Elan lowered the harness over her head. She took Brin by the shoulders and turned her to draw the straps tight across her back. There was no hole far enough along the straps to fit Brin's slender torso. Elan drew her dagger and bore new holes to hold it tight. "It's a very special gift, one that can never be taken from you. Whether or not the Skolani elders accept you for training, know that you've earned this. Believe it and never forget it."

Elan finished with the buckles and turned her daughter to face her. Brin lunged to hug her. It stole her breath. And squeezed her heart. Elan returned the embrace, feeling her beautiful girl's strength, unable to keep the achy smile from her lips. She looked up to find Amaga staring. It was the first time Elan had ever sensed anything resembling approval from the woman.

Elan gathered her resolve, drew back from the embrace, and gave her daughter a last look and a firm nod. "Arise, Blade-Wielder. The time has come. There is much yet to be done. Your new life begins now."

THE FIRST THUMP of the ram hit the palace doors. Vahldan looked up through the windows high overhead. The sky had gone gold with the setting of the sun. He wasn't surprised. They'd only agreed to allow a retreat. The mobile reserve would never leave this till morning. At least the fallen had been retrieved—the wounded taken into care and the slain laid to rest in safety. All those he'd convinced to seek to stay alive were in the catacombs with the women, children, and servants.

He'd tried to order them all to go to the dungeons, to vow to submit once the palace fell. It was akin to commanding them to accept a life of slavery—the gods only knew of what sort, perhaps even an existence of torment and drudgery. Those who complied well knew it. But it was also a commitment to hope—to a future place in a world that was neither strictly of the old ways of the Tutona nor a Tiberian version of civilization, rife with decadence and corruption.

To his relief, many had listened. Many had gone to be with their children. To live.

The dozen Rekkrs who stood with him now were those who had refused, disobeyed. To Vahldan's great annoyance, Arnegern was among them. As was Ermanaric.

Still, Vahldan knew the stubbornness of his two remaining guardians was rooted in loyalty and love. It was too late for condemnation. The ram continued to thump the massive wooden doors. He stood on the empty dais at the far end of the entry hall and beckoned them to gather. "My brothers, this is it. We face an overwhelming foe. There is little doubt as to the outcome. I would plead with you all once more. I would have you go and stand with the others. I would have you commit to hope for the coming restoration of the futhark and the ascension of the Gottari people. For though we may be all but beaten, ours is not a lost cause."

"No, my king," Ermanaric said. "If our cause is Urrinan, I—for one—would wish for our glory to shine, to serve as a light for those who remain." Several nodded and murmured their agreement. "There can be no honor found in abandoning our king. We know that you must fight on and we know why. So I must stand and fight with you."

"Aye, my king," Arnegern said. "You said yourself that they mean to take you to humble you before the world, to crush the spirit of the Tutona. That we cannot abide."

"Yes, we vowed to stand with you, King Vahldan." Another Rekkr stepped forward and knelt. "We belong to you. We belong to destiny."

All of the others followed suit, dropping to a knee. "We belong to you!" they called. And it became a chant, echoing in the hall, drowning out the thumping of the foe at the doors. *"We belong to you! We belong to you!"*

Vahldan leaned heavily on his axe, working his jaw, swallowing back emotion. The near crippling pain in his body faded from the forefront. In spite of his many faults and failures, he had always loved these men. And they him. In a sense, he had done as Angavar had bidden. In spite of it all, he had brought the Amalus back to glory.

The Bringer had brought Urrinan.

The world would now change. His duty was almost done. His rest and reward were near.

Only the loud crack of splintering wood brought his most loyal lions to silence. They stood and grimly took their positions, raising their shields and forming a semicircle around him. Vahldan nodded to these ardent followers. "Thank you, my brothers," he said. He raised his axe, stepped to the edge of the dais, and drew another deep, painful breath.

The time had come. His doom was upon him.

ELAN CRESTED the hill that overlooked the vale. "This is it. That's the stream."

Brin caught up to her, breathing heavily, pulling the horse through the deepening snow. Amaga sat staring into the distance, cradling her sleeping son. The first qeins hadn't spoken much since they'd last stopped to rest.

Elan had pushed hard to arrive here in daylight, utilizing back trails and even deer paths in order to stay off the main road. The snow had not only slowed their progress, it had exhausted them and their only horse. Now they'd run out of cover. The vale below was snow-covered but seemed relatively free of drifts, at least. The roadway was visible, cutting across the barren vale to their left. She saw no new tracks on it. Using the road would still speed them. It would be level and firm. They could angle across the open vale to meet it at the stream's ford.

They were running out of light. Approaching a Skolani camp in the dark was dangerous. Elan had been watching Brin's gait. Her daughter's legs were as wobbly as a newly foaled colt's. Brin had kept up without complaint, even after their water skins had run dry. Eating snow was too chilling, and starting a fire was impossible. They all needed water—particularly the horse.

"There's no sign of them," Brin said. Her daughter squinted, scanning the distance, her brow crinkled with fret. Elan understood. There wasn't even a wisp of smoke. "Is that next ridge the place you spoke about—the one the Skolani retreat to?"

"Skolani don't make themselves apparent," Elan said, veiling her own concern. "There's also no sign of the Tibairya," Elan added.

"I doubt they'll make themselves apparent either," Brin retorted.

Smart girl. Elan nodded. "Good. You're thinking like a Blade-Wielder."

"How will we find them? The Skolani, I mean."

"We won't. They'll find us. On their terms." The setting sun cast the vale in the long shadows of the trees on the western hills. "We need to get moving," Elan said. She scanned the forest's edge, focusing on the spot where the road hit the treeline, heading back to Pontea. She saw nothing. "I'm going first. Stay put till I get to that thicket." She pointed to a patch of sumac and stubby swamp cedar. "Then come behind me. Head for the spot where the road meets the stream." She swiveled her pointing arm to the ford. "I want all three of you on the horse."

Brin's frown matched Amaga's. "Will he be able to carry us?"

"All three of you together weigh less than the man he's used to carrying. Here, let me help you." Elan lifted her daughter till she got her leg over to sit behind the saddle. She stretched the reins on either side of mother and child and gave them to Brin.

"You're sure about this?" Brin asked. "That's a long way in the open."

"It is as it shall be," she said.

"What if we meet Skolani before you catch up?"

"Then do as you've been taught," she said. "Keep your hands in the open, bury away your fear, speak only when spoken to." Her daughter sighed. "Now what?" There wasn't time for this.

"I'm just worried. About you."

Elan huffed a laugh. "A legend's not a legend till it ends, baby girl."

"Let's hope this one's almost over," Brin said, gazing warily ahead.

"It won't end by sitting here." Elan drew an arrow and nocked it. Her arm throbbed from the effort. "Wait for my signal. Then ride out to the stream. Let the horse drink, but don't dismount. I'll fill the skins. Use the road to get to the far ridge, then get out of sight. I'll be right behind you."

Brin pressed her lips tight. Amaga didn't bother trying to hide her terror. Luckily the boy continued to doze. "Understood?" Elan added.

"Understood," Brin said. It wasn't as convincing as last time but it would have to do.

Elan set out downhill. The drifts gave way to windswept, ankle-deep snow on flattened grasses. The footing was too poor for her to run. She looked back at the treeline as she went, keeping herself low and small. The ground under the snow grew spongier as she moved into the cedars. She sought some cover and turned, surveying the scene behind. She stepped into the open and waved her arm for Brin to follow.

The horse hit the shallower snow and finally started trotting. "Come on, girl. Gallop," she said under her breath. As if Brin had heard, she kicked her heels and the exhausted horse reluctantly began to canter, bouncing his riders as he came.

Elan turned and ran to the stream. She found a bit of firm footing near a sandy flow, set aside the nocked bow, and pulled out the first skin to fill it.

Over the soft gurgle of the cold water, she almost felt it first. It built. A rumbling.

Hoofbeats.

Horses. Several horses.

Elan tossed aside the skin and snatched up the bow.

The Equites broke from the trees in three, no, four different spots. They came in groups of three or four at various angles. They had already gotten their horses to gallop and were closing in. Elan's charges bumped along, slogging through the snowy grasses seemingly at half the speed of the Tibairya.

Elan ran to the thicket. Brin had spotted the hunters. "Mother! What do I do?" Brin cried as they passed by Elan's position.

Her daughter's terror struck like a slap. Elan couldn't bear it, couldn't bear the thought of any harm coming to her baby girl. The future of her people sat on the back of that poor horse. She waved, redirecting them to the roadway ford over the stream. "Ride! Get to the road! Ride as fast as you can! Don't fall and don't stop! No matter what."

THE PALACE DOORS BURST OPEN, one of them knocked off of its hinges. The Tiberians came through the doorway behind long, rectangular shields, fanning out into the hall on both of the Gottari's flanks. Vahldan's Rekkrs readied their weapons in response. It seemed both sides were too exhausted to charge, creating a strangely peaceful interlude.

As the imperial phalanx spread to the width of the hall, one of them called a command and the shield wall parted at intervals in unison. Standing on the dais, Vahldan spotted them coming through the gaps first. "Crossbows! Shields up!"

He whipped his own shield around as their bedamned contraptions rattled and snapped, slinging scores of darts into the space. A dart thumped into the lower half of his shield and many of the Gottari tumbled to the floor, most with darts in their unarmored legs. Half of his remaining men had fallen already. Vahldan took heart in knowing most could survive such wounds.

The crossbow archers swiftly withdrew and, at another guttural command, the center of the imperial line opened up. In through the doors rushed a small group of men with golden shields emblazoned with crimson eagles and wearing crested helms. The Equites, Vahldan knew. Although they weren't now mounted, these were the mobile reserve's most elite warriors, trained for battle from boyhood. The Equites barked in reply to each call from an officer. They moved in precise unison.

They came fast, parting his Rekkrs before they could form up for a unified counterattack. The imperial regulars moved in their wake, three abreast, creating a parting two-sided shield wall that divided the hall in two. Spears bristled from the imperial formation, jabbing out at any attempt to rush them from either side.

Vahldan watched it all play out from the dais. It was dreamlike. His men were too exhausted to rally. There was no slowing the foe's momentum. This was a heartless war machine, its gears clicking perfectly, grinding toward resolution.

It had all been carefully crafted. The Equites were coming for him.

Vahldan raised his shield and limped to the edge of the dais. Raw pain shot through his leg and up his back with each step, emanating from his new hip wound. He hefted the axe, laying it on his shoulder, waiting for those who came for him.

Ermanaric charged from his right, only to meet a half-dozen spear thrusts. The Rekkr's cry seemed more born of passion than pain. A moment later, the Rekkr Sigisar fell to his left.

The surging wedge of Equites were within a spear's length of the dais when Arnegern leapt out in front of him. "For Urrinan!" his dear friend called, swinging his sword.

The front of the wedge parted and a spear darted out, striking Arnegern's sword arm even before he landed his blow. Arnegern's sword flew from his hand and his momentum carried him to stumble forward. Something flashed from the right, flying down at an angle. A cudgel struck Arnegern on the side of his helmeted head, instantly knocking him sideways. Vahldan's first and most loyal follower flopped to the floor, insensate. Arnegern's helm fell off and Vahldan glimpsed the blood in his hair.

His own cry erupted in wordless anguish, filling his head. His axe raised, he flung himself from the dais. His blow hit the shoulder of the man with the cudgel, who'd raised it again. The imperials at the fore separated and, using their shields in concert, pushed Vahldan back and forth until he hit the floor. Someone kicked him. The Equites encircled and hovered over him. No blades pierced him. Instead, the foe struck his sides, back, and shoulders with boots and cudgels.

Each blow was painful, but worse, they kept him from getting back to his feet or swinging the axe again. Still, no blow struck his head and no metal pierced his flesh. Even in the midst of the agony, Vahldan knew. This was a careful immobilization of a targeted victim. One they intended to take alive.

Just when it seemed they might accidentally kill him after all, a commanding voice called out. His tormentors stopped striking him and backed away a step, still tightly surrounding him. Vahldan shook his arm to shed his shield. Using his elbows, he crawled to Arnegern. No one impeded him. "Brother?" he wheezed and reached to shake Arnegern's shoulder.

Arnegern didn't move. His eyes were closed and the side of his head was a mass of gore.

The hall grew silent. Vahldan rolled to scan the imperial boots surrounding him. Gottari bodies lay scattered on either side of the hall. The stricken Gottari wounded wore pinched, grim faces, but none cried out.

Footsteps approached, riding boots clicking on the hall's tiles. Vahldan raised his head.

A lone man stepped through the parting Equites. Vahldan strained to roll to his side and found himself face to face with Vernius Stallicus standing over him. His nemesis stood tall, but he wore simple burnished armor and had a plain helm under his arm.

"And so it ends, my worthy rival," Vernius said in Hellainic. "Finally."

THE BEDAMNED Equites riders closed in fast. Too fast.

Worse, the lead foursome of Tibairya had chosen to target Brin. Elan's charges wouldn't make it. Getting them to safety was her sole remaining duty. Elan ran, fleeing at an angle to get within bow range of those targeting the horse and riders. Her side ached and her throat burned. Her feet and her wounded arm were numb, but her limbs still seemed under her command, at least.

Elan ran through cattails, snow, and mud sucking at her boots. Relying on the sound of their hoofbeats, Elan drew her bow as she ran. She twisted and fired as she ducked behind a cluster of scrub cedars. She glimpsed the lead rider falling as she reloaded. Elan continued to push herself, running on across the marshy ground. She paused every half-dozen steps to take two more shots. She dropped at least one more of the four who rode after Brin's horse. The two hits seemed to cause the remaining two riders to hesitate, slowing their pace and taking a wider berth of her in their pursuit.

A second foursome was clearly targeting Elan rather than the fleeing horse. Elan ignored them and ran on toward the roadway, following the best angle to cover Brin's flight. She kept her focus on the remaining two pursuers as they splashed into the stream just moments after Brin was across. Elan took a shot, hitting one horse's rump, causing it to neigh and buck.

Still, the last bedamned hunter from the first foursome rode on after Brin's mount.

Elan's instincts shrieked for her to turn. Her instincts were right. The second foursome bore down on her, moments from impact. The first to arrive raised his sword, his horse's hooves throwing clumps of muddy snow. Elan dropped the useless bow and pulled her belt dagger. She flung herself to the side as she threw, avoiding the rider's swing. The dagger buried itself in the windpipe of her attacker's horse. The beast screamed and reared. The Tibairya tumbled to the slushy turf nearby. Elan gained her feet before the fallen Eques. She stomped his wrist into the slush, kicked the sword from his hand, and bent to snatch it. Her opponent lunged to grab her ankle. She grasped the hilt and swung, smacking the side of his helmeted head.

She pulled her leg away and set herself, waiting until the second pursuer's horse was right over her. Elan spun, whipping the stolen blade around, swiping the horse's fetlocks and ducking its rider's spear thrust. The horse tumbled and she leapt over its back, landing with the tip aimed, plunging it under the chin and into the neck of the thrown rider. The impact drove the blade into the soft ground beneath her victim.

The last two came on. Elan left the sword and scrambled to her feet to run again. Something jolted her, knocking her backbone and sending her sprawling. A jolt of searing pain shocked her, forcing a howl from her lungs as she landed on her hands and knees in the slush. The third rider's momentum carried him past her. He reined in to circle back.

Elan sensed the fourth rider's nearness and lurched onto her side. The move brought an awful realization. Something was stuck in her. Something big. Her pathetic flop and flailing managed to cause the fourth rider to miss and ride by. She couldn't stand or run. She reached to find a bedamned rod protruding from her back. She managed to rise up onto her knees, readying herself to parry as the rider galloped back for a second strike.

The bedamned Eques had already drawn a sword and was nearly upon her. It was the dandy with the horse tail on his helm. Gods, this smirking snake was like a curse. She loathed the thought of losing to him.

The moment seemed surreal—the white bowl of the vale, the cattails swaying, and the blazing sunset sky behind her despised attacker. She felt the wind in her face, saw it all happening so slowly—the snake's snarl, the flash of his raised blade.

Elan wanted to fight—needed to fight—but couldn't seem to do anything. Dizziness washed over her. Her arm grew floppy. She doubted she could even parry.

The ground shook. A cacophony of war cries pierced the wind in her ears. Was her people's goddess coming for her? "Horsella?" she asked aloud.

Hooves pounded, splattering her with slush. So close now. Her executioner's arm started its downward arc.

And then the Tibairya's severed head tumbled to the ground before her, the horse tail helm still strapped to it.

Her attacker's body slumped, slid, and thudded with a jangling sound nearby.

Elan tried to turn and see. Instead, her head lolled and she contorted and fell to her shoulder. From the ground, she looked up as a great Skolani warhorse reared over her. Horse hooves thumped to the ground nearby. A mighty Blade-Wielder shrieked and swung her broadsword, once, then twice, trading blows with a mounted imperial soldier. Another Eques hit the mud-churned turf with a grunt, no more than three span away. The Skolani goddess who'd saved her growled as she surveyed the field and then galloped from view.

Elan lay gasping, a new shockwave of pain jolting her with each breath. She wanted to get up, to reach and pull the bedamned thing out of her back. But she found she could no longer move any of her limbs. And yet, she laughed as realization washed over her.

Her savior hadn't been Horsella. "I think that was Anallya," she said. "How ironic."

∽

VAHLDAN HAD KEPT his grip on the battleaxe shaft, but intense pain told him he didn't have the strength left to raise it, let alone swing it. The Equites who surrounded him had their cudgels poised to swing. Behind them, another row of soldiers held spears at the ready.

"I thought you and I would get another go," he said. "But I'm afraid I can't move."

"Thank the gods," Vernius said and chuckled. "We both know who would've won."

"I suppose it is over, then," Vahldan said. "It's over for us anyway." He supposed the smile he attempted looked more like a grimace. Especially when his breath hissed through it.

Still, Vernius returned it with a smile that managed not to look smug. "Yes, for us anyway." The imperial general said a few words in his own tongue to another officer, who stepped into the circle of soldiers with a chain-linked set of manacles.

Vahldan tried to rise up but the effort made his head swim. "Wait." He heard his father's voice as Angavar's words flowed from his own mouth. "Grant me a warrior's death." He pulled the axe up and cradled it to his chest.

The officer with the manacles stopped. Vernius shook his head. "Not just yet, I'm afraid. You are to be given the opportunity to see Medicia, and the honor of meeting our emperor before you die."

Vahldan squeezed his eyes shut. "To be strangled before a cheering crowd? To make your pathetic emperor feel as though it was he who vanquished us? It was you, my worthy rival. Your chest that stopped my blade. Your wit and will that kept us in retreat."

Vernius's gaze hardened. His adversary nodded. "It is not mine to decide."

"It is," Vahldan hissed. "Grant me a warrior's death." A spasm of pain caused him to contort. He pried his eyes open. All of the surrounding Tiberians stood frozen, transfixed. "Our sons," Vahldan said to Vernius. "Our two sons... They can make the world whole... Our kin, in the new age, they can fight side by side... with honor. No more tribes or empires... A whole people. If you take me to your city, there can only be disgrace... Not just for me. For them... For us..."

He could hardly breathe so he lay gasping for a long moment, eyes closed. He had no idea if his adversary understood. He held the axe to his chest, caught his breath, and tried again. "Grant... me... a warrior's... death," he pleaded, suspecting it would be for the last time.

Vernius drew in a breath and slowly exhaled. He said something in Tiberian to his men and the eyes of the officer with the manacles went wide. Vernius sharply repeated his command.

Vernius looked down, his expression stern, but Vahldan saw respect in it—even a bit of sadness in his adversary's eyes. "I leave you now in the hands of your gods, Vahldan of the Gottari. If you choose to resist my men, I have commanded them to dispatch you. Swiftly and decisively. If I do not see you again, know that I will keep an eye to the new age, and to our kin's place in it."

Vernius bowed his head and put his fist to his wounded chest in salute. Vahldan's worthy rival then spun on his heels and strode away, boots clicking back to the palace doors.

Icannes leapt from the saddle, ran, and dropped to her knees. The snow surrounding her near-sister was red with blood. Swiftly and as gently as she could, she braced Elan's back and pulled the spear out. Elan's agonized cry pierced Icannes's very soul. She shed her cloak, wadded it, and pressed it to the open wound. She sat and gathered Elan in her arms, cradling her.

"Hold on, dear heart," she urged. "Ursellya is coming."

Elan's contorted expression softened as she found focus on Icannes. "You came."

"Oh, my darling. I only wish I'd gotten here sooner." She gripped Elan's hand. It was so cold. Icannes bit her mitt to pull it off and laid her hand on her beloved's chest, then caressed her face. "Tell me, my love. Why? Why didn't you keep running? Why did you turn and fight?"

Elan huffed a laugh, causing a puff of steam and a wheeze of pain. "The girl?"

Icannes nodded. "Brin made it. They're all safe. Thanks to you."

Elan somehow smiled again. "My dream—it was him... and them. It came true... My destiny." Her dearest coughed, then grimaced and shuddered. Icannes pulled her close and held her tight.

VERNIUS'S FOOTSTEPS FADED AWAY. A wave of pain rolled over him. Vahldan remembered his father's bravery in facing this moment. He gripped the axe and nodded. One of the Equites holding a spear returned the nod and the officer with the manacles stepped back.

With all of his remaining strength, he rose up and lunged with the axe, swinging feebly toward the Eques with the spear. Vahldan instantly knew. The man's strike was swift and true.

It would be enough.

He hardly felt the spear-tip sliding in. But he felt his heart jolt. He gasped. The words burst from him in a fervent cry. "Elan! I'll find you!"

Another spear struck, the impact pushing him to the floor. "Elan..." His love's name left his lungs along with his last breath. He found he couldn't draw another. A sleepiness overcame him. The hall grew dim.

Elan was shaking, gasping for breath now. Icannes was seized by the greatest and most terrible fear she'd ever experienced. She cradled her dear heart tighter and looked over her shoulder. "Ursellya! Hurry!"

Elan's gaze found focus on her again. "Oh, my love. It's too late... Say the prayers... For both of us. He... he said he'd find me. But... we need you to say..."

Elan's gaze grew distant. Her breath came as fast panting, but her eyes smiled. "No need. I see him..." Elan's hand weakly rose, her finger pointing.

Just then, a raptor screeched overhead. It hovered directly over them. A kestrel. A male.

"No!" Icannes cried. "Not yet!" She looked back down. "Elan, please, stay with me."

"I see..." Elan whispered. Then Icannes saw the light go from her dear heart's eyes, heard the sigh of her final breath.

Icannes bent to kiss the love of her life and gently closed her eyes. Then she started to sob.

CHAPTER 29
PASSAGES

"The story of my life has really been two stories of two lives—the one before I first entered the Pontean Pass and the one after I passed through to the other side.

One can never really prepare for the changes that come with the great passages of our lives. But every so often, a traveler—if they search their soul, come to know what they stand for; if they are diligent and persevere, even in the face of great setback and sorrow; if they truly believe, not just in themselves but in something greater—finds what their heart has truly sought upon reaching the far side of that rare passage.

It was foretold that I would be a link between the old world and the new—the only one who truly knows each side. I now see that it is as it was destined to be."—Brin Bright Eyes, Saga of Dania

ICANNES ABSENTLY ROCKED Elan in her arms. She had no idea for how long. Her leggings and boots had soaked through, numbing her. She wished the rest of her would grow numb. Particularly the jagged shards of her heart.

The rider dismounted and came to stand silently by, waiting. It had grown darker. She could only hope it was dark enough to veil the wretch that she'd become. She refused to share even her sorrow with anyone else.

"What is it?" she managed by harnessing her anger.

"Several of the Tibairya have fled into the forest. What do you command?"

Icannes's anger became a seething rage, flowing up from her stomach to her chest. "Hunt them down," she growled. "Not a single one of my sister's killers steps foot from this pass. Nor shall another of their ilk step foot into it without paying for this. Not ever. Blood for blood, from this day forward," she vowed.

Anallya bowed. "As it shall be." The blood-bitch strode to remount and rode off into the darkness. Her war cry was answered by her host. The hunt was on.

BRIN HUDDLED in the blanket they gave her, sitting cross-legged before a fire. As far as she could tell, the sentinels who'd brought them here and left them were the only Skolani in this camp. There were paths of footprints through the snow, but the nearby pavilions stood empty. She and Amaga and the boy were otherwise alone, somewhere in the heart of the Pontean Pass.

Across the fire from her, Amaga had managed to rock her son to sleep. The priestess looked on the verge of slumber herself until arriving hoofbeats startled a gasp from her.

A dozen Skolani dismounted nearby. Elan scanned their shadowy faces and postures. She felt hollow when she didn't find her mother among them. Then Brin saw two of them reverently unload a cloth-wrapped form from one of the horses and carefully carry it into one of the pavilions.

Was her worst fear being confirmed? She couldn't move, could hardly draw a breath.

Brin started to unwrap herself from the blanket. A Skolani

appeared before her. Brin looked up. The warrior towered over her, broad at the shoulders, grim of expression. The Skolani's mass of braids looked white in the firelight. Her eyes were red and swollen. She had blood on the front of her tunic. It felt wrong somehow that this fierce woman was so clearly stricken. It was as if her agony had escaped from within, leaving her no choice but to wear it.

Brin's fear spiraled into wordless despair.

Two other Skolani stood behind the stricken woman, one at either shoulder. One was unarmed and the other was the largest woman Brin had ever seen—seemingly as big as Teavar.

The stricken one stared at Brin in silence, as if words could not be summoned. "Your mother," the woman finally said. "She is dead." Her words were accented and blunt. Still, Brin heard the grief and the pity within them.

Brin had lived with dread for this moment since the war had begun. Her dread had only grown since their flight though the pass had started. It felt like it had always been unavoidable, and yet hearing that it had actually happened was like an icy dagger that pierced her very soul.

Tears sprang from the corners of her eyes. It wasn't just that her father had started the war. Or that the Tiberians had been so relentless. Her mother had always known she'd been doomed. But Elan had always been so sure that her doom would mean something. It left Brin's mind scrambling to figure out what.

Her mother had always been a child of the old ways—of the old world. Elan had been the first of her people to venture into the new world. And yet she had never been at peace there. She and Brin's father had come in war. And now they had died in war.

"She saved us," Brin managed. Her voice sounded so small, so childlike. "Just as she was meant to," she blurted as the realization arrived. Tears dripped from her jawline, unwiped. "I promised her. We are to go back, to protect what she has won."

The stricken woman nodded in solemn response. "As it shall be."

The woman gathered herself and looked at Amaga. "What of her brother? I had hoped that he would be with you."

Brin drew a shaky breath. "Uncle Urias. He…" Amaga let out a whimper. Brin wanted to tell the woman that he'd saved them, too. She wanted to say how brave he'd been, how much his loss meant to her. But she could only manage, "He's dead too." Her voice squeaked and broke in saying it. She clapped her hand over her mouth, feeling abashed for showing so much of herself.

The shock seemed to hit the woman like a physical blow, nearly knocking her over. She stood actually tottering. Her jaw worked behind pressed lips, her hands pressed to her heart as if to stanch a stab wound.

Still holding her chest, the woman turned away. She stopped and spoke over her shoulder. "You will be brought food and drink. Once you have eaten, Ursellya here will show you where to sleep." She nodded to indicate the smaller of the two who flanked her.

Amaga looked tiny huddled in her blanket. The priestess seemed content to be ignored.

The stricken woman walked away. There had to be more said than this. "Please," Brin called. "My mother—she said if anything happened to her, I am to seek Princess Icannes."

The woman stopped. "That person no longer exists." She slowly turned back, her face contorting in an effort to cloak her grief. "In fact, the very last of her has just left us. Forever."

The woman's head dropped and her shoulders slumped. She turned and strode to slip silently into one of the pavilions, alone. The larger of her companions went off toward the only other fire circle in the camp.

The unarmed woman remained. She looked Brin and Amaga over, showing her concern. "As the queen said, I am Ursellya. I am a healer. Are either of you hurt?" Brin shook her head. Without looking up, Amaga followed suit. "Kukida is bringing you food and drink," Ursellya said.

The queen? Brin had expected her to be much older. "I want to see my mother," she said.

Ursellya's smile was sad and sympathetic. "Queen Icannes thought that you might. We have your bedding made up so that you might lie beside her, Brin Bright Eyes."

Brin's tears ran again. She opened her mouth to thank Ursellya but then nodded instead.

"Stay strong," Ursellya said. "It is what Elan would ask of you." Brin nodded again, wiped her eyes, and tried to straighten her face. "Tomorrow she will be laid to rest in our people's sacred bog. It is the highest of honors. Elan, daughter of Ellasan, shall be the first to have left the Skolani tribe and to be venerated in this way."

THE CATACOMBS FELL SILENT AGAIN. Only one lamp yet burned, to save fuel. The women huddled with their children on the benches that lined the smelly old storage chamber. Some were crying. Rohdric, son of Eldavar, stood with his hand on the hilt of his father's sword. Come what may, he would protect his family. Or die trying. If he did die, he would do it with honor, like his father. The Valkyries would come for him.

His mother had her arms wrapped around Aunt Mara on one side and his sister Ufairsa on the other. Aunt Mara sat rocking, both hands on her round belly. Aunt Kemella held his cousin Ragnavar on her lap beside Mara.

Rohdric had never seen the women in his life like this. They were frightened, quiet. It made his insides feel all shaky and jumpy. No one knew what would come next.

His mother and aunts always told him he was the blood of the lion, that he would be brave and bold, like his father had been. Like his uncle, the king, was. Rohdric felt anything but brave or bold now.

On the far side of the old wooden door, the thumping of boots got louder than the dripping sounds from the dark depths. Next came the rattling of keys.

Mighty Teavar drew his broadsword and raised his shield. The giant took a fighting stance between his extended family and the door. Teavar was the only named warrior here inside the locked chamber. There were only women and boys, although at nine, Rohdric was the eldest among the sons. The other Rekkrs and bannermen had all gone to the dungeons with their families, where they were likely to stay for some time.

The door finally swung toward them, screeching on rusty hinges. The first thing Rohdric saw of the Tibairya in the flickering torchlight were their long, rectangular shields—crimson, with black eagles emblazoned on them. Then he saw their crested helms and their hard eyes peering over the shields. They came in carrying spears topped with knife-like blades.

Teavar crouched and backed up a step, raising his sword and settling behind his shield. Rohdric started to draw his father's sword. His mother grabbed his wrist. "Rohdric, no." She pushed the blade back into the sheath but Rohdric kept his hand on the hilt.

Behind the Tibairya with the shields, another man came through the doorway. He was helmless and beardless, had short gray hair and a nose like one of the eagles on the shields. His breastplate was plain, dull. He was calm. His eyes were not cold like the soldiers' were. He seemed curious, like he was waiting to hear the end of a joke while looking down his nose at them like the Hellain tutors did.

"Be at ease, Mighty Teavar," the man said in Hellainic. "It is over now." Teavar lowered his blade and stood straighter but the giant still looked ready to fight if necessary. The man looked past Teavar. "Ladies, I regret to inform you that your king is dead."

Mournful cries erupted from his family. Rohdric swallowed hard. He'd been warned that it would probably come to this. His whole life Rohdric had been told of Uncle Vahldan's coming doom, that it would be a part of the Urrinan. But it still seemed impossible.

He'd been told that he would one day be the man of the family.

He also knew that it was his duty to serve his two young cousins, who would bring their people's ascension to fruition. The thought brought back the shaky feeling.

Beak-nose went on. "Not all of your husbands have been killed. Those who were wounded are being treated. Those who have surrendered will be treated fairly. They have been taken to the dungeons to stay with the others until the terms and specifics of your enslavement are made final." More crying and woeful moans arose from his kin. "I fear it will be some time yet before accommodations can be made for you all. Until then you will remain here. In the meantime I will have food and drink brought. I trust we can abide each other with respect until your assignment to your new lives."

Beak-nose scanned the women on the benches and pointed at Rohdric's aunt, who was holding her babe. "You are Lady Harma, then?"

Harma nodded, her cheeks flushing almost to the color of her hair. Beak-nose beckoned her. "Come with me. Our city's new imperial magister, Anax Malvius, wishes to personally see to your safety and comfort."

Aunt Harma stood and hurried to the leader of the foe, holding her babe over her shoulder. "Whore!" one of the women called. "Traitor," Rohdric's mother hissed.

After Harma was out of the chamber, Beak-nose turned to the door and said, "Nicandros. The manacles." Another finely dressed, younger Tibairya came in holding chain-linked bracelets. Beak-nose said, "Rekkr Teavar. If you wish to remain in Lady Harma's service, you must surrender your arms and submit to a period of captivity."

With a sigh rather than a spoken word, the giant sheathed his sword, unbuckled the sword belt, and handed both shield and belt to one of the soldiers. The largest and most formidable warrior of the Amalus clan held out his wrists to this thin, fancy young man, who then led him away. It reminded Rohdric of a little mummer who'd come to the palace with a trained bear.

"No," someone cried mournfully. "It can't be," said another.

Beak-nose cleared his throat. "Ladies, please know that your men fought bravely and mostly with honor. Trust that your cause was misguided and that our empire is a force for good in the world. Most imperial slaves are well treated. Many work their way to harmony with their owners, and no few eventually earn their freedom. You will be brought from this dreary place as soon as possible. In the meantime, let it serve to help you appreciate where you next dwell."

The Tibairya turned and strode out, and the guards backed out and slammed the door.

They sat for what seemed like days. The last lamp was burning low, sputtering as it ran out of oil. The women reclined against one another in turns and the younger children curled up with their heads on laps to sleep. Rohdric was awake, but most everyone else was asleep when the really scary stuff started.

Aunt Mara began to pant for breath. Then she stopped and hissed, squeezing her eyes shut. Aunt Kemella stood and told her she should lie down. But when Mara gathered herself at the edge of the bench, a gush of water hit the floor under her, soaking the skirts of her frock. She sobbed and said, "Not now. Please."

Rohdric was the man of the family now. "I'll go and tell the guards. She needs a bed."

"No, I'll go," Aunt Kemella said and hurried to pound on the door.

"Help me with her, Rohdric," his mother said, taking one of Mara's arms. Together they pulled his aunt her to her feet.

Aunt Mara walked slowly between them toward the door as Aunt Kemella continued to pound and call for help. Finally, the clanking of keys in the lock came and a lone guard opened the door. The Tibairya came in looking suspicious, holding his spear out ahead of him.

"My sister is giving birth," Kemella said in Hellainic. The guard cocked his head. "She needs a bed, and we'll need water and blankets."

The guard's lip curled and he barked something in Tibairyan, waving his spear in front of Mara. "Can't you see? She needs help."

Rohdric's mother spoke loudly, annunciating each word. His mother reached to push the spear from Mara's face. Kemella stepped over to stand in front of Mara.

The guard snarled and bellowed and made a jabbing motion. It was an outrage. Rohdric couldn't let it stand. Swift as he could, he drew his father's sword and moved out in front of his aunts and his mother.

Quick as a snake, the Tibairya struck, flicking Rohdric's blade to one side and sending him stumbling back as he tried to parry.

The rest seemed to happen in slow motion. Rohdric watched the guard rear back and thrust. The spear tip was coming at his chest. Then Aunt Kemella was there, throwing herself between them and shrieking.

An instant later, the spear tip was right in front of Rohdric's eyes, red with blood, sticking through his aunt's frock. Everything stopped for what seemed a long while.

Suddenly everyone was screaming and scrambling. His mother pulled Mara away and the Tibairya yanked his spear back. Aunt Kemella slumped, like her legs had lost their bones. The guard backed away, yelling his foreign words, and slammed the door. Rohdric dropped the sword and tried to catch his aunt. He couldn't hold her and together they fell in a heap. Warm wetness flowed onto his hands and soaked his tunic. Aunt Kemella stared at him, her mouth wide and gasping like she couldn't get enough air.

Then the light left her eyes. Her body got even heavier and weirdly still.

Rohdric realized in that moment—there in a dim, damp storage chamber beneath the palace of Thrakius—that once again, his life was forever changed. He had only just become the man of the family and already he had failed them.

Rohdric vowed, then and there, that he would never fail them again.

❧

Any hope Brin had once held that she was meant to be a Blade-Wielder was dashed merely by being in their company. Particularly as they traveled. Skolani Blade-Wielders were utterly different. So different they almost seemed to be another species than any of the humans she'd known or had observed thus far.

So different that the thought of becoming one was now beyond her imagination.

The feeling wasn't born simply of their gruff manner; Skolani never exchanged pleasantries. Or their immodesty or harsh physicality; Brin had never been handled, held, or forced to remain in close—and often physical—contact with other humans like this. It also wasn't just their size, muscularity, or ease with weaponry; every Skolani was able to lift Brin effortlessly, and they seemed to never be without weapons. Indeed, Brin's assigned guardian—a dusky, wiry Blade-Wielder named Kunna—even brought her sword and a knife with her into the bedding Brin was required to share with her.

It was all of those things, and more.

The most difficult thing to imagine for herself was that each Skolani was as one with her horse. Brin wasn't too surprised, having witnessed her mother with Hrithvarra. But living around so many of the same sort of pairings really brought the reality into focus. Horse and rider moved as one, ate and drank as one. It was as if they were bound in unseen ways. Skolani stayed in the saddle for ungodly long stretches, adding up to most of their waking hours. Skolani didn't seem to need to steer or prod their horses—it was as if horse and rider decided together where to go and how best to do it. When the rider finally dismounted, they groomed, fawned over, and even had lengthy conversations with their horses, which they referred to as their friends. At first, Brin had thought the conversations were one-sided. But in time she saw the horses were not just responding but were often the ones initiating and leading the conversation.

Although galloping was thrilling at first, doing so for any duration rattled her bones. By the end of each lengthy, jarring stretch in the saddle, Brin found herself longing to be off the horse. Her butt and legs and stomach were so sore that in the moments after she was helped down she could hardly stand. At times, when the horse was walking along the edge of crests or on mountainside paths, Brin's head spun and her stomach twisted.

One small blessing that came of the bewilderment, discomfort, and physical pain of this journey was that she had almost no time to dwell on what she'd lost or even to grieve. Thinking of her parents and of Urias and of leaving Ago—it was just too much to bear, like there were so many tears inside of her that she couldn't allow them to begin for fear they would never end.

Occasionally when the dizzy heights, the pain, the strangeness of her companions, and the constant need to parry the grief got to be too much, all she could do was shut down—close her eyes and bow her head and stay that way while clinging to Kunna and rocking with the gait of the horse. More than once this tactic earned her a scolding. Skolani expected the attention and effort of all, at all times. Brin sensed that their reliance on one another never ended and that no one person would dream of being caught giving less than their all.

At first Brin was embarrassed by Kunna's occasional mocking and laughter at her expense. But that was before she fully appreciated the contempt of the other Skolani. It actually made her grateful for Kunna's lighthearted attitude. Teasing and laughter were easier to take than silent scorn.

Other than Kunna and Ursellya, the other Skolani rarely spoke to her. When they did, it was to bark orders or scold her. They seemed as annoyed by her questions as they were by her not knowing what to do or when to do it. Kunna occasionally seemed embarrassed for her. Brin actually envied Amaga and her babe. Mother and child seemed equally oblivious to the contempt of the Skolani. In response, the Skolani seemed resigned to Amaga's helplessness. Thankfully they'd been paired to ride with Ursellya. She was the only Skolani to show Amaga an ounce of kindness during their trek to Dania.

The thing that made Brin more nervous than any of it had to do with Queen Icannes. Brin's mother had always assured her that a woman named Princess Icannes would look after her. That first night, when Brin had asked after her, the queen had told her that woman no longer existed. She hadn't then, but she was starting to believe it now. This woman with the same name was unwilling to even look at her. It was impossible to believe that Elan would have presumed such a person would care about Brin. When Icannes spoke in Brin's presence, she used the old tongue of the Skolani. The woman often disappeared for long stretches, and when she rode with the group, she stayed far to the fore, alone and never looking back. The only presence the queen seemed to tolerate was her big guardian, Kukida. Such a hard woman.

The Skolani often rode on past nightfall, and on one such foggy night, Kunna reined her horse to a halt and craned to gaze up a steep slope. Brin followed her guardian's gaze to see a dark shape in the last light of the day, atop the nearest peak. The figure turned to reveal a profile. Brin thought it was Icannes. "Is that the queen? What's she doing up there?"

Kunna gave a single nod. "She's getting above the fog. She seeks the lodestar."

"Lodestar?" Brin blurted. Her father had used the term, seemingly about her.

"For guidance. To ensure that we do not stray when we leave the main road tomorrow."

Brin was bewildered. "I thought the Skolani knew the pass better than anyone."

Kunna chuckled. "When conditions are less than ideal, even those who think they know the way can stray from it. The Skolani know that paying our lodestar heed will keep us on course, no matter how difficult the journey becomes."

Brin pondered the words—of Kunna and of her father—long into the night.

When morning came, the Skolani announced they would set off for their sacred bog. The gruff warrior she'd learned was named

Anallya—one of the few Blade-Wielders her mother had ever mentioned by name, never in a positive way—openly argued with the queen. They both looked at Brin several times as they bickered. Brin later gleaned that Anallya was the reason she'd been left in camp when they'd taken her mother to be buried.

Brin had been offered no real chance to mourn her mother or her uncle. She and Amaga were left in the company of two of the youngest Blade-Wielders while the others all attended the secretive burial. Neither of those left behind seemed inclined to speak to either her or Amaga. All day the duo took turns leaving the camp on horseback. Brin had never felt more alone. Her mother's and uncle's absence became a great yawning chasm in her chest. Once she started, she couldn't remember crying for so long, much to the disgust of their Skolani guards.

After the burial, Brin gathered that many of the Blade-Wielders disapproved of her wearing her mother's sword. Kunna whispered to confirm it was so during the next morning's ride. Unless a daughter had already earned a blade in training, the custom was to bury a Blade-Wielder who died in battle with her weapons. But apparently the queen had kept this from happening. Brin supposed out of pity. Kunna flatly informed her that the others would resent her all the more over the issue. Which filled Brin back up again with unshed tears.

By the second day after the burial, Brin sensed they were going downhill more often than up. The snow was getting less deep. The next morning they came to a gateless archway in a crumbling old wall with a spooky tower at one end. Kunna told her as they passed through that she was now in her homeland. Indeed, even the very air was different here—so fresh and clean. The pines and firs on either side of the road were the tallest and greenest trees Brin had ever seen. Even the cold wind from the north seemed cleansing if not quite healing. Soon after they passed the border, Brin beheld a sight that she knew she would never forget. The valley that her mother had so often described opened up before her. It was even more breathtaking than she'd dared to imagine.

Looking down on the wide, greenish-blue waterway carving its way through the valley, Brin finally grasped her mother's claim that the river defined Dania. Brin had never better understood her mother's obsession with waterways and with her potted fir and plants. They were pieces of the home of her heart.

Brin had been across the sea, had sailed up the River Haleez across the desert, had visited the dah's lush court in exotic Anaissa, but none of it had prepared her for Dania. This land was rugged and yet alluring, dreamlike and yet somehow familiar. Even if the Skolani made it clear she did not belong among them, Brin felt as though she somehow belonged here, in this wide, lush valley. Maybe Ago was right about home being in the blood.

The little wooden city came into view soon after they entered the valley. But the Skolani moved east, to a camp in a meadow near a frozen lake surrounded by round, pine-covered hillsides. This change of course was much to Amaga's distress. The first qeins sulked as the Skolani broke the ice and hauled buckets of water. To Brin's astonishment, once the water was heated, the women stripped down and took turns washing one another. Brin tried not to look at their rippled and corded bodies. Still, she couldn't help but notice their scars, welts, and bruises. Her own body was so pale and unmarked in comparison. She felt bony in the wrong places and too soft and smooth in all the rest.

After washing, the warriors paired up and set about a grooming ritual. The Skolani now smiled and spoke in gentle tones to one another. Brin even heard a bit of laughter among them. It was yet another side of them, and Brin was again excluded. It made her long to be talked to and laughed with and touched in a fond way. She'd been handled but it hadn't felt caring or gentle.

Eventually Ursellya seemed to notice her mood, and came sat with her and untied her braids. The healer gently combed out and re-braided Brin's hair. As she worked, she explained that the smelly paste the others applied to one another was meant to cleanse and heal warriors who'd passed through battle. It was offered up as an explanation for Brin's exclusion. It still stung. Brin may not have used her sword but no one could deny that she'd been through a battle. She'd even shot a Tiberian Eques. The image of the man struggling to pull out the arrow she'd shot into him was one that often haunted her thoughts, especially late at night.

At least she fared better than Amaga, who sat alone by the fire, pouting. The waif adamantly refused to even wash and kept her cloak drawn tight. Though once Ursellya brought her a pail of warm water, she did relent and wash her son.

The sun was sinking toward the eastern mountaintops when they set out from the lake camp to ride down to the village of Dani-hem. The village, too, felt dreamlike and yet familiar. Its walls were made of lashed tree trunks rather than stone. The whole of the village was square, so she wasn't sure why it surprised her that the streets were laid out in a grid—even more uniform than the avenues of Thrakius. The smell of wood smoke filled the air as they approached. When they came closer, she caught a whiff of cooking meat in the smokiness.

The bells in the gatehouse rang as they crossed the open meadow between a series of corrals dotted with horses, sheep, or goats.

"Brace yourself to be gawked upon," Kunna said as they approached the open gate.

"What shall I do?" Brin asked.

"Gawk back," Kunna said. "Only meaner." Her guardian laughed. "That always keeps them in their place."

They passed into an open area, like a courtyard, only with packed dirt underfoot. It was about the size of the fountain square outside the palace. And Kunna was right. The area was packed with gawking faces. Hundreds. No, a thousand or more.

And they were all Gottari faces. Other than as an army riding in a column, Brin had never seen so many of her people at once.

Kunna was also right about the Skolani gawking back only meaner.

Most of the villagers wore simple work tunics and leggings. Almost all of them—men and women alike—wore the gray-green rough woolen cloaks that Gottari, and even her mother, seemed to love, despite their itchiness.

Directly ahead was a massive building made of great hewn logs. It reminded Brin of a cargo ship at the quay. She knew this must be the famous longhouse of Danihem. The crowd parted for the Skolani to make way to it. A straight line of Rekkrs, dressed in warrior finery, stood on the walkway under the longhouse eaves. As Icannes dismounted and approached, the men stepped forward, staying in a straight line, and formally bowed. The gesture spurred hundreds among the crowd to follow suit, bowing reverently to the Skolani queen.

Ursellya dismounted next and helped Amaga and the boy from the saddle. Amaga's face was crumpled with emotion as she ran to the line of men with her son in her arms. The waif slung an arm around the neck of the man with the biggest gray beard standing at the center of the greeters. Brin spotted the hilt at the man's hip. It had the familiar bronze-colored carved pommel with a ring that dangled from it. A futhark sword—the mate to her father's. This, of course, was the Wolf Lord. Amaga's father.

The Wolf Lord looked oddly stiff embracing his long-lost daughter. But his emotion was evident as his daughter presented his grandson to him. Thaedan, as usual, stared without crying, looking both curious and terrified at once. Thaedan always seemed to be taking it all in, as if he were secretly an adult who was spying on those around him and feared being found out. During the occasions when Brin was asked to hold her half-brother while Amaga relieved herself, Brin often whispered to him that she knew what he was up to. The cranky way Thaedan always reacted seemed to confirm her suspicions.

Through the father-daughter reunion, other than the queen,

none of the other Skolani dismounted. With the press of so many fascinated strangers watching, Brin found Kunna's strong embrace, holding her in place before her in the saddle, reassuring.

Icannes spoke softly to the Wolf Lord and Brin presumed she was telling him about Urias, whom he considered a brother. Holding his grandson on his hip, the man pressed his lips tight and looked away for a long moment before he nodded his thanks to the queen.

Amaga stood before the men still standing in a straight line, facing the crowd. In the most commanding voice Brin had ever heard from the waif, she proclaimed, "Gottari of Danihem! I bring to you the scion of the lion and the wolf—the long foretold first king of a hundred Tutona kingdoms."

Rather than the cheering Brin expected, the Gottari again bowed as one.

The Wolf Lord held the boy up. "Here before you is my heir. He shall one day sit the dais chair of the Wulthus."

One of the men from the line stepped forward as Amaga had done. Brin noticed for the first time that this was Belgar, her father's cousin. He'd left with his ailing wife after Orithya but before the siege had begun. Belgar was looking right at her and pointed. "What of the girl? She, too, is born of the wolf and the lion. As King Vahldan's firstborn, blood of the Amalus kings of old, should Brin Bright Eyes not be raised as a leader among us?"

A murmur swept through the crowd. Suddenly every pair of eyes in the village was upon her. Kunna's arms tightened around her in response.

"No!" The barked word came as a command. Every gaze swung to Queen Icannes. "The girl is mine," the Queen said. The murmuring only grew. It seemed no one dared argue, not even the Wolf Lord. Queen Icannes took a step toward Brin, her eyes fully focused on her for the first time since that first night. Brin saw the same mournfulness she'd seen in them then.

"I claim her as Skolani, as is my right. Her womb-mother, Elan daughter of Ellasan, was a Blade-Wielder and my near-sister. I claim Brin Bright Eyes for my own."

Brin's heart trilled. Could this really be happening? She sensed the agitation of the other Skolani—particularly Anallya. Brin thought she actually heard the woman growl under her breath. Brin also thought Amaga looked slyly pleased.

"As it shall be," the Wolf Lord finally said.

Arnegern heard voices. Something was different about them. He'd been dreaming. For so long. But these voices spoke Tibairyan. He couldn't really speak the language, so why would he be dreaming in it?

He forced himself to open an eye. Gods, the light, it was painful. His head throbbed from his temple to his ear. This was the worst headache he'd ever had, but it was strangely lopsided, worse on one half of his head than the other. What had he been drinking?

Arnegern began to feel his limbs. He was in a bed but not his own. The voices stopped. A figure appeared, looming over him. "Ah, you are indeed coming to," a man said in Hellainic.

He pushed his eyes to focus. The ceiling was plaster. White. That smell. Tibairyan disinfectant. How had he gotten to the armory? And why was he in the infirmary?

The face leaning over him slowly emerged from the blurriness. Gods, it was Vernius Stallicus. The normally stern general was smiling. "I'm relieved, Captain," Vernius said. "Truly I am. Though I had my best medicus attending you, no one could be sure you would pass through your trial. I'm glad to count you among the living once again."

Memories began flooding back. The last battle. The entry hall. The Equites. The cudgels.

The king.

"King Vahldan?" Arnegern managed. His words were little more than hoarse croaking.

"Dead, I'm afraid. He fought bravely. Both of you did, actually."

The passing of the Amalus reign. "No," he shook his head. "Not if I yet live."

Vernius tsked. "Come now, Captain. It's mostly because of your valiant king's death that I remain here. That and a few... I suppose I'd call them *bargains* that I made. I should be well on my way back to Tiberia, along with my army. Well, the army I formerly commanded. You see, I should be retiring on my estate. Land I would have secured by arriving there with your king as my captive and my son and heir as my companion. But alas, it wasn't to be. It seems my penance for allowing a different outcome, and for seeking a different path, is to be left behind in this forsaken city teetering on the edge of civilization. Your king actually left me in the unenviable position to try to provide the proper nudge, so to speak."

"Penance?" Gods, the side of his head. He reached to touch cloth.

"I'd leave those bandages be. Yes, penance. My penance is the same as yours will now become, Captain. Which is why I'm glad you survived. I need your help."

"Me?"

"Yes, you." Vernius actually laughed. "There is little argument that you were the administrator that your king was not. By all accounts you have long seen to the running of this city. And now I'd like you to help me with the administration of your people."

"My people? Who survived?"

"Oh, hundreds, actually. More women and children than men, but still. Your tribal clan grouping—the Amalus, as you name yourselves—remains quite intact."

"Are we not slaves now?"

"Well, yes. But rather than sending you all to the auction blocks to be sold off as whores, road builders, and field hands, your king devised a plan well before his passing. With the help of Captain Lauterus, who had been your captive and who remains here as well.

They even managed to secure the blessing of the magister, whom I sense was mostly concerned with a chance to secure his wife's son's future. It remains a tenuous plan and none of it would've been possible without all of those who were in on the plot."

"His... wife's son?"

"Yes. Lady Harma's son. Who is also your king's son, as I'm sure you'll recall."

Arnegern sighed. "What is this plan?"

"Your young men are to be trained. Here in the armory. In the imperial fashion. Trained to become Federati." Arnegern frowned. His puzzlement must've been evident. "The primary merit of the plan is that Federati are ever more in demand these days. Increasingly, the foreign units are sent to do the dirty work of the imperial militum. Why send Tiberian sons when foreigners can be sent into the most dangerous war zones first. Dangerous as it seems to some of us, our upper-class citizens even prefer foreigners to be the ones stationed in the most volatile shithole outposts at the far reaches of the imperial borderlands. Whatever the causes for that, it seems there are never enough of these expendable soldiers. I myself had my reservations. But having seen you all in battle, much as I hate to admit it, I've come to believe your fallen king's scheme just might work. And since I'm stuck here anyway, well, I figure I may as well play along."

"Why?"

Vernius laughed again, which was so strange to hear. "Actually, it was something your old friend Vahldan said to me, right before he died. He spoke of honor for our sons." The general went to the window and looked out. "I was the son of a disgraced leader, a man who forfeited his life for his beliefs. It is not a lot in life that I would wish upon anyone, let alone my own son. I have come to see that my father went about things all wrong. He was too stubborn. As was Vahldan the Bold, some might argue. I suppose I'm hoping that I've learned a thing or two from the two of them." Vernius turned back to him. "He was a rare sort, that king of yours, was he not?"

"Rare," Arnegern whispered, staving off emotion. "But what I'm asking is, why should I help? Why should our young men become your expendable soldiers?"

"Because it will keep you all here, together. As a people. And because Federati, more than any other type of slaves, are most likely to win their freedom. Because together, you and I, along with my son and yours and Vahldan's son, we just might have a chance at bringing our two peoples together."

"You wish... for that?"

"I do. Because after this forsaken war, I've come to vastly prefer the idea of the Gottari as allies rather than enemies. Is that reason enough for you?"

Arnegern squinted. "I... I'm not sure yet."

Vernius smiled and absently reached to touch a torc hanging around his neck. "Perhaps, too, after all that's happened, it's that I've come to hope again. I've found a hope that honor can still exist in a world that seems bent upon extinguishing both of them—hope and honor."

Arnegern drew a deep breath and sighed it out. "You mentioned my son. What of my wife? What of Mara? And my babe?"

Vernius's expression clouded. "Your wife, son, and new daughter are well, Captain."

"But?"

"But there was an incident, shortly after the battle. When your wife went into labor. A guard in my command... Well, he became confused and frightened. There was an accident. Your sister-in-law is dead. Your wife has named your daughter Kemella in her honor. It's the sort of tragedy our work together could help to keep from happening again."

"Kemella is dead?" It instantly made Arnegern think of Amaga. And Thaedan. He wondered if they'd gotten away, if they yet lived. But he thought it best not to ask.

Vernius nodded solemnly. "I'm sorry." The Tibairya raised his chin. "So. Can I count on your support?"

"May I ask a question?"

"Why not?"

"If I'm a slave and you're in charge now, can I actually refuse your request?"

This time Vernius's smile was wry. "No, not really."

"Then, General, I suppose you can count on my support."

Brin had no idea what time of night it was when Kunna woke her. "The queen wishes to see you," her guardian said, beckoning her.

Brin unwrapped herself from her blanket, slung her cloak around her shoulders, and followed Kunna through the silent camp by the frozen lake to the pavilion on the far side of the camp's largest firepit. Kukida held the flap open as Brin approached.

Brin ducked inside. The interior glowed with lamplight. It was warm and smelled of the cleansing paste. A brazier glowed within and the queen sat on cushions on the far side of it. Icannes didn't look up.

Not knowing what else to do, Brin stood with her head bowed.

"Sit, please," the queen said, indicating the cushions across from her.

Brin sat. Icannes's gaze rose to take her in. Her eyes were swollen and red.

"I sent for you to apologize."

"My queen?"

Icannes settled back and laced her fingers in her lap. "I realize there's no way you could've known it, but when we lost your mother and your uncle, I lost the only two people in this world that I ever chose to truly love." Brin had no idea how to respond. Icannes went on. "Oh, I have my daughters. And there was my mother. But the love of the blood isn't really a choice, is it?"

"I suppose not," Brin murmured.

"There is something special about the love we choose. So you must forgive me if I have dwelled these past days in the sorrow of my loss. I didn't mean to take it out on you. Nor did I mean to ignore that you are suffering the same loss."

"Of course, my queen."

Icannes leaned forward. "Forgive me as well for speaking out in Danihem without speaking to you first. It was rash of me."

"You are forgiven, of course." Panic swept through her. Brin wondered if she was being sent back to the gawking villagers. She'd been stunned when it had happened, but now she realized she wanted a chance at this life more than anything she'd ever wanted before. Now that she realized it, she sensed it was about to be denied.

"And so, I'd like to speak to you of it now." The queen narrowed her eyes, studying Brin. "It wouldn't be easy, you know?"

"My queen?" In spite of her apprehension, her hopes soared.

"Your mother told me that you trained hard with your uncle. She said that Urias called you a natural, born to be a Blade-Wielder."

Brin looked down, her eyes pricking. "He has... Uncle Urias had a special way about him." She'd never properly thanked him. She would always regret it.

For the first time, Icannes smiled. "That he did. Anyway, I am quite certain that if you choose to seek it, the path would be much more difficult. Your uncle was kind. Skolani trainers are not. You would lag behind the girls your age. You are too thin, your frame too slender. The elders will resist the idea. As it is, you will have to fight for your place, among your peers and within the tribe. To find that same place among the Blade-Wielders would be far more challenging. Life would be miserable for you. For many long years."

"I understand, my queen." It didn't matter. There could be no other life. Brin felt her mother's blood beating in her heart now. She wanted this.

"And you would still seek it? To strive to be a Blade-Wielder?"

"I would... I do."

Icannes nodded. "That is good. But there is more. I would also be asking a favor of you."

"Anything, my queen." Brin instantly wondered if that was a foolish offer. But she realized she'd pay any price for this now.

"There are gifts you already possess. Gifts that are beyond the Skolani. Which has led me to seek my own gift to give you."

"A gift?" Brin had no idea where this was going.

Icannes reached down into a basket beside her. She extracted two items and placed them on the mat between them. Brin gasped, wanting to snatch the inkwell and stylus back. She kept herself from doing it.

"Please forgive us," Icannes said. "Kunna saw them among your things and asked me about them. I asked her to *borrow* them from you. Though I know little of their use, I recognize their importance. I took the liberty of procuring some ink in Danihem and having the well filled. I also got you this." She reached into the basket again and laid out a trio of rolls of parchment. "They're blank, of course."

Brin bowed her head. Her father's words came to her—his hopes for her. "I'm not sure what to say." She really wasn't. How could she ever honor his wishes now, with so many challenges ahead of her? Still, how could she refuse to try?

The queen's smile was arch. "Don't speak too soon. I've yet to ask the favor I seek in return. I have two daughters, you see. Both are younger than you. Very special and yet very difficult destinies await each of them. They will need mentorship. And guardianship. Their struggles would be made less difficult if they knew the tongues of the entire region and the letters of the civilized world. Are you willing to offer them these things? In addition to the great difficulty of your own journey?"

"I... I will do what I can. You're kind to entrust me."

Icannes huffed a laugh. "No. I'm afraid you'll find that I'm not. But that's for another day." She sounded just like Brin's mother. "In regard to the loves we choose, I have another gift for you." She reached into the basket again. She rose, came around beside Brin, and got to her knees.

Icannes held the necklace up between them, spreading the cord in both her hands. The carved kestrel dangled before her. Icannes nodded and gestured, and Brin bowed her head. The Skolani queen drew the cord over her head and laid the charm upon her chest.

"May it always remind you of your parents' choice to love one another. And of how you were born of that chosen love."

Brin swallowed hard. With gentle fingers she caressed the kestrel. "Thank you," she whispered. Her tears rolled freely down her cheeks.

"I hope it might also come to symbolize the love that you and I will come to share. For I wish to choose you, Brin. Will you take me as a second mother, just as I choose to love you as a daughter?"

Unable to speak, Brin lunged to hug her. Icannes wrapped her in strong arms and rocked her. "Welcome home, Brin Bright Eyes. Welcome home."

The End

Of The Sundered Nation Trilogy.
The Saga of Dania continues in The Legacy of Broken Oaths
Trilogy, coming soon.

AFTERWARD AND GRATITUDE:

Here we are again, this time in the aftermath of a complete epic tale. I use the terms *complete* and *epic* in the sense of this being a story that covers an entire lifetime. Throughout my journey of bringing The Sundered Nation into being, a question arose often enough that I feel compelled to answer it here. The question is something resembling: "Must it really end this way?"

By most definitions, this tale is a tragedy. Several well-meaning early readers have wondered if it really had to be so. As with most things in my writing journey, understanding begins with Tolkien, who said: *"The story-maker proves a successful 'sub-creator'. He makes a Secondary World which your mind can enter. Inside it, what he relates is 'true': it accords with the laws of that world."*

The world of Dania and the Gottari unfolded before me as a Secondary World. I have honestly felt more like a scribe for these tales than their creator, merely bringing them to the page and rendering them recognizable to those who are meant to find them.

I hope it also helps to explain why this story has to end as it does when I say that the Saga of Dania is far from complete. You see, I first "met" Vahldan and Elan almost two decades ago, in the form of backstory to the tale of their children—a tale that also features the daughter of Icannes and Urias. In fact, the very first time Vahldan and Elan made themselves known to me was as a memory, in a scene I instantly and vividly pictured and heard. In it, a reluctant and clearly still mournful Queen Icannes relates to her daughter Ainsela the tragedy of her beloved near-sister and the father of Ainsela's new subject, Thaedan. Hence, Vahldan and Elan first came to my attention precisely because of the tragedy of their tale.

I began working through the specifics of their story in 2011 and it took me several years to fully grasp the magnitude of their role as the first to have crossed over to the new world from the old. I was made to understand the importance of the "link" they provided between those worlds, embodied by Brin Bright Eyes. Vahldan and Elan aren't just backstory. They provide the necessary foundation for everything that follows. Because of them, the world is made anew.

Through becoming their scribe, I am made to understand their truth. After having made so many mistakes, having failed and faltered, having betrayed and suffered betrayal, having felt driven to reclaim their bond, and ultimately having sacrificed as they did, I have come to grasp how all of it is rooted in love. Vahldan and Elan have shown me that love underpins our very humanity. Just as they've helped me to perceive the luminance of mortality—how it lends urgency and emphasis to our lives, which are best rooted in love.

In Dania, as it is in our world, it takes the courage and the mistakes, the joys and the sorrows, the sacrifice and forgiveness of one generation to provide the makings of what the next might become. And none of it is possible without the underpinning of love.

Although I still don't have all of the answers as to why or from whom I received the *gift* of Vahldan and Elan's tale, I'm sure that relaying it has helped me to better perceive the right questions—about my life, my world, and the human condition. The journey has kept me striving on the path to enlightenment, which has informed and reinforced my core truths.

I find something very special about the moments after "The End" of each book I finish. Whether I am left unsettled or fulfilled, elated or longing—or occasionally both—I am brimming with feeling. I can only describe it as receiving a strong dose of *what it means to be human*. My fondest hope is to have provided you with some measure of feeling in a similar moment.

With that in mind, I want to convey to you, dear reader, my immense gratitude for your time, interest in, and support of this, the most meaningful undertaking of my life. Thank you.

Remember, this is not so much an ending as an elaborate beginning. I hope to see you again on the far side of the Pontean Pass.

As it shall be,
Vaughn

ACKNOWLEDGMENTS

In this section of books one and two, I listed so many wonderful humans without whom I would not have made it to publication. Without exception, they are all just as vital to this book as they were to either books one or two or both. Writing this story and getting through the publication of the trilogy has been a very long haul, and continuing to strive throughout it all has been one of the biggest challenges I've undertaken. Looking back on the past decade makes me realize that persevering is both vital to the endeavor and one of its most difficult features.

Looking back also makes me realize that the primary component of persevering is sustaining a belief—in the project and in oneself. This I could not have achieved without other humans—those who believed in me and/or helped me to continue to believe in myself. My heartfelt gratitude goes to everyone who has ever read anything I've written and offered advice or positive feedback.

The list of those deserving is far too long to enumerate here, of course, but I would like to specifically acknowledge: The Writer Unboxed community for over a decade of support and encouragement, especially Editorial Director and founder Therese Walsh; my awesome group of beta-readers who buoyed belief through the reading of countless renditions of six manuscripts over almost two decades, especially Deb Wagner and Keaghan Cronin who have a particular knack for suppling faith; and the SFF reviewing community, especially Justin Palmer, Daniel Clouser, Quinn Giguiere, and

Philip Chase, who kept me believing through the publication process —in particular through the murky middle of it.

I also need to single out Isabelle Wagner. Isabelle is so much more than a proofreader. She's a Super Reader. She makes books better, it's as simple as that.

Lastly but most importantly, I have to single out my wife Maureen, who provided the brightest, steadiest, and most enduring guiding flame and whose relentless belief has sustained my own. Thank you for teaching me how immense the power of love can be.

About the Author

Vaughn Roycroft has aspired to write epic fantasy since his sixth grade teacher gave him a boxed set of The Lord of the Rings. He has spent many years striving to be worthy of telling the tale of The Saga of Dania. He lives with his soul mate in a cottage they designed and built themselves near their favorite Lake Michigan shoreline. When he's not writing or editing, you can find Vaughn walking in nature, trying to keep up with his energetic black lab.

www.ingramcontent.com/pod-product-compliance
Lightning Source LLC
Chambersburg PA
CBHW022009300726
48970CB00003B/809